When the Emperor Dies

When the Emperor Dies

Mason McCann Smith

Random House New York

Grateful acknowledgment is made to Crown Publishers,
Inc., for permission to reprint lyrics from
"Johnny, I Hardly Knew Ye," from *A Treasury of
Irish Folklore* edited by Padraic Colum. © 1952,
1962, 1967 by Crown Publishers, Inc.

Library of Congress Cataloging in Publication Data

Smith, Mason McCann.
　When the Emperor dies.

　1. Theodore II, Negus of Ethiopia, d. 1868—
Fiction.　I. Title.
PS3569.M53782W5　　　813'.54　　　81-40222
ISBN 0-394-51458-0　　　　　　　　AACR2

Manufactured in the United States of America

9 8 7 6 5 4 3 2

First Edition

MAPS BY RAPHAEL PALACIOS

BOOK DESIGN BY LILLY LANGOTSKY

TO FRANK DEFELITTA,
who made this book happen

Negus kamotu baman yimmaggotu?
When the emperor dies, whom can one ask for justice?
—ancient Amharic proverb

I would like to acknowledge my gratitude to Alan Moorehead, whose *The Blue Nile* first introduced me to the Emperor Theodore.

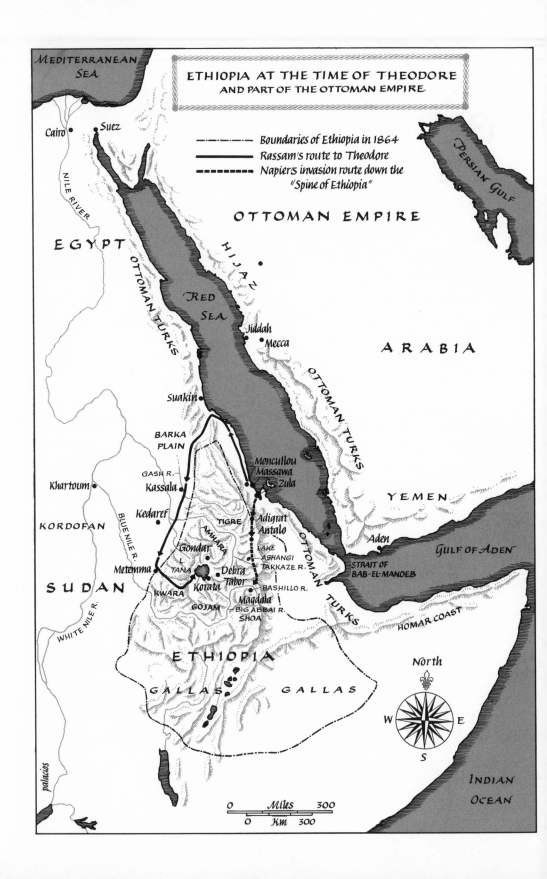

ETHIOPIA AT THE TIME OF THEODORE
AND PART OF THE OTTOMAN EMPIRE

Boundaries of Ethiopia in 1864
Rassam's route to Theodore
Napier's invasion route down the
"Spine of Ethiopia"

MEDITERRANEAN SEA

Cairo
Suez

NILE RIVER

EGYPT

OTTOMAN EMPIRE

HIJAZ

PERSIAN GULF

RED SEA

OTTOMAN TURKS

Jiddah
Mecca

ARABIA

Suakin

BARKA PLAIN

GASH R.
Kassala

Monchoullou
Massawa
Zula

OTTOMAN TURKS

YEMEN

Khartoum

Kedaref

KORDOFAN

BLUE NILE R.

TIGRE

AMHARA

Adigrat
Antalo

LAKE
ASHANGI
TAKKAZE R.

Aden

GULF OF ADEN

STRAIT OF
BAB-EL-MANDEB

Gondar

Metemma

L. TANA

Debra
Tabor

OTTOMAN TURKS

SUDAN

KWARA

Korata

GOJAM

Magdala

BASHILLO R.

BIG ABBAI R.

SHOA

HOMAR COAST

WHITE NILE R.

ETHIOPIA

North

GALLAS

GALLAS

W   E

S

palacios

INDIAN OCEAN

0   Miles   300
0   Km   300

Contents

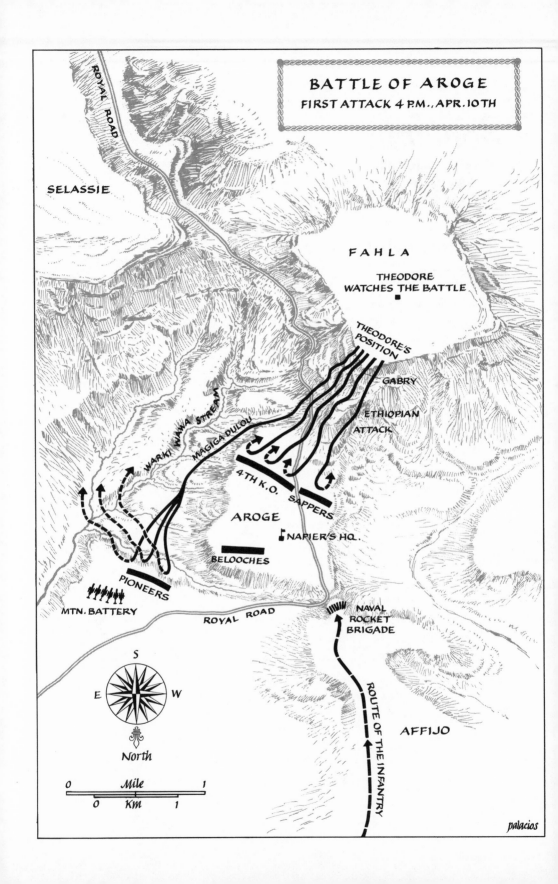

BATTLE OF AROGE
FIRST ATTACK 4 P.M., APR. 10TH

ROYAL ROAD

SELASSIE

FAHLA

THEODORE
WATCHES THE BATTLE

THEODORE'S
POSITION

GABRY

WARKI WAWA STREAM

MAGIGA DULOU

ETHIOPIAN
ATTACK

4TH K.O. SAPPERS

AROGE

NAPIER'S HQ.

BELOOCHES

PIONEERS

MTN. BATTERY

ROYAL ROAD

NAVAL
ROCKET
BRIGADE

S
E   W
North

AFFIJO

ROUTE OF THE INFANTRY

0   Mile   1
0   Km   1

palacios

Author's Note

Fiction makes its own demands on history. *When the Emperor Dies* is very close to historical fact, but I have necessarily embroidered some historical reality for the sake of the novel, and have omitted more for the sake of clarity.

Available firsthand accounts of these events are the work of nine-teenth-century Englishmen: they paint a consistent but oddly uncon-vincing portrait of the Emperor Theodore. I have called my imagination into play in an attempt to portray the Theodore who peeks out at us from between those biased lines. My emperor is neither the ogre of the British nor the semideity of the Ethiopians. The major events of his life, including the prophecy of the Emperor Theodore from the *Fikkare Iyesus*—the Ethiopian book of Jesus' prophecies—are factual. Others, such as his second, essentially political marriage and the birth of a son to that marriage, seem to me superfluous, and so have been omitted from this narrative.

As I told the stories of a few minor characters—most notably John Speedy, John Bell, and Walter Plowden—they began to assume lives of their own. In the end, they may have little resemblance to their real-life counterparts. I hope I have not offended their ghosts by retaining their names: I have come to know them by those names and would have difficulty recognizing them by any others.

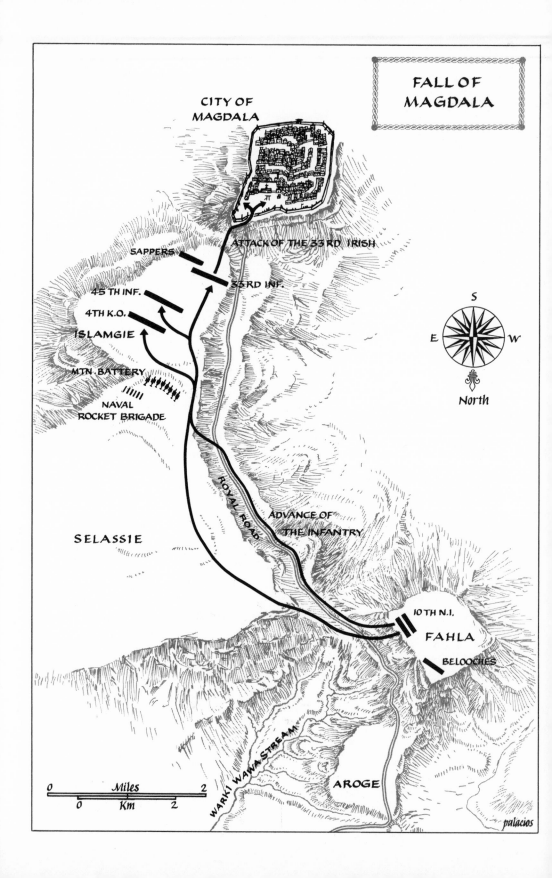

FALL OF
MAGDALA

CITY OF
MAGDALA

ATTACK OF THE 33RD IRISH

SAPPERS

45TH INF.

4TH K.O.

ISLAMGIE

33RD INF.

MTN. BATTERY

NAVAL
ROCKET BRIGADE

ROYAL ROAD

SELASSIE

ADVANCE OF
THE INFANTRY

10TH N.I.

FAHLA

BELOOCHES

S

E   W

North

Miles
0   2

Km
0   2

WARKI WAWA STREAM

AROGE

palacios

When the Emperor Dies

1

June 1864

The Red Sea

As the hot Arabian wind took the locust swarm over the British gunboat *Dalhousie,* one weary locust lighted on Seaman Arthur Pilbeam's shirt. Pilbeam captured it and touched its head to a sheet of metal that was exposed to the sun. The insect began to disintegrate.

The *Dalhousie*'s metal-cased bowels, pressed between the tropical noontime sun and the vessel's own enormous steam turbines, had become a giant furnace. The heat had driven every off-duty seaman into the shade of a striped awning over the stern end of the upper deck. Oozing sweat, gambling listlessly, the crewmen lay half-naked on straw mats in the fragile shade. One end of a concertina slipped from a sailor's hand, bounced lightly and wheezed, but the sailor was already dreaming open-mouthed of misty Scottish mornings. He heard only a distant foghorn. A long time passed between each throw, and even when someone rolled the dice, they lacked their usual staccato rhythm.

"Bloody locusts," muttered Pilbeam, flicking aside the dry, feather-light corpse of the locust.

"Roll 'em dice, Arfur," said Seaman Moses Hoyt.

"Bloody envoy, too, if you ask me." No one had the strength to ask him, so he rose up on one elbow high enough to see over the rail. The coast of Africa, a mile away, looked as desolate as ever. "We left the middle of the sea, where it's cool and breezy, and came here shoreward for that envoy, and I swear we'll be rowing soon on his account. And in this heat."

"Can't very well row 'im out in the middle of the sea," said Seaman Peter Turnbull.

"Like to."

"Roll 'em dice, Arfur," said Hoyt, again.

"Someone stop that concertina making that racket."

"My but you're touchy today," said Master Gunner Ryder.

"Roll 'em bleedin' dice, Arfur," said Hoyt.

Pilbeam grunted. The dice toppled end-over-end across the straw mat.

The great ship began to shiver through her anchoring maneuver. Pilbeam gauged the distance again. "Damned Red Sea. Bottom's so shallow, we've got nine hundred, maybe a thousand fookin' yards."

"Don't bother yourself, Arfur," said Hoyt. "Won't do no bleedin' good." He closed his eyes and rolled over onto his side.

A voice came from beyond the shelter of the awning. "Ready to take a little pleasure cruise, gentlemen?" It was the bosun's mate, from the sound of him no happier than Pilbeam. "You know who you are now, lads, no hiding there in the shade. It'll be dress uniforms for you. You want to give the envoy a rousing send-off, don't you?" The lack of movement in the shade didn't suit him. "That's five minutes!" he shouted. "In your uniforms and on the deck! Now move!" His anger was real enough to send the boat crews scurrying below for their uniforms. They all knew it wasn't directed intentionally at them, but only at them as substitutes for the real target; and since they all shared that same anger, they did not hold it against him.

With half a minute to spare, the crews of the launches, swathed in their heavy woolen dress uniforms, emerged on deck.

They loaded the trunks, valises, and portmanteaux of the envoy and his companion, the doctor, into the first launch, and lowered it to the water. A crew scrambled down the ratlines and started toward the shore. Sweating powerfully, Pilbeam, Hoyt, and the remaining sailors formed an honor guard as the envoy and the doctor—"Queer pigeons both," whispered Hoyt—shook hands with Captain Easterday and climbed awkwardly over the rail into the launch that would take them to Africa.

The envoy and the doctor wore identical white traveling suits and solar helmets, held sun umbrellas over their heads, and carried ebony walking sticks under their free arms. The doctor was a young English gentleman and the envoy was some kind of Asian, but they clipped their words with exactly the same arrogant accent. *Queer pigeons indeed*, agreed Pilbeam silently.

"Man winches!" cried the bosun's mate, and the seamen snapped to their task. As the boat waddled down to the water, the envoy and the doctor sat ramrod straight in the double shade of their helmets and umbrellas.

"I can't be out here in the sun," whispered Hoyt to Pilbeam. "Forgot me brolly."

"I'll take a brolly to your arse." The bosun's mate's voice was close behind, but he was smiling. "Man boat!"

Hoyt spit out his relief. The crew and the bosun's mate climbed down and slid into the launch. The bosun's mate took the tiller, the doctor and the envoy sat on the bench ahead of him facing the bow, and Pilbeam and Hoyt manned the bench ahead of the passengers, eye-to-eye as they took their oars.

"Push away!"

The launch wobbled from the gunboat's metal side, and then, as the bosun's mate called out the cadence, shot across the smooth water. This close to shore there was no breeze at all, and the humid air clung wet and sticky in their lungs. Sweat turned their woolen jerseys into constricting second skins.

Half a mile there and half a mile back. A mile of rowing in this heat because of the envoy and the doctor. Pilbeam's knees were almost touching the envoy's. Their faces were less than two feet apart. Pilbeam's hand slipped across the age-polished oar handle. For a practiced moment, he rowed with one hand, rubbed the other across his leg to dry his drenched palm, squeezed the sweat from his eye sockets with the heel of the hand and flicked his eyebrows dry with his fingers. Then he rowed with that hand and dried the other palm.

Pilbeam had made an art of his hating over the years, defining his objects and refining the keen ache inside his chest. He was not an educated man, nor one with a wide experience of the world off the deck of a ship. He knew there had been voting reform in Great Britain, but no one had offered him a vote. He knew that other men were choosing this nineteenth century to stand up and make demands, but what he mostly knew was that a demand would get him nothing but the sting of the cat. No, Arthur Pilbeam did not know much of what happened off the ships of the Royal Navy, but even he could not fail to hear the murmur rising across the face of the European world, a murmur from the throats of many thousands of little men, no different from him. He was just an isolated, illiterate tar, but he had a sharp, sweet sense of injustice, and he shared the hurt of all those little men.

On principle, Pilbeam hated the envoy, as he hated anyone who neither sweated at his labor nor submitted to another man's orders. In the past, though, it had always been a diffuse, general sort of hating. Now, for the first time, it had a face and it had a name. Pilbeam hated Envoy Hormuzd Rassam with all the hating in his soul.

What made the envoy so remarkably hateable was a simple thing, really: the envoy would not look Pilbeam in the eye. The skin around the envoy's eyes was darker than the rest of his olive complexion, as if someone had laid cobwebs across his lids, and the lids drooped down toward the tip of his nose. The eyes themselves were flinty, cold and clear. Until he blinked, they might have been the eyes of a corpse. Now those eyes swept the shoreline continually, north to south, and in their sweeps they necessarily passed a point at which the envoy's line of sight aligned perfectly with Pilbeam's. Pilbeam, just two feet away, stared into the envoy's eyes to try and force some kind of acknowledgment from him. The envoy's eyes swept through Pilbeam's without a tremor. The envoy was not just failing to see Pilbeam: he was deliberately *not-seeing*. And not-seeing, Pilbeam decided at that moment, was the worst one man could do to another. All the rest, the ordering and the cursing and the whipping, was not nearly as bad as this. The others acknowledged that a man was a man, and therefore at least worth degrading. But this not-seeing . . .

Pilbeam inclined his head toward Hoyt. Their eyes met for an instant, and Pilbeam knew that Hoyt didn't feel as he felt. The angle of Pilbeam's head sent salt stinging into his eyes. He rubbed his face against his woolen shoulder.

Pilbeam's eyes dropped in defeat to his own hands on the oar handle —broad, brown, tattooed hands, glistening wet like glazed hams. His anger became a solid object, as hard and eternal as a diamond.

When he looked up again, something new had entered the envoy's face. It was nothing Pilbeam could put a finger on: a subtle shadow, not from the helmet or the umbrella, but from inside. Pilbeam glanced at the doctor. What the envoy's expression had merely suggested was written clearly enough in the doctor's face for even an illiterate tar to read.

Pilbeam restrained himself from swiveling around to look at the shore. *What kind of hell on earth are we taking these men to?* he asked himself, then quickly snatched back the sympathy: *It's not near bad enough, not bloody near.*

The bosun's mate leaned forward from his tiller. "That bunder doesn't look like it'll take the boat's weight, sir. I'll run her up on the beach."

"Very well," said the envoy, tight-lipped.

As if he has a fookin' word to say about it, thought Pilbeam.

The bunder, an uneven, rickety pier, patched with ill-fitting boards and driftwood, flashed two feet off the starboard beam. The bosun's mate was right: the bunder was wobbling just with the launch's wake, and a touch would have collapsed it. Pilbeam gauged the depth beyond his oar. Half a fathom, smooth sandy bottom.

"Up oars! Beach her, lads! Alive, alive now!"

With a last spasm of energy the sailors leaped into the still, tepid water and hauled the launch onto the sand next to the one that had brought the luggage. Exhausted, they broke discipline without a word and sank to the sand. The bosun's mate let them lie.

"What do you smell?" Hoyt asked suddenly. Pilbeam looked at his friend. A devilish grin lit Hoyt's face. He poked Pilbeam in the ribs. "What do you smell, Arfur?"

Pilbeam raised his head and, for the first time, looked at the shore. Except for the bunder and a small warehouse, the steep, gray beach was empty. Twenty yards from the water, where the ground leveled off, a collection of squalid wooden huts with palm-frond roofs paralleled the shoreline in both directions. Pilbeam sniffed, hawked and spat, and sniffed again. Behind the bewildering, unwholesome mélange from the village, there was another, unmistakable stench.

Pilbeam stood up and stared along the shore. A few hundred yards up the beach, the sand was coated black. Below the black sand, the sea water lay even flatter than elsewhere, and it had a curious, metallic tint. Hoyt looked up eagerly at Pilbeam. "Is that what I think it is?" Pilbeam asked, but Hoyt only repeated, loud enough for everyone to hear, "What do you smell, Arfur?"

Pilbeam could feel every pair of eyes on him. He relished the moment, stretched it out, tangled it up in his mind with his keen hate for the envoy. "I think it is what I think it is," he said, turning his words into a stage whisper aimed at Hoyt, but intended for a larger audience. He ran down the firm sand into the water until it lapped around his waist. He shaded his eyes for them all to see and stared down at the black sand and the metallic water. "It is what I thought it was," he said. He spoke the next word slow and round, as if it were a name of God: "*Oil.*"

Pilbeam thrashed out of the water and ran back onto the dry sand, then slid down on his knees between Hoyt and the launch. "Oil," he whispered. "Oil."

Everyone knew a white man couldn't live for long around the vapors emitted by oil. They clogged the sinuses, constipated the bowels, drove the mind insane. And if it seeped into the drinking water, even in the most minute, undetectable amounts, it would kill.

The muscle-hard cords of Pilbeam's belly began to vibrate, and then he laughed out loud. It was a frightening laugh, maniacal and unconvincing. He cut it off, but it erupted again.

Someone from the first launch called out, "Just like home, i'n't it?" And he roared.

Hoyt began to laugh, and then all the seamen were rolling in the hard, dry sand, throwing handfuls at one another and screaming out their anger until tears rinsed their eyes clean of salt.

They ended up refreshed and strong, their spirits curiously uplifted, not even afraid of what the bosun's mate would do. He was leaning against one of the launches with his arms crossed and an exaggerated look of disgust on his face. "Had enough merriment for the day, gents?" he asked, in an imitation of something higher class, and then he shouted in his best bosun's mate's choler, "Get the lead out, will you? There's luggage to be offloaded and boats to be rowed back to the ship, so lean your arses into it, and don't be all day about it!"

There wasn't a sailor who didn't take note of the fact that the bosun's mate had saved his orders until their laughing was done. They scrambled to the trunks and cases and piled them against the warehouse.

"Where are the inhabitants?" the doctor asked the bosun's mate.

"Inhabi—?" The bosun's mate was pretending he didn't know the word.

"The people who live here," snapped the doctor. "The natives."

"Ah, you mean the natives." The bosun's mate pointed the bronze stub of a forefinger, lost long ago in some forgotten sea battle, at the sun. "Well, yer lordship, it's noon, or close on it. I expect the natives are all sleeping, as the heathen generally tend to do in these latitudes. They likely aren't aware the *Dal'ousie*'s here."

"Isn't anyone here to meet us? Anyone to send for an escort? To carry our luggage?" The doctor was too dignified to notice sailors laughing in the sand, but the filthy hovels and the smell of oil had clearly unnerved him.

"Not likely to find an escort in these parts, yer lordship. Massawa isn't London, you see, and the Turks haven't the same sense of protocol."

"What are we going to do?" The doctor turned to the envoy. To Pilbeam's disappointment, there wasn't a hint of any emotion in the envoy's face. Obviously, he was made of tougher fiber than the doctor.

"I have my orders," said the bosun's mate. "To return to ship when I've offloaded you and your things. I'll take you back to the *Dal'ousie* if you want."

"We shall stay. Naturally." The envoy said it very quickly, before the doctor could say anything more. "We thank you, bosun."

"And I thank you," said the bosun's mate, ignoring the titter that the promotion brought from some unidentified sailor. "My pleasure, sir, my pleasure. May your stay be a happy one." He turned away, and in the brief instant before he barked out the order to prepare the launches for the row back to the gunboat, a pixie's smile streaked across his dour face.

As the crewmen slid the launches into the water, Pilbeam maneuvered Hoyt and himself into the bow bench, as far from the bosun's mate as they could get. They bent to their oars.

They were barely out of earshot of the beach when Pilbeam turned his head closer to Hoyt's and breathed, "Fookin' son of a bitch."

"The bosun's mate? No, he's all right."

"Not the bosun's mate, the envoy fellow. Treats a man like no man at all. No man has the right."

"That's just the way with his kind. You can't bother yourself."

"I'll have revenge on him."

Hoyt nearly missed a stroke. "Coo. What's that you're saying, Arfur?"

"I'll have revenge. I will."

"You're asking the cat a question," said Hoyt, meaning that Pilbeam was inviting the cat-o'-nine-tails to talk across his back.

"No man has the right."

"They do have the right, Arfur, so you can't bother yourself. In the eyes of the Lord, we are all the same."

"And before the Lord I will have revenge."

"You're just talking dramatic, Arfur," said the man on the next bench. "We all know how you like to talk dramatic."

"I'm not talking dramatic. I'm talking true."

Hoyt said, "Revenge, my arse."

Pilbeam tugged savagely at his oar. He lifted his head and looked back at the shore. The envoy and the doctor had moved into the shade of the warehouse. The envoy was sitting on a trunk and fanning himself with his solar helmet. "I will have it," said Pilbeam, "and it will be sweet."

2

June 1864

Massawa, Red Sea Coast

Envoy Hormuzd Rassam sat in the black slash of shadow under the warehouse eave. The sun outside was bleaching the huts and the water and Dr. Blanc into a uniform field of intense, painful white. From the direction of Blanc's voice, Rassam could follow his erratic path as he stormed angrily around. The voice traversed a wide area of beach and bunder, as if Blanc were desperately searching for something. "Is this a city?" cried the voice. "A port? How could anyone, even a Turk, live in a place like this? Hovels and a warehouse? Sand and sun and date trees? And that stench! It's worse than Aden, even worse than Bombay. What in the name of God is that smell?"

"Oil," whispered Rassam, but Blanc hadn't listened to Rassam any more than he had listened to Pilbeam.

"The sheik should have sent an escort. What kind of place is it where a ship can anchor, two launches can come ashore, and no one even comes to investigate?"

"Maybe the bosun's mate was right," said Rassam with an effort. "Maybe no one has seen the ship."

"How could anyone miss a ship of that size? Even Turks have eyes." Then the voice announced, "I shall find someone," and footsteps crunched toward the huts.

He has a right to feel cheated, thought Rassam, in order to excuse Blanc, and at once lapsed back into his own distress.

From shipboard Rassam and Blanc had compared what they had heard about Massawa with what they could see of it, and most of the details had been the same. The first twenty miles to the west of the shoreline was a salty white desert with only a hint of hardy vegetation. For twenty miles the ground hardly rose above sea level, but then it suddenly became a shadowy, fourteen-thousand-foot wall as the salt desert met the vertical eastern escarpment of the Ethiopian plateau. Massawa was a low island snuggling in its own bay of diamond water, and though the channel separating it from the mainland was as narrow as two hundred yards at low tide, Massawa appeared to be perfectly distinct from the desert and the mountains. From nine hundred yards out, looking through the noontime haze, the two men saw a shimmering picture of green groves and whitewashed houses.

On the deck of the *Dalhousie* Blanc had said, "I think we've been misled about Massawa's *genius loci*. I see only the gauzy, inviting aspect of a fairy kingdom. If this first look is any indication, we will find Massawa to be one of those fabled oases of the Orient, a garden of earthly delights."

"Perhaps," sighed Rassam, who knew the fabled Orient better than Blanc. "But I would reserve judgment."

"Reserve whatever you will, but I see foliage and fountains of sweet flowing water and white mansions. I expect enchanted glades, market places brimming with the wealth of two continents, and houris—is that the correct word, houris?"

"Yes," said Rassam. He was straining his eyes to pick out more details of the low island, but either it was still too far away or there was nothing more to see. He glanced back at Blanc. "Yes, houris is right, but you aren't supposed to find them this side of heaven."

"My point exactly," said Blanc, obviously pleased that his little turn of phrase had worked out.

Doubly shaded beneath their umbrellas and solar helmets, the envoy and the doctor had been standing alone in the direct sunlight at the *Dalhousie*'s bow rail. Their costumes were identical, and their mannerisms and speech were so similar that only a man who had been born into them himself could have seen that they were natural for one of the men, and a rather crude affectation for the other. The characteristics and the uniform belonged by birthright to Dr. Blanc, just as they belonged to each of the ten thousand young English gentlemen scattered all over the British empire who could have been substituted for him without sending even a tiny ripple into the order of the cosmos. Blanc was attractive in a pale, delicately carved sort of way. He was tall and slender, his chest was concave, and the slouch in his posture and the angle of his head created an impression of perpetual boredom. He would have been the first to admit, with an offhand pride, that the impression was accurate: he was almost always bored.

He was a product of his social class's system of shucking off the responsibility of raising sons by banishing them to boarding schools, to the university, and eventually to the government service or the army or the church. His fate had never seemed wrong to Blanc, nor right, but only an inarguable reality. Family connections made medicine the line of least resistance. He had never studied seriously and had forgotten much of what he had learned, but he was witty, too good-natured for his own good, and occasionally interested in the less disgusting tropical diseases. A tour of duty in the empire had been the logical next step, and he was assigned to the Bombay Staff Corps. Grandly bored with Bombay and desperate for entertainment, he had allowed himself to be drawn into a short, unpleasant affair with the short, unpleasant wife of General Sir Robert Napier. The affair was so disagreeable, in fact, that Blanc's first reaction, when Napier had walked into Lady Napier's bedroom and found Blanc on the settee, still tugging his riding boot past his heel, was one of relief: whatever might happen to him, at least the affair would be put to death. Blanc's second reaction, after Napier had greeted him as if nothing were happening and Blanc finally realized that Napier in fact did not understand that anything *was* happening, was one of pity for Napier.

The affair had been over for nearly a month before rumors of it reached Napier. The rumors treated Blanc harshly, and Napier treated him more harshly still. Blanc soon found himself on loan to Aden.

Aden was even more boring than Bombay. Where Bombay had at least had a reasonably large British community, Aden was just a hot, dusty little town that was nothing more, as far as Blanc could see, than a refueling stop for steamers and a relay station for the telegraph. He spent his mornings in the European hospital, seeing patients from among the few Europeans in Aden and from the upper classes of Aden society, and the rest of the day lounging in his darkened apartment, sipping a cool drink and watching the slowly rotating punkah fan on the ceiling.

Hormuzd Rassam, the envoy, wore Blanc's costume and mannerisms like props in a play, as if they were what made the Englishman, and not the reverse. He was forty-four years old, slight and short. When he went hatless, he brushed his dark, curling hair too obviously down across his forehead, and no one could miss his object: he was a younger, less commanding version of his personal idol, Benjamin Disraeli, with an unconvincing dash of the upperclass Englishman purposely thrown in. The pathos of that failed imitation cried out *I am the least significant man alive.* Unknowingly, Rassam was responsible for the first impression he made and for the later confirmation of it, but he had spent his adult life trying to overcome it and to achieve some vaguely understood status that he thought of as "being English."

Born in Mosul, in the part of the Ottoman Empire that would someday become Iraq, he had converted his father's money and political connections into an Oxford education and British citizenship. Then he had gone to work for Layard, the archaeologist who excavated the ruins of Nineveh, the ancient Assyrian capital which lay across the Tigris from Mosul. Layard returned to a seat in Commons, and he got Rassam the job of assistant to Colonel Merewether, the political resident in Aden. It was one of the middle-level, dead-end administrative posts that the

English usually farmed out to British citizens of exotic races. Many of these not-quite-Englishmen had been educated in England, and their whole lives centered around their desire to become Englishmen. They emulated the English dress, accent, manners, and values until they became caricatures of the English, and all they succeeded in doing was to amuse the English.

Rassam seemed doomed to sink into obscurity among them. He had attained a moderate importance on paper, but his superiors always delegated the trivial jobs to him. Even Layard had never trusted him with anything more ancient than last month's payroll. He could never hope to succeed to Colonel Merewether's post. When Merewether left, another Englishman would replace him, and Rassam would be that man's assistant, and then the assistant of the next, and so on forever. He seemed to have found his natural level, and to have become fixed there for all time.

Then, so unexpectedly that fate must surely have had a hand in it, the Ethiopian affair had come to release him. As Colonel Merewether's assistant, Rassam had learned the barest details: that Consul Cameron and his people had been seized by the emperor of the Ethiopians, tortured, chained, and thrown into prison. He had seen the penciled note, the first word of Cameron's predicament, that Cameron had managed to smuggle down to Vice-Consul Speedy at Massawa. He had seen, too, the letter that Speedy had written to Colonel Merewether before Speedy quietly disappeared from the Middle East.

What Rassam could not know was how he had been assigned to the Ethiopian mission. Lord Russell at the Foreign Office had more important issues to deal with when Merewether's cable about the situation came to him, and it seemed the kind of affair that might very well resolve itself: the prisoners might escape, or be released, or die. He let the cable slip, unnoticed and soon forgotten, into the loose sheaves of papers on his desk.

Of course, the situation had not resolved itself. In Aden a correspondent of the London *Times* en route to Bombay chanced on a copy of the cable, and in due course it found its way into the pages of the *Times*. The cable had quoted Cameron's penciled note, and the last line of the note—"There is no hope of our release unless a letter is sent as answer to His Majesty"—pointed an especially damning finger. There was an uproar in the country at large, and then in Parliament. Preachers preached, newspapers editorialized, and *Punch* laughed.

The three Whig giants, Palmerston, Gladstone, and Russell, put their mighty heads together. There was only one option that promised to silence their critics and still keep them out of a nasty situation in a faraway land: they must send a man to communicate with the Emperor Theodore from some distant, safe location and to demand that the emperor free the prisoners. This envoy's instructions would be to go up to Ethiopia only with specific instructions from the government. Privately, the Whig giants understood that these specific instructions would never be given.

They drafted a letter for Queen Victoria to sign. The letter thanked Theodore for his past good services, congratulated him on having established his authority in Ethiopia, carefully avoided commenting on his conflict with Britain's Turkish clients, and promised to receive an embassy in London anytime he chose to send one. The last paragraph read:

> Accounts have indeed reached Us of late that Your Majesty has withdrawn your favour from Our servant, whom We sent to you as a token of Our goodwill. We trust, however, that these accounts have originated in false representations on the part of persons ill-disposed to Your Majesty, and who may desire to produce an alteration in Our feelings towards you. But Your Majesty can give no better proof of the sincerity of the sentiments which you profess towards Us, nor ensure more effectually a continuance of Our friendship and goodwill, than by dismissing Our servant Cameron, and any other Europeans who may desire it, from your Court, and by affording them every assistance and protection on their journey to the destination to which they desire to proceed.

The sole remaining question before the Whigs was who should be chosen for the dreary task of conducting the mission to Theodore. The man who sat in Massawa and wrote the letters was not necessarily the one who would go to Ethiopia, if anyone ever did have to go. His role was only to buy time for the government. He must be a careful man, someone who would never act without instructions. He must be a man so inconsequential, so uninspiring, so *boring*, that the public might forget him within a few weeks. He should be so expendable that he would not leave a vacancy that would need to be filled. It was suggested that he should be well acquainted with the eastern world, possibly even an Arab himself. The question was still being debated when another cable arrived from Colonel Merewether: the political resident had someone right there in Aden, conveniently close to Africa, who might be just the man. Layard was called in to express an opinion. Feeling a twinge of guilt at being reminded of how little he had done for his former aide, he was quick to second the suggestion. He described Rassam: adequate, conservative, unexciting, exactly what the government wanted. And so Hormuzd Rassam was selected for the mission.

Rassam didn't know the truth about his selection. He was only certain, the first time he looked down at the envelope, heavy and stiff and sealed with the royal signet, that he was holding in his hands the fulfillment of all the dreams of his life. He would save the prisoners. He might even march boldly into Ethiopia and bring them back himself. Then, he would follow in the footsteps of the great Disraeli, overcome his Arabness as Disraeli had overcome his Jewishness, and rise from common British citizen to the exalted plane of English gentleman.

Rassam and Blanc had only had a nodding acquaintance in Aden, but their relative statuses had been defined automatically: Blanc was superior in everything but official rank, which was only important when something official was happening. Since it was summer in the tropics, official doings were at a minimum. When he heard that Rassam, the curious little assistant to the political resident, was going to Massawa to try for the release of the famous prisoners of the tyrant Theodore, he imagined excitement and prestige, or at least a little activity. He volunteered to go along, to keep Rassam company and to set up a clinic among the natives as a goodwill gesture to the Ottoman government. The request went through channels and came back in very fast time—with Sir Robert Napier's authorization.

Now that they were on government business, of course, their statuses were reversed. They adapted smoothly to the change, at least on the surface. Rassam became the decision-maker, and Blanc became the silent but eloquent judge of Rassam's attitudes, manners, speech, dress, and everything else inherently English. They did not like each other, but friendship was not a necessary condition of their association, and they weren't even aware that they weren't friends. They were two British civil servants isolated in a strange land. That was all that mattered.

The trip from Aden to Massawa lasted three days. Apart from boredom, Rassam found the trip remarkable for only one thing: the sullen, hate-filled glares of a sailor. He was just another big-handed, nut-brown, nameless crewman. Normally Rassam would never have noticed him. They never exchanged a single word, but Rassam knew those looks. *Why does he hate me?* Rassam wondered. *I'm just a man like him, doing my job, trying to get by without stepping on anyone's toes.* To the other sailors, Rassam was a non-person. Privileged, yes, but not a man of the sea and therefore not real. Rassam understood that attitude, but this particular sailor saw things differently. This one hated him, Rassam knew as he let the conclusion rise to consciousness, because Rassam was something other than English. The sailor hated him for defiling the clothes of an Englishman, for profaning the Oxford accent. The English sailor felt superior to Rassam and hated him for his higher status. And Rassam hated himself for having to agree, on a mental level that he nearly always managed to hide from himself, that he *was* inferior; and even the sealed letter and his determination to follow Disraeli could never change that reality.

Rassam groaned to himself when he saw the sailor among the crew of the launch, and when the sailor flew down the ratlines and took the bench opposite him (was there really a moment when the man jostled past another sailor to reach that seat?) then Rassam had set his face into a stone mask to hide his distress. It was a very long nine hundred yards to the shore. He felt the sailor's eyes glued to his as clearly and as painfully as if the sailor had thrust his broken fingernails between Rassam's eyelids. Unseeing, he swept his eyes purposefully up and down the shoreline, making his eyes flow through the sailor's. He only managed to actually see the approaching landscape for a moment. He wondered at its desolation, so unlike Blanc's vision of it, but then the awareness of the sailor's glare shattered his concentration. There was nothing but those eyes.

The boats landed. Rassam leaped out and stepped as far away as he could reasonably go. The next minutes were pure hell. That sailor led his comrades in a fit of demonic laughter. They seemed to be laughing at the deadly, oily shore, but Rassam knew they were really laughing at him. The bosun's mate insulted Rassam and Blanc to their faces. Insulated by his self-confidence, Blanc did not perceive the insult. He only whined in a way that Rassam knew would normally have flayed his flesh and exposed his nerves. Throughout the whole ordeal Rassam suffered quietly and with some measure of dignity, as an Englishman should. All he could think about was sending that sailor back across those nine hundred yards of water to the ship, and then watching the ship sail so far away that Rassam would never have to think about that glare again.

The sailors rowed off at last, and Rassam walked slowly to the little warehouse and slumped wearily onto his trunk.

Through his fatigue, he realized suddenly that he despised Blanc, and that Blanc despised him. And yet Blanc was the man Rassam wanted more than life itself to become. It was a paradox, just one paradox in a life filled with them. His head hurt with the heat, with the straining to see across the water to the ship, with the sailor's hate, with Blanc's careless, stupid anger at a people he would never understand. Rassam would not think about paradoxes now.

A locust sailed through Rassam's line of sight and lit on his knee. He didn't have the energy to brush it away. It rested, then flew off.

Blanc was back within minutes. He dropped onto the trunk without a word and folded his arms. He was sweating, and there was a hint of defeat in the set of his shoulders. They waited.

The first islanders they saw were a bunch of black-skinned, naked children who stared at them from the shade of the huts. Rassam called out to them in Arabic, but they only shook their heads and stayed in the shade. They seemed to find watching the foreigners an interesting pastime.

A pelican was fishing a hundred yards offshore. Its chunky body and enormous head were at odds with its effortless glide above the water. It plunged down with a graceless flattening of its wings. It should have shattered and come up in pieces, but instead it was on the surface again and then flapping clear of the water with a struggling silver fish caught crosswise in its beak. A rat made a brazen expedition across the sand from the warehouse to the bunder, surveyed the bunder and found nothing, and darted back to the warehouse. A sand-colored lizard peeked out from between a leather valise and a trunk, then ducked out of sight again. The children didn't move. They didn't even whisper among themselves. They were totally naked and very dirty, and their eyes were enormous, like great round ostrich eggs.

After about an hour, a man came ambling by. Clothed in a straight white robe and a loosely arranged turban, white with stripes of dusty blue, he must have been the end product of Arabian, Turkish, Black African, and possibly Javanese and Indian bloodlines. He cast a vague look at Rassam and Blanc and then, having found them less interesting than the children did, continued past them to the warehouse door.

Blanc leaped to his feet. "Oh, you fellow! Where is everyone?" The man looked past Blanc to Rassam. Blanc had never learned to speak Arabic, and he tended to forget there were some people who spoke neither French nor English.

"The greetings of the day and the blessings of Allah be upon you," said Rassam in Arabic. His father had insisted on English being spoken in the home, so Arabic was his second language, but it had always come too easily to him, as if it maintained that it should have been his first language.

"And to you," said the man.

"I am an envoy of the Queen of England, here to see your sheik," said Rassam.

The man was unimpressed. He stuck a large brass key into the lock on the warehouse door and jiggled it. The key would not turn. "Who is your friend?"

"He is my traveling companion. He is a doctor."

The man sniffed a surprisingly British sniff, then smiled as the door came open. "I don't know him, perhaps he is a very good man, but already I do not like the tone of his voice. I am the customs official."

"We would like to see your sheik."

"He is in his palace. In the town, that way." The man waved across the island toward the mainland.

"Then this isn't Massawa?" asked Rassam.

The man grinned. "Massawa is a very big town, a very big city. That way."

Blanc had assumed an irritating, disinterested expression. Any conversation that he couldn't follow wasn't worth following. "Massawa is on the inland side of the island," Rassam told him. "This man says it's a very big city."

Blanc said nothing.

Rassam dug an Ottoman coin from his pocket. "Will you deliver word to the sheik that Envoy Hormuzd Rassam and Dr. Henry Blanc, representatives of the British Crown, have landed, and that we would like an escort to Massawa and an audience with His Excellency?"

The man took the coin, studied it for a moment, and salaamed deeply. "It will be my pleasure to serve the *effendi.*" He summoned a small girl from among the children. He relayed the message to her, omitting any reference to Blanc and garbling Rassam's name. She nodded uncertainly and ran off through the huts.

"She is reliable?" asked Rassam.

The man had already entered the warehouse. His voice came distant and muffled. "As reliable as the desert wind. As reliable as corruption. As reliable as a camel's breath. As reliable as—" His voice trailed off; he either could think of no more standards of reliability, or simply lost interest.

Rassam and Blanc settled down for another wait. Finally, the children leaped up and dashed away, screaming and giggling, and after another few seconds a group of men emerged from the village. All but one of them wore nothing but brief leather skirts. The leader, a young Arab in robe and turban, came forward, bowed, touched his fingers to his forehead, and said, "Salaam. I am Abd-ul-Kerim, son of Mohammed Ismail, the sheik of Massawa. He is not sure who you are, since the little girl who delivered your message could not remember. Please, who are you?"

"I am Envoy Hormuzd Rassam, and this is Dr. Henry Blanc. We represent Her Majesty Victoria, Queen of England."

"Ah, English. Forgive me, but you don't look English to me. The doctor, yes, but you, no. Forgive me for saying so."

"I am British," said Rassam, "though not English. I have my papers."

Rassam started to reach into his coat for his credentials, but the young Arab put out his hand and lightly tugged Rassam's wrist. "Of course." When he smiled, two gold emblems appeared, a star inlaid in one of his front teeth and a crescent in the other. There was a wide gap between the teeth.

Abd-ul-Kerim was in his middle twenties. He wore the straight white robe of Yemen, with wide sleeves and pockets in front in which he could hide his hands. His blue-and-white turban, too, was in the Yemeni style. Though it looked as if he had put it together while he was still asleep, it was actually a result of careful, exact workmanship. One fold of it hung down over his ear, crossed loosely under his chin, and reentered the turban at his other ear. The last two feet of the turban wandered down by his shoulder. He spoke with a subtle, ingratiating lisp, and his smile was so open, simple, and disarming—despite the gold inlays—that Rassam did not feel the wounds reopening when Abd-ul-Kerim asked about his race.

There was something else, though, lurking behind Abd-ul-Kerim's comic smile. Rassam was reminded of certain desert Arabs he had known in his lifetime. Abd-ul-Kerim had the same soft brown lover's eyes and the same hawk nose, and though the skin above his scraggly beard was far too pale for a Bedouin, his movements had the same hardness and assurance. Rassam felt sure that this was a man in whom the character of his Bedouin ancestors had resurfaced, perhaps for the first time in centuries. If he was like those other men, then his easy manner might suggest he was a harmless clown, but he would be able to feel a grudge as keenly as any nomad, to carry it with him silently for years, and then to strike out as quickly and savagely as any viper. If he was like those men, then he was a man to fear, and a man to love. Rassam liked him at once.

"Sheik Mohammed has asked me to welcome the British envoy and the doctor to Massawa," said Abd-ul-Kerim, smiling at his very polite, very obvious lie. "He has instructed me specifically to escort you to a house that he has set aside for your use. You are welcome to it until you choose to move to the official British residence at Moncullou, a village several miles inland from the city. Or you may use it forever. As you wish. He also asks you to come to dinner tonight at the palace."

"We shall be pleased."

Abd-ul-Kerim looked around. "Have you no servants?"

"That is rather embarrassing," said Rassam. "They vanished just before we sailed from Aden, and we had no time to replace them. I suppose they were unhappy about leaving their homes."

"Or about coming to Massawa?" Abd-ul-Kerim's flashing emblems invited Rassam to share in the humor.

Rassam smiled. "Or coming to Massawa."

"It makes no difference. We will replace them for you." Abd-ul-Kerim waved his hand carelessly. The half-naked porters headed for the luggage, jostling over the lightest pieces, and then started off through the village. Abd-ul-Kerim, Rassam, and Blanc followed.

"I am a guest in Massawa," said Rassam nervously, "but I am also a British envoy, and I have my duty." He wished he could simply ignore the issue. "I don't want to interfere, but you understand the necessity that my official position places me in. In the matter of servants, I—"

"Ah, your Captain Speedy explained all that to us . . . and then he forgot all he had explained and flew in the face of your government's policies. Your government has made it a mission to suppress the slave trade, and the Sublime Porte in Constantinople has granted all British officials the power to combat the trade everywhere within the Ottoman domains. Well, I assure you that there are now no slaves in Massawa, and no slaves pass through our city." Cheerfully, Abd-ul-Kerim gestured at the line of porters. "These men work for wages and have complete freedom to seek other employment. Any servants we provide you will likewise be free men." The way he told these lies was so blatant that Rassam could read the hidden message line by line: *These porters are slaves,* Abd-ul-Kerim was saying. *Your servants will be slaves. Massawa is still a center for the African slave trade. I invite you—no, I dare you—to exert your influence and end it all. I know, and you know, that you have the power, as close as the nearest ship of the Royal Navy, to do it. But I also offer you a lie that leaves you an honorable escape from your duty if you will not do that duty.* But the hidden message left unsaid the most vital thing of all: why Abd-ul-Kerim was giving this information so openly.

They had been taking a roundabout route through the village at the heels of the porters, and as Rassam was pondering Abd-ul-Kerim's motives, they passed a high enclosure made of hundreds of vertical bamboo poles. The top of each pole had been cut at a sharp angle, so the upper lip of the wall formed a dangerous saw-tooth edge that no man could ever climb. The only opening was a low hole covered with thick woven mats. No sounds came from inside the stockade, but the smell of recent human waste was unmistakable. Abd-ul-Kerim had purposely brought them past a slave pen, empty at the moment, but clearly used to hold slaves awaiting shipment to Turkey.

Those lies, so blatant that they became the most penetrating form of honesty, this walk past the slave pen, had been an exercise in diplomacy, that finest art of the Arabian world, in which the highest meaning is considered too valuable to be committed to mere words, and instead resides in hints and symbols. Rassam's years among Europeans had gotten him out of practice and blunted his skill at this ancient game. Abd-ul-Kerim's smile was saying as plainly as words that he knew a secret and wanted Rassam to guess what it was—and Rassam didn't have a clue. So few words had created a many-layered onion, and Rassam would have to peel away the layers and read the message on each before he could hope to glimpse the secret. Abd-ul-Kerim was talking about slaves. He was talking about Rassam's duty to crush the trade. He was talking about Ottoman weakness and British strength. And he was talking about the nature of Arabian discourse, and the entire world view it symbolized.

Rassam knew these were the topics, but not what Abd-ul-Kerim was saying about them. Perhaps Abd-ul-Kerim was really just talking about Rassam's inability to read the layers of the onion.

On the simplest level, Rassam knew he had to establish some kind of ground rules now, at the very beginning. He ought to enter the competition, state his position on slavery, offer a subtle, veiled warning. But Rassam was unsure of himself; he had not the courage to speak, and the lie was such a convenient refuge that he made only a few meaningless noises as they left the slave pen behind them.

"Massawa is not such a bad place as it must appear at first," went on the young Arab. "I've been in worse. I'm sure you have, too. Take the oil, for instance. I've heard you Europeans have a fear of it, that you think its fumes are deadly. I can assure you they are not in the least unhealthy. Disgusting and unpleasant, certainly, but not harmful at all. And even so, I can assure you that this tiny place is the only spot for many miles around where oil seeps from the ground or gets into the drinking water. As you see, we are fortunate. Allah smiles upon us.

"Your Captain Speedy—though he was the vice-consul, Consul Cameron's assistant, he always insisted on being called *Captain* Speedy—your Captain Speedy had a special aversion to Massawa. He must have told you. He certainly never hesitated to tell us. He was a man of action, a man who must always be moving, doing, acting. There was little for him in Massawa. He left at the first chance."

"Immediately upon receiving Consul Cameron's note," said Rassam.

"Immediately. A dhow was ready to make the run through the Strait of Bab-el-Mandeb to Aden, and he was so eager to be on it that he didn't even take time to pack all his things. He left much behind."

"He still has belongings at the British residence?" asked Rassam eagerly, but as soon as his words were out he saw the innocent little trap that Abd-ul-Kerim had set for him.

Abd-ul-Kerim only smiled his golden-emblemed smile and said, "We could not put a guard over the house forever. The Bedouins and the Shohos come often to the coast to see what they can loot. It is an easy target."

"Of course," said Rassam, and added, by way of admitting his failure, "Dinner with your father ought to be interesting."

"Interesting, yes. I will be there, naturally, and a few other men of the city. They will be curious to meet you."

"We will all be curious."

Blanc had lagged a few paces behind. Rassam turned to him now and said, "I'm sorry, Dr. Blanc. I'm not doing very well as an interpreter, am I? This gentleman is Abd-ul-Kerim, the son of Sheik Mohammed. His father has set aside a house in town for us, and His Excellency has invited us to dinner at the palace."

"That is better, isn't it?" said Blanc. "Please extend my best regards to Abd-ul-Kerim."

Rassam passed Blanc's regards to Abd-ul-Kerim, and Abd-ul-Kerim's to Blanc, and when the smiling and salaaming between the two men was done, Blanc said to Rassam, "But I wonder what will pass for a palace in a pesthole like this, don't you?" And Abd-ul-Kerim said to Rassam, "I don't speak any English, Mr. Rassam, but any fool can tell your friend's meaning by the tone in his voice and the pained look on his face. Why won't he look you straight in the face when he talks to you? Already I do not like him very much." Rassam struggled to keep his voice perfectly neutral, in both English and Arabic, as he begged Blanc to take more care and made a detached, offhand apology to Abd-ul-Kerim.

Blanc, tall and white and proud, was standing at Rassam's right. The umbrella and the helmet shielded his fragile flesh from contact with the sun. He did not have a single doubt about himself.

Abd-ul-Kerim, short and hard and proud, stood at Rassam's left. His turban was a disheveled bundle around his head and under his chin. He was naked under his loose robe, and his feet were dusty and bare. The thin black hairs on his cheeks and that foolish grin gave him a vulnerable look, but he was as sure of himself as Blanc.

Rassam felt a simultaneous attraction toward and repulsion from each —it was that paradox again—and he knew that Abd-ul-Kerim would sympathize with a man caught between two worlds, but Blanc wasn't even aware that such a dilemma could exist. The day seemed to have been chosen as the one on which Rassam would be bombarded with one psychological ordeal after another—and the dinner was still to come. *I won't think at all,* thought Rassam. *I'll just let my mind float free for a while.* But the idea itself had a peculiar flavor, and Rassam realized that his mind had phrased it in Arabic. He forced himself back into English and followed Abd-ul-Kerim on through the village.

The village proved to be an isolated settlement, entirely separate from the city. Once they had left the village, they saw Massawa half a mile away on the mainland side of the island. A high stone wall encircled it, over which loomed the muezzin's minaret and several tall dwellings built of carnelian coral. A shanty town huddled against its southern side. The main gate, a dark square against the pure white of the wall, faced toward the east. The center of the island was barren and sunbaked, and the exact middle was a sink of damp sand that was connected to the sea by a wide channel. At high tide, the ocean would pour in and turn the island into a great crescent around a shallow lagoon. But now sandpipers ran stiff-legged across the sand and young girls, naked except for short white skirts, balanced huge bladders full of water on their heads as they walked along several well-defined paths that all converged on the city. Untended flocks of scrawny brown goats roamed the fringes of the island, searching out the tough, sunburned grass.

"How necessary is the wall?" asked Rassam.

"Very, I'm afraid," answered Abd-ul-Kerim. "The tribes don't always stop at looting. We are only a small outpost of the civilized world, but the tribes think we have the wealth of the Ottomans—compared to them, I suppose we do. The Bedouins and the Shohos and even the Beni Amr from the Barka Plain have tried to storm Massawa at one time or another, but our valiant army has stood firm. Our garrison is small, only fifty men, mostly Massawans and Albanians. But fifty men is quite a large number for this region, and their discipline and firepower make them the match of five or six times their number in nomads. They would crumble before British troops, certainly, but against nomads they are close to invincible. Their commander is Captain Rashid ibn Ali. He came to us from the center, from the very heart, of our glorious Turkish empire. He was sent by the high staff of the Sublime Porte . . . But come, we enter my city."

He led Rassam and Blanc through the gate and into the wedge of shade beneath the wall. It was cooler there, but the human stench turned their stomachs.

I need to rest and organize my thoughts, said Rassam to himself as he picked up more barely hidden messages. There was the suggestion that British troops would be able to defeat the Massawans, of course, but even more vital was the depth of hostility he noticed when Abd-ul-Kerim said the name of the Turkish officer. The young Arab made no effort to hide his hate—in fact he made certain that Rassam saw it. Rassam thought he had Abd-ul-Kerim's measure by now. His kind of man would hold this sort of biting anger under a firm rein until it was time to lash out. One of the victims of that lashing was sure to be Rashid ibn Ali.

It was always a delicate subject, here in a world where an arrogant, history-burdened Arab race was dominated by the Turks, but Rassam decided to explore a little, to make his own feeble entry into the game. "You are an Arab, aren't you?" he asked. "Not a Turk?"

"Turkish?" Abd-ul-Kerim spat out the word. "I am descended from the purest stock of Mecca and Saba. My second cousin married the daughter of a *sherif.*" Abd-ul-Kerim referred to the highly respected lineal descendants of the Prophet himself. He went on to list some of the proudest families in Islam as his ancestors.

"I am honored to know you," said Rassam, and he did not have to pretend to be impressed. He had rarely met an Arab of such distinguished blood. "Has your family been long in Massawa?"

"An ancestor of mine was the first Arab to set foot on the island of Massawa. He came as a refugee from the persecutions in Mecca, while the Prophet made the Hegira to Medina. I am descended from the son of his first wife, a woman of Saba. He took a local woman as his second wife, and he converted the local population to the way of Islam. When the early battles were being fought, he led a few men across the Red Sea to Arabia, and when those battles had been won, he joined in the conquest of the world and journeyed in arms as far as Shiraz. And when he was old and wanted a place to rest, and an inheritance to pass on to his sons, Ali ibn-abu-Talib himself gave my ancestor Massawa and the nearby regions to hold as his sheikdom. My family has lost Massawa twice, one time for almost two hundred years, but we have the right to it, given us by Ali ibn-abu-Talib, and we have always held it or struggled to regain it. We are Massawa, and Massawa is my family!"

"And the Turks haven't interfered?" asked Rassam. It was the dangerous question, the one that would tell Rassam more than any other. There were very few Arabs who had been left in their high positions unmolested.

The question struck the nerve in Abd-ul-Kerim that Rassam had sought: another little victory. Abd-ul-Kerim kicked a stone with his bare toe and watched the stone rattle away. An emaciated chicken pecked at it where it came to rest.

"We are still in Massawa," he said at last. "It has been a very long time, and we are still here. The world has been very different under the Turks. There have been compromises, untold compromises lost in the mists of time. Some I would not have made, if they had arisen in my lifetime, but—" He shook his head and brightened suddenly. "We will discuss it some other time. I promise you, you will hear more about my family and Massawa than you want to hear. Come, I will show you your house."

He turned and started quickly down a narrow corridor through the huts. The Britishers furled their umbrellas and hustled to keep up. The huts were squeezed so tightly together that the streets were just twisting alleyways framed by slapdash, unchinked walls. There were hundreds of people: naked, black-skinned children playing in the dirt; slender, high-breasted women with bronze nose rings; women in black purdah; a few robed and turbanned men—every possible mixture of the Ottoman races—who paused to salaam the newcomers. The heat, the rising stink of poultry and rotting thatch, the garbage and human filth, the noise and the suffocating barriers all around were almost too much for Rassam to bear. Blanc was overwhelmed by it.

Rassam took the doctor by the arm and helped him on. Blanc would normally have pulled away, but now he leaned gratefully against Rassam.

"Come on, now, buck up," said Rassam, pitching his voice low enough that Abd-ul-Kerim might not hear. "We British have to put up with all kinds of nuisances, don't we? A small price to pay for empire, I should say, wouldn't you? I imagine our people have endured worse."

"What could be worse?" Blanc said it so loudly that Abd-ul-Kerim turned to look back and smiled, and then pressed on.

"Remember Calcutta, the Black Hole."

"I wasn't there," moaned Blanc. "I'll never be able to stay in this place. It's worse than Bombay, even worse than Aden."

"It's not so bad," said Rassam. Blanc was beginning to bother him as much as the heat and the stench.

Abd-ul-Kerim stopped in the first tiny open space they reached. It was barely twenty feet on a side, but Rassam and Blanc clung to the absolute middle of it like shipwrecked sailors clinging to a raft.

Far too soon for either of them, Abd-ul-Kerim led them away.

In a few hundred more yards they reached their house, a two-story coral stone structure, hemmed in tightly by huts. The shutters were sealed, and the air inside was stale, but it was cooler than outside. They paused for a minute to let their eyes adjust to the darkness. The downstairs was a single big room, empty except for their luggage against one wall. A ladder led through an opening into the second story.

"I hope we aren't putting anyone out of their home," said Rassam.

"It is a vacant house," said Abd-ul-Kerim, "unused since the ones who lived here died during the last fever season."

Blanc had settled onto a trunk, leaned his head against the wall, and closed his eyes. Rassam passed Abd-ul-Kerim's information on to him.

"What did they die of?" asked Blanc, showing mild suspicion.

"The cholera," said Abd-ul-Kerim.

No doctor in Aden could fail to learn at least that one Arabic word. "Oh, my God," murmured Blanc, and then he was racing through the room flinging open the shutters. Hot air and white light poured into the room. He shouted an order to Rassam: "Get the cholera belts from my medical trunk!" But before Rassam could start to move, Blanc had thrown open the locks on the trunk and found the cholera belts: two broad bands of flannel fitted with buckles. He cinched one around his own waist, over his coat, then fastened the other around Rassam. Rassam submitted to the operation with good humor and exchanged a slightly embarrassed smile with Abd-ul-Kerim. Blanc stood back, surveyed his work, and breathed out his relief.

"What are these?" asked Abd-ul-Kerim.

"For the cholera," said Rassam.

"To cause the cholera, or to cure it?" The young Arab's eyes were laughing, but for once he held his mouth in a tight, serious line.

"To prevent it, I believe. I will ask the doctor." Rassam began to conduct a discussion with his two companions on the merits of various European and Arab medical techniques. Blanc plunged into the conversation with the confidence of an all-knowing expert. He explained the cholera belt, which was in vogue among British doctors in India and China. Abd-ul-Kerim favored other methods. One was to write a few lines from the Koran on a slip of paper, wash the ink from the paper into a glass of water, and drink the water; another was to stitch the Koran-inscribed paper into a small square of red leather and then to apply this square to the afflicted area. He pulled an amulet from beneath his robe and showed it to Blanc. It had been blessed by a *sherif* from Suakin, and it was especially effective in warding off the evil eye. Blanc's face turned florid as he tried to dent the Arab's faith in unscientific medicine, and at last, unaware that Abd-ul-Kerim was taking pleasure from the argument and not caring at all what Blanc thought about amulets and Koranic cures, could not take anymore. "I shall explore the upstairs," he announced. He climbed the ladder with a loud clatter and disappeared through the hatch. His footsteps rang hollow through the ceiling.

Rassam spread his hands. "I am sorry—and ashamed for him."

"He does not understand."

"No."

"I know that he doesn't understand, but I still don't like him."

"No."

"Do you?"

Rassam spread his hands again, and said nothing.

Abd-ul-Kerim waved a locust off Rassam's coat.

Blanc's voice, high-pitched and urgent, echoed from the second floor: "The most malevolent black cloud I've ever seen is heading down from the north. I think it will blot out the sun."

At the same instant, Abd-ul-Kerim froze. He seemed to sniff the air and feel it with his flesh. Outside in the sudden stillness a door slammed. Someone in the nearest row of huts muffled an anxious cough behind his hand; a mule brayed nervously. Only the constant locust hum remained. The city braced itself for something.

Rassam felt a galvanic tingle in his arms. "What is it?"

"A storm," said Abd-ul-Kerim. "Don't be worried. At this season, they are very frequent, every two or three days. I'll leave now, to reach the palace before it hits." He salaamed and turned. From the door he called back, "Close your shutters." His white robe flapped around his ankles as he ran off through the huts.

"Batten down, Blanc, would you?" called Rassam.

"I think we'll be safe enough from the cholera if we let the house air out for a day or two," Blanc called down. "Wouldn't you rather risk getting wet than getting cholera?"

"It doesn't really feel much like rain, does it?" said Rassam, and at that instant the foggy sunlight went midnight black. Shutters began to slam upstairs. Rassam pulled on the downstairs shutters as quickly as he could, but the storm crashed into the house before he had secured the last one on the southern wall. A powerful wind reached around the house and clutched, hot and dry and penetrating, through the open window at Rassam. The temperature soared by twenty degrees. A solid curtain of black sand slammed down. Rassam tugged at one shutter, but the sand-heavy wind pressed it tight against the outside wall. Sand slashed across his cheeks as, blindly, he yanked at the shutter. It loosened, then closed. He groped for the other, found it, pulled it, dropped the latch.

Blanc found a jar of soothing ointment in his medical trunk and rubbed it gently into Rassam's raw face and hands. Then he found rags and plugged the chinks in the shutters where the sand was sifting through. He was quite cheerful, now that Abd-ul-Kerim was gone and he had something to do.

The storm beat against the house for half an hour, and then it was over as quickly as it had come. Blanc swung open the shutters. "There, that's better, isn't it?" he asked, as if he had prescribed the cool sea breeze that wafted through the house. He straightened his collar. "Cheer up, Mr. Rassam. We won't be here long. God willing."

"Theodore willing, Dr. Blanc," replied Rassam. "Theodore willing."

3

Early summer, 1835
Kwara Province, Ethiopia

The teacher of sacred knowledge, the *debtera*, had located his sacred community here at the uttermost verge of the Ethiopian world, here where the last dampening ripple of the Ethiopian highlands vanished into the flat waterless Sudan, because it was an immutable law of God's universe that the Coptic Christian Church should reach out her gentle arms to embrace every least member of the Ethiopian race; and so— at this point in the peroration the *debtera*'s terrifying, yellow-rimmed eyes would fix each of the boys for an eternal instant—and so the *debtera*'s unruly young students would please God (and the *debtera*) if they would only stop complaining about the fate that had stranded them in a land not fit for human existence.

He put such fear into the boys that, after he was gone, they would not even dare to whisper among themselves that, since they were west of the last ripple of Ethiopia they were actually not even in that country, and for a few days the complaining would be stilled.

The world of the village was divided between two dominating physical features that embodied the opposing principles of God's universe: light against dark, God against Shaitan, Christian against Moslem. The first was the cliff, ivory-white clay and sandstone, that rose unbroken as far as the eye could see to north and south. Two paths led to the top, a hard switchback south of the village and a gully to the north. The cliff was the first step in the broad stairway from the Sudan to the high Ethiopian plateau, only true home of the Ethiopian race.

The other feature of this world was the clay plain of the Sudan, dry and white as crushed bone, baked by the sun and bruised by the sirocco. It offered nothing but salt and scorpions and Arab slavers.

The East attracted and the West repelled. The boys, trained for the Church and grown one by one to young manhood, inevitably ascended into the highlands to seek a different life.

The gully that pierced the cliff was narrow and deep as the cut of a spade. It ran into a dry, shallow wadi that shot straight across the plain toward the western horizon. The village—a church, a school and eighty huts, dusty thatch cones over mud cylinders—lay across a slight pregnant swelling of the earth that served as protection against the summer rush of water that had been known, perhaps once in a man's lifetime, to flood the plain.

The *debtera* always suspended classes for a few hours in the middle of the day. In these last weeks, the boys had used that time, and then again the brief interval between the evening meal and darkness, to sow their seeds and to clear the furrows that would tap the wadi's flow. Now, they had nothing to do but wait for the water from Ethiopia.

They spent their free hours lying in black wedges of shade. Their dogs squeezed into the shade beside them. The only sounds were the boys' hoarse, weary whispers, the chatter of pet baboon babies, and the drone of locusts. The only movement in the village was that of an older boy named Kasa, who threaded his way slowly through the maze of huts. He wore white trousers and a long, loose white shirt, a *shama,* which he flapped idly to create a breeze as he walked. His head was shaved, and though his skin was nearly as black as the heathen Sudanese, his nose bore a great Semitic hook and his lips formed a thin, tight line. He was very tall, still slender but starting to fill out in the chest and arms with the promise of future power. He walked with an arrogance that was unusual even for his arrogant race.

A knot of fuzzy-headed boys, their sharp black knees and elbows jutting like acacia spines from their white garments, the blue strings or *matebs* of Coptic Christianity slack around their necks, were sitting in the shade of a hut. Their flinty eyes traced Kasa's approach. The oldest of the group rose, placed himself in Kasa's path, and bowed formally. The boy, Gabry, was more a chicken than a human: shaved head wobbling at the end of a long sinewy neck, silly birdlike eyes, sharp nose, awkwardly akimbo elbows. Kasa answered the formal bow with an equally formal, "God's blessing on you." As he heard his own voice, Kasa was aware again of the inner turmoil that had haunted him these last few months. This new voice, unsought, unwanted, had come to him suddenly. It was an instrument so full of assurance that it could influence, coerce, urge, comfort, soothe or arouse. His walk was more insolent than ever. People watched when he walked by. And his stare could hold a classmate's eye against the boy's will. And, of course, there were the dreams . . .

Kasa sensed his life swelling toward some critical moment, when everything must change. He feared that coming crisis. He told himself he hated the changes in himself that were leading him to it. But he was intrigued and excited by it, too.

Kasa's faith told him that nothing in God's universe is devoid of meaning. Why, he asked himself, had he become different, if not for a purpose? And who could have such a purpose, if not—Kasa tried to shut the thought out, but it wouldn't be denied—if not God Himself. The answer was terrifying, and yet satisfying at the same time.

Gabry looked up from his own clay-whitened toes and whispered softly, uncertainly, "If you aren't busy, could you spend some time with us? Tell us a story, or help us with the poems we're composing, or . . ." His voice trailed away.

"What's wrong?" asked Kasa, too low for the other boys to hear.

"The young ones are frightened of the soldiers," said Gabry. "You can make them feel safer."

"There have been armies before. There will be armies again."

"But never Ras Ali's men." The words tumbled out. "They're worse. They come all the way from Gondar, and they've never been beaten, and Ras Ali is crueler than the other lords." Then, more softly: "Or so we've heard."

"Are you frightened, Gabry?"

"No, not me. Just the little ones." Gabry's head wobbled as he lied. Gabry had no idea that his fear was so obvious.

"I'll tell a story," said Kasa.

He ducked his head as he entered Gabry's hut, and paused to let his eyes adjust to the windowless interior. Goatskins covered a sleeping platform of hardened mud. Kasa lowered himself onto it and tucked his legs up under him. He took the water jar that Gabry offered him, tipped it and let a drop of water touch his lips. This was a Sudanese custom: the host was obliged to offer water, the guest to take just a token sip. Kasa could vaguely recall his childhood years in the water-rich highlands, and both the scarcity of water and the pagan water customs irritated him, continually reminding him that this province of Kwara was not really part of his homeland. He was certain that whatever purpose was attached to his life had to lead him out of this limbo into the cool, airy heights from which he had fled as a small boy.

The hut wasn't large enough for all the boys to sit down, and several of them had to stand against the wall. Nearest to Kasa was the youngest, an emaciated, pot-bellied five-year-old named Wolde, who did not yet comprehend that his parents, killed by scavenging bandits, would never come to take him home.

"What will you hear?" asked Kasa.

A long pause, and Gabry suggested history.

"History, then. One of the oldest stories of all, the story of how the Ark of the Covenant left Jerusalem and came to Ethiopia." Wolde's head was bent, and Kasa stroked the downy scalp.

Kasa tried to give his voice a soothing undertone. It must have been effective, because he could sense the boys relaxing, their muscles loosening and their heartbeats slowing. The story he told was the familiar one of how Makeda, the Ethiopian Queen of Sheba, had been converted to the religion of Israel by Solomon, and then had borne Solomon's son; how this son, Menelik, had returned to Jerusalem to visit his father; how God had willed that Menelik should carry the Ark away with him when he returned to Ethiopia; and how he, Solomon's oldest son, had become the first ancestor of the house of Ethiopia's emperors.

The story held profound meaning for the older boys, who enjoyed hearing about contacts between Ethiopia and the broader outside world, contacts that were mythical to a landlocked people surrounded down through the centuries by unrelenting religious enemies. The story ended, and the fears of the boys at least temporarily forgotten, Kasa rose to leave. As he stooped to pass outside, he motioned for Gabry to follow him.

"How old are you?" he asked, placing his hand on Gabry's arm and drawing him close.

"Fifteen."

Kasa spoke in a conspiratorial tone. "You're older than these others. They look up to you."

"They do?"

"Yes. They try to follow your example." This was a kindly lie, since even the smallest boys looked on Gabry as an affectionate fool.

"The village isn't in any real danger," Kasa went on. "Ras Ali's men won't dare to violate the sanctity of our village. I know this, and you know it too." Gabry nodded his head importantly. "But I think you're right: the little ones are frightened, especially Wolde. I'm depending on you to help him keep his spirits up. Show them all that you aren't afraid, and they won't be afraid, either. Will you do that for me—and especially for Wolde?"

Gabry nodded and bowed quickly, his body blending into the blackness inside the hut. Kasa suspected that Gabry's evident fear was partly responsible for the boys' panic. He was pleased with his solution.

He hurried on through the village until he found the *debtera* in the farthest corner of the sown fields, working in the little plot that he cultivated for his own use.

The *debtera* was old, but not nearly as old as he appeared. The sun had dessicated his skin, and his eyes were moist and yellowed. He had laid aside his *shama* and wore only white trousers and the untidy turban that was the mark of a priest or a *debtera*.

Kasa walked up to him, dropped to the ground and, as was the custom, kissed his master's foot.

Without a glance, the *debtera* handed Kasa the leather pouch of *tef* seed. Kasa followed a step behind as the *debtera* skillfully pierced the earth with his digging stick, dropped in floury pinches of the tiny seeds, and pressed the clay back over them with his big toe.

They sowed in silence for a while. The *debtera*'s digging stick disturbed a snake which, camouflaged against the wrinkled ground by its pattern of purest white and purest black, had been invisible. It fled like a whip and then, the instant it stopped, was invisible again. The *debtera* did not see it.

"The children are very frightened," Kasa said at last.

The *debtera* reached a scaly hand into the pouch for more *tef* seed.

Kasa went on: "Ras Ali's scouts are only a few miles north of here, spreading out below the cliff, sweeping everything before them. They've sworn to kill every Christian in Kwara. Refugees have been passing on the road to the south. There was fighting last night, and our province governor—the *dejazmatch*—had to pull his soldiers back past us to Dungur. We're completely open to Ras Ali and his Moslem soldiers."

"Why are they fighting?" asked the *debtera*. His voice was weary.

"No one seems to know. Why do Ethiopians fight?"

"For any reason, for no reason. In this matter, Christians are no different from Moslems." The *debtera* had very little interest in the subject. They turned again. As they did, Kasa tried to catch his eye, but the old man's gaze was aimed downward. "This wadi will be full of water in another week," the *debtera* went on. "Perhaps it has already rained on the highlands. The waters will travel down the river courses toward Egypt and the northern sea, thousands of miles away. It is a great thing, this flowing of the waters. It is a wonder of God. And yet, in the midst of the destiny of the waters flowing past our eyes and on into distant lands, God will divert some water for us, the least significant people in the least significant corner of the world. It will pass by our own field, and we will capture a little of it in our humble furrows so that it will give life to the *tef.* And the rest of the water will flow on into the Sudan, where the pagans will drink it and mix it with clay to build their huts. After it joins the Mother of Rivers, the Moslems will drink it and water their cattle. It is the will of God that the water should be used by Christians and pagans and Moslems alike. I could dam the wadi, but the will of God is far too great. The water would overflow my feeble dam and wash it away. What man can thwart the will of God?

"Many centuries ago, God willed that the Romans and the Ethiopians should rule the world together. He then willed that we should lose that empire and be surrounded by enemies, so He sent the Prophet of Islam. But He willed that we should live on as the only true followers of God and His Son, as His Chosen People, so He softened the heart of the Prophet of Islam toward us, and the Prophet of Islam said to his people that there was no *jihad* against the Ethiopians. What man can thwart the will of God?

"Now God wills that the land should be ruled by war lords who find delight only in killing, and that one Ethiopian should fight another. And I ask you again: what man can thwart the will of God?"

After so many years under the *debtera*'s control, Kasa was well at-tuned to his dogmatic, semantic logic: have faith, take the tenets of the Church literally, all will be as it is meant to be. That way of dealing with life lacked any hint of the real poetry that comes from the soul but nonetheless, for Kasa, struggling with the contradiction between his own self-importance and the inevitable proofs of his own insignificance, the unalterable black and white of the *debtera*'s answers had a certain attraction. As a young boy he had adopted the teacher's logic as his own, but now, suddenly and for the first time, a peculiar inspiration led him away from his teacher. Kasa sensed too much at stake—even more, much more, than the safety of the children—for him to accept the *debtera*'s words blindly. Afraid he would falter if he hesitated, he blurted out rapidly, "You're wrong. We should hide the children." He swallowed hard and braced himself for his master's wrath, but the *debtera* said nothing, and kept his eyes on the ground. Kasa wanted to demand an answer, but the words wouldn't come.

They finished sowing that row and the next. The black-and-white snake whipped away again and vanished once more into the tortured ground. The *debtera* still hadn't seen it.

Finally, the *debtera* turned to face Kasa. There was no anger in his eyes, only curiosity and bemusement, and behind them another more disturbing emotion.

"Seventeen is not such a great many years," the *debtera* began, but he dropped his eyes before his student's persistent stare. Kasa turned away. The *debtera* continued, still scoffing but less sure of himself: "You are little more than a child yourself, and yet you would protect the children from the armies."

Kasa looked suddenly back at the *debtera*. "Why are you afraid of me?"

"I don't fear you."

"It isn't fear, exactly. It is closer to awe, or disbelief. I see it in your eyes, I hear it in your voice, I feel it in the air between us."

The *debtera* reached out and fingered the *mateb* that encircled Kasa's neck, withdrew the hand and touched his own. "We Ethiopians wear the *mateb* as a sign that we are different from the Moslems, from the Jews, from the worshipers of trees and rivers and the sun. But you, Kasa, you are different from the rest of us who wear these blue strings. I don't understand what I see when I look at you."

"I am a Christian, too."

"A Christian, yes, but unlike the other boys. Perhaps it is because you are the descendent of *rases* and *dejazmatches*. The great Meru was your father's uncle."

"My whole family was destroyed by Ras Ali. I'm alone, no different from the other orphans who are here."

"But different blood flows in your veins. You may even carry the blood of David and Solomon. And who else among the boys has felt the urge to travel into the Moselm lands? To learn to speak Arabic? To learn to ride a horse and shoot a gun?"

"These things came naturally to me," mumbled Kasa. He had never told the reason, and could not speak of it now.

"You've always been unique. As a young boy you brought a great spirit of submission to your faith, but it was always mixed with so much pride that I couldn't understand how you reconciled the two within yourself.

"Lately, your words have carried an inner certainty. You walk like one too sure of himself, or like one who knows more than the rest of us, who knows that he has reason for his sureness.

"The others have always admired you. When you left for the Moslem lands, it was almost impossible for me to keep the rest from following you. But you are too distant for them to love you. You have no friends, and I doubt whether you ever will, though you could have all the devoted followers you might desire.

"That blue string marks you as a Christian, but I think it means something else for you than for the rest of us. I believe there is a chance that God has marked you. Do you think you've heard the Voice of the Spirit of Prophecy?"

Startled that the *debtera* should know enough to ask that question, Kasa let the bag of *tef* seed slip from his hand. He knelt quickly and collected his thoughts as he scooped the powdery seeds back into the bag. "It speaks to me sometimes," he said at last as he rose to confront the *debtera*. "I hear it when I walk alone on the cliff, and in my dreams. It usually only confuses me, but I always have the feeling that in time I will be wise enough to understand it. I understood it clearly only once, and that time I obeyed it, and traveled to Khartoum and Kassala and Kordofan with the caravans. As I traveled, the Voice drew my attention especially to the works of the Egyptians—their magnificent towns, their garrisons, their armies and cannons. I saw, too, how the Europeans helped them, and I wondered why our emperors do not make use of the Europeans." Kasa hesitated. He was afraid that if the *debtera* thought he was presuming too much, then the master would refuse to share his knowledge with him. Kasa felt a desperate need for that knowledge, so he attempted to convey an impression of humility by averting his eyes and shuffling his feet. He studied the chalky folds of the *debtera*'s turban. "I've heard the name 'Theodore' many times. Once I had a dream in which I saw myself walking. There were great mountains all around, and a deep river gorge, and a lake many miles across. I was in the highlands. A fog rolled around me and obscured my sight, and when the fog lifted, I was away from the lake, but there were still the mountains and the river gorge. I saw myself on a flawless white horse. There were silver drums before my legs on either side of the horse. A man held a red parasol over my head, and another held a banner with a crowned lion, the Lion of Judah."

"The regalia of the emperor."

"I recognized them. There were thousands of people following me. I wore a white robe with a band of scarlet at the hem. The robe covered me up to my eyes. I knew that my name was no longer Kasa, but Theodore."

"Have you heard of the prophecy of the Emperor Theodore?" asked the *debtera*.

"I may have. I've heard hundreds of prophecies. I can't possibly remember them all."

"It is written in the most ancient of all books, the *Fikkare Iyesus*, that the Lord Iyesus promised that after a time of war and corruption and the rule of infidels, He Himself would bring to power a Christian emperor named Theodore, who would rule Ethiopia in peace and righteousness. During Theodore's reign, the wrath of God is to be turned from the nation. Joy, contentment, and the fear of God are to return to the hearts of men. Ethiopia will move into a new age of prosperity.

"There are those who claim the time of war and corruption is the *Zemene Mesafint*, and they look for the reign of Theodore to begin soon." The *debtera* was referring to the "Age of Princes," the name that was already being given by Ethiopian historians to the past hundred years of Ethiopian history. The power of the emperor had fallen to less than nothing, and mighty feudal lords, called *rases* (among whom the Moslem Galla, Ali, who controlled the current emperor like a puppet, was supreme at the moment), ruled their own fiefs and constantly warred on one another. "Perhaps it is now, after a hundred years of the rule of the *rases*, that Our Lord intends to bring Theodore to power. Perhaps the Voice of the Spirit of Prophecy is telling you that you are to become the Emperor Theodore."

Kasa's impulse was to pretend that he didn't believe what the *debtera* was saying, but that was all a protest would have been—pretending. In his mind, the prophecy of Theodore tied all the mysteries together. He knew he was to become the Emperor Theodore. It was as if he had heard the prophecy long ago and then forgotten it, and the *debtera*'s retelling had brought it back as clearly as ever. "What should I do?" he asked.

"Do? Why should you do anything?" asked the *debtera*. "You are only seventeen. It is a young age, an age for patience. The *Zemene Mesafint* has waited a century already, and it will wait another century if it has to. God has many years in which to fulfill your fate, whatever it is to be, and He has many years to reveal His Theodore. If you are indeed the Chosen, as we may suspect but may not know, then He will speak to you in His own time."

"Should I seek the Voice?" Kasa didn't dare to tell the *debtera* that he had been fasting for five days in hopes that his hunger, like Iyesus' hunger in the wilderness, might somehow bring him closer to the mystical experience he sought.

"God will speak to you in His own time," said the *debtera*. He took the bag of *tef* seed from Kasa and began to walk toward the village.

"But what about the children? What should we do?" called Kasa, and he caught up with the old man in a couple of long strides. "We should hide them in the groves above the cliff. The soldiers won't leave the road, and the children will be safe."

"Has the Voice of the Spirit of Prophecy spoken to you of the children?"

"No, but we should protect them."

"We will trust in the protection of the Lord," said the *debtera*, "as we always have and always will. If you are to be Theodore, then you must learn to wait and to trust in the will of God—for I ask you once again, what man can thwart the will of God?"

Kasas said: "God helps those who help themselves." He knew how feeble his response was.

"The church and the school are inviolate," said the *debtera*. "No one would dare harm us, for the wrath of God would be upon them."

"But they aren't even Christians," insisted Kasa, though he knew it was useless. "They're Moslems. They've sworn to kill every Christian in Kwara."

"God softened the heart of the Prophet of Islam toward us, and the Prophet of Islam said to his people that there was no *jihad* against the Ethiopians. By the power of God, the rain will fall, the waters will come, the *tef* will grow, and we will suffer through one more year on this hard earth." He started to walk away.

Kasa knew the teacher's insulated world of predetermined fates and helpless men. He had never thought to disagree with the man before, but now he knew the *debtera* was wrong. God determined fates, but men must bring them to pass through their own decisions, courage, and actions. There was room for conviction. Taking the children to safety would have been an act God would have favored.

That first moment, when he realized that he was right and the *debtera* was wrong, opened up a new world of possibilities. It was a world where he had to make his own decisions and take responsibility for his choices. He felt his manhood beginning too suddenly and too soon, but he was confident, with the confidence of a proud seventeen-year-old, that he was ready to handle anything.

Kasa followed the dry wadi toward the cliff. The ache in his stomach had stopped on the third day of his fast, and the mental urge to eat was gone, but as he climbed up into the narrow gully his head was light, and he saw in the black shadows fireflies that weren't there.

At the top of the sheer wall of the gully he came out onto level ground. Sparse groves of ebony, bamboo, banana trees, and coffee shrubs meandered along the cliff's upper edge. He settled himself in the shade of a low bamboo arbor.

His perch allowed him to look down on the village. A cross of ostrich eggs topped the church; white dust formed a patina over all the thatched roofs. He did not see anyone, but heard the soprano voices of the boys in the school. They were learning to recite one of the Psalms in unison.

Mirages drowned the deadly level whiteness of the Sudan. The wadi disappeared into such a mirage, reappeared a dozen miles away, and then vanished forever into the distant clay. The hazy line of the horizon blended without interruption into the blue-white sky. A black vulture floated overhead in gentle ellipses, its splayed-gap wings and neck forming a rude cross. Its patient circles took it farther away until it was a black spot moving against the sky.

Kasa was dizzy from his rapid climb up the gully. He could easily separate the voice of the *debtera* from those of the boys as they chanted down in the school. His hearing seemed to be more acute than it had ever been before. He found that he could focus on one particular voice: Gabry's. Then he heard Wolde's, and then one he recognized as belonging to a boy named Mamo. The sound was unnaturally clear. If he concentrated, he was sure he heard the sizzling heat of the sun on the clay plain, the oily friction of each stiff feather of the vulture's wings.

He pressed the palms of his hands hard against his thighs, worked to relax his muscles, closed his eyes tight and watched the bursting stars on the inner surface of his eyelids. The sounds diminished in an instant and were gone, the red stars blinked out, and he was isolated inside a shell. He waited for the vision to come to him. He tried to stretch out toward it, to grasp it and pull it in, but there was nothing to grasp, and his mind's tentacles closed on emptiness. There was no vision.

There was a word, however, though not really a word, either, for it seemed to enter his mind through his eyes and nose and skin as much as through his ears. The word was: TWELVE.

"Twelve what?" he heard himself asking. The answer came from all around, or perhaps from inside: TWELVE DISCIPLES.

Kasa did not move for some time after the state of readiness for a vision was gone. "What does it mean?" he asked at last. His own voice echoed hollowly and sounded unfamiliar to him.

There was no answer except the constant buzzing of the insects. The bamboo rustled sharply in the breeze.

The state of readiness seemed to have lasted mere minutes, but when he opened his eyes the first thing he saw was the crimson half-sun dropping below the horizon. His eyes turned to the village, and for a long moment he was certain the Spirit was distorting his sight. The clay plain, reddish-gray in the quickly waning daylight, lay below the cliff as level and as distant as ever. The wadi was a straight line of black shadow. In that last instant before he realized what he was seeing, the twists of smoke reminded him of columns of bubbles rising from the bottom of a cauldron just before the water boils.

The village had been leveled. Even the church was nothing but a pile of rubble around a pit where the sunken inner sanctum had been. The fires had consumed nearly all the thatch, and the smoke was only a reminder of what the flames had done.

Then the choking stench hit his nostrils. He felt an iron band pressing against his chest.

He was on his feet instantly, cutting across the level ground to the gully that fed into the plain. He plunged over clay ledges and around boulders on his way down, moving in a heedless delirium. All the time he was praying, not for his classmates and his *debtera,* but for himself: *Lord God send Your Spirit to be with me,* he prayed, *Iyesus, show me what to do.*

"Kasa!"

He jerked to a stop.

"Kasa!" A close-cropped head stuck out from beneath a shrub above him, and Gabry's eyes stared down.

"Stay there, Gabry," commanded Kasa, and the head was sucked turtlelike into the bush. Kasa took a run at the wall and snatched at a shrub to pull himself up. Five boys huddled among the ebony trees. One of them was crying softly, the side of his white *shama* soaked with blood.

Kasa pulled the cloth away from the wound, a thin, shallow slice across the ribs. It was very clean, and with luck there wouldn't be any infection. The boy, Abebe, was more in need of sympathy than medicine. Kasa tore long strips from his own *shama* and wrapped them around Abebe's torso and over his shoulder. "This will be your first battle scar," Kasa said as he worked. "You aren't a true Ethiopian until you've got at least one or two scars. I've got one, too." He pulled back his sleeve to show the jagged white line on his wrist. "From a nomad attack on a caravan, when I was traveling."

The tears finally stopped, and Abebe's clenched fists relaxed.

"We were in the fields," said Abebe, "just a few of us, looking at the wadi, wondering when the water would come. The soldiers came down the road. We ran to the cliff, and we climbed. They rode their horses right to the bottom of the cliff. They threw spears at us, and one hit me. Gabry pulled me up to the top. We hid in the trees, and they didn't bother us any more."

"Are there any others?" asked Kasa.

"We don't know," said Gabry.

"What about Wolde?"

Gabry dropped his eyes. "He was in the village."

"Stay here," Kasa ordered. "I'm going down to see if anyone is there."

Sobs welled up from deep inside Gabry. In a matter of seconds the others joined him, as if they had only been waiting for his cue—all except Abebe, who bit his lip to keep from crying.

Kasa talked to them softly until all their tears were gone. "You aren't boys anymore," he said. "You're men, and you'll have to act like men. I will need you to help me now."

He was certain, though, that it would be he who helped them, gave them courage, made their choices, guided them into the roles they were to play in the destiny they would share with him. He felt like a man pushing through the last branches of a forest in which he has been lost, knowing he is about to break clear onto the path that will carry him straight to his destination. He felt a sudden twinge of guilt at perching safe on the cliff while his village was destroyed, but he didn't allow himself to ask whether it was fear that had led him up there. No, he told himself, it was merely a preordained step toward whatever it was that awaited him beyond those last obscuring branches.

He slid into the gully and climbed down to where it let out into the plain. He held up a hand to shield his eyes from the last rays of the sun. A small dog was sniffing around the fringes of the village. Vultures wheeled patiently.

He crossed the fields and walked onto the higher ground of the village. A chicken flapped out of his way and a dog slunk past him in terror, but otherwise the animals had all disappeared. Only a few wispy columns of smoke remained. The huts had been pushed inward, and he walked between piles of crumbled mud and thatch ash. The wounds in the bodies of his classmates were jagged and gaping where iron spearheads had been thrust in and yanked free, and clean and thin where swords had slashed them. In the failing light, the dried blood appeared as black as their skins—invisible on flesh, darkly inescapable on their white clothing. Some of them were still moving, and one murmured Kasa's name, but they were beyond his ability to help.

The bricks of the church lay in a high, wide ring where the walls had been. The sunken inner sanctum, where the sacred *tabot*, which represented the Ark of the Covenant, had been kept and into which Kasa had never been allowed to see, was a waiting grave.

At the threshold of the church, which Kasa and his classmates had knelt to kiss whenever they entered or even passed by, Kasa found the priest and the *debtera*. A single spear thrust had cut down the priest. He lay coiled on the hard ground, still clutching the ornate iron cross he had always carried. Except for the massive cavity in his chest, he could have been asleep.

The soldiers had taken the *debtera* alive and cut off his hands and feet. His eyes were glazed, but the muscles in his dried-out forearms were still twitching.

"You wouldn't do anything," said Kasa fiercely. "You wouldn't let me hide the children, and now half of them are dead. You would only wait." He knew there should have been tears in his eyes, or at least a lump in his throat, but there was nothing but hollowness. The rapidly failing *debtera* was merely an object that would soon require dealing with; the razed village was just a pile of smoking rubble. The reservoir of feelings inside Kasa had been drained away. *I have no more life of my own,* he thought. *I am just an unthinking instrument.* The idea gave him some comfort. He wondered for an instant whether this emptiness was the natural condition of those selected for sainthood; whether the possession of a man by the breath of the Lord meant that there was no room left inside that man for his own humanity.

He pushed the thought away almost as soon as it formed itself, and again addressed the dying *debtera:* "It is all God's will, you said. But I tell you now, though you cannot hear me: this horror is a sign to me that I, Kasa who will become Theodore, should interpret that will. I will never again wait for anything or anyone. I will never trust anyone's judgment but my own. I will make up my mind and act. The responsibility is mine and mine alone."

He broke away from his teacher and sought out a low moaning that came from beyond the rubble of the church.

Three of the youngest boys had been captured alive. They lay on their backs. Dark streams against the white clay between their legs showed what had been done to them. Two were quiet, their young lives having flowed with their blood, but the third, Wolde, was still alert.

He cried out and tried to lift himself toward the arms of the white-clad, black-skinned angel that stalked the smoky haze and the human wreckage as passionlessly as any of God's servants.

The body was featherlight in Kasa's arms, and aroused no emotion in him. He could sense inside himself no shock, no anger, no pity. "God's most cherished," he said in the proper voice, soothing and comforting. "Beloved of the mother of the Lord Iyesus." As he carried the mutilated child out of the ruins of their sacred community, he kept repeating words of endearment. Wolde held on tight to Kasa's neck and pushed his face into Kasa's chest.

Kasa found the switchback trail to the top of the cliff. "Hold on," he said before he started up the dark, sandy trail, and Wolde's hands pulled at his neck, then relaxed and fell away. As he started up, he whispered, "I'll never leave you, little one. You'll always have a home with me."

Wolde's head slumped back. Kasa pressed his ear to the boy's lips. The even breathing told him that Wolde had just slipped into the most welcome sleep of his life.

From the top of the switchback to the gully was a quarter of a mile. What Kasa had to do seemed perfectly natural to him, as if someone else made the decision and performed the action. "My warriors!" he cried in his deepest, most mature, most resounding voice. "My young lions! My men! My brave ones!" He began to walk along the lip of the cliff above the village, crying out as he went, using the same kind of expansive phrases the *debtera* had always used.

Wolde never stirred, and Kasa's eyes never wavered from the dark line of the gully, but as he passed along the cliff he heard the rustling of branches, light footsteps, low whispers. He did not turn to look, but in his mind's eye he pictured crop-headed, frightened boys peeking out from under bushes and behind trees, moving out of their hiding places to fall in behind him.

The noise grew as he neared the gully. At the sound of his voice, Gabry and his four companions came out of the ebony grove toward him. Kasa laid Wolde in the bamboo arbor, then finally turned to face the boys. There were around fifty of them, more than half the population of the village. The number of bodies by the huts had seemed so great that Kasa was surprised to see so many gathered here. They ranged from five-year-olds to a gangling nineteen-year-old with a nervous tic who had purposely put off the last stages of his priestly training because he was afraid to depart alone to the highlands. Kasa had never been able to remember his name.

"We need food and water," he said. "Especially food, since water from the highlands will reach us soon. Who will go?"

Several of the older boys, but not the procrastinating priest, volunteered.

"Go up the gully to some of the higher villages. They'll be willing to help. If you have to, go as far as the monastery at Mirab Dibba, but don't fail to bring us food."

The night swallowed the boys, and the sounds of their careful footsteps soon faded away.

"Everyone should try to sleep. We march as soon as we have food. Gabry, stay on watch."

With three more of the older boys, Kasa descended through the gully and crossed to the village. Two of the boys climbed down into the inner sanctum of the church and began to scrape away the debris from the hard earth floor. Kasa and the third boy, a stocky, silent youth named Dengel, began carrying the stiffening corpses to the church and laying them side by side on the cleared ground. Some of the bodies had already been mauled by scavenging hyenas and jackals, and Kasa noted Dengel's stolid acceptance as they lifted their burdens. He did not flinch even when they carried to the church the boy who had shared Dengel's hut since they were both small children.

As they covered the village in their search for bodies, they found that the fires had skipped over half-a-dozen huts and one large storage building, and though the walls had been crushed, the thatch of the roofs was still light, dry, and brittle. They carried armfuls of it to the church, and when they had built a huge mound over the row of twisted bodies, Kasa blew a glowing bed of coals into fresh flames and lit the mound.

One of the boys had found the remnants of the eggshell cross that had surmounted the church, and as the flames spread through the pyre Kasa stepped close and laid the cross on the *debtera*'s body. He paused reverently until the flames, spreading slowly but evenly through the thatch, drove him back. His thoughts were not of his old master, but on the impression he must make on his three companions—how they would see his lack of emotion and his self-control, how they would tell the other boys, how the first beginnings of awe would be planted in their minds.

The hyenas and jackals scattered as Kasa and the boys walked out of the village, and then the scavengers closed behind them, chattering angrily as they hovered close around the food they could not reach.

The three boys joined the others on the top of the cliff, pulled their *shamas* tight, and drifted off into exhausted sleep. Kasa went to sit at the edge of the cliff. The fire had reached its highest point; it crackled yellow at the pinnacle, but the bottom, just at the level of the bodies, was a liquid crimson. There were dull bursts and flashes of brilliant light as superheated skulls exploded; white balls of fire shot into the air and vanished instantly. The entire plain was black, but almost directly over-head the flat white moon shone clearly. Kasa hoped to hear the Voice of the Spirit of Prophecy, but was not especially disappointed when he heard only the breathing and shifting of the boys and the snapping of the great fire. He still felt empty inside, and he was sure that there was nothing he as an instrument could do now except follow the inclina-tions, certainly inspired by God, that came to him. This lack of personal control was reassuring.

Footsteps crunched behind him. Someone sat on the ground.

"How is Wolde?" asked Kasa, without turning.

A long silence, then Gabry said, "Still asleep."

"You can't blame yourself," said Kasa. "I asked you to cheer him up, not to protect him. There wasn't anything you could have done."

"I shouldn't have left him."

"If it worries you, you'll have a chance to redeem yourself before long."

Beyond the limits of the firelight, the road below was invisible. It was not much of a road, little more than a caravan track jumping the wadi and bypassing the field and village, and paralleling the cliff for several hundred miles in both directions.

"The soldiers came down the road from the north," said Gabry, evi-dently seeing Kasa's head sweep along the line of the road.

"Did they go on to the south?"

"I suppose. I was hiding. We were all hiding."

"How many were there?"

"Very many. A hundred, maybe more. All on horses. Some had guns . . . What's that sound?"

"The water."

They listened. Within a minute, the distant trickle that Gabry had first heard mounted to a hissing, roaring wave of sound. It came nearer, and then it was beyond them, and still behind them, and everywhere along the course of the gully. The plain was becoming visible under the light of the moon. A straight black snake with a foaming white head appeared, and slithered away until it filled the wadi for as far as they could see.

"Look at it!" cried Gabry. He was at the very lip of the cliff now, pointing down to where the water had already overflowed the irrigation furrows and submerged the field. "That ground has been dry ever since I came here. There's never been enough water to reach that far."

"There's never been this much water in our lifetime," said Kasa. "There was never this much water in the *debtera*'s lifetime. No one since Noah has seen a flood like this one will be."

"You knew the water was coming tonight." Gabry, realizing it suddenly, sounded almost accusing. "You told us it would come. You *knew*."

"I knew," said Kasa mildly, though he wasn't sure whether he had. "Watch how it floods the whole plain."

Gabry sat down again closer to Kasa, as if whatever power Kasa had could protect him.

The water churned in the wadi. Beyond the flooded field white fingers of water oozed out, formed swirling pools on the hard clay, made contact with other streams. Water filled the low ground between the cliff and the village and made a shallow lake. Another lake had formed in the plain beyond the village, and the two lakes hesitantly joined together, a union that turned the village into a subtly glowing island. The vast clay plain of the eastern Sudan had become a six-inch-deep sea.

"I've never seen that much water," breathed Gabry. "I didn't know there was so much in the world."

"The flow will ease off soon," said Kasa, "but it will be a day or two before the flood goes because the earth is so hard. The soldiers will find high ground and stay there."

"The soldiers? What about the soldiers?" Gabry's voice was a confusion of emotions.

"Get some sleep," said Kasa. "The food will be here soon, and then we'll march."

"March?"

"Sleep now, Gabry. Sleep."

Looking down on the great waveless ocean, Kasa prayed for guidance —not for the next two days, which he was sure he already saw clearly, and for which all the decisions had been made, but for the misty time beyond.

When the boys returned from the higher villages with sacks full of fruit and bread, they asked Kasa where they would be going.

"South."

They nodded their approval. "South," repeated one of them, and it was plain that they had discussed it and reached the same conclusion. After a long, wondering look at the watery plain, they stretched out on the ground to catch a few hours' sleep.

Kasa began waking the boys two hours before dawn. Gabry passed out food as they brushed themselves off and shook their stiff arms and legs. Kasa went to the bamboo arbor and broke off four bamboo poles, two long and two shorter. He lashed them into a rectangular frame and stretched his *shama* and Gabry's across it to make a crude stretcher. As he worked, the boys crept near. They watched him patiently. Their whispering was like an uncertain wind through the bamboo. One low voice was particularly insistent. It belonged to Mamo. He was retelling a story, part of which he must have heard from Gabry: he reminded the other boys of how Kasa had told them the water would come down, though it was still fifty miles up the gorge; how he had told Gabry what a great flood it would be. In the retelling, the story took on greater dimensions than it had really had. Eyes turned toward Kasa, then glanced quickly away.

So this is how legends begin, thought Kasa. The creation of the man named Theodore would have to begin in just such a way. He marveled that it happened so easily and naturally, and how completely removed he felt from the person about whom Mamo was talking. This Kasa who had predicted the flood was some distinct other person, just as Theodore would be someone else.

Gabry brought Kasa a loaf of bread. Kasa only shook his head and waved it away. Gabry stammered that Kasa had to eat. Kasa waved it away again. Gabry slipped off.

"He doesn't eat," came Mamo's persistent whisper. "What happened to him?"

Kasa lifted Wolde onto the stretcher. Wolde moaned and twisted, but slept on. Kasa and Dengel took the poles and started toward the switchback trail. They descended to the plain slowly. The stretcher bumped and jolted, but Wolde, still in his deep sleep, did not move. The trail was bone-dry and gritty, but their last step was into ankle-deep water. It was pleasantly cool, and not even the tragedy of the previous afternoon could affect their enjoyment as they splashed themselves and one another.

Kasa passed off his end of the stretcher to Gabry, dipped his hand into the water, and brought it to his mouth. It was foul with the rotting debris that the torrent had washed down from the highlands, but all the springs of the plain would have been polluted by the flood, and this thick, bitter liquid was all they were going to have.

They marched in an elongated wedge, with Kasa, Dengel, Gabry, and the stretcher always in the lead. Sometimes the water barely covered their feet, sometimes it was up to their waists. After the moon set, they went on by starlight. The sun teased them at first, letting them know it had risen long before it finally cleared the shadow-gray cliff and shone down on them at full strength. It warmed their skin, then started them to sweating. It sizzled through the day, and its broken white reflection strained their eyes.

They held the stretcher up all day long. Wolde was jostled constantly and once, through a clumsy exchange of carriers, was almost dumped into the water, but he didn't stir. Gabry confiscated *shamas* from other boys and shielded Wolde from the sun with them.

They couldn't see the road, but it was easy to follow. Kasa had followed this route with the caravans, and he knew it paralleled the cliff for many days' journey. The cliff was a constant wall fifty yards to their left, with only occasional wadi gorges to break its smooth sandstone face. By late afternoon, the cliff dropped in height and became less steep. The contour of the land led more water to this region each year, and the groves of bamboo and ebony and banana trees thickened above the cliff and in places even extended onto the plain. The first baobab trees grew here. The sun approached the horizon, and the boys tilted their heads toward the cliff to rest their bloodshot, weary eyes.

Just when Kasa knew the troop of boys could not go much farther, when the first feathers of doubt began to tickle at his certainty, he saw the faint, shimmering haze for which he had been waiting. Though it was at least two more miles ahead and very dim, it was unmistakeable.

Gabry was at Kasa's elbow like an eager hound. "Why are you stopping?" he asked. He strained to follow Kasa's line of sight, but, not knowing what to look for, he couldn't see anything. "What do you see?"

"They're up ahead," said Kasa, and his words were repeated in a hushed, rolling murmur and taken as another sign of his singularity.

"What are we going to do?" asked Gabry. As he put the question into words for the first time, he finally seemed to realize what they had come to do; but Kasa surprised him and said, "We're going to sleep."

Kasa and Dengel clambered with the stretcher up the slope into the thickest forest that most of the boys had ever seen. They swallowed hasty mouthfuls of bread and then sank to the ground. There had been no tears or complaints from anyone all day, not even from the youngest. They accepted the order to sleep without questioning what tomorrow might bring. Kasa was sure by now that they would follow him blindly wherever he led.

When all of them were still, Kasa started south along the cliff. The moon had not yet risen, and the trees around him were just darker segments of the night. It was not easy to pick a safe path, and he went slowly.

Someone stumbled behind him, pushing through the low branches. Dengel materialized out of the gloom and stopped three paces away.

"It's been a long day," said Kasa. "You should sleep."

Dengel angled his head toward the faraway glow that showed through a break in the trees. "You aren't sleeping."

"That's different."

Dengel didn't move.

"Come on, then," said Kasa, and they started off again.

The cliff dwindled until it was just a gentle slope rising by easy stages toward the east. The flood had been absorbed into the dry ground, and the plain was muddy. The soldiers and their horses had found a dry, comfortable place on the bare crest of a low knoll. A thick fringe of trees encircled the knoll except on the eastern side, where the horses had been picketed. The campfires glowed like red stars through the trees.

Posting sentries was not a common precaution for Ethiopian soldiers, and such a small detachment as this would not bother with them, but Kasa and Dengel still crouched low and darted from one place of concealment to the next. They swerved around to the side farthest from the horses and then crawled silently on their bellies through the trees.

As Kasa had expected, Gabry had exaggerated the size of the Moslem force. There were barely twenty soldiers around the campfires, drinking from skins of *tej* and talking in low voices. Their weapons, mostly spears and swords with only two or three flintlock muskets, had been left carelessly around, usually out of easy reach. Among the Egyptian armies that Kasa had seen, such lack of discipline would have been unthinkable; these soldiers would have been an easy mark for well-organized troops.

When Kasa and Dengel were far beyond earshot of the knoll, Dengel whispered, "Are those the same ones who burnt our village?"

"Yes."

"How do you know?"

How do I know? Kasa asked himself, and the only answer he could find was that they *must* be the same ones.

And if they were not? It made no difference; it would all turn out as it was meant to be.

"Trust me. They're the same."

"What are we going to do?"

"Wait until the darkest time. Between moonset and dawn."

"Soldiers don't fight in the dark." It wasn't a protest, only a statement of fact.

"When we are soldiers," said Kasa, "then we won't fight in the dark. But for now, we are child monks out for vengeance, and we know no rules."

The moon was well up in the east when they passed an abrupt granitic formation, at the base of which lay an immense pile of crumbled rock. Dengel palmed a jagged hunk of rock twice the size of his fist and slapped it appreciatively into his other hand.

"We must remember this place," said Kasa.

On the walk back, Kasa suddenly felt his hunger and his fatigue, as if they had been lying in wait for him behind a shadowy bush and leaped onto his back as he passed. White balls of fire danced and burst, and his knees started to fold under him. He leaned into Dengel's solidness and let Dengel hold him up until his strength returned.

"You have to eat," said Dengel.

"I can't," said Kasa.

"We're all depending on you now."

"Not yet. Soon." He had had no vision, but his five-day-old fast still gave him a feeling of being in contact with the Spirit of Prophecy.

Kasa spent the long hours of the night alone. He allowed his thoughts to float around aimlessly, and though he didn't actually sleep he reached the middle ground between sleeping and waking. His aching, hollow body renewed and filled itself as he listened to the night sounds and the sleeping boys.

An hour before the moon set, he went to check on Wolde. The child's breath came like silk dragged softly across a baby's face.

Kasa woke Gabry, and then he watched Gabry wake the others. The moon-silvered forms rose slowly, turned and stretched, chewed a handful of bread and a dried-out piece of fruit, crept forward one by one to where Kasa sat cross-legged beside Wolde. The moon was very low behind their silhouetted heads. Some of them were very small, so tiny and frail that they had never had an angry thought toward anyone in their lives. They had spent their years in a world suffused with mysticism and religion. The language of the *debtera*'s religion was the language they spoke and understood, and the *debtera*'s symbols were the ones to which they would respond. Kasa shifted his position slightly so the moonlight would fall more directly on his face, giving him a vaguely mystical appearance. He timed the moon's setting carefully, waiting until its lower edge touched the horizon. He tried to imitate the tone the *debtera* had used when urging his pupils to work harder at their studies.

"The Lord brought down the greatest flood any of us have ever known," he began, "to keep the soldiers, our enemies, from traveling beyond our reach. He kept them on the straight road, so we could find them. As He caused the sun to stand still in the sky when Joshua fought the five kings, so He gives us a night without moon to do our work." He had timed the setting perfectly, and he knew that as the moon dipped below the horizon the light drained from his face. "He tells us in His book what we should do: 'And if any mischief follow, then thou shalt give life for life, eye for eye, tooth for tooth, hand for hand, foot for foot, burning for burning, wound for wound, stripe for stripe.'"

He knew that the power of his voice had never been greater in him. He was immersed in his own element, encouraging the boys, taking their lives in his hands and preparing to spend them to buy a promise against the future. The silhouettes squared their thin shoulders, tested their muscles, tensed their bodies.

"He gives our hearts courage and our bodies power. Remember Samson, how after the Philistines put out his eyes and bound him between the pillars with fetters of brass, he cried out to the Lord, 'O Lord God, remember me, I pray thee, and strengthen me, I pray thee, only this once, O God, that I may be avenged of the Philistines for my two eyes'; and the Lord strengthened him and he brought down the house on his own head, killing three thousand of his enemies."

"We have no ordained priest to lead us," he said, emphasizing the word *ordained* so he wouldn't have to let the anemic weakling, whose name he still couldn't remember, lead them in prayer and break the spell he was weaving. "But let us all pray that He give us power to avenge our priest, and our *debtera,* and our friends." They all knelt, and an unintelligible murmur floated into the dense night.

Kasa went on to describe the tree-fringed knoll and explained what he expected of them. He divided them into two groups, the twenty oldest to follow him and the thirty youngest to follow Gabry.

They walked in a slow, single-file column. Some of the boys were young enough to be afraid of the darkness, though none had been frightened when they heard what they were going to do. Kasa left Dengel to lead the procession, and he passed up and down the line, urging, joking, praising, jabbering at random. The line stayed together and made steady progress.

From the granite boulder they had a clear view of the knoll. The campfires had burned down to embers, and there was no visible movement. Kasa repeated his instructions until he was sure everyone understood. The boys picked through the rubble until each had a stone of the right size.

To the older boys, Kasa gave a last warning: "Don't fail to take the man you choose." And to the younger boys: "Be sure to yell. Make them think there are a thousand of you." And to Dengel he gave a last-second change of instructions: "Help Gabry with his group."

Dengel tried to protest, but Kasa had made up his mind: he would not risk Dengel needlessly, not now, not yet. "You're needed with the younger group." They faced each other for a few tense moments as Dengel wavered between obedience and anger. "I need you with the young ones," snapped Kasa, and turned away. When he looked back, Dengel had taken his place beside Gabry.

Kasa led the line down into the plain. There was not nearly enough cover for so many boys, but silence was all they really needed. They moved very slowly, one careful step at a time. Gabry led the second group, and far in the rear came Dengel.

With silent hand gestures Kasa positioned the older boys in a loose arc around the western side of the knoll. Behind the older boys, Gabry and Dengel were herding the younger ones into a compact group. Kasa's place was at the center of his boys' arc. He looked to the right and the left. Those within sight were watching for him to move, and he knew that his movement would spread like a wave down to the ends of the curve.

He touched his blue *mateb,* rolled it between his fingertips, crossed himself, waved his arm, and stepped forward into the trees. He felt a connection with the whole line, as if a string ran through them all. They moved forward like spokes converging on the hub of a wheel.

For the minute it took to pass through the trees, Kasa concentrated on picking his way without making a sound. He twisted sideways between two trees, and crouched just inside the clearing. He could see the soldiers now—about twenty of them, lying like dim gray lumps on the ground. He listened: one man snored into his blanket; a few small birds fluttered, and then were still; a bat flapped stiffly overhead; the horses jostled and snorted softly.

One by one, the boys' heads began to penetrate the interface between concealment and open space. They turned toward Kasa, found him, and waited for his sign.

He chose his own man, a long bundle of blanket with a bullet head at one end. The head rested on a block of wood to protect the man's hair, which he wore long and elaborately braided in the traditional fashion of the highland warrior. Kasa was close enough to smell the liquified butter the man had applied to give his hair a stylish sheen. The man's spear lay beside him.

Kasa felt a sudden tightening in his testicles. He couldn't drag his eyes away from that partially covered block of wood, either to look at his man or at his classmates. He began to panic.

The boys were waiting for him to raise his hand and drop it as a signal. His elbows were locked and his weight was on the rock, which seemed rooted in the earth. He knew he'd fall if he tried to lift a hand from it; his whole body was shaking. *I'm going to run,* he thought suddenly. *I'm going to run and run and run until I drop.*

But through the curtain of fear came the awareness of twenty pairs of eyes on him. He no longer belonged to himself, he belonged to those eyes. All those waiting eyes that had felt warm and comfortable before, back at their sleeping place. Now, each one was like a link of chain fixed to his body. There was no running. There was only trembling, and knowing his bowels were about to give way, and watching his legs shove him out without a signal into the open.

No one noticed he'd missed the signal. Twenty boys followed him.

His hands on the rock were the only solid part of him. He stumbled onto one knee, giving his hands enough direction as they fell so that the rock hit the soldier's head, splintering it like an eggshell. His hands, still clinging to the rock, were slippery with butter and hot with blood. They let go of the rock and in one fluid, unwilled motion reached out to wrap themselves around the polished spear shaft. His hands considered the spear's weight and balance. The iron head reflected no light. His legs jerked and he was standing. There was a thing to do now, if he could remember it. It was . . . it was . . . to scream.

Other boys shouted nearby. From beyond the rim of trees, the high-pitched yells of the younger boys rose as they charged and stumbled through the trees. Their voices were the voices of children. No one would be fooled. It wouldn't work. It didn't matter.

Dark figures ran through the clearing. Kasa ran with them. He jabbed into a swirl of gray and black and felt the spearhead hesitate for a brief instant against taut flesh and then break through. His foot slid into a fire pit, but he didn't feel the pain of the burn. He wrenched his foot out, and landed flat on the ground. He was up again, and in front of him were the horses, whinnying in their panic, fighting against their pickets, lacing the air with their hooves.

He turned, heard screams, knew his mistake. The older boys had run beyond the soldiers, and those soldiers who were still on their feet had gathered together against the trees through which Kasa had crept. There were only half a dozen of them left and they would not last long, but for now they were bigger and stronger and better armed, experienced in battle and fighting for their lives. The younger boys, led by Gabry and Dengel and armed only with stones, were plunging blindly out of the trees straight into the soldiers' spears.

There were fewer of the older boys, now, and their movements were unsure and confused. Kasa faced the tight phalanx of soldiers, saw spearheads waving and threatening. By now they must realize they only faced children . . .

Kasa drew back his spear arm and hurled the shaft into the soldiers. A man-sized bit of the turmoil froze, turned slowly, went down. Kasa stepped on a loose spear and almost fell again as it rolled under his foot. He picked it up and threw it, and was looking for another before the first had struck.

His hand found the rhinocerous-horn hilt of a sword. He twirled it as he ran toward the dancing spearheads, thrusting as he ran. The blade hit something solid and vibrated out of his hand. His arm hurt to the elbow.

He heard Gabry's voice nearby: "For Wolde and his never-to-be-born children!" The spearman in front of Kasa went down under Gabry's thrust so slowly that, by the dull gleam of a bed of embers, Kasa saw his expression change from rage to surprise to blank disinterest before he toppled over.

Kasa made no further effort to participate in the fighting. The panic had come back, and he was sure he couldn't move. The battle whirled darkly around him, but he only struggled to keep on his feet and watch it end. Everything became quiet and restful, not just the exhausted quiet that concludes a fight, but an ethereal, perfect stillness.

Fatigue enveloped him. Gentle fingers seemed to pull down his eyelids, to stroke his temples and his aching shoulders. He had the sensation of floating down to lie supine on the ground, then of being lifted and wafted through the air by a wind that murmured with the voice of children.

He expected the Voice, but it was a silent vision that came to him. In the middle of a black sky was a yellow sun. The sun burned with a great heat, but it left the sky and the earth in perfect darkness. It gave no light.

Another sun appeared. Twelve stars hovered around it, and Kasa knew that this sun was himself. The two suns fought a fierce battle, until

Kasa's sun and its attendant stars had chased the solitary sun out of the sky. Kasa's sun rapidly swelled to an enormous size, far surpassing the size of the defeated sun, but there was still no light to spare for the sky or the ground.

Followed by its twelve faithful stars, Kasa's sun hurtled around the sky for a long time. A small sun would appear, and Kasa's sun would dispatch several of its attendant stars to put it out. Kasa's sun or its stars always defeated the challengers, but they could not make a light that would illuminate sky or earth.

Then, from far away, a small pinprick of light appeared. It approached slowly, never hurrying, often hesitating, always coming nearer. It revealed itself to be a great sun, many times bigger than Kasa's. Clouds of tiny stars surrounded it.

A battle was inevitable, and it was just as inevitable that Kasa's sun would lose, but Kasa's sun relished the arrival of its enemy and nemesis, as if this meeting were the purpose of Kasa's sun's very existence.

The twelve stars, full of vain courage, charged forward to confront the new sun, and the myriad tiny stars rushed to meet them. One by one, the twelve stars burst into sparkling flames and vanished from the sky. Within minutes, Kasa's sun was alone. The cloud of stars approached his sun, but before they could reach it Kasa's sun bowed low before the great sun and willingly exploded.

When the sparks and streamers of the explosion were gone, all that remained were the new sun and its thousands of tiny stars, set like sequins against the velvet backdrop of the night. Slowly, then, light flowed from the sun. The sky passed from black to royal blue, and finally to the powder blue of the highland sky. The distant horizon appeared, a pencil-thin line of color. Light unrolled toward Kasa like a carpet, across a gently rolling flatland. An *amba,* a flat-topped mountain, appeared. Below the *amba,* a mud-brown river ran sluggishly through an incredibly deep gorge. The *amba* was a five-tiered monstrosity. A single trail led up from the river gorge to the highest plateau. The *amba*'s other sides were sheer, metal-blue, and at least a mile straight up from the flatland.

Kasa's sun had exploded directly over this great mountain.

For a long time after the vision had disappeared, Kasa lay in total darkness.

At last, he heard the faint rattle of wind through bamboo; smelled bamboo and earth; and when he shifted his weight he felt the coarseness of a blanket under his body. He heard himself whispering, over and over, "My twelve. My twelve."

Someone pressed a gourd to his lips and poured water that dribbled down his chin. He opened his grainy eyelids, and saw that it was Gabry who was trying to make him drink. Kasa took the gourd with his own hand and took a painful swallow. He looked at the twelve boys who stood there: among them were Gabry, Mamo, the almost-priest whose name he now remembered was Engeddah, Wolde. Dengel was not there.

"Something to eat," he said. A boy scrambled away and brought him a piece of stale bread.

They were in the forest where they had left Wolde. It was twilight, and the reddish glow of the just-set sun lingered in the leaves. "How long have we been here?" he asked.

"Three days and two nights," said Gabry. "We carried you here afterwards."

"Have you buried our dead?"

"Yes."

"Theirs?"

"Yes. And we have their horses, blankets, and weapons. We even have two flintlock muskets, but we don't know how to use them."

"I do."

Wolde was still on the stretcher, but he was sitting up and looking as healthy as Kasa had ever seen him. "What are we going to do?" Wolde asked.

"We can't stay here. We'll ride to the far north of Kwara and become *shifta.*"

"Robbers?" asked Gabry.

"We'll do whatever we have to do. The land is better there than any you've ever seen. There is more water, too. We'll stay together, and we'll prosper."

"Will we be warriors?" asked Gabry.

"Do you want to be?"

"I want to be whatever I have to be," said Gabry, but it was obvious that he was a true son of Ethiopia: his first taste of fighting had whetted his appetite for more. There would be others among the Twelve who felt the same way.

"If it is necessary," said Kasa. "This land of ours seems to demand it."

Kasa organized them as well as he could in the swiftly gathering darkness, rigged a comfortable litter for Wolde, and saddled twelve riding horses. Kasa slid onto one of them, but the boys hesitated, their hands on their bridles and their eyes on Kasa.

"What is it?" asked Kasa, but no one spoke.

It was Gabry who broke the tension. He took a few nervous steps to Kasa's side, bowed, and placed his lips on Kasa's foot. Kasa jerked it back. "Not for me," he whispered harshly. "That is not for me."

Gabry would not meet Kasa's eyes. He said, simply, "You have to let us."

"That is only for the priest or the *debtera.*"

"We have no priest or *debtera.* You have to let us."

Slowly, Kasa realized that Gabry was right: to lead effectively, he must take on the symbols of leadership. There was no point in the guilt he felt. He had no right to the homage, but it would be a necessity in their new life.

One by one, each of the boys bent to kiss Kasa's foot. Last came Wolde, dragging himself out of his litter and hobbling to Kasa's side.

Kasa endured the ritual, and then he said, "Let us ride." He turned his horse toward the north. The boys climbed onto their mounts and fell into line behind him.

They traveled in the darkness that first night. The sirocco rose in the morning, and by noon the wind and sun had returned the Sudan to its naturally bone-dry state. Dust filled the air. The sun was a ghostly, muted lamp. They wrapped layers of cloth over their faces and went on under the cover of the dust. What was left of their village drifted by. Through the tumbling dust it was not quite real; it resembled one of the shadowy, smoke-stained icons painted in a hidden corner of a highland cave-church.

In the manner of Ethiopian armies, Ras Ali's troops seemed to have achieved their objectives and then, having tired of the soldier's life for another few months, to have departed. Kasa and the twelve boys began to travel in the daytime and sleep at night. When he woke in the night, Kasa would go to sit on the cliff, from which he could stare out over the moonlit Sudan. The Spirit of Prophecy didn't come, but new reservoirs of strength, physical and mental, grew in him.

He gave much thought to the vision that had been sent to him. Two visions, really: the vision of the Emperor Theodore, and the vision of the suns and the stars. He examined them much as he would have analyzed a theme running through a Coptic parable. In the light of such logic, the two visions were mutually exclusive. Either he would fulfill the prophecy of Theodore and bring light to Ethiopia, or he would fulfill the vision of the suns and the stars and prepare the way for the Light Bringer from far away. One man could not do both.

The path to each future was the same: he must supplant Ras Ali, to whom all the other Ethiopian lords gave their nominal allegiance, and he must become emperor himself. In the tangled genealogies of an Ethiopia that was three thousand years removed from Menelik, the founder of the imperial line, Kasa's supposed family had claimed a distant relationship to the emperor. This was why that family, upon gathering a following of dissatisfied lords, had been so ruthlessly annihilated. If the *debtera* had been right, then the only survivor from that family had been one small son, who had grown to young manhood under the name of Kasa. For this reason, Kasa would have as clear a right to the Lion Throne as anyone.

When he became emperor—as he had no doubt he would, since God had apparently willed it so—then he would learn whether it would be his lot to become the Theodore of the *Fikkare Iyesus,* riding the flawless white horse, with the parasol and the lion-banner and the silver drums, bringing Ethiopia to the age of prosperity and the fear of God; or to die in an explosion of sparks above the great five-tiered mountain. Both fates were distant, prideful, and important. In bowing humbly before God's unfathomable will, Kasa had managed to elevate himself above his fellow men.

June 1864

Massawa

Soon after the sandstorm ended, a procession of porters brought furniture to the house, and with the porters came two personal servants. Dahon was a Massawan who spoke only Arabic. Rafaelo was from Goa, the Portuguese colony south of Bombay; he was a small, lively man who spoke Arabic, Portuguese, French, and Hindustani. Because Blanc lacked Arabic, Rassam took possession of Dahon as his manservant, and Blanc took Rafaelo as his.

Rafaelo and Dahon puttered around the house, pulling furniture one way, then another, unpacking trunks and cases. They spent more time tripping over each other and invoking holy names against each other's souls than in actual work, but gradually a home grew from the sandy, spidery room. It was small and totally lacking in privacy, but clean and livable.

While the servants worked, Rassam sat on a trunk and reread a letter that he kept in his breast pocket with the sacred letter from the Queen. The letter was a careful copy of the original, which had remained with Colonel Merewether in Aden; but Rassam's imagination had no trouble supplying the black ink that had run in spider webs through the creases in the original pages. The original had been written on an odd collection of papers apparently salvaged from a wastepaper basket: telegrapher's notepaper, purser's accounts, stationery with the official letterhead of H.M.S. *Weddington*.

At the top of the first page was a sketch of a man wearing a long shirt and loose trousers, standing in the traditional African herder's stance: one bare foot lodged against the inside of the opposite knee, his weight balanced against the butt of a spear. He had a great Semitic nose, fine lips, intelligent eyes, a high forehead, and long hair arranged in some

primitive style. Under the drawing were three block letters—*BOB*—
and then the letter itself:

29 April, 1864
2:45 A.M.
Aden Harbor, aboard H.M.S.
Weddington

Colonel Merewether,

My famous luck has held. I've parlayed my vice-consular credentials into
passage on a ship—and not just any ship, no dhow or sailing clipper, but
a modern steamer-of-war. That means I will not even have to wait out the
tide to make my exit. By the time you receive this letter, this dismal corner
of the world will have been obscured from my sight by distance and a black
cloud of coal smoke.

I know you were depending on me as your Ethiopian expert, but diplomacy—excuse the delicate phrasing—*turns my stomach.* I requested the
formal dissolution of my assignment to Massawa from Fitzgerald in Bombay. Assuming that I intended to use my release from Massawa to help you
here in Aden, he released me from service to the Government. Thus freed,
I will disappoint you all, and depart.

Sir, I pity Consul Cameron's plight, of course—do not misunderstand.
He is too good a man for the death that awaits him. We had a few hearty
laughs together. He was generous with his tobacco and liquor. He had
some courage. I ask no more of any man.

Cameron is the aging career officer who abandons the army, but will not
go home—a pitiful fixture of this British Empire. He was a hero in his
younger days—Kaffir War, Natal War of '52, Crimea. You had your exploits,
too, Colonel Merewether. The Beloochi sector in the Mutiny, wasn't it?
Brave men, but where are you now? Captain Cameron became Consul
Cameron, went to Ethiopia, waited patiently for a year and a half, and
wound up in chains. Colonel Merewether became political resident and
wound up in Aden—my God, man, do you want to spend the rest of your
days in Aden?

Well, as for me, Captain Speedy became Vice-Consul Speedy and waited
in Massawa for eighteen months, and when I die I hope to find hell a more
exhilarating place than that. So, I will become Captain Speedy again.
Gallantry suits me better than diplomacy. I rather fancy a cavalry charge
at dawn, sabers high, hooves thundering, savages fleeing left and right. I
am for New Zealand. They are fighting there, either for the Maoris or
against them, can't remember which, and I mean to be a part of it.

"The *Weddington* sails in an hour. What I can put down on paper may
be of help: I may be the only living Englishman (apart from those wretches
in the prison of Magdala), who has traveled to the Ethiopian highlands,
learned the Amharic language, and personally met the fantastic emperor
of the fantastic Ethiopians.

In '57, I found myself in an enviable position—a comfortable income
from a very proper family who were glad to see their black sheep on the
other side of the world, and no immediate attachments to either the
military or the foreign service. I decided to head into Africa to see the
sights and to bag a few elephants, lions, and buffalo. I left from Massawa
with fifteen Arab porters, bearers, and servants, and with a train of fifty

camels. I ran into a few Arab merchants, and sometimes we traveled together, for company and for protection from the Bedouins. The most common travelers in those parts of the Ottoman territories are agents of a merchant from Massawa named Paniotti. His men deal in every salable commodity in northern Africa—salt, hides, ivory, coffee and spices, precious woods and stones—everything except the most African and most valuable: slaves.

Curiously, this very evening I ran into one of Paniotti's people. I knew him in Khartoum, but tonight he denied he'd ever seen me before, that he'd ever been in Khartoum, that he'd ever heard of Paniotti. I suppose he was on secret business. That isn't uncommon in these parts.

I met Paniotti himself in Massawa. He is the most mysterious man I've ever met. He is a Greek, though no one knows precisely where he comes from. He lives in a mansion within the city walls. He is rarely seen, and no one is ever allowed into his house. His servants are from every place except Massawa. After a few months they vanish, and other, equally mysterious men take their places. Paniotti, too, sometimes departs without a word to anyone, no one has any idea where, and then reappears, months later, without notice or explanation.

I spent several months in Khartoum, where I heard fantastic stories about the Ethiopians. I was sure they were exaggerations, since the lowland Moslems have hated the Ethiopians (who claim to be Christian) for hundreds, perhaps thousands of years; but I was so intrigued that I decided to visit that strange land.

I exchanged my Arabs for Ethiopians and my camels for mules in Metemma, and I started up toward the source of the Blue Nile. I will not bore you with the geography of Ethiopia, pausing only to mention that the terrain is so convoluted that the country is perfect for the operation of small, private armies. It is said in Ethiopia that the man who cannot find a hiding place *deserves* to be captured and killed.

The sketch at the beginning of this letter is of the Emperor Theodore. I labeled it "BOB." The Europeans in Ethiopia—for there are a few, the occasional explorer, the rare demented missionary—among themselves call the emperor by that name. For some, it is a jest. For others, deadly serious, like a magical incantation to ward off the power of evil. Bell and Plowden used it when they were alive. Consul Cameron took it as a joke and used it in all his dispatches to me.

Theodore began his career as a common provincial robber chieftain, gained control of the country through alliances and treacheries, and forged a genealogy that gave him a claim to the emperor's throne. He was crowned in the mid-'50's.

Two Englishmen, Messrs. Bell and Plowden, had joined Theodore while he was on his rise to power. I was acquainted with them only slightly. They kept mostly to themselves and would never answer questions about their lives. They knew much of engineering and were engaged in several projects for Theodore—in fact, they had designed the fortifications at Magdala. They had great influence over the emperor. Mr. Bell was some sort of grand chamberlain and secretary to the emperor. Mr. Plowden had communicated with Whitehall, and just at the time of my visit, the Foreign Office had appointed him consul to the Ethiopian court.

I myself spent some months in the service of the emperor, trying to teach discipline to his troops. It was impossible. The Ethiopians are an ignorant, savage race of people. Most of the stories I had heard in Khartoum turned out to be true: the Ethiopian eats raw steaks cut from the flanks of living cattle. He desecrates his churches with wild dancing and singing, and I've heard that their solemn religious festivals often turn into drunken orgies. The Ethiopian only works hard enough in his fields to get him through another year on the verge of starvation, and then spends the rest of the time at his real life's work, the making of war on anyone and everyone.

The Emperor Theodore is exactly the kind of man you would expect to rise out of this morass of barbarity. He has the savage's love of pomp and ceremony and finery. He is cunning and suspicious. He reacts with violence to anything that he perceives as a threat to himself.

A single example may serve. As you know, I am a very large man, eighteen stone, and very powerful through the arms and chest. Years ago, an Arab comrade-in-arms gave me a fine sword of Damascus steel. The blade has such a temper that I've taken it through the thick of battle without so much as a nick or a scratch. And yet it sharpens so perfectly that I've copied the demonstration that Saladin gave Richard the Lion Heart: tossing a silk handkerchief into the air and slicing it in half with one gentle stroke. Some time after I had been given the sword, a Turkish officer challenged me to a contest to compare our strength. The contest consisted of hacking as far as possible through the body of a living sheep, *horizontally,* from chest to tail. The contest was a favorite among these Turkish soldiers (have you ever known a Turk who wasn't crude at heart?), and this particular officer was their champion. Needless to say, his blade stalled down in a hideous mess somewhere before the sheep's croup (do sheep have the same part-names as horses?), and mine slid through like a knife into butter, leaving hardly a speck of blood on my sword.

I've performed this feat on a few occasions since, when I needed to impress one particular audience or another. There are, dear Colonel, many people who respect such things. I split a sheep for the emperor of the Ethiopians, and he was so awed by my ability that he took me into his service at once and set me to the thankless task of trying to train his soldiers.

The Emperor Theodore is an insane despot, capable of any outrage against humanity, without conscience or scruples or dignity or knowledge of the laws that govern all civilized men.

And yet he is not without a certain charisma and presence. At the time of my visit, he was the undisputed ruler of his country, and he resided in the midst of a great ever-moving tent-city of his followers, numbering no less than one hundred thousand, of whom thirty thousand must have been fighting men.

I can add little to your knowledge of recent events. In 1860, Mr. Plowden set out en route to England with a letter from the emperor to the Queen. The contents of the letter were that Theodore wished to exchange envoys with Great Britain and to become the friend of the Queen. On the journey, Mr. Plowden was waylaid and killed by rebels. Theodore marched to avenge the death, but he stumbled into an ambush, and Mr. Bell, riding at the emperor's side, lost his life. Theodore captured the entire rebel band and put all of them, some sixteen hundred, to death.

At this time, with the completion of the canal through the Suez not long in the future (as they still tell us it is not long in the future), the Foreign Office was pursuing a policy of establishing friendly relations along the Red Sea; since Mr. Plowden had already opened the door to Ethiopia, the F.O. decided to send Consul Cameron to replace him. Consul Cameron reached Theodore's court in July 1862. At the same time, I took up residence in Massawa as Consul Cameron's assistant, with the title of vice-consul. Consul Cameron presented the emperor with a gift from the Queen, a brace of pistols, each with a silver plate engraved, "Presented to Theodore, Emperor of Ethiopia, by Victoria, Queen of Great Britain and Ireland, for his kindness to her servant Plowden." Theodore assumed that the *"kindness"* referred to the deaths of sixteen hundred rebels to avenge Plowden's murder.

Theodore drafted a second letter to Queen Victoria, and Cameron promised to take it to Her Majesty. For the sake of continuity, and because I have an English translation of the letter in my possession for which I have no use in the world, I insert it here. If the Ethiopians worried about such things, it would have been dated sometime in August 1862:

> To Victoria, Queen of Great Britain and Ireland, Beloved of God, from Theodore, Emperor of the Ethiopians, King of Kings, Lion of Judah, Heir of David and Solomon of the Hebrews, Slave of God.
>
> I hope Your Majesty is in good health. By the power of God I am well. My fathers, the emperors, having forgotten the Creator, He handed over their kingdom to the Gallas and the Turks, and the rule of it to pretenders. But God created me, lifted me out of the dust, and restored this empire to my rule. He endowed me with power and enabled me to stand in the place of my fathers. By this power I drove away the Gallas.
>
> Mr. Plowden and my late Grand Chamberlain, the Englishman Bell, used to tell me that there is a great Christian Queen, who loves all Christians. When they said to me this: "We are able to make you known to her and to establish friendship between you," then in those times I was very glad. I gave them my love, thinking that I had found Your Majesty's goodwill.
>
> All men are subject to death, and my enemies killed these my friends. But by the power of God I have exterminated those enemies, not leaving one alive, that I may get, by the power of God, your friendship. I was prevented by the Turks occupying the sea coast from sending an Embassy. Consul Cameron arrived with a letter and presents of friendship. By the power of God, I was very glad hearing of your welfare and being assured of your amity. I have received your presents and thank you much.
>
> I fear that if I send ambassadors with presents of amity, they may be arrested by the Turks. I wish that you may arrange for safe passage of my ambassadors everywhere on the road. I wish to have an answer to this letter by Consul Cameron, to whom I am entrusting it, and that

he may return to conduct my Embassy to England.

Do you see how Islam oppresses the Christian?

Before Cameron had left for England, he received instructions from the F.O. to go down to Kassala in the Egyptian Sudan to inquire after cotton. It seems that the war in the United States had caused a shortage, and Cameron was to see whether African cotton might be a substitute. Now, Kassala was the home of Ethiopia's blood enemies, but Consul Cameron, good old soldier that he is, never protested. He sent the emperor's letter by messenger to me at Massawa, and then went merrily off to the Egyptians. I forwarded the letter to Earl Russell at the F.O.

Consul Cameron returned to Ethiopia after seventeen months in the Sudan. He sent word to me that the emperor was enraged and suspicious, but that he was looking forward to an answer to his letter, and that letter should restore Cameron's position. A young Irish gentleman, Laurence Kerens, brought the next dispatches to Cameron. There was no letter from the Queen, but there was an instruction for Cameron to abandon the mission to Ethiopia and return to Massawa.

I did not hear from Cameron until 22 April, one week ago today. A courier, a young Ethiopian lad in Consul Cameron's employ, smuggled out a note. The note reported that Cameron, Kerens, and all their people had been seized, tortured, put in chains, and thrown into the prison at Magdala.

After a month, Theodore seemed to have vacillated, as if he had suddenly realized that he ran the risk of bringing down on his head the armed might of the British Empire. He told Consul Cameron that he would release the prisoners if the consul would sign a document promising that Great Britain would take no vengeance on him. Cameron, our honorable, good, dull-witted old soldier, refused to sign.

Soon after this, the note arrived. I've passed it on to you and do not have a copy, but I recall the closing line exactly: "There is no hope of my release unless a letter is sent as an answer to His Majesty." Two points drew my immediate attention. First, Consul Cameron is in such fear for his life that he did not dare to refer to Theodore as "Bob." In the manner of men without the imagination to create their own jokes, Consul Cameron never failed to use the nickname. Secondly, I do not believe that anyone could have smuggled a note out of Ethiopia. Consul Cameron apparently thought he could manage it, but I have to think that Theodore, for some obscure reason of his own, wanted that note to reach my hands at Massawa. I leave you to cogitate upon the mystery.

For the first time in nearly two years, my duty and my desires were the same. I left Massawa at once and delivered the note to you.

I hear the steam whistle, signaling for visitors to disembark. A few last comments: the Ethiopian soldier is famous for his cowardice and his lack of discipline. He usually has just a spear or a sword. The few firearms in the country are flintlock or matchlock muskets. I would suggest that a cavalry regiment of our own brave lads should be able to reach the prison of Magdala, release the captives, and return to their starting point, either Khartoum or Massawa, within a matter of weeks.

But the nerve for this adventure will surely fail, and diplomacy will be decided upon. In this case, a soldier or an engineer should be sent as envoy. The emperor will respect no one else.

Now to find a boy to act as messenger, and then to find the stern to watch the Middle East sail away in a cloud of smoke.

One single parting word, Colonel Merewether. I do not know how this word relates to British captives and Ethiopian emperors, but I have an intuition that it is a word for you to remember. That word is: *Paniotti*.

Until we meet again, Sir, as we most surely will, I remain your humble and obedient servant,

Capt. J. Speedy.

Led by Rafaelo carrying a torch, Rassam and Blanc reached the open square in front of the sheik's palace. It was just a torchlit space of flattened dirt swarming with children, but coming into it was like standing in the full glare of daylight after many hours in a dark cave. The palace was a blocky, three-storied building made of the same coral rock as their own house. The story-high wall surrounding it left just a few feet of clearance between itself and the palace. The two guards at the gate had been playing chess in the dirt, but they snapped to attention as Rassam and Blanc passed them. A doorman, the first truly black African they had seen in Massawa, answered Rafaelo's knock. Sending Rafaelo down a side corridor to await his masters, the doorman led them down first one hall, then another. Each of them was lushly carpeted and hung with crystal chandeliers. A fountain played in a cool inner courtyard, and they could smell the fragrant flowers of tamarind trees.

They descended a winding staircase, then started back along another hall which ended in a small dark anteroom hung with somber tapestries. Another door lay ahead; the doorman indicated that they should take off their shoes and leave them with the others that already lay there. He gave them soft slippers to wear. They put them on, but the doorman still hesitated. Rassam knew the reason: they were to be delayed in this gloomy chamber in order to make the room beyond seem even more splendid than it was.

The doorman finally rapped softly on the door.

It swung open instantly. Brilliant light haloed an enormous shape. The man inside stepped away slowly, and they entered.

"It's like the *Arabian Nights*," breathed Blanc.

The intricate, mind-twisting patterns of Moselm art cascaded down from the ceiling and spilled across pillars and walls to end on the floor in swirls of interlocking designs. Incense and tobacco smoke misted the air. Low divans formed a circle on the floor, and a dozen men, all in robes and turbans, reclined or sat cross-legged on them. Baby-faced eunuchs with enormous thighs and tiny feet stood against the walls and slipped forward soundlessly to tend the guests and keep the hookahs filled with tobacco.

Like someone approaching through a dream, Abd-ul-Kerim came to greet them. His eyes would not quite focus, and his lisp was even more pronounced than usual. One of his cheeks was swollen, and when he leaned close to kiss Rassam's cheek, the envoy caught the pungent smell of *kat.*

He led them to an older Arab whose mouse-gray beard flowed over his white robe, and who held the mouthpiece of a woven hookah tube in his finely manicured fingertips. Beneath the beard, one cheek bulged like his son's. He touched the mouthpiece to his forehead in a lethargic salaam. "I welcome you to my humble home."

Rassam bowed formally and held out the packet of credentials he had brought for the sheik, including letters of introduction from the Egyptian viceroy and from Colonel Merewether. Sheik Mohammed took the packet in his free hand and set it aside without a glance.

"Sit, sit," he said in Arabic, his voice muffled as he spoke around the wad in his cheek. "Do not be so British. Always on your feet, saluting and bowing." He waved them down to divans beside him. "Your Captain Speedy, now, was not so British. He would smoke a bowl or take a glass with anyone."

Rassam introduced himself and Blanc. The sheik submitted to the passing around of formal compliments, but as soon as he could turned to a more agreeable subject. "Do you chew the *kat?*"

"I do, with pleasure," answered Rassam. He looked past the sheik to Blanc. "The sheik wonders whether we would like to chew *kat.*"

Blanc gave him a curious look. "I'm afraid I don't know what that is."

Rassam was amazed that anyone who had lived for any time at all in Aden could not know about *kat.* "It's a drug, somewhat like opium," he said. "I will chew it, because I enjoy it. You are not under any obligation to try it if you don't want to."

"Are these gentlemen chewing it?"

"Yes, but no one will think badly of you if you don't."

"I will try it," said Blanc. "Want to start off on the right foot, you know."

Eunuchs brought them small, leafy branches of the *kat* bush. Rassam showed Blanc how to strip off the tiny red leaves at the tips, the tastiest ones, and form them into a wad in his cheek. Blanc winced at the acidic taste. Tubes that connected to the hookahs in the center of the circle were handed to them, and Rassam settled himself into the quiet reverie shared by all the men—tobacco smoke, *kat* leaves, resiny red wine. "*Allah kerim,*" said the sheik as he poured himself a glass of wine; "Allah forgives."

The *kat* took effect slowly, pleasurably. Rassam felt light and detached; the room became smaller and warmer; the colors began to melt and glow. He looked across at Blanc. Blanc's eyes were glazed, and he was exaggerating the movement of his hand to hookah stem or wine jug.

Rassam roused himself. "I thank you for the use of the house, the furniture, the servants."

Sheik Mohammed waved away the thanks with his hookah stem.

"I am told that storms like the one this afternoon are frequent along this coast," said Rassam.

"Was there a storm?"

"A sandstorm. In the middle of the afternoon."

"I was unaware."

Rassam noticed movement beyond Blanc now, and a high-pitched, wheedling voice said, "The sheik was occupied with governmental business this afternoon. When he is busy, he is often unaware of what happens outside." The man's body was so immense and pliable that it molded perfectly into the curve of the divan, and great folds of smooth flesh hung over onto the floor. It was impossible to judge his age: somewhere between forty and sixty-five, Rassam would have supposed. The voice identified the man as a eunuch; his accent was Turkish.

"This is Ismail Tasfay, my administrative assistant," said the sheik.

Ismail Tasfay salaamed with a dimpled, glittering hand. His eyes were filled with the drowsy superiority of an Egyptian cat goddess.

Rassam knew the relationship between the two men at once. Sheik Mohammed had the hereditary right to Massawa, but Ismail Tasfay ruled it. Ismail Tasfay would have been sent from Constantinople itself; most likely, deputies of the Sublime Porte had been ruling Massawa for generations, perhaps for centuries. Those were the compromises at which Abd-ul-Kerim had hinted so bitterly.

"Such is the burden of power," said Rassam to the sheik. "Ruling Massawa must be very demanding."

"Very," agreed Sheik Mohammed, and Ismail Tasfay added: "The sheik works very hard. He is very concerned for the wellbeing of his people."

"Is there great trouble with the locusts this year? Are they affecting food supplies?" asked Rassam.

Sheik Mohammed stroked his beard and stared at the floor like a schoolboy caught with his lesson unlearned. Ismail Tasfay inclined his bulbous head forward and answered for him: "We are bringing shipments of food from Jedda to help feed the people." Ismail Tasfay's overblown politeness held an undercurrent of hostility toward Rassam. "If you have any difficulty getting sufficient food, or of good enough quality, I hope you will allow us to help you."

"I will."

"We wouldn't want you to be uncomfortable in our city. If there is anything at all we can do—"

"I will ask."

"Please."

Rassam turned his head and found Abd-ul-Kerim across the circle of divans. He was staring at Rassam with a look that said, "Do you see?"

The sheik introduced each man around the circle to Rassam. Beyond Ismail Tasfay was Rashid ibn Ali, the Turkish commander of the garri-

son, the man Abd-ul-Kerim hated. The way he leaned close to hear
Ismail Tasfay's words, the way he nodded at each sentence and aped the
giant eunuch's expression, told Rassam all he needed to know. The man
was a fawning creature of Ismail Tasfay. In any Massawan equation, he
would rank only as an unthinking pawn.

The relationships were all too obvious, Rassam decided. Two men, a
civil and a military leader, had been sent to rule Massawa. The nominal
sheik had accepted them completely, but his son had too much fire in
his blood to take the situation calmly.

Rassam wondered when Abd-ul-Kerim's anger would burst into
flame, and who besides the two Turks would be burnt.

The rest of the guests were minor officials and merchants of various
races, plus one thin, heavy-browed European whose turban struck a
discordant note above metal-framed eyeglasses. The massive lenses
magnified the eyes, which were as gray as fog, and sucked them right
into the belly of the glass. He was introduced as the mysterious Panagiotes Paniotti. He bobbed his head in greeting and turned those enormous eyes away. He was neither smoking nor chewing *kat*, though he
sipped at a glass of wine.

The sheik snapped his fingers suddenly, and the evening meal arrived. The eunuchs set down silver platters of fruit, bread, cheeses, and
bowls of stew with fatty chunks of lamb in a spicy sauce. Each man spat
his wad of *kat* onto an empty plate provided for the purpose.

The arrival of the food had shaken Blanc loose from his dreams. He
watched the men spitting out their *kat*, and copied them reluctantly.
The bad manners appalled him. Still imitating the others, he scooped
up a piece of lamb with a flat disk of bread and tasted it. He was
pleasantly surprised. Rassam was amazed that Blanc could taste at all,
after his *kat*. "Mr. Rassam, if you would be so kind," said Blanc. The
words came out very slowly, evenly spaced along a pre-set trajectory.
"Tell the sheik that the beauty of his palace is exceeded only by the
savor of the meal he provides."

Rassam relayed the message to the sheik.

Sheik Mohammed laughed and said, "Please tell your friend that his
eloquence is exceeded only by the film of *kat* across his eyes."

To Blanc, Rassam said, "The sheik thanks you, and is pleased that you
approve." Then, in Arabic, he told the sheik, "I must agree with Dr.
Blanc. I've never seen anything to match this room, except possibly in
Damascus and Constantinople itself."

"In such a dreary place as Massawa, in such a distant part of the
world," said Sheik Mohammed, "one feels the need for a little luxury,
a little ostentation. No one knows this part of the palace exists, except
for a few chosen friends and my servants."

"I feel honored to be included among your friends so quickly."

"Of course. The secret adds to the beauty of the place, don't you
agree? It is a little piece of the old Ottoman empire, a fragment of the

glory that was and will never be again." He pitched his voice low. Ismail Tasfay angled his head across Blanc to hear more clearly, but he could not. The sheik seemed to be excluding the eunuch, not because he was afraid to express opinions about the Ottoman empire and the Turks, but because it was a private reflection that he wished to share with Rassam alone.

"But the Ottoman empire lives on," Rassam protested, though he knew as well as Sheik Mohammed that "the sick man of Europe," as the empire was often called these days, was only being held up by the vagaries of the European balance of power. Because Europeans expected every nation of the world to be like their own countries, the Ottoman empire had always been beyond their understanding. They wanted the Ottoman empire to be a political nation, and they wanted its ruling class to govern in the European sense: that is, to enjoy rule in exchange for fulfilling certain obligations to the masses, from whom their power ultimately derived. The Ottoman empire simply refused to fit European preconceptions, because it was not, never had been, and never intended to be a political state.

There was no sense of nationhood in this part of the world. A man belonged not to Egypt or Turkey or Arabia, but to Islam. The empire was only one of many threads running through the all-encompassing fabric of a world religion. The only functions of the ruling class were to tax the masses, to perpetuate itself, and to pursue power for its own sake. In such a political vacuum, it did not matter who the rulers were. A foreigner could rule just as well as a native, and a slave could rule as well as a free man.

The Ottoman concept of slavery had very little in common with, for instance, the slavery of the Americas. Slaves were freely used as laborers, servants, and concubines, but far more important was their use as soldiers and rulers. By the tenth century, the armies of Islam were composed entirely of men who had been enslaved as boys and raised as professional cavalrymen. They received the finest training in the empire, both physical and mental. They were proud of their status, for it was the only avenue toward wealth, power, and prestige. It wasn't uncommon for a slave-cavalryman to include in his name the price that had been paid for him.

Such a system is riddled with inherent dangers. The Imperial slave-troops, the Janissaries, who were taken from annual boy-levies among the Balkan Christian subjects of the empire, came to wield immense influence with the Turkish sultans. At the peak of the empire, in the sixteenth century, nearly all the important posts in the empire were held by Janissaries, and the sultan's grand vizier almost always came from their ranks.

The case of Egypt was even more extreme. The Mamelukes were first introduced to Egypt by the Kurd Saladin, who fought Richard the Lion Heart in the Holy Land and then ruled Egypt. Purchased as boys from their parents in Circassia and the Balkans and even in Turkey itself, the Mamelukes held absolute power in Egypt for six centuries. Having been raised parentless, they had no interest in family life. Their sexual pleasures were almost exclusively homosexual, usually with Mameluke boys. They perpetuated their ranks by purchasing new generations of boys. Their interests centered around the pursuit of power, and it was always the most ruthless Mameluke who ruled the Nile.

There was another hardly less important group of slaves within the ruling elite: the eunuchs. Castrated as boys, they were originally used as guards and attendants in harems, later as teachers, finally as administrators. The extinction of their sexual desires, or so the theory went, eliminated distractions and left the eunuch hungering after power alone. Palace intrigue became their hallmark. It was possible for a eunuch, with the right combination of bloodthirstiness, suavity, and luck, to rise to the rank of vizier, or even, once or twice in a century, to grand vizier.

These, then, were the politics of the Ottoman empire, not a nation-state, but a complex religious world in which curious groups of men followed their own paths, independent of other groups. The Arab explosion had fizzled in the first hundred years after the Prophet, and Islam's warrior and ruling class had come to be taken from other, northern races. The focus of empire had shifted from Arabia to Syria to Baghdad. After the Mongol Tamerlane sacked Baghdad in the 1300s, it shifted once again, this time to Constantinople. Egypt had been independent from Constantinople for hundreds of years, and though it became an official province of the empire in 1517, the sultan never had any real power over the Mamelukes and pashas of the Nile. In this nineteenth century, Egypt had shown herself to be more vital than her crumbling parent. Constantinople had lost the northern Black Sea coast to the czars and all the Balkans to independence. It still held most of the Northern African coast, Crete, Cyprus, Mesopotamia, the eastern Red Sea coast, a few outposts like Massawa on the western coast, and Egypt, but its hold on all these territories was growing increasingly tenuous. It had taken the French and English, worried over the growing power of Russia, to save the Crimea for the Ottomans.

In that same sixty-four years of the nineteenth century, Egypt had shucked off its Mamelukes; extended its control into the Sudan, where it had established the Pashalik of Sudan around Khartoum; and, using new slave troops from the Sudan, temporarily pushed the troops of the empire out of Syria and the Hijaz, the Arabian province containing the Holy Cities of Mecca and Medina. Egypt had relented in 1840. Syria and the Hijaz and Egypt had been Ottoman since then, and Massawa had been back under the administration of the Viyalet of the Hijaz, but Egypt still loomed as the most vigorous part of the empire.

Even Egypt, though, was coming more and more under the influence of the French and the English, and it looked as if it would be only a matter of time before the whole Arabic-speaking world was a European colony.

"Even now the empire is hardly more than a puppet of the new powers of the world," said the sheik. "France, Germany, Russia, Italy, your Great Britain, hold it in their greedy hands—and rightfully so, for they are the future. As we saw in the Crimea, it is only the desire of each to keep the empire out of the hands of the others that keeps the empire alive at all. They are the stronger, they have triumphed.

"It is only right that the empire should fall, but when the powers are through I fear the sum of the pieces will be less than the whole. Some good things—much bad, but much good, too—will be lost. Even I, as Arab sheik in a Turkish empire, will regret its passing. This"—he indicated the room and his world—"will be just a memory."

"And you, as an Arab sheik in a Turkish empire, will regret the passing of that empire?" asked Rassam. "Isn't it possible that it will mean independence for the outlying regions, including the Arabian lands?"

"That is impossible," said the sheik, "though there are those—you have talked with my son, of course—who might disagree. It is a simple fact of history that an Arab empire has never, and could never, survive. The nature of Arab civilization is purely abstract and moral and religious, never applied. A thousand years ago, we overran vast tracts of the world in an explosion of feverish activity, but we neglected that empire through aversion to routine. We had to seek the help of conquered subjects and outsiders to administer the provinces we had won. The Turks gained their foothold in this way. First they were our servants, then they became our rulers.

"The political theory of the Turks, I will readily admit, is as crude as that of the Mongols. They have tried every way they could to *uncreate* the Arabs. They legislated Arabic out of official existence. We Arabs could only serve by becoming Turkish. And yet we've never succumbed. We would not give up our fertile Arabic for their sterile Turkish. We have made a homeland of our language and our religion. We never forget that only we, the Arabs, are qualified to understand and practice Islam.

"To stay alive in the empire, some of us have had to compromise, to placate, or to put up no resistance, so that the powers that wish to oppose us will sweep harmlessly past. We have never lost our Arabness, but neither have my ancestors, and I despised our connection with the Ottomans, who were as inevitable in their time as the European powers will be in theirs. So I find it easy to say, truthfully, that I, even as an Arab sheik in a Turkish empire, will regret the passing of the life I have known and the substitution of one that may be no worse, but will certainly be no better."

"If the empire ever fails," said Rassam, lying diplomatically, "the world will be poorer for its passing."

"Yes, it will be a poorer place."

The sheik lapsed back into the *kat* lethargy, and Rassam took the opportunity to look around the room. Paniotti's unwavering gray eyes were fixed on Rassam; as if it would be death to alight for an instant, his hands moved unceasingly in hummingbird foldings and unfoldings.

Abd-ul-Kerim, next to Paniotti, was whispering to him. Paniotti listened without commenting or even looking at the young Arab.

"You are not English." The sheik was stating a fact.

Rassam tore his eyes from the avian hands. "British, but not English. I was born in Mosul, but I have been British all my adult life. I am almost completely British now. Though I recognize the proud history of the Arabs, I have chosen to attach myself to the equally proud history of the English."

The sheik was a better judge of character than Rassam would have given him credit for. He smiled indulgently. "And yet you seem to be quite at home here, Mr. Envoy of the English Queen, with your *kat* and your wine and your lying on a low couch being served by eunuchs. And I see that you take pleasure in letting your English friend appear a fool, by translating his stupidities exactly. An Englishman would never be so . . . subtle. The English have many virtues—conviction in their own rightness, determination, industry—but they have no subtlety, no grace, no sense of humor. I think you are still more a man of the East than you realize."

"Less than you think, perhaps," said Rassam.

"In any case, and in spite of my somewhat gloomy opinion of world affairs, it is pleasing to have a permanent British presence in Massawa again."

Rassam reverted to his careful business voice. "I apologize if there has been a misunderstanding about my status, Your Excellency." Ismail Tasfay shifted his bulk forward a few inches, and Rashid ibn Ali shadowed the movement. Rassam included them in his words. "I carry letters from the Egyptian viceroy and from the British political resident in Aden to you, asking your assistance in my duties, as you will see when you read my credentials. But I am not assigned to Massawa. For the present, the permanent consul for this area is still the consul in Suakin."

"Then, my dear new friend, what duties has your ever-imaginative government dreamed up for you to do?"

"I carry a letter from Her Majesty Queen Victoria"—his voice quavered slightly as he pronounced the sacred name—"a letter from Queen Victoria herself to the Ethiopian Emperor Theodore. My instructions are to do whatever may be necessary to secure the release of the British subjects he has made captive at the fortress of Magdala."

Obviously relieved, Ismail Tasfay rocked his bulk back. Rashid ibn Ali imitated him. The eunuch was visibly pleased that Rassam's assignment was Ethiopia—or was he pleased that the assignment was not something else? Rassam wondered what that something else might be.

"From Magdala?" asked the sheik. Stars gleamed suddenly in his cloudy eyes. He started to laugh, then frowned. "To secure the release from Magdala of the British subjects?" He turned toward the Greek merchant. "Paniotti!" he cried, unnecessarily loud. The vast gray eyes swung toward him. The hands still flew. "Paniotti, these men are not for Massawa. Can you guess what the British government has ordered them to do?"

Paniotti's accent was Greek, his tone mocking. "The British government is sending them to fetch back their fellow countrymen from the hands of the mad emperor of the mountaintops, of course."

The sheik cried: "Oh, Paniotti, you man of wisdom, you're always so far ahead of the game! I suppose you have already made plans to take money from these poor martyrs." He turned to Rassam. "You must take care with this Paniotti. He is a great merchant, a very great man of commerce, and a famous thief. His business connections encompass the world. He may even have contact with the Ethiopian tyrant."

"I do," said Paniotti.

The sheik placed his fists over his ears. "The Ethiopian is the enemy. I do not want to hear things that I must not hear."

Ismail Tasfay and his creature were very relaxed now, and they seemed to be enjoying themselves.

"You have nothing to fear from me, Mr. Rassam," said Paniotti. "I never steal from the dead."

"A little melodramatic, don't you think?" said Rassam.

"Less so than you might imagine," said Paniotti. "That applies only if you go up to him, of course."

"Mr. Rassam, what are they saying?" said Blanc, his voice thick. "I can tell they are talking about us."

Rassam explained what Paniotti had said. "Tell him he gives too much credit to a savage chieftain on top of some mountain or other," Blanc said. "Tell him the emperor will not dare harm envoys of the British crown."

Reluctantly, Rassam translated the words into Arabic, though he had the feeling that Paniotti understood English.

Speaking carefully in Arabic to hide from Blanc the drift of what he was saying, Paniotti told Rassam, "He is a fool. And if you agree with him that the British crown means so much to the emperor, then you are ill-informed, or you have too glorified an impression of British prestige in the hinterlands of the world . . . or you too are a fool. Many pardons, but I must speak truthfully." Rassam nodded agreement, but felt anger welling up inside. "Have you not heard the stories about him?" asked Paniotti. "If you ask the Massawans, they will say he can hear what anyone says about him, no matter how far away."

"It is true." Each of Sheik Mohammed's words was emphatically visible, as smoke leaked from his lungs and floated away in a chain of word-puffs. "He is listening to us right now."

"Do you really believe that?" asked Rassam.

"It is true," repeated the sheik, and Rassam saw that he did believe. Other Massawans around the circle were also nodding agreement.

Paniotti went on: "His fortress, Magdala, is supposed to be on top of a mountain so high it is lost in the clouds, so high the eagles dare not try for it. The sides of the mountain are perfectly vertical, smooth as glass.

"The emperor never sleeps or eats or drinks. His God—the God of the Ethiopians, the Christian God—has made him holy and taken all human needs from him. He has twelve disciples, invincible in battle, the wisest men since Solomon. Like other men, he prays to God; but God speaks back to him, answers his questions, sings songs to him, sometimes plays chess with him. He is a direct descendant of David and Solomon, and so a member of the house of Jesus Christ. An ancient prophecy, two thousand years old, foretold his coming. He is more than a man, barely less than a god."

"Have you seen him?" asked Rassam.

"A delicate question among Ottomans."

"I do not hear your words." No word-puffs appeared. The sheik was less sure, less comfortable. He shifted on the divan. Ismail Tasfay and Rashid ibn Ali were not even listening.

"I have seen the emperor," said Paniotti. There was a general intake of breath among the secondary members of the circle, as if Paniotti was claiming communication with the demon with which their mothers had threatened them—which, of course, he was. "The emperor is an imposing man, very handsome in the manner of the Ethiopians, tall and strong, charismatic, with an aura of greatness and power and insanity. If I were God, I would choose just such a man to fulfill my prophecy." The enormous eyes and the flat, guarded voice revealed nothing more than the words themselves, no emotion, no bias, not even conviction. "Picture an African king, the descendant of a civilization older than the Roman, who identifies himself with Alexander the Great to the extent of imitating Alexander's famous gaze with the head and neck slanted to one side and the eyes turned heavenward. Picture an African king who has revived, in this modern day and age, the ancient Greek battle cry, 'Alalalalalai!' He has unified a country that has never known peace; he has decimated whole provinces. He has stopped the plunder of the countryside by the imperial army, equalized tariffs and taxes, improved administration, eliminated corruption, encouraged commerce and put an end to the slave trade; he punishes rebels by cutting off their hands and feet and leaving them in the sun to die. No army has ever stood against his might, but now his power is eroding for reasons only an Ethiopian could ever truly understand."

"He is the incarnation of Shaitan," said one of the Massawans.

"He is a madman," said the sheik.

"True, and yet only half the truth," said Paniotti. "The emperor is a very complex man."

And so are you, Mr. Paniotti, thought Rassam. "Has our mission no chance of succeeding, then?"

"Like any madman," said Paniotti, "the emperor is unpredictable to those who do not share his particular madness. One moment he may decide to let his captives all go free, and the next he may decide to kill the lot of them. And any decision that he makes will be perfectly logical. I can give you no better answer."

In these few short minutes Rassam's straightforward mission had become tangled and even dangerous. In the relative comfort of Aden, Rassam had only pictured his triumphant return from Ethiopia, never the possibility that he might actually have to go there and put his head in the noose. That thought was still distant enough to ignore, so he pushed it away. There would be time enough later to be afraid.

"What is your plan?" Paniotti was asking.

"I won't carry a letter from my Queen to the emperor unless he has invited me to attend him. So I will send a letter from myself informing him that I am in Massawa with a letter from my Queen, and that I desire to come to him with it. In my letter I shall also demand that he release the prisoners at once, unless he wishes to incur the wrath of the British crown."

"If I were you," said Paniotti, "I would not make any demands on the emperor. You might subtly hint that it would please your queen if he sent his prisoners—no, you had better call them *honored guests*—if Theodore were to send his honored guests to Massawa or Khartoum."

"Will I have any trouble hiring messengers?"

"You will not be able to find any messengers," said Sheik Mohammed.

"I can pay them well. My government has provided me amply."

"For anywhere else, there would be no problem," said the sheik. "For Ethiopia, no amount of money will buy a messenger. I, the sheik of Massawa, could not find you a messenger. It would take someone with more influence than I." He swung his filmy eyes toward Paniotti.

Eyes shut, Paniotti was cleaning his glasses on the hem of his robe. At last, obviously savoring the effect he was making—the first human response Rassam had detected in him—he replaced the glasses on his face, feigned momentary surprise that all eyes were on him, and said, "I have already arranged for a messenger to carry your letter. To ensure that your letter reaches the emperor through such a troubled land, I would advise sending two or three copies of it by different routes. I will find these messengers if you desire them. They will cost a great deal."

"Thank you, Mr. Paniotti," said Rassam.

Coldly Paniotti said, "I pray to Allah, to the Christian God of Great Britain and Ethiopia, and to the Greek gods who were in Massawa and in Ethiopia before them both, that the Emperor Theodore refuses you permission to go to him."

"I appreciate your concern for us," said Rassam, "but where our duty lies, we must—"

"I pray this not for your sake," interrupted Paniotti in his even, penetrating voice, "but for the sake of Theodore."

"What a curious thing to say! What do you mean?"

But Blanc, speaking thickly, each word treading clumsily on the tail of the last, said: "I say, Mr. Rassam, can you tell me *what is going on?*" Then his eyes closed slowly and he slid off the divan to lie there spread-eagled and still, one hand in the remains of his dinner.

Abd-ul-Kerim held the torch and led the way back to the house. Rafaelo and three of the sheik's eunuchs followed, carrying Blanc. The good doctor nearly woke up several times, frantically mumbled something about chasing red-and-yellow butterflies—he called them *flutter-bies*—through a meadow, then slumped back into limp, loose silence.

Rassam expected to fall asleep at once, but Blanc's mumbling kept him awake for a long time that night. When he finally slept, he dreamed. The dream took place in the sheik's *kat* room. The endlessly repeating patterns of the mosaics had lost their real-life sheen and had become muted and misty. Rassam and half a dozen other men lay on the divans. The men who lay on the divans were men whom Rassam was sure he ought to know, but he didn't recognize any of them, and the next morning he couldn't remember anything that might give him a clue to who they were. They were all stark naked, and there was something wrong with their bodies; after studying them he realized that it was the size of their genitals: the penis of each of them was as small as a newborn baby's. Rassam looked down at his own naked body and saw that he was as underdeveloped as the rest of them.

The rustle of silk drew Rassam's attention to the opposite end of the room, where a partition concealed a door leading to the kitchen. A very small woman was walking out of the kitchen into the room. Her hands were pale and doll-like, and she wore a European gown, black for mourning. An opaque black veil hid her face.

A high-backed chair had appeared against the wall. It had a red-velvet cushion on the seat, and the wooden armrests were carved in the likeness of lions' heads.

The tiny woman walked into the center of the circle of divans. The mourning gown trailed on the floor, but the toes of her black slippers peeped out as she stepped forward. She halted in the center of the circle. The men on the divans watched her closely. She bent down and pulled off one slipper and then the other. Her feet were bare, and very small. She remained where she was in the center of the circle, but she turned slowly, pausing to face one man, then shifting slightly to face another. Whenever she faced Rassam, he knew she had come for him, and not for the others. Her toenails were perfectly manicured, and her feet were very white. Rassam found the daintiness of those feet strangely erotic.

She brought her hands together in front of her as if she was going to pray, but instead her fingers undid the buttons at her wrists. She reached one hand to the throat of her gown and felt under the lower edge of the veil for the top button. She twisted her hand slightly as she released it. Her other hand remained demurely at her side while she undid one button after another, clear to the hem of the gown. She took a sleeve in one hand and shrugged one shoulder free of the gown, then the other shoulder, then she let her arms fall behind her and shook the gown completely off. It made a pile of blackness beside her slippers on the mosaic. Her arms were plump and dimpled and white. She wore a number of mid-calf-length petticoats over a corset that covered her to just above her breasts. The corset bound her into a single contourless column, and was fastened with a series of buttons down the front; in the back it was cinched by an array of laces and eyes, all secured with a great bow at the top. As she turned away from him, his eyes were drawn to that bow and all its possibilities. She still turned slowly, facing each of those faceless, almost genital-less men before she turned to the next. She reached her hands down to one side of her waist, undid two or three buttons, and stepped out of her first petticoat as it rustled to the floor. She caught it on her toe and swung it gracefully toward the gown and slippers. She dropped another petticoat, and another.

Several of the men had started to lean forward from their reclining positions. One reached out a tentative hand toward her tiny foot, but she skipped away. Another put his hand to his crotch and groaned as he felt the impotent, childlike sex organ there. Rassam did the same. He was mentally aroused, but his little boy's penis was ignorant of what the woman was doing to the rest of him. She had dropped her last petticoat. She wore baggy white bloomers that reached her knees and extended up under the lower edge of the corset. She still wore the black veil.

She walked toward Rassam. He could hear the flat moistness of the soles of her feet against the cold tiles. She turned and knelt so that the bow knot was in front of him. He reached for it hesitantly. She waited. He pulled on the two ends, and the knot fell away. He ran his hand down her back and pulled the laces out of the eyes. She walked away from him, leaving the long lace in his fingers and her scent in his nostrils. As she turned, he saw that her body had flowed out to its natural shape. Her waist was still tiny, but her breasts were disproportionately large. The first three inches of cleavage showed at the top of the corset, just below the veil.

Go on, go on, give it to me now, he thought frantically, but he knew that even if she did offer him everything, he wouldn't be able to take it. The frustration of his emasculation pounded at him.

She touched her fingertips to the top button of her corset, drew it away teasingly, and then quickly unfastened it. She undid the rest of the buttons in a single motion, pulled the corset loose, and threw it onto the pile of petticoats. Her stomach was a little puckered where the draw-string of her bloomers had been tied, but otherwise it was flat. Her breasts were round and desirable, the nipples so pale they blended into the smooth flesh around them. Her body was that of a woman in her forties, but it was still firm and beautiful. She came to Rassam, knelt down just two feet away, held out her hands to him, and said, "Come, take me." Her voice was husky with desire. Her accent was the purest Queen's English. Rassam hesitated. He reached out his arms for her. He wanted her more than anything he had ever wanted in his life. His hands hovered inches short of her breasts; he fondled the air in front of them. Her hand shot suddenly down to his crotch and touched his tiny penis. He couldn't feel her touch. With her hand still there, she began to laugh. The veil waved like a flag in a storm. Her shoulders shook. She stood up and backed away. She was still laughing when she yanked off her veil and tossed it toward him. The veil fluttered and settled across his crotch to hide the source of her amusement.

The woman's hair was a mousy brown, parted in the exact middle and pulled back severely from her wide forehead. Her eyes were tiny and bitter, her mouth a thin, angry line. The creases from her pointed nose around the corners of her mouth were very deep, and the skin under her chin hung in loose folds. Even when she laughed there was no joy in her face. She walked, still laughing, out of the circle of divans, which had somehow become empty without Rassam noticing the other men leaving, and went to the high-backed chair with the red-velvet cushion and the lions'-head armrests. Rassam did not know why he hadn't recognized it as a throne. The woman was Queen Victoria. Rassam was aware that he had known it all along.

5

June 1864

Massawa

To Theodore, Emperor of the Ethiopians, King of Kings, Lion of Judah, Heir of David and Solomon of the Hebrews. May you be in good health.

I have the honor to inform Your Majesty that I arrived at this port yesterday, bearing a letter to your address from Her Majesty the British Queen (may God protect her!), and, as I am desirous to deliver the said letter into your hands, I shall await your answer here.

Should Your Majesty acquiesce in my coming to your parts for the purpose of consigning the letter to you personally, my desire would be fulfilled, as I am most anxious for the honour of seeing you, and of enjoying the gratification of being at your happy Court. In that case, I shall feel obliged if you would send one of your followers to escort me to your city, the defended of God.

But should you not deem it advisable for me to come to you at present, owing to it being the rainy season in your country and the consequent difficulty of traveling, I hope that you will oblige me by sending Consul Cameron and his companions under your protection to this place.

Will you be pleased, further, to send a trustworthy person with the Consul, to whom I may deliver the Queen's letter above mentioned.

I am directed to acquaint you in the event of your wishing to send an embassy to England, as you intimated in your letter addressed to our Queen, Her Majesty will be glad to receive it. If you are able to send the Mission down before my return to Aden, I shall take care that it is forwarded to England in safety.

I trust that Your Majesty will favour me with an answer, as I long to have the pleasure of perusing its gratifying and gracious contents. May you be evermore preserved!

From Hormuzd Rassam, Envoy Extraordinary and Minister Plenipotentiary of Victoria, by the Grace of God Queen of Great Britain and Ireland."

The opiate *kat* produces a state of lethargy that dissolves into dreamy sleep. The user wakes with a complete memory of everything that happened to him while he was under the drug's influence, and without any aftereffects at all.

Blanc was up very shortly after first light. He poured out a basin of water to wash himself, dressed carefully, slicked down his hair and combed his side-whiskers, polished his boots, and tightened his collar.

Rassam woke while Blanc was moving around the single downstairs room. From his low bed, he watched the doctor. Neither of them spoke.

When he was finished with his morning ritual, Blanc called Rafaelo and told him they would be spending the morning in a tour of the city and the island. He paused in the doorway and turned at last to Rassam. His voice was even and tightly controlled. "I'll be back . . . when I come back, I suppose. Have a lot of decisions to make, you see, and no time like the present. Where to put the clinic, things like that." He slapped the top of his solar helmet in salute and walked off into the morning with his Goan servant. Rassam couldn't see through Blanc's composure far enough to tell whether he had been embarrassed by his experience of the night before.

Abd-ul-Kerim appeared at the door later in the morning and offered to help Rassam compose the letter to Theodore. He made himself at home on a sofa beside Rassam's desk, his bare feet dangling over one end of the sofa, and his hand resting carelessly on the back of Rassam's chair. Rassam read aloud as he wrote out the letter in quick Arabic strokes on sheets of foolscap, and Abd-ul-Kerim made frequent suggestions on phrasing and content. Rassam accepted all of Abd-ul-Kerim's suggestions without question, and finally signed his name and his title —*Hormuzd Rassam, Envoy Extraordinary and Minister Plenipotentiary of Victoria, by the Grace of God Queen of Great Britain and Ireland*—with as great a flourish as he could give the Arabic characters. It looked ridiculous, and he decided that he would write it more simply on the copies he sent to Ethiopia.

"This letter states my purpose well, I think," said Rassam to Abd-ul-Kerim.

"But stating your purpose, my dear Rassam, and achieving it are two quite different things," lisped Abd-ul-Kerim. "Paniotti doesn't think Theodore will answer your letter at all, let alone release the prisoners or ask you to come to him. Perhaps I shall enjoy your company for longer than you think."

"That wouldn't displease me," said Rassam, surprised at his own honesty. As he began to make a formal copy of the letter, he felt the indistinct pressure of Abd-ul-Kerim's hand on his shoulder. He couldn't remember the last time another man had touched him without apologizing, except for the brief, distasteful British handshake. He knew that Blanc would have been horrified. That hand on his shoulder—could Abd-ul-Kerim possibly sense what it meant to Rassam?—was a breakdown of the rules that maintained proper relationships between individuals and made civilized life possible. That hand was very non-British, very non-Victorian, very Eastern. It reminded Rassam of a young man in Mosul who had worn loose, flowing clothes, who had looked out of simpler eyes at a world in which there was always a right and a wrong, who had dared to tell his most intimate secrets, of which there were many in those days, to his closest friends, of whom there were also many.

During his university days in England, Rassam had taken a week's trip to London. He had walked one day through a district of furniture stores and jewelry shops near Hyde Park. London energized him with the knowledge that he was at the center of a universe of the mind and the soul. He tipped his hat to ladies he passed on the footpath. Carriages rumbled close by, the horses puffing out great clouds of steam that melted into the mists. He rounded a corner and came face to face with another man. Both of them had turned too sharply, and they stopped just short of running headlong into each other. In the brief instant before Rassam recognized the stranger, he absorbed the man's appearance: his topcoat was buttoned to his chin, and a scarf peeked out from under it. He wore a top hat. His muttonchops and mustache and the way he carried his walking stick were perfectly contemporary, but his adoption of English styles couldn't disguise the fact that he did not belong in London. He was from somewhere in the Middle East, and he would never be the Englishman he pretended to be. Rassam felt a swell of pity for a man who could delude himself so completely, and who could fail so miserably at deluding others. This all took less than a second, and then Rassam noticed the gilt frame around the man and realized that he had nearly walked into his own reflection in a mirror that was standing on the pavement. A van had pulled up close to the side of the street, and two men were carrying pieces of furniture into the shop at the corner.

Rassam stumbled away in confusion, sure the moving men had read his mind.

He had forgotten the incident almost instantly, as a man will do with the most painful events in his life, and the memory of it had never once entered his mind in all the years since then. But now two images presented themselves to him while he copied the letter: one the image of what he had been during those days in London; the other, the young Arab behind him on the sofa, the living image of what he might have been at that same age if he had never left Mosul. Copying the letter was a simple task that took only half his mind. The other half wondered what these images had to say to the forty-four-year-old man he had become. He knew there was some truth in what the sheik had said, that he was still very much a man of the East. This place, where even the Europeans wore turbans and spoke slow, razor-sharp Arabic, had already dragged him back to places he never let his thoughts travel anymore. There was something frightening about these thoughts, something threatening to the things he held dear.

"You will be more isolated from Europeans here in Massawa than you were in Aden," Abd-ul-Kerim was saying. "Will that bother you, do you think?"

"If you are asking whether I'll go back to the turban and the robe," said Rassam, "the answer is a confident *no*. I'm British now, completely and forever."

Abd-ul-Kerim only puffed on his cigarette.

"I'll be able to send these letters off today?" asked Rassam.

"Of course," said Abd-ul-Kerim. "Paniotti has promised. He gave me a message for you. He has left Massawa for a time, maybe as long as several months, but the messengers are waiting at his house. We can send your servant Dahon to Paniotti's house with the letters, and the messengers will set out at once. To tell you the truth, I agree with my father: it is a minor miracle that even the infamous Greek was able to find couriers for you. I suspect some mischief on his part."

"What sort of mischief?"

"Oh, there is always mischief with Paniotti. Perhaps he threatens their families with slavery in Constantinople. Perhaps Paniotti is a spy for Theodore."

"Or perhaps the couriers are doing it for the money I am paying them. That is the logical answer."

"What is logic? That is a foreign word that has very little to do with Massawa, even less to do with Paniotti, nothing at all to do with the mad emperor. And I tell you again that it makes no difference whether or not your letters go to Ethiopia. You cannot influence Theodore."

"And you would advise?"

"That you enjoy the pleasures of Massawa, wherever they present themselves. To remain cool inside a sand-proof, darkened house. To drink soothing juices. To avoid the afternoon sandstorms and the floods when they come. To avoid water from the island wells. To ride today with me to Moncullou to see your British residence. It is not too far, and the heat is not so great in Moncullou as here in Massawa. And it is something to do."

"Very well," said Rassam, busy over his penmanship. "I meant to see the residence soon, anyway, to decide whether to move out there or to remain here."

"You should move," said Abd-ul-Kerim. "In Moncullou, you will be more alone, it'll be just you and your servants and your English friend. You will pretend you are in England."

Abd-ul-Kerim's bantering tone brought Rassam around to face him.

"You will be able to pretend," Abd-ul-Kerim continued, "that you are living on an English country estate. The only reminder that you are not in England will be me. I will come to visit you. We will play billiards. I will bring my little Eastern vices with me. I will corrupt you subtly. Massawa will corrupt you. You will learn to feel again."

"I do feel, and I will not be corrupted," said Rassam. "The British are incorruptible. That is one of the traits that make us great."

Abd-ul-Kerim flashed the star, the crescent, and the gap. He folded his hands across his taut belly. Rassam turned back to the copy of the letter.

The four horsemen galloped across the Massawa plain at breakneck speed. For the first time, Abd-ul-Kerim let free that Arabian hardness that Rassam had been sure was there beneath the surface. The wind curled the turban back from his face. The hem of his robe flapped smartly against the horse's croup. His rifle, a wicked-looking, muzzle-loading English Enfield, was bound tightly to his back. He rode with a casual grace, as if he belonged on the back of a horse. His seat was firm and natural, his hand movements barely visible.

Two young Arab bodyguards, their bodies as rigid as those of stalking cats, followed close behind, shadowing his every move. They were stoic-faced men, scarred and burned by the sun, silent, not long from the deep desert. Their eyes picked the horizon apart.

Rassam stayed by Abd-ul-Kerim's side except when they raced single-file down the narrow, tortuous paths through the valleys. Rassam was not nearly the rider the others were, but his horse ran so smoothly and answered so readily to the slightest twitch of the reins that the speed seemed easy. The rushing wind exhilarated him.

Their horses' hooves beat a tattoo against the salt-hard ground. A troop of fifty chacma baboons appeared three hundred yards ahead. Abd-ul-Kerim angled away and passed them, closer than Rassam would have dared alone, at the gallop that was the only gait the Arab seemed to know.

Moncullou was four miles north of Massawa, and a mile from the sea. The village, a thousand huts partially sheltered from the winds by a girdle of twisted trees, appeared first. Abd-ul-Kerim led them directly toward the huts, and they thundered through the open center of the village. People scattered around them and cursed good-naturedly, calling Abd-ul-Kerim by name. They left the village behind. The residence lay a quarter mile ahead. It was a one-story, whitewashed house built on stilts, with a set of stairs leading up to a roofed-in porch across the front. It had been built of wooden planks which Rassam knew could only have been brought at ridiculous expense from India to Aden, and then to Africa. Thirty sycamores, the tallest shade trees for hundreds of miles in any direction, surrounded the house. They, too, must have been brought almost fully grown from Aden.

A crew of fifty men, all of them black-skinned and dressed in the short leather apron that was the uniform of the lowest sort of Massawan laborer, were already at work around the residence and its yard. Abd-ul-Kerim, Rassam, and the bodyguards slipped to the ground before the porch. One of the workers came for the reins, and before Rassam had a chance to say anything, Abd-ul-Kerim had taken his arm and was leading him toward the men beyond the outbuilding.

The Arab was talking quickly, as if he were anxious to keep Rassam from asking any questions of his own. "There is a substratum of volcanic rock at a certain depth everywhere along the coast and on the island of Massawa," he explained. "It traps rain and flood water, and a well dug to that depth always produces fresh water. After a few years, though, salty sediments gather in the bottom of the well and turn the water brackish and unpalatable. On the mainland, there is room to dig a new well, and that is what I have these men doing for you."

The old well, an unwalled hole ten feet across, was only a few yards from the new one. The old well plunged straight down into the white earth for thirty or forty feet. The new well was only as deep as a man's waist so far, but the men were working at it feverishly despite the extreme heat of the midday sun.

"As soon as they get the new well down to the water," Abd-ul-Kerim went on, gesturing at the mound of dirt they were creating between the old well and the new, "they will fill in the old well with the dirt from the new well. Otherwise, we'd have a plain covered with holes and hills."

Abd-ul-Kerim took Rassam's arm again and led him toward the house. They crossed the porch and passed into the cool interior. The house was made up of one big room across the front and two rooms in the back. The floors were bare tile. The furniture was simple and too heavy for a Bedouin to carry away on camel-back. The bulky, blanket-shrouded shape of a billard table dominated the front room. Men were dusting and sweeping out the sand that had filtered into the room through chinks in the shutters. One man proudly opened a blanket and revealed the two halves of a snake he had killed with a shovel. Rassam looked at it more closely. It was a horned viper, not very big but no less deadly for its small size. "Where did you find it?" he asked.

The man pointed toward the open door that led into one of the back rooms. A bed and a bureau were visible through the door. "It was under the bed, very comfortable and cool," he said. "We found scorpions, too."

"Enough," cried Abd-ul-Kerim. "We don't want to hear about your little pests . . . come, Rassam, this is what I came for. I ordered them not to touch the billiard table. Who knows what damage they might have done?" He slid the overhead markers along their wires, and a faint waterfall of dust drifted down onto the blanket that covered the table. The dust was so thick on the markers that they were all the same color.

"Are you responsible for all these men?" asked Rassam.

"It was the least I could do," said Abd-ul-Kerim, who clearly knew that was not what Rassam had meant. He peeled off the blanket carefully to keep the dust and sand from draining onto the felt. Someone brought a towel, and Abd-ul-Kerim wiped off two cue sticks and each ball himself. "There is nothing we can do for the table itself right now," he said. "I'll have someone pull the felt and beat it and restretch it properly . . . but for now—" He set the cue ball on the table, stroked the stick, and broke the racked balls. No balls fell, and Rassam studied the table automatically. His posting at Aden had turned him into a very good billiards player. He sank three balls in a row, but then he over-stroked on the tricky, dusty surface and missed his shot.

One of Abd-ul-Kerim's bodyguards was leaning against the wall watching the game. His rifle and Abd-ul-Kerim's had been laid on top of a table, and his hand rested on the table close to them. The other bodyguard had remained outside on the porch, sitting crosslegged with his rifle cradled in his arms.

As the nearly naked men worked to make the house livable, Rassam and Abd-ul-Kerim worked over the table. Rassam was a much better player than Abd-ul-Kerim, but the condition of the table helped to even out their abilities. They had just set up the rack for a fifth game when the bodyguard on the porch whistled softly. The bodyguard who had been watching the game was out the door instantly, his own rifle in one hand and Abd-ul-Kerim's in the other; Abd-ul-Kerim was close behind him.

Rassam was not afraid as he followed them onto the porch, but he felt a vague anxiety and a mildly resentful curiosity at their prearranged signals and their secret purposes. The two bodyguards had taken up positions against the house, as far under the eaves of the porch as they could squeeze. Abd-ul-Kerim had stepped past them onto the ground and had walked a few paces into the full sunlight. Rassam knew the reason for their alignment at once. The sun was shining over the house and striking Abd-ul-Kerim's back. It would glare into the eyes of anyone who faced him and would make the bodyguards almost invisible. The workmen had all stopped what they were doing. They were watching Abd-ul-Kerim now. That, too, appeared to be part of the plan.

The whole situation—the laborers at the residence before Rassam arrived, the casual positioning of the man on the porch, the quick movement of the other man and Abd-ul-Kerim through the door, their defensive placement at the front of the house—had all been too obvi-ously orchestrated. A dozen horsemen were galloping across the plain toward the residence. The man in the lead wore the blue uniform of the Ottoman cavalry and the tight white turban of Turkey. Those who followed him were strung out without pattern.

Rassam went to Abd-ul-Kerim's side. He felt suddenly vulnerable out in front of the house with the horses racing toward him. "Who are they?" he asked.

"There is no need to worry," said Abd-ul-Kerim. "It will all be clear before long."

"There is a purpose behind all this," said Rassam, his anger rising faster than his fear. "Am I being manipulated?"

A curious smile was playing across Abd-ul-Kerim's face, as if he had looked forward to this for a very long time, but now it dissolved into an expression of hurt. "I'm sorry, dear Rassam," he said. "I wouldn't do anything to injure you. You must have faith in me until you understand. You don't know what this means to me."

"Are you manipulating me?" repeated Rassam.

"Yes, of course I am," said Abd-ul-Kerim. "There is no other way."

"No other way for what?" demanded Rassam, but the riders were almost into the yard and there was no time for an answer.

Rassam recognized the leader: Rashid ibn Ali, mustache flowing, scimitar clanking against his horse's haunch. The men behind were members of his garrison, local recruits dressed in mismatched costumes and armed with flintlock muskets that rolled loosely against their backs. As they reined up savagely in the yard, with a total disregard for the pain they caused their horses, they would never have scared an Arab nomad, but they frightened one Mesopotamian envoy.

The dust cloud passed over them and settled around Abd-ul-Kerim and Rassam. Rashid ibn Ali turned his head angrily, glared at the groups of idle workmen and then down at Abd-ul-Kerim. Uncertain of what to say, he only sputtered impotently.

"You are a little late, aren't you, Rashid?" asked Abd-ul-Kerim. "But aren't you always late?" Rassam wouldn't have believed a voice could convey so much triumph.

Rashid ibn Ali's lips quivered with rage, but he held himself in check and salaamed smartly to Rassam, then to Abd-ul-Kerim. "I heard you were riding out here," he said to Rassam, "and I thought to see whether you needed any assistance. But I see that Abd-ul-Kerim has already provided you with help." He looked around at the workmen again.

"He has been most helpful," said Rassam.

"Of course he has," said Rashid ibn Ali. To Abd-ul-Kerim, he spat out in a suddenly vicious tone, hardly more than a whisper, full of malice: "We had an understanding, didn't we? Ismail Tasfay and I with you? For your good as well as ours. Would you throw everything away?"

"Throw what away?" Abd-ul-Kerim was full of sweetness now.

Rashid ibn Ali chewed on his lower lip and looked again from one group of workmen to the next.

"They won't disappear," said Abd-ul-Kerim. "But my friend Rassam has accepted their help, don't you see, Rashid?" He was handling the garrison commander like a child. "Haven't you accepted the help of my laborers, Rassam?"

Rassam nodded unsurely, as he started to see where Abd-ul-Kerim was leading them all—*where,* yes, but once again no hint of *why.*

"You accepted their help, Mr. Rassam?" asked Rashid ibn Ali, confused by Abd-ul-Kerim's sweetness.

"He has," said Abd-ul-Kerim. "You see, Ismail Tasfay has nothing to worry about. You can report that all is well under control. I am trustworthy. Rassam is trustworthy. You can trust your men to tell their wives and friends the truth that Rassam has accepted the help of my laborers."

"Then you really are for Ethiopia, Mr. Rassam?" asked Rashid ibn Ali. Suddenly delighted, he was falling innocently into the child's role that Abd-ul-Kerim was blocking out for him. "You really are for Ethiopia, and not to suppress the slave trade? You won't interfere in Massawa?"

Rassam started to answer, then swallowed his words. Abd-ul-Kerim whispered, "Thank you, Rashid."

Rashid ibn Ali's smiling face crumbled. He looked uncertainly, questioningly to Abd-ul-Kerim, who clapped his hands and started to laugh, then in confusion back to Rassam—and then his gaze shifted nervously into the black shadow of the porch and for the first time he noticed the two watchful, armed men standing guard in anticipation of his rage.

"Is there slave trade in Massawa?" asked Abd-ul-Kerim innocently, raising his voice. "Are these laborers slaves? Is the stockade in the village near the bunder a slave-holding pen? Do Ismail Tasfay and his eunuchs keep tiny children in slavery and commit unspeakable acts with them? Does Ismail Tasfay let his whipping boy Rashid ibn Ali have free play with them when the eunuchs have had their fun, and does Rashid ibn Ali drench his filthy hands in their young blood? I didn't know. I'm shocked."

"You've done this on purpose," said Rashid ibn Ali, almost inaudibly.

"Done what?" lisped Abd-ul-Kerim.

Rassam heard two metallic clicks behind him on the porch: two rifles cocked.

Abd-ul-Kerim seemed as calm as ever, a little excited in anticipation, perhaps, but not in the least tense. But Rashid ibn Ali was building toward a towering rage. He tried to speak, but the words wouldn't come. Sweat beads rolled across his forehead and off the ends of his mustache. He began to jerk his bridle hand back and forth, and his horse, a big bay, moved side to side with the jerks. The horse tried to shake its head in protest, but Rashid ibn Ali only yanked harder. The horse pawed at the ground, stumbled to the right, then back to the left, inching forward with each turn.

The cavalrymen behind Rashid ibn Ali sat uncertainly on their mounts. They had seen the two Arabs on the porch with their rifles cocked and now, Rassam was sure, leveled at Rashid ibn Ali. Their own antique weapons were still unloaded and on their backs. They were confused by this conflict between their garrison commander and the son of their sheik. There was not a man among them with the courage to choose.

Rashid ibn Ali's great bay horse was staggering as it covered the ground toward Abd-ul-Kerim. The bit was cutting deep and blood was leaking from the edges of the horse's mouth, mixing with the foam, hanging in long pink threads from the horse's neck. The horse tried to pull away from Abd-ul-Kerim, pawed at the ground, shook its mane, nearly touched its knees to the sand, but Rashid ibn Ali kept driving it nearer to Abd-ul-Kerim. The horse came close enough to Abd-ul-Kerim for the young Arab to reach out and touch the muzzle. Abd-ul-Kerim's face was utterly calm. He knew the Turk would never reach him.

Rashid ibn Ali realized it too, suddenly. He raised his head and looked down the black barrels of the Arabs' rifles. He glared at Abd-ul-Kerim for one more moment, then pulled on his bridle. Freed of the seesaw jerking, the horse turned eagerly in that direction and sprang away across the desert. The cavalrymen fell in behind Rashid ibn Ali, and they all dashed away and were swallowed at once in their own cloud of white dust.

Abd-ul-Kerim sighed and smiled at Rassam, but Rassam turned on him. "Why did you subject me to this? These games aren't necessary— it would have been enough to tell me what you wanted me to know, wouldn't it? But no, you insist on subjecting me to this dangerous, embarrassing stage production, and on dropping oblique hints at every chance. Will you please tell me what you are doing, what you expect from me?"

"I am sorry, dear friend," said Abd-ul-Kerim, and he really did look sorry. "But I've waited all my life for this chance. I've waited for you. It hurts me to have to use you. I honestly don't want to hurt you, but I can't let you slip away."

"But why me?" asked Rassam.

"Because you are strong."

"I'm not strong," said Rassam. "I'm as weak as it is possible to be."

"You are as strong as your Royal Navy," said Abd-ul-Kerim. "Look around you. Who else has that kind of strength? Or any strength at all? My father and I bow before a Turkish eunuch. Rashid ibn Ali grovels before him. And Ismail Tasfay, even if I don't stoop to hollow sexual symbols, is as vulnerable as any. You are the only strong one here, Rassam, and I have to use you."

"You own slaves yourself," said Rassam. "You know I have a duty to free them and the power to do it, and yet you want me to know about them. I don't understand."

"It is so simple," said Abd-ul-Kerim. He put out his hand and touched Rassam's arm in an intimate gesture, but Rassam angrily shuffled away from it. "I will tell you how it is with me. My father has followed in the ways of our last few generations and let the eunuchs from Constantinople rule him. My father is a man worthy of nothing but contempt. Ismail Tasfay rules him like a puppet on a string. When Ismail Tasfay moves his smallest finger, my father dances.

"I would have to dance, too, if I stayed in Massawa until I am the sheik. Massawa is a part of me, but I won't allow my vital forces to be sapped by Turkish eunuchs. I will leave before I become my father. But first, I have the need for a little revenge. What can I do to the eunuchs? I could kill Ismail Tasfay, but another would take his place, and the one is the same as the other. What can I do, I ask, to Ismail Tasfay and all his successors? All I can do is to make Massawa as unpleasant a place as I can for them.

"There are really very few slaves in Massawa. If the trade ceases, several merchants will simply go into other commodities, and a few laborers will be paid in coin instead of being supported by their masters. Very little will change for anyone, except for the eunuchs. They have always been the major slaveholders in Massawa. Their slaves are mostly young boys and girls who are forced to perform the vilest acts for the pleasure of eunuchs who aren't able to perform the acts themselves. Prostitutes of all sexes and ages can always be hired, of course, but it is well known how badly the eunuchs and some of their friends, such as Rashid ibn Ali, treat them: how they hurt and bleed and often die. No, no one would willingly become a eunuch's prostitute, so they must depend on slaves. It is an old way of life. You know the details as well as I.

"You are the instrument for whom I have been waiting, Rassam. Captain Speedy could not be bothered—he loved the pleasure provided by Ismail Tasfay too much to interfere. Consul Cameron was not here long enough. I think you will be here long enough, and I think that you will act, now that the troopers will tell everyone that you know there are slaves in Massawa. You may not act at once, but I think the time will come. And when it does, I think we will conspire together to make Massawa the most miserable posting in the world for the eunuchs of the Sublime Porte."

He paused, but Rassam said nothing.

"Do you understand my need?" asked Abd-ul-Kerim. "I am honest with you. I admit that I have manipulated you. Will you forgive me and remain my friend?"

"I think that you should go back to Massawa," said Rassam in a whisper.

"We will go back to Massawa together."

"I will stay here, but I think you should go back to Massawa now," said Rassam. "I will be all right here alone."

"Are you angry with me?"

"Disappointed."

"I will send Dahon out to you," said Abd-ul-Kerim.

"Do that—but now I think you should leave."

Abd-ul-Kerim and his two bodyguards set out toward Massawa at a furious gallop, and the fifty slave laborers followed in a loose company on foot. Rassam watched them from the yard until they were out of sight among the huts of Moncullou village, and then went back across the porch into the front room and lost himself in a solitary game of billiards. He felt very offended and very English.

6

1842

Tigré Province, northeastern Ethiopia

A single rock spire, a quarter of a mile high, jutted out of the flat gray plain. Just below the summit, a dark cleft pierced the stone.

Kasa and five of his closest followers, in answer to the summons from Madhani, the famous holy man of this monastery of Bihaylu, had driven their horses and themselves to the point of exhaustion for seventeen days, but now they were forced to wait. They sat at the base of the spire throughout the afternoon, and camped there for the night. At last, in the morning, a wicker basket bobbled out the cleft and fell toward them. A rope caught it, and it danced into Kasa's hands. Stretched out for so far, the rope looked as delicate as a silken thread. A turbaned head appeared in the cleft and a voice fluttered down the rope: "The priest will come first, and then the *shifta* chieftain."

Outwardly, Wolde was no different from any boy of twelve, but he was set apart by two events he didn't share with his peers: one, his castration, barely remembered after seven years, was his alone; the other, puberty, would belong to everyone else but him. The knowledge of how the future would treat him had made him older than his years. *My little man,* Kasa had called him one day when he was nine and had made some perceptive comment, and Wolde had replied, with no trace of bitterness, "I'll never be a man, of course. A physical impossibility. What will I be, then?" He wasn't asking for an answer, so Kasa let him ponder. At last, Wolde said, "I'll never be a man, so I'll never make a soldier. But I do want to have some value to you, so I had better become a priest." Now, three years later, Wolde had completed the first stage of holy orders.

Wolde climbed boldly into the basket, but he muttered a prayer under his breath. The rope tautened, and his feet lost contact with the ground. He circled slowly as the basket rose toward the cliff. Finally, hands pulled him in, and the basket dropped again.

Each of the young men who were to be left behind kissed Kasa on both cheeks. He squeezed into the basket and rose by sickening jerks. In vain, he prayed against the fear. Finally, he reached the cleft and the priests pulled him in, basket and all.

Wolde had already been led away. Kasa followed a priest along winding corridors, carved from the living rock, lit by narrow fissures through the ceiling to the sky, past tiny cells where priests and monks and *debteras* sat in solitary prayer, up stairways smoothed by untold priestly footsteps. Exquisitely detailed religious paintings covered many of the walls.

The priest did not speak; clearly, Kasa was expected to be silent, too. There were occasional voices elsewhere down the corridors, but whenever Kasa and the priest went by, all conversation froze.

The priest led Kasa to a cell, pushed him toward the opening, and padded away.

Kasa ducked his head and entered the cell. His eyes adjusted slowly to the gloom. The holy man, Madhani, was sitting on a straw sleeping mat, the only furnishing in the room. His head was a dome of drum-tight skin over a tiny face with minute, intense eyes. He wore a white loincloth.

Kasa prostrated himself on the icy stone floor and kissed the holy man's bare feet. "Why have you called me here, holy father?" asked Kasa, prepared for any miracle the monk might perform.

"To teach you to live, and to teach you to die." Madhani's eyes drooped with fatigue. They sat in silence for more than an hour, Kasa afraid to move or make a sound. "To live," said the monk at last, "some people need only to breathe and eat and drink and sleep and fornicate. But others need more. They are the ones who fulfill the will of God. They know what is expected of them, but it is vital to know when to act. I am to give you the signs by which you will know when to do the great deeds of your life." Carefully the monk began to recite the events of Kasa's life-to-come. For each deed that Kasa would perform, the monk told Kasa the signs that would tell him the time was right: changes in the weather, appearances of certain animals, eclipses, telltale phrases spoken by the correct individuals.

The telling of the deeds and the signs lasted through that day and the next. The holy man paused for hours at a time, and then took up exactly where he had left off. A priest brought bread and water to Kasa in the evening. The monk sipped the water, but he didn't touch the bread. They slept in the cell, the monk on the straw mat and Kasa leaning against the cold, hard wall. The priest brought bread in the morning, and again on the second night. Madhani ate nothing. Kasa only left the cell once or twice to relieve himself. The monk never left his mat.

The next morning, Kasa ventured a question: "When I have observed the signs and performed the acts, I will have fulfilled my prophecy of the sun exploding over the great mountain, in submission to the Light Bringer. But what of my visions of myself as an emperor named Theodore? What of the prophecy from the *Fikkare Iyesus?*"

"I know that prophecy," said Madhani, "but I have not seen you in it. This perplexes me. All I can tell you is that the prophecy of the Light Bringer is a true one." He fell silent.

At nightfall of the third day, when the priest brought Kasa bread, Kasa asked Madhani, "Aren't you eating?"

Madhani studied Kasa's face, then said, "I told you that I would teach you to live, and to die. I have taught you the signs you need for your life. But your destiny involves death, too: the extinction of your sun. I will teach you how to die."

"It's a sin to take your life," Kasa spat out.

"Normally a sin, surely, but not for a purpose of God. Our Lord Iyesus died on the cross. Do you think He could not have saved Himself? He gave His life to us. I give mine to you, to teach you the way of death, to show you that death is not a thing to fear, but rather to welcome if it answers the will of God."

The death by starvation of the holy man took another thirteen days. The only communication between Madhani and Kasa consisted of the monk forcing the bread into Kasa's hands and pressing the hands toward his mouth. Madhani sat unmoving during the daylight hours for as long as his strength lasted, and after that lay still on his straw mat. During the last five days, Madhani was too weak and too inward-directed to notice whether Kasa ate or not, and Kasa entered upon a total fast.

When Madhani was finally dead, Kasa stretched out his cramped legs and walked into the corridors of the monastery. A priest found him wandering lost and led him to Wolde. The twenty-four-year-old *shifta* chieftain and his twelve-year-old eunuch priest surveyed each other warily. Kasa felt a need to confide in someone, but that someone was not this child-adult, though Wolde was one of the dearest persons in his life, nor was it anyone else he knew. He felt the weight of prophecies and signs and loneliness.

First Wolde, then Kasa, descended to the ground in the basket. As they began their journey back to Kwara, bells pealed deep within the spire of Bihaylu, and voices rose in the wavering, haunting death keen.

Thousands of men came to Kasa in those years. Some left within days, others stayed for the rest of their lives. Some were refugees from the Ethiopian wars, some had been rescued from Arab slavers, others came because they had heard that Kasa was a man of holiness or that he was a fierce fighter. Of all of them, none was less likely, and none proved more loyal in the end, than the young Greek boy who wandered one night into the light of Kasa's campfire at a Sudanese caravanserai.

Kasa was traveling through the clay desert with half a dozen of his men. They had halted for the night at a tiny oasis, joining three or four caravans and a contingent of Albanian cavalrymen from Khartoum. Around their fire Kasa and his people whiled away the early hours of darkness with the greatest of all nomad arts, the telling of centuries-old stories. Kasa was reciting a legend he had heard around many a caravan campfire, that of a man from the Northern Sea named Alexander, who was brought down by his belief in his own divinity. While he was telling the tale, a shadow appeared out of the night and slipped into the firelight, unnoticed except by Kasa: it was a fourteen-year-old boy, fair-skinned, whose blond hair hung down in ringlets and whose luster-less eyes blinked in the weak light of the fire. Europeans were not entirely unknown in the Sudan, but it was unheard of to find a European child following the caravans. It was unusual, too, to find any European who understood the Amharic tongue, but the boy obviously did, because he tucked himself into a dark place and listened intently to Kasa's story.

Kasa reached the part of Alexander's life where the hero, having conquered Egypt, set out across the desert to find a famous monastery of the Lord God, whose son Alexander had convinced himself he was. "And in search of his supposed father, the Lord God," Kasa said, "Alexander mounted his camel and set out across the Libyan desert toward the setting sun. There was a monastery of God somewhere out in the desert, or so this Alexander had been told, and there he could come face to face with God."

"Was Alexander a Copt?" asked Wolde.

"He was a great man," mused Kasa, "so he must have been a Copt. I cannot imagine it otherwise."

"Nor I," said Wolde.

But the blond child had been squirming nervously and now he couldn't contain himself: "Alexander was no Copt, nor any kind of Christian." The voice was high and anxious, but full of conviction. The Amharic was fluid, heavily accented. "He wasn't Jewish or Moslem or any man of the book. *He was a Greek.*" Then, suddenly, he seemed to recognize the danger of speaking up in a gathering of strange men of the desert. His eyes blinked, his hands fluttered quickly like butterflies, and he shrank back into the darkness.

The Ethiopians only stared, too astonished to raise a hand against him, until Kasa laughed out loud and ordered, "What imp is that, contradicting me from the shadows? Bring him to me."

Strong hands dragged the child into the firelight. He raised a hand to shield his weak eyes from the light.

"Tell me, boy," said Kasa, "what do you know of Alexander?"

"He's only a child," said Gabry, still holding onto the boy's collar. "What could he know?"

"Children have knowledge, too," said Kasa. "Come, boy, tell me what you know of Alexander."

The boy gulped, then said, "Alexander was no Christian of any kind, sir. He lived too long ago for that, three hundred years and more before Christ was even born. Alexander was a Greek. A Greek like me."

"Tell me about your fellow Greek, then," said Kasa. He gestured obliquely at Gabry, and at last Gabry let go the collar.

Nervously at first, then with more assurance, the boy told Alexander's life, from a childhood in Macedonia through the conquest of a world. As he talked, he accepted water from Kasa's woven container and small bean cakes from Kasa's saddle bags. One by one, Kasa's people slipped off to sleep, but Kasa stayed riveted to the boy's story.

When the boy had finished and Alexander was dead, and the empire divided into thirds, Kasa remained absolutely silent for long minutes, transfixed by the story he had heard. At last he shook his head to clear it and said, "Now you, boy: what is the story of this other Greek?"

The boy told his own story. It was a tragic fourteen years that he had seen, but not exceptional for the violent Sudan. His name, he said, was Panagiotes Paniotti. His father had been a Greek merchant. A bandit raid on their caravan had orphaned young Paniotti and bound him into slavery, but he had escaped in the confusion of yet another raid. For two years, he had survived by following the caravan routes, begging, stealing, selling whatever he had, his body not excluded. He told it with a cold detachment, like that of someone who has had all the emotions crushed out of him.

"Do you know anything besides stories of Alexander?" asked Kasa.

"I've been to schools," young Paniotti told him quickly. "I know geography, history, politics, commerce, languages."

"Do you know anything of me?" asked Kasa.

For the first time, Paniotti allowed himself a laugh. "I know who you are," he said. "I know that the Ottomans have put a price on your head, and that that troop of Ottoman cavalry would love to know who you are. I know everything about you, I think. In fact, I've been meaning to meet you for a very long time."

It was Kasa's turn to laugh.

Paniotti straightened up in anger. "You shouldn't laugh," he said. "I mean what I say, every word of it. If I hadn't happened across you, I'd have gone in search of you. I'm young, I know, but I've heard you have a thirst for knowledge. I have more knowledge of the world than any man in this Godforsaken desert. I remember Greece. I've seen Athens and Salonika, the Mediterranean, Constantinople and Medina and Mecca. I've traveled these deserts, and I've been to schools. I speak Greek and Arabic and Amharic and pagan tongues from far south in Kordofan. I could teach you if you'd take me with you."

"You are quick, I can see that clearly. But why do you want to come with me?"

Paniotti's voice was very soft, almost a sob. "I heard you have dreams, that men will follow you. You sound like Alexander to me. And I am alone."

Kasa lifted the boy into his arms. "Travel with me," he whispered. "You aren't alone any more."

Paniotti did travel with Kasa for the next eight years. Kasa purchased books whenever he was able; Paniotti would read them and transfer the knowledge to Kasa.

After Paniotti had laid the contents of his mind at Kasa's feet, Kasa told him that he had a purpose for him. He needed an agent outside Ethiopia, a rich man with connections all over the world, someone to provide him with information, someone to support his interests abroad.

To Paniotti, becoming a rich man seemed impossible, but Kasa told him, "Is that any more impossible than for me to become emperor of Ethiopia? And yet you have no doubt that someday I will sit on the Lion Throne. I tell you that you will go into the world, and you will become a rich man, and you will serve my purposes."

Makeda, the fabled Queen of Sheba whose son by Solomon had begun the Ethiopian imperial line, had gone from Ethiopia with a caravan bearing gold and sapphires. Kasa could only afford nine camels loaded with sacks of coffee beans. Even so, he nearly bankrupted himself and his followers to do it. There was discontent that he had favored Paniotti this way, but Kasa's chief spokesman, Mamo, talked to the people and eased their anger. This caravan was all Kasa could give Paniotti to start his fortune, but he promised the Greek an eternal source of manpower.

Paniotti went out into the Ottoman world, where he struggled to turn his nine camels into a fortune. Somehow he succeeded—whether it was through God's will or Kasa's influence, his own skill or simple luck, Paniotti never dared to ask.

The transformation of a simple *shifta* into a man who led armies and ruled a country was a miraculous accomplishment, achieved in twenty years of methodical, unflinching progress, one improbable step after another until it looked as if nothing would ever truly be impossible again. Many things made it happen: Kasa's unswerving intentness on a single goal; his patience, his charisma, his commanding voice, the religious mystique that grew around him; the huge number of displaced *shifta* who roamed the fringe of the empire; knowledge of Egyptian military techniques that helped him to enforce discipline such as had never been seen in an Ethiopian army. But if someone had asked Kasa himself, he would have replied that it was just the will of God, that he had succeeded because he had followed the signs given him long ago by a dying monk in a remote Tigréan monastery. The signs had never failed him.

By 1848, his *shifta* band had swelled to eight thousand, more than half of them fighting men. Their growing numbers threatened Ras Ali's control of Kwara, so Ras Ali sent a force against them. Traditionally, Ethiopian armies had no intelligence-gathering capabilities, but Kasa had learned the value of spies from the Egyptians. With three days' warning, his warriors stormed out of ambush and pushed their enemies into a dry wadi where they stumbled and fled or were killed. This stunning victory left Kasa unchallenged in the province.

Kasa's future now became linked to Egypt's ambitions. Since 1840, the Egyptians had been extending their control eastward along Ethiopia's northern border, across the Barka Plain, in order to connect Khartoum with the Red Sea. Their control was still tenuous, but Arab, Egyptian, and European slavers were raiding freely into Ethiopia. Rebellions in the highlands prevented Ras Ali from defending the border himself. The situation was rapidly growing serious.

It was at noon of a day during this time, in the year 1848, that Kasa saw an eagle gliding below a totally eclipsing sun. Madhani had said: "This sign will signify a marriage, and the marriage will give you claim to the Lion Throne."

Two days later, an embassy came from Ras Ali with an offer: Ras Ali would give Kasa the hand of his daughter Tawavitch in marriage and the post of *dejazmatch*, or governor, of Kwara, in exchange for Kasa's defending Ethiopia's northwestern border against the Egyptians. The Egyptians, recognizing Kasa's importance in the balance of power, had already made offers to him. Many of Kasa's advisors urged him to choose the Egyptians over the dictator who had tried to destroy them. Kasa's own inclination would have been delay, to play the Egyptians off against the Ethiopians, and see how events developed. But he overruled his advisors' counsel and his own, obeyed the sign, and rode to claim his bride.

Kasa's guard consisted of two hundred men, every one of them convinced they were riding into ambush. Those who were natives of Kwara were astonished by this march into their race's heartland: the sheer *ambas,* the river gorges, the abundance of water, the lush green forests, the blue of the sky so deep it made their Sudanese sky seem white. It was as he was coming over a pass in the mountains, looking down for the first time on Lake Tana, thirty miles across, blue and flat and perfectly round in the midst of rolling farmland, that the marriage, in an unexpected way, gave Kasa his claim to the Lion Throne.

Kasa's family origins had always been a question mark in his life. The *debtera* of the monastic village had believed that Kasa was the son of Haylu, the nephew of Maru, who was a cousin of the emperor. Kasa remembered only vague snatches from his childhood, nothing that would substantiate the *debtera*'s belief. But the sight of Lake Tana brought memories back to him, a whole series of images almost as clear as a vision.

He saw himself as a child. He saw a fine square palace of stone, with a high wall around it and crenelated battlements on the roof.

Servants in bleached white *shamas* padded silently through the rooms. Kasa, according to Ethiopian custom, had been given suck until past his third year, and then weaned very harshly. He was still angry from this weaning. He had no clear image of his mother, but he could picture the twin swellings beneath her robes that were now denied him. His father was there, a tall, slender man with a hook nose like Kasa's, a keen, clear eye, a saber scar across his cheek, and three black braids hanging down his back. There was also an uncle, a brother of his father.

For many days there had been a commotion outside the walls. Kasa leaned from an upstairs window and looked to where many tents had been pitched. Someone pulled him back and scolded him for leaning so far out. His father and uncle and all the men from the tents disappeared one day, and all was quiet again.

At length his father and the army returned, though the tents did not cover quite so much ground as before. His uncle did not return. He heard his father talking with officers, and he heard the name "Ras Ali" over and over again. Even at that age, Kasa could tell they hated this Ras Ali.

Not long after this, the army and his father left again, and this time it was only a single man who returned. Kasa was at an upstairs window when the man arrived, riding his horse furiously across the open field and through the gate, and then running into the palace. Kasa was transfixed by the sight of the horse standing there below, its sides heaving, its legs wobbling, its muzzle and body covered with white foam. The horse's legs gave way, and it tumbled to the ground, tried to rise again, could not, lay still.

He heard shouts downstairs and huddled in the corner of the room. One of the servants found him and carried him, struggling and screaming, down the stairs. His mother hugged him, pressed him against her breasts for the last time, and he saw tears coursing down her face. Then she was gone, and an old man was leading him by the hand out of the palace. They stumbled along until dark, and then they slept beneath a baobab tree. The old man's fear leaped like sparks through the air to Kasa, and he couldn't sleep. Still, he did not ask any questions, and the old man was too preoccupied with saving their lives to offer answers to unspoken questions. They walked for days, until they reached the monastic school and village. The old man told the inhabitants that the boy's name was "Kasa," and then he walked off. From that day, the boy answered to the name "Kasa." He never saw the old man again.

In the next days in Gondar, Wolde sought out and spoke with men who had known Haylu. There could be no doubt that the man Kasa had remembered was his father, and that Kasa was remotely, but sufficiently, related to the imperial line of Solomon and Menelik.

As two hundred of Ras Ali's warriors escorted them into Gondar, the greatest city of Ethiopia, Kasa's men wondered at the cobblestone streets, the tall houses, the bazaars and palaces, and the massive, spired cathedrals.

Ras Ali was a small, dark man with hawklike eyes that turned from face to face, searching constantly for treachery. In the three days of feasting and conferring that preceded the wedding, Kasa learned that Ras Ali was a typical Ethiopian warlord—cruel, suspicious, clever without vision, grasping for power for its own sake. They signed formal agreements and made promises that neither intended to keep—to defend each other against their enemies and, someday, to join together to drive the Egyptians from the Sudan.

The wedding celebration lasted another three days. The entire city and the surrounding countryside put away regular business and erupted into one vast, drunken festival. Kasa had given orders that his men were to drink only moderately, and certain of them, one in five, were to abstain entirely and stay on their guard. Still expecting treason, the men obeyed. Kasa, a temperate drinker and light eater, suffered through those sleepless days and nights as well as he could.

On the second day, Kasa entertained Ras Ali and many male guests at the palace that Ras Ali had lent him. And on the third day, Kasa was married to a fifteen-year-old girl whom he still had not seen.

Kasa's wedding procession took the longest possible route through the city. Thousands of people watched, mostly in silence, from balconies and rooftops. Before Kasa went musicians on foot and heavily armed, horseback-riding warriors. Kasa's special attendants, his *arkees,* were Wolde, Gabry, Mamo, and his closest war leader, Magiga Dulou. They were rich with jeweled pins and brass neck ornaments and fine brocaded *shamas,* but Kasa outshone them all.

In the parade ground before Ras Ali's palace, fifty of Kasa's men and an equal number of Ras Ali's threw up a cloud of dust with their *fakkering,* the sham battle that was symbolic of friendship. When those who had been dragged from their horses had been helped off the field, Kasa joined Ras Ali inside the palace.

Kasa was seated on a couch under a white canopy in a large feasting hall. The nearby rooms were crowded with Kasa's men, Ras Ali's friends and relatives, and soldiers and servants, and with many more men who had simply sneaked in under cover of the confusion—but there were no women, since the sexes were kept apart during a wedding.

Kasa and Ras Ali ate one more ritual meal and downed one more horn of *tej,* the honey liquor of the highlands, and at last it was time for Kasa's first contact with the bride. In Ethiopian custom and in Kasa's own mind the bride was the least important part of this wedding, which was primarily a contract between father and groom. Reports about her had come to him, of course, but he had paid little attention to them. She was a devout Christian, following her Christian mother and not her Moslem father, the rumors said; she was a pretty child, a careful weaver and seamstress, quiet, with few thoughts in her head and few opinions on her lips.

The chair in which she sat was carried into the room by her maids. A plain muslin cloth covered her, so that not even her toes showed beneath the hem. The chair was placed in front of Kasa. A priest stood between them, facing Kasa, his back to the bride. The ceremony lasted mere seconds. "Do you desire to marry this woman?" asked the priest. "By the grace of God, yes," answered Kasa. "Then I make you husband and wife, under God," said the priest. Instantly, the maids snatched up the chair and hurried away with Kasa's bride.

After Ras Ali had presented Kasa with his wedding gifts, carried in one by one by servants, and after another ritual meal, Kasa joined Ras Ali and a hundred warriors on the parade ground in a *deball*, a frenzied war dance with shields and spears. Hundreds of spectators shouted encouragement from rooftops and balconies.

The dance lasted halfway through the night. At last, so exhausted he could hardly stand, weaving from the *tej* he had been forced to drink, Kasa was led by his *arkees* into the palace. They passed down a very long, almost dark corridor. Gabry swung open the door at the end. The room beyond was so black that Kasa could only see a vague image of a small human figure under a blanket, lying on an *arat*, a low wooden frame with leather stretched tightly over it.

Someone shoved him into the room and slammed the door behind him. He stumbled to his knees, then struggled back to his feet. He thought he might fall again. He felt his way forward as carefully as he could, but he banged his shin against the *arat*. He limped back a step or two, pulled off his clothing, lowered himself slowly onto the *arat*, and found the naked body of his wife.

The *arkees*, as custom decreed, shouted ribald comments and encouragement through the closed door. Kasa had never seen this girl and had no particular desire for her, and he was too exhausted to have any interest in sex. She lay still, silent, hardly breathing, while he made love to her as quickly and gently as he could.

When it was over, Kasa slipped off one side of the *arat*, his bride off the other. A door other than that through which he had come in opened, and she was gone. Kasa dressed, then called for his *arkees*. They threw the door open, carried the *arat* through the palace, and propped it up in the parade ground so that everyone could see the small spot of blood on the creamy-white leather. Strong hands pulled Kasa out of the palace, and he danced until dawn.

Kasa and Tawavitch left Gondar by separate routes in the morning. Kasa could hardly keep in the saddle. When he and his escort reached the meeting place, the tent of the bride and groom had already been raised on the top of a high hill. The tent was an enormous pavilion, sky-blue, twin-peaked, thickly carpeted. It was a gift from Ras Ali, who had admonished Kasa to live his life in the saddle and to always sleep in tents as he guarded Ethiopia's border.

Tawavitch's maids fled in panic as Kasa entered. For the first time, standing there in the doorway of their pavilion, Kasa looked upon the face of his wife: *café-au-lait* skin, smooth as a baby's; straight, delicate Amharic nose; curious, bold smile on wide lips; immense, antimony-darkened eyes that did not turn away in pretended awe. Truly, she was a prince's daughter. Kasa lightly touched her cheek, said, "Good, my girl," sank past her onto their *arat*, and was asleep at once.

He woke in the night. Sitting on a stool beside the *arat*, she was watching his face. He stretched his neck, sat up, and took a swallow from a water jug. "Let us talk, you and me," he said.

They conversed through the rest of that night. Though she was only fifteen, half Kasa's age, she was already a strong-willed woman, practical, intelligent, more perceptive and knowledgeable about people than Kasa would ever be. It was customary for a new wife to transfer all her loyalty from her father to her husband. Within minutes, Kasa trusted her, and within an hour loved her. The experience, as exquisite and unexpected as any vision, welling up from somewhere inside his chest, amazed him.

That first night, he told her more about himself than he had ever told Wolde, even more than he had told Paniotti. Before dawn, she knew everything there was to know, except for one part of himself: though he told her there were signs that ruled his deeds, he could not tell her what they were.

The pavilion had walls two layers thick, but early in the morning those closest to the tent heard Kasa's bass laugh floating through the night, and Tawavitch's tinkling counterpoint. By first light, every man of Kasa's two hundred had stolen close enough to hear how this fifteen-year-old girl, this daughter of their enemy, had made their solemn, serious leader laugh. And when Kasa and Tawavitch emerged, hand in hand, two hundred men covered the face of the hill, dropping their breakfasts and their currycombs and whatever they were doing. They swarmed around Kasa and Tawavitch, clapping their hands and banging their spears against their shields, cheering until tears ran down their faces.

Four years later, while walking alone across a grassy field, Kasa stumbled onto the den of a pack of wild hunting dogs. Luckily, the pack was away on the hunt. He managed to kill one bitch and then to hold off the other with his spear—but not before he had counted three wide-eyed balls of fluff in the grass. Three canine pups in a scene of carnage: the sign to break alliances and invade the highlands.

Tawavitch had grown in beauty—if not in fact, at least in Kasa's eyes. And she had grown into his closest advisor. He went to her immediately and told her that he had seen a sign, that now he must move against

Ras Ali. Her eyes gleamed. "Ah, yes," she breathed, "at last the time has come." She did not mention Theodore, the emperor on the flawless white horse, but he knew that that prophecy was on her mind.

They ate their evening meal alone in their pavilion, and talked late into the night. These long nights were legendary among Kasa's people. He never acted before he had talked a night away with Tawavitch, and, emboldened by her, he almost invariably acted afterward. When word passed around, as it always did, that the lamps burned late in the pavilion of Kasa and Tawavitch, then the men would sit through the night, sharpening their spears, whispering in excited tones, retelling the good fights they had had against the Egyptians.

On this particular night, for the thousandth time, Tawavitch told Kasa everything she knew about Amhara, about Ras Ali, about Ras Ali's armies, about the people close to him. At some time in the night, she told him again about Ras Ali's English engineers. These two men, who had come to Ras Ali two years before her marriage to Kasa, were without doubt mercenaries, crude adventurers with no commitment to anything on this earth but to their own advancement; nonetheless, they had skills such as had never been seen before in Ethiopia. Ras Ali gave them precious little chance to display their skills, since he was suspicious of things he didn't understand, but they had built a bridge near Gondar that was a marvel. The bridge was so sturdy and wide that wagons could cross it with ease; it spanned a gorge a thousand feet deep and connected two villages that had been, though within shouting distance, a three days' march apart. "Try to save them," Tawavitch advised that night, "for they are so skillful, so clever, that I believe they could build a bridge to heaven."

Kasa, stunned for the second time that day, made her stop and repeat the phrase. *A beloved person will speak of a bridge to heaven,* Madhani had said. And he had said, *You will not trust the builders of that bridge, but show them mercy and keep them very close to you.*

Kasa threw his entire army, ten thousand men, into the highlands. He had no way of knowing it, but it was the perfect moment. Ras Ali was staggering back to Gondar with his army in disarray after a Pyrrhic victory over Tigréan rebels. Kasa caught his father-in-law at Djisella, scattered his army, and saw his men bring him the corpses of Ras Ali and the puppet emperor of Ethiopia. Kasa had the two Englishmen brought to him, lifted them gently from the ground where they grovelled in fear, and watched their faces light up when he asked them to join him.

John Bell and Walter Plowden, childhood friends from Leicester, had served seventeen years with the Royal Engineers in India. Apart from their dubious ability to read and write they were uneducated, but they were quick-witted and retentive, always watching for that one golden opportunity. By the time they took their unofficial, unannounced leave from the army, they had acquired between them a fair knowledge of military engineering. What one of them had never seen done the other usually had, and so together they formed an almost-complete engineer.

They had departed from Bombay quietly, at night, through a window. Seventeen years in India had earned them nothing more than the calluses on their hands, and the future promised nothing but a fortune in calluses to come, so they were ready for changing scenery when curious rumors reached their ears. The very beautiful, very bored wife of their commanding officer, General Sir Robert Napier, was trysting with a Russian general. The rumors told of a horde of Russian imperials, carelessly embezzled from the Russian consulate; of a secret hiding place within the Napiers' residence; of plans for a pair of lovers to flee India for more exciting climes.

It was quick work for two enterprising Englishmen to bribe native servants, track down leads, substantiate rumors. It was all true, except, perhaps, for the beauty of the lady involved.

When they departed Bombay through their window, the Russian general had been left, trussed and gagged, in his underwear behind the settee in Lady Napier's boudoir; Plowden wore a Russian general's uniform that fit so perfectly it might have been tailored for him, but which was loose by the time he reached Ethiopia. Bell had darkened his skin, put on a turban and a servant's outfit, and cast his voice, slaughtering the Hindustani language, so low that no one but his supposed Russian master could hear more than a murmur. They exchanged a cache of imperials for pounds sterling at a Portuguese banking firm in Goa, and set sail for Aden. Their identities were nearly uncovered in that city when a delegation of Russian officers arrived to inspect the new London-to-Bombay telegraph. On a clear, still day, the dhow on which they made their escape foundered in a sudden mishandling of sails. Two days later, a French naval steamer en route to Massawa rescued them from their perch on the overturned hull. There were Russians in Massawa, too, and in a filthy, narrow alleyway deep within the maze of the city, panting after a frantic dash, Bell had said, "Well, Wally?"

"Eh?" Plowden, leaning against the wall of a hut, brushed thatch from the top of his head and strained to catch his breath.

"Well?" repeated Bell. They had been together so long that simple words spoke volumes.

"I think we ought to find someplace where there aren't any Rooskis," said Plowden thoughtfully, when he was breathing normally again.

"Either that, or you'll have to take off the uniform."

"I've grown to fancy it, John." Plowden fingered the gold braid on his midnight-blue shoulder. "It's a comfortable garment."

"Must say, it does suit you."

"Thanks for saying so."

"Then we'll have to be on our way. Can't stay here. Have you heard of that Ethiopia?"

"Aye."

"And?"

"Do they speak Arabic there?"

"I'd expect they do. Everyone at this end of the world seems to."

"Doesn't matter anyway, does it? Neither of us speaks a word of it. Not likely to find any Rooskis there, I shouldn't think."

"Not bloody."

The year had been 1845. It took them until 1847 to realize that the language they were learning was Amharic, not Arabic, but by then they had insinuated themselves into the favor of Ras Ali, the Moslem Galla prince who owned the emperor and ruled, more or less, the Ethiopian empire.

Ras Ali, no man of vision, had not seen much value in their talents: they had never felt secure with him. Within a week of the battle of Djisella, Bell was able to remark, "I think we've done the cat trick again, Wally," and Plowden could answer, "Aye, landed on our feet again."

As always, they sized up their new circumstances, observed keenly, compared and checked and rechecked their observations. Things couldn't be better, they decided. Kasa, their new master, though he trusted them little, valued their skills. When they brought a new proposal to him, he would let his excitement run free, and it would infect them in turn. In their own limited way they came to respect and, perhaps, even to love him.

1855

Though the air was not as thin or cold as it had been when they were coming over the two-mile high Wandaj and Santara passes, it was still as crisp as a bite from a chilled apple. The planet dropped away toward the Ethiopian plateau proper on their right and more drastically down into the Great Rift and the Red Sea littoral on their left. The scouts trotted ahead, vanished into the blue distance, reappeared beside a faraway hilltop church, waved their spears and signaled with mirrors to show that all was well on the road ahead, then set off again. The column itself cantered and jostled, brayed and jingled. The soldiers' chanting was more lively than ever, sometimes only a few muted voices from the rear guard, then a vocal challenge from a whole company near the van, then an answer somewhere else, but then the whole column would join in a single roaring verse that set the animals into a frantic gallop. Traveling for once without their women and children, the army was small, only eleven thousand strong, but it was the trimmest, most efficient, most disciplined fighting force that Ethiopia had ever produced.

Eight days before, they had swept down into the natural bowl of Lake

Ashangi, with the sun just peeking over the mountains into their eyes, the circular lake still black with the night, the trees leaping out at them through silver mists, the hooves muffled to eerie silence by the lush, dewy grass. They had surprised the enemy, who fled empty-handed in odd directions or just stood stunned and groggy where they had been sleeping. Water birds flapped away like tents in a wind as hundreds of men waded into the lake to hide behind a blanket of fog, or stumbled into the mangrove swamp. There was little fighting, no noise at all until a crocodile closed its jaws around a thin black leg. An abrupt scream broke through the fog. Hordes of dripping men thrashed back to shore and gathered in a vast, squatting group.

The defeated army had been the combined strength of the Ethiopian provinces of Lasta and Wajerat to the west of Lake Ashangi and of the Asubo Gallas to the east. With them disarmed and sent home, all resistance in the eastern part of the empire had crumbled. In the next days, local chieftains had come in voluntarily to throw themselves on the ground and kiss the foot of Ethiopia's new ruler.

This had been the story for the last three years. Djisella had given Kasa instant, undisputed control of Amhara, the spiritual heartland of Ethiopia. All that remained was to subdue the provinces. Efficiently, ruthlessly, Kasa had accomplished in three years what Ras Ali had struggled in vain to do for a lifetime.

In its turn, each conquered province had paused, caught its breath, and suspiciously examined the first months of peace it had known in a century. The nation considered a while, then seemed to decide that it could endure peace, at least for the moment.

After Lake Ashangi, the army had continued to follow the ancient caravan route along the spine of Ethiopia toward the southern, mostly Moslem provinces of Shoa and Gojam. These provinces, the last to come under his sway, promised hard fighting. For an Ethiopian soldier, particularly one who had just been disappointed by the bloodless victory at Ashangi, no fight could be more welcome than a fight against the Gallas, their hostile fellow countrymen.

Kasa, at thirty-seven, was hard-limbed and lean; his hair was arranged in the three long buttered braids of a highland warrior, and, radiating health and confidence, he rode at the head of the column. As was his habit, he rarely spoke. Staff members formed a loose, constantly jockeying cluster around him like lesser baboons around the dominant male. There were his Englishmen: Plowden, still clinging to his faded, patched Russian uniform, bald as an ostrich egg, so tall his bare feet nearly scraped the ground when he rode one of the small Ethiopian horses, hopelessly dependent on his steel-rimmed glasses, yellow with the fever that never gave him a minute's peace, and yet with an inner strength that sustained him through any hardship; and Bell, totally at home in his new environment, wearing Ethiopian clothes and blond buttered braids and a *mateb* around his neck, holding a spear across his pommel. And there were Kasa's Ethiopians: Wolde and Mamo and others from the twelve, and Kasa's military right hand, Magiga Dulou. Gabry, as leader of the rear guard, was supposed to remain far back in the line, but he kept finding excuses to race to the front to spend a few minutes among the privileged. Kasa's valet of ten years, Samuel Aito, was always near at hand, as were couriers and officers and servants of the staff.

In the eighteen months since Djisella, the Englishmen and the Ethiopians had made an uneasy alliance. The Ethiopians resented the *feringi* for their lack of religion, for their doubtful commitment to Ethiopia, for their foreign ways, for the influence they had on Kasa. The Englishmen had no choice but to tolerate the Ethiopians, but they made no effort to hide the fact that they cared little for Ethiopia and only clung to it as an immediately promising venture. Mutual acceptance only blossomed when the Ethiopians realized that the goal of both parties was the same: the complete subjugation of the entire Ethiopian empire under Kasa's rule. And so, though the Ethiopians relished conquest for its own sake and the Englishmen desired it for the wealth and security it might bring them, they made a fragile peace.

The year 1855, then, had come in a burst of glory. Twenty years had passed since the razing of the village, thirteen since the death of Madhani. In all those years, Kasa had never experienced another vision of the sun exploding over the great five-tiered mountain, nor of himself as Theodore astride the flawless white horse. During those years of waiting, there had been times when these two prophecies, the things they demanded of him and the tearing, grinding contradictions between them, had crushed his mind and his will. But in these last years, as his world changed, so had changed the way he saw the prophecies.

Kasa's Ethiopians, especially Gabry and Mamo, had taken to looking back through the ancient prophetic literature. Kasa was beginning to look like the predicted Emperor Theodore. It startled him when they first suggested he might be the object of the prophecy. There were his Englishmen, too. They had begun to feed his pride with a less prophetic version of the Ethiopians' theme: that with their skill and his power they could do almost anything, all the things that Madhani would have said should be done by the Light Bringer. Kasa's eyes lit up at each new suggestion, each new project to make life better for the people of Ethiopia.

The successes in battle, the suggestions of the Ethiopians, the ideas of the Englishmen—all these formed a compartment in Kasa's mind into which he could place things he did not care to face, but it was Tawavitch who gave him the lock and the key. There were times when he knew she had spoken with the Ethiopians or the Englishmen and had carefully timed her gentle insinuations to coincide with theirs, but he knew, too, that all she did was out of love for him. Kasa was totally immersed in a real world of actual, physical, day-to-day problems. The signs that Madhani had given him were so bound up with this existence that he could easily separate them from the mystical prophecy to which they had been attached. The suns and the stars were distant from him; he pushed that prophecy into the appropriate compartment and turned Tawavitch's key, which was his love for her. He retained the vision of Theodore, and he retained Madhani's signs. Now, when his Ethiopians mentioned Theodore, he only smiled a secret smile; when his Englishmen proposed some new idea, he gave it all his enthusiasm; and when Tawavitch, on their *arat* at night, talked to him when he was sleepy, barely able to hear more than the soft, rhythmic sound of her voice, he would tease her a bit and then, inevitably, agree with whatever she suggested.

Kasa hated bloodshed; his successes gave him little pleasure. What had been a period of delirious sensual gratification for his followers had been, for him, a grim time he endured in order to reach the better times beyond. He waited on those times and looked forward with faith and hope. It was only on certain occasions—usually when he was in solitary prayer in the wilderness—that he felt the touch of a delicate hand on his shoulder, reminding him of something he had thought safely locked away.

On the eighth day after Lake Ashangi, on Kasa's decisive expedition to the east and the south, the head of the column ascended such a long, barren rise that, with the ground dropping off to right and left and sloping gently upward before them, they seemed to be climbing to the top of the world. Three scouts waited at what appeared to be the crest. Usually, scouts either stayed far ahead or came racing back with information, and so the staff grew curious as they drew closer to the scouts.

One of the scouts pointed to something still out of sight and shouted back at them, but the breeze tore his words away. He shouted again, and finally one indistinct, windblown word reached them: *Magdala!*

The staff echoed that word in one whispered exhalation: *Magdala.*

The scout had named the famous *amba* that guarded the approach to Shoa and Gojam. Even Bell and Plowden had heard stories about it. In a land studded with the monumental, glassy-sided cores of dead volcanoes, Magdala was mythical. The evil done there, the vengeances plotted and the heroes destroyed, were legendary. The list of armies that had dashed themselves to pieces against Magdala's walls through the centuries would fill many pages of foolscap in the *debteras'* books of records.

Eager for their first sight of the *amba,* the whole staff heeled their horses into a canter. The *amba* unfolded from top to bottom as they cleared the summit of the rising ground. They didn't need the scout's outstretched hand to know Magdala.

The horses shuffled and neighed.

"Holy b'Jesus!" whispered Bell in English.

Plowden found himself assessing the mountain with a military engineer's eye. Kasa was as silent as ever, his face an unreadable, rigid cypher.

The tremendous scale distorted any reasonable sense of perspective. Two miles ahead, the Bashillo River gorge split the plateau. Grayish mists shrouded the far edge of the gorge, another three miles beyond.

Towering above the mists, the mountain was formed of five giants' steps, ascending in order away from the gorge. The first two steps were imbedded in the body of the mountain. The third and fourth were powerful, freestanding *ambas*, but the last, Magdala, dwarfed them all. A winding track led from the lip of the gorge, across each of the steps, to Magdala. The sides of the mountain were so sheer that there could be no other route. The scout was reciting the place names along that track: the Gumbaji Spur from the gorge to the Affijo plateau and the Aroge plateau, the *amba* Fahla, the *amba* Selassie, and then the saddle Islamgie, two miles long and one mile wide, leading to the base of the *amba* Magdala.

Elsewhere, the far side of the Bashillo River gorge gave way to hills that billowed like a becalmed sea to the foot of lofty mountains another forty miles away to the south. Magdala towered like a lone schooner over the billows.

As an engineer, Plowden saw the crude wooden palisade rimming Magdala's summit as a personal offense. It might stop an Ethiopian army, but a single cannon could have reduced it in an hour. "To misuse a spot like that—"

"It's a crime," agreed Bell, who was thinking along the same lines as his friend.

Without removing his eyes from the distant *amba,* Kasa started his horse forward to the gorge for a better look. After a hundred yards he realized that his staff, his scouts, and his entire army were following him. He waved them back and went on alone.

"What's the matter with Bob?" asked Bell. Between themselves, the Englishmen referred to Kasa as *Bob,* in a mostly fond, mostly respectful tribute to Lieutenant-General Sir Robert Napier, G.C.S.I., K.C.B., the man they had followed through years of peaceful public works and unnecessary fortifications in western India, and through the vicious Sikh wars of '45 and '48. Napier and Kasa were very different leaders. Where Kasa was daring and inventive, Napier was a solid engineer and soldier, conservative and thorough and by-the-book, but both of them were the kind of man to have in command when the enemy drew near. There were times—admittedly few—when Bell and Plowden almost regretted having left the Russian general in a position that might cause Napier a scandal.

"Bob's certainly got something on his mind," said Plowden, watching their Ethiopian commander ride off alone to look at the great *amba.* "Very distracted, like. Say, John, since we're probably going to be asked the question: how would you go about reducing that fortress?"

"Looks like a nut, doesn't it?" mused Bell. "I think the question ought to be: how would Sir Robbie have reduced it?"

"Quite."

Kasa rode the two miles to the edge of the Bashillo River gorge and looked down at the brown river so far below, across at the giants' steps, up at *amba* Magdala. It was the best place he had ever seen for a fortress. It was an ideal place to await an enemy from far away, an heroic place to die. He had never been in this part of the country before, but he had already seen Magdala.

He felt as if he had been in the eye of the storm, surrounded by a tempest but unaware of it, but now the hurricane had moved and engulfed him. He could not think. He could only look at Magdala, mentally record its size and texture and color, and recognize it as a reminder of a well-forgotten memory.

Kasa allowed his horse to set its own ambling pace on the return to the army. When Kasa finally halted in a semicircle of staff and scouts, he asked, "Has the fortress submitted yet?" His voice was remote and colorless.

"On your orders, we offered them terms," said a scout. "They threw spears at the messenger from the top of the wall."

"We'll avenge the insult," snapped Gabry, slapping his shield for emphasis.

"They aren't important," said Kasa. "We need Magdala; the people are insignificant. Offer them another chance to surrender. Offer them safe-conduct to anywhere they please, guaranteed on my honor, if they will only leave the fortress and their weapons and go home." Three scouts started away. To the Englishmen, Kasa continued: "Can you take the fortress for me quickly?"

"We've thought of a plan, but it will involve burning the walls down. They would have to be rebuilt from the ground up. Given a little more time, we might be able to—"

"I want it taken quickly," said Kasa. "I don't want to wait here any longer than I have to. Besides, it will be just as well to burn it now as later."

"You can't leave a place like that unoccupied," blurted out Bell.

The merest breath of irony played with the corners of Kasa's mouth. "Can you rebuild it so that it is impregnable?"

"That wouldn't be hard. It's the most naturally defensible place we've ever seen."

"I want it able to withstand cannon fire."

Bell and Plowden exchanged a questioning glance. "There's not a cannon within two hundred miles of here," said Bell.

"I want Magdala as my southern capital. I want it to be Ethiopia's strongest fortress. I want it stronger than a cannon blast. You will have as many laborers as you need."

"Very well," they answered in unison, triumphantly. They looked across the seven or eight miles to what would be the crowning project of their brief careers as master builders. Forgetting Kasa for an instant, Plowden's eyes lit up with sudden excitement, and he said in English, "Sir Robbie himself never had such a spot to build from scratch."

"I'll need a better road through the gorge, too," said Kasa.

The two Englishmen measured what they could see of the gorge with the practiced eyes of men who had wielded pick and shovel on hundreds of miles of road through all kinds of terrain. The near side was hidden, and the far side seemed to be nearly vertical. "It would never be a good road," said Plowden thoughtfully. "It's too steep, the footing could never be good, in the rainy season it would never be useable, and each dry season it would have to be repacked and reshored. But we could widen the existing track, cut switchbacks through the hardest places, lay some sort of gravel surface, and then go right up that cross channel beyond the gorge." He pointed to a slash of black shadow against the far wall of the gorge, a narrow cut that led a stream down from Selassie into the Bashillo River.

"The Warki Wawa," interjected the scout, hovering just within earshot.

"The Warki Wawa," repeated Plowden. "We could take the road up the Warki Wawa to the top of the gorge, and then on up the Gumbaji Spur to Affijo Plateau."

"How long would it take?"

Plowden tried to estimate how much Kasa wanted the road. He asked for twice as many men as they'd ever had before. "With a thousand men, three weeks for the road alone, perhaps a month."

"Could it be made to accommodate cannon?"

Plowden had been expecting the question, though he didn't know why. It was a curious request, after all, since Kasa had no cannon and no way to get any. "It would take a better engineer than I—better, I think, than there is in Ethiopia." His voice trailed off into a question.

Bell took over from his friend. "Of course, there was a general who proved that cannon could be taken anywhere. His name was Ethan Allen, and he was an American officer during the American Revolution. In the dead of night—"

"I will worry about transporting the cannon," interrupted Kasa. "After you've taken Magdala, just build the fortress and as good a road as you can for me. You will have three thousand laborers and everything else you need. If you do your jobs well, I will make you both *rases.*" He turned his horse, and the army began to move toward the gorge and the great mountain. Kasa had never been so abrupt with them. And he had never offered them so much.

"*Rases,*" said Plowden, but there was more caution than joy in his voice. "He'll make us *rases.*"

"Something's wrong with Bob," muttered Bell, with the concern of a man whose very life depends on someone else's good humor.

"I feel like I'm walking a tightrope," said Plowden. "There's a reward at the end, but one misstep and we're dead."

"We'll have to take special care, won't we?"

"And look at the blighters there," said Plowden, "so overcome with admiration they're not even aware that something's the matter with their lord and master." He gestured toward the Ethiopians, who were pushing close to Kasa, their faces and voices revealing to Bell and Plowden nothing but the usual adoration.

Twilight overtook the army on Aroge, the second imbedded plateau. The main body of troops camped there, while a vanguard climbed through the darkness to the first freestanding *amba*, Selassie, to secure the camp against a nighttime sneak attack. Campfires dotted the flat, nearly circular plateau of Aroge. A few cloth tents stood out among the low leafy bowers the common warriors had built for themselves to sleep in on the march.

Gabry's tent had been pitched intentionally near the edge of the plateau, only a short stumble down a rocky slope to a dark, overgrown gully. The Ethiopian habit of eating raw beef gave rise to a nationwide, perpetual epidemic of tapeworms. The native remedy for this was an herb called *koso,* which acted as a powerful purgative.

There had been no lull in the action over the past two weeks, and none seemed likely in the near future, so Gabry decided that this part of the march was as good as any other for a purge.

He was just returning to his tent from the gully when Wolde came walking into the firelight from the opposite direction. Magiga Dulou was already there, sitting on a stone close by the fire.

Wolde squatted near the fire and accepted a long sliver of raw beef from one of Gabry's servants. He grasped one end in his mouth and sliced the beef off close to his lips with his knife. "Purging, eh?" he remarked.

"I hope it works, by the death of Christ," said Gabry, throwing himself down across the fire from Wolde. "The last time, I had to go through it three separate times before I lost the worm."

"I will pray for your worm."

"I'm the one who needs the prayer," muttered Gabry. "The worm can take care of himself."

Magiga Dulou flipped his knife into a tree stump. He asked. "Do you know what is troubling Kasa?"

"He doesn't tell me everything," said Wolde. "But it was obvious that something happened today: look at how he reacted to Magdala; how he wants the *feringi* to rebuild the fortress; how he wants a road through the Bashillo gorge to transport cannon. *Cannon!* The only time I've ever seen a cannon was when we went against the Turks at Kedaref. I hope I never see another one."

"Amen to that," said Gabry.

Wolde mused for a few moments. "It worries me, how he seemed today."

"Worry for us," said Magiga Dulou. "We depend on his judgment."

"I haven't seen him in such a mood since before he married Tawavitch," said Wolde. "Somehow, seeing Magdala has disturbed him. I don't understand it."

"What is there to worry about?" asked Gabry. "We've met nothing but success. The rest of the country will be ours within weeks."

"I only wish I knew why he is concerned," Wolde repeated.

"Will he have himself crowned emperor?" asked Magiga Dulou.

"Of course he will," said Gabry. "And then: the Turks!"

"That's something he hasn't told me," said Wolde to Magiga Dulou.

"But you can guess," urged Magiga Dulou.

Wolde was silent for a minute, chewing and staring into the fire. Then: "I think he will. He has no choice other than to become emperor himself, or to appoint a puppet to the throne. He despises weakness so intensely that the idea of a puppet will disgust him. Besides, he has as strong a claim as any."

"The claim of military might," said Gabry.

"The claim of birthright," corrected Wolde. "Kasa has changed many things, but tradition is still tradition. The emperor must be from the lineage of David and Solomon and Menelik. Kasa is as close as anyone alive."

"And after he is emperor," said Gabry, "we will march against the Turks."

"We will never march against the Turks," said Wolde.

"But why not?"

"Kasa has other dreams than conquering the Turks. Don't you ever wonder why he keeps the *feringi* so close to him?"

"For their usefulness, of course. Their knowledge can help us defeat the Gallas, and then the Turks."

"They are useful, but they are also symbols to Kasa of his dreams. When Ethiopia is a unified empire again, then he will do things such as you have never thought of. It will be a new country, a better place to live. Have you seen how he loves to watch children at play? He has a way of saying it: 'It is all for the children,' he says. 'All for the children.' "

"But all I want is to defeat the Turks. I don't care about a new country."

"Then you will be left behind."

Gabry rose halfway to his feet in anger, glaring at Wolde across the fire; then he straightened up and said in a tightly controlled voice, "My worm is calling me." He stamped away down the dark slope to the gully.

you were planning to set up your southern capital farther into Shoa, toward the confluence of the Big Abai and the Guoler. Magdala is an admirably defensible *amba,* but others are also good and at the same time more central to the south. Magdala is so far to the east that—"

"It will be Magdala," The decision was final. "Are you unable to capture the fortress, or to build the fortifications and the road?"

The road they had followed through the gorge had been a monstrosity of random design. It plunged straight down incredibly steep cliffs and made no use at all of the contour of the gorge, and it had crossed the Bashillo at a spot where the water ran swift and deep, when a natural ford was only a hundred yards upstream. The gorge was deeper than Plowden had imagined, too, the river being at least a mile below the elevation of the plateau. He had revised his estimate of construction time to two months or more, but he was still confident that a decent road could be built—though not good enough for anything less sophisticated than a European army to transport cannon. Bell had taken the fortress as his responsibility. He was more excited about building it than he had ever been about anything in his life. "No, we're ready to start building as soon as we take the fortress. But why are you concerned about making the fortress strong enough to withstand cannon fire, and why the concern about bringing cannon across the Bashillo?"

"Times change. There may be cannon someday."

Plowden laughed softly. "So you're going to be close-mouthed about the whole thing? Well, it occurred to us that there may be a way to make your own cannon."

"My own cannon?" Kasa breathed the astonishing words.

"If we pool our knowledge, we should be able to set up a reasonable forge."

"And if we have a forge, then we ought to be able to cast a cannon."

"I expected no less from you," said Kasa, though the fantastic idea of casting his own cannon had never even entered his thoughts. The cannon he had been thinking about would belong to someone else, would be brought to Magdala from faraway, would be used to destroy Magdala. *His own cannon!* The first cannon ever cast in Ethiopia. The first ever owned by an Ethiopian soldier. With cannon, he could storm any *amba* that housed rebels. He could keep the peace. He could secure his borders. He felt the thrill pulsing in his fingertips. *His own cannon!* Another step into the modern world.

He knew that just listening to the Englishmen was a commitment to continue along the path he had been following, to ignore the coming of the Light Bringer. But: *His own cannon!*

Another thought came to him. "Are there weapons known to you that fire projectiles that explode in great masses of sparks and flames, high in the air?"

The Englishmen were stumped. "Not that I know of." "Nor I."

"There are exploding shells, but they don't really send out many sparks."

Magdala with explosions of sparks and flames overhead, and his sun vanishing in the glittering inferno. The picture was still vivid after all these years. But there was no such weapon, and these Englishmen promised to cast cannon for him.

The Englishmen could not know exactly what they had done with such a few well-chosen words, but they could see the sudden delight in Kasa's expression, and the joy with which his hands waved in the air. His mystical, inward-looking mood was dispersed. He was the practical, safe man on whom they had come to rely.

"I've sketched a map of Magdala," said Bell. "Would you like to see our plans for taking the fortress? With luck, not a single life will be lost."

"Not a single life?"

"With luck, not one on either side." Plowden struck one of his precious European matches and set it to a lantern he had brought with him from the camp. Bell spread out a large sheet of paper on which he had drawn a map of Magdala and diagrams of some new piece of machinery.

Kasa leaned over the paper, and Bell and Plowden began to explain to him the simple idea, borrowed from medieval European warfare and the American frontier, of building one or more huge mangonels, giant crossbows capable of hurling twenty-foot-long arrows for great distances, and fitting them with fire-arrows that would lodge in the wooden palisade and burn it down around its defenders—and, if it was constructed properly, the mangonel could be dismantled and carried along with the army to the next wooden palisade, and the next.

When Kasa had endorsed the project, the Englishmen set off in the direction of other favorites: a fleet of wooden boats for Lake Tana; a bridge across the Big Abai to link Gojam and Amhara for the first time; government-owned storage bins for the collection of grain to tide the nation over the occasional locust famines; draining the Ghish Abai swamp and turning it into lush farmland.

The shock of seeing Magdala was gone, forgotten, sloughed off. The thing that stuck in Kasa's mind was the beginning of a story: "This general you started to tell me about, who carried the cannon—who was he?"

And the Englishmen told Kasa the story of how Ethan Allen and his Green Mountain Boys had dragged their cannon straight up the cliffs to Fort Ticonderoga one dark night and caught the British garrison napping.

"You build your road through the Bashillo River gorge," said Kasa when the story was over, "and I, like this Ethan Allen, will transport the cannon."

Later that night, John Bell remarked to Walter Plowden, "You know, I do believe old Bob could drag cannon straight down into the Bashillo gorge and right out again, if he only had the cannon."

"I do believe he could," agreed Plowden, mumbling into the rug in which he had wrapped himself. Then, lifting his head, he said, "Thank the good Lord it won't be the British against whom this heathen Ethan Allen—" He liked the sound and repeated it: "this heathen Ethan Allen drags his cannon."

"I say, Wally," said Bell, "do you really think we can forge cannon that work?"

"Don't see why not, my man, don't see why not." And Plowden rolled back into his rug and fell asleep with only the distant chatter of an angry hyena to disturb him.

7

1855–1862

Magdala

Kasa returned to Magdala a month before the beginning of the rainy season to have himself crowned emperor of Ethiopia, taking the throne name of Theodore. John Bell's gray, thick-walled fortress still lacked a southern wall to guard against any Gallas who were foolhardy enough to try to scale that glassy cliff, but a city of conical thatch-roofed houses, churches, and granaries had been erected within the horseshoe of the three finished walls, and another temporary city had been thrown up below the *amba* on the Islamgie saddle. The banner of the Lion of Judah fluttered over the walls, and everything had been gaily decorated. The main entrance to the fortress had been laid out in a short zigzag that would require attackers who managed to force the iron-bound gates to break stride as they negotiated the passage into the city. Kasa took up a post just outside this gate, overlooking the last hard climb up from Islamgie, from which he could watch the whole route except for a few hours of the ascent from the gorge and up the Gumbaji spur. At any given time during the day, he could pick out a dozen separate caravans along the road, and at night the fires of those who had halted along the roadside formed a carelessly dangling necklace of red stars. He personally greeted all travelers, and led them into his new city. The city was not remarkable by the standards of Gondar or Tigré, but it was amazing considering its remoteness and the short time in which it had been built. If anyone was not impressed, they didn't let Kasa know.

For himself and his empress-to-be, Kasa had had a large, comfortable house constructed, not the palace they would have had in Amhara, but easily the largest dwelling in this backwater region. After such a long separation, Kasa's reunion with Tawavitch at the main gate was a spectacle that everyone in Magdala turned out to share. Scouts had been stationed at the top of the distant rise, and they gave the first news of her approach with their flashing mirrors. Kasa called for his fine German telescope and watched her come into view, leading her party mounted sidesaddle on a perfect white mule. Messengers came the next morning to make the formal announcement, but even before they arrived, crowds had filled the narrow level space between Islamgie cliff and the fortress wall and had overflowed down to fill up the saddle. The only empty ground was the corridor of the road across Islamgie and a wide, respectful circle around Kasa.

No stranger to pomp, in her element with so many thousands of eyes on her, Tawavitch was every inch an empress. She wore an ankle-length shirt of calico. Henna stained her hands and feet, and silver necklaces and anklets jingled in time to her white mule's stately walk. One hand held the reins loosely, the other held the leash of a baby gray monkey from Lake Tana, which clung to her shoulders as if she were its mother. She stared impassively ahead, as if the throng bored her.

Conscious as always of the impression he had to make, Kasa stood alone in the middle of the empty circle. He stood very tall, his face impassive, his head tilted slightly as Alexander's had tilted. He was the *negus negast*, the king of kings, but once again as he watched his empress approach, he recognized that he was not what he seemed to be. Tawavitch's expressionless face, her restrained bearing, came naturally and easily to her, and she could still communicate a private smile to him with her eyes. Meanwhile, he stood there straining to be the *negus negast*, feeling his knees shake, masking every speck of humanity, keeping his eyes away from hers for fear of letting the crowd get even a glimpse at Kasa, the mortal man. He had been leading others for twenty years, but he still died a little death whenever he felt expectant eyes on him, or rode into battle, or gave an order that changed men's lives.

She halted before him and gathered up her monkey in her arms. Kasa stepped forward, swept her down from her mule, and carried her through the zig-zag entrance into the city. A cheer erupted, and men and boys shouting the high-pitched *"Alalalalai!"* chased after them and swirled around them. Measuring his steps carefully, Kasa carried his wife through the city to the house that would be their first imperial palace. He set her down at the edge of a vast expanse of carpets in front of the house. She took his arm and they walked under a velvet canopy to the door. People pressed up to the limit of the carpets, but not a single foot profaned them. For the benefit of his people, Kasa said in a loud voice, "I laid the carpets for you myself, inside and out." He struggled against the desire to wrap his arms around her and hold her.

"You honor me, my lord," said Tawavitch. She was giving nearly all her attention to petting her gray monkey, but glanced up and quickly wrinkled her nose at him. He looked away and opened the door. She walked in, he followed her, closed it, and then leaned back against it for a minute with his eyes shut, trying to relax, trying to break the hold of being the emperor.

Tawavitch had shed her formal façade the instant the door closed. It was a knack that Kasa envied, but one he knew he would never learn. Tawavitch stroked his temples and whispered endearments. The tension left him slowly, and suddenly it was gone and he felt the urgency of Tawavitch's nearness. He opened his eyes and reached for her, but the monkey was on her shoulder between them. As he pulled her toward him, the monkey screeched. Tawavitch stepped back and let the monkey fall. It scrambled between Kasa's feet. Tawavitch danced back, and as he went after her the monkey's trailing leash snagged around his ankle. The monkey screeched again, and Tawavitch turned and ran. Kasa stopped long enough to kick the leash loose, then ran after her.

She had found their bedroom; the calico shirt was already halfway over her head. He teased himself by just looking at her for a few seconds. Without clothes and without her formality, she was really quite small. Her skin was the color of milky coffee, deliciously taut and smooth. Her neck was long, her shoulders fine-boned and rather wide. She was holding her shirt against her breasts, but he pictured them small and perfectly round, with tiny black nipples that stood far out from the breasts themselves. Her hips and legs were thin, her feet planted far apart. Her tightly curled pubic hair was so short it emphasized the subtle folds of her groin.

Simultaneously Kasa started toward her, the monkey streaked between his feet, and Tawavitch threw the shirt at him. Kasa landed on his knees and came up laughing and lusting for her. By the time he reached her, she was stretched out on their *arat*, the wooden frame laced with rawhide and covered with blankets. He lay half on top of her and touched what he wasn't covering, her breasts and her neck and her shoulders and her groin, and he felt all the rest of her body pressed against him, and though he wanted to go slowly his need was too great. But she was ready and breathing hard, and he shifted his body on top of hers and pushed into her and before he'd even started to move he burst in an explosion of stars in a black night.

He lay on top of her and in her for another few minutes, then rolled off and wrapped his arms around her. "I've slept on the floor or the ground ever since I left you," he said. "I've saved our *arat* for a time when we would be together."

"You always do," she said gently.

"It's been too long."

"For me, too."

"Two months since we were together last."

"Yes, two months. We must make love often now."

He murmured agreement and dreamily fondled her full breasts.

"More often than ever," she said, as if he didn't understand.

"Why?" he asked.

"To strengthen the child."

For a moment, he didn't know what she was saying. Then, he saw it: "Are you with child?" Everyone knew that frequent sex helps an unborn child to grow, and when Tawavitch nodded Kasa screamed out for Wolde and Gabry and Magiga Dulou.

Tawavitch had barely time to draw the blankets around her naked body before the house was filled with the men he had called and twenty more that he hadn't.

"In three days, I will be emperor," he shouted, "and in . . . in how long?"

"In seven months, of course."

"And in seven months, I will be a father."

"An heir?" "A son to carry on?" "By the grace of God, this is a many-blessèd day."

"My lord?" begged Tawavitch.

Kasa waved the men out of the house, and when they were alone again whispered, "Let us work once more to strengthen our son."

"If we must," said Tawavitch, but her eyes were gleaming, and this time Kasa was able to take the act more slowly and bring Tawavitch to her climax seconds before he reached his.

When they were done, he laid his head on her breast and said, "My belovèd, how many times have I wished you were a soldier and could be with me on the march?"

She stroked his head and kneaded the tense knots in his shoulders. She said, "I'm no soldier, and I can't be with you. So, be my eyes and ears." Kasa told her everything that had happened to him since they had been together, and everything he had seen and heard and thought.

The celebration in the city continued past sunrise the next morning, but neither the emperor-to-be nor his empress-to-be appeared outside their palace.

Though this coronation of the new emperor and empress by the Abba Salama could not possibly compete with those in the past that had drawn on the vast resources of the cities of Amhara, it was still such a magnificent occasion, with feasting and dancing and horseback races and rituals so old their meanings had been lost for a thousand years, that it was the keystone event in the lives of several thousand poor southern peasants. The relative humility of the coronation was not as important to Theodore, né Kasa, as the fact that a Magdala coronation would make it clear to the southern provinces that he meant Shoa and Gojam to be more than invested territories, that he meant to bring back the old empire of those long-ago times before the darkness of the *Zemene Mesafint*.

The first months of Theodore's reign went well—too well, perhaps. In the fifth month came the first reverse: the child, a boy, was stillborn, and Tawavitch died from internal bleeding. Theodore absorbed his grief as he always absorbed his emotions, and no one saw in him more than the outward forms of mourning that custom demanded. But the pain had to surface somewhere, and within a month a thing had happened that, always after, made him shudder with the pain of remembering. There was a *shifta* chieftain near Antalo, a cruel, small man who led only a hundred men or so, but whose stronghold atop a difficult *amba* was very nearly impregnable. Captured once on a raid against a peaceful village, the *shifta* had submitted to Kasa and sworn to live within the law. Captured a second time, he had explained that he was completely apolitical and so his marauding should not be taken as disloyalty to Kasa; he again swore to stop his illegal activities. Within weeks of Tawavitch's death, Kasa's soldiers surprised him in the act of looting another village. When word reached Kasa, he came at once and beseiged him in his *amba*. After two days of fierce fighting, Kasa's men breeched the palisade and captured the *shifta* chieftain. Kasa intended to have the *shifta* flogged and thrown into prison, but when he confronted the man's smug, insolent smile, Kasa's rage boiled over.

He remembered nothing of it. As if no time had passed, he found himself standing over the dismembered corpse of the *shifta*. Wolde told him about it later: as Samuel Aito bathed his flaming forehead with water and tried to calm him, he had raved and screamed and ordered his men to torture the chieftain. Wolde had tried to stop him, but Kasa had turned his own sword against his most loyal follower and driven him away. Kasa's soldiers had flogged the *shifta*, chopped off his hands and feet, ripped his limbs out of their sockets, thrown what remained of him on a bed of coals. Kasa himself had handled the whip and hacked off one of the man's feet with his own sword. Such things had been commonplace under Ras Ali, but they had never, never happened under Kasa.

Kasa experienced a second violent blackout several weeks later, and Wolde only survived it because Magiga Dulou hurled himself onto Theodore and tore the sword out of his hand.

Theodore's guard was thrown into confusion by the conflicting orders, those screamed out in fury by Theodore and those demanded, almost begged, by Wolde and Magiga Dulou. The captain of the guard dared to solve the dilemma by ordering his men to restrain all of them, Theodore and Wolde and Magiga Dulou. When he regained his senses, Theodore swore everyone to secrecy, rewarded the captain with the chieftaincy of Theodore's bodyguard, and commanded that he was always to be surrounded by members of the bodyguard who, when his orders were in conflict with Wolde's or Magiga Dulou's, were to follow the orders of his underlings. The bodyguard served well in the next two blackouts, but in the third Wolde and Magiga Dulou were nowhere near and the captain did not realize what was happening until four men were dead and another mutilated. From that time on, Wolde or

Magiga Dulou stayed within shouting distance of Theodore at all times.

But if one didn't know about Theodore's blackouts—and there were barely twenty men who did—then one would have said that Tawavitch's death was the only unhappy note in the first five years of a reign of such glory that few in history have matched it for progress, for peace, for loyalty from a populace with a penchant for disloyalty. It wasn't easy for a conservative people to accept the many radical changes Theodore made, and history said that, even without change, rebellions were inevitable: to the surprise of everyone but Theodore, the new administration began to take hold, and there was almost no large-scale violence within the empire.

Gabry provided the main outlet for all those frustrated warriors. He sealed off the northern border so effectively that the Turkish slave trade ground to a halt, and the Turkish slavers were forced to roam farther afield, to Kordofan and Darfur and beyond, in pursuit of their commodity. Gabry struck into Turkish territory, too, freeing hundreds of Ethiopian captives and annihilating the slavers.

The *feringi*, Bell and Plowden, had a few failures, but their successes were more than enough to keep them high in Theodore's favor, and even to earn the grudging respect of most Ethiopians. They dug new irrigation systems and introduced new agricultural methods, some of them borrowed from a two-hundred year-old English almanac they had found among a dying missionary's belongings; teachers of the new agriculture began to crisscross the countryside distributing knowledge and seeds; new roads connected the largest cities in Amhara; the equalization of tariffs and the encouragement of new industries, which Bell and Plowden had observed in India, released a steady stream of caravans through the empire and down to Massawa and Khartoum and Kassala and Kedaref to trade the leather and coffee and tobacco of Ethiopia for trade goods from around the world.

Among Theodore's pet projects, the only great disappointment was the casting of his own cannon. Plowden and Bell built a fairly modern forge at Gaffat, and they turned out the finest plows that Ethiopian farmers had ever seen, but whenever they tried to cast a cannon, it split when it cooled or it exploded into great sizzling hunks of flying metal when they fired it. They tried every trick they had ever heard of, and a few that were entirely original, but their cannon were never anything but spectacular failures. At last they decided they must be skipping some vital step, and without it there was no point in going on.

Plowden dropped his glasses one day and shattered the lenses. He glued them back together, but his vision was seamed and blurry, and he suffered terrible headaches. His fever had not improved, and there were times when Bell feared for his friend's life. In the previous year, Bell and Plowden had written, as well as they could, a small book about their experiences in Ethiopia, and Plowden had sent along the manuscript to a publishing house in London, in hopes of putting a few pounds in an English bank. They had not heard from the company, and feared that their book had been stolen. Bell suggested Plowden should return to England for a while, to inquire after their book, to learn to cast a cannon, to get a new pair of glasses, and to regain his health.

By this time, the Englishmen were permanently settled in Ethiopia. They had been given the titles of *rases*. Both had married highborn Ethiopian ladies, and Plowden had fathered two daughters. The highlands was their home now, and Plowden was reluctant to leave for a year or more, but there were just too many reasons why he had to make the trip.

But how, they wondered, could he return to England without facing penalties for desertion, for assaulting a Russian general, for theft, for all the other crimes that could be dredged up against him? They consulted for a long time on the question. The only answer was for Plowden to travel as an Ethiopian subject and the emperor's envoy, and therefore protected by diplomatic immunity. Theodore was overjoyed at the thought of becoming friends with the Queen of such a modern Christian nation. He gave Plowden huge sums of money, letters to the Queen, safe conducts and letters to the various rulers Plowden might meet on the way, and sent him off with his blessing and an heroic fanfare.

Plowden's wife had stitched him a reasonable facsimile of an English gentleman's traveling suit from white muslin, to replace the remnants of the Russian general's uniform, though he would have to wait until he reached more civilized climes before he found shoes and a proper hat. Then, properly dressed and equipped, accompanied by fifty of Theodore's finest warriors, he began his journey. His path took him through Tigré toward Massawa, on a direct collision course with the first of the Tigréan rebellions that would plague Theodore for the rest of his life. Plowden's party blundered into an ambush. His new suit was riddled with musket-ball holes and drenched with his own blood, but he was spared for ransom. Theodore sent a fortune to the rebels, but Plowden had already died of his wounds.

Wolde gave the news to Theodore. He expected the worst, but Theodore only nodded his head in grim resignation and went off alone to pray for a few hours. Then he took command of a force that Magiga Dulou had been gathering for some purpose or other and led a march for revenge, the first time he had taken the field since his coronation. Bell rode at Theodore's side, and in their haste they rode into the same ambush that had taken Plowden.

It was all too quick for anyone to be really sure of what happened. With so many intense feelings involved, especially the emperor's, it wasn't surprising that everyone chose to believe the story that reflected the most glory on the emperor and his martyred Englishman. The caravan route they were following had wormed around a sandstone maze of sheer-walled wadis, too deep to see out of without climbing to the top. The scouts had gone on ahead and not returned, caught in ambush out of hearing to those among the deadly wadis. A last turning in the maze revealed a path into a thick grove.

As Bell and Theodore rode forward, a puff of gray blossomed in the heart of the grove, and a shot echoed against sandstone and sky. A small band of warriors stepped from the concealment of the foliage. As they busied themselves with reloading their matchlock muskets, always a tedious task, one of them thought to fling his spear at the emperor. Bell's eyesight had been failing, too, and this may have had something to do with what he did, for courage was not indicated by the deeds of his life: he turned his horse into the spear's path. The horse took it in the neck, lifted one forehoof, and went down. Bell rolled free and drew his pistol. Theodore discharged his musket, and a man looked up from reloading his own gun, then toppled backward. One of the rebels aimed his rifle at the emperor. Bell coolly raised his arm and shot the man, just as his enemy's final, post-mortem shot whistled close by Theodore's ear. Someone hurled a spear, and the head of it split Bell's lowest rib on its way through his body.

As more of the emperor's soldiers jostled out of the wadi, the rebels melted into the trees. Theodore threw himself down on the ground beside his dying engineer. Bell, for some obscure reason, was suddenly concerned with how the Ethiopians would remember him.

"My lord," he groaned, "by the grace of God, I am happy to see that you are saved. By the death of Iyesus Christ, I can die in peace, knowing you will avenge me." In Amharic, the speech sounded quite genuine. No one understood the delirious curses that took over as he died in pain. Some said they were English prayers, some nonsense. Theodore wept over him and gave him a hero's funeral.

Theodore's troops surrounded the grove in which the rebels were hiding. Theodore had a reputation for leniency with captured rebels, and the rebels gave themselves up as soon as it was obvious they were outnumbered and trapped. Theodore did not lose his mind with rage, as Wolde expected him to. He gave every sign of being in complete control of himself as he calmly ordered that every one of the sixteen hundred rebels should have his hands and feet cut off, and then be left in the grove to die and rot. He declared the grove anathema, and posted guards around it for a month to keep relatives from retrieving the bodies of their dead.

The massacre of the rebels was not a particularly violent episode, as far as the Ethiopians were concerned. It was merely a throwback to the way Ethiopians warriors usually behaved. It cracked the myths surrounding Theodore. It shook Ethiopia out of its lethargy, and re-minded the empire of what its business was. Rebellions broke out simultaneously in Shoa, Gojam, Tigré, and most of the rest of the country. Tawavitch's death had been a personal blow to Theodore, and he had almost been able to withstand it; but the deaths of Bell and Plowden and the uprisings in a land he had thought ready for peace were blows at something greater than himself. For a month, he fought back with the vigor for which he was famous. He led striking forces into Tigré and Shoa and put down the rebels more ruthlessly than he had allowed his troops to fight for five long years. And then, just when it looked as if he could really succeed in forcing the lid back onto the pot, he sank into a fearful depression. He screamed in the night. He had always been a temperate man; now he tried to find forgetfulness in *tej* and *arak*. He had frequent blackouts, and Wolde, hovering just out of reach, was often in danger. Theodore's bodyguard followed Wolde's orders for a day or two, but as Theodore remained consistently bloodthirsty it became harder to disobey him. He ordered prisoners killed and rebellions put down with needless violence, after which he would retreat to his tent and go into a sullen, drunken spell that might last a week or more.

In a month he blackened the name he had worked so hard to make. The laxity of his rule joined with the rumor of his insanity, and the rebellion became joyfully universal, with the single exception of the Amhara heartland. No one emerged from among Theodore's followers with enough power, skill, and charisma to check any of the rebellions, except for Magiga Dulou, who pacified Shoa and then moved north-westward to beat down Theodore's home province of Kwara. In the far north, Gabry retreated nearly as far as Gondar, and Engeddah, who had never developed into a strong warrior, could do nothing against the Gallas of Gojam. Theodore's punishment of the sixteen hundred Ti-gréan rebels had catalyzed a chemical reaction, and without a stronger hand than Theodore's it could not be stopped until it had burnt itself out—and in Ethiopia, which had thrived on a century of uninterrupted warfare, that could take forever.

In this moment of desperation, Wolde sent an urgent message to the only man who knew Theodore better than Wolde did: the nearsighted, tight-lipped Greek, Panagiotes Paniotti. The messenger who tried the Tigré route was never heard from again, but the one who took the longer Metemma route reached Massawa safely, only to learn that Pani-otti had just sailed for India. His servants (who were, after all, Theo-dore's servants) sent two messengers of their own after him. He came at once and traveled as fast as his money and his strength could carry him, but it was still six months from the time Wolde sent the message to the end of Paniotti's journey.

At last Paniotti slid down from his mule onto the carpets before the emperor's pavilion, the one he had shared with Tawavitch. There were soldiers nearby, but they hung back from him, for he was as much a man of mystery here as he was in Massawa: in Ethiopia he was somehow tied in with evil omens, bewilderment, and disharmony. He wasn't an Ethiopian, but he wasn't *not* an Ethiopian, either. He breathed in Ethiopian air and breathed out his own, and things never quite meshed together when he walked among them.

Wolde and Paniotti embraced each other silently, and Paniotti walked ghostlike across the carpets and slipped through the tent flap. The muffled voices of the emperor and his servant, raised high and angry, floated through the cloth of the tent. Most of the words were too muted to be understood, but a few key phrases leaked into the ears of the nearby soldiers, and more rumors were born about their fated Emperor Theodore.

The emperor called for his guards, but Wolde stood in their way with his arms outstretched and wouldn't let them pass.

At the end of twenty-four hours, Paniotti, haggard and drawn, emerged and conferred briefly with Wolde. Servants ran away and came back with provisions wrapped in two canvas sacks. Paniotti and the emperor of Ethiopia, the *negus negast,* the Lion of Judah, each hoisted a sack. The emperor's subjects looked on in utter silence as the pair disappeared on foot into a wild tract of hills inhabited only by mountain goats and hermits. Many of the emperor's subjects stood and stared after them, even when they were long gone from sight, until a rainstorm drove them under cover.

For seven days, the people of the tent city huddled out of the rain that slashed the earth, winced at the lightning, and waited. No one, not even Wolde, knew whether their emperor would return. The news spread from Debra Tabor in widening circles of breathless rumor, swelling into fantasy at the fringes. Those curious absurdities from the perimeter would form the basis of legends that itinerant storytellers would preserve into the next century—tales of their emperor's passage, aided by a saint from beyond, through the cleansing fire of the wilderness.

When they returned, Theodore's tread was lighter than it had been in many months. For some time now he was not to suffer any further blackouts, nor would he touch a drop of liquor. To the casual observer, he had returned to the Theodore of the glorious early days of the reign, before the deaths of Tawavitch and the Englishmen, before the rebellions.

Only Paniotti, and Wolde, and perhaps Magiga Dulou, knew that the Emperor Theodore had not come back from the wilderness at all; that all Paniotti's speeches and prayers and arguments had failed to save the Emperor Theodore, who would lead Ethiopia back into a Golden Age; that the emperor had been abandoned in a musty, bitterly cold hermit's cave in the desolation of those barren hills. Only those three knew it was Kasa who had returned with Paniotti, Kasa the hopeless young boy of the exploding suns and the Light Bringer, a Kasa who recognized that he had nothing to offer except his death.

In Kasa's eyes, the world had shifted. Now it fitted perfectly into that vision of the Light Bringer. It seemed to him that the world had always fitted that vision, but he had not known how to see it. The rebellions proved that the reign of the Emperor Theodore was a perversion. Now there was to be no peace, no progress, no tomorrow, but only the running from one place to another quenching enemy suns and stars until that one enormous sun, surrounded by its myriad stars, came to destroy him at Magdala.

In 1862, two years after Bell and Plowden died, one year after Theodore was lost in the hills, a man came from far away. His name was Cameron, and he was a consul from the British Queen. He might have been a likely man to be the Light Bringer, since he came from far away and represented a Christian nation over which the sun must surely shine, but he didn't exhibit any of the signs that would identify the Light Bringer. So Theodore imprisoned the Consul Cameron and his people, tortured them, chained them, threw them into prison on the *amba* Magdala, and allowed them freedom to write despairing letters to their fellow countrymen in the Turkish domains. And Theodore waited for the British Queen to answer this challenge by sending another man, one who might indeed be the Light Bringer.

8

September 1864

Massawa

Rassam's Massawan months gradually passed. Blanc joined Rassam at Moncullou at first, but within a week he moved himself and Rafaelo to a collection of large canvas tents on the mainland beach just north of the island of Massawa. He had decided to set up his clinic there, he said, and so he ought to live there, too. As Abd-ul-Kerim told Rassam, it was a true reason, even if it was incomplete.

Rassam slipped into a pattern of living that might see him through a lifetime as easily as a year, that demanded the barest minimum of effort to get through each day, that established no permanent ties but only loose, easily broken connections with the land and the people. His days had a scheduled simplicity that gave him the impression of daily accomplishment, even when he accomplished nothing. Sometimes he went into Massawa to visit the sheik's *kat* room or to stroll around the open-air market, but mostly he withdrew into his own little world in Moncullou and avoided what meager society Massawa had to offer.

Blanc and Abd-ul-Kerim, visiting him in Moncullou, were his main source of human companionship. His contact with Blanc was rigidly regular. The London *Times* arrived in the diplomatic packet each month, and Blanc made a habit of picking it up from the warehouse by the bunder and bringing it personally to Rassam. Rassam read one newspaper each morning, a consistent twenty-one days late, and in the afternoon he sent the newspaper by Dahon to Blanc, who read it the next morning. Blanc worked in his clinic five afternoons a week. On Wednesdays and Sundays, he rode out to Moncullou with his rifle or shotgun, and he and Rassam spent the afternoon blasting away at the wildlife. Their communication was limited, ritualistic, and unsatisfying, but the pattern was reassuring in its familiarity.

Abd-ul-Kerim visited Rassam several times a week, too, studiously missing Wednesdays and Sundays and the monthly newspaper delivery, but otherwise completely without pattern. He also was a regular subscriber to the London *Times*, but his copy came to him through other, speedier channels. He would receive it about a week before Rassam and Blanc, and would have an English-speaking clerk pick through all the issues at once to find news items that might interest him. He played along with the Britons' game, though, and pretended he hadn't seen a particular article until Rassam had had a chance to read it for himself. He kept an accurate log of the days and always knew what Rassam had read each morning. Then he would appear in Moncullou with a dozen questions, often too complex for Rassam to answer, about what it all meant. But he also brought an increasingly skillful hand with the cue stick and his own favorite addiction, the great books of Eastern literature. He delighted in reading those books aloud deep into the night. Rassam's interest would wane as the wicks burned low, and he usually awoke the next morning in the chair where he had fallen asleep, with his boots off and a blanket tucked close around him. Neither Rassam nor Abd-ul-Kerim mentioned the slaves of Massawa again.

The prisoners still languished in Magdala, so far away it was hard to believe they really shared this flesh-and-blood world of human experience. Consul Cameron's second message, his first since the one Captain Speedy had received, arrived in Moncullou three months after Rassam had settled in. It had rained in the Ethiopian highlands, and during the day a deluge had covered the plain and gurgled between the stilts of Rassam's house. By nightfall, the plain was barely passable for a man on foot, so Rassam was surprised to hear a stealthy, unsure tap on his door in the middle of the night. In his nightshirt and nightcap, he answered the door himself. By the yellow light of the lantern he held he saw a shabby Ethiopian, slightly darker and more slender than most Arabs, wearing a long white shirt over muddy trousers. The Ethiopian stared wide-eyed at Rassam's nightshirt. Rassam couldn't see anything so unusual about himself until he realized that the nightshirt was identical to the Ethiopian's long shirt. The Ethiopian thrust a folded and sealed letter at him. Rassam led him into the house and sat at his desk to read it. Cameron had addressed it, curiously, to "Mr. Rassam, or whoever else may represent the British Government in Massawa." Rassam had no idea how Cameron, in prison, would have learned his name. The letter gave no clue, either. It stated that the prisoners remained in chains. Cameron had had his ankles and wrists tied to long ropes with which gangs of Ethiopian soldiers had competed at tug-of-war until he thought his joints would rip apart. He was beaten into unconsciousness with hippopotamus-hide whips. His wrist chains were attached to his ankle chains in such a way that he could not stand upright or stretch out on the ground. Theodore gave them no food or drink, and they had to buy their own. They were running short of money, and if Rassam did not send some they would soon starve to death. Cameron said again that nothing but a letter from the Queen would set them free. "But for God's sake," he wrote, "do not come up here; he will cage you sure as a gun, as he thinks that while he has us in his hands he is safe from attack, and, of course, with a swell like you in addition, matters would only be better for him." He urged Rassam to send the letter from the Queen by messenger.

Rassam fed Cameron's messenger, paid him well, gave him a place to sleep for the night, and sent him back to Cameron with a bag full of Austrian Maria Theresa dollars (the minting of 1728, the one showing the most cleavage, which was the only money recognized in Ethiopia) and a message of encouragement; but since the emperor had sent no answer to his letter, and since Paniotti's couriers had not returned, Rassam would not send the Queen's letter. As he later explained to Abd-ul-Kerim, "It would not be becoming to impose on the emperor a letter from the Queen when the emperor, by his inaction, has indicated for all the world to see that he does not want it."

Instead, Rassam wrote another letter to Theodore:

> Be it known to Your Majesty that it is now three months since I arrived here, bearing a letter to your address from her august Majesty, our British Queen; and the day after my arrival I dispatched a letter to you by two messengers, named severally Mohammed Abawas and Mohammed Sa'id; but up to this time I have received no answer thereto. I hope that the cause is propitious.
>
> Different reports reach me daily regarding this delay, and a rumor has been current that the messengers did not succeed in reaching you, owing to some people on the road having intimidated them against approaching you. [This was Abd-ul-Kerim's idea.] It is also suggested that perhaps the letter was handed to some individual who failed to deliver it to you. For this reason, I now write to you again, and enclose herewith a copy of my former communication which may not have reached you, in order that you may learn its purport.

During the next five months, Rassam received three more notes from Cameron. They described more severe tortures and ever-pressing problems of finance. Rassam sent back bags of dollars and letters of encouragement, and the next note from Cameron always acknowledged them.

There was no reply from the emperor.

Paniotti had returned from his trip in Rassam's second month at Moncullou, and during the next few months Rassam had seen him fairly often, at the sheik's *kat* room, in the market place, meeting a boat at the rickety old bunder. At Paniotti's suggestion, Rassam, Blanc, Abd-ul-Kerim, and the Greek merchant had spent a week touring the coast by camel as far south as the hot springs at Adulis, near Annesley Bay. Paniotti impressed Rassam with his energy, his casual self-confidence, his refusal to use two words where one would serve. He was a valuable

compendium of trivial information; he pointed out geological forma-
tions, constellations, and empty river beds that he warned could turn
into deadly torrents in a matter of minutes. He made a point of instruct-
ing Rassam in the most vital bits of travelers' lore, so that after a few
days in his company Rassam fancied that, equipped with camel and
proper gear, he might have made any solo desert crossing in perfect
safety and reasonable comfort.

Despite this contact, Paniotti remained as mysterious as ever. He
would not talk about Ethiopia, nor about himself. Abd-ul-Kerim whispered to Rassam that it was believed that Paniotti's parents had come
from Greece to Jiddah with him as a small child, and from there he had
appeared in Massawa twenty years ago, already famous and rich and
obscure. More than this, no one seemed to know.

Paniotti disappeared without a word again in December 1864,
Rassam's sixth month in Moncullou, and this time he was gone for four
months. Even Abd-ul-Kerim had no idea where he was, and the sheik
could only wave his hookah stem and say, "Who knows where Paniotti
goes? To Nubia and the caravan routes to Egypt? Down the Mother
River to the Mountains of the Moon? He flees in the night, and then one
day he is back as if he had never gone. He doesn't talk about his trips,
his servants won't talk, his camels are silent. The only evidence that he
has been gone is that he is even richer than before."

As Captain Speedy had written, Paniotti surrounded himself with
faceless men from all over the East, and when he was gone they continued to inhabit his house and run his business affairs. They were men
without ties or friends in Massawa, men who never spoke without need,
who appeared one day in Massawa and might disappear, never to be
seen again, a week or a year later. *It is just Paniotti,* the Massawans
would say, *it is just Paniotti.*

It was one of those faceless men, a small, quick-eyed Yemeni, who
knocked at Rassam's door one morning. Dahon led him in to Rassam.
The man smiled around yellow, broken teeth and said, "My master
wishes that I should invite you to English tea. He suggests that there is
someone you may wish to meet."

"Who is that?" asked Rassam, though the question was less intriguing
than the invitation itself: to Rassam's knowledge, no one but the faceless
men had ever been inside Paniotti's house.

"My master urges patience and an open mind," said the Yemeni, and
he salaamed and started back to Massawa.

Paniotti's house was an undistinguished coral stone building, nearly
as large as the sheik's palace. The door swung open the instant Rassam's
knuckle touched the polished, unpainted wood. Rassam stepped past
the servant into the foyer and stopped, even more amazed than he had
been at the sheik's *kat* room. The interior of the house was not Arabian
or Turkish, but rather had been modeled after an English country
mansion. A wide stairway, cleverly proportioned to create an impres-

sion of vast distance, rippled down at him like a rush of marble cata-racts. Mirrors reflected dozens of Rassams, glittering in rainbowed sun-light that entered through a high window and refracted through a crystal chandelier. The furniture was Louis Quinze, finely kept, obvi-ously genuine, ugly, out of place, and incredible.

"This way, please." The doorman gave the soft Arabic syllables a tone of officious command, like that of an English butler in his master's home.

Paniotti was waiting for Rassam in an English drawing room: grand piano, velveteen curtains, white porcelain dogs by the absurdly inap-propriate fireplace, gas lamps in brackets. Paniotti engulfed him in the traditional Arab embrace that no one but Paniotti ever had enough zeal to perform. "Welcome, my friend, welcome."

"Your home—" gasped Rassam, stepping away from Paniotti and turning for another look.

"You will embarrass me," warned Paniotti.

"But it is magnificent. Unexpected."

"It is comfortable. You should feel comfortable here, too. Are you well, Rassam? The climate of Massawa is too dry to be unhealthy, and you are not of the fragile English type, but I still worry for you."

"I am very well."

Paniotti's eyes, hidden behind the thick lenses, revealed as little as ever.

"Your trip?" said Rassam. "It was successful?"

Paniotti gave no information. "How does one measure success? But come, I have news for you. And someone for you to meet."

Rassam realized that a man was standing close behind Paniotti. He was diminutive, the size of a boy of ten or eleven, with the white *shama* and trousers of the Ethiopians, the *mateb* around the neck, and a floppy, dust-white turban. In his hand he held a device of iron that was so intricately worked that Rassam needed a hard look to recognize it as a crucifix. The man had the straight nose, thin lips, and café-au-lait skin coloring of the Ethiopians. Rassam could not make even an approxi-mate guess at his age: his dress and confident stance indicated that he was a man, but his size and his smooth, beardless face were those of a boy.

"This is Mr. Hormuzd Rassam, the envoy of the British Queen Vic-toria, of whom I have spoken," said Paniotti to the Ethiopian. "And this is Wolde, a Coptic priest from Ethiopia. I have known Wolde for many years, and when I heard that he had traveled down from the highlands with a caravan that had come to trade for salt and lead, I thought immediately of my dear friend, Mr. Rassam, who is so desperate for news of Ethiopia. So I invited Wolde to visit me."

Wolde touched his fingertips to his forehead. "By the power of God, I have heard much about you, and I am happy to see you at last." His Arabic accent was strong and unfamiliar to Rassam, and his voice was abnormally, unpleasantly high-pitched, vaguely reminiscent of Ismail

Tasfay's. Rassam knew why he had not been able to guess Wolde's age: the man was a eunuch, castrated as a child, certainly many years older than he looked.

Rassam nodded in his smartest British manner. "Pleased."

They seated themselves, and Paniotti clapped his hands for tea. While a barefoot servant brought in a silver tea service and poured, Paniotti said, "Wolde has informed me that all your letters have reached Theodore, that he has read them and set them aside. That is the only news, I fear, from the camp of the emperor."

"He made no comment?" asked Rassam.

"None." Wolde made the sign of the cross over his tea with his iron crucifix.

"May I ask, what is your relationship with the emperor?" asked Rassam.

"Relationship?"

"By that I mean, do you know him personally? Do you often see him? What is your source of information about him?"

"I am a priest attached permanently to his army. I serve his soldiers and their families. I travel where he goes, though I am only one of many priests. I see him often, but he knows me little."

"I thought Wolde might tell you the story of the founding of Ethiopia's imperial lineage," said Paniotti. "It is an interesting tale, and it tells quite a bit about the Ethiopians."

Patience and an open mind, the messenger had said this morning. "I would be pleased to hear it," said Rassam. Feeling uncomfortably manipulated, as he had not allowed himself to be since he had withdrawn from the mainstream of Massawan life, Rassam prepared to try to decipher all the hidden meanings in Wolde's story.

"I would be pleased to tell it," said Wolde. "It is the favorite story of my people. In the time in which Solomon was building the Great Temple in Jerusalem, the Ethiopians ruled a far-flung empire that included all of Africa and Arabia, but these Ethiopian empire-builders, though powerful, were ignorant men who worshiped pagan gods. Our queen was Makeda, called in the Bible the Queen of Sheba. Solomon sent out heralds to all the world, asking to buy the things he needed for the construction of the Temple. Makeda herself led a great caravan of seven hundred and ninety-seven camels bearing red gold and sapphires and hard black wood and gifts for Solomon himself.

"Makeda stayed many months in Jerusalem. Solomon so impressed Makeda with his vast wisdom that she gave up the worship of the sun and the moon and began instead to worship the God of Israel.

"Now Solomon desired to raise up many sons in many parts of the world, in order that they might rule the heathen lands and throw down the false idols, and so he determined to plant his seed in Makeda. She, understanding his wisdom, allowed him to have his way with her.

"While he slept, Solomon had a dream. In the dream the sun came down to Jerusalem and shone very brightly, but then it left Jerusalem and went southward to Ethiopia, and Jerusalem was left in darkness."

Wolde stumbled occasionally over the translation from Amharic to Arabic. He punctuated many of his words by stabbing the air with his heavy iron crucifix, but there was little life in the words themselves. Rassam had been paying very close attention to both the story and the storyteller, but now he decided that the hidden messages must be in the story; Wolde himself was notable for being a eunuch, an Ethiopian, a man who had seen Theodore, and for nothing else.

"Makeda returned to Ethiopia, bore Solomon's son, and named him Menelik. When Menelik was grown to the fullness of manhood, he journeyed to Jerusalem to see his father. Solomon rejoiced to see him, for God had granted him so far only one other son, Rehoboam, who was then only seven years old.

"Solomon annointed Menelik with the holy oil of kingship and passed a law that only Menelik's heirs should ever rule in Ethiopia. Menelik asked his father for a piece of the fringe of the covering of the Ark of the Covenant, and Solomon promised that he should have it. Solomon sent for his counselors and officers, and said to them: 'I am sending my firstborn son to rule in Ethiopia. Send your firstborn sons with him to be his counselors and officers.'

"When the time came to leave, Azariah, the firstborn son of Zadok, the high priest, was inspired by God with a plan by which these firstborn sons could take with them the Ark. He went to a carpenter and, giving him the dimensions of the Ark, told him to make a raft of that size. In the dead of night, Azariah took the raft into the Temple. The Angel of the Lord opened the doors of the sanctuary for him. Azariah took the Ark and put in its place the raft and covered it with the three coverings of the Ark.

"The next day, Solomon ordered Zadok to give Menelik the outer covering of the Ark. Menelik and the firstborn sons of Israel then set out in a caravan of wagons, and God made it so they skimmed a cubit above the ground and covered thirteen days' journey in a single day. When they reached Egypt, Azariah told Menelik that they had brought the Ark with them, and Menelik rejoiced. Menelik went on to Ethiopia, where he ruled, and his sons after him, and where the firstborn sons and their sons after them were the emperors' counselors and officers.

"After Menelik had left, Solomon told Zadok about the dream of the sun which had shone on Jerusalem, but then had left for Ethiopia. Zadok said: 'I wish you had told me of this dream before, for I fear that the Ark of the Covenant is gone.' They went to the sanctuary, took off the coverings, and found the raft. Solomon wept and rent his garments, but the Spirit of Prophecy spoke gently to him and said: 'The Ark has not been given to an alien but to your own firstborn son.' These words comforted Solomon and he ordered all his counselors and officers to keep secret that the Ark was gone.

"Years later, Balthazar, the king of Rome, who had no son, sent to King Solomon and asked for one of his sons to marry his daughter and rule over Rome. Solomon sent Adramis, his youngest son, and with him the youngest sons of his counselors and officers. Rehoboam ruled over Judah, Menelik ruled the lands to the south and the east, and Adramis ruled the lands to the north and the west, and so the prophecy that the seed of David and Solomon would rule the world came to pass.

"Then, in his later days, Solomon dreamed another dream. He saw the sun come again to Jerusalem, but the Jews hated the sun and tried to destroy it, and it departed to Rome and Ethiopia. This prophecy came to pass when the Jews slew the Son of God, and only the Romans and the Ethiopians worshiped Him. Then again, in later years, the kings of Rome were led astray and came to believe that Our Lord had two natures, one divine and one human. Only the Coptic Church has remained faithful to the truth that Iyesus' manhood was absorbed in his divinity, and so it is now only the Copts who are the heirs to the promises of God to man. That is the story of how the Ark of the Covenant came to Ethiopia, and how the Ethiopians became the chosen people of God."

Rassam had listened to Wolde's story with growing impatience. Try as he might, he couldn't figure out any reason why Paniotti wanted him to hear it. This was his first chance to talk to an Ethiopian who could really provide him with solid, firsthand information about the emperor, and he spent the time listening to a fairy tale! "What can you tell me about the emperor's mood?" he asked. "What is he like?"

Wolde poured himself another cup of tea, made the sign of the cross over it, and drank it down. He returned the cup to the tray and said, "There is an ancient prophecy in Ethiopia, in the *Fikkare Iyesus,* our most venerable book of prophecies, that there will come a *negus negast,* an emperor, who will be named Theodore. That our Lord Iyesus Christ Himself will bring this Theodore to the throne of the Lion of Judah. That Theodore will reign after a time of war and hate and neglect of God. That he will bring peace, prosperity, and the fear of God to Ethiopia."

"Is the current Theodore supposed to be the Theodore of the prophecy?"

"He is."

"Do you believe it?"

Wolde shrugged. "Many believe it. Many more believed it in the past. You see, for a few years when he first came to the throne, there was peace such as there had never been before. A man could carry his wealth openly in his hands and walk from one end of Ethiopia to the other, and no man would disturb him. The churches thrived, and there was ample food for everyone. Then, the rebel chieftains rose up against him in a moment of his weakness, as they have always risen up in the past, and their successes and his losses have caused many to doubt.

"But I, I am his man. I was with him from the beginning and saw the miracle of his rise to power, and I have seen the generosity in his heart and the grace in his soul. He is the Theodore of the prophecy. He will put down the rebels, and we will have the prophesied reign of peace and the fear of God."

Another tack, thought Rassam. *Anything to draw him out of his fantasy world and make him give me something more real than prophecies.* "Do the rebels make him angry?" Rassam asked. "I've heard horror stories about the way he deals with them when he catches them."

Wolde smiled at some bitter, private joke. "In war or rebellion, everyone suffers. The rebels make him angry, certainly. He roars that they are ungrateful, which is true. He warns them to lay down their arms, he begs them to return to him and help him bring peace to the land. They keep on fighting, and he captures them with loss of life on both sides. They promise to obey him, and he releases them. They fight again. He captures them once more and cuts off their hands and feet. What else can he do? The prophecy must take precedence over human life, but I can say this: he has never taken a life without suffering himself for the loss of that life, and he has never—he would never—*castrate a five-year-old boy.*"

That childish voice emanating from the thin-lipped mouth, talking so simply about killing, set Rassam's nerves on edge. He asked stiffly, "Why has the emperor deprived the consul and the missionaries of their rights, violated diplomatic immunity, thrown them into prison and tortured them?"

"It is an easy thing to understand," said Wolde, his smile never flickering. "Theodore is a great emperor, justifiably proud. He hopes to be a friend to the British Queen. He was very glad when Consul Cameron said he could make friendship between them, but there was no answer to his letter. For a year and a half, there was no answer. That is a very great insult to a proud monarch, is it not? And instead of delivering the letter by hand, Consul Cameron went to the Sudan, to Kassala, to visit the Turks, the emperor's enemies. *Why did he do this?* the emperor asks. This too is a very great insult.

"The emperor has many reasons for disliking Cameron. Cameron told some of the emperor's subjects that Theodore was a murderer for avenging the deaths of Bell and Plowden. This angered the emperor, but the hope of the letter from the Queen was so great in Theodore's heart that he kept Cameron in his favor. It was only when the letter did not come that the emperor allowed his anger to reveal itself, and he put Cameron into prison at Magdala with all his people."

"Do the Ethiopians support him in these actions? Don't they think he's been too severe with them?"

"No. Cameron is a very evil man. He has insulted the emperor, and through the emperor all Ethiopians."

"Does the emperor know that I mean to be his friend, that I would like to repair things between our two countries again? That I carry a letter from the Queen?"

"I understand that he knows."

"Why hasn't he answered my letters?"

"Are you a Christian?" asked Wolde.

The sudden change of topic caught Rassam off guard. "I am."

"Coptic, or Roman?"

"Neither. Church of England."

"Well, that is not too bad. Are you a soldier or an engineer? Can you cast a cannon, build a road, lead an army? Are you a priest or a man of great learning?"

"I am a diplomat."

Wolde pondered this for a moment. "But what can you do?"

"I was involved in archaeological excavations for some years," said Rassam hopefully, feeling that he was on trial, hoping he did well.

"What is that?"

Paniotti explained to him what archeology was.

"It is not very useful," said Wolde.

"Why are you asking these things?" said Rassam.

Wolde brushed the question aside. "I am only curious as to what kind of a man your government sends to deliver a letter to our emperor. Your friend, what is he?"

"Blanc is a doctor, and a captain in the army."

"A doctor. And a soldier."

"He is not a soldier, only a doctor attached to the army."

"A doctor is still good."

"Have I any chance of getting an answer from the emperor?"

Wolde wagged his head thoughtfully. "A soldier or an engineer would have a better chance. The emperor likes to have soldiers and engineers come to him. Do you think your government may decide to send a soldier or an engineer in your place?"

"Unlikely. But I, do I have a chance?"

"You must be patient," said Wolde. "More than that, I don't know. If you like, I will take a letter to my superiors in the Church, and they will offer it to the emperor. He is a very religious man, and if they bring it to him, he will read it more carefully and give it more thought."

"I thank you," said Rassam.

I hope Your Majesty will pardon the liberty which I am taking in addressing you this third time upon a matter which has given me much anxiety.

More than eight months ago, I wrote and informed Your Majesty that I had been sent here by the British Government as the bearer of a letter for you from our Queen. After having waited about three months for a reply, I was compelled to write to you again, as I feared that the first two messengers had not delivered my letter safely to you.

Neither to the first nor to the second letter have I as yet received an answer, and the very thought of knowing that the two letters have reached you long since makes me the more anxious to learn the cause of your silence.

I beg to inform Your Majesty that the sole duty on which I have been sent is to convey to you our Queen's letter. I have nothing else to do but to deliver it to you, and to assure you of the sincere wishes which our Sovereign entertains for the welfare and prosperity of the great country which the Almighty has placed under your rule.

It is rumored that some evil-disposed persons, who do not wish to see England and Ethiopia on the best terms, have misrepresented the object of my mission to you. I can confidently assure you that the British Government takes a sincere interest in the welfare of your Empire, and would greatly deplore any unfriendly feeling taking place between the two countries through a mere misunderstanding.

The delay makes me feel this painful suspense the more, because I am at a loss what explanation to give my Government as to its cause. Moreover, the rainy season is now fast approaching again, and, if Your Majesty will not honor me with an answer soon, I shall be obliged to return to my duties at Aden."

"I wonder whether you have the sense of being judged, Mr. Rassam?" asked Paniotti.

"Exactly," said Rassam. "Every time I venture out in public, I feel like a bug under a microscope, with a whole class of leering medical students sharing the lens. I know my every word and gesture is being judged and evaluated. By Blanc, by Rashid ibn Ali, by Ismail Tasfay, by my superiors in Aden and Bombay and London, by the sheik and by you."

"And by Theodore?"

"No doubt. By everyone except for Abd-ul-Kerim, and that's only because he understood me so completely the moment we met that he has no further need for evaluation. Yes, I am like that bug under the microscope—or like a prisoner in the dock surrounded by his bewigged and pitiless judges."

"Do you see how the roles are reversed, too?" asked Paniotti. "That to us you have been sent as a judge, with far more power over us than we have over you. The Ottomans need British favor. The eunuchs need your indulgence. Abd-ul-Kerim needs your friendship."

"Do you think I'm not keen enough to know what's going on around me?" Rassam snapped. The idea that everyone hung on his judgment was actually new to him, though he wouldn't admit it. "Why do you ask?"

"I only wondered," said Paniotti, and after a perfectly neutral pause he added, "How did Wolde strike you? What feeling did he give you?"

Rassam chuckled bitterly, swiftly. "He was a simple, uncomplicated man, wasn't he?" His tone was purely sarcastic, but then he continued seriously, like a beaten man. "He put me off guard with that fairy tale. He convinced me that he had no imagination or skill. There was so little remarkable about him that I wouldn't have recognized him the next time I saw him, unless, of course, I heard him speak. He asked such meaningless questions, and then he excused himself and ran off so quickly. He left me with a nagging suspicion in my mind, but the sensation grew during the day, and in the middle of the night I bolted awake suddenly, drenched with sweat and trembling, and I knew what he had done. Without my even being aware of it, he had flayed me alive, drawn out my insides and examined them and learned everything there is to know about me. He didn't care what the answers to his questions were. I suppose he already knew them." Paniotti nodded softly, but Rassam was talking so fast that he didn't notice. "He was simply watching my gestures and the way I drank my tea, listening to the tone of my voice. He could interpret them all. And that remark of his about the castration of five-year-old boys: he gave me an invitation to ask about the most personal parts of his own life, to do some probing of my own, to show him my own skill, and I didn't have the courage to ask the questions. He will report to the emperor, won't he?"

"Of course."

"And he has already left Massawa."

"I will see that your letter catches up with him."

"Naturally. I didn't really expect to have a chance to try for him again."

"That sounds like the voice of resignation," said Paniotti.

"It is my Massawa voice," said Rassam. "Only my Massawa voice."

9

August 1865

Massawa and London

Rassam had been in Africa for fourteen months. Five months had passed since his third letter had started into the Ethiopian highlands with Theodore's eunuch priest. One more highland dry season had nearly ended, and the salt desert around Massawa had reached its most parched condition of the year. Blanc had prepared a brief treatise on Massawa's endemic diseases for the British medical corps, and it had been filed away and forgotten in Bombay. The American war was over and the American president was dead, but that was news from another world. Nothing else had changed.

One morning an Ethiopian boy entered the city. He had been walking so long that the dust of the road had become an almost permanent patina on his clothes and body. He was conspicuous because of his Ethiopian trousers and *shama,* so he attracted some unwelcome attention as he wriggled through just as the gates slammed shut for the night. He sought out his destination at once, to assure himself he hadn't forgotten where it was, but then passed it by with barely a glance and walked until darkness gave him some small measure of concealment. Then he abandoned his random wandering and headed straight back to his destination. He circled around the rear of the two-storied coral house and found a cramped cul-de-sac that ended against the encircling wall. With a quick look to make sure no one was watching, he leaped up and scrambled over.

He made a fast search around a back door and found the key he had known would be hidden in an ornamental cornice. He unlocked the door, pushed it open, and padded silently down darkened halls to Paniotti's English drawing room. He paused in the doorway and saw again the absurd velveteen curtains, the porcelain dogs, the brittle, gaudily carved furniture, and the useless fireplace.

Paniotti, who was reading by candlelight, felt his presence and looked up to see the boy watching him.

"Seraphiel!" cried the Greek. "Come, Seraphiel, come." He was on his feet at once, leading the boy into the room, clapping his hands loudly for a servant, waving the boy toward a chair. Seraphiel shook his head at the chair and squatted on the floor. Without a word, he folded up his trousers leg and began unraveling the thread that secured a wide inner cuff.

"Was the journey hard, by the grace of God?" Paniotti spoke in the musical Amharic tongue, in which it is nearly impossible to say anything without a reference to the deity.

Seraphiel grunted. "God has made Kassai very strong in Tigré province. I started down with my brother Ayalu. Kassai's people took him near Senafe and killed him."

Paniotti gave a typically Amharic sound, enough to show his sorrow, little enough to not embarrass Seraphiel.

The servant brought a jug of *tej,* the powerful honey liquor of the highlands. Seraphiel went on worrying his cuff, finally pulling it open and extracting a thin packet of brown papers that had become molded to the shape of his calf. Only then did he pour a glass of *tej* and drain it in a single gulp.

Paniotti smoothed out the papers on the floor. He read:

> To the much beloved friend of my heart, with the love of Iyesus, from Theodore.
>
> I pray to the Lord God that you are well, Paniotti, as I am well. Wolde delivered to me the letter from Rassam, and he told me what he observed of this man. I have heard the observations, too, of the men who delivered the letters from the Consul Cameron to Rassam, and of other men as well. I have seen also the letter that you yourself sent by Wolde to me. I thank you, my most cherished, for the honesty you have given me. By the death of Christ, honesty and frankness from others have not often been my share.
>
> You tell me that Rassam will be my death if he comes to Ethiopia. You tell me that we all seek death, each in his own way, but that only God may decree the proper time, and so we should live each day as if we have a million more to live. You tell me that I should not seek death by allowing Rassam to come to me. You tell me there still remain the good things that I should do. But I tell you, Paniotti, that God decreed my death to me thirty years ago.
>
> I have called myself the slave of God, but I have neglected my obligations to the Lord. I thought that I was greater than the Word of God, and I tried to do in my lifetime the things the Voice of the Spirit of Prophecy told me I would not do, but that would happen after my death. I sinned in my excessive pride, but God is merciful. He forgives. He grants Theodore, His slave, another chance.
>
> I will not do the good things, because God wills it not so. But by my deeds —by my death—they will come to pass. I welcome the coming of Rassam, and whatever fate he brings with him. Take heart: perhaps he is not even the one for whom I wait.

Ever, I have trusted you. I listen to your words with my heart, and to this extent I follow them: I do not address my letter to Rassam by his name. If he is not the one, then I am certain, as I have faith, that God will inspire the hearts of his people to send another, who may be the one I seek.

As you have ever been loyal to me and served me well, send Seraphiel and Ayalu to Rassam with my letter, and see that he or another comes safely to me.

LONDON

Ten Downing Street was just one of a row of shaky houses, one hundred seventy years old, badly built by the profiteering contractor whose name the street bore. In the second-floor study, the prime minister towered behind his massive oak desk and leaned across toward the men who, in the name of Queen Victoria, ruled the British empire. Blue veins formed a web under the bleached whiteness of his forehead, and a tremor shook the long finger he aimed first at Sir Austen Layard, then at Lord Russell. Henry John Temple, Viscount Palmerston, the prime minister, was past eighty now, and he could not last much longer, but the mere pointing of that long, quivering finger still brought to mind an angry God demanding; "Hast thou eaten of the tree, whereof I commanded thee that thou shouldest not eat?"

Layard examined the carpet, Russell his own hands. Russell's face, still youthful despite his seventy-three years, wore such a look of schoolboy remorse that Palmerston barely suppressed a smile.

Sitting at his ease with pipe smoke wreathing his head, Gladstone exchanged a brief, knowing glance with the prime minister. They formed an exclusive club now, these two, the once and future rulers of British destiny, and there was a grudging understanding between them.

Palmerston settled his old bones into his chair and folded his hands on the polished oak.

"It is not," he began slowly, "a question of blame. With a general election in two months, the question is how we are to salvage an unfortunate situation, this—what are the newspapers calling it?—this 'Ethiopian imbroglio.' Gentlemen, I believe we have three alternatives." He counted them off on his fingers. "One, I announce that I have perfect faith in this Arab person, this Rassam, and let him go on up to Ethiopia and join the rest of those fellows in chains. Two, I have the Foreign Office replace him with someone more acceptable, who will do the same. Three, I give immediate orders to prepare for war."

"For war?" croaked Layard, who lacked the genius ever to be a member of this inner ruling circle.

"Does anyone know whether Mr. Rassam is a Whig or a Tory?" asked Gladstone.

Layard whispered, "One of them. A Tory. Idolizes Disraeli."

Gladstone said, "Then by all means, send him."

Layard took out his pipe and began working a cleaning tool around the inside of the bowl with jerking, nervous movements.

"That would neither assuage our consciences nor help us in the election," said Russell.

Since Consul Cameron's imprisonment, a year and a half before, the English press had supplied the public with a steady stream of information on the 'Ethiopian imbroglio.' Things had reached the point where the Whigs could not afford to be accused of concealing facts; reluctantly, they had been releasing every communication from Cameron to the press. Each pitiful message set off a new round of public outrage.

Palmerston's Whigs had stifled debate in Parliament on the ground that Theodore might have the English newspapers read to him and take out his anger on the prisoners. But, this very morning, Benjamin Disraeli, leader of the Tories in Commons, had violated the loose prohibition and denounced the government in round, clear terms. The occasion of his speech was a critical one. The letter from the emperor to Rassam and Rassam's request for instructions had both been received by Whitehall the previous day, and released at once to the press. After elaborate, highly religious salutations, the letter had launched into a presentation of the emperor's grievances against Consul Cameron.

"Cameron, who is called consul," Theodore wrote, "represented to me that he was a servant of the Queen. I invested him with a robe of honor of my country and supplied him with provisions for the journey to deliver my letter of friendship to the Queen. When he was sent on his mission, he went instead and stayed some time with my enemies, the Turks, and returned to me. I spoke to him about the letter I sent through him to the Queen. He said that up to that time he had not received any intelligence concerning it. What have I done, thought I, that they should hate me and treat me with animosity? By the power of the Lord my Creator, I kept silent." At last, after much more of the same, the final paragraph read: "Be it known to the bearer of the letter from the British Queen that there exists just now a rebellion in Tigré, the northernmost province of my empire. By the power of God, come round by way of Metemma. When you reach Metemma, send a messenger, and, by the grace of God, I will send people to receive you."

Rassam reported that he had sent an answer to the emperor saying that the rainy season and the resulting fevers on the Barka Plain would make travel dangerous until October, so he and Blanc would delay their departure until then. Meanwhile, Rassam was requesting instructions.

When Disraeli rose in Commons, it was no secret that he was making an election speech. He condemned the government for all the blunders that had led up to Cameron's imprisonment; for allowing the prisoners to remain in captivity for twenty months; but most of all for putting in charge of the mission an undistinguished middle-level bureaucrat, a man who was not a soldier and so could not command the respect of a fighting chieftain, a man who was, most importantly, *not even English.* Disraeli pointed out that Theodore's letter had not mentioned Rassam by name, but had only called him "the bearer of the letter from the British Queen."

Across the aisle, Layard had risen to try to explain that an Oriental such as Rassam would be better equipped to understand the intricate working of the emperor's mind. He suggested that negotiations in the eastern world were a time-consuming process, and that the members should be pleased with the achievement of even such a bitter, ambiguous letter from the emperor.

Layard's speech was typically weak. Many newspapers, including the *Times,* would carry the entire text of Disraeli's speech without even mentioning Layard's defense.

Palmerston, behind his massive desk, turned his eyes to Layard. "Can you tell me what Mr. Rassam has been doing for the past year? Why hasn't he achieved any more results?"

Layard, who was held responsible for the original choice of Rassam as envoy, mumbled something unintelligible.

"Speak up," commanded Palmerston. "This isn't church, is it? Or Parliament?"

Layard cleared his throat and started again. "Takes time for these matters in the Orient and Africa. Isn't at all like Europe. Given a little more time—or allowed to go up to Ethiopia—"

"What has he done?"

"Sent letters to the emperor."

"I have read those letters. They are weak. They make no demands, offer no threats. Why hasn't he gone into Ethiopia, or at least sent the Queen's letter up?"

"If you recall," Russell answered, "it was never intended that he should actually go up to Ethiopia. His instructions were to stay in Massawa and avoid trouble. And he considers it unbecoming to send the Queen's letter without a request from the emperor. Rassam is very correct about protocol."

"So the mad emperor of the Ethiopians may have respect for British protocol, and the rest of the world may laugh."

"Rassam has been caught in a bind," said Russell.

"From another angle," continued Palmerston, "has he occupied his time with any adventures? Done anything that justifies support for him? Something we can throw up to the public and say, 'See, he hasn't gotten the prisoners freed, but he *has* done this and that.' Has he done anything about fighting the Arab slave trade, for instance? Slaves are always a popular cause. Plenty of Englishmen have made their careers on a few daring raids against slavers. Has he done anything at all to save his damned neck?"

"No," said Layard.

Gladstone said, somewhat mockingly, "Most men would try to stir up a little excitement for themselves after a year of waiting. But perhaps your envoy thrives on boredom."

"As I said, blame is not the question," said Palmerston. "What would you suggest, Sir Austen?"

Layard studied the great man's folded hands. "Perhaps someone more forceful—"

"More forceful."

"Someone with more prestige."

"John?" In all the years since before Waterloo, only Palmerston had ever called Lord Russell by his given name.

"With nothing to show from Rassam, we are in an awkward position," said Russell. "If the prisoners were released, we might risk sending Rassam to deliver the Queen's letter and fetch them out. But without any kind of assurance from the emperor, we would surely be making a mistake. We could never risk it.

"In lieu of results, then, I think we must recall him, and then either replace him or prepare for war. A more forceful envoy might make a peremptory demand for the release of the prisoners, and if Theodore refuses or doesn't answer, we could send an army after them. That ought to satisfy just about everyone."

"He would kill the prisoners," said Layard, his voice a frail squeak. "He is a madman."

A tense silence lingered, until Layard realized that his role in the conclave had ended. He lowered his head and gripped his knees.

"There are advantages to war," said Russell. "It would serve notice to the world that we are still willing to back up our honor with force. A successful campaign would please the army—that cannot be overlooked: morale has never recovered completely from the Crimea and the Mutiny.

"Lines of command and the transport services have been overhauled in the last few years. An Ethiopian campaign would strain our ability to feed and clothe the troops. The lines of supply would be incredibly long, the logistics complex. I have already heard from a general or two who would welcome a test like Ethiopia."

Palmerston liked what he heard, as Russell had known he would. A show of military might appealed to him now, with his career and his life nearly over. Just one more good show.

Gladstone, chancellor of the exchequer, disagreed. "Think of the cost, Lord Russell. It would run into millions. Where would the money come from? War might please the public now, before the election, but we will have to live with them afterward, when it is time to pay the bill."

"Mr. Gladstone," said Russell, "what price will the English people place on English honor?"

Acidly, Gladstone said, "Would Lord Russell be advocating quick, decisive, dramatic, expensive action to cover past mistakes?"

Russell snorted. "Hardly fair, sir."

"Gentlemen, calm yourselves," said Palmerston. He spread his hands out on the desk, and almost without considering what he was about to say, announced, "I think I shall agree with Lord Russell: an unmeetable demand and then war. I would like Lord Russell to recall Mr. Rassam at once and to appoint someone else, a soldier or an explorer. Your choice must be someone who will do the job properly, and excite the public at the same time. Someone famous and . . . thrilling. Instruct him to send one demand to release the prisoners, or beware the consequences. Contact the secretary of war. In perfect secrecy, he is to prepare a budget and detailed plans for a campaign into Ethiopia." Then, almost reluctantly, he added: "If Mr. Rassam reports any more progress, by which I mean nothing short of the release of the prisoners, we may reconsider."

For four weeks after he sent the emperor's letter on to Merewether at Aden, Rassam oscillated between jubilation and despair. London had to change his instructions now and send him on to Ethiopia—they *had to*—but there was no guarantee, and there were so many things that could go wrong. He never thought about Consul Cameron any more. He rarely thought about Ethiopia itself, about what going there would mean. It was only the exact instant of departure that signified for him now, that moment when the camels moved toward the Barka Plain and left Massawa and all considerations of Englishness behind.

Late on a torrid afternoon, a sandstorm rolled down from the north to engulf the residence for one claustrophobic hour, and it left behind an evening so calm, soft, and silent that from the porch Rassam and Abd-ul-Kerim could hear children laughing in Moncullou, and a herdsman calling after his goats. Inside the house the only sound from the outside was the gentle sifting of sand over the roof. Rassam lay on a sofa, watched the wraiths of smoke from the two hashish pipes drifting yellow and ghostlike through the corners, and listened to Abd-ul-Kerim's prattle.

Eventually Rassam pulled his eyes down from the smoke and noticed Abd-ul-Kerim's foolish, dreamy smile. The Arab's voice was lisping and utterly relaxed. These were two warning signs that his mind was functioning at its keenest level.

Rassam watched a segment of smoke that took on the shape of a horse's head, and then slid through Ismail Tasfay to become, for one fleeting eyeblink, Queen Victoria. A year before, it would have been impossible for Rassam to see Queen Victoria in a yellow puff of hashish smoke. Now, he only let her dissipate away and then forgot her.

Abd-ul-Kerin was discussing some new and complex theory. Rassam's attention floated in and out of the lecture.

Abd-ul-Kerim's theory had something to do with a dynamic, eternal conflict between the eastern world and the western. "The Levantine peoples," Rassam heard him say, "the Persians, the Jews, and Moslems, the early Christians, have always worshiped God: they are religious. The Europeans—the Greeks, the Romans, the Celts and Germans and Franks and English—have only paid lip service to gods who are more mythical conveniences than religious deities. Truly, they worship only Man: they are humanistic. That is why the Europeans have never invented a religion worth exporting."

"You are being ridiculously profound," said Rassam, who had wandered back for the last bit of Abd-ul-Kerim's lecture.

"Wait, I will be ridiculously historical," answered Abd-ul-Kerim. And for an hour or more he discussed the heart of his theory: that there is a certain innate balance in the world, a delicate philosophical equilibrium, expressed on the battlefield as often as in the church, synagogue, mosque, or temple.

Rassam settled himself deeper into the sofa and said, "You are talking historically, as you promised, but it still sounds like philosophical double-talk to me."

"I am coming to the point of all my double-talk, Rassam," said Abd-ul-Kerim. "We learn that the forces that operate the world are greater than mere men—greater even than mere gods. These forces are as passionless and as irresistible as the forces that turn the tide. The balance will be maintained. Darius will be defeated, Alexander will die, the tide will flow and ebb."

Rassam had only been half listening to Abd-ul-Kerim. "But what does it all mean?" he asked.

"It means that my father can wait calmly for his way of life to end," answered Abd-ul-Kerim, "as he told you, because he knows the forces that will end it. Men die and others are born. Everything changes. Nothing changes. Nothing matters to him."

"A dismal outlook. What about you?"

"I will pass, too. Like all men, my life on earth is just a ripple in time. I can hang onto a descending world, go out with the tide: or I can seek another time, join myself to an ascendant and rise with it. My family has a certain amount of wealth, of course. I can go to any city in the Arab world and live in comfort and honor, dividing my time between hashish pipe and harem, never noticing that I am sinking. I can go into the desert and suffer and deny myself and live just as meaningless a life. Or I can find a message and cling to it as it rises, and float like a balloonist over the top of the world."

"I don't follow you at all," murmured Rassam. "What kind of message?"

"You understand the Arab disposition well enough to know we'll follow anyone with charisma and a creed. There have been forty thousand prophets, and their broken faiths litter the boundaries of the desert. They are born in the cities and the crowded places, but an unfathomable yearning draws them into the desert. They pass through the fire. They return with their messages complete and clear. They are black and white without a sliver of gray, as colorless and unambiguous as Massawa under the noontime sun. We Arabs have no use for doubt or confusion. We choose to know, and so we always come to know. I honor other faiths, but I choose to know there is no God but Allah and that Mohammed is His Prophet. I am a Moslem, but in this world of Turkish Moslems and African Moslems and Javanese Moslems, I search for another message, something more."

"Something to turn you into a balloonist?"

"Exactly. You understand me."

"I understand that you are talking nonsense."

"True. But I do search for my message because I cannot remain for long in Massawa."

"Oh? When will you go?" asked Rassam. There was a long pause. At last Abd-ul-Kerim said, in so low a whisper that Rassam had to strain to hear it and so heard it more clearly than if Abd-ul-Kerim had said it at a normal volume: "When you have set the slaves free."

"I will set no slaves free," said Rassam. He surprised himself with his own quiet anger. "I am here for Ethiopia."

"And I am here for myself," said Abd-ul-Kerim evenly, "and I will leave for my message. Have you seen Ismail Tasfay recently?"

"No." Rassam had withdrawn from Massawa as completely as he could, but not so completely that he shouldn't have run into Ismail Tasfay every month or so. On Abd-ul-Kerim's invitation he occasionally went to the sheik's *kat* room, and there he might see the sheik, Paniotti, various other businessmen of Massawa, once or twice a sullen, suspicious, unforgiving Rashid ibn Ali, but he had never seen Ismail Tasfay again.

"You've shown no interest in Massawa's slaves," said Abd-ul-Kerim, "and so Ismail Tasfay has no interest in you. He has been avoiding you. He was frightened of you for a while, but now he has grown confident and complacent. He gloats behind your back and calls you a spineless creature. If you had planned it, you couldn't have manipulated the situation better. A blow against the slavers will be more shattering than ever, and after you've freed the slaves, the Sublime Porte will have no other choice than to recall Ismail Tasfay to a life of obscurity in Constantinople or in some meaningless provincial capital." He spoke matter-of-factly, as if he were answering a question Rassam had asked.

"I'm not going to free any slaves," Rassam protested weakly. "I am only for Ethiopia."

Abd-ul-Kerim said, "When all is lost, when you don't know who you are, when your life is at its lowest point, then I think you will strike. You will strike out at them in righteous anger as you would want to strike out against yourself. And by acting, you will discover who you are."

"You are talking nonsense. My life isn't at its highest point, but it is far from its lowest."

Abd-ul-Kerim laughed softly. "Lower than this?" And then he said, "You feel no guilt, do you?"

"Of course I don't." That was all Rassam had meant to say, but the words started pouring out. "I've been to the village at the bunder to meet our steamers a couple of times, but I never go near the slave pen. I don't consciously think about avoiding it, but somehow I just never happen to go near it. Wherever I go, I never see any slaves. I never think about them. I don't feel any sense of duty undone, any guilt, anything. The slaves are not my affair. They don't worry me."

"But somehow you never go near the slave pen in the village," prompted Abd-ul-Kerim.

"Why do you remind me?" begged Rassam.

"You know why," lisped Abd-ul-Kerim. "You know why."

They were silent then for two or three hours. Some of the villagers had gathered together to sing away the spirits of the night. Their voices floated across a quarter mile of nighttime desert.

Rassam said at last, "You talk about the desert." He had not said anything in so long that the words caught in his throat and came out as a croak, and he had to repeat them. "You talk about the desert as a fire through which the prophets must pass. And here I've been for more than a year. Some nights, I feel the loneliness of it all. I hear the voice of the wind whispering across the salt flat, and it isn't hard to believe it's the voice of God. The bats creak by like demons. Serpents glide like slippery tongues across my porch and roof. I don't know who I am anymore. I'm not English, but I'm not Arab, either. The desert has taken me away from myself, burned my old self away, but it hasn't given me anything in return."

After a minute, Abd-ul-Kerim said, "Remember: when it is time, I'll be here."

"My dear Mr. Rassam," began the dispatch. The normally dour political resident had never before used anything so sentimental as "my dear Mr. Rassam." It was an immediate clue that all was lost. It was Rassam's first warning, in fact, since he was still two days short of reaching Disraeli's speech among his stack of newspapers.

"I have some distressing news for you," the letter continued. "You have been recalled from the Ethiopian mission by the F.O. The telegram came two weeks ago, on August 6. I put off letting you know for these two weeks while I made enquiries, but I have no positive explanation. At this point, I would guess we never will have one. As far as I am concerned, you have done a commendable job, cautious but firm, always well within the guidelines of your instructions. Until now, I have heard nothing from London to lead me to believe that F.O. did not share my feelings. There has been the inevitable sniping at a civil servant in a sensitive post. I am sure you have seen it in the press. I am certain, though, that the F.O. would not bend beneath so little pressure, and so it must be the political appointment of someone else. I am certain that it has nothing to do with you or with the job you have done.

It must be particularly painful though, coming as it does in the wake of that letter from the emperor. It looked as if you were almost in Ethiopia, didn't it?

"I suggest that you return to Aden at your earliest convenience, as I have more than enough work for you to do here." The letter was signed "W.L. Merewether."

Rassam handed the dispatch and the telegram to Blanc, who had brought the diplomatic packet from the bunder to Moncullou. "That *is* bad luck," said the doctor. "You had rather placed your hopes in this mission, hadn't you?"

"Rather."

"I had hoped to see Ethiopia myself," said Blanc. "After more than a year of Massawa it would have been a well-deserved reward. Massawa is boring. Life itself is a bore. But *Ethiopia!*" He shook his head in resignation, and for the first time in over a year thrust out his hand to Rassam. They shook hands solemnly. "Send the *Times* over, will you?" Blanc asked, and then he was on his way.

Rassam sat down on the edge of the porch. He watched the guinea fowl bumbling around in the brush, and he thought them as useless and stupid and misguided as he was himself. There was no meaning to their existence, no reason they should live, nothing to keep them going, but, like Rassam, each of them must be sure it was the most important creature alive. Dahon brought him tea. He drank cupfuls of it through the long August afternoon and evening. Shadows lengthened, the shadow image of the house became a vast angular wash across the sand and brush and trees in front of him. The guinea fowl congregated in the branches of one of the trees for the night. After dark had fallen, a lion roared somewhere nearby.

Dahon came onto the porch to collect the tea service. He paused in the doorway as he re-entered the house. "The vipers will be out, master," he whispered.

Rassam didn't move, only stared out into the darkness.

"You must come in, master," Dahon said more insistently, touching Rassam's shoulder. "It isn't safe to sit in the dark. Come in now, I've prepared dinner."

Rassam got up, brushed off his coat, and patted down his hair. "I don't think I shall eat tonight," he said. "Thank you all the same." He found his hands involuntarily tugging his tightly cinched collar higher against his throat to make certain it was in its most proper and uncomfortable position. He went into the house, hesitated for an uncertain moment by the billiard table, then went into his bedroom and dressed for bed while Dahon shook out the bedclothes and checked for scorpions. After Dahon had blown out the lamp, Rassam tossed for a few minutes in bed. He remembered how Abd-ul-Kerim had told him he would free the slaves when he reached his lowest point. He experienced a certain small amount of satisfaction that he would prove his friend wrong: he was at his lowest point, but he had no intention of freeing anyone. Then he slid into an exhausted sleep.

"What would you make of a man like that?" asked Rassam. "From the first moment he sees you, he glares at you with hatred. He seems to take pleasure from his hatred, to sharpen and refine it, to make it into a work of art. He was just a common seaman. We never exchanged a word, but it was clear that he hated me as if I were the devil himself."

"Perhaps you were," said Abd-ul-Kerim.

Rassam stopped walking, and Abd-ul-Kerim, sensing that Rassam was not following any more, stopped too and looked back. Dressed in his flowing white robe, with one hand raised as if in benediction, Abd-ul-Kerim stood as still as an icon among the leafy shadows of the ravine bottom.

"You think I am the devil?" asked Rassam, bewildered, slightly awed.

Abd-ul-Kerim moved at last. His face reappeared from the green shadows. The golden emblems gleamed in his mouth. "We all have our own devils, do we not?" he lisped. "Who knows what devils possess this man?"

It had only taken Rassam the one day following his recall to pack all his belongings, and now the Suez-to-Aden naval steamer, due the next day, would take him and Blanc back to their old lives as exiled mediocrities. Abd-ul-Kerim had come to Moncullou on the morning of Rassam's last full day in Africa and, refusing to reveal their destination, had led Rassam for nearly five miles across the plain in the direction of the Ethiopian escarpment, which now loomed ahead of them in the early morning light. They had left their horses in the shade at the mouth of a narrow ravine, from which a shallow stream of warmish water flowed out onto the plain, only to disappear into the sand a hundred yards beyond the last sheltering vegetation. The path wound through tamarisk and thorny acacia trees. The stream sometimes split into tiny channels, sometimes spread into a marshy expanse. Abd-ul-Kerim carried his rifle.

"Why would I be this sailor's devil?" Rassam pressed Abd-ul-Kerim. "I used to think it was because he was English and I wasn't, and he hated me for the color of my skin and my accent—but now I am not so sure."

Abd-ul-Kerim answered without stopping or turning his head. The close-hanging greenery muffled his voice. "I can only guess, but I would say it's exactly the opposite. You thought he hated you for your inferiority; I think he hated you instead for your superiority. The lower orders are usually color-blind, but they are always keenly aware of the distribution of power. Has there ever been a man who didn't hate those who were more powerful than himself? To him you are not an Arab. You are a man of position, influence, dignity, even wealth. You answer to no one that he can see. You can look anyone in the eye. While he . . . he follows the orders of a hundred other men. You say he rowed you to shore—

wouldn't you resent someone who could demand labor of you? Did you give him a choice? Did you pay him? Did you thank him? You were his master, he your slave. You held the power over him to make him do whatever you wanted. Of course he hated you. And of course he would be you if he could."

"Couldn't I ever earn his respect?"

"You have it now. He hates you, but it is hate permeated with respect." Abd-ul-Kerim stopped beside the stream and tested it with his hand. He motioned for Rassam to do the same. The water was very hot. Abd-ul-Kerim said, "Aren't you the same as he? Don't you have the highest respect for the English, and yet hate them at the same time?"

Rassam had never thought of his feelings in exactly that way before, but he realized that Abd-ul-Kerim had described them with perfect accuracy.

"Yes," he said. "I've loved them ever since I can remember, and I've hated them almost as long. My father was one of the great men of Mosul, one of the wealthy merchants. We were an Ottoman city, just on the verge of the Arab world, but while I was young it was the English business interests who were the real force behind our existence. My father groveled before them, curried favor, let them walk all over him. Much like your father with the Turks"—Abd-ul-Kerim had walked on, but now he turned his head far enough around to give Rassam a sympathetic nod—"and yet different, too. Your father hates the Ottomans and so salvages some of his dignity. My father loved the English. We never spoke Arabic or even Turkish at home. I learned English as my first language. I wore English clothes, went to the schools of the English children, grew up with English friends who could barely tolerate me.

"I recognized what kind of man my father was when I was about fifteen years old. I realized how little dignity he had kept, and I swore I would never be like him. Outside the home I became a perfect Arab boy. Those were really glorious times for me, those next five years, but then I realized, slowly and painfully, the truth: that an Arab boy might grow up to become an Arab man, but in Mosul that was nothing. All doors were closed to Arabs: Turks and Englishmen held all the keys. I knew then that power was everything, and I swore to become the most complete Englishman in the world. I understood who I was in those days. I knew where I was going. I studied at Oxford, worked with Layard, did all the things a young Englishman like Henry Blanc might do. And now I realize that I have been just as wrong these last twenty years as I was those five as an Arab boy in Mosul. I am not Arab. I am not English. I am neither Abd-ul-Kerim nor Henry Blanc. There doesn't seem to be a place for me at all."

"You are my friend," said Abd-ul-Kerim softly. "That isn't a place like Mosul or Massawa or London, but it is something, isn't it?"

He stopped and turned then, and his expression was so hopeful that Rassam had to laugh. "Yes," he said, "it is something."

"Ah, I've made you laugh," sparkled Abd-ul-Kerim, and then he was running on ahead through the winding pathways. Rassam jogged after him, and they laughed as they ran.

They had caught their breath and were walking again when Abd-ul-Kerim said, "What will you do?"

"Return to Aden. Go on as I was before."

"Do you feel cheated?"

"Yes, of course. But that is the way politics works. Once again, I have been a victim—of power, I suppose. I have too much to suit common seamen, and yet not enough to suit myself."

"It is a paradox."

"Yes."

"An eternal paradox."

"An unsolvable one."

"Not necessarily," said Abd-ul-Kerim.

"How solved, then?" asked Rassam.

"Through politics, through deceit. Play a game that isn't expected of you. Tell me: what is it you want to have happen?"

"To go to Theodore as envoy."

"What is it that would convince them to send you?"

"I couldn't use deceit."

"Just play the game with me. What is it that would convince them?"

"My instructions were never really to go to Ethiopia," he admitted. "I've hidden it from everyone, even from myself, but I was only supposed to deal with Theodore from Massawa. I know now that I was never intended to go to Ethiopia."

Abd-ul-Kerim had slowed. His tone was apologetic. "I knew it."

"Naturally. So . . . I've placed myself outside the situation and tried to analyze the thinking of everyone involved. They know in London that Theodore has told me to come to him with the Queen's letter, but they know he didn't call me by name, and they may use that as an excuse for replacing me. They know that he is still holding the prisoners at Magdala. If they were willing to take a risk to free the prisoners, I think they would allow me to go to Ethiopia. Since they are recalling me and replacing me, I assume they aren't willing to take the risk at all. Ergo, I can only imagine that the replacement has orders simply to send an ultimatum to Theodore and once he has refused it, they intend to send an army to defeat him."

"You think they are planning that?"

"It's ironic, I suppose," said Rassam, "but I'm both close enough to the English mentality and far enough removed from it, so that I can usually dissect English thinking more accurately than an Englishman could. It's the same as your ability to dissect my thinking."

"Exactly."

"I am certain those are their plans," Rassam went on, "and the only thing I can think of that might interrupt them would be if the emperor released the prisoners, and announced that he was waiting for me, *personally, by name,* to come to bring them down. That he would chain them again, or even kill them, if I did not come to him with the Queen's letter."

"Then tell your superiors in Aden and Bombay and London, tell everyone who will listen, that that is what has happened. If you must, forge a letter from the emperor. Then, before the trick is discovered, leave for Ethiopia and accomplish your mission. Cling to Ethiopia as to a rising message. Rise with it. Return to England a victorious balloonist. Be welcomed a hero. Be English if you still want to be, or spit in their eyes."

"It cannot be done."

"It cannot? Or you will not?"

"Cannot, will not, it is the same thing, isn't it? For me, anyway. It is another paradox. I still want to be English, and therefore I cannot violate the moral code of the English which condemns lying. But if I do not lie, I shall not become English."

"I would lie," said Abd-ul-Kerim. "It would not be the first time, nor the last."

"I am not you," said Rassam.

"Nor I you . . . but here we are."

They passed out of the jungle and found themselves at the edge of a glassy-smooth, sandy-bottomed pool. The opening in the foliage overhead let in vast amounts of sunlight that gave the steamy air a gauzy texture. The sand glinted underwater.

Abd-ul-Kerim yanked off his turban and whisked off his long robe. Absolutely naked, he stepped down to the water, tested it with his foot, and slid in. He rolled onto his back and floated away, kicked awkwardly, then let his body sink to the bottom.

Abd-ul-Kerim's easy nudity stunned Rassam's Victorian morals for a few seconds, but within a minute he had undressed, piled his folded clothes neatly on top of a dry log, and joined his friend in the hot, relaxing water.

10

August 1865

Massawa

The steamer anchored off Massawa the next afternoon, too late to chance the treacherous sand bars and reefs until morning brought sunlight and the high tide. The captain of the ship—which, by chance, was the gunboat *Dalhousie*—sent word to Rassam at Moncullou that launches would be waiting for him and Blanc at the bunder at dawn.

The previous morning, before Abd-ul-Kerim had come to take him to the hot spring, Rassam had read the *Times* of August 5. As always, he had read it exactly on schedule, an even three weeks late. In that edition of the paper, he had read the text of the emperor's letter to him. If it had been intentional it would have been cruel, but he knew that reading that hopeful letter on that dismal morning was a meaningless coincidence, and he had shrugged it off. Then, this morning, he had read the *Times* of August 6. The newspaper carried an account of Disraeli's speech in Parliament. It had been so long since the prisoners were chained and there had been so few results that Rassam could understand Disraeli's concern—but Disraeli had gone on to talk about Rassam himself. Rassam's hands began to tremble as he held the page. He read the article once, then again, more slowly. *A man who is not even English,* Disraeli had said. Those words had been spoken before Parliament, printed in the *Times* and every other newspaper in the British empire, had been read by every person whose respect Rassam had ever hoped to win. Those words had been spoken by Disraeli, Rassam's saint and god and idol, the man who had overcome his own racial heritage to become the consummate Englishman. *A man who is not even English!*

Rassam spent the whole day on the porch. There was nothing else to do. Dahon could fetch porters—slaves—from Massawa on three hours' notice. Blanc could handle his own arrangements for meeting the steamer in the morning. Abd-ul-Kerim didn't come to visit, as he might have done on Rassam's last day in Africa.

It was getting on toward evening when Rassam realized that Abd-ul-Kerim must have already read Disraeli's speech. Yet he had not come to Moncullou to see his friend. For several hours, Rassam hated Abd-ul-Kerim for leaving him alone in his misery, but then he began to wonder how long ago Abd-ul-Kerim had read the speech. Rassam had not read about Lincoln's assassination until May 5, twenty-one days after it was reported in the *Times;* Rassam knew from a slip of the tongue by Abd-ul-Kerim, forgotten at the moment but remembered later after Rassam read that Lincoln was dead, that Abd-ul-Kerim had been at least seven days ahead of him. Rassam counted back the days. It was just six days ago that Abd-ul-Kerim had predicted that Rassam would free the slaves at the lowest point in his life. He had already seen the speech, and he had known that Rassam would read it on this particular morning. He knew about Rassam's feelings for Disraeli. Rassam knew, then, why Abd-ul-Kerim was staying away. Abd-ul-Kerim's ability to see inside Rassam's mind was uncanny. *But no,* thought Rassam, still hating his friend, *I won't do it. Never. Never.*

Several hours later, lulled to sleep by an overworked brain and the gentle warmth of the August night, Rassam nodded off. At dusk, the guinea fowl had gathered in the branches of their usual tree. When he woke, Rassam went through the front room into his bedroom. He dropped off the carpet slippers that he had not taken off all day long and put on his boots, cinched a high white collar tight around his neck, and put on his woolen traveling jacket. He slipped handfuls of shells into his pockets, hoisted his shotgun to his shoulder, and went outside. Dahon muttered protesting noises as Rassam went by him, but Rassam ignored him and walked out into the brush. Shadows loomed around him. He could barely see his feet. He pushed through carelessly, not noticing how the thorns ripped his clothing and scored his face and hands.

The moon had risen beyond the tree and silhouetted the bare branches and sleeping birds. Rassam stopped a dozen paces away, loaded his shotgun, and blasted a gaping hole among the birds. Three guinea fowl dropped, fluttering and screeching, to the ground. The moon shone through the hole. The birds around the hole jerked, scrambled, jostled stupidly until they had filled it again. One of them tottered and fell. Its neighbors pressed together and filled its space. So much for a meaning to their existence, or a reason they should live. Rassam reloaded and blasted more of them out of the roost. They jostled again.

Behind him, Rassam saw Dahon, outlined by the light inside the front room, standing on the porch. Rassam felt cruel, passionless, above all moral judgment, like a wrathful God Whose creations have not behaved the way He, in His arbitrary glory, has decreed they should. The world had treated Rassam unfairly. It no longer made sense to him. The things he had held dear were chimeras. He released himself from his antiquated laws. He fired and fired and fired, until the tree was empty, scarred and torn, branches hanging, swaying in the Red Sea breeze, the ground littered with the carcasses of dead or wounded birds, some still squawking in confusion and pain.

He wandered around in the brush for a few hours after he had killed the guinea fowl. Some change in the moisture of the air or some alteration in the sounds of the night told him it was just minutes short of first light before he started back to the residence.

The lamp was still burning in the front room, and Dahon was still standing in the doorway. As he entered the yard, though, Rassam saw two horses tethered at the side of the house, and he knew it was Abd-ul-Kerim, not Dahon, who had been watching him from the doorway. He realized that he had known it all along, and that he had intentionally stayed out in the brush to make Abd-ul-Kerim wait.

Rassam stopped in front of the porch.

They examined each other. Abd-ul-Kerim's face was a mass of soft shadows. For the first time this far from Massawa, he had no rifle, nor was there a weapon on either of the horses.

"Are you ready?" the young Arab asked, his voice soothing, his lisp exaggerated.

Rassam stepped onto the porch. Abd-ul-Kerim made room for him to pass through the doorway. Rassam laid his shotgun on the billiard table and followed Abd-ul-Kerim to the horses. They cantered across the plain toward Massawa, the first time Rassam had ever seen Abd-ul-Kerim ride at anything less than a gallop. The tide was in and the channel was wide, but there were men to hold the horses and a boat to take them across. They stepped onto dry sand only fifty yards from the city wall. Abd-ul-Kerim led Rassam into the blackness hard against the western wall. Rassam followed obediently. Yellow threads of light outlined a small postern gate Rassam had never noticed before. Abd-ul-Kerim tapped a short code against the gate, and it swung silently inward. One of Abd-ul-Kerim's young Arabs pressed himself against the wall within to make room for them. He held the only illumination, an oil lamp. Beyond him a narrow brick tunnel angled downward and vanished into the darkness.

"I don't have to see them. I know all about what happens to them," Rassam whispered hoarsely. Then, more truthfully, "I don't want to."

"You should see them," commanded Abd-ul-Kerim. "You are going to do this out of pure selfishness. There's nothing wrong with that—oh, no—but you should see their abused little bodies, so degraded and so ruined, and know you are doing a worthy thing. That knowledge may help you later." He ducked through the gate, took the oil lamp, and started down the tunnel. Rassam hesitated a few seconds longer, then ran after him.

The tunnel descended for a long distance. Finally, when it must have been a whole level below the sheik's basement *kat* room, it stopped its descent and it made two quick turns to the right to send it back the way it had come. Down this deep the tunnel was dank and cool. Water dripped from the low ceiling, and the wall and floor were slick with wet mosses. There were heavy iron-bound doors with massive locks. "Armory," Abd-ul-Kerim would whisper as they passed a door. "Treasury." "Escape route to the mainland." The tunnel branched a few times, but Abd-ul-Kerim led the way without pausing. At last he halted in front of one of the doors and drew Rassam very close. His voice was barely audible. "These tunnels were my playground when I was a boy, as they've been for untold generations of my ancestors. The Turkish eunuchs have always thought their subterranean secrets were their own, but I'm sure there's never been a male of my line grown to manhood who didn't know them all."

He produced a key and set it into the lock, and before he turned it he blew out the lamp. The door whispered open and let out a faint, centuries-old commingling of the scents of hashish and wine and perfume and sweat.

They stood in the doorway long enough to let their eyes adjust to the darkness. After a few minutes, Rassam realized the darkness wasn't total. Past the door was a passageway so narrow that one man couldn't pass another. At intervals of twenty feet or so along one wall, at about eye level, were small lattice panels. Light shone dimly on the panels and reflected brighter on the opposite wall.

Abd-ul-Kerim stepped forward and pulled Rassam after him. Rassam found that the floor was thickly carpeted and the walls were draped with blankets to deaden sound in the passageway, so as to make the observer safer from detection. Abd-ul-Kerim's face appeared for an instant as he looked through the first panel. He shook his head and went on to the next, and the next. Rassam followed. Abd-ul-Kerim found what he wanted at the fourth panel and guided Rassam up to it.

The room behind the panel had obviously been intended to imitate and outdo the sheik's *kat* room. The walls were hung with fine tapestries depicting all kinds of hedonistic pursuits. Between the divans were the remains of a late meal—a dozen empty plates, wine, and hashish. Ismail Tasfay lolled naked on one divan and watched through drowsy eyes. The other eunuch, one of the servants from the sheik's retinue, wore a short shirt of red silk. His legs were bare. From his divan he directed the entertainment.

There were four children in the room, aged between thirteen and fifteen. A European boy, totally naked, his blond hair curled into lank ringlets around his temples, lay on his back on a divan between Ismail Tasfay and the other eunuch. An Arab girl, also naked, fine-featured, thin-limbed, with small, pointed, raisin-tipped breasts and bony buttocks, knelt on the cold floor beside him and worked at his penis with her mouth. Everything about the couple, the slow rise and fall of her head, the bored look on the boy's face, the way his hand dangled limply off the side of the divan, suggested resignation. Neither was getting any pleasure from the act, and if the eunuchs were getting any pleasure it could only have been in their ability to force weaker persons to perform for them against their wills. It was slavery for slavery's sake. The eunuch with the red silk shirt held a thin whip in one hand and idly snapped it as he urged them on. The girl already had welts across her back and buttocks. Beads of blood formed a criss-cross necklace across her dark, smooth skin. Even so, she couldn't answer the eunuch's urgings with any more enthusiasm.

In a far corner cowered two Africans, a boy and a girl, fully clothed, a year or two younger than the others. Wide-eyed, they were watching the eunuchs and the other children, but they weren't taking any part in the performance. New arrivals, not yet used, perhaps, not yet burned out, learning the things that would be demanded of them.

Rassam pulled away from the panel. Abd-ul-Kerim guided him into the main tunnel, closed the door, relit the lamp, and led the way back to the distant postern gate.

What Rassam had seen wasn't particularly shocking in a world where the exercise of raw power was just part of the game that everyone played. But he agreed with what Abd-ul-Kerim had said: it was better for him to have seen with his own eyes.

Outside again, they started around the city walls, and Abd-ul-Kerim said, "It is a good morning for it. The traders have at least fifty or sixty slaves in the village pen."

Rassam accelerated his pace. The tide was high, and the inrushing sea had turned half a mile in a straight line into a two-mile-curve. It took them more than twenty minutes to get around the crescent to the village by the bunder.

The sun, low over the Red Sea, shone in their eyes as they left the shelter of the village and walked out onto the beach. Two launches and their crews were waiting for Rassam and Blanc on the beach fronting the village, between the bunder and the oil slick. A bosun's mate stepped forward and saluted them languidly, but Rassam commanded: "I am Envoy Rassam. You will take my friend and me to the ship. At once. Without delay."

"Your luggage, sir?" asked the bosun's mate. He had looked more closely at Rassam and noticed his torn clothing and the ragged stripes of blood on his hands and face.

"Damn my luggage!" cried Rassam. "At once!" He had never spoken this way to an Englishman before, not even to someone with as little status as a bosun's mate, but it made no difference. The old values were so remote and trivial now that Rassam could hardly believe he had ever followed such nonsense at all.

"Aye, aye, sir." The bosun's mate drew himself up and responded to the kind of order he was used to receiving. "At once."

The cadence that the bosun's mate called out was far sharper than that last time, more than a year before, and the oars dipped and tugged at the water with a sound like clapping hands.

Rassam wondered for a moment whether this was the same bosun's mate who had let the sailors laugh at him and Blanc, and whether that one sailor who seemed to hate him was among the crew, but his mind was such a riot of distracted, conflicting emotions that the wondering disappeared almost immediately. The launch slid alongside the *Dalhousie* and bumped with a metallic echo. "I'll send the men above to drop the hawsers, sir, and we'll haul the launch aboard," said the bosun's mate, but Rassam just sniffed at him—he borrowed one of Blanc's disdainful sniffs for a sailor who knew the meaning of English sniffs—and pushed aside the oarsmen, who were starting to pull themselves onto the ratlines. His leather-soled boots slipped across the thick, tarry ropes, but he pulled himself up with his hands and scrambled up toward the deck. Abd-ul-Kerim was a shadowy white phantom floating effortlessly at his side. From below, Rassam heard a rough voice whisper, "The blighter's not wearing nothing underneath. I always wondered." And another voice said, "Look at 'im, flopping in the breeze." But Rassam only felt a tiny surge of pity for these English slaves who were making fun of his proud Arab friend.

The first mate was on the metal deck to greet them, but Rassam interrupted his salute: "I am Envoy Rassam. Is Captain Easterday still commanding this ship?"

"Yes, sir."

"I will see him at once. A matter of importance."

Lines of command between an envoy and a first mate were more certain than between an envoy and a common bosun's mate. "Aye, aye, sir," said the mate, and then they were fairly running through the maze of corridors toward the captain's quarters.

Captain Easterday was still asleep, but the first mate opened his door and shook him awake. Rassam and Abd-ul-Kerim pushed into the minuscule cabin behind the first mate. There was barely room for all of them.

"What is it?" moaned the captain, rubbing sleep from his eyes. One side of his great gray mustache flared up toward his eye, and the other side trailed down limply across his chin. He found his wire-rimmed glasses and put them on. Not quite believing what he saw, he looked from the bloodstained envoy to the turbaned Arab.

"I am Envoy Hormuzd Rassam," said Rassam, dragging out of storage his most formal diplomatic tone of voice.

"I remember."

"I am empowered, as are all diplomatic representatives of the British crown, to make use of all British forces in combating slavery and the slave trade everywhere within the Ottoman empire. There is a thriving slave trade passing through Massawa. There are slaves being held right now in a disgusting pen in the village by the bunder. There are slaves in the palace of the sheik of Massawa. Captain, I request that your marines come ashore this morning, at once, and put an end to it."

The captain's expression was one of sleepy resignation. Slavery meant little or nothing to him, but he knew his orders and Rassam's authority: the lines of command between an envoy and a ship's captain were even more certain than between an envoy and a first mate. "Exactly where will we find these slaves?" he asked, but then he thought better of the question. "Benson," he said to the first mate, "give this gentleman whatever he needs in the way of marines and naval support. Plan on holding the ship over for as long as this business takes. It's your show, all right? Don't hash it up."

"Sir."

"Well, get on with it." Captain Easterday pulled his glasses off, hid them carefully under his mattress, rolled onto his face, and went back to sleep.

Within fifteen minutes, fifty British marines, scarlet-jacketed, solar-helmeted, armed with long muskets, had been drawn up in battle order on the deck. They were all young, and somehow they had all found time to shave as they dressed in their combat finery. Their freshly scraped faces were baby-smooth and rosy-pink. Rassam's own cheeks, after twenty-four hours without shaving, were as blue-black as the marines' gun barrels, as flinty as the reputed sides of Magdala *amba,* but now that contrast made no difference. Rassam snapped off jarring orders to all these Englishmen.

Blanc had climbed out of his launch onto the ship. He stared around in confusion at the marines, but after Rassam had explained it all to him, he laughed, "It'll be a jolly crack, won't it?" and to Rassam's surprise he was ready to go. Final orders were given, and all the ship's launches raced across the flat water toward the beach. Minutes later, the fifty marines were drawn up exactly as they had been on the ship's deck, the only visible change being the sand on their shiny boots. They could not keep the excitement from showing in their faces. Slavery meant nothing to them, either, but a "jolly crack" meant the world.

The sergeant major of marines barked out an order that carried far along the beach in the still, dry air, and he and Blanc set out at a jog at the head of a file of ten marines toward the slave pen. The lieutenant of marines barked out an order, not quite as authoritatively as the sergeant major, and the remaining forty marines, with the lieutenant, Rassam, and Abd-ul-Kerim in the lead, set out running in perfect symmetry, with a polished, even, energy-conserving, high-stepping pace and crisp jingling of equipment, through the village and around the crescent-shaped island.

Across the lagoon, the main gates of the city had just been opened for the day. As he ran, Rassam could pick out a few members of Rashid ibn Ali's garrison at the gate, but, busy about their leisure, they didn't see the marines until they were within three or four minutes of reaching the gate. The guards fled without even trying to close the gate or fire a shot. The marines jogged on, still in perfect order, still not hurrying, hardly breathing, through the gate into the city. The forty marines split up into two equal squadrons. One set out with Abd-ul-Kerim and a sergeant toward Rashid ibn Ali's barracks. The other fell in behind Rassam and the lieutenant, and Rassam led it at that jog through the narrow alleyways. Though it was slow and steady, the pace was wearing Rassam down. His boots seemed filled with sand, and his breath came harsh and shallow, but those footsteps behind him were still perfectly in time, like the tattoo of primitive drums, swelling his heart, urging him on.

They burst into the square before the palace and instantly formed a line facing it. Two of Rashid ibn Ali's guards were at the opening in the wall that let onto the front door. One of them bolted into the house. The other started to follow, hesitated, then brought his flintlock musket up to his shoulder and pulled the trigger. The bullet flew harmlessly overhead. For a brief moment, Rassam registered amazement that any of Rashid ibn Ali's men had taken his duty seriously enough to have his weapon loaded, let alone use it against twenty armed men in defense of the palace. The man wavered before the door, trying to decide whether to reload and fire again or to run, then trying to figure out why no one had returned his fire. Bedouins and Egyptians would have fired back randomly, and they probably would have missed him. The silence was unbearable. The terror of not knowing hypnotized him, froze him like a rabbit before a snake. The lieutenant of marines gave an order. The square echoed with metallic clicks. He gave another order. The marines' rifles fired so closely together they made a single report. The bullets splattered against the wall and the front door and the man, chips of stone and dust and wood flew, and when the smoke drifted away the man had become a rudely flung rag doll lying twisted and broken across the steps. The lieutenant called out more orders. The marines reloaded, their discipline so great that they performed each step exactly together. Another order, and they jogged, still not hurrying, across the square and vanished in pairs through the front door. Breathing raggedly and glad of the chance to stop running, Rassam walked slowly into the square. There hadn't been any shots from the barracks or the slave pen. A few curious Massawans crept timidly toward Rassam. They stared at the blank face of the palace and listened, but they didn't ask him any questions.

The people of Massawa, as anonymous to Rassam as Paniotti's faceless men, would go on living their heedless lives of desperate poverty as if nothing had happened. No act of Rassam's, no simple emancipation of slaves, would ever make a bit of difference to them. Rassam remembered some simple words of Abd-ul-Kerim. He had been referring to his father, but he could have been speaking about Massawa herself:

"Everything changes. Nothing changes. Nothing matters to him."

Rassam realized that those words might refer to himself, too. Then, as his heartbeat slowed to near normal, he had the leisure to be truly terrified.

Rassam spent the rest of the day wandering aimlessly around Massawa, sampling reactions to the British attack. First, for no particular reason other than that he was walking in that direction, he strolled into the palace. There had been five full minutes of deathly silence from within. He paused in the doorway: no one, not a sound, nothing disturbed or out of place. He walked into the vast foyer, and down a long corridor. His footsteps rang loud and slow and hollow as he walked. He didn't encounter a single person or see a sign, besides this eerie emptiness, that anything had happened. A rich, familiar scent reached his nostrils from beyond the *kat* room door. He tugged off his boots and pushed his feet into slippers, then shoved at the heavy door. The sheik was lounging on a divan. A servant was kneeling on the floor in front of him among a collection of containers, burners, pots, and utensils, going through the exacting, time-honored process of preparing coffee: fresh coffee beans roasted, then ground up in a mortar with three grains, no more nor less, of cardamom; the ground-up mixture boiled, tapped down, and strained through a palm-fiber mat to remove all the grounds from the finished product. The sheik had always enjoyed having his servants make a deliberate, graceful ritual of it. He was following his servant's movements now, but when Rassam pushed open the door he smiled and waved for him to enter. Rassam took the divan beside the sheik's and watched the servant finish straining three cups of coffee. The servant handed two of the cups to the sheik and Rassam, then took the third to the far end of the room, squatted by the wall, and began to sip it with obvious pleasure.

After a few minutes, the sheik laughed softly. "So, my clever son finally got through to you, didn't he?" he asked. "I've been wondering what took him so long."

"He'd have done it sooner," said Rassam, "but it had to be done with his own kind of style. That took a little longer. You aren't angry with him?"

"Of course I'm angry. Enraged. Furious. I shall never speak to him again, but he is my son, and I'll take him back if he asks my forgiveness."

"He'll never ask it, I think," said Rassam. "He is too proud."

The sheik gave a quick nod of agreement. "You are right. He'll never ask it. But perhaps I'll take him back without it, one day. Who can tell the depths of love in a father's heart? Give him my blessing, will you?" He set the cup down on the tile floor and said, "Do you see how things have changed because of this morning?"

"The cup of coffee?"

"Yes, the cup of coffee. I have no more slaves, so I must pay my servants. For this one, a cup of coffee from his master's urn is payment enough, at least until he has time to think about it. A simple thing, isn't it?"

"Simple."

"But who can tell? Perhaps it will not matter, or perhaps it will end this whole way of life forever."

Rassam went off into the palace hallways again and passed along corridors he had never walked before. In some areas he found servants milling around, unsure of what to do but not afraid, and in other areas he found marines standing guard at seemingly random locations. He ran across Ismail Tasfay in one of the tamarind courtyards, sitting beside a tinkling fountain of silver water, lost in thought. This morning was the second time Rassam had seen him since that first night in Massawa. The eunuch felt Rassam's presence and glared at him with silent, impotent rage. Rassam took a tentative step toward him, but he could think of nothing to say, and Ismail Tasfay hoisted himself up to his feet and glided away. A latticework door closed behind him, and a lock clicked shut.

Rashid ibn Ali, when Rassam found him in the street near the barracks, sputtered at him. Where Ismail Tasfay would not talk, Rashid ibn Ali could not. He worked a drop of saliva onto his lip with the intention of spitting it at Rassam, but he couldn't control his mouth and it only dribbled down his chin.

The British authority was limited to halting the possession or trade of slaves. It was up to the Sublime Porte to punish its own, and so Ismail Tasfay and Rashid ibn Ali were under no censure from the British. There was no doubt, though, that their Massawa careers were over. They disappeared that morning, and it was presumed they had taken passage aboard a northbound dhow that stopped at the bunder to take on a consignment of fifty slaves that never appeared.

Paniotti was everywhere that day, standing at a safe distance, watching it all. Rassam tried to press him for an opinion, but, as if afraid of giving away some secret, he wouldn't say much.

Abd-ul-Kerim appeared out of the labyrinth of Massawa's alleyways. He was carrying his rifle, and his two Bedouin bodyguards were with him. He grasped Rassam in a tight hug and said, "So, I see you've finally emerged from the cleansing flame of the desert. I see you standing there radiant as a prophet of doom, with religious certainty in your mind and the deadly sword of justice in your hand."

"Don't make fun," said Rassam.

"You know I don't."

"I think I understand what your father means by the cleansing flame," answered Rassam. "By the way, your father asked that I give you his blessing. I'm sure he'll forgive you as soon as he can without appearing to condone what you've done."

Abd-ul-Kerim acknowledged it with a faint nod and a smile. "We understand each other, he and I, our mutual contempt and hate and love. There are no problems between us. As for you, my friend: contact me through Paniotti."

"Through Paniotti?" asked Rassam.

"Yes. I'm leaving too. I'm going to my own desert."

"To seek your balloon?"

"Don't make fun," said Abd-ul-Kerim.

"You know I don't," said Rassam.

Abd-ul-Kerim smiled. "Paniotti will know where I am. Keep your billiards game sharp, and read a book or two to remember me by, eh? And for the sake of our friendship, tell a couple of little lies." He hugged Rassam again. Rassam held him close, unwilling to see him walk away. Abd-ul-Kerim broke away gently, then reached out to touch Rassam's cheek with his fingertips. In disbelief, Abd-ul-Kerim stared at his fingertips for a moment, and Rassam realized that both of them were crying shamelessly. Abd-ul-Kerim hugged Rassam fiercely for one last instant, and then he and his Bedouins were gone.

That afternoon, the British marines set up camp in Rashid ibn Ali's barracks in order to take over the regular defense of the garrison, which, leaderless and afraid, had already dispersed; and also in order to enforce the new way of things in this corner of the world. The young marines were overjoyed at trading the boredom of life aboard the *Dalhousie* for the excitement of garrison duty in an exotic port. Rassam and Blanc laughed at that.

The citizens of Massawa gathered in gossiping groups throughout that first day. After all, it was not often that British marines assaulted the sheik's palace and set loose in their midst nearly a hundred Africans who, for the most part, did not speak the language, did not even know where they were, and for whom there was no place in the community. But by the second morning the freed slaves had somehow disappeared or been assimilated, and the Massawans went about their business as if nothing unusual had happened.

"It was just something I've been meaning to do," Rassam said, when Blanc asked why he had chosen this particular time to move against the slave trade.

For many reasons, Rassam had been most curious about Blanc's reaction. He had thrown himself into the adventure with a will made keener by a year of boredom, and now he laughed at Rassam's answer. "Just something you've been meaning to do. Well, Mr. Rassam, if you decide to hold any more of these little escapades, I really do hope you'll invite me along. I've never had so much fun in my life."

"By the way, I've had news from the emperor," Rassam went on, hardly flinching at all. "A messenger came down from him last night and delivered an oral message—seems the letter itself was stolen along the way. The emperor has freed the prisoners from Magdala, pending my arrival in Ethiopia to work out the details of a friendship agreement between him and the Queen. The emperor told the messenger to seek me out. Mentioned me by name this time. Apologized for the omission last time, but the messenger had forgotten whether the emperor ever told him the reason for it."

"Then the government has got to reinstate us," cried Blanc.

"Us?"

"Yes, *us*, naturally. You wouldn't think of going off adventuring without me, would you?" Blanc was still drunk with the morning's excitement, and perhaps didn't know exactly what he was saying.

"We will have to let the *Dalhousie* go on to Aden without us, and take the soonest ship heading toward Egypt."

"Toward Egypt! Wonderful."

Rassam didn't feel the slightest twinge of guilt about what he would come to think of as "my little lie."

He and Blanc took passage to Jedda on a dhow of the tiny *sambuk* class, high-sterned, low-bowed, awkward, unseaworthy. It took five days to cover the 450 miles to Jedda. Wrapped in their Smyrna rugs, they slept on the deck among crates, chickens, goats, and other passengers: Arabs, Turks, Africans, dervishes, and Greeks. The wind blew fair from the south, cool and gentle. Blanc took possession of a stack of red-dyed leather skins as his daytime chair and nighttime bed, and by the time they reached Jedda the constant sweaty contact had dyed the back of his white suit as red as the leather. He wore the stain as a badge of accomplishment.

For the first time in twenty years, Rassam dealt with an Englishman without the least need to impress the man, to imitate him, to become him. On that five-day trip, he forgot why he had ever disliked Blanc, and they actually came close to being friends.

From Jedda, they cabled their news to London, and then traveled by British steamer to Suez and by train to Cairo. Colonel Merewether cabled his support of Rassam to London. In England, Layard finally found his voice. He told Palmerston, Gladstone, and Russell that he thought removing Rassam would endanger the ex-prisoners, and he rose in Parliament to urge the Members to rally behind the man who had achieved this first vital step toward freeing the prisoners and restoring British honor and who had struck such a bold blow against the slavers of Massawa. Disraeli declined Layard's invitation to respond. When the London newspapers reported the news, public opinion reversed immediately. Reading the *Times* of the next few days might have given Rassam some self-satisfaction, but he had given up the habit, probably forever, of reading the English press. In England, Whigs united behind him, and Tories walked about very quietly or spoke on other issues.

In Cairo Sir William Gifford Palgrave, Lord Russell's choice for Rassam's replacement, was more interested in an exploration of the upper Nile than in the mission to Ethiopia. He gave Rassam the presents he had purchased for the Ethiopian emperor—a fine telescope, several crystal chandeliers, mirrors, a rifle, two cases of Curaçao—and with a hearty handshake and a "Best of luck, my good fellow, and thanks very much for relieving me of the burden," he departed up the Mother River.

A naval steamer was specially commissioned to transport Rassam and Blanc back to Massawa with their presents and their supplies, and by September 25, 1865, they were temporarily settled in Massawa once more. Cameron and the missionaries had been prisoners in Ethiopia for nineteen months. Rassam and Blanc had arrived in Massawa for the first time fifteen months ago. Now they prepared to begin their journey into Ethiopia.

11

October 1865

Bombay

Rassam had only departed for Ethiopia a month before. It would be more than a year before the civilized world learned whether he had succeeded or failed, but in the mind of one particular man in Bombay the military campaign against the emperor of the Ethiopians had already begun. In his mind the preparations were unfolding as steadily as the punkah fan revolving over the governor of Bombay's table, as deliberately as the stately dinner plodding along beneath the fan.

The punkah groaned. Servants padded softly along the walls. The windows were very tall; ships' lanterns twinkled down below in Bombay harbor.

A dozen dinner guests were wandering through their usual fog of forced gaiety, suffering in the humid heat, waiting for the short but blessedly dry interim between the summer monsoon and the winter monsoon. Seymour Fitzgerald, civil governor of Bombay and host of this party, had assigned the seating in a careful continuum of interests. At the frivolous end of the table the conversation flittered over rumors and scandals and fashions. At the serious end the voices stayed low, as if to avoid disturbing the guests at the other end. Colonel Dunn was asking, "Am I correct in understanding you to say, Sir Robert, that you would turn down an offer of troops from Cairo?" Dunn had the thinnest black mustache, curled up into points that nearly stabbed his eyes, that had ever been seen in India. His eyebrows were unnaturally perfect, as if they'd been plucked. No one but the London craftsman who made his toupees had ever seen his receding hairline. His monocle hung from a green silk ribbon that was tangled among the medals on his scarlet chest. The medals were arranged to leave a deliberate little space of red around one: his Victoria Cross. Besides being a dandy, Dunn was widely known as a military incompetent. It was that incompetence that had won him his Victoria Cross and made his career. He had won it as the leader of the fatal charge of the Light Brigade at Balaklava, the charge straight into the face of the Russian guns that had ruined an entire brigade, electrified a nation, and inspired the poet Tennyson. Dunn's was the only Victoria Cross awarded in the entire Crimean fiasco. With that distinction on his chest, his career was secure. He was now a thirty-seven-year-old colonel, and commander of the 33rd Foot, the Duke of Wellington's Own infantry regiment. He leaned forward earnestly, tapped the tabletop for emphasis, and said in a voice that was meant to suggest that he knew more about military strategy than any mere general, "You would actually turn down troops?"

General Sir Robert Napier, military governor of Bombay, was in his fifty-seventh year, pale and slight, black-haired, with great bushy eyebrows, an enormous mustache, and a long weasel's nose all hanging off the front of a fragile skull. He seemed out of place in the scarlet tunic that bore the decorations of so many campaigns, including a Victoria Cross of his own, won against the Sikhs. He seemed out of place, too, in the company of other human beings. He appeared to hide in his own world of inanimate objects and mathematical equations, to be attending with only half his mind, as he murmured, "Precisely."

"Sir, I've served in Egypt, trained Egyptian troops, accompanied an Egyptian expedition into the Sudan." It was a young Cornishman, Major Briggs of the Sind Horse, so eager to please that he stumbled over his words. He had become Dunn's protégée, and he was trying to imitate his master in everything. He was in the process of cultivating a mustache like Dunn's. He wore a monocle on a silk ribbon, pale green to complement the darker green of his clumsy frock coat, which was the Sind uniform, and he tried to tap the table exactly as Dunn had. "It's true enough that the Egyptians aren't on a par with our troops, or even with Sepoys. But Cairo could easily send ten thousand of them up the Nile and into Ethiopia through Khartoum. Correct me if I am wrong, sir. They might only trip over their own feet and walk in circles and get lost, but ten thousand troops must surely be a diversion worth having."

Napier mumbled, "There will be no Egyptians in my expedition." Slowly, searching like a lawyer for exactly the right words, he said, "There is, of course, to be no expedition to Ethiopia, as you gentlemen are well aware. A diplomatic mission has been dispatched to bring the captives home. That mission will succeed. There will be no offer of an Egyptian diversion."

"But aren't you making plans for an expedition?" asked Dunn, with a superior smirk. "Haven't you been gathering intelligence?"

Even less restrained, young Briggs smiled and said, "All the officers have been talking about it. We're eager for a fight."

Napier blinked at Briggs, but his expression was unreadable. "It is common knowledge that I have been putting some thought into a hypothetical African campaign," said Napier. "There's no reason to deny it. But there is not actually going to be any such campaign, and it would be presumptuous to assume that I should lead it if there were. I am engaged in an academic exercise, to keep my skills sharp, to help me pass the time, to provide a written framework for an African campaign should one ever, at any time in the future, become necessary. It is only a contingency plan, one of hundreds I have developed. That is all."

What Napier had said was a blatant lie, but of course he'd had to put the lie on the public record. Everyone knew the diplomatic mission was going to fail. Everyone was anxious for war. Everyone knew Napier was the obvious man, in terms of prestige and personal connections and military experience, to command.

The one thing that everyone did not know was that Napier knew, absolutely, that there would be an expedition and that he would be the man to lead it. He had received secret instructions from the secretary of war to make these preparations, but it was even more than that that made him so certain. Others might find out about the instructions in time, but no one would ever find out about the other proofs he had.

Dunn winked at Briggs and said to Napier, "Then perhaps you could tell us, Sir Robert, just for the hypothetical instruction of two younger officers, why you would not accept a hypothetical diversion by Egyptian troops during your hypothetical expedition?"

Irritated, Napier said, "I have been doing quite a bit of reading about the Ethiopians. I found a book by an interesting fellow named Walter Plowden." Napier spoke Plowden's name slowly, very clearly, and then waited for someone to remember.

"Wasn't he the English engineer who worked for the emperor?" asked Fitzgerald from the head of the table.

"Worked for Napoleon?" asked Lady Seymour, who hadn't really been listening.

"Not emperor of the French, dear. Of the Ethiopians," scolded her husband, and the lady and the colonel at the frivolous end of the table tumbled their laughters together.

Twelve years before, if anyone had mentioned Bell and Plowden in Napier's presence, there would have been smiles and badly suppressed laughter, but most of those at the table had arrived in India since then, and Fitzgerald had apparently forgotten. Napier rarely showed a hint of emotion, and no one knew his relief. "This Plowden wrote a small book of his experiences and his observations in Ethiopia," he continued. "Plowden was not a particularly literate man. As I read the book, I had the feeling that he had written it to show to the emperor and thereby curry favor. His praise of the emperor is extravagant and not to be believed.

"In many other details, though, I am willing to place more faith in his judgment. He made an interesting observation that might pertain to

Egyptian troops accompanying an English campaign into Ethiopia. I quote as accurately as I am able: 'To a foreign conquest little resistance would be offered, for the Ethiopians are too imaginative to dream of patriotism. This spirit, which is entirely lacking, has always been supplied in their contests with the Mohammedans, their mortal enemies, by fanatical excitement.' " Napier forced his seemingly lazy eyes to focus around the table, and he appeared to be displeased to find that everyone, even those at the frivolous end, were listening to him. Among imperial Englishmen, there was always an air of being involved in history, but this conversation was beginning to sound like something more than the run-of-the-mill, day-to-day making of history: this might have the makings of a Grand Event. Like the Ethiopians, Napier had too much imagination for patriotism, and he despised those who did not. "I may form a minority of one among the military men at this table," he continued, "but I have tasted quite enough fanatical excitement to last a lifetime."

"So have we all," said Fitzgerald quickly. The only real skirmish of his life was now thirty-five years in the past, but he never missed a chance to remind people that he had been a soldier.

"Save all the glory for the English," said Briggs. "That's what I say."

"Save as many English lives as possible," said Napier.

"Sir?" said Briggs, but Lady Fitzgerald, a pudding-faced woman with bright red hair, interrupted, "How can this Mr. Plowden call the Ethiopians imaginative? I should have thought they would lack an imagination, being savages. They are savages, aren't they?"

Napier said, "The Ethiopian, Madam, in common with his dusky-skinned cousins all across the globe, will surely be found to have an amazingly active imagination. The world of the native is occupied by demons and spirits that may be invisible to you, but which are certainly clear to him. Ideas percolate through his mind. He has only a tenuous grasp on reality, but his mind ranges far." Napier had fought too many years against too many non-European races, and he was too rational and objective and imaginative not to have gained more respect for Chinese, Indians, Arabs, and Africans than was common to his own people. "One has only to look so close to home as Ireland," he said. "The skins of the Irish are as fair as our own, but no matter: they are hardly more civilized than the Ethiopians, and so they will do for an example. Who can deny that their imagination puts our own to shame? Who hasn't heard of leprechauns? Or of the pagan holdovers in the popish religion? Walk down a Dublin street and listen to the grimy urchin who begs from you. He has too much imagination to simply ask. He invents a new dodge every day. Enter an Irish pub—"

"I would not!" said Lady Fitzgerald.

"But if you did you would hear language that glitters, ideas dropping from the mouths of common laborers that would put to shame the dull-witted talk of an English pub."

"And you propose, sir," said Dunn, "that the imagination of the primitive Ethiopians—and the dull-wittedness of the English—will defeat the Ethiopians? I admit I don't follow your argument."

"Having an imagination," Napier went on, "the Ethiopian lacks discipline. He lacks dedication to a national symbol. What man in his right mind would march unquestioning into a line of fire for fourpence a day if he were able to imagine the pain of a bullet wound? Would an English soldier risk his life for his beloved Union Jack if he could imagine Lord Palmerston with his pants down on the commode?"

Ladies gasped, Dunn and Fitzgerald looked away in embarrassment, but Briggs laughed out loud. Napier fixed him with another of those unreadable stares. With difficulty, Briggs stifled a laugh behind his fist, but his eyes were still smiling directly into Napier's. Napier continued: "No army can operate effectively when a common soldier has an opinion. That is the trouble with Irish troops: splendid when we need derring-do, miserable when we need a solid line. We will surely find that to be the weakness of Ethiopian troops. The Ethiopian will not be melded easily into a unit of a greater whole. How the emperor has managed it as well as he has is beyond me. He must be a very great leader.

"The common English soldier, on the other hand, is a born follower. He hasn't got an idea in his feathery brain, and so he will bend himself easily to discipline. On this lightweight bedrock is built the British army. It is this difference between the British army and the Ethiopian that makes it impossible for the British ever to be defeated by the Ethiopians. By the terrain and the elements, perhaps, but never by the Ethiopians."

"You have been doing your homework, haven't you?" said Fitzgerald. "Sir Robert is the most prepared man I have ever known. We all know there is to be no expedition to Ethiopia, but I shall be surprised if he has not already had scouts roaming the African mountains and spying on the emperor's harem."

The ideas about the different armies were interesting to Napier, but he had finished talking about them, and he had no intention of talking about anything else. Just now, he was directing his distracted gaze toward the mousse that an Indian servant had slid in front of him. He answered in a barely audible voice. "Matter of fact, I've had two men, on the Red Sea. Scouting out a base camp. Should one ever be required. Merewether and Phayre."

Colonel Merewether and Lieutenant-Colonel Phayre, seated across from each other, exchanged a pleased, conspiratorial glance and then tried to transfer the glance to Napier, but he was still staring dubiously at his mousse and didn't even see them. Phayre wore military scarlet, Merewether mufti. Phayre was short and plump and red-faced and clownish, Merewether tall and very serious.

"What are your conclusions, gentlemen?" asked Fitzgerald.

"We've only just returned," Merewether said carefully. "We haven't had time to report in full to Sir Robert. Perhaps we shouldn't say anything."

"Oh, I'm sure Sir Robert has no objections," said Fitzgerald. "Have you, Sir Robert?"

Napier didn't seem to hear. Fitzgerald took that as consent and waved Merewether on.

Merewether was not certain whether he had really been given permission to speak. Fitzgerald was not widely respected among military men, and Napier had said nothing.

"Go on," urged Fitzgerald.

"Well, it's a desolate place, if ever there was one," Merewether began slowly. "I've served as political resident at Aden for six years, and Aden, as dry and barren as it is, is a Garden of Eden next to the western shore of the Red Sea."

"Can a British army survive there?"

Merewether looked again to Napier, but Napier was apparently lost in his own reflections. Merewether hesitated, and Phayre began quickly, "It is barren, mostly salt desert from the sea to the mountains, but we found plenty of water in natural catch basins and in streams flowing steadily down from the Ethiopian escarpment." Merewether tried to stop Phayre with a warning look, but Phayre, perhaps expecting it, kept his eyes away from his superior officer. He was obviously delighted to have the center stage, and didn't care what secrets he let out. "The water table is quite high. Away from the sea the underground water is fresh, and a man can dig a decent well in an hour. There is no food, but there is a good harbor, Zula. Very shallow, but long bunders can be built, condensors established, supplies off-loaded, and a base camp set up. Sir Robert is prepared for all that construction, of course.

"From Zula to the escarpment is just ten miles. A railroad could be built across this stretch. Sir Robert has made plans for this, too. The ascent is then very steep. Four miles reaches Komayli at 1100 feet. Thirteen more miles reaches Suru at 2600 feet, and another thirty miles reaches Senafe at more than 8300 feet." Phayre reeled off the figures with a schoolboy's pride. "That may not sound like much, but there are many places that are very hard. However, there is a caravan route up it that shouldn't be too difficult, even for elephants. It may be hot at Zula, but at Suru it always dips below freezing at night. Zula will not be a comfortable post, but it will be liveable for Sepoys and coolies, and for a few days for Englishmen. As Sir Robert has said, the British army is invincible in battle: the challenge will be getting the army to the battle, and getting them there well-fed and in good health."

"No more Crimeas, eh?" asked Fitzgerald, though he hadn't served in that Phyrric victory of British arms and Russian ineptitude.

"That is exactly what we shall not have," said Napier, abruptly shaking himself awake, stunning the dinner guests with the sharpness of his words. "Not in Ethiopia and not ever again. This expedition will be run in a way that will be remembered and emulated. It will be organized in the manner of a business firm. Supply and transport will receive the highest priorities. You will see an expedition that is slow, deliberate, very expensive, very boring, and very successful. The world will see the new British army in action for the first time."

The only guest who was not English was a businessman from Philadelphia who had been placed, for lack of information about his preference, midway between the frivolous and serious ends of the table. "That's a phrase I keep hearing but don't understand," he said. "What do you British mean when you talk about your 'new British army.' I don't mean to be rude, but your soldiers are still wearing those splendid red uniforms that gave our revolutionaries such fine targets. Your drill, so far as I've seen, hasn't changed since Waterloo. You're still using the basic square that absorbed Marshal Ney's cavalry, aren't you? What I mean to say is this: to my untrained eye, your army seems old-fashioned—that is, tradition-minded at the expense of modern efficiency—next to the armies that fought in the American war."

There was a rustle of discontent among the British officers, but very quickly, before anyone else had a chance to object, Napier said, "You are exactly right, sir, quite right, and I applaud your knowledge of military history. The drill is the same, the uniforms are still bright. But our problems are very different from those of the American armies. If we were to fight in Ethiopia, we should have to gather an army on an inhospitable shore thousands of miles from either England or India, and then we should have to march hundreds of miles through uncharted deserts and mountain ranges, through territory full of hostile natives, combating unknown medical hazards and severe changes in weather.

"The Duke of Wellington never allowed a change in the army; after all, it had defeated Napoleon. The great man died just before the Crimea, and there we learned how inefficient our logistics were. All that is different now, sir. The army which we would see in Ethiopia would march along trailing an umbilical cord, stretching all the way back to England, composed of ships, railroads, telegraphs, horses, mules, and elephants, storage depots and command posts. And it is that umbilical cord, sir, that will allow our unimaginative, disciplined, invincible army to defeat the emperor of the Ethiopians."

"You make it sound quite uninteresting," said the American.

"Had you the opportunity to participate in the American war?" asked Napier.

"I was a captain in the Federal army," said the American. "I fought at Vicksburg and Chattanooga."

"And did you find those battles interesting?" asked Napier. "Or did you find them uncomfortable, cold, wet, and bloody?"

"Your point is well taken, Sir Robert," conceded the American.

"I thank you," said Napier. "If you would care to see a modern British army in action, I invite you to accompany us to Magdala. That is, if we were to send an expedition to Ethiopia, naturally."

The heart of the British complex in Bombay was a wide, cobblestoned square. Dozens of tiny, carefully sculpted gardens were set at random throughout it. Fountains splashed and gurgled. Gas lamps were yellow pools in the pale gray of the square. On the rare rainless night like this, Sarah Napier would have enjoyed strolling, seeing the people she knew, sitting in a garden listening to the splash of water. But when she strolled in the square it was always on the arm of some young officer, never on her husband's. In fact, Napier had never once walked across the square, though for fifteen years he had occupied the sandstone mansion of the military governor of Bombay, one thousand yards from Fitzgerald's, with this wife and with the last. Napier looked at every event with an engineer's eye. To him, if a place was worth going to at all, it was worth going to in the most direct, fastest, cheapest way, with the least possible expenditure of energy. Sarah Napier would have preferred to walk to Fitzgerald's, but she knew that if she could wheedle and threaten her husband into going out at all, it would not be on foot. It was this way with Sarah, and it had been this way with the last wife.

On the drive home from Fitzgerald's, they sat shoulder-to-shoulder in the fine lacquered darkness of their carriage. Napier, isolated as usual in his own world, satisfied with his own excellent company, sat with his head tilted back, his eyes closed. Sarah examined his profile. There was no sign of anything extraordinary in his sharp, long nose, his sprouting eyebrows and mustache, his drooping pipe, but she was certain there was greatness in him. It was for this she had pursued him and married him.

"What was said after dinner?" she said.

Napier blinked his eyes, smacked his lips on the pipe stem and drew no smoke; he busied himself relighting the tobacco he had let go out. Finally, out of a cloud of swirling smoke, he asked himself, "After dinner? Hmmm, after dinner." The first Lady Napier had never cared very much for the affairs of men, but Sarah had to know everything. He always answered honestly and at length, but not before he had pretended that it was difficult for him to focus his mind on the question.

At last, he began, "After dinner, when we had retired for brandy and tobacco, we talked of the normal things. The governor has a new brandy, excellent. I asked him for the name of his merchant, and he promised to write a letter of introduction for me. I was a bit bored, and I suppose I slept off and on until the American left. He turned out to be a quite reasonable man, and of course he was very perceptive about the British army, but I did not feel I could speak in front of someone not a countryman, do you see? Then, after he had left, I told the others that I am certain there will be a campaign to Africa, that I know I will lead it, and that I expect to be ennobled as a result of it."

"Robert, you didn't say that," Sarah gasped. "You simply did not say those things. You've ruined us." Sarah sank back against the seat, pulled out a handkerchief and began to sob into it. Between sobs, she said in a quavering voice, "I'll never be able to face anyone again. Never. We shall have to leave India."

Secretly, Sarah was thrilled at what her husband had said. Finally, he was moving in the direction in which she had always hoped he would go. But she was putting so much heart into her tears that she was sure he thought they were authentic. Napier leaned back and puffed at his pipe, enjoying the performance, content in the game he had created out of his domestic life.

The tears stopped in the minute it took the carriage to clatter through their gate and sway to a halt at their front door. "Come with me." She almost snarled the words under her breath as she took the footman's hand and glided out of the carriage and into the house. Napier followed slowly, handed his hat and cane to someone who stuck out a hand for them, and wandered into the salon to pour himself a brandy. When he came back into the hall, Sarah was glaring down at him from the top of the wide marble stairway. He climbed up and followed her to her rooms. He slid into an overstuffed armchair; she closed the door and sat on her canopied bed. "Explain yourself, Robert," she said, then smiled in a way she thought was pretty. "Please. I know you couldn't have said those things."

Napier sniffed at the brandy, whirled it around in the snifter. "Yes, I'll explain," he said. "Wouldn't want you to worry for no reason." Then, for a moment he slipped off into a hazy recollection of how this room had looked when it had been his first wife's. Sarah had changed nearly everything. The only thing that remained the same was a love seat, blue velvet set in carved rosewood, ugly in the manner of the time. Sarah had wanted to get rid of it, but for some reason of his own that even he couldn't fathom, Napier had urged her to keep it. The velvet, he remembered, had been scarlet when he had found the Russian general tied up behind it. Napier seemed to remember the velvet as lime green when he had found Henry Blanc sitting on it, collar askew, his hair mussed, the late Lady Napier sitting flushed on the bed. Now, the velvet was blue, but it was still the same love seat. Funny that this love seat should be the only piece of furniture, probably the only inanimate object, to which Napier had ever had an emotional attachment.

Napier had spent twenty-seven years with his first wife, and he had been contented. After the smallpox took her, he had been contented with widowerhood. It had never been his intention to remarry, but after he married Sarah, he was contented with her, too.

Sarah, the eighteen-year-old daughter of a British merchant, was outwardly plain, and she hadn't seemed to have much to compensate, but he had discovered that inside she harbored a smoldering ambition. The wife of the military governor of Bombay was not a big enough role, in itself, to attract her, but she had been convinced there were greater things in store for the woman who married Napier, if that woman had the talent and drive to shake him loose from his decade-long lethargy. She had spent the first year of their married life trying to goad him into action, and he had allowed her to believe she had failed miserably. Her feelings now, when she heard him talk about a campaign and ennoblement, were mixed: delight at the thought, fear that he might fail if he were not guided by her.

"So, after the American left," Napier continued, between sips on his brandy, "this Major Briggs, a rash young sort, asked me point-blank whether I thought there would be an Ethiopian campaign. I told him, yes, certainly there will be an Ethiopian campaign. This diplomatic mission is a charade. It is designed for failure. The government, either this government or a Tory government, will have to wage war, sooner or later. Major Briggs asked me whether I should lead it, and I told him, yes, I am the logical choice for it, and I want it badly. And then it was Colonel Dunn, I believe, who made the characteristically unsubtle remark that the man who leads the campaign to Ethiopia will surely be rewarded. Laurel wreaths, he said, glory for British arms, nonsense of that sort. And Fitzgerald said, no laurel wreaths for that man. Fitzgerald said, that man will be an earl. The others agreed, and young Briggs asked me, again point-blank, mannerless, bold, whether that should please me. Sarah, you know I cannot lie."

"I know that, Robert," said Sarah, still hiding her feelings behind a mask of grave concern.

"I told Briggs, yes, that should please me, certainly, but it should please my young wife far more than me. I promise you, I said nothing to reflect badly on us. I told them, 'I am fifty-seven years old, I have a beautiful young wife, and soon I will be ready to retire. I was born in Ceylon, lived practically all my life in India; in fifty-seven years I've spent a total of thirty-three months in England. I have served long and well. I believe I deserve the chance to command this last campaign, to win myself and my wife a peerage, a seat in Lords, and an honorable retirement in that English homeland I've hardly known.

"I've been ordered to make plans for it. That by itself is no guarantee, but I'm planning the campaign in such a way that no man but me, no one without my skills as a military engineer, could possibly carry it off.

"I know my reputation, Sarah. I'm considered politically naïve, but that isn't true at all. I've cultivated friends in high places. I will have this expedition. I didn't say anything those gentlemen hadn't thought out for themselves."

Sarah was staring into her folded hands, trying to hide her eagerness. Napier went on: "I talked about the nature of such a campaign. 'Some of you here will be involved in this expedition,' I said, singling out Major Briggs and Lieutenant-Colonel Dunn 'There may even be those present who will die in the African highlands. My aim—our aim, gentlemen

—must be to please the government, and what will please the government will be that the expedition should be deliberate, expensive, and perfectly successful. I will command as if I were directing the digging of a canal, as if I had all the time in the world. When the campaign begins, the English nation will be ecstatic. The English people are desperate for a symbol to replace the Crimea, the Mutiny, even that piddling war against the Americans in 1812. They no longer want to convert heathens to Christianity as they did at the beginning of this century, though they give conversion lip-service. They don't need or want more colonies. They just want to crush someone, and then to be washed clean in an orgy of self-congratulation.'

"Major Briggs, who is quite an enthusiastic, idealistic sort, asked, 'But what about the poor captives, languishing in their prison?'

"I like this young Briggs, Sarah. Dunn is a perfect ass, of course. The 33rd is too good a regiment for him. All those Irishmen are wasted on him. And Phayre is no better, but he is Lord Russell's cousin, and I cannot touch him. The American took our army to task for the buying and selling of commissions, for our preferring money and connections to military expertise. He might have something, too. I wish there were some way I could replace Dunn and Phayre.

"But Briggs, though he bought his commission like the rest of us, has a certain boldness, a certain flair, that I especially like. He has much more imagination than I. He would be good to keep close to me, to temper my caution, to relieve my boredom. I think I may gather together a collection of rash young officers like him and keep them busy with adventures."

"What did you answer him?" asked Sarah.

"I told him the truth, the sort of truth that no one under a certain age understands. 'As far as I am concerned,' I told him, 'and as far as the government is concerned, the prisoners, including this new Mesopotamian envoy, are already dead men. The invasion will be nothing but an outburst of racial pride. No savages will get away with shaming the British crown. No foreigners are going to say we cannot handle the heathens.' "

"I don't have to know more," Sarah interrupted. "I'm sure you handled yourself with your usual care and dignity, and I am sorry I doubted you." Napier leaned back comfortably, sipped the last of his warm brandy, and thought about his plan for a band of courageous cavalrymen dashing boldly across the Ethiopian plateau. They might not help the campaign, but they would certainly help to relieve the boredom. "I have another question," said Sarah.

"Hmmmmm?" he asked.

"Who was Walter Plowden?"

"Plowden? As I said, he was an English engineer who worked for the Ethiopian emperor. He wrote a small book. He died in '60, or thereabouts."

Sarah sniffed. "You know how we ladies have so little of substance to talk about when you gentlemen are away, so we clutch at straws and dissect every nuance of the dinner conversation. Usually, our talk is mere drivel, but sometimes we make impressive conjectures. This evening, all the ladies had the impression that you were waiting to see whether anyone knew Plowden's name. As if he should have been known to us. Who was he?"

Napier did not answer, and Sarah watched him sitting there with his sharp nose deep in the empty brandy snifter, and she did not ask again.

Napier, truthfully, had felt some attraction drawing him toward Ethiopia ever since he had heard that Henry Blanc was marching into the same remote country that had sheltered Bell and Plowden. In his whole life, only those two hints of scandal—Blanc and the Russian general—had ever touched him. Outwardly, he was a perfectly emotionless man, but those two incidents had seemed to smash against the walls of his isolation, to threaten the man within. Behind those walls, hidden even from himself, was a fragile man who had nearly been crushed by those two incidents. He could go gliding carelessly through bloody seiges and attacks, look down on the mutilated corpses of men he knew; yet those assaults on his dignity had very nearly killed him.

From the first moment he had heard about Blanc's journey to Ethiopia, Napier had known that he, too, would be going there. The coincidence was too obvious, too elegant, for it to be anything but a masterful play by his grand opponent, in this game into which he had made his life. He knew there would be an expedition to Ethiopia, and that he would lead it.

While Napier sat in his armchair, thinking about Bell and Plowden and Blanc and that band of courageous young cavalrymen—and pretending not to notice his wife—Sarah dimmed the gas lamps and prepared herself for bed. She pulled off her gown, her corset, her shoes and stockings and petticoats and bloomers, and, totally naked, stood in front of Napier for one full, hopeful minute, letting her long hair down and running a silver-backed brush through it. Her face was flat and plain, but her body was almost perfect: pale creamy skin, long, graceful legs, round, full breasts that rose and fell as she brushed her hair. Napier did not look at her, only stared into the brandy snifter. She was desirable and eager, but he was fifty-seven and Victorian and more interested in pouring over Merewether's report than over his young wife's body. She pulled on her shift and curled up in her bed. After another ten minutes, Napier got up, brushed her forehead with his lips, and wandered off toward his own rooms.

12

October–December 1865
The Sudan

"Whatever happened to *le Comte* de Bisson?" asked Paniotti. "Did he manage to establish his holy kingdom in the desert?"

"You know his story," said Kozika. "You were here."

"It is instructive," said Paniotti. "I wish our guests to hear it."

"Very well," said Kozika, touching his fingertips to his forehead as if he were submitting himself to Paniotti's will.

Paniotti, Rassam, Blanc, Abd-ul-Kerim, and Kozika, Paniotti's agent in Kassala, were sitting cross-legged on the earth floor around Kozika's low table eating a meal of flat bread, a stew of vegetables and gristly lamb in a common pot, and red wine full of sediment—a meal fit for a king, the weary travelers thought. Kozika was a short, fleshy Athenian, burned dark as an Arab and dressed in fez and robes.

"That one, that poor misguided fool," he recalled softly. His voice never rose above a whisper, but he rattled along in Arabic as if he were afraid he would die before he finished. "Such an unfortunate man he was—still is, I imagine. Have you heard of him?" he asked Rassam, and without waiting for a reply he began the story: "*Le Comte* was a man of sixty years, a Frenchman originally, I think, healthy and handsome and very ambitious for the future. He was an officer in one of the Italian armies, perhaps the Neapolitan, and married a young girl for the sake of her father's money. With his inheritance in hand, he launched his long-cherished scheme. He and his bride came to Kassala last year, before the Nubian mutiny, and they brought along an army of fifty Europeans, the worst rabble he could find in Cairo. 'I have come to colonize the Barka Plain,' he announced to the captain of the Egyptian garrison. 'I will turn the Bedouins into good Christians.' We all tried to reason with him. 'They are already good Moslems,' we said, 'happy in their faith. They are like the will-o'-the-wisp: you will never see them, or if they choose they will steal upon you unawares and kill you all.' But he wouldn't listen. 'They will fall down before my power,' he said. 'They will welcome the true God and acknowledge my rule over them.'

"The saddest thing of all is that he seemed to truly believe that he had a mission to bring the light to the Bedouins. He thought he was doing a worthy thing.

"With extravagant promises he recruited a hundred Arabs from Kassala, possibly an even worse rabble than his Europeans. He dressed his Arabs in European uniforms and gave them rifles, which he taught them how to fire. He tried to teach them European drill, but they weren't very interested in discipline. Still, he was undaunted.

"It was a wonderful sight when they departed. A gallant Austrian captain, riding a camel and playing a march on his trumpet, led the way. Next came a French officer, de Bisson's second in command, mounted on a fiery white stallion. Then came the European soldiers, marching in file. *Le Général le Comte* de Bisson and his wife were next, riding side by side on camels and waving at the crowd that had gathered to jeer at them. De Bisson wore a general's uniform—from which army, I do not know—and his wife wore the kepi and red uniform of the French Zouave. Last came the Arab soldiers, ridiculous in their ill-fitting uniforms, struggling to keep in step, many with their rifles across the wrong shoulder.

"I fear that de Bisson did not very much understand Africa. He was defeated without fighting a single battle, without taking a single Bedouin life or converting a single heathen soul. The Bedouins of the Barka simply persuaded de Bisson's Arabs to desert from his army. De Bisson awoke one morning to find his army shrunk by two-thirds. It was a tragic group that returned to Kassala. *Le Général* wore civilian clothes. He had lost all his Arabs, half his Europeans, and all of his pride. The handsome Austrian captain had died of a fever, the French second in command of the bite of a horned viper. Only the wife was smiling as they entered the city. She had had a wonderful adventure, and she waved to the crowd just as she had on their departure.

"De Bisson tried to collect damages from the Egyptian government. I don't know what charges he made against them. They laughed at him. He and his lady left for Europe, leaving behind those of their Europeans who were still alive. Some of them are still here, with nowhere to go. They might have fought during the Nubian mutiny, the first soldiering they would have done in Africa, but most of them just hid until the fighting was over. There is nothing for them to do here, but there is nowhere else for them to go. They wander the streets, waiting, I suppose, to die. It is a sad story, very sad."

The only route from Massawa to Ethiopia that did not cross rebellious Ethiopian territories went generally westward along the southern boundary of the Egyptian Pashalik of the Sudan, then southeastward up into Amhara. The caravan had taken twenty-two days to cover the 245 miles from Massawa to Kassala. Often they had set out across country where even their local guides couldn't find the caravan tracks. They had traversed the ranges of Bedouins who spoke pure Yemenese Arabic, and the lands of black nomads, where they had to sleep in shifts in order to guard their camels. They had crossed sandy deserts and hilly districts and valleys choked with tropical forests. And always there had been the vaguest hint of mountains just over the horizon to their left, to the South, toward Ethiopia.

Paniotti had decided to accompany them as far as the route lay inside Ottoman territory. The trip would give him a chance to look after his business interests, he said, but the usual hidden motives were lurking close behind. He came reluctantly, as if he had been ordered against his will to see that they reached Ethiopia safely. He was often sullen, and he volunteered even less information than before.

Abd-ul-Kerim had appeared suddenly on the third day from Massawa. He, too, would go as far as the limits of Ottoman control. He had some new, mysterious connection with Paniotti, but he wouldn't talk about it, and Rassam was afraid to press him. Otherwise, the young Arab was as lively and happy as ever.

The caravan had started out with thirty camels and fifty mules loaded high with supplies, equipment, and the bulging packages that were the chandeliers and other gifts for Theodore. A hundred porters and servants accompanied them. Dahon was among them, but not Rafaelo, since the Goan had conveniently sprained his back on the day before departure. The camels had been hired for a certain distance, and the owners refused to go any farther. Left to themselves, Rassam and Blanc would have been stranded, but Paniotti's influence was visible everywhere along the road. They never understood the reason for his accompanying them, but Rassam knew they couldn't have made it without him.

Rassam suffered from the sparse diet and the constant riding, from the daily thunderstorms, from the severe heat of day and the bitter cold of night, and he soon contracted a fever. He wasn't able to hide his pain, but he had too much pride to do less than his share. Abd-ul-Kerim and Paniotti offered to stand his watch at sentry. He refused, but one of them always went with him to watch over him and keep him company.

On one incredibly hot day, he finally let Abd-ul-Kerim talk him out of his solar helmet and collar and traveling suit, and into a turban and loose robe. He was amazed at how much cooler he was in his new, but very familiar, clothes.

Paniotti was an experienced caravaner, and he simply accepted the inconveniences of the journey. In the daytime, he did the work that had to be done and rested when the sun grew too hot; at night he rolled himself quickly into his rug and didn't stir until dawn.

Abd-ul-Kerim followed the Greek's lead in all things, and he seemed to get along as comfortably as in Massawa.

Surprisingly, it was Blanc who thrived. The instant he had realized there was no gentlemanly way of getting out of this journey "into the very teeth of death itself," he had been perfectly reconciled to it. Each day, eager for new adventures, he rose long before anyone else. At noontime, even the Bedouins would lie panting in the shade, but Blanc seemed impervious to the heat. Wearing his thick traveling suit, his patent leather shoes slipping on rocks and filling up with sand, sweat pouring off his nose and his chin, he walked endless miles through the brush. He always came back with game to supplement their diet, or, if it were too large to carry, sent porters out to retrieve it. Blanc was an excellent backwoods doctor, too, considering his limited medical knowledge and the few medicines he had brought. He treated everyone, and though it was the end of the fever season, not a single man died during the entire twenty-two days. He even realized, finally, that some people will never learn English or French, and he began to form an adequate Arabic vocabulary. Arabic had been a constant presence in Aden and Massawa. Though he had never paid any attention to it, much of it had penetrated and remained floating close beneath the surface, only waiting for some concentration to turn it into language. He would practice with Rassam and Abd-ul-Kerim and Paniotti until they would have nothing more to do with him, and then—the thing that shocked Rassam most of all—he would talk with the servants and the Bedouins.

They sent messengers ahead to announce their approach to Kassala, and Kozika and the whole Egyptian-Albanian garrison came several miles up the road to meet them. There had been rumors in Cairo and Massawa of a mutiny of native troops in the Sudan, but the travelers weren't prepared for the desolation they encountered in the last two days before Kassala. The fields had never been prosperous, but now they were deserted and burnt, and the mud houses stood open to the gusting wind and sand.

The inhabitants of Kassala who remained walked silently, listlessly, through the streets. Among them were a few ragged Europeans who looked up in quick interest as the caravan entered the city, then continued walking.

"Great sickness in the city after the mutiny," Kozika had explained. Of all the people in Kassala, only Kozika and the garrison still looked well fed. "The Nubian troops had not been paid for two years, and they requested a portion of what was due them. The Egyptians only laughed. They have a cruel sense of humor in these parts. So, in July, the Nubians rose in the night and killed their officers. A few Egyptians managed to hold the arsenal until the Egyptian and Albanian soldiers could come from Khartoum and Kedaref to raise the seige. More than a thousand Nubians were killed in the fighting, and another thousand were captured and executed. Those who escaped fled into the desert, and their eternal enemies the Bedouins tracked them down and killed them. Very bloody business. With unburied bodies all over Kassala, the diseases started. The people of the city who had not been killed in the fighting died of the sicknesses, or they ran away. It was once a great city, a very beautiful city, with gardens and children and laughing people. I am sorry you weren't able to see it as it was, my friends."

"Will the city be reinhabited, do you think?" asked Rassam.

"As always," laughed Kozika. "With any luck at all, with better people than before. I'll just sit here and wait and do business, and the city will grow around me."

"Will we be able to get fresh camels?" asked Paniotti.

"It will be very difficult," said Kozika. "The Bedouins are the only ones alive who still own camels. They have had a great deal of blood-sport recently, and now that there are soldiers in Kassala again, they are afraid to come too near. But . . . we shall see whether there are any beasts to be had."

With Paniotti's help they got fresh camels and Bedouin riders. They continued their journey, striking almost due south from Kassala toward Metemma, the village that straddled the traditional border of Ethiopia. Two days out of Kassala, the fever hit Rassam even harder than before. For a few days, he rode a mule instead of a camel, because it was a shorter fall from a mule, but soon even that was too much for him. His head swam, his vision blurred, his body ached, and he couldn't concentrate on keeping his seat. Paniotti hung a hammock on a pole and beat the bearers with a stick until they took up the ends and carried Rassam. Blanc and Paniotti walked on either side of him. Blanc bathed Rassam's forehead with wet rags, but when Rassam was swallowed up in his delirium and shouted that he wanted to be left behind to die in peace, it was Paniotti who held him tight in the hammock and told him in a voice that sliced through the haze, "You're going on, Mr. Rassam. You've come this far, there's too much depending on your going on now, and you will go on."

Rassam was riding again by the time the caravan reached Metemma. Behind them lay the deadly flat plain of the Sudan, but beyond Metemma to the south and the east began the ridges that terraced into the Ethiopian highlands.

Metemma, situated on low ground with a stagnant stream running through the middle of the village, was an unhealthy place. They sent a messenger ahead to announce their arrival. While they waited in Metemma, Blanc was swamped with pleas for medicine. He dispensed and treated so many that he was afraid he would run out of supplies before they even crossed the stream into Ethiopia, so he sealed himself into the tent he shared with Rassam and refused to see anyone else.

On Christmas Day, their messengers returned from the highlands with greetings from Theodore, and with instructions from the emperor to Sheik Jumma of Metemma, who officially recognized both the Ethiopian monarch and the Egyptian pasha, to provide them with camels to Wochnee, a village a few days farther up into Ethiopia. According to the message, Theodore would send down a few people to meet them in Wochnee.

That night, while Blanc and Abd-ul-Kerim led their Moslem and pagan camelteers in a ragged multilingual riot of Christmas carols, Rassam found Paniotti alone in his tent. Paniotti looked up from where he lay and said, a little sadly, "I was expecting you to come." They walked slowly along the Sudanese bank of the stream until the fires were a dull glow in the distance and the singing just a hoarse whisper. Rassam's next-to-last pair of shoes had given out in Kassala. He was saving the last pair for his meeting with the emperor, so now he went about in thin-soled leather sandals. His feet had toughened so much he didn't notice the gravel that gathered between foot and leather. His fever was gone, too, and he was beginning to sense a new, unfamiliar strength growing inside him, a confidence that he could survive anything.

Rassam squatted comfortably, Bedouin-style, on the bank. Paniotti turned his slender back to Rassam and looked across the stream. Moonlight traced Ethiopia's upward curve in silver. At last he said, questioningly, "Yes?" He filled that one syllable with a wealth of implications: anxiety, suspicion, defeat. During the whole journey, he had acted as if he was accompanying Rassam against his will, but at least he had been civil. In the last few weeks, ever since the first Ethiopian ridge appeared hard against the horizon of the flat Moslem plain, he had withdrawn into himself. When the rest of the company celebrated the messengers' return, Paniotti had brooded alone in his tent.

Rassam let a handful of sand pour in a gritty waterfall from one hand to the other. He didn't know what to say to this unfamiliar Paniotti.

"You came to me," the Greek accused him. "Speak."

"I thought we should talk," started Rassam. "I wanted to ask you certain questions."

"Ask."

"I thought perhaps you might have something to say . . ."

"Parting thoughts? Encouragement in your mission? Best wishes for the emperor?" Coming from the emotionless Paniotti, the sudden harshness was like a curtain parting around a sick bed to reveal him feeble and helpless. His thick lenses had always been a wall between him and the world, a source of strength, but now they were just to help his weak eyes see. Rassam had never noticed before how fragile his body really was, how the fluttering of his hands was really a sign of fear.

"Why did you come with us?" asked Rassam. "To protect me? To make sure I reach Ethiopia? Why don't you want us to reach the emperor? What are you to him?"

"Why haven't you asked before?" asked Paniotti.

"You wouldn't have answered."

"And you think I'll answer now?"

"I think so." Rassam stood up to face Paniotti. Somehow Paniotti had seemed so small that Rassam expected to tower over him, but they were exactly the same height. He stared into the gray shadows of Paniotti's face until Paniotti turned away and looked up at Ethiopia again.

"You are more perceptive than before," Paniotti muttered.

"You said once that you worry about what the emperor will do if I come to him," said Rassam. "Maybe if you explain yourself to me, I'll be able to share some of your worry, take greater care with him. You said long ago that I bring ruin to him. Maybe I can protect him, if I have some idea of what ruin I can possibly bring . . ." Rassam had spoken quickly, but his voice trailed off uncertainly as he realized how little he really knew about either Paniotti or the emperor, and as he remembered for the first time in several months what he might face in Ethiopia.

Still gazing up at Ethiopia, Paniotti said, "I never cease to marvel at a government that sends out envoys who know absolutely nothing about their destinations. With the roles reversed, what would your Viscount Palmerston and your Mr. Disraeli think of an ambassador to England who had never heard of Wellington and Nelson?" Paniotti did not wait for an answer. "When you first came to Massawa, you knew nothing of Ethiopia. I fear you know no more now. I was sure you were the wrong man for the mission. Oh, I sent your letters faithfully to the emperor, never fear. But I had my reservations, and I told the emperor my opinions about you."

"You told the emperor? Your two trips from Massawa?"

Paniotti refused to hear the question. "The only quality you have that recommends you is persistence. I thought you would go away, but you stayed, and stayed, and stayed. I think you would never leave."

"Never," said Rassam, too forcefully, and he thought: *Go away? To where? To what?*

Paniotti asked, "What did you learn from the story of Makeda and Menelik?"

Rassam pondered, tried to figure out what Paniotti wanted to hear. He finally answered, truthfully, "I learned that the Ethiopians have as superstitious a body of oral literature as any primitive people. Besides that, very little. Wolde told it mostly to get me off my guard, I think, so he could judge me. He had me preoccupied with bringing him back from his fairy tale to reality, and so I was unaware of what he was really doing."

Amazed at Rassam's stupidity, Paniotti shook his head. "You missed it all," he said. "To hear that story from Wolde's lips is an opportunity such as few men have ever had, and it was wasted on you. It was like hearing Homer himself recite the *Odyssey*. Ethiopians will walk hundreds of miles just to hear Wolde's voice—and all you heard was a fairy tale."

Rassam started to speak, but Paniotti turned abruptly and stilled him with an upturned hand. "This Ethiopia," he said, "is different from anywhere you have ever been. The edges of that Ethiopian plateau mark a different world. Below in the deserts are Negroes and Arabs, paganism and Islam, but in the highlands you find a quick, lively people, Christian for fifteen hundred years.

"The Arab who invades the plateau from Massawa or Khartoum or Somaliland complains of the cold and the wet, and his camel freezes in the chill of the mountain nights and dies. The Ethiopian who descends from his plateau succumbs to the fevers, his mule collapses from the heat, and he soon retreats to his mountain home.

"This is how it has always been, and always will be. The Prophet of Islam had so much respect for the Ethiopians that he declared there should be no *jihad* against them. So the Ethiopians, who had fought in Troy and traded with India, have remained alone on their plateau ever since, cut off from the rest of Christendom, surrounded by religious enemies, protected by their mountains.

"Think of it, Rassam. To forget for a thousand years that the rest of the world exists!

"But the mountains, at last, proved no protection against the Moslem Gallas, wild tribesmen from Somaliland. More than a hundred years ago, they began to invade Ethiopia. They seized control of the emperor, and so began the *Zemene Mesafint,* the 'Age of Princes.' Every man who could command the loyalty of ten others thought he was a feudal lord. The emperor was a figurehead in the hands of the Gallas. It was a time of rape, plunder, death. Moslem and Christian armies destroyed the countryside and killed indiscriminately.

"And then there rose a man to put an end to it all. The Emperor Theodore was a rebel chieftain of great charisma, a leader of men, a master tactician. He used every bit of luck and leverage and influence wisely, aligned himself skillfully, and when the time was right he swept through the highlands, brought peace to Ethiopia, and had himself crowned emperor."

Paniotti paused, and Rassam said, "Who are you?"

"Only one of the emperor's faceless men," said Paniotti, brushing the question aside. "In the beginning, he was a great ruler. In a land that sustains itself on warfare, prophecy, and myth, he was a pacifist and a realist. He is the only patriot Ethiopia has ever known. He was the first Ethiopian leader to pay his armies, so his were the first soldiers who did not have to live by pillaging the countryside. He put an end to the slave trade. He set an example of temperance and piety for his subjects. He observed the fast days like a priest—and in Ethiopia there are more than two hundred partial fast days a year. He had the marks of greatness, almost of divinity. He was an Alexander. His troops went into battle with Alexander's battle cry on their lips.

"He was flying as high as man ever flew. He called himself 'the slave of God,' but he was as close to a human god as ever lived—and then it all came tumbling down around his head. Peace gave way to violence. He was in despair. All seemed lost, when Cameron came to him and promised to bring him to the favor of the British Queen. He placed all his hopes on the letter that your government never sent."

He said this last in a bitter, accusatory tone. Rassam only bowed his head.

"Now, the rebellions have taken all but the heart of the country. He drinks sometimes—not so often as once, but sometimes—and he falls into fearful, blind rages. In his rages, he orders killings, and when he awakes and realizes what he has done he scourges himself with guilt. Every step he takes, he bears the burden of prophecies that call him, soon, to martyrdom."

Rassam asked, "Is his insanity the reason he imprisoned Consul Cameron?"

"Theodore," said Paniotti, punctuating each slow syllable with a forefinger in Rassam's chest, "is not insane. This may be difficult for you to understand, but the Emperor Theodore is the only rational man in Ethiopia.

"Theodore and his subjects believe in the story of Makeda and Menelik, in the ancient prophecies, in the Voice of the Spirit of Prophecy speaking to men, but these are not simple beliefs. They are reality itself. When you talk about bringing Wolde back from his 'fairy tale' to reality, you have lost sight of reality.

"The emperor is a man of his people, and these things are as real to him as they are to his subjects; but he also believes in pragmatic, realistic policies to govern Ethiopia as a modern nation. Even now, he never acts without a reason. He is enormously cunning."

"I should like to ask a question, Mr. Paniotti," said Rassam. "I should feel foolish even thinking to ask it, but I must."

"Ask."

"It is the same question I asked Wolde: Is Theodore the Theodore of the prophecy?"

Paniotti moved his hands in a way that implied the question made no sense. "There are prophecies and there are prophecies," he said. "There are prophecies about Theodore that even Wolde does not know. But I am a merchant, a man of numbers and measures. I deal in cold facts. The fact is that he is a great man, greater by far than anyone you have ever seen. If you meet him, search his face for the marks of that greatness. Treat him with respect and caution. Keep in mind that there are those of us who pray for him to recapture what he had. Remember that he is Ethiopian, not English, nor Arab or Turkish. Take care, Rassam, take care."

Without another word, Paniotti started toward the glow of the campfires. Rassam stood for another minute, listening to the singing and the night sounds, less certain than ever about what he was walking toward, until a shuffling across the gravelly sand behind him sent him scurrying after Paniotti.

Abd-ul-Kerim wept the next morning when Rassam and Blanc left him and Paniotti behind and started up toward Wochnee. Sheik Jumma of Metemma and most of his subjects waved good-by as the caravan lurched across the stream, and several of the local militia fired off independent salutes. From the top of the first ridge Rassam turned in his saddle and looked back. The locals had dispersed. Abd-ul-Kerim and Paniotti stood alone now, their heads close together, talking earnestly. Rassam realized that, while Paniotti had made the Emperor Theodore into a nation, Abd-ul-Kerim had made him into a balloon on which to rise and float over all the world. Rassam hoped his young Arab friend would find what he sought in the service of the emperor. Just before they disappeared below the ridge, Abd-ul-Kerim put his arm across the Greek's shoulder, and the two men walked back toward the encampment.

After fifteen months of waiting in Massawa and three months traveling through the Sudan, the ascent into Ethiopia seemed to Rassam and Blanc like a journey into a magical kingdom. The path to Wochnee undulated through high, swaying grasses, scattered with thorn trees and baobabs. They encountered the first real cultivation they had seen in two years in Africa; the villages seemed prosperous and comfortable. The peasants' café-au-lait skin, hooked noses, and dark, wavy hair were like those of the Sudanese Arabs, but, as Paniotti had said, they were a totally different people. They wore the Ethiopian *shama* and white trousers. Even when they were working in the fields, the men kept their weapons—sword or spear, and small round shield—within easy reach. They walked with lighter steps and worked with more energy than the lowland peoples. A round, thatch-roofed church perched on nearly every hilltop, and companies of turbanned priests came out to watch the caravan go by.

When they left Kassala, Kozika had given Rassam two precious books, accounts of Ethiopian journeys, one by the Scot James Bruce, who had visited Ethiopia in the eighteenth century, and one by the Englishman Mansfield Parkyns, who had made his trip in the 1840s. Rassam's fever had prevented him from reading them before, so he read them now on camel-back. He looked up from his books whenever he came across something interesting and shouted it across to Blanc. The books painted an incredible picture: feasts of raw beef cut from the flanks of living cattle, wars and savagery, wild religious celebrations.

Blanc listened politely, but he tended to notice other things. "It doesn't seem to be particularly unhealthy," he said. "There are some of the expected diseases of a primitive place, of course, but just from the way the natives walk, you can tell they're healthier. Of course

. . . hand me the Parkyns book, will you?" He leaned out and took the book from Rassam, thumbed through to a certain page, and read: " 'Local bleedings, such as the natives practice, are often highly advantageous; and firing with a hot iron at their recommendation may also be adopted. For severe inflammation of the bowels, when you cannot bear to be touched on the part, some boiling water poured on it will be a ready and effective blister—a wet rag being wrapped around in a ring to confine the water within the intended limits.' "

"Please, Dr. Blanc." Rassam wasn't actually turning pale, but he was squirming a little in his saddle.

In all his life, Blanc had felt he was a misfit. He saw other people following their own individual pursuits, interests, loves and hates, but he'd never found anything that could hold his attention for long. He had gone into medicine because it was the family profession, though he had never felt drawn to it. He had entered the army because it was the expected, usual pattern, but he had never felt at home there. But here, separated from all the normal realities he had known, wandering alone for long hours in the wilderness, looked to by the others as the source of their health, besieged in villages along the way by people praying for medicines and salvation from the doctor whose fame had preceded his arrival, he felt strangely at home. His medicine took on a new meaning. He applied himself to studying native remedies: he didn't believe in most of them, but for the sake of scientific curiosity he interviewed Ethiopians and recorded their cures in a notebook.

He had been forced to walk around barefoot for a few weeks now in order to save his remaining pair of shoes; it felt perfectly natural. His white complexion had first turned red, then had peeled, and was now a freckled bronze. The food was coarse and the ground at night was hard, but there was never any real lack of anything. His mind and body toughened.

He found himself enjoying the company of people in ways that were unfamiliar to him. There weren't any real Englishmen around, but he discovered to his surprise that a Mesopotamian wasn't nearly as far from being English as he had thought, nor a Greek, nor an Arab, nor even a filthy Bedouin camel driver. He was thriving, and he had never been happier.

On the fourth day, the head priest of Wochnee met them at the outskirts of the village, the largest they'd seen since Kassala. The emperor had sent word, the priest told them in Amharic through Dahon, that they were to wait in Wochnee, and he would send a small number of people to escort them onward, as well as mules, since their camels were useless farther ahead where the terrain got difficult.

They pitched their tents among the sycamore trees outside the village. During the four days they waited, Rassam finished the Ethiopian travel books Kozika had given him, and also shot the elephant for which Blanc had been hoping for more than three months.

It was a tremendous bull with one tusk snapped off in a jagged mess of ivory splinters. Together, Blanc and Rassam had stalked it and cornered it against a lake. Rassam dearly wanted Blanc to have it, but the elephant ran in such a way that there was a dense grove of trees between itself and Blanc. Rassam, two hundred yards away from Blanc, fired a wild shot, caught it exactly in the heart, and sent it tumbling down to die.

On the morning of the fourth day in Wochnee, the "few people" from the emperor arrived. Dahon saw the escort first and came running to the sycamore grove. "They're here!" he cried. "The emperor's people are here!"

Blanc and Rassam came out of their tents and started toward the trail, but Dahon put himself in their way and said anxiously, "There is something you should know, masters. There are many of them. Very many. Horse and on foot. I didn't know there would be so many. I didn't know you were so important to the emperor. Forgive me. The horsemen will greet you by *fakkering.* As if they do war. It is not to frighten, not to harm, only to greet. Please, don't be afraid."

Blanc sniffed and went on toward the trail.

"Thank you," said Rassam softly, though he didn't know what Dahon was trying to tell them. "It's always nice to be prepared." He had put aside his turban and robe here in Wochnee, and he was wearing his woolen traveling suit and solar helmet. It was still very hot in Wochnee, sweat was dripping down his face, and his feet were dirty-gray in their sandals. He missed the cool softness of his turban, and felt a little ridiculous in this costume without shoes. "Come," he said to Dahon, "we'll go and see them."

"There are very many," repeated Dahon, tagging along at Rassam's side.

"Then the honor will be greater," said Rassam.

The three men positioned themselves where they could see the track coming over the next ridge. Before the emperor's people came into sight, the sound of them, rumbling, murmuring, like a volcano about to burst, was audible.

Rassam turned to Dahon to ask a question, but he saw Blanc standing firm and strong, and he was silent. Facing the unknown with courage, standing aloof from danger, was part of what made Blanc an Englishman. For the first time in several months, Rassam found himself worrying about what Blanc thought of him. He realized, too, that he was afraid of that approaching rumble.

The first man appeared. He was riding a short, shaggy horse. He held a small round shield on his left arm, and a naked sword dangled from his right hand. His black hair was long and glistening.

Another horseman appeared, and then another, until there were a dozen of them, riding slowly in a loose rank.

"Not so many," whispered Rassam.

Another dozen appeared. And then the men on foot began to come over the ridge. They were all dressed in the white costume of Ethiopia, and they had shields on their arms and spears over their shoulders. They didn't march in any particular order, but just seemed to follow the horsemen in a general way, overflowing on either side of the caravan track. There were mules among them, some carrying bundles of equipment, some unladen. There were more than a thousand marching men and a hundred mules.

"If it isn't a royal welcome, Mr. Rassam," laughed Blanc, and his laugh sounded perfectly genuine, "then it's time to break out the last bottle of cognac and drink it quickly. Isn't it?" Rassam, pale and shaking, didn't answer.

"I don't see any chains among them. Do you?"

Again, Rassam didn't answer.

The horsemen began to gallop, their horses' hooves tossing up brown grass and loose dirt as they raced down the long slope. All the swords were suddenly out, waving in the air. One man screamed, "*Alalalalai!*" and the others joined in until they were all screaming it. Their voices drowned the dull thunder of the unshod hooves.

Blanc felt Rassam starting to faint. "Stand firm," he cried, and he held tight to Rassam's arm and held him up. "Let us be a credit to our Queen."

Rassam tried to straighten up, but Blanc still had to support most of his weight. Rassam heard Blanc cry, "God save the Queen!" The man might bend so far as to talk as an equal to Bedouins, but he never forgot for an instant who he was.

The horsemen were fifty yards away now. Their swords were waving like blades of brown grass. Rassam could see the spit fly from the men's screaming lips, the foam on the horses' muzzles. The horses pounded toward them, to the point where they should stop, past the point of no return, so close now they had to trample the waiting men. And then they stopped short in a great confusion of hooves and steel and grass and sweat, more quickly than any cavalry maneuver the Britishers had ever seen.

The leader leaped from his saddle and landed two feet in front of them. He was short, powerfully built, and his face was a web of white saber scars. He salaamed briskly with the hilt of his sword and began to speak rapidly in Amharic.

"Dahon," ordered Blanc, and the servant was instantly at his elbow, translating: "This man is Magiga Dulou, very famous. This other man is Gabry." He indicated a second man who had followed Magiga Dulou forward and was now standing beside him. "They are both generals of the emperor, and Gabry is one of the emperor's Twelve Disciples. It is a great honor to be met by these men."

"Did Magiga Dulou say that, or do you say it?" asked Blanc.

"It is what Magiga Dulou said, but it is very true. The Twelve are very great men in this country, very holy and blessed by God. Magiga Dulou says he is very happy to see you, hopes you are well. If you can make yourselves ready this afternoon, then he will be pleased to begin the trip to the emperor's court."

Just beginning to breath properly again, Rassam asked, "How far are we from the emperor?"

"Twenty days. A very difficult journey."

The men on foot had caught up with the horsemen, and they surrounded Rassam and Blanc and Dahon in a tight mass of pushing, talking, pulsing, breathing humanity. Blanc felt himself the core of a thing greater than himself, the focal point of great events that were about to happen. In all the months since he and Rassam had left Aden, this was the first time he had had any sense of the importance of this mission. He looked at Rassam, who had straightened up as if he too sensed their central position and found in it better medicine than Blanc could prescribe for him. *What does this all mean to Rassam?* Blanc wondered.

The caravan, minus the last Bedouin camelteers but now swelled by a thousand Ethiopian warriors, progressed by very short stages, mostly because the escort spent so much time getting ready each morning.

It turned out that Magiga Dulou spoke very adequate Arabic, but he was a man of no unnecessary words in any language. Rassam asked him why he had made them speak through Dahon on the first morning, and he replied truthfully, "To judge you and your people, as I was told to do." He was the ideal image of the proud savage: honest, stoic, silent, self-contained, probably cruel and ruthless.

Though he spoke only Amharic, Gabry was Magiga Dulou's complete opposite. He kept Dahon with him all the time they were on the march, and through him he constantly jabbered away to Rassam and Blanc. All the Ethiopians but Magiga Dulou deferred to him as an important man, but it was soon clear to Rassam that he was totally lacking in common sense. Most of Gabry's talk was about the emperor, his bravery, his wisdom, his generosity. Magiga Dulou kept a close eye on his fellow-general, stayed near him all the time he was talking to the foreigners, and snarled out a warning in Amharic whenever he thought Gabry was straying onto forbidden ground.

In camp on the first night, Dahon disappeared after dinner and didn't reappear until after midnight. Waiting for Dahon to return, Rassam realized how little he knew this man who had been such a devoted servant. Rassam had been expecting Dahon to disappear this way. He wondered what messages from Paniotti he was giving to Magiga Dulou, what intimate information about Rassam and Blanc.

Word of their coming preceded them, and in each village crowds of peasants and priests swarmed around Blanc shouting, *"Medanite, abeit, medanite."* "Medicine, lord, medicine." Blanc tried to help as many as he could, writing down descriptions of the various illnesses he found here, observing to Rassam again and again that the general level of health was improving as they gained altitude, but before too many days had passed he had to resume his old practice of hiding in his tent after they had set up camp. Magiga Dulou instructed the soldiers to keep the peasants away from Blanc, and after that it was only the important men of each district who were allowed access to the doctor and his medicines.

On the seventeenth day, they emerged through a high, narrow pass and saw the plateau below, stretching out to the horizon, dotted with freestanding *ambas* and round lakes, still rising gently toward the east but now, suddenly, a true tableland.

In the center of it all lay Lake Tana. In the tone of a teacher explaining something to an ignorant student, Gabry pointed out the Ghish Abai, the swamp south of the lake from which the Little Abai River flowed in a dark ribbon into the lake, and the place several miles farther to the east where the Abai, or Blue Nile, flowed out of the lake in a broad band toward the southeast, cut into the plateau in a winding, widening gash, and began its great swing to the south and then to the west and north.

The promontory of Zagé lay on the south bank of the lake between the two rivers; and Theodore had expected to be encamped there by the time their party reached the plateau.

Magiga Dulou sent messengers ahead that night, and throughout the next day messengers were constantly leaving for the emperor's camp or returning from it. As the brief highland twilight descended, they pitched their tents on a hilltop overlooking a stream of clear, cold water. A dozen scrawny cattle were waiting for them by the stream. "A gift from the emperor to his welcome guests," Gabry explained. The soldiers didn't cut steaks from the flanks of the living cows, as Mansfield Parkyns had reported they would, but they did butcher the cows and eat the flesh raw. Dahon roasted a huge portion, and the envoy and the doctor ate well, if a little queasily.

On a hilltop in the distance, perhaps two miles away, they could just make out a large red pavilion surrounded by smaller white tents. As night came on, they could see the fires on the hilltop, and by the time it had grown dark a vast glow had spread over the surrounding landscape.

"It will be tomorrow," said Rassam. "At last, it will be tomorrow."

"I wonder what he'll be like," said Blanc. "We shall have to have our wits about us."

"Yes," answered Rassam, "we shall."

13

January 1866
Zagé, Ethiopia

Rassam put on his blue "diplomatic suit," Blanc his scarlet officer's uniform. Rassam tugged on stockings and squeezed his feet into his shoes. When he stood, his feet spread out as if they were still in sandals, and they hurt until he mounted his horse and took his weight off them.

Magiga Dulou and Gabry led the way, Dahon rode just behind Rassam and Blanc, and their escort, swollen during the night to a noisy mob of three thousand men, followed.

As they forded the stream that ran at the foot of their hill, Gabry pointed out a black-and-white falcon that was perched high in a mimosa. The bird stared curiously down at them, blinked, ruffled its shoulder feathers, and was still.

Magiga Dulou explained in Arabic, "It is the gaddy-gaddy, an important omen for travelers. Watch him as we go by. If he flies away, he predicts ill for your journey. If he stays and watches, he predicts well."

Rassam wasn't a superstitious man, but deep down, against his will, he needed the omen to be real, and he needed the falcon to stay. Looking back, he saw the huge mass of men and mules and horses, jostling, shouting, spreading out to make elbowroom for themselves. They passed under and around the mimosa. Dust swirled high, water splashed, and the tree shook as a mule bumped against it.

The falcon swayed on its slender branch. It lifted its wings, fluttered them for balance. Rassam raised his bridle hand toward the bird and whispered, "Stay." The falcon lifted its wings again, but its talons clung tight to the branch.

"Excellent," said Magiga Dulou in Arabic, then leaned toward Gabry and said it again in Amharic.

"I'll choose to believe this omen," said Blanc lightly.

Gabry opened a saddlebag and took out a thick falconer's gauntlet and a lure. He wheeled his horse away from the column and up. At the top of the hill, he swung the lure and whistled quickly, three times, then three more. Stiff-winged, the falcon glided in over Rassam's head, circled the contour of the hill, came back into view as it rose up beyond it, towered high over Gabry, and stooped to the lure. Gabry tugged it in, and came riding down the hill with the hooded falcon on his gauntlet. He was grinning proudly.

"That's all it was?" said Rassam, disappointed. "Just a trick?"

Magiga Dulou looked at him curiously, not understanding. "It was a favorable omen. The gaddy-gaddy stayed."

"It wasn't a real omen," said Rassam.

"The gaddy-gaddy is real," said Magiga Dulou. "See." He reached out and stroked the bird on Gabry's fist.

"Gabry made it stay."

"The gaddy-gaddy is real. It stayed. The omen is good."

"An omen can't work if it's planned ahead of time. It doesn't work if you manipulate it and make it happen."

"That's a curious thought," said Magiga Dulou. "Is that the way with omens in your country?"

The column had stopped while Gabry rode to the top of the hill. The horses had milled around, and Rassam looked past Magiga Dulou into Blanc's smiling face. His Arabic might not have been good enough yet for him to catch every word, but he was able to understand the gist. He was laughing softly, listening for Rassam's reply.

"Well, we don't actually place much faith in omens in our country," Rassam said. "But it isn't logical for a man to be able to make an omen happen, and have it still predict the future."

"What isn't logical about it?" asked Magiga Dulou.

"I can't explain," said Rassam, knowing he was defeated. "It just doesn't seem logical to me."

"It seems perfectly logical to me," said Magiga Dulou. Then, politely, "I can't explain, either."

They started again. The path they took kept to the low, marshy ground between the hills, even when it might have been faster to take a higher route. There were signs of abandoned campsites everywhere, but not a single tent or horse or human being. The reason for picking this way soon became clear. They could never see farther than the next hilltop, so they were becoming disoriented. Rassam was reminded of the short, deliberate wait they had had in the dim anteroom to the sheik's *kat* room. They were being prepared for some sort of impressive display. Knowing what was being done to him didn't make it any less effective. Rassam felt his tension rising.

At last, Magiga Dulou turned from the valley bottom and led them up a broad, gentle ridge. As they came up to the summit, Magiga Dulou slowed their pace to less than a walk. They moved forward two feet, then paused, then moved forward three, then paused. The silver-and-crimson lion pennant appeared first, high up, fluttering all alone in the amazing blue of the highland sky. Then the red pavilion appeared. It was still half a mile away, but from here they could see that its diameter was at least fifty yards. The entire front was open.

As they moved onto the crest of the ridge, the slope below the pavilion came slowly into view. A patchwork quilt of carpets, as wide as the pavilion itself, led down to the base of the hill. The hill and the valley bottom between were covered with a solid mass of humanity. Ethiopian soldiers were everywhere but on the avenue of carpets; not a single toe touched the carpets themselves. A narrow alley with ruler-straight sides led through what must have been ten thousand mounted warriors to the base of the emperor's hill, where a tent of yellow silk had been pitched. A silk Union Jack, with slightly off-color reds and blues, hung above the yellow tent.

The sun had cleared the tops of the hills, and shone directly down into the valley. The body heat from thousands of men and horses, the stench of so many animals, was a solid mist surrounding Rassam and Blanc as they started through the alley. The warriors' horses were adorned with richly decorated bridles, and many of the warriors held shields encased in solid silver. They wore their hair in long buttered braids, like Magiga Dulou, Gabry, and the rest of their escort. The butter had flowed in long streaks down their bodies.

The ten thousand horsemen raised their spears and swords and flintlocks. They began to shout, *"Alalalalai!"* and banged their weapons against their shields. High-pitched women's voices began to warble somewhere in the background.

The farther Rassam rode into the alley, the narrower it seemed to be, the tighter the horsemen seemed to press in on him, the louder the noise became. His senses were having trouble finding any kind of anchor. He clung to his horse, letting it find its own way.

The piercing yellow of the tent finally rose in front of them. In the wide empty space around it, Rassam felt less claustrophobic and got himself under better control. Magiga Dulou helped him down from his horse and led him into the pavilion. Someone let the tent flaps fall. The shouting outside ended in an instant, and silence echoed harshly through the valley. Rassam walked over beautiful Oriental rugs. The sun shining through the yellow silk imparted a yellow glow to everything.

Three men were waiting inside the tent. One was a tall warrior, dressed more simply than any of the thousands of soldiers outside. Something about his bearing gave him an aura of power and grace, and made his simple clothes more impressive than the finest garments. He stepped forward and salaamed deeply to Rassam and then to Blanc. "I am Mamo, the emperor's chamberlain. I am of the Twelve." Though they had to wait for Dahon's translation to understand the words, it was clear that this man had spent years training his voice to match his station.

Rassam salaamed as deeply as Mamo, and found that his hands were shaking. "I am honored to meet another of the famous Twelve of the Emperor Theodore," he said. "I am Mr. Hormuzd Rassam, Envoy of Her Majesty Queen Victoria, and this is Dr. Henry Blanc of the British army."

"By the power of God, I hope you are well," said Mamo. "And you also, Dr. Blanc."

"Yes, I am well."

"Very. I hope you are well, also."

"I am, thanks be to God most high," said Mamo through Dahon. "This is Samuel." He indicated a spry, elderly Ethiopian who stepped forward. "Samuel is the personal servant of the emperor. The emperor has made him your *balderaba*, your announcer and servant for the time you are in our country."

Dahon gasped with surprise before he translated, and when he had finished repeating Mamo's words in Arabic, he said quickly, "You cannot know what an honor this is."

"What is a *balderaba?*" asked Rassam.

"The *balderaba* is an Ethiopian custom," said Dahon. "A host offers one of his own servants to an honored guest. The servant, the *balderaba*, becomes the man of the guest. He announces him on formal occasions, serves him all the time. For the emperor to give you Samuel as *balderaba*—it is too great an honor. I had no idea. Samuel has been the emperor's personal, closest servant for ten years."

Rassam had always known that Dahon was more than the simple servant he seemed. It had been too easy for Abd-ul-Kerim to find an Amharic-speaking servant in Massawa. His talks with Paniotti on the journey and with Magiga Dulou on the first night had confirmed the suspicion. Still, Dahon had always been an excellent servant, perfectly loyal, and Rassam had overlooked his being a spy. Now, certainly, it was obvious by his tone of voice that he was to be trusted in this matter: Dahon was indeed surprised, and being given Samuel as *balderaba* was a tremendous honor.

"I am overjoyed," said Rassam. "I thank the emperor."

"And this is Wolde," said Mamo. "The emperor's personal priest. He also is of the Twelve." This was said in a perfectly serious tone, without a hint of the absurdity of introducing Wolde to Rassam.

Wolde stepped closer. "By the death of Christ, I am happy you have made your journey safely," he said in Arabic. "Are you very well?"

"Very well," said Rassam. "I am pleased to see you again."

"And I you."

"The emperor will see you in a little while," said Mamo. "First, he desires that you should eat and drink and rest."

They sat in a circle on cushions on the floor, except for Samuel and

Dahon, who crouched against the wall of the tent and whispered together. Other servants, on a signal from Mamo, brought flat loaves of coarse bread, dishes of a paste with pieces of beef mixed in it, and glasses of milky liquor. The paste was peppery to the taste of the Britishers, almost too spicy to eat, but the liquor, which Mamo explained was the famous *tej*, was faintly reminiscent of honey and very soothing.

The conversation during the meal fell into a pattern that was quickly becoming familiar in Ethiopia. Mamo and Wolde requested the minutest details as to the well-being of Rassam and Blanc, and discussed Rassam's fever at great length. Obviously, health was a matter of great concern to the Ethiopians, as well as being an innocuous topic of discussion.

At last, the meal over, they were left alone with Samuel and Dahon.

Still crouching by the wall, Samuel told them, "I am pleased to be *balderaba* to the envoys of the British Queen. We have been waiting for you for a very long time. By the Immaculate Conception, I will do whatever you ask, for I am now your servant."

"When will we see the emperor?" asked Rassam.

"Soon. Very soon. He only desires that you should be made comfortable before coming to see him."

Rassam was eager to ask Samuel about the captives, about Theodore's disposition, about anything Samuel could tell them, but he knew he wouldn't believe answers from the emperor's personal servant, and he was sure Samuel would instantly report everything he said to Theodore. "That will be all for now," he said, though he did not know what tone of voice one used with one's *balderaba*.

Samuel nodded and started toward the tent flap, then turned and said over his shoulder, in slow, unsteady Arabic, "A *balderaba* in Ethiopia is a man for trusting. I was the emperor's man; now I am yours. I have no ties to him anymore. If you wish to know anything, I will tell you gladly. Such is my sacred duty."

Rassam only looked at him. Samuel seemed so sincere that Rassam wanted to trust him, but he couldn't be sure. He was starting to feel dizzy. The yellow that permeated everything inside the tent was too strong; the smell and sound from outside leaked through the silk walls, and the pressure of that slow ride through the alley of horsemen was still too recent. He didn't say anything.

"I shall be near," Samuel said. He slipped out and the tent flap fell behind him.

Rassam lay on his back on the carpets and pulled a cushion under his head. Even through his eyelids he could see that intense yellow. He worked at regaining control of himself. Across from him Blanc leaned against cushions and watched him. Rassam's anxiety was obvious. It was true that he didn't have to carry the burden of the mission like Rassam did, Blanc thought, but even for a timid man this moment shouldn't hold such depths of terror. There must be more to it all in Rassam's mind than was apparent on the surface—and if those hidden anxieties were ruling Rassam at the thought of approaching a heathen king, then what would happen to the mission, to Blanc, to the captive consul and missionaries, if Rassam were in command during a real emergency?

After a while, Rassam seemed to regain some control over himself. He sat up, neatened his collar, and smoothed down his hair.

Just to fill the gap, Blanc started rambling. "Have you ever noticed how professional people try to make themselves more impressive than they really are by separating themselves from other people? I don't mean separating in a social sense, though they certainly do that, too. I mean in a physical sense.

"A judge doesn't enter a courtroom by the same door everyone else does. To get to a doctor or a solicitor, you have to pass through layers of people. They always have someone else to greet you. Often you have to talk to two or three people before you actually are admitted into the *presence.*

"They may not know exactly what they are doing, but they have set up their physical surroundings in such a way that it removes them from their clients. That makes them seem more important, less human, when you finally do get through to them.

"That's what the emperor is doing here. The stage management of all this day is too perfect to be unintentional. Look at all the layers we've come through: Waiting in Metemma. Waiting in Wochnee. Gabry and Magiga Dulou and their escort. Waiting that last night within sight of the red pavilion. The new escort this morning. Passing through all those ranks of men on horses. Meeting the next layer of the emperor's ministers, Mamo, Wolde. Waiting here in this tent.

"Layers. Many, many layers. There are sure to be more layers to penetrate, and we may never get all the way through to him at all. He may be a savage and a heathen, but I have to hand it to him: he understands the theory of layers. He is an excellent stage manager."

"You may be right," said Rassam. He still felt weak, though his strength was returning slowly.

"Of course I'm right," said Blanc. "Now, I wonder when we'll be admitted to the *presence?*"

The time of their audience was announced by a slowly swelling clamor from the hordes surrounding their tent. Samuel appeared and said, "Your escort is coming in state down the hill. Do you need anything to prepare yourselves? Can I bring you anything?"

"We are perfectly ready," said Rassam.

"Have been for months," Blanc muttered in English.

Samuel threw open the flaps of the yellow tent, and on the crest of rippling cheers an escort of four—Magiga Dulou, Gabry, Wolde, and Mamo—reached the tent and waited for Rassam and Blanc. The Britishers brushed off their suits for the last time and stepped into the brilliant sunshine. The men of their escort were mounted on flawless white horses. "A sign of highest honor," Dahon whispered to Rassam, "to them and to you." They had brought two more perfect horses with them. Rassam and Blanc stepped onto their low mounts. Dahon and Samuel got onto mules.

The long wait in the hot sun had only intensified the excitement of the massed army that covered the valley and the hill. Their thousands of polished metal weapons were raised high above their heads, and the sun, now shining straight down, turned them into a million mirrored surfaces.

When they reached the carpets, they dismounted and began to walk uphill. Here, finally, there was plenty of elbow room. Laid directly on the tall grass, the carpets sunk down under each step. The hill was steep and the surface of the carpets made the climb exhausting. "Just another layer," Blanc whispered to Rassam, hoping to keep his companion's courage up, "just another layer."

The top of the hill was perfectly flat, like a miniature *amba*. The scarlet pavilion had been pitched in its exact center.

The Ethiopian escort stopped at the point where the slope leveled off. Rassam and Blanc waited with them. "It is part of the ritual of an audience with the emperor," Samuel told Rassam. "To wait within his sight for his signal to approach."

"How long will we have to wait?" asked Blanc, leaning toward Samuel. Blanc was afraid that Rassam wouldn't last if they had to stand here for long.

"An hour," said Samuel. "Maybe more, maybe less. The greater the honor of the guest, the shorter the wait. We can only wait and see." He turned and looked back toward their yellow tent. "The gifts you brought for the emperor are being brought up," he said. "It will be proper to give them to His Majesty during the audience."

A group of warriors were carrying the crates, still unopened, marked with penciled descriptions of the contents, up the hill. They were not nearly as efficient in their carrying as porters in Massawa would have been, Rassam noted, because they had to carry their shields and spears as well as the crates. It was inefficient, but that was the basic difference between there and here. There were no slaves in Ethiopia. Every man was a warrior.

The men set the crates down behind Rassam and Blanc, then sat on them and waited.

The pavilion, as they were now able to see more clearly, was a great square tent with a peaked roof, large enough for a hundred men to sit in comfort. A long awning extended toward them. Under the awning, room for twice as many. The interior of the pavilion was so dark that they could not see into it.

A warrior was standing at the very edge of the open side, looking steadily into the pavilion. Barely ten minutes after they had stopped, he seemed to receive a signal from inside. He turned and raised his hand. A band of soldiers just down the hill fired off a clean, resonating salute with their flintlocks, and every other musket in the valley cracked off a ragged shot. A cloud of brimstone engulfed the hill, and in an instant there was no sound at all except for the echo of the shots.

Samuel took the lead across the carpets under the awning. Rassam and Blanc followed, and Dahon and the four Ethiopians came behind. They walked the length of the awning and then stopped before entering the pavilion itself. Within the shadowed interior, nine white-clothed men, each holding two double-barreled pistols, stood in a line against the far wall, fifty yards away. In the middle of their line the emperor sat on a low wooden platform. He wore a voluminous white robe, bordered with a wide scarlet band. The robe hung down around the platform, covered his hands, and extended up past his chin, so all they could see of him was his head above the level of his mouth and one bare foot that hung down from the platform. To one side of his platform, two silver kettledrums rested on the carpet. The warrior closest to him had a double-barreled pistol in one hand, and with the other held a parasol over the emperor's head.

Samuel indicated with a movement of his hand that the others should wait for him, and he swept forward and prostrated himself on the carpets, crawled the last ten feet, kissed the outstretched imperial toe, and then retreated back to Rassam and Blanc. He faced the emperor and made his announcement in a loud, formal tone across those fifty yards of carpet. He spoke for five minutes or more, but Dahon, clearly as awed as Rassam, did not dare to translate for his masters.

After the announcement, the emperor leaned slightly to one side and, without looking in that direction, spoke in a low voice.

The officer to that side came forward and whispered to Samuel, who in turn relayed the words in Arabic to Rassam and Blanc. "The Emperor Theodore wishes you welcome. He asks if you are well, and if you have had a difficult journey to come here. He wishes me to say also that he desires to honor you, in the manner of our country. If strict protocol were to be followed, it would be necessary for you to crawl to him and kiss his toe before you would be allowed to enter his presence. He does not wish to impose such a ritual on you, as he knows it runs contrary to your custom, so he will conduct the audience from this distance."

Rassam was nearly overwhelmed by the deliberate presentation. Just as Blanc had suggested, the emperor's costume detached him from the realm of mankind, and the extra distance imposed between them by this relaying of the words was equally awe-inspiring. Rassam found himself thinking in contradictions. The vast army of warriors. The solid row of heavily armed, ruthless officers. The barbarism of the whole display. The Oriental splendor. The isolation of the Buddha. Theodore wasn't giving him an audience, but a chance to look on god-in-the-likeness-of-man. Knowing what was being done to him, how the illusion was being created, did nothing to lessen the visual effect it produced.

"We are well," he said dryly. The little speech he had prepared months before and practiced a thousand times came out by itself. "The journey was long and difficult, but we have been sustained by the hope of meeting such a wise and famous Christian monarch as the Emperor Theodore of the Ethiopians. I bring a letter from Her Majesty Victoria, Queen of Great Britain and Ireland, to Your Majesty."

He handed the Queen's letter to Samuel. The moment the precious document left his fingers, it seemed as if an electrical impulse was trying to draw it back into his hand, but Samuel had the letter and was translating Rassam's words into Amharic for the officer. The officer listened carefully, then took the letter and the words to Theodore. The emperor indicated with a subtle nod of his head that the letter should be placed on one of the drums.

He spoke again to the officer, who spoke to Samuel, and Samuel told them, "The emperor asks you to be seated. It is a very great honor." Servants brought wooden stools, and they sat on them where they had stood, still fifty yards from the emperor. The conversation went on for nearly an hour in the same tedious vein, the words passing from Theodore to the officer to Samuel to Rassam, and then back through the same roundabout route. This process obviously strained out much of the meaning of what was being said, and it made any real conversation impossible—which was exactly what was intended.

"I am very happy to see that my British friends have arrived safely," said the emperor. "I have long anticipated the pleasure of seeing you."

"We have anticipated the chance to see Your Majesty."

Compliments and the usual questions about each other's health became the topics of conversation, until Theodore abruptly changed direction and said, "Long ago, I had friends among the British. Their names were John Bell and Walter Plowden. Were they known to you?"

Rassam answered, "Their names are known, but I did not know them personally."

"They were very good men. They helped me to build roads and bridges, and they told me they could make me a friend of the British Queen, who loves all Christians everywhere in the world. This made me very happy. But it was the will of God that they should be killed.

"The Consul Cameron came to me later, and I was very pleased, for I thought he could make me a friend of the British Queen. But he betrayed me. He went down to my enemies the Turks, and he did not deliver my letter to the Queen. This Consul Cameron is not my friend, he is my enemy. Now that you have come to be my friends, I hope you can make me a friend of your British Queen."

Long ago, Rassam had decided that the safest policy would be to remain as neutral as possible in regard to Cameron. "It was unfortunate that you came to doubt the friendship of the Queen," said Rassam. "When you have read the letter I have brought, you will see that she is most eager to be your friend."

"I am eager to be her friend, also."

"I can assure Your Majesty that nothing is dearer to the hopes of our Queen than to be your friend."

"I hope all will be well between our countries again."

"I am sure it will. In hopes of showing my goodwill to you, and the goodwill of our Queen, I have taken the liberty of bringing a few small presents to you."

"Are these gifts from you, or are they from your Queen?" asked Theodore.

"I chose them at the instructions of my Queen."

The emperor nodded slightly. "Then I shall be pleased to accept them."

The warriors who had carried the crates up the hill began to pry them open. Servants from the emperor brought each present in turn to him for his inspection, than laid them out in front of him. They made a quite impressive display. The emperor sent back formal thanks after each item, but the distance was so great and the process of translation destroyed so much meaning, that Rassam couldn't tell whether the gifts had made any impression on Theodore at all.

After more formal compliments and mutual assurances of goodwill, Theodore told them, "After your long journey, you are surely tired. You may go now, and I will speak to you tomorrow."

They remounted their horses, and their escort led them past the yellow tent and around the hill. "The emperor has selected another site for your tent," Samuel explained.

As they rode through the valleys, with Ethiopian soldiers running along beside them, scrambling up above them for a better look, Blanc pulled his horse close beside Rassam's and said in English, "When the presents were opened, I thought his eyes would pop out."

Rassam looked back at Blanc curiously.

"I mean that he appeared to me the typical savage," said Blanc. "Despite all the artificial display. If you understand about layers and look at him objectively, he seemed just like a child at Christmas."

"From that distance you could see so much?" asked Rassam.

"Clearly."

"I thought he was most dignified."

"Dignified?" asked Blanc. "Never. Just like a child."

Rassam wondered how he and Blanc could have such widely divergent views of what they had seen. He was still feeling an intense emotional response to the emperor's manner, to the setting, to the religious aura around him. Blanc seemed to have seen exactly what he planned to see.

"I think the idea of threatening him with British might is still the best," said Blanc. "He should respond to that."

"I shall treat him like a sovereign," said Rassam.

Rassam awoke to an insistent hand on his arm. Samuel, close to his ear, was whispering, "Master Rassam, Master Rassam."

Rassam only murmured.

"The emperor is waiting for you."

Rassam opened his grainy eyes. It was still dark, but Samuel had brought into the tent a low-burning lamp that cast his face in weird, warm colors.

"Come quickly. He waits."

"Now?"

"Yes, now. Dress quickly.

"Dr. Blanc as well?"

"No, just Master Rassam. Come quickly."

Rassam rubbed cold water into his face, pulled on his diplomatic suit and his shoes, and followed Samuel into the black, dewy night.

Rassam and Blanc had been given a huge white silk tent that was pitched on a hilltop facing the emperor's compound—the red pavilion, it had turned out, was only a ceremonial tent and not really the emperor's living quarters. The emperor's compound consisted of his own great sky-blue tent, and another twenty tents of various colors and sizes that housed close ministers and their concubines, offices, and a chapel. An empty strip fifty yards wide surrounded the emperor's tents, and a similar empty strip surrounded the tent of the Britishers and the smaller tent shared by Dahon and Samuel.

A winding journey of several miles had led them from Theodore's ceremonial pavilion to their own tent. It immediately became apparent that the soldiers who had greeted them had not constituted the whole army, but were merely a small honor guard. Thousands more flocked to watch them pass as they moved through the camp, and then the realization that this was not just an army, but a complete city, struck them. There were not only soldiers, but old people, women, and children. Thousands upon thousands of dark-skinned, naked children screamed and pushed for a look at the *feringi*. An escort of mounted warriors hovered close around Rassam and Blanc, but the children still swarmed underfoot like locusts and cut their progress to a crawl.

In the evening, endless lines of women passed on their way to fetch water from the many streams that ran through the camp. They were handsome, swaying, high cheeked women, wearing flowing robes of white muslin or Manchester calico. Their feet and hands were darkened with henna, and their eyes were rimmed with black antimony. Many had blue crosses tattooed on their foreheads and bare arms. Silver anklets jingled as they walked. As they looked up at the *feringi* on the hill, their glances were bold, curious, intelligent. They chanted atonally, but in time with some silent rhythm they all shared. Rassam found their voices strange, but appealing.

It was not long before cooking odors began to fill the air, and late into the night music, shouts, and laughter floated across the hilltops.

Rassam had the impression of watching a vast beehive full of lively, intelligent, happy people. How large the population might be, he couldn't guess, and Samuel didn't know. Samuel told him that the whole camp would be making a "progress" the next day. Rassam thought that might give him a better opportunity to judge the size of the encampment.

More servants had been added to their retinue. Samuel sent some of them to Rassam and Blanc with dishes full of the meat in the same spicy paste they had already tasted, and many other foods, along with alcoholic drinks, sour milk, and woven jugs full of water. It was another great honor, Dahon explained, since this was food from the emperor's own table.

After dark, Samuel appeared, leading two mules that staggered beneath bulging saddlebags.

"This is for you," he panted. "A gift from the emperor."

They opened the saddlebags and found them full of Austrian Maria Theresa dollars, the minting of 1728.

"It is five thousand dollars," said Samuel. "He says, too, that he will supply your servants with food and other necessities for as long as you are his guests. He suggests that you use some of this money to hire more servants and to buy beasts of burden, but he emphasizes that this is only a suggestion from one friend to another, and that you may use the money in any manner that is agreeable to the Lord Iyesus."

"Agreeable to the Lord Jesus?"

"Jesus, Iyesus, the same. Those were his words."

Thinking that he might be able to draw Samuel out on the subject of Theodore, Rassam asked, "The emperor is a very religious man, isn't he?"

"Ho, very religious," exclaimed Samuel. "A very great man of God."

"I've heard he has a special relationship with God."

Samuel knew instantly what Rassam was trying to do. He drew himself up proudly and said, "Master Rassam, I beg to explain something to you. I have been assigned by the Emperor Theodore to be your *balderaba*. The traditions that are attached to the role of *balderaba* are very strict in Ethiopia. As your *balderaba*, my allegiance to the emperor is severed, and I have become your man. As if I were your vassal, I will give your orders a higher priority than those of the emperor. It is forbidden on pain of death for me to report to the emperor or to anyone else the things I hear you say or see you do. Even after I have returned to the emperor's service, it will be forever forbidden for me to speak a single word about you. You may have perfect faith that I will not spy on you, nor carry any tales.

"But neither will I carry tales about the emperor, who has been my master for ten years, and who is the greatest man in our history since the days of Menelik, son of Solomon, son of David. Anything else you want to know, I will gladly tell you, but I will not speak to you of the emperor. Anything that he wants you to know about himself, he will tell you." Samuel's whole body was shaking with emotion.

Rassam believed him. He salaamed as gracefully as he could to the old man and said, "I thank you for the explanation, Samuel. I am sorry I placed you in such a position. I did so out of ignorance."

Samuel forgave the error immediately. He stayed with Rassam and Blanc through the evening, answering their questions about Ethiopia until they couldn't think of anything more to ask.

Samuel and Dahon had both been stunned by the amount of honor that the emperor had heaped upon the Britishers. Again and again during the night, they returned to that topic. As far as either of them could remember, no one had ever been greeted in a manner approaching this.

Samuel had slept with the other servants in the smaller tent, but long before dawn a messenger from the emperor awakened him, and now he led Rassam swiftly through the sleeping tent city. Sentries paced the dark aisles at wide intervals, but they recognized Samuel and the *feringi* and let them pass without a word.

They went beyond the outer boundary of the tent city and the last loose line of sentries. They topped a shallow rise. Samuel stopped and pointed. A white-robed shape stood out against a black line of trees.

Rassam walked on alone, stumbling once on a log hidden in the knee-high grass. He made a great deal of noise as he approached, but the emperor did not move. Theodore was alone at the edge of a grove of trees. He wore ankle-length white trousers and a plain white *shama*. His arms were bare, thick and well-rounded, and he stood half a head taller than Rassam. His right foot was tucked against the inside of his left knee in the African herder's stance, and he balanced easily on his left leg and on the shaft of a spear that he held in his hands. It was the exact position that Captain Speedy had drawn nearly two years before.

Theodore was gazing out across a wide, downward-sloping vista toward the east. His face was obscured in darkness. He was a human this time, and not a semidivine bundle of clothes speaking words like an ancient oracle, but the mystery of the early-morning summons and the dark isolation of the place caught Rassam off guard again. Also, something about the emperor's comfortable stance created an aura around him of power, of confidence—and of something else that Rassam could not name. Perhaps it was serenity, perhaps religious certainty. He did not have the look of a man who expected to die soon, as Paniotti had suggested. Rassam thought again of the Buddha.

The emperor turned his head slowly, regally, like a lion. He spoke flawless, Yemeni-accented Arabic. His voice was sonorous and powerful. Theodore began without greeting Rassam, as if the ideas had too great a need to be spoken to waste time on preliminaries. Rassam, standing half a dozen paces from him, was in his spell instantly. "I have read the Queen's letter," he said. "It is a good letter. I think she wants to be my friend. Also, I like the presents that she has sent by you. The Queen has asked that I release my prisoners. She is subtle and does not call them 'prisoners,' but we are men of honesty and can speak truthfully. Consul Cameron and his people and the missionaries are my prisoners. Their usefulness to me is over, and so I have already sent an escort to bring them to you."

"I thank Your Majesty," said Rassam. All he could think about was that everything he had aimed at for so long had just been granted. He could leave with the captives.

The emperor turned to gaze down the slope toward the east. He was silent for a moment. Then he said, "I asked you to meet me here for an important reason. You are a man of some intellect, or so I have been told. I wish to tell you certain things that I have told no man for many years. They are things that I cannot tell my own advisors, not even Magiga Dulou or Wolde, for they would not understand. Do you know why I met you yesterday in such state, with armies, wrapped in an imperial robe, unable to talk directly to you, unable to have you come near me?"

"It is the custom of the country, I thought."

"It is, but I find it—have always found it—repugnant. I met you that way because my people expected it. I am their emperor, their leader, the focus of their world. I carry the weight of them on my shoulders. So, I carry on charades for them. But I cannot speak before them, for they would not understand. Mr. Rassam, what do you think is the enemy of Ethiopia?"

"I've heard you consider the Turks your enemy, though—"

"Not the Turks, though my people will tell you that. No, it is a fact of history that we are invulnerable to them here in our mountains, just as they are safe from us. But my people need the Turks to be their enemy, so I play that charade, too. No, the Turks are not the enemy. The enemy is ignorance. The soil is rich here. There is plenty of rain. There are forests full of good, hard wood. There are animals whose skins would make good leather. There are thousands of men who can read and write. But despite all this there is no prosperity. And the reason is ignorance.

"The cities and roads were built three hundred years ago by the Portuguese. They haven't been repaired since. There are no industries. We could irrigate to open up huge areas of new farmland, but we don't know how. Our educated men could learn these things and teach the rest of us, but they spend their whole lives poring over the holy books and writing useless poetry.

"The greatest problem of all, the greatest sign of our ignorance, is war. The peasants are afraid to grow more than they can eat, because the armies will come and take it.

"The true enemy of Ethiopia is ignorance. There is no light in our country."

He lapsed into another long silence.

Rassam considered what the emperor was saying. There was nothing of the mystic here, nor of the madman. Theodore was a perfectly rational, supremely perceptive, pragmatic man concerned about the future of his nation.

The time that passed in silence was made comfortable somehow by the emperor's serenity. Theodore finally broke the spell. "Plowden and Bell came at a time when I was ready for them. It was remarkable that these men came from so far away, and yet devoted themselves so completely to our country. There are those who will say they were only interested in their own gain, that they were mercenaries, but that is only slander. They never wanted anything but to help me bring Ethiopia into the light.

"They brought new ideas that I, in my ignorance, would never have had. We worked together. We had a dream of an Ethiopia that might exist someday: roads, cities, bridges, industries, teachers, schools, trade with other countries, peace. We built a few roads. We set men to work improving the cities. Plowden worked to establish friendship between your Queen and me. But things went slowly, because Ethiopia is an ignorant country. We had patience, and Ethiopia was mine for a few years as it had been no man's for centuries. There was peace. They helped me make changes in the laws, too. I ended the slave trade. I sent out my own officers to govern the provinces. I encouraged caravans and pilgrims to other nations. We were happy in those times, though we were displeased that my people did not seem to understand what we were doing.

"But then God turned against me. My wife, Tawavitch, died. Bell and Plowden were killed. Rebellions began to rise up against me in all parts of the country. I felt alone. I often drank liquor until I lost control of myself. I know people still remember those days, and they tell stories about what an evil man I was. Well, I will tell you, my friend, that I did many evil things during those times. But those times were past before Cameron came to me.

"When he came, I hoped he would take the place of Bell and Plowden, but he was a man of words and nothing else. They say I put him in prison because he did not deliver my letter to the Queen, and because he visited the Turks. That is what I told my people, that is what they believe. But those weren't the true reasons. I knew he had sent my letter. I knew he was not betraying me with the Turks. Tell me, do you believe in prophecy?"

Rassam gulped at the sudden question. "Yes," he said, though he did not.

"I tell you, then, that God promised me long ago that a man would come from far away, and he would bring light to my country. This man, I knew, was neither Bell nor Plowden, since they did not match the signs that had been foretold. But still I thought that with their help I could bring the light to my country, and so we worked for Ethiopia until God turned against me and killed them. Was it a sin, do you think, for me to try to bring light to Ethiopia without waiting for the prophecy of the Lord to come to pass?"

"Not if your intentions were good."

"It was a sin of pride, a sin of lack of faith. I should have waited calmly, prepared the way. I should have had the faith to wait. When Cameron came, I hoped for a few vain days that he might be the promised one, the Light Bringer, but he was not. For a few days, I actually doubted that God had ever spoken to me. I thought I had invented the prophecies in my own mind. But then I realized, in a revelation, that Cameron had been given to me not to *be* the Light Bringer, but to bring that one to me. *I knew it was true.* I was being given another chance. I prepared myself to accept and welcome the Light Bringer when he came. God had told me long ago, through an ancient monk, the signs for which I should watch. I humbled myself before God each morning, and I told Him over and over again that I would not impede the promised one, that I would accept him and fulfill my fate. Do you find all this hard to believe?"

"God works in mysterious ways," mumbled Rassam, somewhat unoriginally. This new direction in the emperor's monologue had confused him, upset his opinions.

"When Cameron made me angry, I realized that I must use him to bring the Light Bringer to me. I put Cameron in prison, but I treated him well. I allowed his messengers to travel freely through my domain. I knew your government would send someone else to try and release him. They sent you. I waited for long months, waiting for the signs that would tell me you are the Light Bringer. One of the signs appeared while you were in Massawa. Another appeared when you were in Wochnee. I now await the others."

Rassam suddenly realized what Theodore was saying. "Me? You think I'm the one?"

"You. I have already seen two of these signs. I await the others in order to be sure."

"What kinds of signs?"

"I had waited for the signs to appear for nearly two years after you arrived in Massawa, and none had appeared. I tired of waiting and sent for you to come to me, and immediately one of the signs was revealed to me. The Light Bringer is to set people free from bondage. In Massawa you rose up boldly and crushed the slave trade.

"Elephants will fall before the Light Bringer. In Wochnee you shot an elephant, and he surely fell before you.

"The other signs, the ones I am awaiting, I cannot tell you. I watch for them."

Rassam felt all the easy gains slipping away, felt himself being swallowed up by an impossible situation. "What can I do?"

"It is not for you to do anything, until the time of the Light Bringer. It is only for me to watch for the signs."

Confusion interfered with Rassam's thinking. "How could I bring light to Ethiopia? I know no industries, no crafts, nothing about farming or building. I cannot do anything."

"You are a great man in your country," said Theodore. "Perhaps it is through your great influence that you will bring the light. As you said, God works in mysterious ways. A great man like you could cause artisans to come. There are many things you could do."

Rassam felt the urge to shout, *I am not a great man. I am the least significant of men.* But he could not. He bowed his head in silence.

Theodore was also silent. The first ray of the sun appeared through a cleft between two distant mountains. Theodore looked straight into its light, and Rassam studied his profile. His face was that of a man born to lead men, who would have risen to leadership wherever he was born, no matter how high or low, no matter how he tried to expedite or hinder his rise. It was the face of a man who *knew,* and through this knowing, whether it was true or not, could become a Christ or Mohammed or Buddha, a great thinker or a martyr.

"Our people worshiped the sun at one time," whispered Theodore. "They thought the sun was a god. They worshiped the moon and the stars, too. In the Bible you can read how Joseph had a dream in which stars, representing his brothers, made obeisance to him. Solomon had a dream of suns. And I, the Emperor Theodore who was a boy named Kasa, I saw a vision of suns and stars. My vision foretold the future for me just as surely as the dreams of Joseph and Solomon foretold their futures. What the dream prophesies for me, that I must do . . .

"Cameron and the others are of no use to me now, so I give them to you and your Queen. I release them, and you are free to do what you will with them. I ask that you make me a friend of your Queen. I ask that you arrange for an embassy to travel with safe conduct to England. And I ask that you, Mr. Rassam, will be my friend."

Theodore held out his arms, and Rassam fell into his embrace. "I have waited long to see you," said Theodore.

"I've waited long, too," said Rassam, though he didn't know whether Theodore was referring to him as Rassam or as the Light Bringer.

"You may go now," said Theodore. "We will progress this morning, and for the next several days. We travel often, for no one area could feed so many people for long, but on this progress we shall pass near Lake Tana. You will be carried in boats across the lake, and in Korata you will await Cameron and the others."

Rassam bowed formally to the emperor, and he made his way back through the grass to where Samuel was waiting for him.

The meeting had affected Rassam strangely. The emperor was an amazing man, a heady mixture of solid pragmatism and religious zeal, practical one moment and mystical the next, so simple and yet so complex, so strong and yet so fragile. *Signs.* Theodore was watching for signs: when he spoke about them, it was hard to disbelieve. Rassam's impressions were confusing, but one thing was clear to him: odd as it might seem, he *liked* the emperor.

Standing on his left foot, leaning his weight against the shaft of his spear, Theodore remained alone after Rassam left him. The rising sun gentled the plateau to life. Tiny birds darted through the trees and the grass and challenged each other in shrill voices. Gazelles grazed close enough for him to see their lustrous eyes, and then spotted him and trotted away with fluid steps. Ants marched across the imperial foot, and a fly lit on the imperial eyelid. The gorge of the Big Abai, the Blue Nile, ran across his field of vision to the east, and Lake Tana lay to the north. He could not see them, but distinct cloud patterns, ruddy in the early morning light, pinpointed their locations.

The question of signs filled his mind. Identifying the Light Bringer was to be the critical act of his life. For this identification, there were not the usual one or two signs. There were five.

The first sign, as Theodore had explained, was that the Light Bringer would set people free from bondage.

The second sign was that elephants would fall down before the Light Bringer.

These two signs had already been fulfilled.

Though it was not one of the foretold signs, Theodore had added his own to the list. It was appropriate that the Light Bringer should come to him accompanied by thousands of men, to represent the myriad stars. Since it was his own sign, Theodore did not feel he had seriously violated it by providing those thousands himself.

There remained three more signs to be fulfilled.

The Light Bringer would accept Theodore's help through a difficult place.

The Light Bringer would usurp Theodore's rights in Theodore's presence.

The Light Bringer would blame Theodore for what Theodore had done, and even when Theodore humbled himself publicly and begged forgiveness, the Light Bringer would never forgive him.

Theodore felt as if he were nearing a destination toward which he had been traveling for many years. The Light Bringer was in Ethiopia. Three signs remained. The illumination would begin, and Theodore would be dead. It would be a glorious death, certainly, there to the south, atop that flat-topped mountain, in the great fortress that his long-dead *feringi* had built for him, exploding into flame, preserved forever in the memory of his people, but death in all its terrifying majesty nonetheless.

A nerve deep inside his cheek twitched, but, as always, his surface remained as still as a monument.

All this for Rassam? That timid man, the Light Bringer? To die to make room for Rassam?

14

January-March 1866
Lake Tana

Samuel had hired four Ethiopian boys as servants, and had purchased three pack mules. By the time Samuel and Rassam returned to their tents, the boys were already working. The tents were being expertly folded, tied, and fastened to the mules. It was obvious from the way the boys sang, laughed, and ran back and forth through the campsite that they were brand-new employees, eager to please. Blanc sat in the middle of it all, barefoot, bareheaded, dressed once again in his worn traveling suit, sipping a cup of something hot.

"Is that coffee?" asked Rassam. Its rich aroma dominated all the other pungent morning smells.

The Arabic word for coffee is identical to the Amharic. Two of the boys heard him and raced to bring him a cup. Grounds were floating in it, and it was so thick it would almost have made a meal in itself.

"Why so early?" groaned Blanc. "In the middle of the night the tent started coming down around my head. Right around my head. 'Samuel orders,' the boys said. They'd obviously learned the words by rote, don't speak another word of Arabic. Nothing but 'Samuel orders, Samuel orders.'"

Samuel looked up from checking the knots on one of the mules, and called out, "It is essential to start early. You will see why when the progress has begun." He walked back and forth like an elderly weasel, urging the boys to work faster, tightening ropes and redoing saddles, always trying to speed things up. He motioned Blanc off the trunk on which he had been sitting, then waved them both away. They walked out of the camp and watched from downhill.

"Where were you so early?" asked Blanc.

"The emperor wanted to see me." Somehow, Rassam didn't want to tell Blanc any more than that. He knew he could never explain the things the emperor had said in such a way that Blanc wouldn't laugh at them.

"And?"

"The captives. They've been set free. We made a good impression, I suppose."

"Set free? Marvelous."

"Yes," said Rassam. "This progress will take us toward our rendezvous with Consul Cameron."

Samuel waved at them from the top of the hill and called, "We are ready to begin, masters. Come."

"Anything more?" asked Blanc, as they started up the hill toward Samuel.

"No, it was a short audience."

"When can we start for home?"

"A few days."

"Marvelous," repeated Blanc, but Rassam only nodded and said softly, "Marvelous."

They adjusted their clothing and settled their solar helmets on their heads, took their walking sticks and parasols firmly in hand, and mounted their horses. Halfway to the outskirts of the camp they discovered the reasons for Samuel's urgency. There were dozens more people and animals on the trail ahead of them, and more were filtering in from every side. Before they had gone another hundred yards, the jam-up locked them into place. Circumventing the trail was out of the question; there was nothing to do but wait. The sun had begun to bake the mud, and dust filled the air. Blanc and Rassam choked on it. The noise was overwhelming.

By noon they had barely reached the outskirts of the camp. Herds of cattle and sheep that had been grazing outside the camp joined the progress, adding their stink and noise and dust.

"I tried to get us moving early," said Samuel with a toothy, unconcerned grin, "but our boys weren't quick enough. Perhaps tomorrow we can get away before the rest of the emperor's people. It is not so dusty in front."

They had been standing in the same place for more than an hour when a small group of horsemen came prancing down the sheer slope toward them, the ponies struggling hard to maintain their footing, the soldiers perfectly confident and relaxed in the lurching saddles.

Magiga Dulou was in the lead. "I have been searching for you," he shouted to Rassam. "The emperor wishes you to be escorted to the front of the progress, out of this confusion and dust."

He threw out a sharp command, and his horsemen began to shove the people and animals ahead of them off the trail. People went down into the mud and came up cursing and shaking their fists.

Rassam started to protest, but Blanc shouted, "Oh, jolly good, wonderful fellows!" and jammed his heels into his horse to get it jogging down the cleared trail. Samuel seized the halter of one of the pack mules and followed Blanc. The servants rushed into line, and Rassam's horse followed by itself.

Magiga Dulou's pace was slower than that he would have taken on a normal journey, but they worked their way steadily through the hordes and into the countryside. The road turned into a gently undulating downward slope where they had somewhat more elbowroom, and they began to pick up speed. At the bottom of the slope the progress was pressed up against a narrow but swiftly moving white-water stream. Most of the people were pushing their way toward the wide ford, and so the ground before it was crowded and hard to get through. Many of the riders were shoved into the deep water, where their animals foundered. The onlookers stopped to laugh and applaud, further adding to the confusion.

Magiga Dulou and his men struggled through to the ford, and Rassam and Blanc and their people followed, inside a protective wedge of warriors. They lurched across the stream and broke into a canter away from the direct line of travel beyond.

Several thousand people had already got past the ford, but here at least they were able to spread out over the wide meadows and proceed at a comfortable pace. After an hour or so, however, the progress came up against another obstruction. The entire horde had stopped, and the jostling crowd was constantly growing. Magiga Dulou stood up in his saddle and looked ahead, then sent his warriors on to clear a passage through the crowd.

They finally discovered what the problem was: another stream, wider and slower than the first, flowed through the bottom of a shallow ravine. A crescent-shaped line of foot soldiers were holding people back from the stream, but they parted long enough to let Rassam's party into the wide arc of empty space behind them.

A wide series of terraces had been cut down to the ford, and on the far bank a company of soldiers was working with shovels and spades to construct another series of terraces from the ford out of the ravine. A tall, well-muscled man, naked to the waist, shovel in hand, was directing them with shouts and gestures, digging and sweating along with them.

Rassam stared at the man, thought he might recognize him, but the sun was shining too brightly for him to see clearly. He swung his pink parasol out and snapped it open, then angled it over his head so it blocked the sun's rays. Yes, the sweating man directing the workers was the emperor.

Theodore saw Rassam and his party, smiled in recognition, and began to wave them across the stream—but his hand froze in midair. The smile vanished, turned to anger, then slid into amazement.

Rassam shrugged his shoulders. wondering what was wrong, and at that instant Samuel was at his side. "Put down your parasol, Master

Rassam," he whispered harshly. It was a definite order, no tone Rassam would expect from a servant. Rassam hesitated, and Samuel repeated, more urgently, "Put it down at once."

Rassam collapsed the parasol and tucked it back under his arm. "What is the matter?"

"The parasol," said Samuel, "it is one of the emperor's insignia." His voice was filled with dread. "No one but he may use the parasol. It is like wearing a crown in the presence of a king."

"My God," muttered Rassam. "Thank you, Samuel. Please do me the favor of going to him at once and telling him I didn't know, that I apologize."

"At once," said Samuel. He flew down the terraces to the ford and started across. Halfway across the stream he bowed down so low that his face touched the water, and he kept it there, almost submerged, until he reached the bank. Sliding out of the water on his belly he writhed like a salamander up the terrace to Theodore. He reached the emperor and kissed the mud on Theodore's foot.

Without looking down at his old servant, Theodore snapped his fingers and said a single word. Samuel leaped upright and bowed, then talked for a long time.

Too great a distance separated Rassam and Theodore for the envoy to be able to see the emperor's eyes, but from the angle of his unmoving face Rassam knew the emperor was staring hard at him. He wilted under the pressure of that gaze.

The emperor's lips finally moved. Samuel spun around and came running back down the terraces and through the stream.

"The emperor says he understands your intention was not to insult him," Samuel said. "He forgives." Samuel leaned panting against Rassam's saddle. "He asks you to join him. Both of you."

Rassam kicked his horse a few steps nearer to the first terrace. The mud was wet and deep. He looked up dubiously at Theodore, who waved him to come across. Rassam let out a sharp breath, pointed his horse's muzzle at the stream below, and gave it a vicious kick in the ribs. It took half a step, then locked its knees. Rassam kicked again. It whinnied, braced itself, and would not move. Theodore called out, and Samuel shouted and slapped the horse. It jumped forward, then found itself too close to the edge to stop. Its hooves sank into the mud, and it jerked and slipped down the terraces to the stream. Rassam almost lost his seat, but then they were safe on the gravelly bank of the stream. The horse stopped.

Rassam looked up. The soldiers had halted their work and were watching the crazy *feringi*'s first encounter with the independence of an Ethiopian horse. Alone among them, Theodore was not laughing. He was waiting patiently now, watching Rassam closely, with a look of knowing what was about to happen.

Rassam prodded the horse into the stream, which was wide but only inches deep at this point. Surprisingly, he made it easily to the other side, but the horse refused to start up the terraces, no matter how Rassam urged, begged, or kicked.

Finally, disgusted, Rassam swung down and started up on foot.

His leather boot soles slipped in the mud. One boot stuck, and he fell to his knees.

The soldiers again began to erupt into laughter, but Theodore silenced them with one angry gesture.

Rassam got up and tried again. He slipped and fell. One of the soldiers started down toward him to help, but Theodore shouted frantically and waved him back, and then he himself clambered down the terraces to Rassam. "Be of good cheer," he said, extending his hand. "Do not be afraid."

"I thank you," said Rassam, "but Your Majesty does me too much honor by helping me."

"Have I a choice?" asked the emperor as they reached the top together.

Rassam knew he was missing something. "Of course."

Theodore shook his head wearily. "In some things, none of us have choices," he said.

"I don't understand."

"Signs," said Theodore. "We cannot escape them, much as we would like."

"What about signs?"

"Two more have I seen. You usurped my rights in my presence. I helped you through a difficult place. One sign remains."

"One?" breathed Rassam. *One more.* The confusion rose like a hollow ball in his chest. *One more sign, and then?*

Blanc got across the stream, and his horse lurched easily up the terraces. Blanc dismounted and tipped his hat to the emperor. "Your Majesty."

The emperor seemed momentarily shocked by the casual salute, then burst out with a laugh. He salaamed to Blanc.

"Beastly hot," remarked Blanc.

"Beastly hot?" asked the emperor. "Hot like the beasts?"

Blanc had translated "beastly" into Arabic literally, and the phrase had no meaning. Rassam explained the misunderstanding.

"Ah, I understand," said Theodore. "And yes, I must agree that it is indeed beastly hot, by the power of God."

Rassam's party found a shady spot under a huge baobab tree, and from there they watched the warriors digging their terraces. Theodore led by example with his shovel. He dug like a man possessed, as if trying to lose himself in physical labor, and his followers picked up their rhythm from him. They began a fast, impelling chant.

Occasionally, during a lull in the chant, Theodore stood up from the mud, wiped his brow, and looked at Rassam. But he did not seem to actually see Rassam the man, perhaps seeing instead Rassam the idea, Rassam the long-awaited. Something in his look said that all doubts in the world had been removed, that a supposed future was now a certainty. Rassam felt that he was out of his territory, wandering lost and at the mercy of unknown forces.

He looked back up the meadows. Indistinct, hazy movement far in the distance told him that more people were still joining the crowd around the ford. Clouds of dust were rising beyond the farthest limits of sight. How many people were there?

At last the terraces were done, and Theodore waved the nearest ranks down to the stream, across, and back up to the level ground. They went slowly, with many slips and false starts and balks by the animals, but they finally got there. Theodore was on the terraces to help them, crying out encouragement, carrying small children in his arms, offering a firm hand to an old woman, slapping the rump of a reluctant mule.

When it was clear that the terraces would do their job, Theodore and his personal escort threw their *shamas* about their shoulders, mounted their horses, and started toward the front of the column, which was already winding into the next series of hills. Theodore waved Rassam and Blanc up to join him. They traveled together for the two hours that remained until dark.

This was a different Theodore from the man Rassam had seen at the pavilion or outside the camp at dawn or in the mud of the terraces. Rassam wondered which was the real Theodore. There was neither formality nor moroseness nor religious fervor about him. He spoke cheerfully on a wide range of topics. He amazed Rassam both by his curiosity and by his understanding of the world beyond Ethiopia. Though his sources of information were scanty, he knew a little about all the main events in world affairs. He asked dozens of questions during those two hours, and Rassam, far removed from newspapers, was only able to answer a few of them: *Was the American war over? Why had they fought? Had England taken sides? Why had the English fought the Ashantis? Would the Egyptian Viceroy fight the Turkish Sultan? Would Garibaldi try to seize Rome by force?*

At the top of a very high ridge Rassam turned in his saddle and looked back at the masses of people who had crossed the stream and the thousands who were still approaching it. It was difficult to estimate such incredible numbers, but Rassam did his best to visually break down his field of vision into squares, to judge the number of people in each square, and to arrive at a total figure. He decided at last that he could see one hundred and fifty thousand people. Clouds of dust were still rising in the distance.

"Have you ever counted your people?" he asked Theodore.

It was the prophet Theodore who answered: "There is a Biblical injunction against numbering of the people. Do you not recall how

David ordered his captain Joab to number the people, and how the Lord was angry and brought pestilence to the land?"

Rassam swiveled around and looked again at the progress of the emperor's encampment. Since he had turned away, even more must have appeared over the most distant visible ridge. One hundred fifty thousand people. One in five a fighting man, in this warlike land where every able-bodied man was a warrior. That comes to an army of thirty thousand men. Many of them armed with flintlocks, but even armed with spears an army of thirty thousand men . . . And Theodore must be able to call on thousands more from the rest of the nation.

"How are so many fed?" asked Rassam.

A shadow crossed the emperor's smiling face. Rassam realized he should have known better than to ask such a question. "As the emperor," said Theodore, "I receive tribute and taxes from all my vassals. It is a vast amount of food, material, and gold. I receive tribute that my army, which is necessary to the peace of the nation, should eat."

Rassam recalled how Paniotti had explained to him that Theodore was the first Ethiopian leader to pay his soldiers, and so to stop them from pillaging the land; how Theodore was able to pay his soldiers because he collected fair tax from each of his provinces.

The rebellions in the border provinces must have reduced the amount of tax money that was coming in. Theodore's answer might have been true in the past, but it could not be true now. Rassam wondered how he managed to continue paying and feeding his hungry, nonproducing army and their families.

A partial answer came at sunset. Rassam's party had pitched their tents on a gentle rise near the hill chosen for the emperor's compound. Though some of them were still ten miles away, all the emperor's horde stopped where they were the moment the emperor's banner first fluttered over his tent. Samuel explained that the emperor would remain where he was for a day or two, until everyone had caught up, and then he would make another stage.

Thousands of tents of all sizes and colors went up all over the countryside to the limits of sight, and certainly far beyond that. Then, as campfires began to send up wraiths of thin smoke, wraiths that soon joined into a single, vast cloud, hundreds of men headed out from the route of travel into the nearest fields. Something had disturbed Rassam about the countryside, and now he realized—such an obvious thing, and he had overlooked it entirely—that there were no local people anywhere, only the people of the emperor's horde.

The emperor's followers now stripped the deserted fields of their crops, looted the villages along the way, and brought back what would have been gathered in earlier, happier times through even-handed tribute collection, spread out across all of Ethiopia and so made easy for everyone instead of devastating for a few.

It was the old way, the way armies had been supported throughout the centuries before Theodore—and now it was the way again.

While Blanc commented in a low, secretive tone on the barbarity of it, Rassam could only wonder what pain this grim necessity must cause a monarch who gave every indication of loving his subjects.

Rassam sat on the Lake Tana shore one evening and watched a band of warriors build the entire imperial navy. They cut down bulrushes, wove them into two thick mats that were six feet wide by twenty feet long, rolled the mats up and tied the ends—and two boats were lying on the shore.

They departed for Korata, where they were to wait for Consul Cameron, just after dawn the next morning. Rassam and Blanc, one in each boat, sat on bundles of bulrushes, rolled up their pants, and held on while their paddlers towed them into the lake. On the shore Samuel and Dahon waved good-by while the Ethiopian boys struck the camp. The servants were going to take the roundabout land route to Korata because, as Samuel explained, being brought across by boat was too great an honor.

The paddlers, stark naked, knelt in the bow and stern. They propelled the boats by slapping the water with long sticks, sending great fountains over their passengers. The boats moved sluggishly through the water, and wallowed deeper as each hour passed. The paddlers were afraid to get very far from dry land, so they set a sinuous course through coves and around long peninsulas. The lake shore was a thick rain forest of acacias, banyons, lily pads, and baobabs. Wide streams oozed into the lake. Quick gray monkeys ran through the branches, and everywhere were blue starlings, fish eagles, black-and-white kingfishers, and giant toucans. Pythons swam around the boats and draped overhead from branch to branch.

It took twelve hours to skirt the lake to Korata, by which time one of the boats had three inches of freeboard left and the other was entirely submerged except for the stern and the tip of the bow. Korata appeared as a walled city low on the lakefront, glowing red in the sunset, studded with ostrich eggshell crosses. The shore was crowded with an unruly mob of priests, monks, and *debteras,* with iron crosses in their hands and turbans on their heads. They had come to meet the famous *feringi,* and they let out a cheer. Crosses waved in the air like weapons, and the holy men pushed down to the water and thrashed into it so eagerly that Rassam began to wonder whether this reception was friendly or not— but Samuel appeared like a black angel out of the crowd, shouted until he could be heard, and formally announced Rassam and Blanc. Then he led the Britishers out of the crowd and away from the city.

The servants, Rassam learned as they walked to their tents, had taken seven hours to ride to Korata. They had set up camp, prepared dinner, and still had several hours left over to rest before Rassam and Blanc arrived. But Samuel was quick to remind Rassam and Blanc of what an honor it was to have been brought across the lake by boat.

Cameron was at least three weeks away, so Rassam and Blanc settled into their newest temporary home to wait. They rose early each morning and hunted until the heat drove them back to their tents. There were wooded regions nearby where they shot giant toucans and pythons and hippopotami. Deep in the foliage, masked by distracting branches, the toucan was a fairly challenging shot. Pythons and hippopotami were ridiculously easy. They shot the useless pythons out of some inborn hatred for serpents, and watched them uncoil slowly from the branches and quiver as they dangled down. Hippopotami wallowed just under the surface, and they found that a first shot would almost always bring the giants thrashing to the top where a shot from Blanc's large-bore elephant gun would send them bubbling, bleeding, back into the muddy depths.

In the afternoons, Blanc pursued his study of Ethiopian diseases and cures. Rassam studied Amharic with a crippled old priest who spoke passable Arabic.

Gifts for Rassam arrived daily from Theodore. The gifts were sometimes precious, sometimes filled with honor: a brace of partridges shot by the emperor himself and brought at a dead run by a relay of horsemen while they were still fresh; a pair of fine antique pistols; a white robe with the Lion of Judah embroidered on it in gold thread. According to Samuel, this robe was the highest honor a man could receive from the Ethiopian emperor. Rassam wrote back thanking Theodore for the gifts, complimenting and praising him, saying the bland nothings he thought the emperor would want to hear.

There were isolated moments when Rassam felt himself distrusting the emperor's promise, when he remembered the business of the signs, and then waves of helplessness would swamp him. But these moments were infrequent. He usually allowed himself to be lulled into what even he knew was a false sense of security. For the most part, he was more confident and cheerful than he had been at any time since he had read Disraeli's speech in the London *Times,* five months before.

The days were pleasant enough, and the nights were cold but bearable beside a roaring fire on the beach or bundled up in a thick Smyrna rug in his tent. Time stood still for this long moment, trapped between all the events of the past and the uncertainty of the future.

After a little more than three weeks, on March 10, 1866, the Magdala prisoners arrived in Korata. A Goan servant appeared in camp and asked in stumbling English for permission to approach, and while he was running back up the path Rassam and Blanc dressed carefully in their uniforms. Then they strode out to meet the consul.

There were two Europeans in the midst of fifty Ethiopian warriors. All were riding, and were accompanied by heavily laden pack animals.

The ritual of meeting fellow-Europeans in a savage land had a long and inflexible tradition behind it. As befitted his higher rank, Rassam slowed his steps and halted entirely, so it would be Cameron who came to him. A gust of wind caught a rag hanging from a pole held by one of the Europeans, and a handmade Union Jack fluttered out.

Blanc called, "God save the Queen." His voice was choked with emotion.

The one who held the flag answered, "God save the Queen."

The Magdala party stopped twenty paces from Rassam and Blanc, and the older European, the one without the flag, dismounted and walked toward them. He wore a solar helmet and a faded blue suit with tails. His beard, which was very short and neatly trimmed, was a mousy brown, and so were his tiny eyes. His steps were short and deliberate, full of fatigue and hinting at poor health.

He stopped two paces away, tapped his solar helmet, fiddled nervously with his walking stick, and coughed. His eyes darted to Rassam's, then sneaked away.

Cameron had come to them, and the ritual said he was supposed to introduce himself, but there was only a brittle silence, another cough, then more silence.

At last, Rassam said, "Afternoon, sir. I am Envoy Rassam. This is Captain Blanc." He put out his hand.

Cameron's rodent eyes took in the hand, then leaped away. He started to stick out his own hand, but it only got halfway to Rassam's before a compulsion took control of it. His hand jumped up and pulled at his beard with the intensity of a frightened child stroking a blanket. "Mmmmmmm, Envoy Rassam," he whispered. He worked the hand away from his beard, touched Rassam's hand for one fleeting instant, and let his hand return to his beard. "Delighted. Mm, Captain Blanc." He touched Blanc's hand. "Good of you to come."

"Our pleasure, sir," said Blanc, and while Cameron was staring into the distance, he quizzically raised his eyebrows at Rassam.

"Are you in good health?" asked Rassam.

"Not very," said Cameron. He seemed suddenly able to make the mental leap from wherever his mind had been wandering to the here-and-now. "Come and meet our enthusiastic young patriot, Mr. Kerens."

Laurence Kerens was twenty-two years old, ruddy-faced, with the pale, downy mustache and goatee of an adolescent boy. He smiled eagerly at Rassam and Blanc, and could hardly limit himself to a brief, dignified handshake. "Very pleased to meet you at last, sirs," he laughed.

"Have you heard the news, gentlemen?" asked Rassam.

"Nothing," said Cameron.

"We shall all be going home soon. I have the emperor's promise."

"A promise—" muttered Cameron, and his eyes drifted away.

"So that's the lake," said Kerens. "I've been in this country I don't know how long, and I've never seen it. Rather like an ocean, isn't it?

Has it a tide?" He looked along the shoreline to the tents. "This is a jolly place to stay. You can see forever, over the water. You'd be surprised at how a man longs for room to let his eyes sprint ahead when he's surrounded by high walls. Are there crocodiles in the lake?"

"A few," answered Blanc, who had recognized a man of his own kind immediately. "There are more hippos. Pythons in the jungle, too."

"Have you a gun?"

"Several. Do you shoot?"

"Of course. Oh, what fun."

"Well, then, time is flitting by," said Blanc. "There are still a few hours of daylight left."

"We can shoot now?"

"Come with me. If you will excuse us, gentlemen."

Kerens looked at Rassam. "Oh, I'm being rude. I shouldn't run off when we've just met."

"Not at all," said Rassam. "The consul and I need to have a talk, in any case."

Kerens and Blanc dashed off to the tents to get Blanc's guns.

"Amazing," said Rassam. "After all he's been through, and he's still more interested in shooting a hippo than in hearing what is going to happen to him."

"The resiliency of youth," said Cameron, in a crisp voice that announced he was back to the real world again. "The whole thing has been an adventure to him. Never a thought about the danger. All he wants from the future is to be able to grow a decent beard. I was like that once."

"Would you care to bring your people down and have them start setting up your camp?" asked Rassam.

"Yes. Of course."

In addition to Kerens, Cameron had with him half a dozen servants. They began to establish a campsite next to Rassam's.

The status of Cameron and Kerens—whether captive or free—was not clear. All but ten of the Ethiopian warriors turned their horses back and began the return trip to Magdala at once. The remaining ten pitched tents at a little distance from Cameron's, and then proceeded to ignore the Europeans. Neither Rassam nor Cameron knew whether their orders were to protect the British, or to keep an eye on them.

While the tents were going up, Rassam took Cameron for a walk along the shore.

"I've waited for you for a very long time," said Cameron. "I expected you during the last dry season." His tone was not accusatory, but Rassam felt a twinge of guilt.

"Diplomatic protocol," he murmured. "Never forgot about you."

"Naturally. It has been a very long time, though."

"Has your imprisonment been miserable?"

"Hard enough. Not as bad as it could have been," said Cameron. "I've

been ill, but that's no fault of the prison. Other than that, not so bad."
He began to ramble along, one word tumbling quickly after the last
without a pause to catch his breath, and Rassam couldn't tell whether
his mind was here on the shore, or wandering, or half here and half
away. Cameron pulled continually at his beard with his right hand.

"When I came to Ethiopia, the emperor was eager to establish relations with Great Britain. No, *eager* is too mild a word—he was fervid,
frantic, as if establishing diplomatic relations was the only thing standing between him and death. I had but to make a suggestion, and he
would leap at it. He had presents actually prepared and waiting to send
with his embassy to England, as soon as the Queen's letter arrived.

"I tried to explain the situation to London, but the distance is so great,
and there is such a gulf between the English and the Ethiopians, that
I couldn't make them understand. I knew it would anger Theodore if
I went down to Kassala, but those were my orders. What else could I
do? I clung to my faith that the Queen's letter would turn his anger into
joy. I was still sure the letter was coming, you see. It had to be coming.
There was no reason on God's earth for it not to come.

"I assigned Mr. Kerens the task of waiting in Massawa for the packet,
and when it arrived, he hurried up to Ethiopia with it, still unopened.
If he had opened it, he might have saved himself a great deal of grief.
There was no letter in the packet. I have no hesitation in blaming F.O.
for all that has happened to us."

"Those are the reasons for your imprisonment?" asked Rassam,
remembering what Theodore had told him.

"Those are the reasons," answered Cameron. "I cannot fault the
emperor for his anger, nor for the treatment we've received. The top
of the *amba* Magdala is surrounded by a stone stockade that can repel
any Ethiopian invader. It would even give a modern army difficulty. It
was built by Theodore's pet Englishmen, Bell and Plowden. Within the
stockade is a permanent community of several thousands, plus a large
garrison of soldiers. The prison for Theodore's political prisoners, three
or four hundred in number, is in Magdala, too. It is to Theodore's credit
—many's the time I've heard it remarked—that those prisoners are still
alive at all. They are mostly rebel leaders who were reconciled to
Theodore two or three times before he finally imprisoned them. Any
of the previous emperors would have put them to death when they
were first captured. Their situation is not especially bad. Those who can
afford the luxury have their wives and servants with them. They are
somewhat crowded, but they lack for very little but freedom.

"We lived in a separate compound in several huts. Our most painful
day-to-day torture was our leg irons." Cameron stopped walking long
enough to lift his cuff and show Rassam a broad band of callus around
his ankle. "You cannot imagine the pain of this the first month. It bled
constantly. I wrapped it with rags during the day to ease the chafing,
but I had to unwrap it at night to let the circulation through. But it is

vital to understand that chains are not considered a torture by the Ethiopians. They are only an expedient way of keeping a prisoner from escaping.

"I was beaten during the first week, but after that I was treated well. Thanks to your Maria Theresa dollars, we never lacked anything. We grew our own vegetables. We had a flower garden full of songbirds, and our servants bought us meat, water, liquor, tobacco, whatever else we needed."

"It doesn't sound as onerous as I had expected," said Rassam.

"It was, at the beginning," said Cameron. "I think the emperor ordered it so, so I would write despairing letters to our people on the outside. For some reason of his own, he wanted me to write those letters. Did you not wonder how I knew your name, the first time I wrote to you?"

"I did."

"He himself told me your name. It was his messenger who took the note to you. I could have written a graceful, long letter, full of truth, but my despair was great. Can you blame a man for wanting to be free? And when my imprisonment had eased, I made up tortures to put in the letters. They served their purpose. They reached the London newspapers. What other forum did I have, when F.O. wouldn't listen?"

Rassam said, "I must say I admire you for holding by your honor when Theodore asked you to sign the document promising that Great Britain would take no vengeance on Theodore if he let you go. Englishmen everywhere were inspired by your courage."

Cameron tugged viciously at his beard. "Mr. Rassam, I put myself and my good name in your hands," he whispered. "It is easy to be honorable when you are healthy and strong and courageous. It is easy to refuse to sign documents that would embarrass your country when you can still stand on your own two feet without wincing from the pain of your ankle irons. It is easy then to stand tall and cry 'God save the Queen.' I'm not a coward, Mr. Rassam. I faced the Kaffirs. I was in the Natal War, the Crimea. I don't have to prove myself to anyone." His voice was barely audible. "Six months ago I sent a message to the emperor asking him whether he would release us if I were to sign the document. I begged him to let me sign it. I would have done anything to be out of that prison, to be on my way home.

"He came to me himself, a ride of more than fifty miles through the roughest terrain in the world. He came to Magdala to see me, though he was busy putting down a rebellion in the south. He came into the fortress and directly to our little compound, and he walked up to me and fell down on the ground at my feet and begged me to forgive him. He could not release me, he said, and it cut him to the quick to keep me a prisoner. He had nothing against me, he said, but he had no choice. He had a purpose, he said. These are his exact words: 'I have a purpose, a purpose that I cannot tell you, but it is a purpose greater than either of us. And so, though it hurts me greatly, I cannot let you go.' I was stunned by his sincerity and his dignity, even as he lay at my feet and begged me to forgive him.

"I forgave him, of course. He went away, and he left behind a broken man, an empty shell, a man without honor.

"The only things I have left now are a desire to enjoy pleasant company and a desire to go home. I will enjoy your company if you can still speak to me after everything I've said, but I have absolutely no faith in your ability to free us. I will never leave this country, and Kerens will never leave, and you will never leave." Great sobs began to bubble out of him.

Rassam touched his shoulder, and Cameron threw himself into Rassam's arms. Rassam embraced him lightly, distastefully. "No one could have done anything else," he said, though he knew his tone was not comforting. "I understand. I understand."

15

March-May 1866
Lake Tana

The emperor of the Ethiopians will beg the Light Bringer to forgive him, but the Light Bringer will refuse: by this sign the Light Bringer will be known.

Significant occasions demand public validation. The red ceremonial pavilion had been set up on the wide summit of a long, gentle hill. The open side of the pavilion faced northward, and from his low wooden throne at the back Theodore could see the entire hillside, the shoreline, and Lake Tana, glittering silver and green in the noontime sun. Carpets had been placed on the hillside from the pavilion to the lake at a width of nine carpets—the holy three times three.

Theodore was wearing the voluminous formal garment that covered nearly all his body. The silver drums were at his right hand, and someone was holding the red parasol so close over his head that its forward fringe prevented him from seeing any of the ceiling. His advisors and his servants were with him, but he had summoned none of his armies. The camp lay mostly behind the red pavilion, and there were no people visible in front of the pavilion except for Rassam and his party.

Theodore could pick them out easily, though they were still down near the water: Rassam, Blanc, Samuel, Dahon, the boys, Magiga Dulou and the fifty-warrior escort, the mules already loaded for the trip to the Sudan. They came across Theodore's line of vision from the east, moving slowly along the shore. Rassam, Blanc, and Samuel dismounted at the edge of the carpets and began to walk up the hill toward the pavilion.

Two days before, Theodore had brought his vast tent city to the lake. From his hilltop compound he could see Korata across the water, gleaming white in the daytime and glowing faintly at night, and he could see the camp of the Europeans as tiny drops of color on the bone-white beach or as fierce pinpricks of firelight in the dark.

The next morning, he had sent a messenger around the lake to Rassam.

"From the slave of God, His created being," the letter read, "the son of David, the son of Solomon, the King of Kings, Theodore.

"To my most beloved Rassam. I understand that your health has held well. I am thankful to God for this news. By the blessings of Iyesus, I am well also.

"I have established my quarters at the shore of the lake near the Big Abai. Your tents are visible to me, and I saw your campfires last night. They are a very pretty sight across the water.

"I have fulfilled half my promise, with the arrival in your presence of Mr. Cameron and Mr. Kerens.

"Now, I wish that all your belongings should be made ready to begin your journey to Khartoum. In the morning, Cameron and Kerens may begin their journey around the north end of the lake. I wish you to come around to say good-by to me, after which you may continue around the south end of the lake. You may rejoin your fellow countrymen at Wochnee. My people will accompany both your groups to guarantee your safety."

There was no apparent strength in Rassam's stride as he led his two companions up the hill of carpets. Theodore already had word of Rassam's parting from Cameron. One of the warriors in the Ethiopian camp near the European camp had watched through Theodore's own German telescope, and then he had ridden fast to describe it to the emperor. Cameron had been crying, the man reported, and when it was time to set out he had had to be lifted onto his horse. Rassam had made a feeble effort to calm the consul, but the spy was sure he had been near tears himself.

And it was for this Rassam, weak, uncertain, frightened in Theodore's presence, concerned only about getting home, that Theodore was supposed to die at Magdala.

It was almost a joke. Rassam couldn't possibly be the one—and yet the signs were so clear!

It was inevitable now. Rassam would refuse to forgive, and there would be the solemn journey to Magdala, and then there would be the exploding sun.

In the past months, Theodore had thought about all the things that were to be left undone, all the things that could have been accomplished if there had only been time, if only the Light Bringer had not come and if only the country had not crumbled around Theodore's head. So much had been within his grasp, and it had all fallen away. The momentum was with the rebels now, and the day of the Light Bringer was here. That Theodore who would bring peace and the fear of God, who would rule for forty years, did not exist. He was now simply Kasa, the Light Bringer's *balderaba*, John the Baptist to Rassam's Christ.

Theodore had felt his doom approaching. The terrible purpose had drawn near.

He had suffered the pain of having lost his dreams, and the pain of awful fear. He was afraid of not having the courage to do what he had to do; he was afraid of making a mistake and dying for no reason—indeed he was afraid of death itself.

The advice of his council had been predictable. Gabry was loud in favor of torturing all the Europeans to death to show the British government that it couldn't insult the Ethiopian ruler and his people. Magiga Dulou agreed. Wolde favored swallowing pride and sending them back to Massawa, then asking Rassam to send craftsmen and engineers and soldiers to help Theodore regain what he had lost. From a great distance, Paniotti supported Wolde's point of view, and the rest of the council was almost evenly divided between these two opinions.

Theodore had not commented on their advice. He had simply sent the letter which would bring Rassam to him and give Rassam the chance to refuse forgiveness.

The long years of pain had so numbed Theodore, that he felt almost nothing as he watched Rassam walk up the hill, then stop at the proper distance and wait for the signal to approach.

Immediately, Theodore waved his hand, and one of the servants signaled to Samuel.

Obviously astonished at the immediate response, Samuel said, "Go ahead, Master Rassam."

Rassam started toward the jet-black shade of the pavilion. As he walked under the shelter of the awning, he was able to make out the same line of dim, white-clothed figures he had seen at his first formal audience with the emperor. All of the emperor that was visible was the upper part of his head, his hands, and the one bare foot dangling below the garment. Rassam halted at the entrance to the pavilion, but the emperor raised one hand and waved him on, and Mamo, the emperor's *balderaba*, cried, "Rassam only to come forward."

Before he could take his first step, Rassam felt a hand on his elbow. From behind him Samuel's voice came low and very urgent: "If you go into the presence, you must prostrate yourself and kiss the foot."

Blanc's voice came fast, a single biting word: "Never."

Samuel's voice whispered: "He must."

"An envoy of the Queen kneels to no man. Ever."

"He must."

"Never. Keep that in mind, Mr. Rassam. Keep that in mind."

Rassam shook off the hand and the voices, and stepped into the pavilion. The breeze lightly ruffled the fabric overhead. His footsteps were eerily silent. All eyes were on him. He seemed to be moving unnaturally slowly, as if in a dream. That voluminously robed human dominated him completely. He started to wonder whether he would indeed prostrate himself and kiss the foot, but his hands were trembling and his knees were shaking and his mind wouldn't quite focus on the question; he saw the foot from a distance and couldn't pull his attention away from it, and then without having realized that he was getting any closer he had reached the throne and the line of frowning warriors. Without making a decision, he sagged to his knees. The carpets absorbed them soundlessly, and he rolled forward to rest half his weight on his hands. His eyes were riveted to the emperor's bare foot, and his mind was a perfect blank except for the mental image of Blanc's glare drilling a hole just under his solar helmet at the exact place where his spine connected to his skull. The bare foot disappeared into the folds of the garment, then winked out as the emperor flowed quickly off his low throne and leaped toward Rassam. Rassam's body kept rolling forward, his elbows bending, his knees straightening, but just as his chest grazed the carpet he heard a sudden sharp sound like a rifle shot over his head—an urgent, imploring *"No"*—and felt the emperor's strong hands on his shoulders pulling him back to his feet, and he knew the rifle shot had been the emperor's desperate handclap.

Back on his feet, the first thing Rassam saw was the warriors' faces. Gabry's was bending into fury. He was trying to lift his double-barreled pistol toward Rassam, but two other men were holding him back. Wolde was staring in disbelief at the emperor, and his jaw had dropped —for a fleeting instant, Rassam thought how it was the first time he'd ever really seen a person's jaw drop. The other faces were filled with rage, astonishment, worry, embarrassment.

Theodore saw Rassam's eyes flicker across the faces of his people, then turn to meet his own. For the first time in his life, he was glad of the awkward formal garment that hid his face. Even so, he was afraid Rassam would see from the attitude of his body, the way he clenched and unclenched his hands, how tired he was and how amazed at himself for the impulse to leave the throne and pull Rassam up. He threw all his effort into concealing his confusion, stepped slowly back until his calves touched the throne, and stood there forcing his hands to hang open and relaxed.

He and Rassam stared at each other. Rassam had no idea what had just happened, and Theodore knew he would stand there without doing or saying anything until Theodore had given him a clue.

Theodore lowered himself onto the throne in as dignified a manner as he could. "You are my friend, and you never have to prostrate yourself in my presence," he whispered, struggling to keep his voice even.

Rassam didn't move.

There was a noise among the warriors, shallow breathing, a foot scraping across the carpet, a moist hand squeaking on a pistol butt, and there was a low, distinct curse from Gabry.

Theodore slashed his hand out viciously, and Gabry choked back a second curse.

Theodore began to talk, though he hardly thought about what he was saying. "My friend John Bell once told me the Christians of England are not blessed with so many prophecies and visions as we Ethiopians are. At that time, I agreed with him that prophecies are a blessing. But now I think they are a curse. They haunt you every day of your life. They won't let you go for a single minute. They turn you into something less than a man. I hate the prophecies of my life, but I know they are true, and I have to follow them.

"Rassam, I swear to you by everything holy that I've never done anything without a good reason. I am not an evil man. I have never hurt anyone without a cause. I had a reason for imprisoning Cameron and Kerens. You must believe it hurt me to have to do it. I want you to forgive me for what I've done to them." There came that brittle sound from his warriors again, but he let it go. The humiliation of this moment was greater than he had imagined.

Rassam started to raise his hand and step forward to comfort the emperor, but he caught himself in time. His words came out in a painful croak. "It isn't for me to forgive you, Your Majesty. I'm not worthy to pass judgment on you. My opinion doesn't matter."

"It matters," said Theodore. "Forgive me."

Rassam shuffled his feet helplessly and didn't say anything.

Theodore rose again. He felt numb, but he knew tears were gathering in his eyes. He started to take a step, couldn't make his legs move. He willed his body to throw itself onto the carpet at Rassam's feet, but his body wouldn't cooperate. The men behind him didn't matter anymore, but his own pride was like a length of chain holding him back. Slowly, deliberately, he forced himself down to his knees. "For Christ's sake, forgive me," he said in a shaky voice, and then all at once he threw himself onto his belly. Into the carpet he said, "Forgive me."

He heard Rassam's voice, fragile and quick, as if from a long distance. "Your Majesty, for everything, for anything, I forgive you."

Theodore lay face down for another unbelieving minute. Then he pushed himself up to his knees. Rassam had dropped down to his own knees, and they faced each other there. The tears welled out of Theodore's eyes. There were tear-streaks on Rassam's cheeks, too, and Theodore realized that this Mesopotamian was so utterly foreign to him that he couldn't even guess why the man should cry.

What had brought the tears to Rassam's eyes was the sight of Theodore humbled. Rassam didn't understand it all, but he was sure this humbling meant that another personal idol was about to let him down. Remembering Disraeli, he wept.

Theodore could only think, over and over, *Rassam is not the Light Bringer!* A weight disappeared from his back, and then he groaned as he realized that he would have to repeat the whole agonizing process, watch for the signs in another man, once more approach his own death.

Theodore stretched out his long arms and gathered Rassam into them. "You will forgive me?" he asked, still not sure he'd heard correctly.

"I do, I do, Your Majesty, and I swear to you that I will do whatever I can to help you. If you write a letter to Queen Victoria, I will take it with me and personally see that it is acted upon. If you want engineers and workmen, I'll see that they come to you."

Rassam seemed to be offering Theodore a way back to his path. For one short moment, Theodore dreamed he might be able to return to it, but in the next moment he knew he would not, and he knew what he must do.

Rassam had not even had that moment of hope: even as he spoke, he had known how useless his suggestion was.

"I will send you away before the rains," Theodore said, though both of them knew he was only saying that to fill in the terrible empty space before the inevitable happened. "But for a few more days, you will stay with me."

"I will," said Rassam, and he felt the pit opening under his feet.

Cameron and Kerens rejoined Rassam and Blanc at twilight of the next day. Blanc went halfway down the hill to greet them, but Rassam just sat in his camp chair and watched as Cameron led the weary procession up the hill to the British tents, dismounted, waved his hand to show the servants where to pitch his tent, and dropped without a word into a chair beside Rassam. He and Rassam didn't say anything or even look at each other. Cameron was already pulling at his beard and gazing northward across the lake. Silently, Dahon appeared with a pipe for Cameron and lit it with a glowing twig from the fire.

Blanc and Kerens came up the last bit of the hill together, talking rapidly. "They've been turned back, Mr. Rassam," Blanc called ahead. Rassam had only told him the emperor's version—that they would be sent down before the rains—and hadn't told him the truth that both he and the emperor knew.

Kerens and Blanc took chairs with the others, and Kerens accepted a glass of his favorite sherry from Dahon. "Show him the letter," said Blanc, and Kerens handed a folded sheet of paper to Rassam. It had the single word *Cameron* in Arabic characters; its red wax seal had been broken. Rassam unfolded it, turned so his body sheltered it from the wind and read aloud: "I have been angry with my friends and with those Englishmen who say, as it is reported to me, 'We depart for our country and are not yet reconciled with this emperor of the Ethiopians.' Until I consult what I will do, therefore, I have given orders to my people to take hold of you, but not to make you uncomfortable or afraid, and not to hurt you. I am sorry. Be of good cheer."

"Gibberish," spat out Blanc. "Damned savage. Lunatic." He looked for agreement to Kerens, but the young Irishman was just enjoying his sherry.

Cameron set a file of perfect smoke rings marching between Blanc and Kerens.

"They've excellent tobacco here in Ethiopia," said Rassam, very softly.

"Aye, more flavorsome than at home," said Cameron, though his mind was obviously not on his words. Rassam remembered how Cameron had boasted about the heroic things he had done as a young man, but Rassam couldn't picture him as anything but the broken shell of a man he was at this moment.

"Have you any idea what the emperor is planning?" demanded Blanc.

Rassam considered telling Blanc the entire truth, but instead he said, "At the moment, he is under pressure. To let us go is to lose face with his own people. To keep us is to risk a British invasion. I think he is still considering what to do."

"Then it's maybe back to Magdala," laughed Kerens. His humor was genuine, completely out of harmony with everyone else. "I'll be a hundred years old before I'm ever back to Londonderry."

Cameron pulled his gaze in from the lake, glanced quickly at Kerens, and said in a cruel tone that Kerens didn't seem to notice, "At least you should have your beard by then."

"I should," said Kerens. "I say, are those the emperor's tents?" Without a glance at Dahon, he held out his glass for the Goan to refill.

A wide, gentle saddle connected their hill with the next. Beyond this next hill was the lake. The saddle was empty except for a few stray goats. The hilltop was covered with the emperor's tents and people, and his lion banner flew above everything. Blanc turned to Cameron, saw the clear hopelessness, gave up on him and turned to Kerens. "I shouldn't worry much about being turned back," he said. "Mr. Rassam has things well under control."

"Has he?" asked Kerens.

"He had an audience yesterday with the emperor and wrapped him around his little finger. It was a miracle of diplomacy. The emperor called Mr. Rassam into his presence. Samuel whispered that Mr. Rassam would have to prostrate himself and kiss the bloody emperor's foot. I said *no*, no envoy of the British Queen could ever humble himself like that. If you can imagine, that cheeky old African and I had an argument about it, right there under the emperor's awning. But Mr. Rassam never had a second thought: he walked right up to the emperor, and threw himself onto his knees."

"Wrapped him around his little finger, you said?"

Rassam avoided Kerens's eyes.

"Right onto his knees," Blanc went on. "I was humiliated. But the emperor leaped off his throne, pulled Mr. Rassam up to his feet, and told him in front of everyone that Mr. Rassam should never have to humble himself before anyone. And then the emperor threw himself onto the ground, right on his belly, and begged Mr. Rassam to forgive him for everything he's done to you and Captain Cameron. Mr. Rassam refused to forgive him, the emperor begged again, and Mr. Rassam finally relented and forgave him. Mr. Rassam knew what he was doing all along. He played the emperor like a lyre."

"Just excellent, Mr. Rassam," said Kerens. "My congratulations, sir."

"The emperor may be considering what to do, but surely that's only to save a little of his own face before he lets us go," said Blanc. "Mr. Rassam can steer him in any direction he likes."

Blanc had been so secure in his own vision of what had happened that he hadn't noticed Rassam hadn't said a word about it. The constant praise had hurt Rassam as badly as an insult. Now, Rassam said quietly, bluntly, "I hate to disappoint you, Henry, but you don't understand. Theodore is considering what to do, but he doesn't actually have any choice. He can't let us go. We'll all be at Magdala, just as soon as he makes up his mind. And as a matter of fact I did honestly try to humble myself before him, but he wouldn't let me." Rassam turned to Cameron. "We've both tried to humble ourselves," he said, "but he wouldn't accept either of us. Neither of us is the right man, and we'll stay here until the right man comes." Again to Blanc, "He wasn't asking forgiveness for past crimes and insults. He was asking forgiveness in advance for what he's going to do."

"You're saying we'll be imprisoned?" asked Blanc.

Rassam nodded, and Cameron whispered, "You're in prison already."

"Do something about it," said Blanc.

"There's nothing to do," said Rassam.

"You've given up hope?"

"There is no hope."

"Use your diplomatic skills. Isn't that your job?"

Very slowly, very softly, Rassam said, "I couldn't sway him. He has no choice. Besides, he terrifies me."

Kerens stifled a laugh.

Blanc stood up and looked across at the emperor's tents. His narrow back was to Rassam. "You've let me down," he said. "You've betrayed me."

To himself, so quietly that Blanc couldn't hear, Rassam said, "I know the meaning of betrayal, too."

The emperor's tent city remained in the same location along the southern shore of Lake Tana for the next two months. According to Samuel, this was almost unheard of: the tent city normally traveled every week, or every two weeks at the very longest. From the hilltop Rassam saw the emperor three or four times, leaving or returning on horseback. Once, the emperor and an escort passed directly below the British hill. Rassam sat in his camp chair and watched him go by, only forty yards away, but the emperor didn't look up. Rassam received no messages or gifts, and Samuel seemed just as confused about what the emperor was doing as the rest of them.

They had perfect freedom to walk or ride anywhere in the tent city, and Blanc and Kerens sometimes hunted several miles beyond the line of sentries, but they were so far inside Ethiopia and so recognizable that they might as well have been in chains.

Rassam was almost alone during these two months. Blanc never said a word to him and wouldn't even sit near him. All his newfound vitality, humor, and strength had been erased by that one betrayal. Kerens didn't care very much about Rassam, but Blanc forced the young Irishman to make a choice between Blanc and Rassam, and there was no question of whom it had to be. Rassam didn't count this as much of a loss, since Kerens' cheerfulness was turning out to be his only good point: he wasn't very bright, and he never had an opinion on anything. There were even times when Rassam saw a fleeting look of irritation on Blanc's face, and Rassam was sure it was becoming an effort for Blanc to put up with his insipid friend. Cameron had no complaint with Rassam, but he was in no condition to be company. He spent his days sitting in a chair staring at the lake. He ate very little, coughed up bloody phlegm into an old rag, and grunted when someone talked to him. He was a man utterly without hope, and Rassam didn't expect him to live much longer.

The first driving torrent of the rainy season came in the middle of May, nearly a month early. Before this there had always remained the feeblest chance that they might be allowed to leave; now the rains would seal off the country for the next six months, and there was no hope left. That first rain came down across the lake at breakfast time. Black clouds punched through the blue sky, the lake surface churned into white foam, and the first drops made hand-sized craters in the dust on their hilltop. The rain lasted throughout the morning. By noon, they were outside the tent in their usual seating arrangements, but now their hilltop was an island connected to the emperor's by a narrow isthmus.

By late afternoon, a man could wade from one hill to the next. There was some activity in the emperor's compound. A group of the emperor's people came onto the saddle just below the emperor's compound and spent half an hour setting up a peculiar lavender-colored tent, very small, open on the side facing the British camp, with carpets for a floor but without any carpets outside, and without an awning. The lion banner went up at one corner, and the emperor's throne and signs of rule disappeared inside.

"What is it?" Rassam asked Samuel, who was squatting nearby and watching.

"It is the emperor's judgment tent," said Samuel. "He sits within when he is trying the cases of criminals. Today, he will try a group of rebel chieftains from Tigré. As he ordered, the common warriors were disarmed and sent home, and the leaders have been brought to him for judgment."

"What will he do with them?"

"That isn't for an old man to say. That is up to His Majesty. But in the past he has scolded them fiercely. A scolding from the emperor is a fearsome thing. His voice in anger can curl a man's hair, or loosen his bowels, or make his penis fall off. I've never actually seen a man's penis fall off, but I've talked to others who have. And after he has scolded them, he makes them promise to be loyal to him, and he sets them free. If a man is brought to trial a second time, he will likely be set free again, and if he is brought to trial a third time, he will be sent to imprisonment at Magdala. It is an enlightened policy, is it not?"

"It is," said Rassam.

"Look, there are the prisoners."

Rassam followed Samuel's pointing finger, and saw a troop of warriors on horseback come splashing up toward the saddle. In their midst walked six men, looking half naked without their weapons. Their braids had been loosened, and they dragged their ankle-chains through the wet grass. They reached the lavender tent, and all of them, prisoners and escort together, squatted on the ground. The prisoners did not seem particularly worried. Cameron was staring at the lake, but the other Britishers were all watching the rare activity.

At the end of an hour, the Ethiopians at the lavender tent were growing visibly restless, but none of them had moved.

At last men began to scurry among the emperor's tents on the hilltop. Rassam recognized several of the emperor's key people. Gabry came down to the lavender tent with a long brown whip coiled in one hand. He exchanged a few words with some of the squatting men, but he was too far away for Rassam to hear any of it. He let the whip uncoil onto the ground. It was twelve feet long, as thick as a man's wrist at one end, tapering to the width of a little finger and blossoming into a flower of loose thongs. Gabry lashed out with a subtle, effortless motion, and the whip ripped through the air and boomed as loud as gunfire. He cracked it five or six times, then coiled it up and squatted comfortably among the warriors.

Before Rassam could ask, Samuel said, as if he were eager that Rassam shouldn't get the wrong impression, "It is a hippopotamus-hide whip, very dangerous. The tip can easily kill a man; the rough edge can rip one's flesh open. But it is only an ancient symbol of the emperor's power of life and death. It is never used, at least not by this emperor. There is a proverb in Ethiopia. It is very ancient, but it has been more true with Theodore than ever before. In Amharic it is, *Negus kamotu baman yimmaggotu.* In Arabic something close to, *When the emperor dies, whom can one ask for justice?*"

Wolde was on the hilltop near the emperor's own tent. He conferred seriously with a tall turbaned Ethiopian whom Rassam had never noticed before: "Engeddah, one of the Twelve," Samuel answered, in reply to his question. Wolde went into the emperor's tent, came out again to talk more with Engeddah, then re-entered the tent. People swirled around on the hilltop, and Rassam had the very distinct, definitely uncomfortable feeling of a ritual gone wrong. It seemed as if an everyday routine, one that everyone knew by heart, had been suddenly complicated, and no one knew exactly how to deviate from the traditional way of doing things.

Finally, Wolde and Theodore emerged into the fine gray daylight. Theodore towered two full heads above his little eunuch priest. He wore his usual white trousers and shirt, but he was carrying a ceremonial spear, a gold head mounted on a silver shaft with golden tassels at the head and at the butt. The emperor's other hand lay heavily on Wolde's shoulder. They walked toward the lavender tent. Engeddah started to walk with them, but Wolde, with an almost furtive gesture, waved him off. Engeddah and a small body of scribes and bodyguards followed them at a few paces' distance. Theodore's steps were leaden, and he swayed as he walked. Wolde struggled under the weight of his emperor.

Samuel had watched them when they came out of the tent, but now his head was lowered and he was covering his eyes with one hand.

It was Blanc who said in a loud voice to Kerens, "I believe he's tipsy," and then called in Arabic to Samuel, "Has His Majesty been drinking?"

Samuel looked up at Blanc and said weakly, "I've been here. I haven't seen him."

Blanc sniffed and directed his attention back to the emperor.

Rassam leaned closer to Samuel and whispered, "How long has he been this way?"

When Samuel lifted his head, Rassam saw tears streaking through the dusty creases of the old man's cheeks. "I am humiliated," Samuel said. "You should have known him when he was younger. He was a lion." He lowered his head so Rassam couldn't see the tears. "Wolde told me to tell you everything, in hopes you know more than we, but I was too shamed to speak. He has been drinking today since the rain began this morning. Wolde was with him. At the first drops, he stepped out of his tent and felt the drops on his palms and said, 'So, our fates are sealed.' Wolde didn't understand what he meant."

"The rain," Rassam said. Rassam's emotions had been stretched so tightly for so long that the rain hadn't meant anything to him. All he felt was pity for Theodore, nothing at all for himself. "He means that the rains make it impossible for him to let us go. Now, he is committed to keeping us here as prisoners. How has he been these last two months?"

"Very bad," said Samuel. "Moody. Depressed. He prays alone late into the night. He has been drinking sometimes, once or twice a week."

"Violence?"

A long pause, and then a whisper: "You know about those horrors?"

"His Majesty told me himself."

"Master Rassam, he hasn't hurt anyone yet. But Wolde is worried that he may. Anything might set him off—or nothing at all."

"I haven't got a solution," said Rassam. "He's a cornered man. I feel sorry for him."

"I, too," said Samuel. "It is not an easy thing to be emperor."

Wolde and Theodore had reached the lavender tent. Theodore disappeared inside, and Wolde remained outside with everyone else. Gabry took his place at the end of the tent's open side, away from Wolde. He snapped his hippopotamus-hide whip twice to get everyone's attention, then shouted out a short speech. The British heard the whip clearly, but were too far away to catch Gabry's words. It had begun to rain, and Dahon draped a blanket over Rassam's shoulders.

In answer to Gabry's shout, one of the prisoners got to his feet and shuffled forward. He dropped to his hands and knees, crawled the last yards to the lavender tent, and then pushed himself up into a kneeling position facing it.

The British were watching a pantomime. Rassam called for his telescope. The kneeling prisoner was listening to the emperor. Several times, apparently in answer to questions, he himself spoke. His head bobbed when he talked, but his hands stayed rigidly at his sides. Finally he simply knelt there on the wet ground with his head bowed and listened to the emperor. Through the telescope Rassam could easily detect the cringing of the man's shoulders. When the scolding was done, Gabry cracked his whip. Two of the emperor's men helped the prisoner to a low boulder. He sat straddling the stone while the men chiseled at his ankle-chains. When they had fallen off the man rubbed his ankles gratefully and rejoined the others. His entire trial had lasted ten minutes.

Gabry cracked the whip again and called for another prisoner. As far as Rassam could tell through his telescope, this man's trial was identical to the first. So was the third. All ended with stone, hammer, and chisel.

A hard rain from the lake was extending past the shoreline. It had drenched the fourth prisoner's clothing, so that his black skin showed through the fabric.

This man was different. He was hardly bigger than Wolde, but even with his ankle-chains on he had a way of swaggering as he walked. When he crawled forward on his hands and knees, it wasn't a humbling action. He hadn't learned from the example of the others. He was too proud. Rassam worried about what could come out of a meeting between two excessively proud men.

The man knelt at the proper place, but instead of listening with bowed head to the emperor, he began to talk. He gestured sharply with his hands, and once he even raised his palm as if he were ordering the emperor to be quiet and listen.

"He's trying to defend himself," Samuel muttered. "The fool." He turned his head toward Rassam. "There is no defense in a trial before the emperor," he said. "There is only the submitting and the forgiveness." And Samuel lowered his head and began to pray in a rapid, musical voice.

"Go ahead, tell the bastard a thing or two," It was Kerens's voice, aimed at the prisoner. Blanc echoed him: "Tell the bastard."

From out of the emperor's sight, Wolde clapped his hands to get the prisoner's attention. The prisoner turned his head. Wolde waved his hands, warning the prisoner to stop. The prisoner shook his head, looked back at Theodore, and kept on gesturing and talking.

Gabry, at the other side of the lavender tent, was watching eagerly, like a cat eying a bird. His whip snaked back and forth a few inches above the ground.

Suddenly, the prisoner put his palms on the ground and used them to push himself up to his feet. His ankle-chains tripped him. He went down in a heap, and rose halfway up again.

Plunging out of the tent, Theodore was just a blur of white at the top edge of the telescope lens. The ceremonial spear was in both hands, like a medieval fighting staff. He smashed the silver spear shaft like a club into the prisoner's back. The man skidded on his face through the slick grass.

Wolde reached for the spear. Theodore slashed around at him without looking, and Wolde went down. Theodore took a step toward the prisoner, but Wolde scrambled after him and threw himself into Theodore's legs from behind. They both collapsed. Theodore came up first. He raised the spear over his head and brought it down in a silent arc. It hit Wolde's upper arm, just above the elbow. Wolde tried to crawl away.

Theodore turned and found the prisoner, curled into a ball. Theodore shouted at Gabry, and the whip flashed out. The flower-tip touched the man's shoulder blade, a delicate caress. It opened the man's back deep into the muscles. The man leaped up. Gabry swung the whip again. The edge touched the man's side between his ribs and his hip. It dug into the soft flesh like a rip-saw. Through the telescope Rassam saw the broad band of frayed, bloody cloth, as if the man had been cut in half. The man turned a full circle as he fell onto his knees, balanced there for five more seconds, then collapsed onto his face and lay still.

Seen through the lens from such a distance, with the rain and the deepening twilight and the silence, it seemed just a fiction put on for Rassam's entertainment. He found Wolde in the telescope. The arm was hanging off at an unnatural angle, and the sleeve was already soaked through with a pink mixture of blood and rain. Engeddah sat helplessly beside him.

Rassam pulled his eye away from the telescope. Samuel was lying face down on the ground. His arms were outstretched, and his hands were pulling up tufts of grass. Blanc, emotionless as ever, was on his feet, craning his neck as if that would help him see. Kerens was sitting in his camp chair, calmly sipping his sherry, ignoring the rainwater dripping off his solar helmet into his lap, shielding the sherry from the rain with his hand. Cameron hadn't noticed that anything was happening.

The prisoners and warriors were a roiling crowd of men. They had all surged to their feet at once, but some had slipped in the mud or tripped on their chains. Rassam saw Theodore running through the middle of the crowd, waving his ceremonial spear and shouting. Prisoners and warriors alike tried to leap out of his way. No one seemed to know exactly what to do.

Theodore spun and shouted orders. He pointed at a man, one of the prisoners he had already pardoned. A warrior pushed the man's chest, and the man, not struggling, only stunned, let himself float backward onto the ground. More warriors grasped one of his arms. A sword went up and came down. The warriors let go the arm, and the man waved a bloody stump.

The warriors were experienced at their task. They went at it quickly: the other hand, a foot, the other. The mutilated man lay still. Rassam could see his ribs rising, falling, rising, breathing desperately.

The other two prisoners whose chains had been removed tried to run. One was too deep inside the crowd, and a sword stroke chopped him down. The other made it into the open. He sprinted down the hill, high-stepping, his feet sending back sprays of water, with Theodore and two other warriors in pursuit. The prisoner's feet slipped out from under him. He fell, then was up and running, but he had lost his lead. Theodore cocked his spear arm back, dug one foot into the ground, and let his momentum carry him through a high-armed javelin throw. Rassam followed the spear's trajectory in his telescope. The point made contact with the man's bottom rib, just beside the spine. Thrown down by the force of the blow, he pitched forward immediately, landing on the hillside. He glided over a steep drop and plunged out of sight.

The three other ankle-chained prisoners waited passively among the warriors. They were thrown down and their hands and feet cut off.

Theodore stood above the little drop in the hillside and looked down at the man he had killed. After a minute, he sank to his knees and raised his head to look out at the lake. His people watched but did not approach him, and he was still kneeling there alone when night fell.

Inside Rassam's tortured dream, drops of water splattered against his hot face, sizzled the instant they made contact, and danced around. He smelled rancid butter, and the sour reek of *tej*. He heard the muffled nonsense sounds, very close. The water drops kept splattering, but now they were cold; they dripped down his chin to gather in a pool in the hollow of his neck. There was a light pressure on his chest, and water rushing in the far distance. It was not a dream. He lay in the darkness of the tent, gripping the edge of his Smyrna rug tight in his hands, feeling the pulse in his neck on both sides of the pool of water. He had no way of knowing how many minutes passed this way. At last, he pried two fingers loose from the rug and stretched them out to explore the darkness. Half an inch, and the nails encountered a solid object, cloth-covered, soaking wet, cold. An arm. The pressure on his chest, a hand.

He put his hand up, found the shoulder, traced the bristly, quivering jaw. The man didn't move.

So softly he wasn't sure whether he actually made a sound, Rassam whispered, "Theodore."

The hand pressed harder on his chest, then pulled away entirely.

Rassam sat up in bed, reached out with his hands, and made contact with the man again. "Your Majesty," he said.

There was no response. Rassam slid past the man and fumbled around in the dark until he found a candle and a box of matches. The moisture on the ceiling and walls glittered in the candlelight.

Head bowed, Theodore was kneeling beside Rassam's low *arat*. His braids had come loose in the rain and fell below his shoulders to the carpet. Rassam sat on the carpet and watched him. Finally, Theodore raised his head. His eyes were lifeless, his lips a straight line. "Someone is always watching me," he said. "Always, always." All the emotion had been drained from his voice. He spoke a few sentences in Amharic, too complex for Rassam to understand. Then he said, "A favor. I need a favor."

He paused, as if he were trying to recapture his train of thought, and Rassam said, "What favor?"

A brief light crossed Theodore's face. "Wolde. My people can't do anything for him. They think he'll die." His voice trailed off into emptiness again.

Rassam asked, "Do you want Dr. Blanc to see him?"

Theodore nodded his head slowly. He might have said "Blanc," but a gust of rain-filled wind gripped the tent at the same moment and muffled the sound.

"I'll go for him," said Rassam. He dashed out of the tent.

A quick, unexpected movement caught his eye immediately. He gasped and looked. Between Blanc's tent and that of Kerens, four men were standing close together in the rain, staring at him. In the dim light, and as terrified as he was, Rassam could only see one of the men clearly. It was Gabry. The hippo-hide whip was coiled in his hands. The rain had molded his white clothing to his body, and he appeared to be emaciated. His face was a puzzle of grays and blacks, but there was no mistaking the hatred in it. The three men behind him were just shadows. They didn't move, and at last Rassam turned away and strode deliberately to Blanc's tent.

He hadn't brought a candle, so he had to grope through the blackness until he found Blanc's *arat*. He shook Blanc gently. Blanc murmured, then leaned up on his elbow and asked, "Laurence?"

"No, it's me," said Rassam. Those were practically the first words he'd spoken to Blanc in two months. Blanc didn't respond, so Rassam rushed on: "The emperor is in my tent. He says the Ethiopian doctors can't help Wolde."

"Murderer." Blanc spat the word out. "The bloody savage."

"Not for Theodore," said Rassam. "Do it for Wolde."

Blanc was silent, but Rassam could feel cold anger flowing from him.

"It's vital," said Rassam. He let himself beg. "Please, Henry. Please do it." He nearly choked on the unfamiliar name. Using it was more humbling than anything he had done in Ethiopia.

At last, in the haughtiest voice Rassam had ever heard, Blanc said, "For the priest, then, *Mr. Rassam*. But I'll not have anything to do with the emperor."

"Theodore's in my tent. Just dress and walk straight to his camp, and you won't see him at all."

Rassam backed out. He went to the servants' tent and woke Dahon, who hurried out to accompany Blanc across the saddle.

On the way back to his own tent, Rassam glanced again at the sheltered alcove between Blanc's tent and Kerens'. The men were still there, motionless, glaring.

Rassam plunged through the flap into his tent. It took him a few seconds to find Theodore. The emperor was at the far end of the tent, almost outside the candle's hard yellow light. He was lying on his side in a fetal position, exactly like the prisoner before Gabry had whipped him to death. His loose hair was a wide black halo around his head. Rassam laid a blanket over him. He didn't seem to notice, though his eyes were open. In the half minute that Rassam hovered over him, the eyes didn't blink. Rassam sat cross-legged on his *arat* and watched Theodore all through that long, rainy night. Theodore's self-pity didn't diminish Rassam's feeling of the emperor's majesty. It was fitting, he thought, that a man so far above other men, so aloof and emotionless, should break down so much harder than a mortal man.

Rassam himself knew no emotions that long night—no fear, no sympathy, not even the familiar sense of betrayal. After the first few minutes, he only knew boredom.

Several times during the night Theodore shivered under his blanket and cried softly. Once, in the middle of a crying spell, he raised his head and said, "I can't let you stay near me, Rassam. I'm afraid I'll hurt you." Later, he said in a voice so smooth and rational that it chilled Rassam, "I used to hear I was called a madman for the things I did, but I never believed it before. Now, I think I really must be mad. But I still understand some things clearly. I've never meant harm to anyone. Whatever evil I do, I've got no choice. There is always a purpose. I have to do it. I have to." And then again, he said, "One day I think you will see me dead, and while you stand over my corpse it may be that you will curse me. You may say, 'This was a wicked man who shouldn't be buried. Let his remains rot above the ground.' But I trust your generosity, Rassam. You will bury me."

When morning had turned the yellow light into a soft blue, Theodore finally pulled himself up. He waddled on his knees to Rassam and wrapped his arms around him.

He whispered, "Do you understand me?"

Rassam answered, "Yes."

Theodore asked, "Do you forgive me?" and Rassam said, "Yes."

Theodore said, "Do not be afraid." He turned quickly and ducked through the tent flap.

Rassam went outside, sat in his camp chair near the fire, and took a cup of coffee from Samuel. He watched Theodore climb the saddle, now unnaturally empty, and enter his own tent.

Later in the morning, a dozen warriors appeared on the next hill behind the British camp. Rassam had never seen any of them before. The leader dismounted, waded through the marshy low ground between the hills, and walked up the hill to Rassam. He salaamed gracefully, and spoke in an exaggeratedly respectful tone. "Excuse the interruption, sir, but by the Mother of God I have no choice but to bother you. I have orders from His Majesty to escort you to the *amba* Magdala. How soon can you be ready to travel?"

"This afternoon," said Rassam.

16

August 1867 - January 1868
London and Africa

Palmerston's Whigs won the general election of 1865, but "Old Pam" died late in the year. Lord Russell succeeded him as prime minister, but he lacked the spark to follow the great man. Gladstone, waiting patiently in the Exchequer for his own chance to rule, couldn't save him. The government fell over the Reform Bill, and in June of '66, almost at the same instant that Rassam was having the leg irons pounded tight around his ankles, the Whigs resigned. Queen Victoria asked the Earl of Derby and her beloved Disraeli to try to form a minority government. Derby became prime minister, Disraeli took the Exchequer, and Derby's son, Lord Stanley, took over the Foreign Office.

These Tories were the party of social reform, of government by the aristocracy for the good of the masses, of imperialism. Where the Whigs had been cautious about Ethiopia, Derby and Disraeli would have sent in an army at once, but even they had to admit this wasn't the moment for a war. England was consumed by more urgent problems: riots over the Reform Bills, war between Prussia and Austria, financial crisis in the City, cattle plague in the English countryside. Tory control of English politics was tenuous; the situation was perilous, and they had been out of power so long their courage was blunted. They sent two mild letters to Ethiopia through a certain Red Sea merchant, a Greek named Paniotti who had offered his broad commercial contacts to Colonel Merewether in Aden. There was no reply. At last, after fourteen months of delay, they had sharpened their courage and were ready to act.

*　　*　　*

The Secretary of State for Foreign
Affairs to His Majesty Theodore,
King of Ethiopia.

Many months have now elapsed since the Queen, my Sovereign, on the
4th of October 1866, and Her Majesty's Secretary of State for Foreign
Affairs, by command of Her Majesty, on the 16th of April of this year,
appealed to Your Majesty in order to obtain the release from the captivity
in which they have for a long period been most unjustifiably held, of
officers sent to your Court on public matters.

But Your Majesty has disregarded these successive appeals, has made
light of the remonstrances and representations of the Queen, and has
rejected the friendly overtures which have so repeatedly been made to
you by Her Majesty's command.

It is impossible for the Queen any longer to endure such conduct on the
part of Your Majesty, and Her Majesty has, therefore, given orders that a
military force should without delay enter your dominions and obtain from
you by force a concession which you have hitherto withheld from friendly
representations.

For the result of this measure, whatever may be the consequences of it
to your throne and to your country, Your Majesty can alone be held responsible throughout the civilised world; and, although the Queen would fain
hope that, even in this last hour, Your Majesty may be induced to listen
to words of peace, and avert by full and immediate concession the attack
which in a short pace of time will be directed against you, I am commanded by the Queen to warn Your Majesty that the course of action
which I now make known to you is irrevocably determined on, and that
the only means of preserving your country from war, and your own power
from overthrow, will be found in the delivery to the commander of the
British invading army of all European prisoners in your keeping; and it is
the earnest desire of the Queen that this last opportunity which Her
Majesty offers to you may be taken advantage of by Your Majesty, and that
peace may be so preserved between England and Ethiopia.

Having thus fulfilled the command of my Sovereign, I bid Your Majesty
heartily farewell.

Your sincere friend,
Stanley

By this time, the invasion belonged to Robert Napier. The elegant,
elaborate plans over which he had labored were designed in such a way
that no man without Napier's engineering expertise could hope to carry
them out. To choose another man would require a complete revision,
which could take months. Nor had Napier neglected the politics of war.
The Whigs had seemed firmly entrenched in power, but Napier, ever
methodical, ever thorough, had not ignored Disraeli and his Tory com-
patriots. It hadn't been hard to cultivate them, since their vulnerability
was obvious. They were the party of imperialism, and though he was
an apolitical man, he easily convinced them that he stood for everything

in which they believed. When an invasion was at last being decided on, a curious assortment of politicians and civil servants and military men, Whigs and Tories and Radicals, were surprised to discover that they all favored him. On the same day that Stanley sent his ultimatum to Paniotti, he sent Napier orders to make final estimates and to begin preparing for war. To Napier, it was just a confirmation of something he had known for two years.

European warfare was changing. The technology of war was growing vastly more sophisticated, while the administrative machinery needed to support it had not kept pace. Though conventional wisdom still refused to admit it, the most successful general was the one with the firmest grasp of logistics. Napier, the ideal military mind for his time, sat down at his desk and prepared the most deliberate war in history. Never had the military generated such extensive, elaborate paperwork. It dealt with the transcendent and the mundane, the macrocosm and the microcosm. As if invisible strands of steel-hard spiders' web connected these great heaps of paper in Bombay to the real world, thousands of men in all parts of the globe were set into frenzied activity.

There were to be four thousand European and nine thousand Indian troops. Sir Robert chose most from his own Bombay regiments, but as a gesture of goodwill to the other Indian presidencies he included one brigade each from Calcutta and Karachi, two companies of Madras Sappers from Calicut, and a regiment from Vingorla. The Royal Navy wasn't to be excluded, either. There was going to be a brigade of rocketeers from the navy, and Captain Fellowes, the commander of the brigade, was swamped with volunteers. European officers and soldiers were considered too valuable to do anything but fight, so their servants had to be included, as well as muleteers and camel drivers, railroad gangs and laborers, Indians, Persians, Egyptians, and Chinese. The estimates quickly rose to thirty-two thousand men and fifty-five thousand animals.

To transport the army and its equipment, the British hired two hundred sailing vessels and seventy-five steamers from India and England and points between.

Each officer was to have two servants, a *khansamah* to watch after him and a *syce* to watch after his horse.

Each white soldier was issued seven pairs of socks, two pairs of boots, a solar helmet, a cholera belt, and a canteen.

Each regiment of Sikhs was to have eight hundred pounds of borax and a similar amount of *ghee* to wash and dress their waist-length hair, plus specified amounts of rum and opium.

There were to be forty-four trained elephants to carry the heavy guns and to terrify the Ethiopians. They required two specially converted ships, and were taken aboard in slings, then placed in compartments that had been reinforced with shingle and stone. During a cyclone in

Calcutta harbor, they proved just how devastating a seasick elephant can be.

Hiring commissions were dispatched to the Mediterranean and the Near East to arrange for mules and camels and men to handle them. Animals and men from as far away as Spain and Persia began to converge on the Red Sea.

The first reconnaissance by Merewether and Phayre had been in October, 1865. They arrived on the western Red Sea coast again in October 1867. Their original impressions were confirmed: barren, hot, unappealing, but plenty of potable water. They made a firm decision on Zula, a derelict village on the site of the ancient Greek settlement of Adulis, as their port.

A contingent of Indian Sappers, plus several thousand Chinese coolies, had come with them. They off-loaded a few thousand tons of supplies and equipment, and then set to work. Within three weeks, they had built a seven-hundred-yard-long pier to make a connection to deep-draft ocean-going vessels, constructed trestles across several wadis, and laid the beginnings of a railroad from the shore to the escarpment.

In early November, three things happened in rapid succession. First, Africa fought back. Merewether and Phayre hadn't been aware that October was the end of the highland rainy season. The wells that were so adequate in October dried up in November. The coast grew miserably hot. Dust devils twirled through Zula. Great blankets of sand driven by gale force winds came down from the north.

Second, the officers left. Merewether went up to Suru to begin distributing to the native chiefs a proclamation that stated the purpose of the invasion and promised not to interfere with peaceable Ethiopians. Phayre went up to scout the route. Every other officer who had enough rank to order someone else to cover for him invented an immediate task that demanded his presence in the cool, healthy, water-rich highlands. They migrated en masse, and eager, inexperienced young subalterns took over the army's base camp.

Third, the army began to pour into Zula.

Ships off-loaded their passengers and cargo onto the pier. The arriving officers organized their men and the listless laborers, then summed up the situation and started after Merewether and Phayre.

Thousands of mules were set loose on the beach. The first muleteers in Zula had been recruited from the slums of Bombay and Calcutta, and most of them had never handled a mule before. The mules wandered around for a few days, and then they began to drop from thirst.

A system had just been devised for feeding and watering them when fever struck. Mules and horses frothed at the mouth for an hour or two, then they fell, trembled, and died. There were no veterinarians ashore, and the Indians, pleading the laws of their religion, refused to help clear away the rotting carcasses. Their stink, combined with the stink from the undisciplined sanitary habits of the men, was awesome.

One night an unusually high tide washed up and damaged supplies on the beach. A subaltern ordered that the supplies be moved farther from the water, and then as a further precaution supervised the building of a long, high dike of sandbags and stones on the shoreward side of the supplies. On the night his creation was finished, an unseasonable deluge flowed down the escarpment. The entire desert was covered with half an inch of water, reflecting the stars. The flood backed up three feet deep behind the dike that was supposed to prevent the flow of water from the opposite direction. Thousands more tons of supplies were ruined, along with the pride and hopes of one young subaltern, who, through the honor of British officers, remained forever anonymous, though never forgotten.

Napier's second-in-command, Major-General Sir Charles Staveley, reached Zula in early December. As his steamer chugged up to the pier, Staveley overheard the whispered remark of the French army observer, Captain d'Henrecourt, to the French naval observer, Commandant Galli-Passebosse: *"Encore la Crimée!"* Staveley said nothing.

What faced him was definitely reminiscent of the Crimea, though it was different in its own, African way. There was a low, shimmering, bone-white shoreline, and, ten miles away, the escarpment. There was one finished pier, and another half done. The Hadas River was merely a wide depression in the sand, without even a trickle of water. The troops were camped north of the river, their dusty tents set up at random and interspersed haphazardly with storage depots.

South of the river the Chinese coolies had erected low bowerlike shelters, piled high with branches and blankets. For all its meanness, it had a more homelike permanence than the camp across the river. The first stage of the railroad led through the middle of their encampment. No work was going on, neither on the railroad or anywhere else in sight.

During the following weeks, Staveley's strong hand forced order from the chaos. The second pier, nine hundred yards long, was completed, and a third was started. Condensers were set up on the ends of the piers and connected through long pipes to holding tanks on the shore. They added one thousand tons of water per week to the ten thousand being brought by steamer from Aden.

The Chinese coolies were set to completing the track across the ten miles of salt desert to the mountains. A telegraph line already ran from Suakin to Khartoum to Cairo, and from Cairo to England. Sappers tried to run a line from Zula to Suakin, but they had to give up when white ants ate the poles. The English and Indian tents were moved into straight rows, all facing the same direction. Sanitary regulations were announced and strictly enforced.

The only place for bathing was off the piers at low tide, when the shallow water forced the ships to stand off in deeper water. At those times, pink-skinned generals and colonels wallowed and splashed alongside Cockney artillerymen and Irish foot soldiers. Mules and horses were fed and watered immediately upon reaching shore, and then packed and sent forward up to Suru. They struggled up the escarpment on their sea-weary legs, but at least they were spared the fever and the thirst, and most of them survived.

Once things were under control in Zula, Staveley turned his attention to the approach to Ethiopia. Phayre's report had said that the caravan route from Zula up to Suru was steep in places, but not too difficult. What Staveley found was one of the most treacherous trails he'd ever seen, often less than ten feet wide, hemmed in by vertical cliffs. For a single man on a horse, if the man were willing to dismount and lead the horse through the hardest places, it wasn't too difficult. But for an elephant, an artillery battery, a supply cart, or a file of a thousand men, it was impossible. With two months already invested in Zula, Staveley could not abandon it and search for another route: he ordered the Sappers into action. They began blasting paths through solid granite and leveling the steepest places with ramps of gravel and mud.

By New Year's Zula had taken on the appearance of an established army camp: boring, homelike, disciplined. Upon being pushed into motion, the ponderous, efficient British military machine couldn't help but be what Napier expected. The machine was building up momentum. Nothing and no one could stand before it without trembling.

It was noon on the sixth of January, 1868. The blazing sun set the entire salt desert shimmering. Great ranks of troops, blocked off into rectangles by the color of their tunics—scarlet, blue, green, black—and by their headgear—turbans, solar helmets, puggrees, waist-length black hair—stood and sweated on the beach. Cavalry maneuvered on the plain beyond the Zula camp. Pennants fluttered. Trumpets, bagpipes, and elephants blared. At a secret signal big guns fired a distant salute from the base of the Ethiopian escarpment. The commander-in-chief had arrived to take over personal control of his expedition.

Rocketeer Arthur Pilbeam stood at close attention in the first rank of the naval rocket brigade aboard the steamer *Octavia*. Like his companions he wore the sailor's uniform that had been modified for those seamen who were going to march into Ethiopia, and across his shoulder he held a sun-hot metal rocket tube. He felt well-fed and rested after six weeks of special training in Aden and three weeks of duty-free leisure on the *Octavia*.

Captain Fellowes was directly in front of Pilbeam, at a right angle to his rocketeers. Fellowes's chin was tucked down so hard that it had disappeared into his chest, and his body was so perfectly straight and rigid that a strong gust would have toppled him like a tree.

Pilbeam studied the African coast. Underneath all the display and pageantry, it was Africa and nothing else. He knew the continent well, from all the years he'd skirted it, from Alexandria to Gibraltar, the Gold Coast to the Cape, Mombasa to Aden to Suez. But he'd never penetrated more than ten miles, and to him the interior was nothing but a mystery: he supposed it was all mountains, deserts, and jungles, all Boers and Berbers and Blacks. He'd never been much interested. The only thing about the interior that was important to him was that the envoy was somewhere on the other side of the mountains.

In the two years since Massawa, Pilbeam had carefully refined his anger into a delicate, quivering thing that always hovered just outside his body, at rest like one of the rockets still in the tube he carried, but already connected by invisible wires through the air and past the horizon to its target. It hovered in silence, waiting for those wires to pull it skyward, waiting to fly, streaming sparks like a piece of metal dragged fast along a cobblestone street, waiting to explode over the envoy's head.

When the envoy had come aboard to take the *Dalhousie*'s marines ashore to free some slaves Pilbeam had been in the engine room shoveling coal. The engine room wasn't his usual assignment, but he had had to replace an injured sailor. It had been painful to be that close, and yet not to see the envoy. He had made Hoyt tell him every detail, over and over, until Hoyt refused to talk about it anymore.

It seemed to be fate at work, then, when Captain Easterday announced the call for volunteers to learn to fire the new rockets, in order to join an overland expedition to free Pilbeam's envoy. Pilbeam was not surprised when he was selected to represent the *Dalhousie:* fate had willed it so.

Hoyt tried to reason with his friend, but Pilbeam would not be moved. For the first time in two years, Pilbeam wouldn't even talk about the envoy. Hoyt watched sadly as his friend hoisted his sea bag onto his shoulder and clumped down the gangplank onto the Aden pier.

Pilbeam stood at attention among the ninety-eight sailors who were to march to Ethiopia, and who were expected to terrify the natives with their rockets, bursting like exploding stars high up in the air. The other sailors were proud of their unusual weapons and their special training, their new uniforms, their role in this monumental event. They were even glad to be part of a band of ninety-eight faceless cogs in a machine. Pilbeam merely felt isolated from his companions, felt nothing in common with the thousands of uniformed figures waiting rank upon rank on the shore. He was only Pilbeam, a man alone, a man with anger in his breast.

The rocket brigade was acting as honor guard for the disembarking commander-in-chief. Sir Robert Napier, trailing a dozen aides-de-camp, walked to the ship's rail. He had a distracted air about him, as if he were not quite sure where he was; he dismissed Captain Fellowes, straining to be noticed, with a single glance.

Standing a little apart from the other aides were two officers. Pilbeam had seen them often enough, in Aden and on the *Octavia*. Captain Speedy, the general's Amharic interpreter, was close to Pilbeam's size:

six feet three, two hundred fifty pounds. He wore a bushy handlebar mustache sprinkled with gray, a scarlet tunic, shiny black riding boots, and a floppy white turban. His cavalry saber's sheath was embossed in silver leaf, but the hilt was wrapped in dirty cord and stained reddish-brown around the hand-guard, proof that it had felt its share of blood and bone. Major Briggs was only a couple of inches shorter than Speedy, but so slender that he looked like a young boy beside him. He had abandoned his imitation of the foppish Colonel Dunn, and now imitated Speedy in nearly everything. He had let his pointy mustache go wild, he wore a muslin turban and a scarlet tunic, he walked with a roll to suggest that he was more comfortable on horseback than on foot. He wore a cavalry saber like Speedy's, too, but there was something about it or about Briggs himself that made Pilbeam sure he had smeared dirt on the hilt to make it resemble his new master's.

Speedy and Briggs were the leaders of an elite troop of cavalry. They and their twenty men, all officers, had spent their time in Aden dashing across the countryside, waving their swords and shooting their pistols and ruining their fine Arabian stallions. On the ship they had paced the deck impatiently for three days and talked loudly about all the glory they would win in Africa.

The trumpets and bagpipes on the shore were suddenly silent, though one stubborn elephant kept up its bellowing. A band on the pier struck up "Hail the Conquering Hero Comes." Soldiers on the pier snapped to present arms. Captain Fellowes, at the head of the gang-plank, stabbed his hat brim with the slice of his salute, and froze into position. But Napier only leaned against the rail and stared toward the escarpment. The band reached the end of the piece. The aides-de-camp exchanged bewildered glances, but none of them did anything. The conductor looked around for a clue as to what to do, then waved his baton. The band launched into "Hail the Conquering Hero Comes" for a second time.

Speedy elbowed his way through the aides to Napier and said, "Sir Robert, perhaps we should go ashore."

Napier started. "Ashore? Ah, yes, we should go ashore, shouldn't we?"

"The army is waiting."

"Well, away then." Sir Robert returned Captain Fellowes's salute and started down toward the stone pier.

The naval brigade paused in Zula only long enough to regain its sea legs. After dinner, the sailors began the nighttime hike across the salt desert and the ascent to Komayli, a trip of fourteen miles. Their equipment and their rockets were making the journey on a mule train that was going to follow immediately after them, but nonetheless they were uncomfortable walking on dry land in heavy boots. The caravan track from Zula to the defile had become a smooth, clear road. A full tropical moon, shining bright as a beacon, lit their path and glinted off the half-completed railroad that paralleled the road. They proceeded slowly in single file up toward Komayli. By the time first light began to tint the walls of the defile, all Pilbeam could recall of the night was that the trousers of the man in front of him were gray in the moonlight and black in the shadows, and that his tarred queue bounced on his back-pack.

The sun was well up before they reached Komayli, which turned out to be a cool, green bowl buried deep among pine-spotted cliffs. More miles of climbing loomed ahead before they could reach Suru, but they debouched willingly into Komayli for the daylight hours. Several fresh-water springs poured out of the surrounding hills, ran a few hundred yards through the bowl, and then disappeared back into the ground. There had been signs of the work of the Indian Sappers all the way up the defile, and they had been here, too. Very neat catch basins of stone and mortar formed watering pools for the animals, and there were separate fountains for the men.

The sailors drank and filled their canteens, staked out a place of their own, and prepared a late breakfast. The bowl was a temporary home for hundreds of other men, both soldiers and civilians. An army on the march might have been commonplace to soldiers, but to the sailors it was something new and fascinating. While they ate, they stared at all the curious men and unfamiliar uniforms. There were at least twenty different uniforms. The 33rd, the Wellington's Own, was made up of seven hundred Irishmen in scarlet tunics and black trousers. The 4th King's Own, four hundred fifty strong, wore uniforms the dusty color of the surrounding hills. There were representatives of several native Indian regiments, their skin colors ranging from the rich bronze of the Sikhs to nearly jet black, their uniforms a mis-matched combination of European and Indian: scarlet jackets, white loincloths, turbans of white or claret brown, forage caps wrapped in puggrees of green or blue. A contingent of the Sind Horse ignored the trail and went crashing through the trees at the edge of the bowl. Their horses were ugly, raw-boned creatures, and their uniforms were just as ungainly: long green frock coats, green trousers, red sashes around the waist, red turbans, black leather sabretaches clanking along beside their sabers.

By the time they had eaten, the sleepy sailors were ready for their tents and bedrolls, but there was no sign of the mule train. Not particularly surprised, since no sailor would ever depend on a mule, they lay in the soft grass under the trees. With their greatcoats for pillows, they fell asleep.

The mule train still had not arrived at sunset, and Captain Fellowes finally learned from a passing courier that it had been spotted milling around in confusion at the bottom of the defile six hours before.

The sailors cooked another meal from the supplies in their packs, and then scattered in different directions to find entertainment. Most of them ended up joining a group of English soldiers chasing baboons through the hills.

Pilbeam wandered thoughtfully across the bowl to the source of a queer, reedy music, which had been playing all day, in and out of his dreams. It was coming from a crowd of Madras Sappers, Irishmen of the 33rd, and Punjab Pioneers. The musicians were a quartet of Punjabis. They were concentrating so hard on their music, almost as if it were a religious ritual that could not be stopped for fear of breaking a spell, that they seemed to be utterly unaware of the crowd that surrounded them.

An Ethiopian minstrel, an ancient, frail man in the white garments of the highlanders, wandered by the group and climbed a few yards up the hill. He sat on the ground, strummed his curious lozenge-shaped guitar, and began chanting in an odd, singsong voice. Pilbeam and a few of the Irishmen walked up toward him to listen. His words were perfectly unintelligible, of course, except that they were able to pick out references to "Theodore" and "Magdala."

"Your man-o there would be singing in our honor, I suppose," said the Irishman next to Pilbeam. "In honor of the damned English army."

"D'ye suppose?" asked Pilbeam.

"I suppose, young fellow, for whatever it's worth," said the Irishman. He spoke with the singsong accent of County Cork. *Young* was *yoong*, *fellow* was one syllable: *yoong flah*. He was a small man of about forty-five, puffing on a curved-stemmed pipe. Shaving discipline had been relaxed in Zula, and all the European troops had sprouted beards. This Irishman's was black, just past the stage of bristles. He had shaved his head, too, and his forehead and scalp were tanned and seamed like mahogany.

"Queer-sounding music, if ye ast me," said Pilbeam. "Do you feel honored?"

The Irishman fiddled calmly with his pipe. "Do you?"

Pilbeam grunted.

The song the Ethiopian was playing seemed to go on forever without a break. After a while, all the other Irishmen drifted away to a low-branched baobab tree. The embers of their pipes glowed out of the darkness.

Pilbeam's Irishman found a cigarette in a pocket. Pilbeam nodded his thanks and leaned over to light it from the Irishman's pipe. They smoked and listened to the song, which by now was ten minutes old.

Hoofbeats clattered through the Komayli bowl. Captain Speedy trotted out of the twilight. Major Briggs and several more of their band of adventurers were close behind. They stopped within a few yards of Pilbeam, as if they were looking through the gathering night for their path.

Briggs saw the sailor and the Irish soldier, and demanded, "Where is the water for the horses? We were promised water here. And fodder, and the road to Suru?"

"Water and fodder are that way," answered the Irishman in a controlled, neutral voice. "The Parsees are seeing to it. They'll set you on the path to Suru."

Without a word, Briggs turned his horse, but Speedy caught Briggs's bridle. To Pilbeam and the Irishman he said, "Do you gentlemen have any idea what you are listening to?" He didn't wait for an answer, didn't care whether they had one. He continued to Briggs: "He is singing about the certain destruction of the British army against the walls of Magdala, and our defeat at the hands of the invincible Emperor Theodore. He's singing the praises of the emperor's Twelve Disciples, and he's telling how they will mow our troops down like wheat." He said a few quiet words in Amharic to the Ethiopian, who snatched up his guitar and ran into the hills on his spindly legs.

The cavalrymen cantered away.

"Feel the perfect idiot?" asked the Irishman. *Idiot* was *ee-jit*.

"Not a bit of it," said Pilbeam, puffing comfortably at his cigarette. "A smoke and a soft bit of grass to lie down on and no bosun's mate hanging over your shoulder make all the difference. I don't give a damn."

"I hear you," said the Irishman. "My name is Irion. Geoffrey Irion, from Bantry, Ireland. Long ago, from Bantry."

Pilbeam enveloped Irion's small hand in his own enormous one and introduced himself: "Arthur Pilbeam, from Folkestone, England. Long ago from Folkestone, as you say."

Night was falling. The Punjabis had started their queer Indian music again, and a troop of the naval brigade had started to dance the hornpipe on the grass, struggling to adjust their steps to the music.

"You don't join your friends," observed Irion. He was lying back, propped up on his elbows.

"I'm not much for dancing," said Pilbeam.

"For talking?"

"Sometimes."

"You tars are all volunteers for this expedition, aren't you?"

"Aye."

"Why did you volunteer?"

"The monsoon was ending when I volunteered," said Pilbeam. "It's awfully hot on an ironclad steamer in the Indian Ocean outside monsoon. It's cool here. Green. I haven't often seen so many pines, nor so many people. What about you?"

"I? I go where the regiment goes. One place is the same as another, provided there's plenty of food." Irion waggled his pipe at Pilbeam. "But I'm curious about you. You aren't a jolly jack-tar like the others. You're too thoughtful. You aren't the type to volunteer."

Pilbeam stubbed out the butt of his cigarette with a wetted fingertip and dropped it in his pocket. A little defensively, he said, "You're Irish." It was more a question than a statement.

"I am Irish."

"And you fight for the English."

Irion sat up cross-legged to face Pilbeam. "It's the Irish way, Arthur," he said. "It is my people's history. You can't escape your history. You look at me like I'm talking nonsense, but I know of what I speak. I was something of an educated man, once. I was studying for the priesthood, I was, at Maynooth. You may have heard of it."

"No."

"But the famine . . . aye, the famine. The Dublin docks were crowded with fat Irish cattle waiting to be ferried across to fill English bellies while Irish children starved. English landlords evicted millions of Irishmen from the land they had held for generations. On that whole beautiful island, where there were three Irishmen twenty years ago, there is one today. We're still recovering. We may never stop recovering.

"A man has to eat. I joined the English army. It's always been the way. We Irish have always had our finest moments in the service of others, but when it's time to show our colors on our own behalf, the well is dry. We cannot organize ourselves. Every Irishman wants to be the leader, no one wants to be the follower.

"Bantry is ages ago, another lifetime. My home is the Wellington's Own. We're a curious regiment. The generals never seem to know what to do with us. We get nervous in something like that celebration at the beach in Zula, standing in great faceless rows. But we're a good regiment, the very best for some jobs. We worked like slaves down in Zula, alongside the coolies and the Beloochees and the Sappers. When the army moves south from Antalo, we are to be rewarded by marching in the van. We're proud of that."

"I don't understand," said Pilbeam.

"Nor I," said Irion. He cleaned and filled and relit his pipe, and he dug out another cigarette for Pilbeam.

"What about you?" asked Irion. "The truth now. No cooling breezes."

Pilbeam felt an awkward kinship with this small, stubbly-bearded Irishman. He was able, for the first time since he'd talked to Hoyt, to tell someone about the envoy. He didn't have Irion's command of English, and he struggled to put his feelings into words, but Irion seemed to understand.

"What do you plan to do with him, if you have your chance?" asked Irion. "Explode a rocket over his head?"

"I don't know," said Pilbeam, admitting the singular weakness in his scheme. "Aren't we a lot alike, you and me? I'm marching to rescue the man I hate most of all in the world. You are part of the army of the English, whom you hate."

"You misunderstand, I fear," said Irion. "You put sentiments in my breast that aren't there. I hate no one, not even the English."

"But the famine?" said Pilbeam. "How can you not hate the English?"

"I am a scholar," said Irion, "and almost a priest. I don't hate, I analyze. And my analysis tells me that I have a home as long as I follow Sir Bob."

"Sir Bob? You mean the commander?"

"Aye, Sir Robert Napier. Haven't you heard him called Sir Bob?"

Pilbeam muttered a negative reply.

"I'll give you a word of information. Sir Bob is a queer fish, but he's the man to follow in a pinch. It doesn't matter much to him if a man is English or Irish or Indian. Another thing that's been remarked upon: the Ethiopian emperor, the one they say is the madman of the mountains, has the name Theodore, but the captives at Magdala have always called him 'Bob' in their letters. So we have one Bob marching off to fight another Bob. Queer, isn't it?"

"Confusing," said Pilbeam. "I've hardly given any thought to the purpose behind this expedition. From down here it doesn't seem to matter much."

"I've come to think it's all a game of cards," said Irion, "and we are the cards. Someone else makes the rules and shuffles the deck, and we turn without a clue at what all the other cards are doing."

"I wonder what the view looks like to the general?"

"Or to the emperor?"

A bugle rang across the bowl.

"That's our muster call," said Irion, rising reluctantly. "We're to march up to Suru tonight."

"We're waiting for our baggage to arrive from Zula," said Pilbeam. "It looks like a night in a greatcoat."

"There are worse ways to spend a night," said Irion, looking up at the unnaturally bright stars in the clear tropical sky. "I'll be surprised if a night such as this in a greatcoat is the worst we encounter."

"Will I see you again?" asked Pilbeam. "Whatever you say, I think we have a lot in common. Maybe you could educate me."

Irion laughed softly. Then, "You won't have any trouble finding me. The 33rd marches in the van, and I'm sure our patriotic tars won't be far behind. The navy won't be hard to find. Out of an army of shaved heads, I'll look for the black queues."

"Who aren't Sikhs," added Pilbeam.

"I'll look for the hornpipe danced to Punjabi reeds."

They shook hands, and as Irion walked away, Pilbeam could hear him singing to himself:

> "Pat may be foolish and sometimes very wrong.
> "Paddy's got a temper but it won't last very long.
> "Pat is fond of jollity and everybody knows
> "There never was a coward where the shamrock grows."

The first human casualty of the expedition occurred at sunset that same evening. In the middle of the afternoon, Colonel Dunn, commander of the 33rd Foot, the Duke of Wellington's Own, had climbed into the hills around Komayli to try for a few partridges. He wore his usual scarlet uniform with his own personal flourishes. His hands were encased in soft kid gloves, his violet silk handkerchief hung carelessly through his epaulet, and a gauzy green veil fluttered off his solar helmet and shielded the back of his neck from the sun. The only medal he wore was the Victoria Cross he had won at Balaklava. He was armed with his German twelve-gauge shotgun and a six-shot Colt pistol. He was accompanied by a little troupe of aides-de-camp, similarly armed, and a bigger crew of Indian bearers who followed at a discreet distance.

After an hour or so, an aide pointed out a nearby ridge to Dunn, and the colonel called a halt to look. Three mounted Ethiopian warriors were on the crest of the ridge. The Ethiopians who had come into Komayli had all been inoffensive, unarmed boys and old men, but these three were a different matter. Their horses were small, shaggy, and stocky, ideal for maneuvering through mountainous terrain. The warriors were dressed in white shirts and trousers. Their feet were bare, their hair was glossy and braided. They had sabers hanging from their saddles, and they carried flintlock rifles across their pommels. "Still as statues," said a young major. "Like bloody pirates," said a subaltern. They were close enough to see one another's faces clearly. One Ethiopian had a web of fine scars across his cheek. Another bore a puckered saber cut that ran from his hairline, through a hollow eye socket, across the end of his mouth, and off his jaw. The third, the youngest, was still unmarked. Almost without blinking, they stared at the Englishmen, who stared back.

After several minutes, Dunn said, "This is pointless." He started off again. The aides and bearers followed. The Ethiopians watched until they were out of sight. Dunn and his people hunted all afternoon. The colonel brought down four fat partridges for the pot, the young major shot two, and a lieutenant, as befitted his rank, made a bad kill on one. They made a loop of seven or eight miles, getting two miles from Komayli at the farthest. The same three Ethiopians appeared again, watching silently from a nearby hill, later joined by a fourth warrior. The next time, a dozen observers appeared. There was never any attempt at communication by either side, only the staring and ignoring.

Dunn led his party on the walk back to Komayli. Walking straight into the setting sun, Dunn didn't see the snake, a small and harmless type of boa constrictor, until he planted his foot on top of it. The snake writhed and coiled around his ankle. He leaped away, fell onto his side, and slid headfirst down a gravelly incline. His shotgun went off at point-blank range, the pellets tearing away his violet handkerchief, ruining his Victoria Cross, and ripping open the right side of his rib cage. He was dead before anyone could reach him.

His aides were still standing helplessly over his mutilated body when they heard the frightened Hindustani voices of the bearers. The young major shoved the lieutenant, who scrambled up and pushed his way through the bearers. The dozen Ethiopian warriors were all around him. Their expressions were absolutely neutral. The lieutenant didn't know what to do, so he just stood there with his shotgun dangling loose in his right hand.

The Ethiopian with the web of scars looked across at the young, unmarked warrior and said a few words. The young warrior slipped off his horse, handed the bridle to the lieutenant, and climbed up behind the scarred warrior. The Ethiopians turned their horses and cantered away.

The aides draped Colonel Dunn's body across the Ethiopian horse and carried him through the twilight back to Komayli.

When Lieutenant-Colonel Phayre had staked out the layout of the Zula camp in October, he had assigned headquarters to an area at the edge of camp farthest from the shore, flanking a long, sandy depression that ran northeastward toward the sea. The bottom of the depression was hard-baked sand. Brittle sand-colored reeds stood in a few places in the sand, and the only real trees anywhere near Zula grew along its borders. If a man had to live in Zula, this was the most homey place.

Napier's own tent had been pitched a few yards inland from the depression, on a shallow knoll. The tent was a lavish affair. On the outside, it was waterproofed canvas, each side painted into an enormous Union Jack. An awning extended out from the front, and that entire side could be rolled up to expose the interior. Inside, it was lined with yellow cotton, and curtains of the same material could be drawn across to form a large dining room in front and several smaller rooms in back. It was carpeted with Oriental rugs and hung inside with tapestries. A crew of servants needed two hours to take it down or put it up, and it required a train of ten mules to carry it.

On his third and last evening in Zula, Napier was working in one of the back rooms while servants in the main room cleared away the remains of his nightly dinner party. With him were two staff officers and his military secretary. The night was unbearably hot, but none of them had loosened a button or a collar. Insects buzzed around the yellow oil lamps and slapped softly against the tent walls.

From beneath the awning a Welsh aide-de-camp said, "Beg pardon, sir, but the merchant is here. He's brought some Arab or other with him." Napier looked up from his desk. The tiny merchant was hardly visible beside the tall figure of the aide. The man wore huge, steel-rimmed glasses and a turban, and his nervous hands fluttered like butterflies. Behind him stood a willowy young Arab. Napier waved his hand for the merchant to enter and dismissed the officers and the secretary with a distracted, "Later, gentlemen. Please." Paniotti and Abd-ul-Kerim wove their way among the servants, ignored the curious, angry glances of the officers, and stopped just outside the alcove. Paniotti and Napier appraised each other with a cool, wary gaze. There was no secret that each of them was intensely interested in the other—as men, as personalities, as players in a game. The merchant's hands moved nervously, but his eyes, big and gray behind the lenses, were calm and inquisitive.

Napier finally stood up, and waved them toward chairs. Abd-ul-Kerim did not move. Paniotti hesitated as if he had been caught halfway through a thought. Still standing, he said in romantically accented English, "I saw your elephants as I came through the camp."

"Yes, we have war elephants," said Napier. "We're an Indian army, you see."

"Yes, of course. I've been away at Massawa for a week, and I was a little surprised to see them. It hadn't occurred to me that you would have elephants." He waggled his head, said, "Oh, well, never mind," and sat down, teetering on the edge of the chair. Abd-ul-Kerim sat beside him.

Napier stared hard at Paniotti, shifted his gaze to Abd-ul-Kerim. The Arab stared calmly into Napier's eyes. Napier did not let his eyes drop, but without meaning to do so began to chew on the end of his pencil.

Paniotti broke the silence. "This is Abd-ul-Kerim. He is the son of the sheik of Massawa. While Rassam was at Massawa, the two of them became very close friends. He speaks no English, but he had a desire to see the English general who is to save his friend from the madman of the mountains." He gave Theodore's popular title a twist of irony.

Napier nodded to Abd-ul-Kerim. Then, to Paniotti, he said slowly, "Lieutenant-Colonel Phayre's quartermaster branch informs me you've been of great help in, hmmm, procuring certain supplies. Your business connections are said to be excellent. I asked you here this evening to thank you personally."

Paniotti stared for another few moments, then gave a subtle English sniff, looked up at the ceiling, and began to recite in a monotone: " 'I met Paniotti himself in Massawa. He is the most mysterious man I've ever met. He is a Greek, though no one knows precisely where he comes from. He lives in a mansion within the city walls. He is rarely seen, et cetera, et cetera.' And again: 'One single parting word, Colonel Merewether. I do not know how this word relates to British captives and Ethiopian emperors, but I have an intuition that it is a word for you to remember. That word is: *Paniotti*.' " He let his hands flutter briefly. "I can go on."

Napier let a little smile play across his lips. "It won't be necessary. That is from Speedy's letter to Merewether, isn't it? Probably the only letter written about this Ethiopia affair that never made it into the newspapers. I am impressed, Mr. Paniotti. Impressed."

"I don't care to impress, General," said Paniotti. "I only mean to say, let us not play games with each other."

Napier was so used to dealing with evasive Englishmen that Paniotti's offer of frankness didn't open up their communication, but instead placed a momentary barrier between them. "Let us not play games, then," Napier said cautiously, and waited for Paniotti to continue.

"You have Captain Speedy's recommendation to talk to me," said Paniotti. "You've heard I have some sort of connection with the emperor. You wonder who I am and what I know."

"Yes," said Napier. "All that."

Paniotti looked over his own shoulder. The servants had left. Two soldiers were on guard under the awning. Paniotti moved his chair nearer to Napier's desk and leaned closer. He spoke in a low voice. "I am His Majesty's agent on the Red Sea. More than that, I am probably his closest friend."

As if to delay having to comment on what Paniotti had said, Napier shifted his attention to Abd-ul-Kerim. Their eyes met and locked. Napier was astonished at the merciless hardness in those unwavering eyes. "Who is your friend?" asked Napier, still sparring with the Arab.

"A man of the emperor," said Paniotti. "As you say, he is my friend."

Napier looked back at the Greek merchant. "You are spies."

"I am an observer for your enemy," said Paniotti. "I am supplying your quartermaster branch only to be able to observe more closely. I will report back to His Majesty. Yes, that makes me a spy."

"I should have you arrested. Questioned. Tried by military tribunal. Shot."

"You should."

"What kind of information are you gathering on my army?"

"Your army isn't very important," said Paniotti. "It will utterly crush Theodore. What else do we have to know? Compared to your soldiers, his warriors are only guerrilla fighters. They could pick off hundreds of your men, but they could never turn you back, and Theodore won't let them loose. He wants a head-on confrontation at Magdala. He wants to go down in one glorious battle. You have no particular reason to trust me, General, but you won't have to worry much about defending your lines of communication. They won't be threatened."

"You are well aware I can't believe you," said Napier.

"I know it."

They stared at each other. In a way that Napier had not experienced before, Paniotti's honesty seemed to brush the knights and castles and pawns of Napier's perpetual chess game off the board onto the floor. Paniotti refused to play the game: Napier realized, unpleasantly, that he would have to return honesty for honesty. At last, he said, "The only man I have who has ever seen the emperor is that pompous ass Speedy. He's an idiot, a fool. He's only good for entertainment. Riding around the countryside, waving his sword, slashing sheep in half, irritating the honest soldiers. He wouldn't know a hero if one spat in his eye."

"I saw his letter to Colonel Merewether," Paniotti reminded him.

"Yes, didn't you?" said Napier. "Do you smoke? What are you free to tell me about the emperor?"

Paniotti said, "I don't smoke." Napier found a pipe under a stack of papers, filled and lit it. Yellow smoke wreathed his head. He poured three brandies and slid two across the desk. Abd-ul-Kerim took his and sipped at it. Paniotti took the glass, swirled it, sniffed it, but didn't drink. "There's no point now in concealing anything," said Paniotti, and he began to speak. He went on continuously for more than two hours. After the first interruption, Napier ordered the Welsh aide-de-camp to keep everyone away. He listened carefully, and the few questions he asked were precise and respectful. Paniotti told Napier the story of Kasa's childhood, his years as a *shifta*, his rise to the Lion Throne, the years of glory, and the fall. He would have skipped lightly over the prophecies that controlled Theodore's life, but Napier insisted on hearing them.

At the end, Napier said, thoughtfully, "Now, if I understand you correctly, the emperor expected this Rassam to be his Light Bringer. Only Rassam didn't match all the signs, so it couldn't be him. The emperor is still waiting for a new candidate, and that must be me."

Paniotti nodded. "It's you."

Napier chewed on his pipe and considered what this meant. He asked, "How am I doing on the signs?"

"Very well," said Paniotti. "Or poorly, depending on your orientation. I'll list them for you." He ticked them off on his fingers.

"One, he will free people from bondage. We've all heard how you set free the garrisons that were being held by Tanti Topi during the Mutiny.

"Two, elephants will fall down before him. That is why I was so interested to see your war elephants.

"Three, he will be accompanied by thousands of people, the myriad stars of the vision. Done.

"Fourth, Theodore will help him through a difficult place. If you cross the Bashillo River to get to Magdala, you will certainly be helped by his road through the gorge.

"Five, he will usurp the emperor's rights. Just by marching through his empire and issuing proclamations to his subjects, you are doing that.

"Sixth, and last, though the emperor begs him, he will never forgive. This is the only one you haven't fulfilled yet, but I promise you His Majesty will offer you the chance."

Napier asked, "These signs mean so much to him?"

"Everything," said Paniotti.

"Is there any way to avoid this waste?" asked Napier.

"No," said Paniotti. "There's no way at all. The emperor is locked in. You are locked in. From the moment you landed, he had lost everything. If you come to him, you will crush him. If he surrenders the captives to you and you go away, the rebels will see his weakness and rise all over the empire, and *they* will crush him."

"Are you asking me to take my army home?" asked Napier.

"You could never do that," said Paniotti with a bitter little laugh. "In all the world, five men have known the signs. Madhani, the monk, is dead. The others are Theodore, Rassam, you, and I. I told you so that you will understand him. So perhaps you will think a little about his dreams. So perhaps you will let him die with dignity."

"A fascinating situation," said Napier quietly, around the pipe stem. "An intriguing man. I hope I have the chance to meet him."

"He'll be dead before you ever see him," said Paniotti, without emotion. He rose from his precarious balance on the chair and took a step out of the alcove. Abd-ul-Kerim moved silently, as if he were Paniotti's shadow. "You have more respect than I anticipated," Paniotti said. "You aren't so caught up in your own superiority as the rest of your Englishmen. Theodore will be pleased to hear it."

Napier nodded his thanks.

Paniotti continued, "I have a thing to ask. I wouldn't ask it of any other man, but I think you may be different from others. You know that I am with the Emperor Theodore. Soon after Rassam was put in chains at Magdala, Abd-ul-Kerim traveled to Ethiopia and formally entered the emperor's service. So, we are two spies for your enemy—and also two friends of Rassam. What we ask is this: even knowing who we are, will you let us go with your army?"

"You are asking me to take acknowledged spies along with me?" asked Napier, gnawing at his pipe.

Softly, Paniotti answered, "Exactly."

"But why?" asked Napier, and Paniotti answered, "To be close when the end has come. That is all."

"It may not be a place to wait for a friend," he said. "Rassam's chances are slim."

Paniotti allowed himself a little smile. "Oh, no, Rassam is in no danger. Abd-ul-Kerim has Theodore's word on it, and even without that promise, I have no fears. No, if Rassam is in danger, it is not from the emperor."

Napier considered this, then said, "I shall find some sort of excuse for you to accompany the army, at least until we trim down to the assault force." He ran his finger down a map that was pinned to the pavilion wall beside the desk. "That will be Lake Ashangi. Yes, you may come as far as Ashangi, but you will have to wait there."

"Fair enough," said Paniotti. He spoke in Arabic to Abd-ul-Kerim, who flashed the golden emblems in his smile and touched his forehead in thanks.

"What about you, Mr. Paniotti?" asked Napier. "When it is all over, what will you do?"

The hands fluttered violently. "Be loyal to my cause until it dies."

"Then?"

"Then I will be rich, and useless, and alone, and homeless."

"How homeless?" asked Napier. "A man with your fortune won't ever be homeless."

"A home can be more than a place," said Paniotti. "It can be an idea or a cause. Theodore has been my home for many years."

"You'll find a new home," said Napier.

"Perhaps. A man without a home is a pitiable creature, General. A very pitiable creature, indeed. Mine is Theodore. What is yours?"

Napier bit hard on his pipe. "The army, I suppose."

Paniotti waggled his head. "I doubt it. By the way, your Lieutenant-Colonel Phayre is making a fool of himself up in the highlands. He is the laughingstock of Tigré province.

"He's done poorly here in Zula, too. He located your headquarters, every tent but your own, in a branch of the Hadas River. This depression may be dry now, and the trees may be a blessing, but if there were a rain in the highlands, you would wake up on an island, and all the rest of your staff would wake up on the floor of the ocean." He and Abd-ul-Kerim turned away, pushed through the crowd waiting impatiently under the awning, and disappeared into the night.

17

January 1868
Tigré Province

The route of the march would lead the Anglo-Indian army onto the sharp, rocky spine of Ethiopia at Suru, and then southward along the spine toward Magdala. As the army advanced, it would leave behind many of its units as garrisons, until it unfolded into an elongated pyramid, fat at the bases of Zula and Suru and Senafe, leaner and more efficient the farther south it stretched. At the end, at Magdala, there would remain only the five thousand troops selected for the actual assault.

The first two hundred miles or so were through the province of Tigré. Political Officer Merewether had promised Napier that Tigré was in rebellion against Theodore and wouldn't hinder the invasion. It turned out he had been too cautious. The Tigréans were overjoyed to accept insanely inflated prices from the quartermaster's branch for huge quantities of food and fodder, and Tigréan peasants flocked in from miles around to cheer as the miraculous army filed by. At any moment, they might see a dozen uniforms and half a dozen races, curious instruments of war on carts or animal-back, horses, mules, elephants, and shivering, dying camels. Musicians led every regiment. For as far back as the music carried, the soldiers tried to march in time. The army went by uneven jerks and stops and starts, galloping and walking and resting all at once, every minute of the day. And five times a day the entire army halted long enough for the Moslem troops to bow to Mecca.

Colonel Phayre traveled several days ahead with one hundred fifty British sabers and four companies of Indian Sappers. The army based each day's march on the intelligence reports he sent back. Phayre had a tendency to believe whatever he was told. A competition grew among the Tigré districts as to who could spin the most farfetched lies. When it was all over, the winner was the monk who sent Phayre away from the caravan route into a box canyon. Before his scouts stumbled across the easy route, Phayre's Sappers had spent a week blasting a path through solid granite. The new path would still be in use by the Ethiopians a century later, but no English soldier ever walked its length.

It was only the Irishmen of the 33rd, marching in the van, foundering in Phayre's wake, who determined the real truth. A man who marches for a living develops a keen sense of the distance his feet are logging. The Irishmen knew to within a quarter of a mile how far they had walked each day. Copies of Phayre's reports were distributed to the commanders of all the units. A second, underground set of reports, originating with the foot soldiers of the 33rd, circulated on a parallel course. A few enlightened officers made it a daily habit to read Phayre's reports, then to send a sergeant major out to verify them by asking the troops. More often, even when they knew Phayre's reports were fantastic, the commanders went by established procedure and based their marches on the official intelligence.

When a commander gave the marching orders-of-the-day to his subordinate officers, he would read Phayre's report aloud to give them an idea of what lay ahead. The subalterns would relay the orders and the intelligence to the sergeant majors, who would pass them along to the troops. The official word might be that the march was ten miles of rolling hills with plenty of fresh water. The men might already know it was eighteen miles of steady climb with only two fouled springs. But the British and Indian troops would obediently cinch their pack straps tight, hunker down their shoulders, grumble under their breath, and plod into the march.

Again, it was only the Irishmen of the 33rd, absorbing more lies on each day's march, who objected openly. A lieutenant-colonel named Cooper had been transferred into the regiment to replace Dunn. Cooper tried to lead them like English troops. They bristled at his spit and polish, at his orders that seemed to be handed down from Jehovan heights. Discipline among the Irish had always been marginal. Helplessly, Cooper watched it crumble away day by day.

It was the march from Mai Wahez to Ada Baga, the 33rd's ninth march after Komayli, that finally broke the regiment. They had marched overnight from Adigrat to Mai Wahez. They had been told it was seven miles. It was over fourteen.

Night marches had been comfortable at lower altitudes, when the days were unmercifully hot and the moon was full, but here, at over ten thousand feet, the day was the time to hike and the night the time to shiver inside a tent. Cooper hadn't yet received orders to change over to daytime marches, and he wouldn't make the decision on his own.

The march was up a straight, treeless ridge, with the ground sloping gently away to right and left. The moon was a new, useless sliver, and around midnight a vast cloud cover rolled in to blot out the stars.

Sergeant majors lit lanterns and held them up on their rifles, and the soldiers stumbled behind. Soon after the clouds came in, the rain began, at first as a gentle mist, then as big freezing drops that fell like bullets. The lanterns went out. Each soldier held onto the pack of the man ahead, and they crept blindly up the long ridge through the solid night. Lightning cracked all around, stunned them, and revealed instantaneous images of sheer cliffs next to the trail.

The rain let up at dawn, just as the 33rd was stumbling into Mai Wahez, a sheltered little grass valley. There were freshwater streams, with a monastery and a church overlooking them. The monks came down, bartered briskly, lit fires, butchered fifteen sheep, and set them to cooking. The Irishmen lit their own fires and hung their sopping coats and socks and bedrolls over them to dry.

And then, just as the mutton was coming off the spits, the sergeant majors, badly concealing their own anger, passed the word that the 33rd had lost so much time during the night that they were going to do a double march. Seven more miles to Ada Baga, and there they would rest. The orders came down with a bit of encouragement from Cooper, something about pride in the regimental colors. Dutifully, the sergeant majors repeated it, but they nearly choked.

The Irishmen put their wet clothing back on, took what mutton they could carry in their hands, and started off in a ragged column. Their boots sloshed, their underwear clung wetly. The day was perfect for hiking, but freezing cold for men in wet clothes.

Six miles up, the band topped the crown of the ridge. They had no real hopes of it, but they knew their destination was supposed to be one short mile beyond the summit. Over the top, the band, and then the next company of infantry, looked down into a wide basin, treeless and empty. Five miles away a collection of white tents stood on flat ground below the next line of hills: Mai Wahez. Within five minutes, the entire regiment, all seven hundred of them, stretched back for three quarters of a mile, knew exactly what lay ahead.

The revolt began at the rear and rolled forward like dominoes falling. A forty-year-old Kerryman, a twenty-one-year veteran of the regiment, heard the news from an eighteen-year-old Belfast boy. The Kerryman looked over his shoulder. There was no one behind him, except for a splotch of red dots a few miles back which were probably couriers. He stopped in his tracks and let ten yards grow between himself and the Belfast boy. Then, he took off his helmet, said "Shit" in a loud voice at the boy's back, and threw the helmet so it rattled noisily across a boulder. He tossed his pack onto the ground, sat beside it on the spongy, soaked heather off the trail, and laid his Snyder rifle across his lap to keep it from getting wet.

The Belfast boy had turned at the word "Shit." He took another three steps, wavered, looked back, and then set his pack off the trail and sat quietly beside it.

The boy hadn't made a sound, so the Kerryman cupped his hands around his mouth and shouted up the trail, "Shit!"

The next man turned, and within one step he had thrown himself onto the ground and shouted ahead. "Shit. Oh, Leahy lad, *shit.*" "Great Mother of God, *shit,*" cried the man ahead of him. The one-syllable order rolled forward, and the Irishmen fell out, some alone, most into groups of three or four or ten. They left the trail completely clear. Those who were leading pack-mules staked their animals off the trail, then sat beside them. Sergeant majors screamed at the men. A few tried to drag soldiers up. The men did not resist, but when the sergeant majors let go they went back to sitting on the heather. The sergeant majors congregated into little groups. They stood with their arms crossed and their legs set wide apart. They muttered among themselves. But they were Irish, too, and their muttering was against Lieutenant-Colonel Phayre, and Lieutenant-Colonel Cooper, and the entire British army. The Indian servants formed into their own bare-legged groups and discussed the situation in their usual detached fashion. They were used to being treated like slaves. Double marches were none of their business, even when they shared in the suffering.

The red dots in the distance resolved into Captain Speedy and Major Briggs and their dashing band of swashbuckling cavalrymen. By now they had all learned to wear turbans, their saber hilts were properly blooded, and their mustaches were wild. Speedy slowed his prancing horse as he came abreast of the Kerryman. The trail was clear. The riders walked their horses, still in the casual, independent double file in which they went everywhere. Speedy studied the Irishmen for a clue as to what they were doing. Briggs and the rest watched Speedy for a clue, too.

"Damned sloppy way to fall out," said Speedy to Briggs. He used the absolutely correct tone of voice for talking in front of servants or other people who were so vastly inferior that it didn't matter whether they overheard or not. "Not military at all."

Briggs saw one of the soldiers glowering at Speedy, and he said, "I don't think an officer would have ordered this." He screwed in his eyepiece and said to the soldier, who was sitting alone, "What do you mean, lazing around like this? Hasn't your regiment any pride?"

Geoffrey Irion, who was the glowering Irishman, mouthed one short word, too low to be heard.

"Again?" demanded Speedy.

Irion repeated, round and clear, though not particularly loud, the key word of the moment: "Shit."

Briggs coughed nervously. He had never seen foot soldiers in revolt before, hadn't known they were capable of it. Asking for an answer, Briggs said to Speedy, "He said 'shit.'"

Speedy put in his own eyepiece to give himself a space of time. "I heard him," he said, without his usual bravado.

Briggs decided to take command. "What is your name, soldier?"

Irion said, "Shit."

Angrily, "What squadron is this?"

Again, "Shit."

Briggs craned his neck, saw a group of sergeant majors, and shouted at them.

Irion's non-com ran down the trail. "Sir."

"What is going on here?"

"The men just started falling out, sir," said the sergeant major. "They've walked a very long way, sir, and they won't march anymore. Sir."

"Well, they'll march now," said Speedy, pulling his horse forward against Briggs's, "or we'll cut them down."

The cavalrymen murmured their approval, and one of them said, "Like sheep."

"Cut them down?" said Briggs. His voice was suddenly weak.

"It's mutiny," said Speedy. "Mutiny, plain and simple. The penalty is death."

"Shit," said Irion, and a boy from Mallow, a few yards up the trail in a cluster of his friends, echoed, "Shit." Someone else said it, and it rippled up the trail and over the crown of the ridge. They began to say it in time, once every two seconds. Each of them said it in a distinct, conversational voice. The quiet tone gave the chant a sinister, thoughtful quality.

Colonel Cooper and ten aides-de-camp came pounding swiftly down the trail. They mixed in with Speedy's men. The thirty horsemen milled aimlessly around, muttered under their breath, and cast uncertain, embarrassed glances at the long, uneven line of infantrymen. The Irishmen looked boldly up at the riders.

At the focus of it all, Speedy said to Cooper, "You have mutiny on your hands."

"Resting," said Cooper. He was a sixtyish colonel, impeccably cut from the mold of Bombay colonels, square-chinned, mutton-chopped, absolutely set in his ways. He was very confused.

Speedy said, "Resting, my ass," and Briggs echoed, "My ass."

"It's mutiny," said Speedy, and he repeated it louder to carry over the men's chanting. He found Irion's sergeant major. "Tell the colonel what you told me."

"The men just started falling out. They've walked so far, and they won't march anymore. Sir."

"That's mutiny," said Speedy.

"Mutiny," said Cooper. He had no idea of how to deal with the situation.

"Hang them," said Speedy.

"Hang them," said Cooper.

"Oh, jolly," said Briggs, who liked the idea of hanging them better than the idea of cutting them down. "Hang them."

"Hang them," repeated Cooper. He leaned close as if he was going to whisper, but then he said loud enough for all the riders and many of the infantrymen to hear, "You can't hang my whole regiment."

"Then just a few as an example. That one." He pointed to Irion. "And that one and that one."

"I can't do that."

"Then make them move," said Speedy. Cooper only stared at Speedy, who finally said, "I'll make them move." He crossed his hand to his saber hilt and swept the blade out. Briggs and his twenty turbaned officers did the same.

"Put those away," blurted Cooper, almost by accident. Then, more boldly, he said, "There'll be no bloodshed here."

"We'll make your Irish bastards move," said Briggs, and pushed his horse one jerky step closer to the broken line of Irishmen on the heather.

"No," shouted Cooper. A conflict with common foot soldiers was a baffling mystery to Cooper, but a conflict with another officer was a known quantity.

The cavalrymen watched Speedy for his cue. The colonel's aides watched Cooper for his. Cooper dragged his horse hard into Speedy's, flank to nose, and glared into Speedy's ironbound face. Harshly, he whispered, "I said no, *Captain.*"

Speedy hissed back, "It's clear you haven't the courage to control your own men. If I have to do it for you, I will."

Cooper looked over Speedy's shoulder at Briggs. "Major, you will order your men, including this captain, to put away their sabers, and you will leave this sector. At once." Startled at being singled out, Briggs just stared.

Speedy talked into the side of Cooper's face. "I'm the general's man, not yours, and I see a vital duty undone."

"Major!"

The two intermixed forces on horseback stared uncomfortably at each other, and the tension became so intense that the infantry's chanting ceased in one scattered "shit." Absolute silence hovered all along the trail. The two bodies of horsemen eyed each other, and the Irish were forgotten.

Very quietly, with careful movements, Irion had pried open the breech of his Snyder, pushed in a cartridge, and closed the breech. Into the silence, he suddenly thrust the dull metallic click of the rifle's hammer. He hadn't shifted the position of the rifle across his lap, but now it was ready to fire.

A few yards away another hammer clicked, and then all seven hundred of them, one and a half miles of rifles, clicked into a ready position.

In the following silence Cooper said, "Major, put your sabers away."

Speedy hadn't let his glare leave Cooper's face, even at the sound of the rifles. He leaned forward so his nose almost touched Cooper's cheek.

"If you weren't an old man," he said, "I'd call you out and kill you for dishonoring that uniform."

Cooper gave no sign of even knowing Speedy was there. "Major?" he said.

Speedy yanked his horse away, thrust his saber into the scabbard, and spurred his horse up the trail so suddenly he left Briggs and the rest sitting their horses with their sabers out, feeling like fools. They galloped after him, some still struggling to put their sabers away as they rode.

Instantly, the Irish began their chant again. "Shit." Two seconds. "Shit." Two seconds.

The twenty-two riders kept their chins tucked down and their eyes fixed straight ahead all the way to the crown of the ridge and·down the other side into the Ada Baga basin, until their hoofbeats drowned out the taunting chant.

The infantry's tents were the same *routies* they had used in India: canvas, twenty feet square, double-poled, sloping down from those two peaks nearly to the ground, and then finished off under the protection of the roof in a separate apron. At this stage of the march the infantry's mules were carrying a *routie* for every twelve soldiers. That first evening, even without orders, the men of the 33rd gathered into their usual groupings of twelve and created a line, a mile and a half long, militarily precise, of brown pyramids fifteen yards off the trail, spaced at an almost exact forty yards, all facing onto the path.

Cooper retreated in shame that first evening into a compound of tents at the head of the regiment. Except for a solitary courier heading back toward Napier, he and his officers weren't seen again in the next few days. The servants of the sergeant majors pitched their masters' *routies* across the path from the soldiers' *routies*. There was no communication from Cooper to the sergeant majors, and none from the sergeant majors to the soldiers. No one gave anyone else an order, but the momentum of military life carried the 33rd into its usual ordered existence. The soldiers dug proper latrines and imposed sanitary discipline on themselves. The mules were strung together, fed, and watered. By day, the Irishmen sat in front of their *routies* and watched the army, of which they had been the leaders, plod by. By night, they sat at their campfires and remembered stories of India and Ireland. They were waiting for someone to punish them. They weren't sorry for what they'd done, but it wasn't easy for them to watch the van of the army, their rightful position, getting farther and farther away. The ancient Irish harp, hurriedly painted or stitched from green rags, hung from a few flagpoles, but it never hung without a Union Jack beside it.

The naval brigade made the Mai Wahez-Ada Baga march on the fourth day after the mutiny. Captain Fellowes had given strict orders not to fraternize with the Irish, but the sailors flung cheerfully crude remarks at the soldiers, and the soldiers lilted back friendly replies.

Leading a mule laden with steel rocket tubes, Arthur Pilbeam was near the end of the naval brigade. He searched the faces of the Irishmen as he passed them, and outside the fifth or sixth *routie* he found Irion, caught his eye, and waved. Irion had been watching for him, too. He smiled and lifted his pipe in greeting.

Pilbeam called to a man a few places ahead: "Bosun?" Fellowes had ordered everyone to use shore titles and army terminology, but the entire brigade, even the bosuns (who were supposed to have become sergeant majors), routinely ignored the instructions. In many cases, they had even stretched their imaginations to invent nautical equivalents for land-bound events. "Bosun?"

The bosun stepped away from the path and shouted back, "Aye, seaman? What is it?"

"Bosun, I've sighted a friend of mine to starboard. Request permission to tack this four-legged skiff over close to hail him."

Under his breath, a nearby sailor whispered to another, just loud enough for Pilbeam to hear and ignore, "If that unkindly bastard Pilbeam has one single friend in all the world, for God's sake let him go."

The bosun waited until Pilbeam and his mule had come abreast of him. "You heard the commander, Pilbeam. These Irish're in mutiny. You can't have nothing to do with them."

"Aw, bosun," said Pilbeam, "do me this one. He's an old friend . . . a cousin. He's a cousin on my poor mother's side."

The bosun crossed his sturdy forearms. "Pilbeam, you've got no Paddy kin."

"Do this for me, bosun," Pilbeam said, with a note of pleading in his voice.

The bosun was astonished to hear that note from Pilbeam, who was generally so aloof and self-contained. He started to waver. "You really want this, don't you?"

"I want to see him, aye. Bosun, do this for me."

The bosun spat a dusty crater into the trail and muttered to himself, "Damn." Then he said, "Tack quick away out of sight of the captain, then, and mind you catch us up before we make port." He turned and jogged toward his place.

Pilbeam pulled his mule's lead rope—*painter,* he would have called it—and turned off the path toward Irion. Irion was sitting on the heather with his tent mates. He rose and walked forward to meet Pilbeam. His black beard had grown in beyond the stage of bristles. The top of his head was more freckled and seamed than before. They touched hands, and Irion said, "I'm very glad to see you, boy. Yes, I'm glad."

Pilbeam started to say something, but then he noticed all of Irion's companions looking at him and listening, and he choked on the words.

"Ahh," breathed Irion. He took the mule's rope and led the mule and Pilbeam away from the men. "Don't like so many people, do you?"

"No," said Pilbeam, the man of few words. "Your beard is looking better."

"And my head is looking uglier. I know." Irion stopped behind the *routie*. He found a cigarette for Pilbeam.

"What happened?" asked Pilbeam. "We heard a lot of strange stories."

"I'm a hero," said Irion, "and maybe a scapegoat. I was, by horrible chance, the man on the spot." Quickly, he told the whole story, from the nighttime march from Adigrat to Mai Wahez to his own role in the revolt. "It isn't something I'd have done if I'd had a choice," he said at the end. "But it's what the situation called for. Now every man in the regiment knows me. I'm the almost-priest who said 'shit' to the general's pet swordsman. I'm the one who cocked his rifle. I'm the one who bears the brunt, if someone has to bear it. I'm the most popular man in the regiment. And now, of my own free will, I can earnestly repeat myself: 'shit.' "

"Don't you hate that Captain Speedy?" asked Pilbeam. "I do."

"I don't hate anyone. Honestly."

"What will they do to you?"

"Haven't a clue, my friend, haven't a clue. Sometime soon we'll be ordered back into line. We'll grumble and balk. But we'll do it because we're Irish, and we're leaderless. The lads are trying to make me into a leader, but I won't do it. I haven't the stomach nor the purpose. I wish the whole thing hadn't happened. Fact is, the longer we sit here with no word from Cooper, and no word from Napier, the more we all regret it. Four days ago, with a leader, the regiment would have fought anyone who tried to order us into line. We would have done murder.

"But since we've been sitting here, we've watched the whole damned army walk past. Our place in the van meant a lot to us. We've lost it. Now at best, we'll be brought forward a few stations and left to garrison some insignificant little village. It'll take the regiment years to live down the humiliation."

Pilbeam felt anger rising in him, or perhaps it was only anger masking disappointment. "I wouldn't feel humiliated," he said. "Four days or four years, it wouldn't matter. With a leader or without. If we mutinied, I'd never go back. I'd do my damage, and I'd die doing more."

"Why?" he asked softly.

"Because I hate them," hissed Pilbeam.

"And you hate your envoy?"

"Him most of all."

Gently: "You hate so much. Why?"

"I thought you were a brave man," said Pilbeam. "I thought you were so smart. But you'll march along with them and die for nothing." He realized with shock that he was getting close to tears. He threw the cigarette down, grabbed the mule's lead rope, and dragged the mule at a run toward the path.

Late that night, Colonel Cooper slipped silently from his tent and cantered with just one aide to the crown of the ridge. Once past the last *routie,* he let the horse make its own slower pace, but the way was all downhill and he made good time. The last two hours to Adigrat were in the light of early morning. In a few isolated encampments, soldiers were crawling into the sunlight, dressing, washing, grooming their animals, eating the breakfasts their servants had prepared for them. Very few of them noticed him at all: he meant nothing to them. He passed one major with whom he was slightly acquainted. They exchanged quick, rigid greetings, and the major looked away.

The Ethiopians considered Adigrat a three-church town: probably seven or eight hundred people. It was in a desolate flatness, a small desert at the top of the world inhabited mostly by goat herders. At the moment, the British garrison and the soldiers in transit to the south numbered a thousand or so. The camp utilized space considerably more efficiently than the Ethiopian town, and filled a much smaller space. Coming down on Adigrat from the south, Cooper saw the difference between the huts, radiating out from the three churches, and the crisp lines of the British tents. Napier's Union Jack pavilion dominated the army from a low knoll beyond the camp, but it wasn't the same kind of pure domination as that of the churches over the town in which they were embedded. Cooper skirted the village and the camp to get to Napier's pavilion. To his relief, he didn't encounter anyone who knew him. An Indian manservant in turban and loincloth took Cooper's horse and that of his aide. The tent was open on the side toward the camp. A dining table and a dozen tall-backed chairs were in the front dining area. A vase full of wild flowers was on the table. The curtains to the rooms beyond were drawn.

Cooper had managed to keep himself numb through the long night's ride, but now, so close to Napier, his stomach began to churn, and he was glad he hadn't eaten on the way. To the servant, he began nervously, "Is . . . ah, is he . . ."

The servant gestured around to the back of the pavilion. "Latrine. Master Robert went to the latrine. Back soon."

"Well. I am Colonel Cooper of the 33rd. I shall wait."

"Ah, the colonel of the troublesome Irish," said the servant, with a quick, toothless smile. "Please, you are to wait. Be comfortable."

Any other time, Cooper might have been angry, but now he was so tired he just let the servant herd him into the tent and seat him. The aide hesitated, then wandered away. The servant backed out of sight, and Cooper, with nothing to look at but the vase of flowers, and nothing to occupy his mind but the mutiny, felt his hands begin to shake. Voices intruded on his thoughts, once, maybe twice, but he couldn't concentrate enough to tell whether they were speaking to him, or only about him. There came a splashing of water, and Napier said, "How are you faring, Colonel?"

Cooper rose automatically at the general's voice and turned slowly. Napier was washing his hands in a basin the servant held for him. As he dried them on a towel, he looked into the tent at Cooper and repeated himself. "How are you faring, Colonel?" Cooper was silent. Napier dropped the towel carelessly into the basin and entered the hut. He walked past Cooper to the table and busied himself rearranging the flowers in the vase. He seemed to have forgotten for the moment that Cooper was there.

"General," began Cooper in an overly high voice. He cleared his throat and began again. "General, I rode all night." It disturbed him to have to talk to Napier's back. "General, I came to tender my resignation."

Still fiddling with the flowers, Napier snapped, "Don't want to hear it, Cooper." He looked up with sudden interest. "Have you eaten?"

"Sir Robert, I rode all night. I couldn't bear to face anyone I knew. Haven't seen a soul in four days."

Firmly, Napier asked, "Have you eaten, Colonel?"

"No, sir."

Napier slapped his palms together and called for the servant. The man appeared in the opening. Napier told him, "We shall have breakfast now. The colonel and I. And close the tent."

The servant released the wall, and Napier and Cooper were shut off from the army.

"General, I rode all—" began Cooper again, but Napier deliberately cut him off: "Colonel Cooper, my congratulations on the situation you've created in the 33rd. I couldn't have done better myself. Honestly."

Cooper was stunned. There was no hint of sarcasm in the general's voice, but Cooper knew that that didn't mean anything: Napier's tone rarely coincided with the meaning of his words. Cooper mumbled, "Sir?"

"Excellent job," Napier continued. "Have a seat. Please." He waved Cooper back into his chair. "I thought I was the only officer in the army who understood the Irish, but you've proven me wrong."

"Sir? I don't follow."

Napier ignored him and looked past his shoulder. "Ah, breakfast."

The Indian manservant and another boy brought in breakfast. There were pots of coffee and of tea, wrapped in cosies. Under metal covers were poached eggs, grilled tomatoes, slabs of ham and bacon. In a wicker basket there were rows of soda bread slices, so neat they should have been marching off to war. A little apart from the rest of the breakfast the servants placed a decanter of brandy and two snifters.

"Eat," said Napier, picking up his fork. Through a mouthful of egg, he repeated, more like an order, "Eat."

It occurred to Cooper that Napier was trying to fatten him for sacrifice. Warily, still mystified, he poured a cup of tea.

Conversationally, Napier said, "You'll be wondering about the breakfast. I'm a bit embarrassed by it, actually. Just a bit. Dinner, too, as you will see, is far superior to what is being endured by everyone else this far into Ethiopia. I gave orders to every unit to reduce its personal baggage before it left Senafe. Seventy-five pounds of baggage for an officer. Two officers to share a tent. Twelve soldiers to a tent. That sort of thing."

"I received the orders," said Cooper. "I reduced."

"Naturally," said Napier. "We all did. I gave instructions for my own baggage to be reduced. I excepted my tent, of course, since it is more office than bedroom. But I ordered the rest of my baggage reduced, and I fully expected to eat as badly as everyone else. I have a clever young fellow for an aide-de-camp, however. Name of Scott. Major Scott. He anticipated my order and sent ahead a party of camels to leave strategic, secret depots along the route. The party passed Phayre and his people by nearly a hundred miles. They stashed away beer and brandy and port, tinned meats, dried fruits and sealed preserves, enough to last my guests and me for months."

"Sir?" Cooper's voice was barely more than a whisper.

Napier seemed not to have heard him. "I couldn't let inventiveness like that go to waste. I feel guilty as hell, but I'll eat well from here to Ashangi."

Cooper's hand shook as he lowered his cup and saucer; tea spilled onto the tablecloth. "Sir, I'm sorry."

Napier dropped a linen napkin onto the spill. Then he looked up quickly, hard, into Cooper's eyes. "You had something on your mind, didn't you?"

"I did, sir," said Cooper. "The Irish, sir."

"Ahh, the Irish," said Napier, pretending he had forgotten. "Yes, the Irish. As I said, Cooper, I'm pleased to learn I'm not the only officer in the army who understands the Irish. It's difficult to go into an unfamiliar regiment and take command, but you went in and read the lay of the land perfectly. You realized that you have to treat the Irish differently from Englishmen and Indians. You have to prepare the Irish if they're going to perform. Excellent idea, yours. Drive them through the night and the day until they couldn't go on any farther. Humiliate them in front of the whole army. Take away their cherished place in the van. Put them in the rear. Convince them that they are about to be left as a garrison. Let them walk along watching other units being left behind, and wondering when they'll get the order to fall out. Bring them right up to Magdala before you tell them they will lead the attack. Then watch how inspired they are, how hard they fight. Cooper, you've handled them like a genius. I'll issue the orders to you this morning."

Napier waited for a response. Cooper pressed his fingers onto the edge of the table so hard his knuckles turned white, but said nothing.

"I know it won't be easy," said Napier. "From now until we reach Magdala, you will have to play the weak commander who has lost control of his regiment. The men have ways of finding out everything their officers know, so it will have to remain a secret between you and me. You will always be wondering what your fellow officers are thinking about you, what your men are whispering. But you will be supported by the knowledge that I know the truth. And . . . there will be rewards aplenty when this expedition is over, for those who have served me well." This last phrase almost had the force of a warning.

"Thank you, sir," mumbled Cooper.

Napier gave his attention to spreading jam onto a slice of soda bread. "Curious, but I've always been especially partial to soda bread," he said. "It is an Irish bread, isn't it?"

"I think so," said Cooper. "Sir, about Captain Speedy? I—"

"Captain Speedy is a pure and utter ass," said Napier. "As soon as I heard he had disobeyed your orders, I called him to me and dressed him down severely." Napier put his hand on Cooper's arm. "But Speedy is too valuable to the expedition for me to ruin him. I have a purpose for him. He doesn't know about it, and I can't tell even you what it is. He'll never see the glory he thinks will be his. He won't be happy with his purpose. But I need him—we all need him—and I can't destroy him. Do you understand?"

"Yes."

"Will you have faith in my judgment?"

"I will, sir." Cooper had the feeling, now, that this general, in his own distracted way, understood things better than anyone else, that he had his entire world under perfect control. Cooper sensed the army to be run through with layers of meaning and purpose so complex that only General Napier could know them all.

Napier understood the trust he had inspired in Cooper. He knew that his distracted air had served him again, distanced him from other men, made him seem invulnerable and all-knowing. He remembered what he had told Speedy, when Speedy had reached headquarters by a round-about route on the same night as the incident before Ada Baga, and had stormed into Napier's tent to demand that Napier remove Cooper from command of the 33rd. *"Captain Speedy, Cooper is a fool, but by complete accident he has made himself too valuable to lose. Without having any idea what he is doing, he gave me the opportunity to turn the 33rd into a magnificent fighting machine. As for Cooper: he will remain in command of the 33rd, but at Magdala he will be miles from the action, and he won't have a chance to interfere."*

"Now, Colonel Cooper," said Napier. "You will stay for dinner, won't you? You can ride back to your regiment tonight."

18

March 1868

Magdala

Dinner was served in the common yard in the center of the four individual huts of the British prisoners. The rising moon was big as a beacon, and the evening was crisp and pleasant. The servants, all looking very efficient in their clean Ethiopian white, waited table in the proper, servile manner Blanc had taught them; still more servants formed a relay between the cooking hut at the far end of the compound and the yard. Tonight, dinner began with vegetable soup and continued with fish fresh from the Bashillo River, a leg of lamb, heavy *tef* bread, butter and preserves, and a pudding. To drink there were *tej* and *arak* and coffee. They ate off a linen tablecloth, patched and stained in a few places, but still quite serviceable, using Italian silver and crystal glasses.

The meal, as always, was eaten in complete, uncomfortable silence. As always, too, there were only three of them at dinner. Cameron would eat in his hut, if he ate at all. These days, Cameron never left his hut under his own power. Sometimes his servants would carry his pallet outside and he would lie in the weak sunlight and stare blankly up at the sky, but he didn't seem to know where he was. If someone tried to talk to him, he didn't hear. Everyone assumed he wouldn't live much longer.

Kerens and Blanc weren't speaking to each other. During the ride from Zagé to Magdala, the British had been three unconnected islands: Cameron alone, Rassam alone, Blanc and Kerens together. But a rift had begun to develop between Blanc and Kerens on the day after they reached their prison. On the afternoon when they crossed the saddle of Islamgie and fell under the awesome shadow of Magdala, with its sheer black cliff and its white stone wall so high above, Kerens had explained to Blanc what he should expect inside the fortress, and how he should react. Kerens spoke loudly, an implicit invitation for Rassam to listen in. Rassam listened carefully and tried to prepare himself. Blanc, stunned by the size and power of his prison, wasn't able to pay attention. Most important of all, Kerens explained, was the chaining. The chains weren't intended as torture or humiliation, but only as the simplest means of keeping prisoners from running away. Kerens stressed this point: that they would get the most benefit out of the ordeal by submitting calmly and pretending the chains were just a trivial nuisance. This would gain the respect and approval of their jailers, who had the power to make life in Magdala a boring, pleasant interlude in their lives, or a daily, living hell.

The party passed through the zigzag gate in the early evening, rode between lines of silently staring Ethiopians, settled into their compound with all their servants and baggage that night, and in the morning after breakfast they were chained.

A single warrior, draped in chains, came into the compound and politely but firmly herded them to a flat stone at one corner of the yard. Kerens went first. He sat on the ground and laid his ankle on the stone. The warrior slid the last link of a length of chain onto a heavy iron ring with a wide gap in it, then slipped it around Kerens's ankle, hefted a mallet, and tapped the ring to close the gap. The ring grated across the stone and twisted against Kerens's flesh. He gasped with the sudden pain, then set his jaw into a hard line and didn't make another sound. It took fifteen or twenty blows of the mallet to close the gap on the ring, and the same number to lock a ring around Kerens's other ankle. When it was done, the warrior gently helped Kerens to his feet. Kerens found a Maria Theresa dollar in a pocket and gave it to the man, exactly as he would have tipped a porter in a London hotel, and hobbled away. Two feet of black chain dragged between his ankles. His socks were spotted with blood. He winced with every step, but as he passed Rassam, who was getting ready to be next, he said, as casually as he could, the first words he had spoken directly to Rassam in a long time, "Think about how you will get your trousers off, Mr. Rassam."

Rassam was terrified, but he made an unconvincing little laugh and said, trying to copy Kerens's casual tone, "With scissors, I imagine." The pounding of the mallet on the iron rings was even more painful than it looked. There is little flesh to pad the anklebone, and with every blow it felt as if the bone was splintering. But Rassam lay on his back with his eyes staring straight up at a thunderhead that roiled through the profiles of all his lost heroes and bore the pain as well as he could. When it was over and the warrior had helped him up, he searched his pockets for a coin and couldn't find one, but Dahon appeared instantly at his elbow and slipped a dollar into his hand.

Cameron was next. His servants led him to the stone and sat him down. He seemed unaware of what was happening, and he never winced or made a sound.

Blanc was last. Since he'd first seen Magdala across the Bashillo River gorge, he'd had a preoccupied, frightened air about him. It was clear from his face that the ankle chains terrified him. What terrors did those fetters hold? Rassam wondered. Submission, humiliation, loss of freedom, pain, and how many other hidden fears? Unsuccessfully, Blanc struggled to keep the emotion off his face. He marched forward as if he were walking on eggs, stopped at the stone, and stared down at it. With the mallet swinging in his hand, the warrior waited for Blanc to sit down, but Blanc didn't move. Kerens, sitting next to Rassam, muttered, "Oh, damn it all, Henry."

The warrior touched Blanc's shoulder to guide him, but he slapped the hand away. Then he raised his solar helmet high above his head, lifted his eyes to the sky, and cried in a loud, wavering voice, "God save the Queen." Then he sat down and dropped his leg onto the stone.

Kerens slapped a fist into a palm, and half to Rassam, half to himself, said, "Bloody fool, he'll spoil it for all of us."

The warrior took far less care with Blanc's ankles than he had with the others. He let Blanc struggle to his feet without help, and gave him a rough push in the back that sent him sprawling onto his face, crying out in pain.

That night Rassam heard the two younger men's voices raised in a bitter argument about the chaining: Kerens accused Blanc of endangering them, and Blanc accused Kerens of swallowing his pride and embarrassing them all. They tried hard to act normally the next day, but they never managed to patch the argument up entirely, and within several weeks another event occurred that split them up forever.

The rebellion in Tigré had become so fierce that there was no hope of money reaching them from the coast. No more open gifts of money came from Theodore, either, and it wasn't long before they had spent all they had. Samuel managed to keep them well supplied with everything they needed, and though they never heard from the emperor and Samuel wouldn't say anything on the subject, it was obvious that Theodore was secretly taking care of them. Samuel, using his mysterious funds, hired more Ethiopian servants, both men and women, until there were so many that some of them were never assigned any work at all. It was a matter of pride to have more servants than they needed, Samuel said.

The ankle chains were extremely painful at first. The iron rings had to be wrapped with rags in the daytime to keep them from rubbing the raw flesh, and at night they were unwrapped to let the circulation flow through. The wounds had to be bathed and dressed often during the day. A manservant took on these chores for Rassam, Blanc, and Cameron, but a girl took them on for Kerens. She was about sixteen years old, petite, with large eyes, long legs and small, pointed breasts. From the very start, it was obvious to Rassam, from the tender way she handled his ankles and the soft looks he gave her, that they had known each other when Kerens was at Magdala before, and that they were straining to hide whatever it was that existed between them. Blanc, of course, was so immersed in his British superiority that he remained oblivious to the possibility of anything happening between a Briton and what he would call "a dusky native."

After two weeks of pretending, Kerens couldn't stand the pretence any longer. The girl moved into his hut. Blanc never said another word to Kerens.

Rassam was surprised that Kerens's Ethiopian lover hadn't shocked him, and in the next few months he came closer to developing a friendly relationship with Kerens. But habits of silence between men are hard to break, and all four Englishmen remained separate and unfriendly.

At the end of the second month, Dahon came to Rassam and asked to be excused from the service of the European captives. He confessed that he had always been the emperor's man, and that Paniotti had assigned him to become Rassam's servant. Now, he said, he felt that they were in good hands with Samuel as their *balderaba*, and he desired to be allowed to return to Paniotti in Massawa. Rassam gave his permission, and Dahon left the next day.

Very little else happened during those first months, until one night when Samuel, after hovering nervously around the outskirts of the dinner table, intercepted Rassam and led him urgently off toward the farthest end of the British compound. Rassam's ankles had healed and callused, the rings caused no more pain, and he moved in a quick little jog-step, to the accompaniment of rattling metal. They went past the servants' huts and down the path through the middle of Rassam's flower garden. At the opposite end of the compound was a vegetable garden, the work of the servants; this garden, full of nothing but flowers and songbirds, was Rassam's alone. During the day, the birds that flocked into the garden could be heard, or so Samuel said, all the way to Islamgie.

The garden butted up to the ten-foot high woven bamboo fence that surrounded the entire compound. Along the whole half mile of fence there was only one door, through which, by imperial decree, any servant might pass freely in either direction, but which was never to be used by any Briton.

Samuel led Rassam through the flower garden until they were within thirty feet of the fence. Then he stopped and waited for Rassam to catch up. He held a lantern in two hands as he was offering its light to Rassam. "Master Rassam," he said, "forgive me for making you walk. I have a reason."

"So you said in the yard," Rassam told him softly. Samuel couldn't be made to fit into any of the neat categories of men that Rassam knew— he wasn't servant or master, friend or companion, inferior or superior —and Rassam had never really been able to grasp who this little Ethiopian was. But, in a curious way, he had become very dear to Rassam, and it disturbed him to hear the pleading in Samuel's voice. "I trust your reason to be good, as I trust you."

"It is good," Samuel said quickly. "A letter. I have been handed a letter, and I didn't know what to do with it."

"What kind of letter?" asked Rassam.

Samuel ignored the question. "I didn't know what to do. To whom I should give it. I walked alone all day, wrestling with myself, weighing my loyalty."

"You have always been loyal," Rassam said, trying to be comforting.

"But I have two loyalties," Samuel complained. "To you, because I am your *balderaba*. To Theodore, because I love him. I walked until I came to a small monastery at the end of Fahla plateau, where my face isn't known. I posed the question to a *debtera* there. I tried to make him understand the gravity of the choice, the complexity of it, without telling him to whom my loyalties are given. He had no sympathy for my dilemma. He told me what I already knew, what I needed to hear him say. 'A *balderaba*'s loyalty is given away to the new master,' he told me. 'It is a sacred trust. You have no loyalty to your old master until your new master returns you to him.'"

Gently, Rassam touched the old man's birdlike shoulder. "I wouldn't hold you to that," he whispered.

Fiercely, Samuel shook off the hand and snapped, "You could never hold me to anything. I hold myself to it." He ripped a letter from inside his shama, shoved it into Rassam's hand, set the lantern on the ground, and stalked away into the darkness. A dark shape against the lights of the huts, he stood with his arms folded and his back to Rassam.

Rassam knelt down and held the letter close against the lantern. It was a single sheet of stiff brown paper, folded into thirds, that had been molded round someone's calf. It had been sealed with the silver seal of the Bombay army, though the seal had been torn apart.

He opened it and read:

> To Theodore, King of Ethiopia.
> I am commanded by Her Majesty the Queen of England to demand that the prisoners whom Your Majesty has wrongly detained in captivity shall be immediately released and sent in safety to the British Camp.
> Should Your Majesty fail to comply with this command, I am further commanded to enter Your Majesty's country at the head of an army to enforce it, and nothing will arrest my progress until this object shall have been accomplished.
> My Sovereign has no desire to deprive you of any part of your dominions, nor to subvert your authority, although it is obvious that such would in all probability be the result of hostilities.
> Your Majesty might avert this danger by immediate surrender of the prisoners. But should they not be delivered safely into my hands, should they suffer a continuance of ill-treatment, or should any injury befall them,

Your Majesty will be held personally responsible, and no hope of further condonation need be entertained.

R. Napier, General, Commander-in-Chief, Bombay Army

After he had read the letter, Rassam carried the lantern toward Samuel and stopped behind him. Softly, he asked, "How did this letter come to you?"

Samuel did not turn. He answered mechanically, "Your general hired an Ethiopian boy to take it to His Majesty. The boy took the general's money in good faith and honestly intended to deliver it, but as he made his way through Tigré he heard stories about Theodore, how Theodore had gone insane, how Theodore had killed messengers who brought him unwelcome news. To see whether the letter contained such news, the boy broke the seal, but the letter is in Arabic and the boy couldn't read it. He understood that Theodore would come to Magdala, so he decided to bring it here to give it to me or some other of the emperor's people. He gave it to me, and then fled."

"Have you read it?" asked Rassam.

"I can't read Arabic."

"Who knows about it?"

"The boy, who has fled. Myself. You."

Rassam tried to picture how Theodore would react to the letter. Sending it to him if he were in the wrong mood might ensure the death of all of them. Keeping it might do the same. "What is the emperor doing?" asked Rassam. He tried to make Samuel see by his tone of voice how vital an honest answer was.

Samuel turned to face Rassam. He spoke very slowly, as if it were an effort to drag the traitorous words out. "I haven't heard a single word from him since we came here. He sends money for your needs, but he sends no messages. Neither does he send words to anyone else in Magdala. We only wait to learn his pleasure.

"I have heard from Wolde. He says the emperor prays too much, talks too little. The camp has been at Debra Tabor for two months. The countryside cannot support them for so long. The fields are bare, the peasants are leaving, the camp nears the verge of hunger. He makes no decision, but only sits and waits and prays. There are those of his people who truly wonder whether he hasn't lost his mind.

"As for me, I worry for him. As ever."

Rassam said, "This is a strong letter." He gripped it tightly in his fingertips and wavered around a decision. Along with the fear, he must consider his obligation to the emperor. That obligation, he knew, demanded that he pass the letter on to the emperor. He made a sudden choice. "It is a very strong letter," he said again. He tossed the lantern down on the path. The chimney shattered on the hard-packed earth, and oil flowed out in a serpent of white flame. He dragged himself close to the fire and tried to place the letter in it. The stiff paper fluttered up and away like a wounded butterfly, singed but unburnt. He reached up and caught it in midair. He yanked up a stake that was supporting a dark, flowering vine, pulling flowers, vine, and leaves with it. He used the stake to hold the letter firmly in the flame until it had been consumed.

At the exact moment Rassam was burning Napier's ultimatum to Theodore, an Ethiopian courier, plunging through the darkness into the Bashillo River gorge, felt his horse lurch under him and cartwheel downward into blackness. The courier wriggled free and leaped away. He curled into a ball as he fell, hit the slope in a roll and came to a stop, more gently than he had any right to expect, in thick bushes. Before he even moved, he felt for the pouch he'd carried from Debra Tabor. It was there, still on the strap around his neck. He climbed out of the bushes, checked his arms and legs, found them intact and strong. He took a step. Something was wrong with his left foot: no pain, but somehow its fit with the earth wasn't as tight as it had always been. He hopped on the right foot and wrapped his fingers around the toes of his left foot. Four small toes with jagged nails, and an empty space where the big toe had been. "By the breath of Iyesus," he swore, then quickly touched the blue *mateb* around his neck and mouthed a formula apology for swearing. The loss of a big toe wasn't uncommon, not with the big toes sitting snug in iron stirrup rings. The loss might bother him later, but he had been aiming so urgently for Magdala that for now it only meant a slowing of his pace. Without the toe, the whole left side of his world seemed to tilt. He hobbled down to his horse. It was lying on its side, snuffling softly, heaving. He spat and swore again. It was the third or fourth horse he had killed on the journey. He would remember how many later, after the journey was over and he had time to sleep.

There was a campfire through the brush ahead, and men from that direction were appearing around him. They began to ask questions, but he held a ringed finger to them. "The emperor's lion signet," he hissed. "By the Cross, I need a horse." They started toward the campfire. He stumbled. Someone took his arm to help him, but he struck it away. "A horse!"

He rode awkwardly with one foot loose of the stirrup until he learned to wedge the foot under the saddle strap. The sideways pressure against his leg sent spears of pain shooting through his hip and knee. He steadied his vision on the lights at the Bashillo ford, and after he'd plunged across the river he watched the glow from the Affijo plateau. Unaware of how fast he'd done the trip, unaware that he was far ahead of the murderous, impossible timetable the emperor had set for him, he drove the weakening animal through the night up Plowden's road and across Affijo. Admiring warriors on the Aroge plateau saw the dying horse and the injury and exhaustion written clearly on the courier's face. They understood the signs, and they seated him well on the best horse they had and watched him gallop upward alone, draped low on the mane, wobbling dangerously.

The sun rose as he crossed Islamgie saddle and approached Magdala. The country below was still wrapped in shadow, and Islamgie itself was somber gray, but the sun's rays lit Magdala into a white tower far ahead, and touched the mane so closely that it turned the coarse sweat-beaded hairs into dew-dropped spider silk.

The gallop eased by itself into a walk before they reached the end of Islamgie, and though the courier pounded on the horse and begged and prayed, the animal couldn't even attempt the steep path upward to Bell's fortress. The courier started up on foot. After fifty paces his left knee gave out, and no matter how he ordered it it wouldn't straighten again. Unable to move, he lay on the trail. Silently, he cursed his body for failing him, and he cursed the horse, and even as he cursed the horse he saw it totter on its widely splayed legs, sag down onto the ground, and close its eyes in death.

He had earlier passed the camp of a caravan headed away from Magdala. The caravan guards had cheered him as he raced by. They had seen him fall. Within minutes, they were with him, helping him into the saddle of a fresh horse, slapping the horse's rump to send it onward.

He turned and waved, and the caravan guards sent him off with Alexander the Great's battle cry, *"Alalalalalai!"*

"A message for the prisoners," he croaked from horseback to the sentries at the zigzag gate. "For the *feringi.*" The sentries hesitated. He held up his hand to show the lion signet, and then he slipped off the horse and landed flat on his back on the ground. The sentries threw water into his face to revive him. He couldn't walk, even with assistance, so they picked him up and carried him through the city to the British compound and through the plaited door in the fence. They laid him on the ground in front of Rassam's hut.

Samuel roused Rassam from sleep, and Rassam came out dazed into the bright morning.

Struggling to remain conscious, the courier removed the pouch from around his neck and held it out to Rassam.

"What is it?" Rassam asked in a sleepy voice.

Samuel talked in Amharic with the courier. Then, to Rassam: "The pouch is for you, from His Majesty. It is the first communication of the emperor with Magdala for a very long time. The emperor was very urgent to have this message here as quickly as possible. He allowed the courier six days to make it here. He thinks he made it in four or five, but he's so tired he can't remember. If he made it in four, that will be a feat worthy of minstrels' songs. He killed horses to get here."

"He killed horses?" whispered Rassam, awestruck. "The message is so important?"

"Apparently."

Rassam looked at the unadorned leather pouch in his hands. Killing horses to bring it to him was so incredible that he didn't even wonder what was in it. "What should I do?" he asked Samuel.

"Do? You should open the pouch, I suppose."

"With the courier," corrected Rassam, feeling as if he had been awakened into an unfamiliar world. "Should I reward him with money?" A tip seemed too feeble a reward for what the man had done, but Rassam didn't know how else he could react.

"The emperor will reward him," said Samuel, sounding like his old, efficient, perceptive self again. "But I will give him your thanks."

Samuel turned to speak to the man, but he had already slipped into unconsciousness. One of the sentries felt the pulse at his neck and listened to his breathing, then said a few words to Samuel.

"He will be well after he sleeps," Samuel said. "But now, read the contents."

Rassam took the pouch into his hut to escape the prying eyes of the sentries and the servants.

My cherished Rassam,

It is long since I have spoken to you. I have not written to you the contents of my heart, as it has been essential to great purposes that you seem to the world's eyes to be a perfect prisoner. Believe, Rassam, as Iyesus stands as my witness, that you have ever been close to my heart. It has grieved me to leave you without assurances of my esteem and friendship. I have not even communicated with Samuel, though on his own initiative he has written to inform me that you are well and unharmed. He tells me that you have created a garden filled with flowers and sweet birds. I long to see this wonder.

You know that an invincible English army has landed at Zula on the Red Sea. This army is now marching southward. They expect to meet me at Magdala, there to kill me and to set you free. There are few people who truly know the meaning of this army, to me and to Ethiopia. You know, Paniotti knows, and I.

I receive constant reports on this army. Your General Napier has fulfilled all the signs but one. When he has fulfilled this last, he will be the Light Bringer. I am prepared. I am willing. And Rassam (and this is a thing only you may know), I am terrified.

Unhappy, also. I understood it was the custom in Europe, as in all civilized lands, to send a formal challenge to one's enemy. Does an English general not have enough respect for his opponent, though the opponent be ignorant and barely civilized, to communicate with him? Am I not worthy of such communication? Does he think I am too ignorant to understand his words? I had hoped to be granted the opportunity, in these awful days, at least to write letters to the Light Bringer, and to receive his answers. He will kill me. To this I am reconciled. But I had hoped to have a little knowledge of the man who will kill me. Is that too much to ask?

I have much fear in my breast, but I have lived with fear for all the years of my life. I hate it, but it is known to me, and I can live with it. It is not the fear that tortures these, my last nights of life on earth: it is the failure of your general to communicate with me.

But I should not try to lay upon your shoulders the burdens God has placed on me. I have this day given orders that all the thousands of people of my camp are to disperse and return to their natural homes. I retain only an elite guard of ten thousand troops, who will accompany me to Magdala and die with me there. They think they go to crush the invading English, but you and I know better. I will not steal away their futile dreams of glory.

The messenger who brings this letter to you should reach you before the word of my actions has reached Magdala through any other source. It is a keen desire of mine that you, of all the people of Magdala, should be the first to know I am coming to you. By this letter, I hope you will know how much I care for you, and how it has grieved me to do evil to you. It is now, by European reckoning, the seventh of March, in the year 1868. You will have this letter by the 13th of March, sooner or later depending on the speed of the courier and the will of God. I will be at Magdala by the 27th. Your English army will be at Magdala by Easter, which falls this year on the 12th of April. I shall die near Easter. It is a fitting time to die.

With this communication, I send on the hand of my courier the emperor's lion signet. By this sign Samuel and other of my people have long known that I order you and your companions to be released from your chains. The signet will be seen by my people, and as a sign of my good will you will be unshackled.

As I have perfect faith in you, before God, my dear Rassam, I wish that you should have perfect faith in me. Of all the people in the world, only you and Paniotti understand me. Only you and Paniotti would never betray me, would never do a thing that would cause me injury or grief. I pray that you, alone of all men, should have no bitterness to me, and should remember me kindly. I once told you, in a moment of terror and doubt: "One day I think you will see me dead, and while you stand over my corpse it may be that you will curse me. You may say, *'This is a wicked man who shouldn't be buried. Let his remains rot above the ground.'* " I said on that day that I trusted your generosity. I pray again that you will be generous to me, alive and dead, and never betray me.

As Rassam sat in his hut, crushing the letter in his hands, Samuel brought the lion signet to him and slipped it onto his finger.

It was not true that Theodore had killed messengers who brought him unwelcome news, but rumors were spilling through the country as fast as the mountains and valleys would allow, flowing past each other in the night, sometimes touching and uniting and giving birth to the seeds of new, fantastic legends. No one knew what to believe. This particular rumor had sent most of Theodore's spies in Tigré into hiding and cut his information about the invading British army to an uncertain trickle. All he knew for certain was that the British army was still a hundred miles or so to the north, heading southward on the salt caravan route along Ethiopia's spine. Theodore didn't need any more information to know he would meet Napier at Magdala at Eastertide.

Time was a dream, now, just lingering impressions of life in the mind of a corpse that wasn't yet quite cold. He knew this part of the country, yet it wasn't familiar to him anymore. The British, across their hundred miles of mountains, weren't quite real, either. Nor was one-armed Wolde, riding so close that their two horses' jostling was a constant motion. Nor were the ten thousand men at his back. The army swaggered with some of its old blood lust. Their braids were buttered and knotted with military precision, the weapons were polished, the tack was freshly oiled. The soldiers played their chanting games as they rode. A strange funeral procession, Theodore thought. The fear and the anger were smothered for the moment under a blanket of numbness.

He relived his past in the days of that journey. For some reason that he didn't care to define, it was vital that he crystallize his life, so there would be completion when he died. That was part of a meaningful death: to have a clear image of all the threads of accident and purpose that led to the ultimate meaning. He spent two days of the trip recalling the burning of his village below the Kwara cliff. The most insistent memory was the funeral pyre over the sacred inner sanctum of the church, in which he had immolated the remains of his *debtera*, his priest, and his classmates.

He remembered all his hopes and the ruin into which they had crumbled. It was all a dream, but it made perfect sense.

Magdala, when it rose from the plateau, was a real place. Alone of all the places he'd seen, it bore the imprint of himself. The stone walls, towering high and white above the cliffs, might fall, but the ghosts of the walls would stand forever. And inside Magdala, high above the jingling, chanting procession, was Rassam—the only real man, the only man who truly understood Theodore as a human being. To everyone else, Theodore was more than a man: he was a demon or a god. In these last months, Theodore had finally come to know how that made him less than a man. Only to Rassam, he thought, was he just a man. Rassam was his humanity.

Theodore had ordered no celebration at his arrival, but orders couldn't keep the Magdalans from gathering outside the zigzag gate and on the saddle below to see him and his army. The chanting stopped as the army waited expectantly to hear the crowds. As they walked their horses slowly across the saddle, Theodore experienced an unfamiliar sense of smallness. Islamgie lay all around and swallowed him up inside its naked flatness. Magdala hovered so tall it could easily crush him. Silently, the crowds hung back from him, shuffled nervously.

The people outside the zigzag gate gave a few shouts as he neared them, but the cheers were weak and forced, and when he came close enough to be seen clearly the crowd was silent and simply stared, as if they no longer recognized him.

He slipped quickly down to the ground, and, with Gabry and Wolde close behind, passed through the zigzag gate and walked through the city. Gabry walked directly behind him, almost treading on his heels. The people knew Gabry as Theodore's finest warrior, his cleverest general, chosen by God to be one of the Twelve, to be Theodore's strong right arm, to wield his sword on behalf of Theodore and God. And off to one side of Theodore, half a step behind, skipping every few steps to match his short strides to Theodore's long ones, walked Wolde, Theodore's priest and conscience. There were dozens of legends built around Wolde already, most of them revolving around the burning of the monastic village, many new ones now about the reasons for Theodore breaking his arm so badly that the *feringi* doctor had had to cut it off. He watched Theodore so eagerly that he looked to the crowd like a loyal puppy trotting along at the side of its master. These two, the warrior and the priest, the people understood; but they would never understand Theodore. The crowd inside Magdala stood aside as he and his companions walked through the city.

Theodore remembered how the crowds had cheered Iyesus during His life, then had watched silently at Calvary. The comparison would have shamed him in the past. Now, it seemed natural. He didn't know whether he had been hiding from the comparison all these years, or whether he had been seeking it.

These people all around him were just dream people. A few children came forward, ever so slowly, to touch his *shama* or his feet, the same feet Gabry and Wolde had kissed so many years before at the start of this whole journey. He had always loved children, but now he couldn't quite focus on them. Iyesus had looked inward at the end. He had had His moments of doubt, of wanting it all not to be. Theodore had the right, too.

In the last year or so more and more of the people had understood the peculiar connection between their emperor and their savior, but there was confusion in their minds about it. They knew that Theodore intended to save them, but they didn't know from what. The British, to them, were not a special threat. They were only another army to enjoy fighting, to enjoy destroying.

He wouldn't save them from the *Zemene Mesafint*, certainly. They lived for the constant warfare.

He wouldn't save them from religious mistakes. After all, weren't the Ethiopian Copts already the true believers, the chosen of God?

At the compound of the British prisoners Theodore ducked his head and swept past the guards through the low door. Wolde and Gabry slipped through after him.

Servants scattered as Theodore walked rapidly through them. Blanc, at the entrance to his hut, stood up automatically as Theodore appeared. Someone shouted for Samuel. The *balderaba* came running. He threw himself on the ground and pressed his lips to the emperor's foot.

"Where is Rassam?" asked Theodore.

"Beyond," Samuel pointed. "Tending to his garden."

Theodore waved his hand, and Samuel hurried to lead the way.

Left behind, Blanc eased back down into his chair and unconsciously rubbed his ankles, which had been itching miserably ever since the chains had been removed, two weeks before.

Samuel took Theodore past the cooking hut to the edge of the garden. The fragrance of the flowers and the racket of the birds surrounded them like a smothering blanket. Samuel backed away and let Theodore go on alone. Gabry started to follow, but Wolde put a restraining hand on his arm and held him back. Since the loss of his arm, Wolde had been so fiercely protective of Theodore that even Gabry let the little eunuch priest have his way.

Near the woven bamboo fence, a white turban bobbed between two bushes laden with pale yellow roses. Theodore walked toward it and stopped in the path a few paces away. It was Rassam, on his hands and knees, prying out weeds with a sharpened stick. He was wearing a *shama* and white trousers. His feet were bare. There was even a *mateb* around his neck. Black dust had filled the creases of his face, and laid a black spider web across his cheeks; his flinty Arab eyes had almost a Hindi cast. Theodore called Rassam's name softly. Rassam glanced up, knelt a few seconds more with no expression on his face, rose, remembered the digging stick, bent over and stuck it into the ground, and straightened again. "No one told me you had arrived," he said. There was no surprise in his voice, no question, no meaning.

"Rassam," whispered the emperor. Rassam stepped forward silently and hugged the emperor. It was a defeated, despairing kind of hug. It asked for mercy, but expected none.

The emperor squeezed Rassam back, and then Rassam stepped away. They studied each other. Rassam saw changes in Theodore, changes more vital than the frosting of white where unbraided hair hung loose at his temples. His cheeks had collapsed into his face and left his eyes alone to dominate, two wells in a subterranean lake of cold fire. There was nothing of the world left in them: they were a mystic's eyes. Seeing them, Rassam knew that Theodore was beyond reaching.

"Do you still forgive what has happened to you?" asked Theodore, without inflection.

Rassam understood the phrasing. Events had passed out of Theodore's control. Rassam noticed that Theodore's bare feet were pressed onto the seared, crusty serpent of earth in the path where Rassam had burned Napier's letter in the burning oil of Samuel's lantern. "I do," said Rassam. "I still forgive. I remain constant."

"I came all this way to hear that," said Theodore. "At least there exists one man in the world who understands what life has done to me. One man who knows me as a man, who will remember me as I was, as I could have been. One man who will never betray me."

Rassam nodded. This was the only hero who hadn't betrayed his faith, but Rassam had already betrayed him, and would surely do so again. The man needed Rassam: that was clear. He needed the lie that Rassam gave him. Rassam loved the emperor, and he hated himself for the lie, but he was so deeply submerged in it that there was no way to get out. "I won't betray you," he said at last.

"Alive and dead?"

"Alive and dead."

"Easter is drawing near," said Theodore. "Easter brings your liberators . . . and my Light Bringer." After a pause, he said slowly, "You must miss your home. Where will you go?"

"Aden," said Rassam, only because he had no other answer to offer.

"Do you have family there?"

"Friends," said Rassam. "A few friends."

"It is four years since you have been in Aden," said Theodore. He blinked. "All my invincible Twelve are here . . . the ones my people call my disciples. It is truly a miracle of God that all are still alive, after so many battles, after so many years. There have been saber cuts, broken fingers, small injuries, but all are still alive and whole. All but one, my Wolde." He said this without emotion, without guilt. "The only one of the Twelve who has ever been hurt was hurt by me. Ah, well, what man can thwart the will of God?" He paused a second, as if reflecting on some private joke. "We will only wait for liberation, you and I." He hugged Rassam without feeling.

As the emperor went down the path, Rassam nearly called after him to tell him how he had burned Napier's letter. He wanted to tell the emperor that the British would leave if only he sent the prisoners down to them. He wanted to protest this useless death. He watched until Theodore and his companions were out of sight.

Rassam bowed his turbaned head and prayed, to himself, not to God, that he might have the chance to save the emperor, or at least some part of him. That if he couldn't stop the death, he could at least give the death some meaning. That he might do something for this hero, something that might lift Rassam himself out of defeat. He prayed that if there was an opportunity, he would have the courage to use it.

19

March 1868

Lake Ashangi

The British army made its final pause at Lake Ashangi, one hundred miles short of Magdala. The entire army was to gather there, and by the time it resumed its southward march, it would have been trimmed down to just the five thousand troops who would make the actual assault. There would be no more servants, except for Napier's; there would be no inessential equipment. South of Ashangi, soldiers would sleep in the open, and officers would sleep twelve to a tent.

This gathering at Ashangi was to be the occasion of an event of some importance. A month before, in early February, Napier had received a curious letter.

> In the name of the Father, the Son, and the Holy Ghost.
>
> This letter is sent from Ibrahim, head of the Chiefs of Ethiopia, to reach the Chief of the *feringi* warriors.
>
> How are you?
>
> Very well?
>
> By Christ's grace I have recovered the throne of my ancestors, of Mikael, of Welda Selasse, of Sabagadis, from the pretender Theodore, who calls himself falsely the Lion of Judah. I have recovered the throne of my ancestors, and so now I hold the rule of Lasta and Wajerat, and I am become the greatest of the Chiefs of Ethiopia. The Coptic Church of the Ethiopians, too, has recognized my power.
>
> Of old I am house friends with the *feringi* who have come to this country, with Plowden, Bell, Cameron, and Rassam. I expected to receive a letter from you; but as it has been retarded, I have sent a letter. I know not what you have come for; if I knew, it would certainly please me. I consider you to be my house friend.
>
> I am sending this letter by Muroja, the son of Atu Waiku, who knows my

language and yours. I am sending the contents of my heart to you, and you too should send me your heart. In the year 1868 from Christ in the time of John the Evangelist, in the month of Hadar the 18th, written Wednesday.

Muroja had appeared alone out of the hills and approached a surveying party of Pioneers. The boy was eighteen or twenty years old, tall and skeletal, with smallpox pits on his cheeks and ringworm scars all down his arms and an Adam's apple like a sharp stone knife. He wore a *debtera*'s turban and carried an iron crucifix. He halted his horse a few yards from the surveyors and stared at the ground. The English subaltern who was commanding the party tried to talk to him. Muroja's eyes flashed up, then down, full of terror. He began to babble in Amharic. When the officer tried to speak to him in English, Muroja thrust out the letter, which was in Arabic. The officer had no Arabic, so he sent Muroja to Phayre, who sent him, under guard, to Napier. At headquarters, thirty miles to the north, Speedy tried to question Muroja in Amharic and Merewether tried in Arabic. The boy spoke a bare smattering of Arabic, and it immediately became clear that when Ibrahim wrote that Muroja spoke the language of the invaders, it was because he wasn't aware that there were more languages in the world than Arabic and Amharic.

No one in Phayre's intelligence branch nor in Napier's headquarters wing had ever heard of Ibrahim. The latest information had been that the provinces of Lasta and Wajerat were in turmoil: all the tribes were in rebellion against Theodore, but in the absence of any immediate threat from the emperor they were fighting among themselves for mastery of the region.

Muroja was too terrified to offer much information, and what he gave had the air of being memorized speeches, but from him Speedy and Merewether got the impression that Ibrahim was a chieftain who had recently put down his opposition in that area, and who was preparing, with the blessing of the church, to make war on the Asubo Gallas to the east of Lake Ashangi.

Napier wrote a letter to Ibrahim, congratulating him on his newfound power and inviting him to meet the invading army at Ashangi in a month's time. Muroja rode to the advance guard with an escort of lances, and then set off on his own on a cavalry charger, a gift from Napier, to deliver the letter to his master.

Day by day, the British army crept southward over a range of ten-thousand-foot mountain passes, where rain swept down in solid sheets in the hours of daylight, and where the temperatures dipped so far below freezing at night that the rain froze the instant it hit the ground and formed a free-flowing covering of ice through the entire mountain range. Soldiers broke ankles on the paths at night, and mules slipped over precipices to their deaths.

After the mountain passes, Ashangi was such a relief that many of the units broke into a run down the last steep decline. One continuous wall of thunderheads stood all around, but the sky over low-lying Ashangi was purest blue. The lake was perfectly round, still, and black, set like an onyx in a setting turned bright green with age.

Major Scott, one of Napier's aides-de-camp, had ridden ahead to be at Phayre's side when Phayre began setting up the Ashangi camp. Phayre outranked Scott, and Scott came with no openly revealed orders at all, except to be present in Ashangi before the camp was laid out. But Phayre was clever enough to read the hidden orders, and had so little investment in the trivialities of his own responsibilities that he let Scott plan the camp. By the time the rearguard, the Irish Wellington's Own, marched out of a raging storm into the tranquillity of Ashangi bowl, the army had been distributed carefully into an orderly camp, nestled gently against the hills surrounding the bowl to make a great crescent around half the lake. There were seven thousand soldiers and officers, two thousand servants, five hundred *routies,* headquarters tents and storage tents, neat strings of mules and horses, pens for camels and elephants. Unlike those units that ran eagerly into the bowl, the 33rd Foot trooped sullenly between lake and camp toward their assigned place at the farthest left wing of the crescent. They still felt their place in the rear keenly. By now there wasn't an Irishman in the regiment who wouldn't have traded that moment of glory before Ada Baga for a chance at the vanguard. They had been alone in their disgrace for all the hundred and three miles since Ada Baga, rarely encountering any other units except those who were being left behind to garrison remote outposts, expecting at any moment to be left behind themselves. Now, walking in front of the rest of the army, wet when everyone else had been sitting dry and comfortable in Ashangi for days, they were bitterly aware that they were forced to parade their disgrace. The other units had made them into rebellious heroes, and called out to them now as they passed; but the Irishmen averted their eyes and marched doggedly ahead through the marshy ground.

The 33rd's tents and other equipment were still miles behind and might well not reach them before the next morning. They hung their backpacks and Snyder rifles and sopping greatcoats on tree limbs to keep them out of the wet, and then found bits of dry ground on which to sit and smoke and watch their servants preparing a noontime meal.

To the right of the 33rd was a division of Punjab Pioneers, all in their blousy white cotton shirts and their tight claret-brown turbans, all perfectly clean, with their tents in ruler-straight rows and the grass between cut into a smooth lawn.

Beyond the Pioneers were the naval rocketeers.

As the 33rd marched past, Geoffrey Irion had searched their faces, the only clean-shaven European faces left in the entire army, but he hadn't spied Pilbeam. After his lunch of stew, Bengali *chupatis,* and rum, Irion wandered away from his regiment. He didn't find Pilbeam immediately, so he stopped at a group of half a dozen sailors, snoozing and idly smoking, and asked after him.

One of them screwed open an eye and recognized Irion. "You're his friend. The one he split away to see, that day after you Paddies retired from the military. Got to tell you, we all thought that was splendid. It was all anyone talked about for days . . . that and the fookin' ice storms. How'd you fare through the passes?"

"Why'd you ever start up again?" asked another.

Irion said simply, warning them not to pursue the question, "It's a long walk home. Isn't it?" Then, when the sailors didn't ask again: "Pilbeam? Is he around?"

A young sailor, with skin so sun-blackened and hair so frizzed that from the neck up he might have been a one-braided Ethiopian warrior, had been working hard at whittling holes in a length of bamboo. He put the flute to his lips, blew a piercing note, and set the note quavering like an Indian pipe. He cut the note off suddenly and looked up under his lazy eyelids to be sure everyone was paying attention to him. Around the bamboo he said softly, "Bastard Pilbeam. God rot him." He pushed himself up and walked away, tootling softly.

With a trace of apology, the first sailor said, "You may have guessed Pilbeam isn't the most popular man among us. He likes to be alone, even in a crowd. He's always busy in his brain, but he won't tell the rest of us what it is that busies him. Some, like that young fellah, just take it more personal than others. I'll tell you something: it stunned hell out of us to see he had a singlemost friend in all the world."

"We've been here at Ashangi for a week now," said the second. "He's been down fishing every minute of every day. Bought himself a boat from a native, and he just floats in the lake, alone with his boat and his fish and himself."

Irion walked through the marshy ground at the lake front, past the Pioneers and his own 33rd, toward a swamp of tangled, high-rooted mangroves that blurred the border of the lake for half a mile. Pilbeam's boat was made of reeds, and after a week of use only the tip of the bow and the stern still cleared the water. The surface was black and smooth, as if blanketed with oil. Individual blades of saw grass penetrated the surface. Pilbeam propelled his boat by shoving off the bottom with a pole. It moved so sluggishly and the water was so heavy that it hardly rippled the surface. The blades of grass bowed under the boat, then reappeared behind. Irion watched from a distance. Pilbeam seemed to be steering a repetitive course from a point fifty yards around the swamp to a point fifty yards along the shore, always five or six yards out, never venturing into water deeper than his waist, back and forth between his two invisible points. He stared so intently into the water that he didn't notice Irion. Irion couldn't see a net or a pole or any other sign that Pilbeam was actually fishing, though he was certainly searching for something.

From where he stood Irion could see that Pilbeam wasn't alone at this end of the lake. Seven scarlet-tuniced, solar-helmeted officers were prowling around the shoreward side of the mangrove swamp, out of Pilbeam's sight. Among them appeared a fleeting, milky glimmer of smoke, and an instant later Irion heard the brittle crack of a pistol shot. The officers milled around without purpose. The shot had missed.

Irion waded through the marshy grass until he came abreast of Pilbeam. He called out, and Pilbeam looked up as if he had been expecting Irion. They eyed each other warily, remembering how they had parted the last time, before Ada Baga.

"Come here," said Irion at last. "We can't talk like this, yoong f'lah."

Pilbeam waited another few seconds, trying to make some point, before he shoved at the pole and brought the bow of the boat around toward the shore. It ran aground six feet short of the grass, and Pilbeam slid off the submerged boat and waded ashore. Pilbeam stopped three paces short of Irion. The sailor looked like some kind of swamp monster: he was dressed in khaki, plastered wet to his armpits, glued with bits of grass and mud from the lake. His queue was soaked through, tar dripping in a macadam roadway down his chest.

He looked distantly at Irion. In the last month, Irion had trimmed his black beard into muttonchops in imitation of Napier's, just as most of the Irishmen had done, and he had let his shaved head grow into a coarse stubble. Irion put out his hand. Pilbeam squeezed it, gave it a slight shake, but neither said anything.

Off behind the mangrove, another pistol shot fired. There were shouts, the sound of men crashing through foliage, then silence.

"Fools," said Pilbeam. "Officers. They've all got some idea about seeing who can kill the biggest game with a pistol. There's plenty of game around the lake, up in the hills. Enough wildlife for every one of them to get his share of blood."

"Any decent fish in the lake?" asked Irion.

"I've seen a lot," said Pilbeam. "Big ones, from the looks of them. But I'm not fishing. I'll take a crocodile."

Irion laughed. "I should have known old Arthur Pilbeam, my magical, angry lad, wouldn't settle for mere fish. What are you planning? Barehanded wrestling? Capture it alive and carry it to Magdala in your backpack, and slip it into your envoy's soup?"

Pilbeam didn't hear Irion's laughter. "I've got it all planned," he said seriously. "I bought the boat from one of the Ethiopians who were here before the army arrived. I paid a whole dollar for it, almost a month's wages. But I figure it'll be worth the cost. If it doesn't sink before I get my croc, of course."

"Naturally," said Irion.

"I've got a wire noose in the boat. I bought the wire from one of the Punjabis, over in the engineering branch."

"But why?"

"I just want one," said Pilbeam, suddenly irritated at the question, sensing that Irion didn't share his enthusiasm.

Another shot rang out from the mangroves, much closer than before.

"Because of them?" asked Irion.

"I just want one," said Pilbeam, pouting like a young boy. He brightened suddenly. "Here, I'll show you my noose." He splashed to the boat and returned with a six-foot length of heavy wire, probably stolen by Pilbeam's Punjabi engineer from the telegraph supplies. It had a noose at one end and a wooden handle at the other. Pilbeam demonstrated how he would drop the noose around the crocodile's snout and yank it tight.

"Then what'll you do, lad?" asked Irion, who was beginning to enjoy Pilbeam's excitement.

"I'll hold the handle with one hand," said Pilbeam, miming his action. "I'll slip my other arm under his belly, and I'll lift him up clear of the ground. With his snout shut and his feet off the ground, he'll be helpless. Some of them are fearsome large monsters, but I calculate I'm big enough to do it. They couldn't weigh more than a couple hundred pounds. Could they?"

"I wouldn't know," said Irion.

"I've seen a few since we got here, but I haven't gotten close enough to catch one. I saw one that must have been twice as long as I am tall."

A dozen quick shots cracked very close by, inside the mangroves. Twigs broke as the bullets ripped through the branches.

"What's the biggest they've got?" asked Irion.

"A monkey, this big." Pilbeam showed with his hand that the monkey had stood three feet tall.

Irion said, "Nothing on the order of a crocodile, then?"

"No. Nothing near," said Pilbeam, not realizing what Irion was hinting. "Look, there's a bunch of them, blazing away with their pistols at the swamp, walking around the outside so they won't get their uniforms wet. The one in the lead, the one they all cluster around like planets around a sun: that's Lieutenant-Colonel Phayre, and those are his pet officers. How men can beg for favor before someone else, and then expect to get any respect from the soldiers, I don't know. That Phayre, he's the quartermaster, in command of the advance guard. He's the one who told your Colonel Cooper it was seven miles from Adigrat to Mai Wahez, and seven more miles from Mai Wahez to Ada Baga. Look what he's shot. It's probably put him ahead in the contest." A lieutenant was holding a swan, absolutely white except for a black beak and a few droplets of pink blood on its wings. "And there," Pilbeam shouted suddenly, pointing toward the mangroves, "is my crocodile. Come on, Geoffrey." With his wire noose slapping against his legs, he sprinted toward the swamp.

Irion tagged along a few yards behind. His boots sank into the mud and slipped through the wet grass. Ahead of him, Pilbeam's head bobbed as he ran jerkily across the uneven ground.

Irion couldn't see the crocodile. He didn't particularly want to.

"There he is," said Pilbeam, admiringly. "My crocodile."

Irion stepped to one side and looked. The crocodile was an eight-footer. It had moved twice its own body length beyond the mangroves. Here on the solid ground, down low in the moisture-laden grass, it was an element of the deep earth, of rock and shale and soil and fearsome nightmare pressures. Still as a boulder buried in the earth, its stony eyes stared without blinking, without caring, at the peculiar air-creature Arthur Pilbeam. Twenty feet of undulating grass lay between the crocodile's blunt snout and Irion's boot tip. He wasn't familiar with crocs, didn't know anything about them, but the thing terrified him down to the depths of his dormant religiosity: it couldn't possibly have any speed, but its solidity, its rootedness in the earth, tied it to the old pagan gods of his cold North, made it a being of earthquakes and volcanoes.

"Go behind it and keep it from getting away," said Pilbeam, as still as the crocodile, hissing carefully through clenched teeth.

"Getting away?" asked Irion.

"Go between it and the swamp."

As he sneaked through a wide circle, Irion curiously watched himself playing his assigned role in Pilbeam's farce. The crocodile, too, played its part and didn't move. Irion lined himself up halfway between the crocodile's tail and the verge of the swamp. He wouldn't let his attention flicker, but by a hint of scarlet fog in the corner of his eye he knew the encroaching band of hunters had arrived.

Pilbeam dangled the wire delicately and slid forward. His toes stopped four feet from the snout. The noose hung two feet away, one foot up.

The voices of the officers penetrated Irion's attentive haze, though Pilbeam didn't hear. A middle-aged officer's voice: "My crocodile. I'll beat that damned monkey." Another officer's voice: "Think a pistol shot'll pierce that hide?" And a young voice, cheering on the soldiers, "Go for it, lads. Hold the bastard."

Pilbeam shook the noose, inches from the snout. The crocodile didn't react. "Get it to turn," Pilbeam said to Irion. "Grab its tail. I'll noose it before it gets you."

Irion put out a timid hand, and pulled it back. He clapped his hands, but the crocodile either didn't hear or didn't care. He wrenched up a clod of grass and mud and tentatively tossed it underhanded at the crocodile. It grazed the crocodile's side, and still it didn't move. He pulled up another clod, as big as his own head, and tossed it harder. It arced up and fell fast. It landed squarely at the place the tail joined the body. In that next instant, Irion learned why dragons can fly. The crocodile isn't a creature of the earth. Its element is air, its strength is speed. It knows no gravity. Irion didn't see the turning, only the brief instantaneous flash in his mind's eye of the crocodile bent into a curve, with its tail and snout both aimed exactly at him. There wasn't time to will his feet to move.

Pilbeam moved faster than the crocodile. One step, and he leaped parallel to the ground, hands out with the noose, landing flat on his belly on the rocky back, scrabbling forward with his free hand, digging his toes into the dragon's scales, forcing the noose over the very tip of the croc's snout and pulling it tight. Standing still, Irion looked down on the two of them, spinning in great circles at each end of the wire. Pilbeam held onto the wooden handle with one huge hand. His body skidded across the wet grass and wrapped slowly around Irion's leg. Together, they went down. Pilbeam was up in an instant, and his getting up threw Irion another ten feet away. Irion tumbled as he flew, saw scarlet tunics and black trousers, collided with a pair of black riding boots and brought their owner down with him. Irion pushed himself up to his elbow, and only vaguely aware that his legs were still tangled with the officer's, watched Pilbeam.

It was Pilbeam's performance now, something for which he had waited, and practiced, and worked. Irion and the officers were only the audience.

Pilbeam was holding hard onto the wooden handle. The wire quivered with the tension between Pilbeam and the crocodile, giving out a high-pitched, quavering note. Pilbeam tried to run around behind the crocodile, but the crocodile turned with him. With each of Pilbeam's attempts to maneuver the animal, the noose was sliding farther toward the tip of the snout. It would not hold for much longer.

"Let him go," shouted Irion.

Pilbeam didn't hear. He threw himself around the wire's arc, but the crocodile moved too fast for him to get behind, and the noose slipped down to one corner of the snout, slicing across one nostril and hooking under the ripping teeth of the top jaw. The crocodile shook its head, and the noose scooted another inch. Pilbeam held it tight, and the wire hummed. Pilbeam shifted his weight, then made another run around the arc. The noose was almost loose, but Pilbeam wouldn't let it go. He was facing Irion now, and Irion could see from the rocky set to Pilbeam's face that Pilbeam would never let go until the noose was off and the crocodile had killed him.

Without thinking about it, Irion scrambled away from the fallen officer and threw himself the length of the crocodile's body. He stretched out his hands as he watched the stony hide pass under him, as he realized how much he wanted to not be doing what he was doing, and as his belly smacked hard onto the crocodile's back he wrapped his hands hard, so hard the bones might break, around the snout, a hand's breadth from the end. The noose lay under one fingertip, but almost at once it ripped out from under his grasp, and the wire snapped away, then hung loose in Pilbeam's hand. Pilbeam's bearlike body swallowed up the light. Pilbeam's amazing hands, big as hams, folded over Irion's, and their shoulders ground into each other, rooting the two men together. The crocodile spun again, and they flew away across the wet, slick grass. Irion stopped among the officers' boots, Pilbeam in the open. The crocodile stalked in a tight circle, eying them all.

Pilbeam found the wooden handle. He worked the wire back into a noose and joined the crocodile in its circular stalk. Helplessly, Irion got onto his knees and watched. He felt the presence of the officers close around him. As always with officers, he did not exist.

"Will you shoot it, Lieutenant-Colonel?" asked one.

"You'll only enrage it," said another. "It'll kill that fellow."

Beside Irion, Lieutenant-Colonel Phayre pulled out his pistol and spun the cylinder. His voice was the middle-aged voice that had claimed the crocodile as his own. "Nonsense. I'll take it in a shot."

Pilbeam and the crocodile were still circling each other. The crocodile was responding quickly to each of Pilbeam's movements, not at all to the noose he was dangling out to distract its attention. Irion could tell that Pilbeam was getting very close to the point where he would simply leap forward and take his chances. Pilbeam suddenly stopped shuffling around in a circle. The crocodile became motionless, lined up exactly at Pilbeam. Pilbeam squirmed his feet around in the sod, digging the toes in, getting a firm stance. He leaned forward slightly.

Phayre's pistol rose from behind Irion, hung out beyond Irion's head, and fired with a ridiculous, tinny report. Phayre's scarlet sleeve, with just a hint of white lace at the cuff, leaped out of Irion's line of sight. Fifteen feet away, a black spot appeared in the crocodile's jaw, just under its eye: the bullet had lodged, half in and half out of the tough hide. Pilbeam was midway through tensing for his leap. At the sudden pistol shot, he hesitated, rocked forward and back, and leaped away. The crocodile hesitated, too, leaned in Pilbeam's direction, then turned toward the shot. The tail slapped out as if the crocodile was under water. It flew six inches over the ground into the little crowd of officers. Irion threw himself from his knees into a roll, up to his feet and away. The tail touched his foot. He stumbled, caught himself, and sprinted. The young lieutenant who was carrying Phayre's dead swan bumped into someone's back and slipped in the wet grass. The crocodile went for the one horizontal leg in a field of vertical, running legs. It jaws went round the leg, and the crocodile's entire body, eight feet long, jerked sideways. The lieutenant slid with the crocodile across the grass, then snapped like a human whip as the croc pulled back. The lieutenant's solar helmet bounced like a soccer ball. There was a sound of muscles ripping, a clear, loud intake of breath by the lieutenant, but no screams.

Within seconds, a major was beside the crocodile, pouring slugs from his pistol into it from an arm's length away. He emptied the cylinder into it in an erratic, terrified pattern of shots. The crocodile loosened its jaws, and strong hands pulled the lieutenant away by his epaulets. The crocodile circled itself, glared at the men who stood out of reach, then slithered, apparently completely uninjured, into the mangroves.

The young lieutenant lay on his back in the grass. His pale-blue eyes, opened wide, darted around and saw everything, but other than the eyes and the rolling sheets of glistening sweat, his face lay flaccid and still. His black trouser leg had been ripped off above the knee and pushed down around his ankle. The shin was covered with a loose web of cloth and leather, dyed thickly with blood. The leg stood out from the hip at a crazy angle, and the crocodile had invented a new joint between the lieutenant's knee and ankle.

Phayre burst into the midst of the gawking officers. "You two." He gestured at Pilbeam and Irion. "Run for help. Bring a stretcher and a doctor. Quickly now, quickly. Run along." His voice had an artificially efficient tone, still breathless and hollow from the danger to himself, but not at all concerned with the lieutenant. Phayre tossed a Maria Theresa dollar at Irion, who caught it. "There'll be another dollar if you have help here in fifteen minutes."

Pilbeam swayed on his knees, and his hands folded slowly, unconsciously, into enormous fists. Irion ducked through the officers, grabbed his friend by the arm, and hustled him quickly away. Pilbeam made a feeble effort to hold back, but Irion yanked savagely on the arm and dragged him away. They dog-trotted along the shore toward the camp.

"He lost my fookin' crocodile," muttered Pilbeam as they ran.

"It's not that important," said Irion.

"Not to you, maybe," said Pilbeam. "It was my crocodile. Mine. I've been trying for it for a week, and that Phayre lost me it. He's been steering us wrong through his stupidity every step of the way, from Zula to here, and now he's lost me my crocodile, too. And we're running off to fetch him help."

"Help for the lieutenant," puffed Irion. "I wouldn't walk a step for Phayre."

Pilbeam jammed his feet into the grass, and Irion slid to a stop a few paces farther along. Pilbeam stomped up to Irion. His fists were on his hips, and he looked down into the Irishman's face. "Shit, Paddy," he said. "I'm slow, sure, but I see you anyway. You'll start a beautiful mutiny, so pretty it's like a piece of art, to show them you won't play their magnificent game of war. And then you'll break the mutiny because you want to be at the front of the very selfsame game. You'll run off at the bidding of a stupid son-of-a-bitch like Phayre, catch his goddam dollar in the air, kowtow like some damned Bombay native boy, and say, 'Oh, yes sir. Right away, sir.' "

Irion stared up evenly into Pilbeam's eyes, and Pilbeam's voice melted away. "There's no justice, Arthur," said Irion, coldly. "There's no justice anywhere, not from man nor God. You think we live by rules, that all the rules are fair, but they're nothing but so many farts in the wind. We think we understand, and then a crocodile you've pegged for an element of the earth turns in an instant, right before your very eyes, into an element of the air. It's like this Africa. We don't belong here. We walk along, but we don't actually touch anything, and nothing touches us. We'll be here for a time, and then we'll leave, and there won't be a sign we were here at all." His words trailed off as he realized that Pilbeam didn't understand what he was saying.

Irion placed his hands on the big man's chest. Clearly, Pilbeam wanted to understand Irion, still to respect him. "Look, I don't care about Phayre," Irion went on, "nor any other officer. They don't offer me justice, and neither do my own people. After we mutinied, my friends in the regiment were ready to stone me to death for not leading their mutiny. Later, when they decided they didn't like the thought of missing the assault, they were angry at me for starting it. No, Arthur, a man can't plan on getting justice from any other man, nor from a God who can make a place like Africa and put men like us inside it. A man has to find his own justice inside himself. I want to be in the van of this army, because something amazing, something horrible, is happening here in Africa—can't you feel it?—and I want to see it. I want to get help for that poor broken man back there, because he is a reasonably innocent soul who is suffering pain.

"But all you care about is the justice you're denied by others. You never give a thought to the justice you deny yourself. This magnificent game of war is really just an enormous game of cards, owned and operated and even invented by the people above us. Sir Bob sits at the table, and Phayre, and every other officer in this bloody English army. But you and I, Arthur, we ourselves are only cards, and small cards at that. You are a two of hearts, and I am a three of clubs. With every action of your life, you try to leap out of the deck and sit at the table. You do it by trying to catch 'a fookin' crocodile' with your bare hands. You do it by standing aloof, hoping they are watching, hoping they care.

"It will never happen. You are just a card, and you will never hold your own hand in their game.

"So abandon it. Forget it exists. Let them play, shuffle you, use you if you come up. But play your own games, separate from theirs.

"Arthur, I own my own dignity. I play my own game. I hold my own justice. And that dollar?" Irion held up his open, empty hands. "That dollar burned my hand the instant I touched it. I dropped it into the lake. The water turned to steam."

Embarrassed, thinking slowly, Pilbeam stared at Irion's palms. Softly, he said, "It steamed?"

"Right there in the lake," said Irion, sincerely. "There was a little puff of steam over the place I plunked it in." He touched Pilbeam's shoulder and pulled him gently. "Come on, Arthur. Let's go get help for the poor hurt man."

Muroja, the son of Atu Waiku, brought word down from the mountains to the south that Ibrahim would come into the Ashangi bowl at noon, two days in the future, to greet the English commander, to see his famous army and his miraculously obedient elephants, and to discuss the terms of Napier's passage through Ibrahim's provinces. As soon as he had stammered out the message to Captain Speedy and Napier, he slipped onto his horse and dashed away around the lake. Behind his camp desk, Napier chewed thoughtfully on the stub of a pencil and looked across the still, black water until he saw Muroja, arms flapping, braids whipping out behind, disappear into the forest. Napier set the pencil down carefully, leaned his elbows on the desk, and said, "What is wrong with that fellow?" His tone did not make it clear whether he was asking Speedy the question, or just talking to himself.

"It's just his manner to act that way, I would suppose," said Speedy. "Terrified of us, because we're so far advanced over his people. Wouldn't any poor bugger be frightened?"

"No, it's more than that," said Napier, careful now to make it absolutely obvious that he wasn't talking to Speedy. "It's more, I think." Speedy shuffled his feet for another minute, then wandered away.

Napier continued to look across the lake. He couldn't quite put his finger on it, but there was more than a normal dose of terror in Muroja's stammering. There was hidden complexity here. Napier couldn't follow the gangly priest's Amharic, but he was sure that there was, flowing through those fluid syllables, a hint of rote memorization. The same hint had been there in Muroja's previous visit, when he answered Napier's questions about Ibrahim. It was as if someone had coached Muroja in his speeches. As if Muroja were lying.

Any other man would have missed it, but it slowly became clear to Napier. Behind Muroja was a man with Napier's own sense of gamesmanship, with Napier's own skill at manipulating people.

Napier began to look forward to meeting Ibrahim.

In the way of all secrets, long before Ibrahim's arrival every foot soldier and musician and groom in the army knew Napier's elaborate plans for the meeting. There would be the usual show of military might, of course, the demonstrations of the mountain guns and a parade of the elephants. But even more interesting, even more characteristic of Napier, was the order in which the army was to be drawn up. Napier's staff and every officer over the rank of major would line up in two separate files on the shore before Napier's headquarters. Those officers who were placed in the rank around Napier himself would be the commanders of units that would be marching on beyond Ashangi. Since there were to be no more garrisons left in the hundred thirty miles between Ashangi and Magdala, these would be the units participating in the assault. A second rank of officers would be off to Napier's right, separated from the lucky ones by a few yards. These were the commanders of units that would remain behind to garrison Ashangi. The officers themselves did not know who would be selected and who would be placed in that unfortunate rank off to the right.

A few representatives from every unit in the entire army would be chosen to provide a colorful background between the officers and Napier's tents. Just an hour before one of Colonel Cooper's aides-de-camp moved through the regiment and pointed out five Irishmen for this honor, another astonishing story made its way through the regiment: Napier had given orders to Cooper that four of the Irishmen were to be chosen randomly, or in any way Cooper pleased, but the fifth was to be Geoffrey Irion.

That special recognition from the commanding general threw Irion's status among his mates into sudden limbo. Several who hadn't been particularly friendly to him since the mutiny brought him the rumor, along with tobacco to fill his pipe, and sat around speculating on the mystery. The only one who had any theory to offer was the forty-year-old Kerryman who, at the rear of the column, had been the first to fall out before Ada Baga. With a tinge of malice, he said, "I'll warrant you are to be a sacrifice, Geoffrey."

"How do you mean?" asked Irion.

"You are the educated one here," said the Kerryman. "I'm only a poor *culchi* from Kerry, but you were nearly a priest."

"I'm from the countryside, too," Irion reminded him softly.

"Yes, but nearly a priest," scolded the man. "*Sacrifice.* You know the word."

"We all know it," said Irion, wary about being baited after weeks of hostility from his friends.

"Bu' wha's tha' t' do with him?" asked the Belfast boy who had fallen out next, slurring his fast city accent.

"Just this, my boyeen," said the Kerryman, slowly, like a teacher to a dim-witted student. "His generalship will need a human being to sacrifice to the war gods of the heathen Ethiopians, to show he means business. And our man Irion, being the most infamous man in the army, is the logical pick. Logical." He let a puff of smoke envelop his own head, and out of the smoke he set to drift the two syllables that punctuate all Irish logic: *"Jus' l'that."*

Cooper's aide-de-camp rescued Irion from this irritating little discussion, and soon, in full scarlet battle dress, Irion stood at ease in a long rank of soldiers in all the colors of the army—or, as aptly, all the colors of the rainbow.

Napier had been the first man in place. Appearing very small, he sat gently in his saddle and watched the lake. Purposefully, he had nothing to do with the activity behind him. The decisions had been made. They were irreversible.

The majors and colonels and generals, some already mounted, some holding their own bridles, others horseless until they would call for their patient grooms, milled around on the hard-beaten parade ground between Napier and the varicolored rank of soldiers. Napier's aide-de-camp, Major Scott, was stage-managing the performance. Tall, narrow-hipped, Scott walked among the officers with a list in his hand.

With huge effort, the officers restrained themselves from peeking at the list. In a high-pitched, eager voice, Scott read each name in turn, complete with titles and honors as if he were announcing guests at a formal ball. And after he had called each name, he would find the individual and, struggling to appear like a passionless angel of God, would pass sentence: You to Magdala, you to stay at Ashangi. This one to a place with Napier, this one off to join the lepers.

Irion found Colonel Cooper among the officers. Where everyone else kept in perpetual, anxious motion, Cooper just stood with an arm draped across his horse's neck and stared down at the ground. He was an outcast among his fellow officers, and from the slump in his shoulders Irion decided Cooper knew what the list decreed for him and the 33rd: the Ashangi leper colony. Once, Cooper raised his gray eyes slowly and fixed them on Irion. There was recognition in them, but nothing else, as if Irion were just a familiar face to him, without particular memories attached. Scott called Cooper's name and read quickly through his titles. A glimmer of a smile touched the colonel's face as he swung into his saddle, then vanished as he looked down again at Irion. Before Scott could reach him, he turned his horse toward Napier, away from the lepers.

"Going the wrong way, Cooper," muttered Lieutenant-Colonel Phayre, who was sitting his horse near Irion, but Scott chased after Cooper and led him into a place in the front rank just one space away from Napier.

Then we're for Magdala! thought Irion, and joined eagerly in the handshakes of congratulation among the five Irishmen.

But something else was happening in the front rank of officers. Cooper's horse and the horse next to his, between him and Napier, were jostling each other. Irion craned his neck to see who occupied that space. The horse beside Cooper's reared suddenly, angrily, and its hooves laced the air. The rider turned his head toward Cooper, and beneath the turban Irion saw Captain Speedy's black-and-gray mustache and vicious, flinty eyes. The horse settled briefly, and Speedy's elbow dug, with very little pretence at accident, into Cooper's ribs. Cooper's horse, far more placid than Speedy's, edged away and pushed into the horse ahead. Speedy turned his horse closer to Cooper's. Others around them began to maneuver into position to see what was happening.

Napier turned away from the lake for the first time in over an hour. "Speedy, calm your horse." His voice, surprisingly strong, was powerful enough to calm the horse by itself.

Someone else said, "Look, Ibrahim is here." The horses settled into an uneasy stillness, and all heads, Cooper's and Speedy's last of all, turned toward the lake.

As always, Irion had been a passive, mute observer through the whole performance—and he was sure that *performance* was the right word for it. Somehow, for some reason, it had been designed for him. There was too much cleverness in it for it to be anything else than intentional. It was an overwhelming display for a commanding general to arrange for one small, faceless soldier. The performance told him, and thereby told the entire Irish regiment, that their disgrace was over. Honoring Irion himself, the man who reluctantly bore credit for the mutiny, emphasized the message and made it unmistakably clear. And this business of deliberately putting Cooper next to Speedy was a sign, if Irion interpreted correctly, that Napier hadn't forgotten Cooper's weakness before Ada Baga: that the regiment might be back in favor, but that the regiment should keep Cooper's weakness in mind, just as Napier did.

Protocol prohibited Napier from communicating directly with common soldiers. Perhaps, Irion thought, this was the only way Napier could think of to deliver his messages. Perhaps it appealed to Napier's sense of the dramatic. One thing struck Irion forcibly: of all the Irish regiment, he might be the only soldier with enough education, with enough awareness of symbols, to understand these messages and carry them back to his fellows. Irion's respect for this distracted general expanded.

Scott moved skillfully but mechanically. Obviously, Napier held Scott's strings. What other messages, to what other men in the audience, was this performance delivering? How many games was Napier playing simultaneously? How many feuds was he smoothing over or encouraging? What harvest would he gain from the seeds he planted today? Irion now had a sense of Napier's complexity: he seemed like a master puppeteer, controlling every man in his army by invisible strings, corrupting their thoughts and guiding their aspirations, all to achieve his own ends.

And the day's performance was not yet over. Ibrahim emerged from the forest across the lake. The dark thunderclouds that confined Ashangi, laced with delicate, brief electric spider webs of lightning, opened overhead to a perfect turquoise sky. The mountains' lower slopes burst into sunlit emerald for a few yards before the blackness of the lake. Ibrahim paused for a moment after his horse, the cavalry charger that Napier had given Muroja, cleared the trees. Calmly, he turned his head to survey the orderly Anglo-Indian camp across the water, all the neat rows of tents, the thousands of soldiers in their precise ranks, the elephants and the cannons. At this distance, the noontime sunlight made him into a stark figure, nothing but haloed, shining hair, bleached white clothing, and motionless ebony horse. He swiveled his head slowly, so slowly he must have practiced the gesture. The impression he made couldn't have been unintentional. He had chosen this hour and this entrance to the bowl expressly to create this tableau. But, Irion thought, Ibrahim had misjudged Napier if he thought he could intimidate the commanding general with these cheap theatrics.

The necessity for Ibrahim's performance became clear as his ragged bunch of followers began to follow him out of the forest. Ibrahim himself might impress; his people, never. A priest, Muroja, came behind him. Then came three more turbaned holy men, and then all two hundred of his mounted honor guard.

Ibrahim's torso barely swayed as his horse walked to the lake and dipped its front hooves into the water. The Ethiopian horses of his men were three hands shorter than his cavalry charger, shaggy and unimpressive. His men, too, were shaggy. There was an unruly, piratical look, a meanness, a nervousness, that made Napier wonder again about this new prince of Lasta and Wajerat. Already, Napier was sure he was dealing with a natural leader, a charismatic, a man of the most devious, dangerous type. It was the type of man he had fought in Tanti Topi during the Mutiny. It was the type who might rise to become prince of two provinces, or even—and he hesitated at the thought—to become emperor of Ethiopia. And it was the type of man who would walk calmly into the midst of an English army and gamble on a bluff.

On Napier's side, away from Speedy, Colonel Merewether said, "Rather scruffy lot, aren't they, Sir Robert? I would have expected a more martial appearance, for men who have accomplished so much."

"I shouldn't worry about their appearance," snarled Speedy. Napier stared straight across the water, as if he hadn't heard. Speedy talked across him at Merewether. "You won't ever find Ethiopian soldiers looking much more disciplined than that. Besides, this is only a small honor guard, hardly a fraction of Ibrahim's force. I dare say five thousand of those would appear fearsome enough."

"Perhaps you are right," said Merewether.

"They would appear fearsome, that is," said Speedy, "if you were a smaller band of similar warriors. They won't scare our lads."

Napier turned toward Speedy as if he had only just heard him and said, "Honor guard."

Those two words were somewhere between a question and a statement.

"Yes, sir," said Speedy, not certain, as he never was with Napier, how he was expected to answer. "That is Ibrahim's honor guard."

Napier studied the two hundred warriors across the lake. "He has another five thousand like these hidden in the mountains?"

"Ruling two provinces, Sir Robert," said Merewether. "Preparing to attack the Gallas and drive them out of Asubo."

"Quite a successful man, in his own right," said Speedy.

As if to himself, Napier said, "Five thousand more. In the mountains." Napier made it clear, intentionally, that he was only talking to himself; but he pitched his voice loud enough for officers and soldiers to hear. There was the sense of hidden meanings, the suggestion that Napier knew things that were beyond other men. Everyone within earshot cataloged Napier's tone and remembered it later as an example of

Napier's genius: and perhaps this ability to make other men consider him a genius was itself the substance of Napier's skill.

Napier shook himself loose from his thoughts. "Speedy, I want you to gallop around the lake. Take young Briggs. Let me see the sod fly under your hooves. Give Ibrahim whatever graciousness he expects, and tell him we are going to honor his visit with a demonstration."

Speedy and Briggs thundered across the parade ground, in front of the Naval Brigade and the Punjabis and the 33rd, behind the mangrove swamp, back into view across the water, and within five minutes they were pulling up beside Ibrahim. Aware that every eye around the lake was on him, Speedy threw his hand up in the most elaborate salaam of his life and began to speak. Ibrahim's warriors jostled forward to hear, but Ibrahim angrily waved them back. Speedy talked for several minutes, gesturing in the exaggerated manner of a mime, once pointing at the officers bunched before Napier's tall pavilion. When he had finished whatever unnecessary explanations he was making, Speedy drew his pistol and fired a shot that cracked instantly over the still water and echoed back hollowly from the walls of the bowl.

Napier raised his hand, and the demonstration, first conceived a month before, began. When Napier had laid out the dispositions for the Ashangi camp and sent Scott forward to see that they were carried out, he had had it in mind to create a vast stage along the northern arc of the lake, with units performing from one end to the other to surround an audience across the lake with noise and motion. The demonstration proceeded with the cold precision of an English army in battle. Each unit waited patiently for its cue, then sprang instantly into action, aware that the whole army and the commanding general were watching critically. To Napier's far left, the 33rd threw themselves into a fast, efficient drill, marching right, left, then forward in a tight double file to the water's edge. The front row knelt, shouldered their Snyders, and fired a roaring blast into the forest across the lake, between Ibrahim and the far end of the camp. Working with clockwork timing, they turned their rifles over to dump out the expended brass cartridges and slapped in fresh ones. Halfway through their twelve-second reloading, the second rank, standing behind, fired. Each rank fired three volleys: six fast volleys, six seconds between, the reports mixing with the booms returning from the mountains, the forest half a mile away withering under thousands of bullets.

The Ethiopian horses were no strangers to gunfire, but they were rearing and turning at the speed and volume of the volleys. Only Ibrahim, on his cavalry charger, was still.

Off to Napier's right the elephants marched in a ragged circle to the accompaniment of a dozen Scottish bagpipes. Cavalry maneuvered on the parade ground before Napier. The 4th Infantry fired six volleys from near the elephant brigade into the mangrove swamp beyond the 33rd.

Ibrahim's people held their horses under better control during the 4th's volleys, but then they had to fight with them again when a mountain battery fired three shots from the mountain slope behind Napier's pavilion. The trajectory was so low that Napier and Ibrahim both felt the projectiles flying close overhead.

While Ibrahim's men brought their mounts under control, six sailors slipped down to the water. Three carried rocket tubes over their shoulders. The others adjusted the slow-burning fuses and set matches to them. And every man in the Anglo-Indian army held his breath and waited.

In the style of the rocket technology of the day, the rockets went off separately. The first started a high, screaming arc over the lake toward the forest that the 33rd had riddled with bullets. Sparks dripped off the rocket's stick tail and fell sizzling into the water. Halfway across, the rocket suddenly dipped, fell fast, then leveled off at the last possible moment. It raced crazily just above the water, skittered off the surface, and plunged in a burst of sparks into the darkness of the trees. The second and third rockets went off together, five seconds later. One whizzed over Ibrahim's head, the other over the Naval Brigade. Like exploding suns, they burst simultaneously against the black wall of cloud and, chased by crackling lightning bolts, showered white-hot sparks into the mountain passes.

The little Ethiopian horses bolted into the forest. It was late in the afternoon before Ibrahim could regroup his people and return to the Ashangi bowl.

If Ibrahim felt embarrassed at how his warriors had fled the rockets, he gave no sign of it as he rode proudly across the parade ground with Speedy, Briggs, and his two hundred men. He paused for a few moments to study the officers gathered at the pavilion. His appearance was so striking that every man stared at him. The barest quiver of approval touched the corner of his eyes, and he swung easily down to the ground. He wore the three buttered braids and the ordinary, unadorned white clothing of any Ethiopian warrior, his feet were bare and his flintlock musket remained slantwise across his back, but the resemblance to his men ended there. He was taller—about six feet—and more heavily muscled than was average for his short, slender race. He moved with a cat's flexible, eager strength. His obsidian eyes, set between long, curling lashes, seemed to caress every object they encountered as they moved slowly across the officers' faces. His nose was long and unnaturally straight, his lips thin; his chin was strong, with just a hint of cleft. Taken altogether, his features were too perfect. The smooth, pinkish saber scar on one cheek wasn't enough of a flaw to make him handsome in an honest, human way.

A Bengali *syce* stepped timidly forward through the silence. Without a glance at the man, Ibrahim handed him his charger's bridle. It was a gesture that belonged to the undisputed ruler of his universe. Ibrahim was more than the British expected, and he was well aware of it.

He turned with a question to Speedy, who pointed out Napier to him. Ibrahim's thin lips broke into a smile full of white, even teeth. It was the kind of smile a man used to greet a visitor to his home. He salaamed gracefully to Napier, strode forward, seized the general's shoulders, leaned down and kissed each of Napier's hairy cheeks.

Napier accepted the kisses without visible reaction. Having made such a powerful opening statement with his elephants and Snyders and rockets, Napier was willing to let Ibrahim have the initiative in their conversation. "Welcome to our camp," Napier said.

Speedy translated the words. Ibrahim grinned slyly, only for Napier, and replied. Speedy translated uneasily: "Welcome to my domain. By the grace of God, sir, since I have been prince of Lasta and Wajerat, I have not welcomed such a distinguished guest as yourself to my homeland."

Ibrahim locked eyes with Napier while Speedy translated his words. The shared look communicated more information than any speech. Napier already understood much about this man. For whatever reason —bloodline, training, or heavenly inspiration—Ibrahim was a man alone, chosen for great things. In a situation where he should have been overwhelmed, he remained in full command of himself and his world. He knew no fear.

Ibrahim, too, seemed to understand Napier. There might be fencing between them, but no secrets would last for long. Ibrahim said: "By Iyesus's torment, sir, you must be good Christians, or heaven would not give you the intelligence to make such splendid weapons."

"Our Queen is a good Christian," answered Napier. "We strive to follow her example."

"Ah, that is cheerful news," said Ibrahim. "There are too many infidels in the world. We Christians should all be friends. Don't you agree?"

"I do."

Ibrahim looked past Napier into the pavilion, took Napier's arm in a familiar manner, and said, "Come, we will sit and talk."

"Yes, that is well," said Napier, amused at Ibrahim's invitation to enter his own tent. They went into the pavilion and sat on camp chairs with a low tea table between. Speedy released the tent flap to give them privacy, and then pulled up a chair to one side. Servants brought tea and small cakes. Unconsciously, Ibrahim made the sign of the cross over his tea before beginning to slurp it up. He admired the silver tea service, and they exchanged boring pleasantries for an appropriate amount of time. Napier allowed Ibrahim to control the tempo and direction of the conversation.

At last, Ibrahim set his empty teacup down in a deliberate gesture, signaling a new stage in the talk. "I will speak frankly with you, sir," he said, "as great men should. I am prince of two provinces. You are commander of a great army. There should be understanding between men such as us."

Napier paid more attention to Ibrahim's face and his tone than he did to Speedy's translation.

"I agree," he said simply.

"Then, by God, I will ask you directly," said Ibrahim, "not detouring from the straight path nor hiding my intentions in confusing words. I come to you to ask, why have you come to Ethiopia?"

"We English are accustomed to speaking frankly, and to writing just as frankly," said Napier. "The proclamation which we have distributed explains our purpose."

Ibrahim spread his hands on the low tea table. "I have seen no proclamation."

"Our Lieutenant-Colonel Phayre, who leads the scouts ahead of our army, has been distributing it," said Napier, suddenly annoyed. "You haven't seen it?"

Ibrahim answered that he hadn't.

Napier turned to Speedy. "Has Phayre been passing the proclamation out?"

Speedy shrugged. "Haven't a clue, Sir Robert. Knowing Phayre, I wouldn't bet tuppence on it."

Napier rose in disgust and found an English-language copy of the proclamation in his desk. He gave it to Speedy and told him to translate it to Ibrahim.

The proclamation, which still traveled, undistributed, in Phayre's luggage, read:

> To the Governors, the Chiefs, the Religious Orders, and the People of Ethiopia.
>
> It is known to you that Theodore, Emperor of Ethiopia, detains in captivity British subjects, in violation of the laws of all civilized nations. All friendly persuasion having failed to obtain their release, my Sovereign has commanded me to lead an army to liberate them.
>
> All who befriend the prisoners or assist in their liberation shall be rewarded, but those who may injure them shall be severely punished.
>
> When the time shall arrive for the march of the British Army through your country, bear in mind, people of Ethiopia, that the Queen of England has no unfriendly feeling toward you, and no design against your country or your liberty. Your religious establishments, your persons and your property shall be carefully protected. All supplies required for my soldiers shall be paid for; no peaceable inhabitants shall be molested.
>
> The sole object for which the British force has been sent to Ethiopia is the liberation of Her Majesty's servants, unjustly detained as captives; and as soon as that object is effected it will be withdrawn. There is no intention to occupy permanently any portion of the Ethiopian territory, or to interfere with the Government of the country.

Ibrahim listened carefully, though his expressionless eyes remained on Napier. When Speedy had finished, he asked, "This is true?"

"It is true," said Napier. "Do you doubt our words?"

"No, no, no," said Ibrahim quickly. "I do not doubt you. I knew this must be your purpose, but I had heard nothing. And the rest of your writing, your intention to leave Ethiopia when you have delivered the prisoners from bondage: this too is true?"

"Absolutely," said Napier. "Every word of it."

"By the breath of the Holy Spirit, then, I am pleased," said Ibrahim. "I had hoped as much."

Napier leaned forward and poured tea into Ibrahim's cup. "How does our intention suit you?"

Ibrahim again made the sign of the cross over his cup and said, "It suits me well, indeed. If you take the prisoners from Theodore, then he must fall. My enemy will be no more." He became suddenly expansive, eager to talk freely. "I will tell you the truth, sir. This Theodore is an evil man, a horrible man. Do you know, he has no right to rule, no right to be emperor? He claims he is related to the imperial line, the family of Iyesus and Menelik, but it is a lie."

"I had heard as much," said Napier, softly.

"There was a time," Ibrahim went on, "when he ruled all Ethiopia. It was plain that he had assistance from a greater power. No man could do the things he did. The people said he was with God, but I have long known the truth: Theodore is allied with the devil, with Shaitan himself. I will tell you more: I came to you today to ask for weapons as the price of your passage through my provinces, so I could defend myself from Theodore's wrath after he had destroyed you. I say this in all honesty. I came fearfully, because Shaitan has given Theodore the ability to hear all that is said about him no matter how far away.

"But now I have seen your power, and I know you are with God. You will triumph over Theodore. You will be returning through my provinces, and at that time I may prevail on you to give me the weapons I need to fight our infidel enemy, the Asubo Gallas. I trust to your generosity."

Napier had watched Ibrahim closely and listened carefully to his voice. The man was as brash, clever, and fanatic as Theodore must be, but there was none of the visionary quality that, by all accounts, drove and sustained Theodore. Ibrahim's absolute horizon was the eternal, useless struggle against the Moslem enemy. Beside Theodore's steady star, Ibrahim was a fragile firefly.

"When I return," said Napier, "I may be willing to give you weapons." He chose a new direction in which to probe. "In the meanwhile, will you give me free passage to Magdala?"

"Willingly," said Ibrahim. "I greet you to Lasta and Wajerat with open arms."

"May I tell people along the road that I am your friend?"

"My people will welcome you," said Ibrahim. "But I must warn you against certain evil men whom I have not yet exterminated. They may claim to have power in parts of my domain. They may even claim that

Ibrahim is not the prince of Lasta and Wajerat. You must be proof against such lies. You must be secure in my power and in our friendship. I haven't uprooted all these men yet, but as soon as you give me weapons, I will uproot them, and then I will proceed against the Gallas."

"I will be on my guard against their lies," said Napier. "In the meantime, would it not be wise for you and I to remain in close contact?"

Ibrahim smiled widely. "Yes, for we should be friends, one to the other."

"Then I will send an envoy to your capital city," said Napier.

Ibrahim's face dropped for an instant, the first crack in his composure, and then the cheerful, transparent mask was up again. His new smile seemed to say: I know you are not fooled; but I am who I am, you are who you are, and you will not deny me what I want. "I have no capital city yet," said Ibrahim. "I have only just subdued my realm. I still spend all of my time traveling, consolidating my gains, seeing that my people are comfortable and happy."

"Then I will send an envoy to travel with you and your army," said Napier. He caught Ibrahim's gaze carefully and held it for a long second.

A little nervously, but bluffing well, Ibrahim said, "I would love to have such a man to travel with me, but I cannot allow you to make this sacrifice. I know Theodore's power. For you to lose a single warrior might tip the balance in his favor."

Napier hesitated, holding Ibrahim for a moment longer. He now knew that Ibrahim did not rule two provinces, that the two hundred men of his honor guard were all he had, and that this was just a mad, dangerous gamble to try for weapons that would give him the edge against his neighboring chieftains. Boldness, courage, and luck were the routes to power in Ethiopia, and Ibrahim was playing the game exceedingly well. At last, Napier released him: "Then I shall not be able to send an envoy to you. Despite this, I hope we can be close friends."

"Assuredly, sir," Ibrahim said quickly.

Napier poured fresh tea for Ibrahim and himself. Then, in such a tone that Ibrahim knew it was the truth, he said, "I admire your courage."

"I have no unusual amount of courage," said Ibrahim, also truthfully. "I have much faith that the Lord Iyesus will not desert me."

"That is powerful faith," said Napier.

Ibrahim fingered the blue *mateb* that encircled his neck. He spoke slowly, emphasizing each word with care, "In Ethiopia we believe there are certain of us who are chosen especially by God to rise above the rest of mankind. These men may be identified by a mark, or a sign, or a vision, or just by the power of their deeds. For one of these men to hold back from danger is a failure of his faith in God. It would be a sin. Is it not the same in your country?"

"Perhaps we lack faith as strong as yours," said Napier.

"We are Copts," said Ibrahim. He put down his teacup and spread his hands out on the table again. "We are the chosen race of God, the last true believers. You have your guns and your elephants and your suns that burst with myriad dying stars, but we have the security of our faith."

"A very strong faith," said Napier.

"The strongest faith," replied Ibrahim. "The only faith."

Neither spoke for another minute. This, then, thought Napier, was the power of these Ethiopian warriors: simple faith, the most stubborn power of all.

At last he said, "We will remain in communication as I march southward. You are welcome at the garrison that remains here at Ashangi, and we will renew our friendship when my army returns."

20

Thursday, April 9, 1868;

Good Friday, April 10, 1868

Magdala

Rassam saw a round-framed, unsteady picture of the distant face of the Bashillo River gorge.

"Keep your hands free of the telescope," Theodore told him. "It is so far away, you must let the tripod hold it firm to see."

Rassam took his fingers off the long German telescope, taking care not to touch the eyepiece. The picture solidified. The telescope was focused on a switchbacking segment of Walter Plowden's Royal Road into the gorge. The distance was so great that Rassam could barely make out a file of turbaned Indian infantrymen in full scarlet-and-black battle dress plodding down to the river.

Theodore took over the telescope and redirected it. Rassam looked. English cavalry were bobbing down the trail.

Again, and an elephant swayed awkwardly down with a Bengali *ma-hout* on its neck and two steel-barreled mountain guns harnessed to its gray sides.

Again, and a thousand troops were pitching their *routies* among the reeds and willows on the flat, sandy northern bank of the Bashillo River. The river was brown and sluggish, and a fair number of men were already fishing in it.

Again, and on the plateau across the gorge a high pavilion with brilliant Union Jacks on the sides was being lowered by a small army of servants.

Rassam looked away from the telescope.

"It will be tomorrow that it starts," said Theodore. "They will camp across the Bashillo tonight, and then in the morning, they will attack." Theodore spoke casually, almost as if he weren't involved in the movements of all those men. He was giving off the same calmness and strength that Rassam remembered from their first meetings. "Do you know what they are doing now?" he asked, and he answered his own question: "They are using my Royal Road, which I caused to be built. They are accepting my help through a difficult place. It is one of the signs of the Light Bringer. Your general only has one more sign to fulfill. It is the same one you failed to show me."

"Can you tell me what it was?" asked Rassam.

"It couldn't matter now," said Theodore. "The Light Bringer will refuse to forgive me, even when I humble myself and beg it."

Softly, Rassam said, "I couldn't refuse you."

"Because you are not the one for whom I have been waiting," said Theodore. He pointed out his own army on Fahla, the lowest of the three freestanding plateaus. Theodore and Rassam were above Fahla on the edge of Selassie. Behind them across the Islamgie saddle stood Magdala. Below Fahla they could just see the outer lips of the two embedded plateaus, Aroge one step higher than Affijo. From ten miles away the Royal Road twisted its way into the gorge to the British camp at the river, but on the near face of the gorge it was hidden from Selassie until it reappeared on Aroge. From his one trip through the gorge, twenty months before, Rassam knew the Royal Road followed the course of the stream called the Warki Wawa all the way from the river to Aroge, off to the right of Affijo. The road met Aroge on the plateau's riverward edge, crossed Aroge, skirted Fahla and passed behind Selassie, and finally went on a beeline across the Islamgie saddle. "I brought ten thousand warriors with me from the north," said Theodore, "and Magdala's garrison was almost another thousand." Like ants, the Ethiopian army covered Fahla. The chiefs had their brightly colored tents. The lucky warriors who had arrived first had found enough brush to build low bowers. The rest of the army would sleep in the open. Many of them were congregating on the edge of the plateau overlooking the Bashillo. Polishing their weapons, chatting, wrestling, eating and getting drunk, they were doing all the things soldiers do before battle, but more than anything they were watching the enemy putting together their camp, five miles down on the river. At its largest the British camp would only be half as large as the Ethiopian. The confidence of the Ethiopians was swelling.

"Your army looks formidable," said Rassam.

Theodore threw out his hand in the unconscious, natural gesture of an emperor who will not listen to nonsense. "My army is the greatest in Ethiopia since the Portuguese," he said. "For the first time, every single warrior in an Ethiopian army has a flintlock or a matchlock. But compared to your British army, my men are rabble. Last night, I stood on a tall boulder on Fahla and talked to my people. 'Are you ready to fight?' I asked. 'Will you enrich yourselves with the spoils of the enemy, or will you disgrace me by running away?' One old man, toothless, skinny, shouted, 'We will kill them all, and then on to Jerusalem!' I almost told the old fool the truth. I nearly said, 'Do you know what you're saying, you idiot? Have you ever seen an English soldier? Have you ever in your life heard a cannon, or seen grapeshot sweep across a battlefield? Before you know where you are, your belly will be riddled with bullets.' "

Rassam started to object, but Theodore stilled him. "We should understand each other by now, Rassam. You and I know that your English army will run over my men as if they weren't even there. The saddest thing is that of all the thousands of fighting men, of all the warriors and chieftains, of all the invincible Twelve, of all the educated *debteras* and priests, of all of them I am the only one who knows what will happen tomorrow. I'm the only one who can picture the carnage. I'm the only one weeping inside today, but there will be many weeping openly tomorrow."

Rassam was silent. He could not deny the obvious truth of Theodore's words.

He looked back toward the gorge. A thousand people, all on foot, were walking down the Royal Road. They were strung out across the far end of Aroge, and the leaders had nearly reached the Warki Wawa. They were moving so hurriedly that sometimes the whole troop broke into an ungainly jog. When Rassam had answered Theodore's summons and had started down from Magdala with only Samuel ("Normally," Samuel had said as he explained the complicated rules of Ethiopian protocol, "it would be an insult to have a man of your honor travel unattended; but since you have been a prisoner, Theodore honors you by sending for you alone"), he had passed this body of people on the Islamgie saddle. Samuel had explained that Theodore, for some unfathomable reason of his own, had announced a general amnesty for all Ethiopian prisoners in Magdala. Now, with their wives and servants, the captured rebel chieftains were trying to get off the *amba* and out of Theodore's reach before he changed his mind.

Rassam asked Theodore about them, and Theodore replied, "It has hurt me to have to imprison them, though they gave me no choice. The English, I think, will be so powerful in this country that a few rebel chieftains will not injure them. In the evil of these days, it is good to have the chance to offer liberty to someone." He called for Wolde.

"The letter," Theodore said, and Wolde handed him a stiff sheet of brown paper, folded into thirds, sealed with Napier's silver signet.

Sarcastically, Theodore said, "He finally deigned to communicate with me. After more than three months in my country, he has written me a letter. You cannot know how this hurts me, that he never sent me a letter before." He handed the letter to Rassam. It was written in triplicate on the one page, in English, Arabic, and Amharic. It began without any salutation, which was a major affront in Ethiopia.

> By the command of the Queen of England I am approaching Magdala with my army, in order to recover from your hands the European captives now in Your Majesty's power. I request Your Majesty to send them to my camp as soon as it is sufficiently near to admit of their coming in safety.
>
> General Sir Robert Napier

Theodore said, when Rassam had finished reading, "I can understand how a man might be this blunt if unfriendly letters had been exchanged in the past. But I can't believe it is customary in your country to be so lacking in grace and politeness when one has never communicated before."

"It isn't customary," mumbled Rassam.

"What manner of man is your General Sir Robert Napier?" asked Theodore. He pronounced the full name and title in crazily accented English, obviously having sounded out the signature on the letter, and he said the names and titles with clear bitterness. "I always thought my Light Bringer would be a man of compassion and strength, but he hasn't shown these qualities to me."

Coming down from the *amba,* Rassam had been worried about the state of mind in which he would find the emperor. Theodore exhibited none of the terror of the past, nor the drunkenness that Rassam might have expected. He was almost ethereally calm and rational. Now that the conclusion was so near, his situation seemed to have become more comfortable. Rassam knew there was no chance of changing things, but he had to try.

"Napier is a famous general," he said. "He was involved in the two wars against the Sikhs twenty years ago, and in the Indian Mutiny ten years ago. I don't know whether I've ever heard much about him, though. I don't think he is the kind of general who attracts much attention. I seem to remember that he is a very deliberate leader. I doubt if he has any of your flair for leading an army." Rassam paused, considered, and went on: "Since he is a deliberate leader, he probably would avoid fighting if he could. Even now, if you sent Blanc and Cameron and Kerens and me to him, he would have to call off the attack. Or, I could go and talk to him on your behalf. I could take Wolde with me. We could try to make some arrangement—"

"No," said Theodore, quietly, but so powerfully that the rest of Rassam's sentence vanished from his mind. "No arrangements, no compromises, no surrenders." He noticed Wolde, hanging close to his imperial master with the look of a loyal puppy, and gently sent him outside their conversation. Wolde's face fell, but he walked away. Theodore continued in a low tone: "That isn't worthy of you, Rassam. You know all the reasons that make it impossible. It has gone beyond the will of God, the signs, the prophecies. Now it is impossible.

"Granting the political prisoners amnesty has caused so much grumbling among my warriors that I've had to promise them English blood to quiet them down. My men live to fight. Even if they knew they would all die, they would still go into battle. If I surrendered, they would attack without me.

"If I surrendered to your people, and if by some miracle of God I kept this *amba* and all my warriors, then all of Ethiopia would see my weakness and rise in an instant and engulf me.

"If I offer your general anything less than surrender, he will have to fight me. How could he march his men so many miles, and then turn around and walk away without defeating me? What kind of man, English or Ethiopian, could hold up his head after that?

"No, the die is cast. Tomorrow the British will come up from the river. I won't send any men to harass them as they climb. My warriors will wait with me on Fahla. At my signal they will rush down to their deaths on Aroge." He motioned with his hand to show the rough, steep slope between Fahla and Aroge. "Do you know what day is tomorrow?"

"Beside the battle?" asked Rassam.

Theodore looked down carefully at Rassam. "Tomorrow is Good Friday, the day on which our Lord Iyesus died upon his Roman Tree." He sighed. "It would be good to die on Good Friday. That is a little pride I have allowed myself: the hope that I could die on the same day as Our Lord. But I don't think it will be. It is a long climb up from the Bashillo. The fight will be late in the afternoon. It would be foolish for a general —and especially when he is so overwhelmingly powerful—to press his men too hard through the afternoon. I think tomorrow will see a battle on Aroge. On the next day, Saturday, he will press on to Magdala, where I will die. Or perhaps he will be even more cautious, and wait until Sunday. Easter would not be a bad day on which to die, either."

Across the Bashillo it had begun to hail. Large, heavy rain drops began to splatter the dust around Rassam and Theodore.

"You'd better start back to Magdala," said Theodore. "It is a two-mile ride, and it will surely be raining by the time you get to shelter."

Thunder rolled through the Bashillo gorge, battering equally against the British and the Ethiopians. Theodore was perfectly calm, but he seemed to be trying to decide whether to say something else.

"What is it you want to say?" asked Rassam.

Theodore smiled at the question, then decided to speak his mind. "Truly, I brought you down to speak my heart to you," he said. "But I feel so comfortable here, and I am so pleased to see you are still well and still remain my friend, after all these painful months, that I thought I would not speak. But now I think I will.

"Everything is clear, now. I know that General Sir Robert Napier is my Light Bringer. I know how he will destroy my army, how my twelve stars will burst, one by one, against his myriad stars, how I will die. I know he will bring the light to Ethiopia, as I was never meant to do.

I know all this as surely as I know my own name, as surely as I trust you are my friend, but I can't stop myself from worrying. Rassam, I won't be here to guide events. You can't know how terrible that is to a man who has led a country for all these years. I want someone I trust to be there, someone who can speak to the Light Bringer. I want you to explain to him what I meant to do. I want him to realize that I died for him."

"I understand," said Rassam, promising nothing, but trying to appear to promise everything. He desperately wanted to do this, but he doubted his courage.

"I know you do," said Theodore, retrieving his composure. He put his hands on Rassam's shoulders and stared into his eyes as if trying to see through them into Rassam's soul. He shrugged a confused little shrug, which seemed to say, *I can read other men's eyes. Why can't I read anything in yours?* In a less certain voice, he said, "I don't think you will fail me."

Raindrops were sliding off his buttered hair onto his forehead. "You should go now," he said.

"What will happen?" asked Rassam, not sure to which events, in the entire universe of events, he was referring.

Theodore stood back from him and looked across the gorge. He put his eye briefly to the telescope, then turned and said, "It is hailing powerfully on the English, but they are unaware. They stride forward with confidence, like ancient Greek gods, like Mycenaeans striding into the boats that will take them to ravage Troy. Did you know that there were Ethiopians on the side of Troy in that battle?"

"Paniotti told me," said Rassam.

"Here come my Greeks," said Theodore. "I will fight them on the plains, and I will retreat before them. They will storm my majestic walls and slay me and all my people. It will be a battle to remember, a battle worthy of epics and songs. I wonder, will there be a blind poet to sing my songs?" He turned back to Rassam, back to Rassam's question. "We will fight tomorrow on Aroge. I think the British will halt there for the night, close enough to the place of battle to hear the groans of my people as they die. On the following day I will send you and the other Europeans down to your General Sir Robert Napier. His army will come up to Magdala, and I will die. You will help to guide your General Sir Robert Napier into the path God has chosen for him. All will be well."

"Will that be well?" asked Rassam.

Flatly, Theodore said, "A man once told me, *what man can thwart the will of God?*" He looked past Rassam at Samuel and Wolde. He gave rapid instructions: Samuel to return Rassam to comfort at Magdala, Wolde to come with Theodore to a meeting of the chieftains to plan the battle strategy for the next day.

*   *   *

GOOD FRIDAY, APRIL 10, 1868

Napier had given his orders for the attack. The assault force was to be composed entirely of infantry and artillery. Commanders of the cavalry complained at being excluded, but Napier told them the obvious—that a cavalry charge might be glorious to watch, but there was no room for it on a mountainside—and then he refused to listen to them anymore.

Two thousand infantrymen and gunners, divided into two brigades, were to cross the Bashillo. Lieutenant-Colonel Phayre, with Major Scott in attendance, would lead the First Brigade across the Bashillo before dawn. With its narrow overhangs, the Royal Road up the Warki Wawa gave the Ethiopians an excellent opportunity for ambush, but the Royal Road was the only feasible route out of the gorge. An observation post, equipped with telescopes, semaphore flags, and signaling mirrors, had been established high on the northern face of the gorge, in a place where its observers could detect any movements of Ethiopian warriors and warn Phayre instantly. After the First Brigade cleared the lip of the gorge, it would veer away from the dangerous Royal Road and proceed up the steep, barren Gumbaji Spur across the two embedded plateaus, Affijo and Aroge. Leading the Brigade would be the 4th King's Own, the Beloochees, and the Punjabi Pioneers. Next would come the Sappers, who would make the spur passable for the heavy guns. At the last, the Naval Brigade and the artillery would follow.

The Second Brigade, which included the 33rd Wellington's Own, was to wait at the Bashillo until Phayre and the First Brigade had secured Aroge.

The men of the First Brigade waded the river barefoot, and there was some confusion on the far bank when they sat down to put their socks and boots back on. When the infantry had returned to order, Phayre mounted his charger and gave the signal. The 4th followed him onto the Royal Road, and all the units across the river, except for one, let out a cheer that echoed through the gorge.

The 33rd did not cheer. Irion and his comrades watched the four hundred men of the 4th, resplendent in their dust-brown battle uniforms, marching into battle, and keenly felt how, one more time, they were being excluded. The Irishmen were dressed in their battle uniforms, too, their beautiful scarlet tunics and black trousers. The units on either side of them, also waiting, were fully prepared, but they did not share the nervousness of the 33rd at watching others go into battle. The 33rd had waited so long at the rear of the army for Napier to send them off to garrison some lonely outpost. They had made it this far, and so it was even more anguishing to be dressed for battle and to watch the 4th march toward the enemy.

From the bottom of the gorge Irion could see no more than the first few hundred yards of its southern face, and nothing at all of the mountain above, but everyone in the army knew that the observation post had seen thousands of campfires on the Fahla plateau during the night. The last men to vanish up the Royal Road were the rocketeers of the Naval Brigade. They had changed into the uniforms that had been specially designed as their land battle dress. The uniforms retained a nautical flair, but were not very different from the uniforms of the infantry: blue with scarlet facings on the tunic. Pilbeam had located Irion across the river. Pilbeam had made some sort of unintelligible gesture at his uniform, waved good-by, pulled on the rope of his rocket-laden mule, and started up the Royal Road. The tarred queues of the sailors, hanging out from under their solar helmets onto their packs, were the last sight anyone below had of the First Brigade.

After the sailors had left, the observation post was the only place in the gorge with any visible activity. The observers were watching the gorge's southern face through their telescopes and occasionally signaling mysterious messages down to Napier. Irion tried to relax, but within minutes he found himself pacing back and forth in front of his *routie*. He was not alone in his pacing.

The sailors had grumbled when they were ordered to put on their battle uniforms. They did so reluctantly, complaining about the tightness of the tunics and the unfamiliar weight of the solar helmets. But then they had started to realize how smart they looked, and when they gathered into order for the march, were pleased with the martial appearance of their ninety-eight-man brigade. Even Pilbeam started to feel some of the new spirit that seemed to flow from the uniforms into their pores, through their pores into their bloodstreams. Each man among them, unconsciously, began to understand the invincibility of an English army.

A company of Lieutenant-Colonel Phayre's Punjabi Pioneers served as advance guard. Fifty yards behind, Phayre led the rest of the First Brigade. With him were his own aides-de-camp; one of Napier's signalmen, who kept swiveling in his saddle to see whether the observation post across the gorge had lit a fire to get his attention; and Napier's own aide-de-camp, Major Scott. As at Ashangi, Scott was at Phayre's side without any obvious purpose, except to keep an eye on Phayre. Scott's nature was so gracious that it was hard to find fault with him, but Phayre was beginning to see his presence as an insult. Every time he made a comment to one of his own people, he saw Scott's soft gray eyes on him and knew the young major was weighing every word he said. Scott hung onto him like a leech. Even when Phayre maneuvered to put his own people between himself and Scott, Scott managed to slide back unobtrusively to within a couple of yards; he never said a word, only watched Phayre with those open, disarming eyes, listening, waiting.

The road to the top of the gorge was five miles long, and Phayre did not complete it until ten o'clock in the morning. He surveyed the ground quickly. Napier's orders were for the infantry to lead up the

Gumbaji Spur, off to Phayre's right, and for the heavy guns to follow. From this new vantage point, however, it was apparent that the spur would be more difficult than anyone had expected. The Royal Road to Aroge might be more dangerous, but it would be far easier for the mules pulling artillery and carrying the navy's rockets. The elephants could be made to go up the Royal Road, but Phayre was sure they would never go up the spur. The terrain suited him well.

The advance guard of Punjabi Pioneers was relaxing on the hillside above. The faint aroma of opium smoke reached Phayre. The rest of the First Brigade was stacking up on the road below. Phayre sat on his horse on a flat piece of ground and took a leisurely look around, enjoying the chance to make a decision.

To the signalman, he said at last, "Flag the observation post, and find out whether they've seen any Africans on the Royal Road above us."

"Sir," snapped the signalman, and he spurred his horse up the slope to give himself room to dismount and wag his semaphore flags. He waved a message, then read the reply through his telescope. Phayre was keenly aware of Scott at his elbow, but he carefully refrained from acknowledging him. The signalman waved again, watched a longer reply, and called down: "Sir, no sign of the enemy anywhere below Fahla, neither on the road nor on the spur."

Phayre turned to meet Scott's eyes, and was a little disappointed at not being able to read anything in them. Scott's expression was as bland as ever, as if he were not interested at all in what Phayre was planning.

"The spur is very steep," Phayre said to him, trying hard to mask his eagerness.

"Very steep," said Scott, his voice as bland as his eyes.

"I think it is too steep for the elephants and the artillery," said Phayre. He got no response of any kind from Scott, and Phayre realized that he hated the young soldier. "Don't you think it is too steep for the elephants, Major?" repeated Phayre. The politeness that must always exist between British gentlemen, that politeness which was the glue that held their world together, was barely enough to keep the hatred from boiling out of Phayre and spewing over Scott.

"The elephants might have trouble on the spur," said Scott.

"They will have more than trouble," said Phayre. "They will founder. Only a fool would send elephants up there." There was no response from Scott. "I am going to have the infantry advance up the spur, and the elephants, artillery, and Naval Brigade up the Royal Road."

Quietly, Scott reminded him, "Sir Robert's orders were for the artillery to follow the infantry up the spur."

"I am changing those orders," said Phayre, struggling now to keep his voice under some measure of control. "Sir Robert will surely approve when he has a chance to see the terrain for himself." He waited in vain for a response. "You will ride back to Sir Robert and inform him of the change in plans."

For the first time, Scott let a smile creep through his bland expression. The smile confused Phayre. It seemed to say that he had allowed himself to fall into a carefully laid trap, but, no matter how hard he tried to figure it out, he could not see where the trap lay. It occurred to him that Scott might reveal secret orders from Napier to take over the brigade under circumstances like these. Scott did not reach for any orders. He said, "A semaphore signal to the observation post on the north face, relayed down to the Bashillo, would be faster by an hour. Sir."

"I don't trust the semaphore," said Phayre. "You will be able to give a more accurate report."

In a voice full of mockery Scott said, "You are, after all, sir, the expedition's acknowledged master of judging terrain. With your leave, sir." He tapped his solar helmet, turned his horse's head, and plunged away down the Royal Road into the Bashillo gorge, past the First Brigade.

Napier was not surprised to see Scott come splashing across the Bashillo. Scott changed horses, and he, Napier, and Napier's bold band of dashing sabers, Speedy and Briggs and the rest, started up the Royal Road. They reached the lip of the gorge at noon. The navy, the mountain batteries, and the elephants were all resting, waiting for Phayre's orders to press on. Napier had a signalman get one last confirmation from the observation post that there were no Ethiopians nearer than Fahla, and then he started them up the easy Warki Wawa route. He and his own people forged up the Gumbaji spur in pursuit of the infantry. About four miles up they passed the 4th King's Own, fallen out exhausted on the near edge of the Affijo plateau. Farther up the Beloochees were still climbing wearily from Affijo to Aroge, and when Napier reached the edge of Aroge, the main body of Phayre's Punjabi Pioneers were just debouching onto the plateau.

Napier found the Pioneers' commander and asked him where Phayre was, but the major could only shrug and say, "Haven't seen him since we left the gorge, sir. He went on ahead and left us in his dust."

Napier submerged himself into that meditative state where he seemed unaware of anyone else. His eyes swung around slowly, taking in the terrain. The Aroge plateau, one mile long and almost a mile wide, undulated gracefully southward. A rugged, grassy hillside led up another mile from Aroge to Fahla. Even with his naked eye, Napier could detect the movement of many men near the edge of Fahla.

Far off to Napier's left, across three quarters of a mile of a wilderness of rock, sand, and scrub, seven hundred feet below the plateau, the Royal Road emerged from the Warki Wawa ravine and then made a long loop behind Aroge. Napier followed that loop with his eyes and realized for the first time that he was actually on the road.

Napier drew himself out of his meditation. "What time is it?" he asked, and someone said, "Half one, sir."

"Half one," muttered Napier. "Damn." Then, "Major."

The commander of the Pioneers moved his horse closer to Napier's. "Sir?" The major was a sixtyish career officer, too old to be in the expedition, too experienced to be excited about anything but retirement.

"The mouth of the Warki Wawa ravine is unsecured," said Napier. "You will take your Pioneers and secure it."

"Shall we take the road, sir?" asked the major, resignedly.

"The road head is vulnerable to attack," said Napier. "The artillery will be coming up shortly. If it fell into the hands of the Ethiopians, we should be in a sad position. We haven't time for you to take the road."

"The men are exhausted, sir," said the major.

"The men are Punjabis," said Napier. "They won't complain." He took another look at the high Fahla plateau, bristling with warriors. "The hour is getting late. I want the battle to take place this afternoon, instead of having to spend the night directly under a strong position held by the enemy. You will proceed, major."

"Sir," replied the major, wearily. He turned to give the orders.

"And, Major," said Napier.

"Sir."

"Rest at the road head, Major. But not too much. I think there will be blood this afternoon."

Napier called an aide-de-camp, a captain, to him. "Follow the Punjabis down to the road head," he said. "Have the Naval Brigade proceed up the road until they reach this spot, and then prepare here for battle. Have the mountain guns fix a position near the road head from which they can command the plateau and that wilderness off to the left. The Pioneers are to remain in support of the artillery." He leaned close to the captain and whispered, "Keep a careful eye on that major. I fear he hasn't the stomach for a battle. If he is presenting a danger, take command of the left wing. If he refuses, arrest him."

"And if he and his people refuse an arrest, sir?"

"Then you shall have tried," said Napier. "Now, away."

The aide chased the Pioneers toward the road head.

Napier surveyed the eager faces around him. "Briggs, go down and bring the 4th up at once. Promise them blood if they are up quickly enough."

"Yes, sir." Briggs's voice cracked slightly. This would be his first battle, and he was very excited. He had played at boldness for so long that he couldn't abandon the role when it was really required.

Napier glanced across at the other faces. They were mostly nondescript, without even names to give them character. The only ones he knew well were Scott and Speedy. Scott was exhausted, sitting there on his panting horse. He was practically untested, but he was clever and he would do well. Napier knew he could rely on him.

Speedy was hanging back from the rest. It wasn't fear, Napier was certain: Speedy was far too much of a fool to understand fear. But there was a strangeness in his manner this morning that made Napier distrust him. He was preoccupied with something other than the fighting. Napier was sure he knew what it was. That preoccupation could be useful in its own way, but it could be dangerous in the battle.

Briggs galloped down the narrow path that led from Aroge to Affijo, and then across Affijo onto the Gumbaji spur, pulling up before the 4th's commander, Lieutenant-Colonel Sandwith. He delivered Napier's orders, and together they raced on horseback along the stationary column and got the Englishmen back on their feet. While Sandwith led the regiment, Briggs rode up and down the column, shouting encouragement, telling the soldiers what a short distance it was, promising them a sharp battle if they walked quickly enough and a long, dangerous night if they didn't. The men of the 4th grumbled about the crazy officer, hardly more than a boy, but their feet moved faster in spite of themselves.

Napier and his people searched the northern end of Aroge and found Phayre and his aides-de-camp in the shelter of a great baobab tree, eating their lunch. Napier galloped his horse to the baobab and reined it up fast in front of the picnickers, spraying dirt over their roast chicken and wine.

Napier glared down at Phayre for more than a minute, while Phayre picked slowly, nervously, at his chicken. Behind Napier, Scott had that same confusing smile on his face. At last, very quietly, Napier said, "I will be commanding the Aroge action personally. I would like you—when you have finished your meal, naturally—to descend with all your people into the gorge. You will wait with the Second Brigade until orders arrive for them to come up. I would expect the order to arrive sometime tonight, after the action."

He exchanged a brief, secretive smile with Scott, who had been in on the gambit since Ashangi. Always at Phayre's shoulder, Scott had watched for that one monumental dereliction of duty that would free Napier to take away every responsibility held by Phayre. This picnic in the face of the enemy had given Napier the lever he sought. Phayre was safe from punishment, sheltered by the fact that he was cousin to Lord Russell, but Napier could use the lever to pry Phayre out of the vanguard. And if he complained, then Napier would establish Phayre's incompetence for all the world to see. Napier turned and rode away, leaving behind a lieutenant-colonel who had no idea whether he had been punished or rewarded.

Lightning was beginning to lace the sky, though on the ground the air remained hot and humid. A rain would be good, thought Napier. It would dampen the Ethiopian's powder, while leaving his own brass cartridges unaffected, and it would clear away the smoke and make for clean volleys.

Off to the left of the plateau, the Pioneers were forming a defensive flank. The Naval Brigade was proceeding along the loop of the Royal Road toward Aroge. Behind the Pioneers a mountain battery was being unloaded from the elephants.

The Beloochees had been on Aroge for more than an hour. The 4th and the Madras Sappers were just now coming onto Aroge.

Napier sent his dashing sabers off in all directions with orders: the navy to hurry forward; the mountain battery to establish a position quickly, with the Pioneers in support; the 4th to form a line across the width of Aroge plateau; the Beloochees to wait behind the 4th in reserve; the Sappers to support the 4th right flank, which overlooked a gradually sloping wilderness. The army responded eagerly, despite their exhaustion. They had walked almost three and a half months, four hundred miles, for this moment. They lifted their dusty boots and ran toward their battle stations, they formed into lines, stacked their rockets and shells, fixed their bayonets, and waited.

They did not have long to wait. As the thunder rolled across the plateau and echoed against the mountains, a single pistol shot sounded up on Fahla plateau. Ten thousand voices suddenly began to chant *"Alalalalai!"* The chanting lasted one minute, and then it increased instantly in volume as ten thousand Ethiopian warriors appeared over the crest of Fahla, a mile and a half away and a few hundred feet above the 4th, and charged down the mountain.

21

Good Friday, April 10, 1868

Magdala

A quarter mile behind the 4th King's Own, on the edge of Aroge nearest the river, the naval rocketeers had unloaded their rocket tubes and rockets. A deluge of excitement flowed off the plateaus toward them, swirled around their feet, distorted their vision with a haze of pure emotion. Pilbeam sucked in the haze and felt the excitement fill his lungs.

In twenty years in the Royal Navy, Pilbeam had never been engaged in anything resembling real war: a few small actions at sea, but never a full-scale fight to the death by huge numbers of men. On that climb up the Royal Road, he had never been afraid of what was coming, only curious. There were too many British troops, too well dressed and armed, too capable and efficient, for any one man to feel fear for his own puny life.

The Naval Brigade had been given a good vantage point for watching the battle. They were on a subtle rise, and so they were able to look down at an oblique angle at the 4th, at the chosen battlefield beyond, and at the sharply rising slope down which the Ethiopians would charge. Surrounded by his mounted cavalrymen, Napier had set up his headquarters between the navy and the 4th. In the time the sailors waited, Pilbeam heard a dozen comments on Napier's position: "I wouldn't sit on no horse in front of us. We're dangerous." "I told my rocket, whispered in its little steel ear, to go looking for black Africans, but it has a mind of its own. No telling but what it'll go for generals."

The sailors had long considered it a point of honor that they would be the first troops involved in any battle. The inaccuracy of their new-fangled weapons might prevent them from drawing first blood. In fact, the trajectory of each rocket was so much up to the individual rocket that they had little hope of actually hitting anything. Still, the sailors would be the first men in the army to fire weapons in anger, and even if they didn't injure a soul, they would (or so the theory went) at least terrify the enemy.

Couriers radiated out from Napier, throwing up puffs of whitish dust, sometimes racing to Fellowes, sometimes to the mountain guns and the Pioneers at the mouth of the ravine, sometimes past the navy and down to Affijo. Fellowes tried to talk to his brigade, but in his excitement he had to struggle to keep his voice steady. "We're to wait, lads, until the savages start their attack. They are to start hostilities, so no wayward rockets, if you please. It won't be long now. You can see them preparing." He pointed, and all eyes went up to Fahla. From the number of distant, antlike figures visible at the near edge of Fahla, there must have been a great number of Ethiopians on the plateau. "They will come down the mountainside toward our brave companions of the 4th King's Own. I shall give the signal, and then it will be every tar for himself. We'll want rockets exploding high and frightening the buggers to death. But whatever you do, try to keep them clear of the general and the 4th."

One of the sailors shouted, "I'll find that bleeding emperor himself, won't I, and nail him wi' my rocket."

Fellowes tried to laugh too. He was a good man, with more respect for the common soldiers and sailors of the army than was ordinary among officers, but even he had never been able to shake off the disdain he had been taught to hold for men of the lower orders. "Good spirit," he said, "but I doubt whether you'll have enough accuracy to hit a mountain, let alone an emperor."

"Where will he be, Captain?" asked one of the sailors. "Up there on his mountain, directing the battle like any other general?"

"I wouldn't think so," said Fellowes. "From what I've heard, he'll be leading the charge himself. Forget about him; concentrate on frightening the soldiers racing down the hill. If we frighten them badly enough, it will be so much easier for the 4th to cut them to pieces."

"What'll it be like?" asked a sailor. "I've never fought on land before."

"I've never been in a land action, either," said Fellowes. "We'll have a good view of it here, snug and safe behind the 4th. And . . . what is that?"

Fellowes waved for silence, and the sailors listened. From the Fahla plateau, a high-pitched chant, slow, methodical, was rising gradually in volume and tempo.

"Form triads," shouted Fellowes. His voice cracked and was nearly inaudible, but the sailors leaped into action.

The ten largest men in the brigade had the honor of being tube-holders, the most desirable job. Each of them had two partners: Number One loaded the tube and lit the fuse, while Number Two carried rockets to his Number One. The ten triads spread out quickly into a long, loose line. The remaining sixty-eight sailors, armed with Snyder rifles, waited behind at ease to support the rocketeers if it became necessary.

Pilbeam was the largest man in the brigade. He took his position near the middle of the line and settled the rocket tube, five feet long and six inches in diameter, weighing fifty pounds, onto his right shoulder. His Number One slid a rocket into the tube and adjusted the fuse so it could be lit at will. Pilbeam's Number Two prepared a slow-burning punk for the Number One, and then stepped away.

The Ethiopians came over the lip of the plateau like a flood pouring over a dam. Horsemen led the charge, but most were on foot. Rain fell in enormous drops. Pilbeam's Number One took off his solar helmet to shelter the punk and the fuse.

"Give them a minute to get closer," shouted Fellowes. Pilbeam braced his feet far apart. Fellowes called, "Mind you keep those rockets well over the heads of the 4th, or there'll be the devil to pay. Have at it now, lads."

"Lighting," whispered Pilbeam's Number One. Off to Pilbeam's right, his Number Two said, "Get it off well, Arthur. Take a hundred of the savages. Make 'em shit."

Pilbeam had never had much to say to his partners, nor they to him. He was amazed at the tone in their voices now: they were a team, inseparable, committed to each other.

"Fuse burning, Arthur," said Number One. "Send it high, now."

Off to the left, Pilbeam saw a rocket spring to life in a shower of white sparks, and he heard the strange whining sound of its passage out of the tube.

"Damn," muttered Number One.

"Don't worry," Pilbeam said, surprising himself with his own friendly tone. "Don't have to be first to be best."

The first rocket had exploded in a burst of sparks over the Ethiopians before Pilbeam's fuse burnt down. "Brace yourself," said Number One, and Pilbeam pushed his face down to protect himself from the sparks with his solar helmet. The rocket sizzled hot in the tube. The rocket was suddenly gone with that absolute lack of recoil that never ceased to amaze Pilbeam, free, arcing high, traveling with a mind of its own far beyond the point where its charge should have given out. It spun once and whizzed in a high, straight line toward Fahla. Just over the lip of the far distant plateau, two miles away, it dipped downward and burst out of sight on the surface of the plateau.

Captain Fellowes laughed at Pilbeam's side. "Not so much force, Arthur. We're not aiming for Magdala yet."

"Aye, aye, sir," snapped Number One.

Pilbeam turned angrily on Fellowes, but when he saw their faces he laughed with them. "Aye, aye, sir," he said brightly, and he settled down to fire another rocket at the mass of Ethiopians running down the mountainside at the 4th.

Theodore knew he would not join the dead until all the signs had been revealed. Only one remained: even though he begged forgiveness, the Light Bringer would not forgive him. Theodore knew he had to give his ten thousand warriors their moment against the British, that he must give his invincible Twelve their chance to burst against the overwhelming weight of the Light Bringer's myriad stars. Once that had happened, Theodore could beg.

There was no point in leading the attack, only to walk back to Fahla alone, so Theodore had chosen to remain on Fahla to watch the battle from a distance. Gabry would lead. Nine more of the Twelve would be among the mounted chiefs. Mamo and Wolde would remain on Fahla with Theodore and his reserve of messengers, but he was sure they wouldn't long survive the rest.

At four o'clock in the afternoon, Theodore climbed onto a tall boulder and addressed his ten thousand troops. This day, Good Friday, and the next day, Saturday, were the holiest obligation of the calendar: an absolute fast of forty-eight hours, which every Copt, not just priests, *debteras*, and fanatical emperors, obeyed. The soldiers had drunk only water all day, and they had eaten nothing. Their hunger gave their impatience a keen, metallic edge. Theodore felt subtly lightheaded as he mounted the boulder and exhorted his men for the last time. He told them all the things they wanted to hear, all the painful lies that for thirty-three years he had known were false. He used the powers of his famous voice to encourage them, to hearten them, to fill them with pride and conviction and certainty. He announced that Gabry would lead the attack, and then he turned his telescope toward Aroge. A long, very thin line of men in dust-colored uniforms had formed across Aroge. More men in uniforms of other colors waited behind them. There was little movement on the plateau. The British seemed to be ready.

Gabry began to lead the battle cry that Theodore had learned from Alexander the Great, by way of Paniotti. Theodore let the chant swell, and then he raised one of the pistols he had received from Queen Victoria—those with the silver plate engraved, *"Presented to Theodore, Emperor of Ethiopia, by Victoria, Queen of Great Britain and Ireland, for his kindness to her servant Plowden"*—and signaled the attack with a pistol shot. Thunder boomed close overhead and nearly buried the pistol shot inside its greater power. The ten thousand warriors plunged over the lip of Fahla.

All through that long day of waiting, Theodore had been calm, weighed down by the same feeling of emotional emptiness that had exhausted him in the days after the burning of his monastic village. Death was very close, for him and for nearly all the people who had been with him for most of his life—but death was an abstract thing, difficult to think about.

He climbed off the boulder and sat beside Wolde to watch his warriors bounce down the mountainside toward the British guns. Wolde squeezed close to Theodore, like a chick seeking shelter under its mother's wing. Mamo and the corps of messengers waited some yards behind.

Theodore had to admire the semblance of unconcern among the British troops, the beautiful uniforms, the motionlessness, the orderly set of all those vertical, still rifles. He had waited for a very long time to see a British army in action.

His thoughts strayed briefly to the steep, wild slope off Aroge's left side. A rank of soldiers in scarlet uniforms stood at an angle against the end of the line of dust-colored uniforms. Below those scarlet soldiers was the place where Theodore had tried to pray on the night he first saw Magdala. Bell and Plowden had blundered into his isolation and confused him with their talk of fortresses and roads and cannons. They had cost him additional years of conflict, but that couldn't negate the fact that they had been good men, honest and loyal. They were more than eight years dead, now. Theodore never spent much time looking back into the past, but his thoughts slipped from Bell and Plowden to Tawavitch, and how he had watched through his telescope as she and her party climbed up the new Royal Road out of the Bashillo. He remembered how close to him she had appeared, through the powerful German lens, when she crossed the Aroge plateau.

Out of this memory, the miraculous happened. It was the event that separated this day forever from any day of normal reality. It was as true and as untrue as a staff turning into a serpent, or a sea parting, or a sun standing still in the sky. Some flying creature traced a line of dripping sparks straight up into the air. For the first few moments, Theodore couldn't tell whether the creature was very small and only inches from his eyes, or very large and miles away. When it reached an angle sharply over Theodore's head, it exploded suddenly. He saw that it was still half a mile away, high over the heads of his warriors.

He stared at the hollow place the bursting star had left behind. He watched the sparks still falling, and through the falling sparks he saw another star rise into the sky. It dipped and wavered, and then he knew it was racing toward Fahla.

The star took three seconds to reach Fahla. It headed directly toward Theodore, into his eyes, into his mind. He watched it sizzling closer, and he felt no quickening of pulse, no fear. But it rose a tiny degree in the last hundred yards and passed so close over his head that he could feel the cold-hot sparks against his face.

It burst soundlessly behind him and threw sparks over his head.

He did not move. Wolde was suddenly a real presence, hanging over him. "You're burning," the high-pitched voice cried. Wolde threw himself onto Theodore. They rolled down the slope in a tangle of brambles and arms and mud and white garments. When they stopped rolling, Wolde beat Theodore's chest with his fist. One place on Theodore's upper chest, just under his collarbone, burned with cold fire. Wolde backed away when he had beaten all the flames out. "Your chest." He was crying, softly. "Your face." He reached out his fingertips and stopped just short of touching Theodore's forehead. "Your face."

Theodore sat up and started to brush himself off.

Wolde stood and looked over the bank onto the plateau. He sucked in his breath suddenly. "Oh, Iyesus Lord," he said, and his voice came out in a whistle. "Mamo. Mamo."

The rocket had hit Mamo or his horse. The horse and Mamo lay a dozen yards apart. Mamo's white clothing was full of ragged, charred holes with black edges, and the flesh beneath each hole was a deep, smoldering crater of burned flesh.

Two other messengers had been thrown. One had broken a leg, the other had had his big toe ripped off by his iron stirrup ring.

Theodore waved his hand at the other messengers, who were standing at a distance, watching in stunned silence. "Take care of them," he ordered, and he went back to his observation spot.

Behind, he was vaguely aware of Wolde, through his tears, giving orders. The men moved slowly. They were well aware of what Mamo's death, the first among all the invincible Twelve, signified.

The *"Alalalalalai"* chant that Theodore had taught them back in the early days swelled through the mass of the ten thousand warriors and lifted Gabry's heart almost into his throat. He turned his horse and plunged blindly over the lip of the Fahla plateau. Like a wave at his heels, the army followed and poured down toward Aroge. The chiefs rode two horse-lengths behind him, while the warriors came on foot, for the fighting ground was so torturous that Theodore had made a decision similar to Napier's: horses would only be in the way.

Gabry examined the enemy below. There couldn't be more than a thousand British soldiers on the entire field. It wouldn't take skillful tactics to sweep them away in the first charge.

At the Warki Wawa were the black barrels of half a dozen cannon. Gabry hadn't seen cannon since the useless battle against the Egyptians at Kedaref, twenty years before. There were two hundred men, no more, with the cannon. Those slender, black barrels, like the forbidden cigars of the heathen Turks, frightened Gabry. He was glad that it was to be Magiga Dulou who would lead the attack on the top of the Warki Wawa. He turned to search for Magiga Dulou, and found him at his elbow. Gabry held out his hand, and Magiga Dulou leaned out from his bouncing saddle and placed his palm against Gabry's. "God with you," Gabry said. "God with you," replied Magiga Dulou.

Magiga Dulou and his two thousand warriors turned away from the line of attack and veered off to the right, toward the rougher ground below Aroge's eastern edge.

Gabry aimed all his attention at the line of dust-colored uniforms on Aroge. There were only four hundred or so of them, outnumbered twenty to one by Gabry's people, stretched thin along a line half a mile long—but somehow they managed to make that line look tighter than it was.

Gabry looked back again at the eight thousand men behind him. There had never been, before Theodore, an Ethiopian army like this. Every man had a flintlock or a matchlock musket. The British would have seen Ethiopian armies in the last months, and they would be surprised to see Theodore's army so well armed, so organized. The chanting was growing louder. It would frighten the British until they couldn't hold their weapons steady. They would drop their rifles and flee, or they would be swept away.

Gabry waved his arms and shouted orders. Mounted chiefs echoed them. The eight thousand men slowed to a walk and spread out in a line across the plateau. The line matched the dust-colored uniforms in length, but it was six or seven men deep, solid across the face of Aroge. A fly couldn't have made it through that mass of warriors.

Gabry walked his men onto the flatness of the plateau to rest them before they charged. The chanting stilled, was silent. The men caught their breath and prepared to burst out into chanting as they attacked.

The dust-colored uniforms were motionless; the rifles remained vertical and still. Ethiopian warriors never fought defensively, and the obstinate lack of activity among the British began to bother Gabry. It simply wasn't natural for four hundred warriors to wait for eight thousand to overwhelm them. The Ethiopians were pacing anxiously, eager to begin. Gabry wheeled his horse and raised his arm, then dropped his hand to signal the attack. And just as he lowered his hand, something incredible happened. It was as if lowering his hand were a signal for more than the Ethiopian attack. From beyond the dust-colored uniforms something raced up into the air, shedding sparks as it went. It rose faster than anything Gabry had ever seen, tilted a little as it rose, and then burst in a vast blossom of sparks high against the thunderheads. It filled the atmosphere around the Ethiopians with blinding fireflies. Lightning followed it through the sky.

Gabry hesitated just an instant too long, just long enough to give his men time to think about what had happened. Then he yanked his spooked horse across the plateau, which now appeared, by contrast, black as night. The chanting began, wavered, continued by its own momentum. The Ethiopians swept forward at a dead run.

Gabry concentrated on the line of dust-colored uniforms, half a mile ahead, but he couldn't help seeing another spark-dripping thing rise, and another, and half a dozen more. They burst directly overhead, down in the mud at their feet, in their eyes, behind them. The rain was falling fast now. The dust-colored uniforms appeared, disappeared behind a gray wall of water, appeared again. They were only three hundred yards away. For the first time, Gabry saw that they were white-faced: Europeans. The chiefs rode beside Gabry. They held their horses back to the pace of the running warriors. The chanting had faltered at the first exploding sun. It wavered now as the men preserved their wind on the long run. Engeddah, the smallpox-scarred priest, lank and long, rode off to Gabry's left. His feet nearly dragged on the ground. It was hard to hold the horses off a gallop. Two more of the invincible Twelve were on Gabry's right hand. Behind these four members of the Twelve, and behind all the others of the Twelve along the half-mile long line of running Ethiopians, the warriors pushed and shoved and crowded close together. The Twelve were impregnable. Being behind them gave a sense of greater security, a better chance to get close enough to the enemy. The warriors had always depended on the Twelve. The Twelve were one of their strengths, one of the reasons they had come to rule an empire.

The Ethiopian flintlocks and matchlocks had a range of something less than a hundred yards. Gabry measured off a hundred yards from the dust-colored uniforms. He found the range and planned to halt the line there, to fire a volley into the British. The Ethiopians would unsling their spears, draw their swords, and follow up their volley with a hand-to-hand charge that would sweep the surviving British off the plateau.

Ahead, the dust-colored uniforms were lowering their rifles into firing position, though the two lines were still three hundred yards apart. They would only waste their strength, holding their rifles in position for the time it took the Ethiopians to cover another two hundred yards. The horses were bucking to be free. The excitement of oncoming victory filled the horses and their riders and the thousands of men running barefoot just five yards behind. This was what the Ethiopians lived for.

Just at the edge of his battle haze, Gabry was vaguely surprised when the British rifles let off two hundred puffs of white smoke. The rain beat the smoke away before the bullets reached the Ethiopians. The distance was so great that Gabry's mind wouldn't believe that two hundred bullets had smacked so hard into his people. The sound of the volley reached him later, and then the second volley shattered Gabry's illusions and brought him hard against reality. Before they had covered thirty more yards, the dust-colored line gave off another short puff of white smoke. Two hundred more bullets slapped into the Ethiopians. It wasn't possible, but the British had fired within six seconds.

And Gabry became aware of something else. The right half of Engeddah's pockmarked face was a ragged mass of blood and tissue. Engeddah's muscles slowly turned to jelly. He slumped in the saddle, swayed wildly forward and back, and was gone. The British dust-colored uniforms fired again, thirty yards farther on, and the Ethiopian warriors were still a hundred yards short of being able to fire.

Engeddah's falling had more effect than the rapid, impossible firing. God had left the Ethiopians. Those who were close enough knew what had happened, and their terror spread like waves down the uncomprehending line of running Africans. Exploding stars couldn't stop them. Snyder rifles might not slow them. But one of the invincible Twelve had died, and God was gone from Theodore's army.

Thirty yards farther on, a British bullet entered Gabry's horse's neck. The horse plunged forward in a heap, Gabry flew over it, and Gabry's neck broke in the fall.

On the right side of the Ethiopian attack, the warriors stopped a hundred yards from the British. They were too shocked and confused to think about firing. They waited for one more withering volley to reach them through the rain, and then they turned and ran. There were no mounted chiefs among them.

Through some quirk of randomness, the left side of the Ethiopian line was more densely packed, there were no members of the Twelve to die among them, and their momentum was greater. They made it to within fifty yards of the dust-colored uniforms. Some of them fired off individual shots. No British soldiers were hit, and the Ethiopians fled.

The dust-colored uniforms threw another volley at the backs of the retreating Ethiopians, and then they relaxed.

The fighting at the Warki Wawa was harder than on the plateau. After the Mutiny in India in 1857, the British colonial government had taken the Enfields and Snyders away from the Indian troops. The replacements were the Brown Bess muskets of a half century before. The Brown Bess barrel wasn't rifled. It was cumbersome to carry, slow to load, and generally unreliable. An English Snyder could throw a devastating volley at three hundred yards, and could continue to throw them every twelve seconds, every six seconds with a second rank. A Brown Bess couldn't reach much farther than a hundred yards, and it would take twenty seconds to fire a second volley, more than enough time for an attacking force to reach the line. The Indian troops hadn't shown any sign of rebellion in a decade, but the colonial government still hadn't given permission for them to use anything but Brown Besses.

The ground over which Magiga Dulou and his two thousand warriors attacked was an impossible slanted wilderness of rock and brush. His horse bogged down quickly, and he and the chiefs with him dismounted and led the force forward at a slow, uneven jog.

Rockets began to burst off to their left, over the plateau. The men would have faltered, but Magiga Dulou only cursed at them and pressed onward so patiently that no one hesitated. Eyes were on Magiga Dulou, not on the rockets, not even on the half dozen cannons and the two hundred men in their scarlet jackets and claret-brown turbans. The Ethiopians stumbled through shallow wadis that were racing with rain water. The enemy they faced were tall, dark-skinned men. The hair that escaped from their turbans was longer than the hair of Ethiopian warriors, but it was unbraided.

Six hundred yards away, the six steel-barreled mountain guns fired a volley. The shells flew close over the ground with a sound of rushing wind and exploded when they hit. Warriors fell, but Magiga Dulou pushed his chin forward and led his men on. Three hundred yards closer, another barrage from the mountain guns rushed down on them, and more men flew. But no more than fifty had been killed, and the enemy was clearly within sight now. The Ethiopians ducked into a depression, climbed up to the top of a rise and looked down at the Sikhs, just two hundred yards away. Volleys were flying on the plateau, but they ignored the sound. Magiga Dulou began to chant Theodore's *"Alalalalai!"* The men behind him took it up, short of breath but enthusiastic, clinging to the familiar in the face of a confusing enemy.

One hundred fifty yards away now. The uneven terrain smoothed out and ran gently down to the Sikhs. The mountain guns stuck their round muzzles out through breaks in the ranks of scarlet-garbed Indians. Magiga Dulou raised his flintlock rifle over his head and waved it to encourage the men at his back.

The chanting was a comfort in the storm. The mountain guns fired, six quick bursts of smoke beaten down by the rain, six reports, and everything was chaos. There were no shells, only whistling chains and chunks of metal and all the hideous components of man-mutilating grapeshot. Legs and arms were ripped instantly from bodies, men were torn in half. The chanting died in a breath, but the men continued to run. In the sudden silence the tall, dark-skinned soldiers ahead lowered their rifles and fired a volley. The rifles fired together, more closely than any volley Magiga Dulou had ever heard, but the bullets didn't have any more power than he expected. Momentum carried the warriors forward. There were half as many as there had been, but they still outnumbered the Pioneers by five to one.

The mountain guns were still now. The Sikhs were fixing bayonets to their rifles, standing and lowering their steel-tipped gun barrels.

The Africans started an uneven fire, but they saw that the enemy was prepared to fight with cold steel. This was more to the Ethiopians' liking. They dropped their flintlocks in the mud and loosened their spears and swords.

The two lines flowed together. The faces of the Sikhs were cold as stone, implacable, calm. Their bayonets were a solid wall at chest level. With arm outstretched, Magiga Dulou's sword wouldn't reach over the bayonets and the rifles and touch the enemy. The flimsy weight of the Ethiopian charge couldn't budge those Indian troops. The Ethiopians hesitated, milled around. Bayonets leaped forward into flesh. There was bitter hand-to-hand fighting for thirty seconds, no more.

Magiga Dulou swung his sword and stretched. A bayonet briefly pierced his abdomen. Its owner expertly wrenched it free. Magiga Dulou fell unnoticed under the feet of his men.

The Ethiopians behind pressed on the Ethiopians in the front rank. Someone tripped over Magiga Dulou. More Ethiopians were bayoneted on the ground than on their feet. They absorbed the frustration as long as they could, then turned away and ran to their right down the steep slope of the next ravine beyond the Warki Wawa. The Sikhs pursued them, formed a steady line at the top of the ravine, and fired down at the backs of the fleeing warriors. The Ethiopians splashed through the rising stream in the ravine and tried to scramble up the opposing slope, but the sandstone crumbled under their feet and they slipped back down the muddy cliff. They crawled over each other in the bottom of that trap, while the Sikhs hit them with a deadly fire. Some were torn away by the rushing water and carried off down the ravine. Barely three hundred of Magiga Dulou's troops finally made it to relative safety in the wilderness below the Aroge plateau, just as night fell.

The rain drenched the Irishmen of the 33rd and all the other soldiers of the Second Brigade. The Indian troops huddled snug inside their *routies,* but almost to a man the Irishmen sat outside in the mud and the rain. The river was turning violent now, jumping beyond its banks and threatening the tents. The Irishmen listened closely to the sounds of the battle, far off in the distance, so muted that it was hard to believe men were fighting and dying just a few miles away. They heard the bursts of the rockets, soft and hollow—the sharp cracks of the infantry volleys—the dull boom of the cannon. Their senses were so acute that they could easily tell the Snyders from the Brown Besses.

The Irishmen wore their thick woolen battle uniforms. The wool became sodden in the steady rainfall and began to smell. The uniforms were a mockery to the Irishmen. On the plateaus above the brightly colored, distinctive uniforms might give the fighting soldiers the sense of being part of a close-knit, invincible group, but there in the muddy gorge they only alienated the men from one another. The uniforms were a sign of shame.

Wolde was beside Theodore again before the volleys of the 4th King's Own beat back the charge of Gabry's eight thousand warriors. It was less than a mile from Fahla to the battle ground. When the Ethiopians fell back in confusion, they saw that there were no mounted chiefs among them.

"Maybe Gabry ordered the chiefs to dismount," said Wolde.

"No," said Theodore. He looked at Wolde and gently placed a hand on his shoulder. "Their dead horses are on the field. The chiefs are dead, too. You can see them if you look through the telescope, but I don't have to look to know."

Wolde mumbled a prayer, then covered his eyes with his palm and let the sobs break loose. Theodore put an arm around the little man and pulled him close. They stayed together on the lip of the Fahla plateau all through the long hours of that afternoon. They watched the Aroge force fall back nearly to the base of Fahla, and then slowly, awkwardly, regroup and approach the British line again . . . and again . . . and again. They were a leaderless band of guerrillas. They moved forward in groups of five or a hundred. They crept across the plateau and ran at the British line from whatever cover they could find. They only got close enough to be repulsed again. Some of them tried to go around to the left of Aroge, down the steep slope where Theodore had met so long ago with Bell and Plowden, but the Madras Sappers on the 4th's flank beat them off. There was some hand-to-hand fighting on that flank, and a few Sappers were killed. But many more Ethiopians were left to crawl away among those slippery wet boulders and die.

Theodore and Wolde saw Magiga Dulou's two thousand warriors cut to ribbons by the mountain guns, then pursued and decimated in the ravine by the Pioneers. It was so far from Fahla to the mouth of the Warki Wawa that it was more difficult to tell what was going on there. They only saw isolated glimpses of Ethiopian warriors wandering around in the rain.

Theodore would not take any part in the battle, but Wolde took it on himself to send couriers down onto Aroge to find out what was happening. The only information they could bring back was what was already known—that all the chiefs were dead.

The battle did not end until seven o'clock in the evening, when nightfall added to the rain and closed down visibility on the field. During the last hour, Theodore retreated into meditation, and Wolde was unable to get any response from him. The remains of Theodore's army passed below Fahla in the darkness and headed on foot toward Selassie. There were surprisingly few of them.

Theodore stayed on Fahla for another two hours after the last of his surviving army had gone by, and then he rose without a word and mounted his horse. With Wolde close beside him, he rode slowly up the Royal Road around Selassie, along the mile-long Islamgie saddle, and up the switchback trail to his citadel at the top of Magdala.

As night ended the fighting, it appeared that there must be at least a thousand dead or wounded Ethiopian warriors scattered all over the southern half of the Aroge plateau and in the wilderness on either side of it. Twenty-three Indian soldiers had been wounded, fifteen among the Pioneers at the Warki Wawa and eight among the Madras Sappers who fought hand-to-hand in the growing darkness below Aroge. No Englishmen suffered anything worse than a powder burn.

The First Brigade remained for the night where it had fought. Napier had his pavilion erected where he had spent the battle, midway between the 4th and the naval rocketeers. His headquarters staff and his couriers had their own tents put up around his. The surgeon corps set up a field hospital behind the 4th, well out of earshot of Napier's tent.

The cries of the wounded Ethiopians were a nerve-racking nuisance to the men of the 4th. Torches trooped down the Royal Road from Selassie and wandered around the battlefield. British parties were ordered into the darkness to bring back as many wounded Ethiopians as they could find. The Englishmen passed among hundreds of silent Ethiopian women who had come down from Magdala to search for their men. There were jackals and hyenas out on the plateau, too, but there was too much fresh, dead meat for them to offer any threat to the living.

Despite the rain, the freezing temperature, the cries of the wounded, and the lack of firewood and tents, the men of the 4th turned the night into a victory celebration. The baggage train with their food had not arrived, and most of them had finished the rations they carried on their backs. But Napier himself sent several mules laden with rum. No one thought about sleep until very late into the night.

The headquarters staff met for a late supper in Napier's pavilion. The mood was exultant. Lieutenant-Colonel Sandwith of the 4th was particularly happy, and he had good reason: outnumbered twenty to one, his regiment had beaten off an assault of eight thousand experienced, fairly well-armed warriors without suffering a single casualty. "And shall we press home tomorrow?" he asked from his seat at Napier's right hand. "I think my lads could run up the mountain and storm that citadel in their pajamas."

"With sticks and stones for weapons," shouted someone else, and everyone raised their sherry glasses in a noisy toast to Sandwith.

"Silence, everyone!" cried Merewether. "Listen to them." Muffled by distance, the drunken strains of an obscene ballad came to the officers through the night.

"They've cause to be happy," said someone. "It was a brilliant stand."

"Inspiring," said Napier, very slowly. It was the first thing he'd said in many minutes, the first time he had seemed to be aware of the company, and his guests listened closely. Napier held his glass to Sandwith in salute. "The discipline of the 4th—in the face of eight thousand screaming warriors—was marvelous. And the Pioneers—what little I could see of them—were just as staunch. Discipline in a regiment only stems from the example of its leaders. I congratulate you, Lieutenant-Colonel Sandwith—and you, Major Chamberlain." He rose, and everyone but Sandwith and Chamberlain, who held the seats at Napier's right and left hands, rose with him. The officers cried out congratulations and drained their glasses. Sandwith, an excited man of only twenty-six years, tried to catch Chamberlain's eye to share a smile with him, but Chamberlain, as if bored, stared at the table. Sandwith slipped his stolid mask back into place.

The officers resumed their seats. Indian soldiers, acting as servants, moved behind them and refilled their glasses. Napier looked up at the smoke against the yellow ceiling. In a distracted tone, he said, "The men singing after an action—that is the proof of the pudding. It separates a minor little *action* from a *battle*. At Bahawalnagar, when we'd finally driven the Sikhs off for the last time, when we knew they were not going to come back again—then we knew we had really been in a battle. It was three o'clock in the afternoon, but those few of the men who were unhurt simply crawled into the shade and fell asleep. It didn't matter a bit that comrades were groaning in agony, dying, just inches away." Napier looked at Merewether. "It was the same at Multan, wasn't it?"

Merewether nodded. "Couldn't get the bastards to wake up."

Napier's eyes drifted to the smoke again. "My uncle was with the 23rd at Waterloo, up on the ridge above Hougoumont. They took the attack of the Imperial Guard in the evening, and when the Imperial Guard ran away, the men of the 23rd lay down in their square and were instantly fast asleep. Forty thousand dead and dying men on the field. Thousands of wounded horses. Their own square riddled with cannon shot for six hours, nearly half the regiment dead. And the survivors wrapped themselves in their greatcoats and went to sleep. No Englishman moved a finger to help any of the wounded until they woke the next morning. Waterloo was a battle. Bahawalnagar and Multan were battles. But one can tell from the singing that today was just an action." He looked down at the faces of his guests. There was an uncomfortable silence. He sniffed at his sherry and permitted a rare smile to touch his lips. "Of, course, while it may have only been an action for us," he said, "it must have been—hmmmmm—one—hell —of a battle—to the Ethiopians."

One man laughed, others sighed with relief, and someone else called out, "Well said, Sir Robert."

Briggs cleared his throat. He had done especially hard duty today, and Napier had complimented him for his bravery in carrying orders into the heat of the battle. The thrill of his first fight lingered on, and his courage was great. "Sir Robert, it may be presumptuous for such a junior officer as myself to propose a toast to such a distinguished gathering . . ."

Napier almost allowed himself to laugh. "You have earned the right to speak in any company."

"Long ago, before Mr. Rassam and Dr. Blanc had even been imprisoned," began Briggs, "I was privileged to attend a dinner party at the home of Sir Seymour Fitzgerald in Bombay. I was there with certain other officers of our Bombay army, including our unfortunate Colonel Dunn. You were in attendance as well, and your wife, Lady Napier."

The general murmured, giving no clue as to whether he remembered or not.

"We young officers listened with great attention to your opinions about a hypothetical invasion of Ethiopia. You said certain things that everyone present thought were, if I may be so bold, nonsense. You said that the Ethiopian savage is much more imaginative than the English soldier, and that this imagination would be the downfall of the Ethiopian army: that this imagination among the Ethiopians would make it impossible for them to be welded into a disciplined army. At this time, I would like to congratulate Colonel Sandwith and Major Chamberlain on the discipline of their ignorant, unimaginative troops; and you, Sir Robert, on the imagination of your analysis." He raised his glass, and the officers said, "Hear, hear."

Napier nodded his thanks, but Briggs was not yet finished. "When you spoke that evening, you said you would run this expedition in the manner of a business enterprise: conservatively, slowly, deliberately, without risk. You have done just that, Sir Robert, and today we have seen the power of your ideas."

Napier slackened his jaw as if to speak, then hesitated. Everyone listened. Slowly, Napier looked around at the expectant faces in the soft, saffron light. Of those twenty-five men, only three drew his attention. Briggs and Scott were identical—Scott a few years older than Briggs, but otherwise the same: clear gray eyes, round chins, voices still quivering with excitement. The battle had terrified them both, but they'd never faltered. He knew he could trust them.

Speedy, too, had followed every order exactly, but through the whole day, even while riding close to the line of battle, his turban tucked down low to his charger's mane, his mind had seemed to be somewhere else. Once Napier had caught him looking back toward the Royal Road from the Warki Wawa, from which a sodden regiment of soldiers in scarlet tunics was debouching onto the plateau. It was too far away and the day was too gray for anyone without field glasses to make out individuals or even to identify the regiment from its colors, but Speedy looked as if he were watching, waiting, hoping, for one particular man. Under Napier's stare, Speedy had looked away with a guilty down-sweep of his eyes. And Napier had known, at that moment, what occupied Speedy's mind.

The rest of the officers at that table, even Merewether, Sandwith, and Chamberlain, were merely names attached to faces. They performed their functions adequately, with the expected amount of courage. They had little else to recommend them. They might despise the common English foot soldiers whom they commanded, but Napier had never found any difference between them and those foot soldiers except for a light dusting of education, a heavy dose of manners, and the money to buy a commission.

"Thank you, Briggs," Napier said at last. "I think things have worked out as planned."

The officers gave a polite round of handclaps, which seemed to irritate Napier. He went on: "I have another task for you this night, if you will take it. You've had a long day, a worthy day, but I would have one last message delivered without fail."

Briggs puffed out his chest. "I will deliver it, sir."

"I seem to remember, at that same dinner party, saying that another particular nationality shared in the savage imagination of the Ethiopians. Can you remember who they were, Major?"

"Easily, Sir Robert. The Irish."

"Forming a line against an attacking force of warriors needs discipline," Napier said. "Scaling high stone walls is an act of individual heroism, sacrifice, stupidity. To do a thing like that, a man has to think he is winning the war by himself. I want the Irish to do it."

Sandwith started to protest, then restrained himself.

"I want you to go down to the Bashillo tonight and bring the 33rd onto the Aroge plateau," said Napier. "You should make it by dawn. The 33rd will move into the van and lead the way onward."

Officers muttered as loudly as they dared. "They've been in disgrace, with good reason." "They shouldn't have the honor." "The mutinous bastards."

Napier ignored the grumbling. "You are to take command of the 33rd on the march up, Briggs. I want Colonel Cooper to come up quickly, so I can make certain arrangements with him tonight. Send Lieutenant-Colonel Phayre up with him. Be sure to let the men of the 33rd know they are to take the van. I think you'll see them step lively on the way out of the gorge." Napier sneaked a look at Speedy and saw how hard the man was thinking. It was a complicated situation, one that would need a master's play. Already, Phayre's exile to the Bashillo was a move that had pleased Napier. Napier could not resist adding one more torment to Phayre's purgatory: he planned to keep Phayre moving, through one excuse or another, up and down the gorge wall, from the Bashillo to Aroge and back to the Bashillo, until the poor man could not ride anymore.

Cooper was a completely different matter. Napier had not lied to Speedy, two months before: he had no intention of allowing Cooper to command the Irish in battle. He would divert Cooper off into other, harmless duties. The 33rd would be commanded—and Napier had relished this thought for a very long time—by his own aide-de-camp, Major Scott. It would need an instant promotion to a colonelcy for the young man, and that would cause grumbling on the staff, but Napier had ignored grumbling many times before. With the delight of a father on Christmas Eve, he pictured Scott's reaction when he told him: that boyish grin, almost a visual shout, shining through the desperate attempt to hide his emotions. "Ah, yes, Sir Robert, of course," he would say. "Very well, sir. I had rather fancied spending the battle at your side, sir, learning from your example, but if you think I should be better employed at the head of the gallant 33rd, then I shall be pleased to obey." And Scott saluting, marching in a dignified fashion out of sight, and then leaping into the air and shouting and running through the camp like a lunatic.

These primary pieces of Napier's grand game had all slipped into the

positions which Napier had selected for them weeks ago. He took a
gamesman's pleasure in seeing how easily he had maneuvered them. It
had all been simple, but now Speedy's wandering thoughts were adding
unexpected wrinkles to the game. Napier had taken Speedy's grudge
against Cooper, fed it, encouraged it, built it into a solid monument in
Speedy's brain. It had not been part of the major game, just a series of
moves made far out on the periphery of the board, something to idle
away the boring weeks. Napier had created Speedy's hate, and as its
creator he controlled it. Napier knew Speedy's frustration, rage, and
pride, but he also knew that Speedy, under the bravado, was a coward.
Speedy had no fear of death, pain, disfigurement, or any of the things
by which a man's courage is normally measured, but he did carry his
own particular terror: Speedy knew he was a crude, obnoxious oaf who
had never mastered any of the graces of a gentleman, and he lived in
constant terror of being known for what he was.

Murdering Cooper might have been a solution for Speedy, but in the
confines of the army it was impossible.

Though illegal, a duel might have been a solution, but Speedy knew
he could never carry it off with any dignity. He would do it clumsily,
and then he would be the laughing stock of every man in the army, from
Napier down to the lowest Bombay-beggar-turned-muleteer. That was
more than Speedy could bear.

So, Napier thought, Speedy had no choice: he might twist and squirm
and scheme and tremble inside with rage, but he would never, never,
never do anything to Cooper.

But power that isn't exercised is worthless—a gamesman's skill is
nothing if it isn't tested—so Napier decided to maneuver Speedy
through the night. He would remind Speedy that Cooper was alone, or
nearly so, in the Warki Wawa, tie him down with witnesses, put Speedy
on his horse, and send him out under cover of night where he couldn't
help reflecting on his impotence. Then, in the morning, Napier would
have the satisfaction of seeing Speedy and Cooper together, alive, on
Aroge. These, thought Napier, were the satisfactions that made the
game worth playing.

Briggs had risen to leave, but Napier had ignored him for more than
a minute. "By your leave, Sir Robert," said Briggs for the third time.

"Ah, yes, thank you," said Napier. "I know your fatigue, but I promise
you, there will be time to rest tomorrow, and rewards enough to make
it all worthwhile."

"I've no doubt of it," said Briggs. He saluted, said "Gentlemen" to his
fellow officers, and vanished into the night.

The conversation continued for another hour or so. One by one,
officers left for their tents, and at last Speedy rose. "I think I will catch
some few hours of sleep, Sir Robert," he said. "I am sure tomorrow will
not be lacking in excitement, and I should hate to sleep through it."

Harshly, Napier said, "I've work for you, Speedy."

Speedy had the look of a schoolboy caught in an improper act. "Sir?"

"I'm sure the 4th has posted regulation sentries in front of their line, but I would like more complete precautions tonight. After all"—he spoke slowly, emphasizing each word—"Colonel Cooper is coming up the Warki Wawa tonight, with the 33rd following some distance behind, and we should keep an eye on enemy movements in all directions. I would like two mounted patrols to travel a distance up the Royal Road tonight, toward the next plateaus."

"Fahla and Selassie," supplied Sandwith.

"Yes, toward Selassie."

"I don't think I am capable," stammered Speedy. "I shall fall asleep in the saddle."

Napier was impressed with Speedy's desperation: it must have caused him pain to point out personal weakness in front of a dozen fellow officers. Napier was impressed, also, with Speedy's keen perception of Napier's purpose; he had already tasted the temptation he would endure this night, and he had not liked it. In his cold camp bed he might at least have covered it with sleep, but out in the darkness he would have to live with it. "I think you are quite capable," Napier said flatly. "You will take ten sabers from the 3rd Bombay Light Cavalry. Move with utmost caution up the Royal Road. Pass beneath Fahla and observe whether there is any activity on the plateau beyond, Selassie. Take care against snipers. Scott is to follow half a mile behind with another thirty sabers, to support if needed. When you reach Selassie, wait, join with Scott if you are able to find each other in the dark, and watch until morning. Report to me only if there is any enemy movement. After dawn, you may return and retire in peace to bed."

As always, there was no arguing with Napier.

Speedy's horse protested at the fast pace Speedy set across the dark, treacherous plateau, but Speedy applied his spurs. The ten horses of the 3rd Bombay Light followed more readily, with Speedy's horse to pierce the darkness, and the riders were too eager for action to complain. One hundred men of their regiment were all the cavalry Napier had allowed to cross the Bashillo River. They were glad just to be on Aroge. If they were given a chance to do anything at all, even scouting duty, they would not object if they were led at a foolish pace through the night by a sullen, turbaned captain who answered their sergeant's question about where they were going with a single angry word: "Scouting."

Scott had given Speedy's party a head start of ten minutes, but Speedy's pace quickly lengthened it. The singing of the 4th King's Own, hoarse and imprecise after five drunken hours, retreated into the distance. The rain had stopped, but lightning bolts gave instant, burning images of Fahla on the right and Selassie straight ahead, and thunder rolled down in soft, vast waves.

Speedy halted where the Royal Road began to rise from the broad flatness of the plateau and entered the wilderness below Fahla. The ten horses jostled to a stop behind him. The sergeant was at Speedy's elbow: "Sir?"

Deep in thought that was as dark as the night, Speedy sat motionless for a minute. It ought to have been so simple: Cooper had embarrassed him in front of the entire army. Formal duels were illegal and had been for half a century, but there wasn't an English gentleman alive who would blame him for killing Cooper if the fight were fair, honest, and clean. He expected to face charges, certainly, but an officer and a gentleman such as himself wouldn't suffer more than a monetary fine, and in the long run it would enhance his reputation and aid his career in an army where imagination, boldness, and honor were in short supply. That had been his plan since the instant he'd learned that Cooper was coming up the Warki Wawa; he had never intended to go to bed; Napier had not robbed him of sleep, but of a chance to avenge his honor. It should have been so simple.

Then why, he asked himself, *did he have this vague uncomfortableness about the whole thing? And how had General Napier become mixed up in his mind with his hatred for Cooper?* It was almost as if Napier himself had created this feud, kept it alive by feeding its flames, reminded Speedy and Cooper of it by placing them side by side at Ashangi. *But why would Sir Robert do something like that?* It was too confusing. Speedy preferred his answers hard and fast and simple. Cold steel and bullets flaring through the night were the least complex answers he knew. The thing would be done properly, with a challenge, with witnesses, with honor . . . but above all it would be done. He pushed aside the confusion. A sudden lightning flash lit Selassie, still tall before them. Without looking at the man beside him, Speedy said, "We've reached Selassie. There is no sign of enemy movement."

Nervously, the sergeant said, "Sir, I would swear Selassie lies ahead."

"We've reached Selassie," said Speedy, stating it slowly so the sergeant would remember it. "We've done this much of our duty, anyway. You take the patrol, sergeant. I shall go elsewhere."

"Beg pardon, sir?" asked the sergeant, but Speedy had already started away from the Royal Road toward the eastern edge of the plateau. The sergeant whispered after him, "Sir?" There was no answer. He threw caution to the winds and shouted, "Should we come with you, captain?"

Speedy was already invisible. His voice drifted back, "No, I shall go alone."

"What of us, sir?" called the sergeant.

"What of you?"

"What orders, sir? What would you have us do?"

Speedy's laugh came from a long distance. "Do what you damn well please, sergeant."

Speedy spurred his horse along the eastern edge of Aroge, well away from Scott's route up the Royal Road, identified himself to the sentries of the 4th, skirted far behind Napier's pavilion, and regained the Royal Road where the naval rocketeers were still playing their concertinas and flutes, dancing their hornpipe, and swilling their rum. He followed Briggs's path into the gorge. The road was slick with twenty hours' rain. After they reached the Warki Wawa, the horse splashed through run-off water from the plateaus. Sometimes the wall of the ravine hung so high and close that all Speedy could see above was the gray reflection of lightning against the clouds. Near the lip of the Bashillo gorge, the ravine opened up for a few hundred yards. A loose mimosa grove stood on one side of the road, and a steep slope dropped abruptly off the other. Speedy turned his horse into the grove, drew his cape high around his neck, and settled down to wait.

He spent nearly three hours in the mimosa grove. The first light before dawn was already touching the underside of the clouds. Rain still drizzled, but there had been no lightning for an hour. Riders were coming up the gorge. Speedy leaned out cautiously and caught a brief, unclear glimpse. He made out three: Cooper in the lead, then Phayre, then Cooper's aide-de-camp. Speedy backed his horse another step into the shelter of the grove.

The men passed in front of Speedy. They rode wearily, silently, hunched against the rain. Speedy let the third rider, the aide-de-camp, get thirty feet beyond him. He would make an entrance worthy of his turban and his mustache. Later, Phayre and the aide would describe how he had appeared like a horseman of the apocalypse out of the night, thundering suddenly up the rain-slick road, waving his saber, challenging his enemy in the resonant voice that Speedy had practiced for so many years. It would be a good touch. Gently, Speedy pulled his famous cavalry saber from its scabbard. He drove his spurs violently into his horse's flanks, and the animal sprang out of the grove. Too late, Speedy sensed the fourth rider. A dark shape loomed against his cheek, pressed against his leg and molded tight into his horse's body. Then the shape screamed and reared and spun away into the night. The rider separated from the horse and fell away down the slope. The horse's front hooves came off the track and the slope carried it downward, screaming.

Speedy's horse stood sideways across the road. Speedy knew instantly that he had succeeded in making himself into a fool. Instinctively, he raised his hands in a gesture that was meant to say he was sorry, that he hadn't known the fourth man was there, that this hadn't been his intention, but a sudden flash of lightning gleamed against his saber.

In yet another flash, Speedy saw the third rider turning a pistol on him; Phayre was staring dumbly down the track, and, farthest away, Cooper was fumbling with his holster. The third rider's pistol flash lengthened the lightning burst by a fraction of a second, and Speedy felt the burn across his temple and through the fleshy part of his ear. He reacted without thinking. His spurs dug in, the horse lurched forward, and Speedy was close enough. The pistol fired again, and Speedy felt the bullet wet inside his ribs. His saber sizzled into the man's face, just below the solar helmet. Speedy struck with a loose wrist so the saber would slice clean and come free easily. Speedy's horse's momentum carried them past the aide before the man tottered in his saddle.

Phayre had pulled his horse sideways across the road to see what was happening. His eyes were blank holes. Concentrating on Cooper beyond, Speedy swung at Phayre with the careless disregard of a man pushing through a curtain. Phayre fell backward instantly, carried down by a slash in the neck. Speedy's horse hesitated against the shoulder of Phayre's horse. Speedy kicked with the spurs, and his horse pushed upward.

Cooper had turned his horse to face Speedy's. He had his pistol out, and his thumb was at the hammer. Almost before he was into range, Speedy leaned toward the man he hated and made a short, chopping blow with his saber. The last six inches of the blade touched Cooper's wrist. Still tight together, the pistol and the hand fell into the mud.

The horses were pressed together now, nose to tail. Cooper's shoulder brushed Speedy's. Cooper stared without understanding at the painless stump. Speedy tried to maneuver far enough away to swing his saber, but there was no room on the narrow road. He backhanded Cooper across the face with his saber hilt. Cooper tumbled into the mud below the track. Twenty feet away, he tried to rise. Speedy drew his own pistol, took careful aim across Cooper's empty saddle, and put a bullet in Cooper's back. The elderly colonel pitched forward onto his face.

Feeling the coldness of the rain for the first time, Speedy holstered his pistol, leaned down to wipe his blade clean on Phayre's tunic, and sheathed his saber. Then he started down the Royal Road into the Bashillo gorge. It would be something of a lonely ride to Zula, he knew, but he had ridden alone before. He would have to leave the road, of course, and avoid British patrols, but he knew the language; he had traveled Ethiopia in the past, and he would do it again.

He touched a finger to his ear, which burned. Half the ear was gone. He touched his chest, halfway between his left nipple and his armpit, which burned too, but with an icy-cold fire. His chest was numb, and he did not feel the touch of his finger. The ear might burn, he decided, but it was the chest that should worry him. He must do something about it before long.

He did not anticipate any special trouble when he resurfaced in Aden or Bombay or London, after a year or so of lying low. It had been a point of honor, after all, hadn't it? What matter if it hadn't turned out as he had planned? In the flush of victory over the Ethiopians, who would worry much about him? And by the time he made it home, the event would have receded so far into the distance that he could pass it off as a proper duel, fought with all the gentlemanly niceties, and no one would disagree.

On the way into the Bashillo gorge, Speedy passed Briggs at the head of the 33rd Regiment. Singing songs of the Irish rebellions, the Irishmen were stumbling at a fast pace up the Royal Road. Keeping his left arm folded across his chest and his head tilted away to hide his wounds, Speedy waved to Briggs, called out, "Message to deliver," and pushed the Irish infantrymen out of his way.

Confused by Speedy's sudden departure, the sergeant had decided to take his patrol back to headquarters for instructions. In the darkness he and his men wandered away from the nearly invisible Royal Road and passed a hundred yards to one side of Scott's larger support patrol. Expecting that Speedy had already scouted the road beyond Aroge, Scott led his thirty cavalrymen into the wilderness toward Selassie at a much faster rate than he would otherwise have set, and he did not take proper care to listen and to watch for enemy warriors.

Seven warriors who had been driven far down the western cliff of Aroge by the Madras Sappers were making their way back to Magdala. They were overjoyed to hear hoofbeats coming up the road. They hid themselves in the brush above the road, and as the English cavalrymen were passing they fired a ragged volley at them. In the manner of Ethiopian warriors, always seeking after glory, all of them had aimed their flintlocks at the leader. One ball pierced Scott's temple, and he fell, the first Englishman since John Bell to die at Ethiopian hands.

22

Saturday, April 11, 1868
Magdala

Rassam slept badly that night. Sometime after midnight, he bolted awake out of a tortured, confusing dream to clutch the scaly hand that was shaking his arm. He only let the hand go when he recognized Samuel by the cloudy light of his *balderaba*'s lantern. "What is it?" he asked, fearfully.

"The emperor calls for you," said Samuel.

"Ah, very well," mumbled Rassam, and slipped off his *arat.*

"He wants you to wear the uniform you wore the first time he saw you," said Samuel.

Rassam rummaged around in a rhino-hide trunk and brought out the blue suit he had worn for his first audiences with Theodore. The moisture of two rainy seasons had left it mildewed, and the moths of two dry seasons had claimed one entire elbow. He dressed, then followed Samuel into the night. The ground was cold and slick under Rassam's bare feet, the air biting and pleasantly familiar. "I've enjoyed the weather here," he told Samuel. "The rain, the fresh air, the flowers and birds."

"That is good," said Samuel.

"Whatever may happen," Rassam said to Samuel's back, "I've enjoyed having you serve me. You have been loyal and honest. Above all, honest. I apologize for the times I doubted you."

Samuel stopped, but didn't turn. He murmured, "Thank you," and walked on.

"What happened in the fighting yesterday?" Rassam asked. The sounds of battle had been loud in the British compound. For three hours, Blanc, Kerens, and Rassam had sat together under a leaky bamboo awning and listened, first to the high-pitched chanting of the warriors, then to the rolling volleys of the British infantrymen and the thunder of the cannon, finally to the sporadic fire of the Ethiopian flintlocks. Every free Magdala man, except for their own personal servants, had joined in the fight. There weren't even any guards at the gate of the British compound. Once, Kerens cautiously pushed the plaited door open and peered out into the city. He returned to the awning and announced, in the general way in which the Europeans passed along information, careful not to compromise their two-year-old feud: "I do not think there is anyone but children, women, and great-grandfathers. Every man capable of lifting a weapon must be at the battle." The Europeans could have walked out of Magdala without hindrance, but no one moved, since the only route off the mountain was choked with ten thousand Ethiopian warriors.

No word had yet reached the Europeans from the battlefield.

Without turning or slowing his pace, Samuel said, with an old man's calm, deliberate acceptance, "It was a disaster, worse than anything else in all the *Zemene Mesafint.* The emperor is alive, and so is Wolde. All the rest of the invincible Twelve are dead. Magiga Dulou is dead. A thousand warriors are dead." His factual, bland tone affected Rassam more than tears would have done.

"How is the emperor?" asked Rassam, but Samuel pretended he hadn't heard. They walked half a mile through the quiet, peaceful city and arrived at a long, low house. Rassam recognized it from descriptions he had heard: it was the palace Theodore had built for Tawavitch, his beloved wife. According to what Rassam had heard, Theodore had ordered it to be sealed up after her death, and no one had ever entered it since. Samuel led Rassam to the front door and motioned him inside.

Rassam pulled the door open and paused in the doorway. The only light came through a door, slightly ajar, that led into the next room. Rassam could barely make out ghostly forms, furniture draped with blankets, all the sharp angles gentled with dust. A powerful smell of rat droppings clogged Rassam's nostrils. Rassam walked through the room, pulled open the door, and stepped into the room beyond.

Theodore lay on an *arat.* The dusty, tattered blanket that had protected it for thirteen years had not been removed, and the dust had peeled away from the blanket onto Theodore's white clothing. His eyes were open and he was aware, but one limp hand lay on the floor, and his jaw hung open. The other hand unsteadily supported a gourd of some liquid: *tej,* from the sweet odor that permeated the room and blended unpleasantly with all the other scents. Just above his eyebrows, a fresh coronet of charred tissue and dried blood had been burned into his forehead.

Wolde sat against the opposite wall on a low stool. His heavy iron crucifix dangled down, as if he were too exhausted to carry it anymore. Silently, wearily, he waved Rassam onto a stool beside his own. They exchanged a glance and both understood, vaguely, that they were on the same side.

It was some minutes before Theodore turned his eyes toward Rassam and then lurched up to a sitting position. He wavered, threw himself onto his knees and held a bowl to his face. He vomited into the bowl with great surging heaves, rinsed his mouth out with *tej,* and spat the mouthful of milky liquid into the bowl. He leaned back against the *arat* and whispered, "Please, Wolde." Weakly, the little priest set down the crucifix, took the bowl through another door, and a few moments later returned with it, still dripping clean water.

With his legs curled under him and his hands folded in his lap, Theodore looked very tiny. He gave Rassam the impression of a sheltered child brought suddenly face-to-face with some unimagined horror.

Theodore waited for Rassam to speak, but Rassam would not, and finally Theodore tossed up his hands in a childlike gesture and said, "Do you see how low I've sunk?"

Rassam didn't answer.

Theodore went on: "Yesterday was Good Friday, the day our Lord Iyesus bled out his life on the Roman Tree. The Friday and the Saturday are an absolute fast for Copts. It is the most sacred obligation of the year. We aren't to eat a morsel, nor drink anything but water. Look at me, Rassam." With his hands and his voice, he pleaded for Rassam to forgive him or to punish him, somehow to give him release. "It's all here. Every terror I've ever imagined. Watching my people die. Magiga Dulou, my Twelve—" He remembered Wolde and corrected himself: "Eleven of my Twelve. And all those other thousands of men. I watched from Fahla and saw them all die. They trusted me. I could have sent them away and faced my death alone, but I wouldn't do it. I've been in battle before, and every time I've died a hundred little deaths. I'm not like Gabry and the rest. I've always hated it, seen what a waste it is." He paused, then continued with wonder. "Rassam, I saw the exploding stars. Your people are bringing them. I don't know what they are, but I've seen them before. I saw them in my vision, the day we killed the soldiers who sacked our village. Seeing those stars is like seeing the face of God. I'm not strong enough to look at them. No man is that strong. Rassam, I'm terrified. I can't go through with it." His words were slurred with drink. Tears flowed through the gray dust on his burned face. "Thirty years ago, God told me what He was going to demand of me. He gave me years to prepare, and now that the time is come—I cannot!" Theodore shuffled forward on his knees and reached for Rassam's hands. He squeezed them tightly. "Rassam, go down to your General Sir Robert Napier. Be *my* envoy, now. Take Wolde with you. Stop the bloodshed. Let us live. Stop the British army before it attacks."

Theodore released Rassam's hands.

Rassam flexed them slowly and said, "I will, Your Majesty. I urged this weeks ago."

"You were right," cried Theodore. Then, more calmly, he said, "You still wear the lion signet."

Rassam raised his hand to show Theodore the ring the messenger had brought him.

"It marks you as my envoy," said Theodore. "It gives you free passage anywhere in my domain."

Rassam and Wolde rose and started out the door.

"Rassam," called Theodore.

Rassam stopped in the doorway.

"Whatever you do," said Theodore, "don't tell your General Sir Robert Napier that I want him to forgive me. That is the last sign. It mustn't be fulfilled."

Rassam turned away and left Tawavitch's palace.

Down the trail from Magdala and on the Royal Road past Islamgie and Selassie, Wolde and Rassam guided their horses slowly through a horde of Ethiopians. By the murky light of a damp, cold dawn, a general exodus from Magdala was taking place. Rassam was astonished to see that it wasn't only women, bundling their children out of range of the exploding stars, carrying away on their heads as many of their possessions as they could: there were thousands of able-bodied men, too. As a sign of disgrace, the warriors had let out their braids, but they hadn't left their weapons behind. That these men were escaping—that they would take a chance in the surrounding territory, filled with Gallas who would turn hostile the instant Theodore fell, rather than remain any longer in Theodore's impregnable stronghold—was a measure of how badly they had been crushed on Aroge.

Wolde seemed to be embarrassed by Theodore's condition and by the deserting army. Rassam didn't press him to talk, so they rode in silence.

The evacuees turned away from the Royal Road just below Selassie and headed into the relative security of the steep wilderness to the east of Aroge, in order to bypass the British army. Finally alone except for Wolde, Rassam stopped and studied Aroge from above. Morning campfires were still visible, but it was light enough to recognize several regiments by their uniforms and the regimental colors that hung wetly, like sheets caught on the clothesline in a downpour. At the far end of the plateau, fresh troops were debouching from the Warki Wawa. There were many artillery pieces with them, on elephant-back and behind teams of mules. Directly below them, the British were already on the move. Indian Sappers were coming first, flung out on either side of the road as an advance guard, but the following regiment—scarlet tunics, black trousers, white solar helmets—was marching up the road so eagerly there was hardly any gap between them and the Sappers. Just at the fringes of the morning, a brisk tune reached Rassam's ears. There was no mistaking the favorite, most bitter song of the Irish regiments. Across the sea, the Confederacy had borrowed the tune for its own "When Johnny Comes Marching Home," but for the Irish it had always been, and would never be anything else than, "Johnny, I Hardly Knew

Ye." The song was astonishing in the callousness of its view of soldiering: The chorus told how Johnny had marched off to war and been nearly slain by the enemy. The verses told the story of Johnny's return to wife and child:

> Where are the eyes that looked so mild, hoo-roo, hoo-roo?
> Where are the eyes that looked so mild, hoo-roo, hoo-roo?
> Where are the eyes that looked so mild,
> When my poor heart you first beguiled?
> Why did ye skidaddle from me an' the child?
> Johnny, I hardly knew ye.
>
> Where are the legs with which you run, hoo-roo, hoo-roo?
> Where are the legs with which you run, hoo-roo, hoo-roo?
> Where are the legs with which you run,
> When first you went to carry a gun?
> Johnny, I hardly knew ye.
>
> You haven't an arm, you haven't a leg, hoo-roo, hoo-roo,
> You haven't an arm, you haven't a leg, hoo-roo, hoo-roo,
> You haven't an arm, you haven't a leg,
> You're an eyeless, boneless, chickenless egg.
> Johnny, I hardly knew ye.

So, Rassam thought, the English were sending two groups of their colonial servants, the Indians and the Irish, to finish off the emperor of the Ethiopians.

Cautiously, Rassam and Wolde started down. The Sappers stared curiously at them as they rode through the center of the skirmishing line, and a young English subaltern tapped his helmet and said, without surprise, "Morning, sir."

An officer on horseback, with several aides, was at the head of the Irish regiment. When thirty yards separated them, the officer called a halt to the regiment and trotted forward alone. He was very young, but, as was proper, he showed absolutely no curiosity as he carefully looked over Wolde, then Rassam. His voice was under complete control, and he modulated his accent perfectly: "Brevet Colonel Briggs, commanding her Majesty's 33rd Wellington's Own regiment." The "brevet" indicated that his colonelcy was only a temporary promotion for the duration of an assignment that demanded a higher rank than he actually possessed.

Briggs was the first new English-speaking man Rassam had met in two years. The man's calculated coldness, his lack of interest, his absolute similarity to Henry Blanc, stunned Rassam. He tried to remind himself that every young English gentleman learned to play this role. He struggled to recover and to remember his own English speech and mannerisms, but as soon as the first words had left his lips, he knew he had failed to convince the young colonel. "I am Hormuzd Rassam, Her Majesty's envoy to the emperor of the Ethiopians. At your service."

"Pleased," said Briggs.

Rassam fumbled along. "I am here this morning on a rather curious mission. I was sent by His Majesty, the emperor of Ethiopia, to speak on his behalf to the commanding general. Would you be so kind as to deliver me to him?"

"Certainly," said Briggs. "At once. I shall escort you personally." He hesitated, perhaps remembering that he was in command of a regiment. "I shall have an aide-de-camp escort you, sir."

"I would appreciate that courtesy," said Rassam.

Briggs called two of the aides. "Escort Mr. Rassam and—" he hesitated again, looking contemptuously at Wolde.

"Wolde, the Emperor Theodore's priest and confidant," said Rassam.

"Escort them to General Napier's headquarters."

"Colonel Briggs, I should hold my regiment on Selassie, if I were you," said Rassam. "I believe the words I bring from His Majesty to General Napier will prevent a battle this day. Hopefully altogether."

For the first time, Briggs allowed emotion to show through: he was clearly disappointed, and an echoing groan rolled backward through the regiment as Rassam's words were relayed toward the rear. "Those were already my orders," said Briggs. "To secure Selassie and gather there. Our General Napier is a cautious man."

Near the rear of the regiment, Geoffrey Irion waited for the envoy and the one-armed Ethiopian child-priest to pass. He was disappointed in the man he saw—and he was pleased at his disappointment. The envoy was a perfectly nondescript sort of man: forty-some years old, unshaven, bare feet dangling without shackles, wearing faded blue rags but looking far healthier than a man had a right to look after two years in prison. He seemed absolutely harmless, no one toward whom a sailor should bear a burning hatred for nearly four years. Rassam appeared to be exactly the man Irion had hoped he would be.

There was jostling ahead in the column, and Irion looked toward the front of the regiment. Colonel Briggs was riding, and the regiment followed. Despite all the excitement that his long, sleepless night had seen, Briggs still gave every sign of enjoying himself. It must have been a shock when, an hour after dawn, he had stumbled across the body of Cooper's aide-de-camp, lying on the Royal Road in the rain. They had found the body of Lieutenant-Colonel Phayre on the road and the bodies of Colonel Cooper and the broken-backed aide down on the muddy slope below; they had also found Cooper's hand, rigid around the pistol butt. They had wrapped up the bodies, slung them over horses, and proceeded upward, and though there wasn't an Irishman in the 33rd who didn't know who had killed the four officers, it wasn't until he reached Napier's headquarters that Briggs connected the murders with Speedy's urgent departure down the trail into the gorge. A small company of lances set off in pursuit, but no one expected them to find him.

The regiment was not particularly stung by the loss of Cooper, who had been an ineffectual leader when he bothered to lead at all, but they devoted an enormous amount of verbal energy to discussing the superstitious value of losing two commanders to violence before the regiment had even come under fire.

They overcame their worries immediately when Napier appeared before them at a predawn assembly of the regiment. They cheered wildly and threw their helmets into the air when Napier announced that the 33rd would take the lead on the march toward Magdala, and that they should be making the actual assault on the citadel before nightfall. They had cheered again, with hardly less enthusiasm, when Napier told them that he had put Briggs in permanent command of the regiment. Actually, the regiment felt no great need for leadership of any kind: all they really wanted was someone who would not interfere with them.

They had set out briskly, with a sense of impending final vindication, itching for battle. They were a little dizzy from sleeplessness, but no matter: it served to give their intoxication a keener edge.

To the men of the 33rd, Hormuzd Rassam was far more than a man. He had been a symbol, an excuse to fight, a vague end that justified their African adventure. Very rarely had any of them actually tried to picture him as a real, flesh-and-blood human being. Now, on the last leg of their journey, with their self-respect restored and their weapons primed, they had seen Rassam, a meek, small man who told them they wouldn't, after all, be fighting. On the way up to Selassie they let the Sappers gain their proper distance, and more. Even the sight of Magdala itself, two miles away, towering like a magical castle from stories told by itinerant poets in their childhoods in Connemara and Clare and Kerry, couldn't dispel their sudden gloom. Half a mile onto Selassie they threw their equipment down in the mud, threw themselves on top, lit their pipes, and stared in silence at the unreachable citadel.

Rassam and Wolde and the two aides-de-camp passed other units which were already on the march toward Magdala; the Beloochees, the 10th Native Infantry, the 45th Sherwood Foresters. The 4th King's Own was preparing to march, and behind them the Naval Brigade was already on the move.

Rassam and Wolde were a strange sight, and the sailors stared at them, but Rassam rode looking straight ahead toward Napier's Union Jack pavilion and did not notice the huge, nut-brown sailor whose jaw dropped open as he saw Rassam, and who stopped so suddenly to gape that his mule walked into his back and the line of sailors behind jumbled up. In the excitement of the battle, Pilbeam had entirely forgotten about his envoy, but this new look at him renewed his hatred. He swore again that he would do something to see him in misery.

Rassam and Wolde and the two aides reached Napier's pavilion, and grooms took their horses. Napier, who had already been awake and dressed for four hours, saw them at once. Rassam walked into his presence, tipped his helmet, and said, "Good morning, sir. I am Hormuzd Rassam, Her Majesty's envoy to Ethiopia. At your service." Napier stared at Rassam far longer than politeness allowed, as if Rassam were some object Napier had been seeking, but—like a dead rat in the attic—had hoped not to find. At last he asked, simply, "What are you doing here?" The voice said Napier had no interest at all in Rassam as a person.

Rassam fought back the impulse to answer, as rudely as he could, "What are *you* doing here, sir?" Instead, he said, "His Majesty asked me to come down. He had no idea how thoroughly outmatched he is by a British army. He thought force of numbers would win the day, and he found out that it couldn't."

"What does he want, then?" asked Napier.

"He wants the fighting to stop."

"Is he surrendering?"

"He just wants the fighting to stop," said Rassam.

Napier leaned back in his chair and chewed thoughtfully at the nub of a pencil. Rassam remained in front of the desk, with Wolde to one side. After another minute, Napier asked, "Who is *he?*"

"This is Wolde, Theodore's priest and closest friend," said Rassam. In Amharic, he introduced Napier. Wolde salaamed, and Napier said, "Pleased." Then, to Rassam, Napier asked, "Does he speak any English?"

"Not a word," said Rassam.

"Does he have to be here?"

"Not particularly."

"Does he speak Arabic?" asked Napier.

Rassam nodded.

"I'll send for my Arabic translator, Colonel Merewether," said Napier. "The colonel can show your friend the elephants and the cannons. The Ethiopians usually enjoy seeing them."

Angrily, Rassam started, "I don't think you have enough respect for Wolde, sir. The man isn't one of your ignorant savages—"

Napier held up his hand, and his voice stopped Rassam with a power that Rassam had never heard in any other voice besides Theodore's. "On the contrary, Mr. Rassam. I have too much respect for them. Can't get another man in the army to understand that we shouldn't underestimate them. I want to talk honestly with you, and I can't do it in front of Wolde."

Napier called his secretary and sent the man for Merewether. While they waited, Rassam explained to Wolde everything that had been said. Though he and Wolde had hardly spoken a word on the trip down from Magdala, each of them had a sense of being completely allied with the other, brought together by a common, desperate need to find some sort of release for Theodore. "You will tell me everything that passes," Wolde said, and Rassam told him, "Of course. Trust me."

Merewether appeared in the pavilion's doorway and gave Rassam the first smile he had received from anyone in the British army. They shook hands with pleasure, and Napier gave them a few minutes to chat about matters of little substance, before he sent Merewether and Wolde away.

Alone with Rassam, Napier seemed to relax. He waved Rassam into a chair, offered him a brandy, and asked, "What is happening up on that mountain? Tell me everything."

Rassam savored his brandy, marveled at the absence of pulp in it and the clarity of its taste, and gave Napier a careful, cursory description of the situation. He told the general that most of Theodore's army had defected in the morning, and that the previous day's battle had left the warriors who remained leaderless. At Napier's suggestion, he even sketched a map of Magdala's walls, as well as his limited experience outside the prisoners' compound allowed him to do. Napier listened to all this information, and then he surprised Rassam by saying, "That is all very well—these are things I need to know—but what I *really* want to know is: what is Theodore like? *Who is he?* I've been chasing after him for six months. No, far longer than that, actually—ever since you and Dr. Blanc left Massawa for Ethiopia, and I first knew there would have to be an expedition. I've heard snatches about him from people who've known him, from people who've hated him. He fascinates me. I want to know him."

With an acid edge, Rassam said, "You want to know the victim before you murder him."

"Ah, so he has done it to you, too," laughed Napier. "No one, it seems, can remain neutral with respect to this emperor of the Ethiopians. If a man doesn't love him, he hates him. There is no middle ground."

"He is a great man," said Rassam. He hesitated, stopped by a sudden unwillingness to have Napier know anything about Theodore. He realized that Napier was exactly like Theodore, an overwhelming man, a man one would either have to hate or to love. Napier was the only kind of man who could occupy that middle ground with Theodore: he would neither hate nor love the emperor. That neutrality, Rassam decided, comprised the ultimate contempt anyone could hold for a man like Theodore, for it denied him his greatness. Rassam knew that he hated Napier. "That is all," said Rassam. "Theodore is simply a great man."

"Come, there must be more," said Napier. "Is he still clinging to this belief that I am his—what did Paniotti call it?—his Light Bringer?"

As Napier had intended, Rassam started at Paniotti's name, but he only answered, "His Majesty does not discuss his beliefs with me."

"Something like that must be common knowledge in Magdala," said Napier.

"The Ethiopians are quite secretive," said Rassam. "Remember, I have been a prisoner."

"Is he still looking at my army as the instrument of his martyrdom?" asked Napier.

"His Majesty does not discuss his beliefs with me," repeated Rassam.

"Does his martyrdom require him to resist to the death?" asked Napier.

"His Majesty does not discuss—"

Napier stopped him with a wave of the hand. "No more of this, please, Mr. Rassam. You aren't willing to tell me about him. I can respect that, even if I can't understand it. Will you tell me something else?"

"What is it?" asked Rassam.

"What will happen to his country after he is dead?"

"An old Ethiopian servant of mine told me an ancient proverb," said Rassam. "It is this: 'When the emperor dies, whom can one ask for justice?' "

"And that means?" asked Napier.

"It means that the country will sink back into the *Zemene Mesafint*, the era of lawlessness and anarchy that reigned before Theodore put an end to it. From what I understand, the *Zemene Mesafint* has already returned to the areas where his control is gone. The country is plunging back into the Dark Ages."

"Do you blame me for that?" asked Napier.

Rassam threw up his hands. "It is your fault," he said. "It is Theodore's fault. It is even mine. Or perhaps it is no one's fault, only history's."

Napier waved away the approaching philosophical discussion. "What could prevent it?" he asked. "Don't give me metaphysics. Give me concrete, political, military actions that can save a country."

Rassam said, "You could turn around and leave Ethiopia, and leave Theodore on his throne."

Angrily, Napier tossed his pencil down on the desk. "You know I cannot do that—and even if I could, that it wouldn't save Theodore."

"A strong hand and a modern army, then," said Rassam. He remembered his promise to Theodore. Trying to speak boldly, convincingly, he continued, "If you stayed on in Ethiopia with a small army, you could quell the rebellions easily and bring peace to the land."

Napier thought very hard. "You pose a difficult dilemma," he said slowly. "I will tell you honestly, Mr. Rassam, that I won't stay. I came for a reason, and that reason has nothing to do with staying in Ethiopia, or even in India."

The world seemed to fall away from Rassam. Somehow, against all hope, Theodore's certainty had made Rassam believe that Napier, even if he wasn't a Light Bringer ordained and sent by God, would stay in Ethiopia.

But Napier spoke again. "There are other alternatives. A message to the telegraph at Antalo, and instructions might come back from London in a fortnight."

"Instructions for what?" asked Rassam.

"Someone else to stay on in Ethiopia with troops."

"One of your officers?" asked Rassam. "Merewether?"

"You," said Napier, and he let the word dangle alone for a moment.

"You have been here for two years. You know the country better than anyone. We could create the Crown Colony of Ethiopia, pacify the populace, establish trading posts here. You could serve as civil governor. I could leave you a military governor and a large garrison."

Rassam had no response to make. Napier expected none. Rassam would not accept the challenge, and the responsibility was off Napier's shoulders. If Ethiopia sank back into anarchy as a result of Napier's expedition, it wasn't Napier's fault, but Rassam's.

There was no answer, and Napier changed the subject. "I should write some sort of response to the emperor," he said. He brought out pen, ink, and paper, and wrote:

> Your Majesty has fought like a brave man, and has been overcome by the superior power of the British army. It is my desire that no more blood be shed. If, therefore, Your Majesty will submit to the Queen of England, and bring all the Europeans now in Your Majesty's hands, and deliver them safely this day in the British camp, I guarantee honorable treatment for yourself and all of Your Majesty's subjects.

Rassam read it and put it into a pocket. "But what does it mean?" he asked.

Napier smiled. "Absolutely nothing. There will be a battle. We will storm Magdala. We will win, he will die." Napier lingered over his next words. Cruelly, he said, "I saw your friend Abd-ul-Kerim in Zula. He has been in the service of the emperor for the last year or so. You cannot save the emperor for him, but you do have a chance to carry on Theodore's plans. I think your friend would like that. Consider my offer well, won't you?"

Rassam stood. "Thank you for the brandy," he said, and then he turned in the doorway of the pavilion. "There is something else. Wolde told me this while we were riding down. It is an Ethiopian custom to send cattle to an enemy. The gesture implies that the giver asks forgiveness of the other. It is considered a very humbling gesture. And if the person who has been sent the cattle refuses them, then it is assumed that forgiveness has been refused."

Napier said, "I won't be able to forgive him unless he formally, unconditionally surrenders."

"I am aware of that," said Rassam. "You will wait for him to make up his mind, won't you?"

"Until tomorrow," said Napier. "It is a truce until Sunday morning."

Below Magdala, Rassam and Wolde had ridden past the gathering force of the British army, infantry and artillery and rocketeers, which had continued to mass on the plateau while they were with the commanding general. On the trail from Selassie to Magdala they had had to push their way through the last remnants of the exodus from Magdala. As soon as Rassam and Wolde entered the citadel through the zigzag gate, Rassam realized how perceptive Wolde had been in warning him about the gesture of the sheep and the cows. Just inside the gate Theodore was sitting on a stool in the inner courtyard watching a few of his remaining men herding together a flock of sheep and cattle.

Rassam and Wolde dismounted and went to him. Theodore looked up wearily at Rassam. "I am ashamed," he said.

"There is no need," said Rassam. "I still consider you to be—"

"In front of myself," interrupted Theodore, suddenly fierce. Then, in a milder voice: "In front of my God. With my eleven lost Disciples, all dead on Aroge, I should have known, but I was weak and drunk. Shaitan had control of me. I was ready to fail my God. But He came to me and strengthened me, as He always did in years past. He did not speak, but I could feel the strength flowing into my mind. Now, I will not fail Him."

Rassam hesitated. He didn't know what he had hoped from Theodore, but it wasn't a renewed decision to martyr himself. It was plain that Theodore had lost his empire down on the Aroge plateau, but at least, thought Rassam, the man could live. But once again he seemed intent on following through with his cherished martyrdom. His voice was flat and spent, but determined. There was none of this morning's terror in it: only resignation.

"General Napier sends a message," said Rassam.

"I will hear it," said Theodore, "but it won't make any difference. The stars have exploded. I am doing the last task of my life, sending these cows and sheep. Do you understand their significance?"

Wolde said, "I told him."

"And if they are accepted?" asked Rassam.

Theodore ignored the question, and he said, "Read the message."

Rassam translated Napier's words into Amharic.

"It says very little," said Theodore when Rassam was finished. "What is 'honorable treatment'? Is he offering me my throne? Is he promising not to kill me? Or is he promising to kill me to end my shame?"

"I don't know," said Rassam. "It doesn't matter, does it?"

"No," said Theodore. "All that matters is my shame, and the cruel punishment God is giving me for it." He cradled his head in his hands, and despite the gravity of the moment, Rassam nearly laughed at the emperor's hangover.

Watching Theodore in the pain of his vast, imperial headache, Rassam would not have dared to predict one minute of the future. Theodore seemed committed to death, but he had changed so often, so mercurially, that he could do anything at any moment. He might proceed as he planned, or he might surrender to Napier, or he might—and Rassam shuddered at the thought—go into one of the violent blackouts that always seemed to come at times of greatest stress.

Rassam stayed with Theodore and Wolde until Theodore's men herded the cattle and sheep through the gate and started down to find

Napier. Leaving them sitting close together, all alone, he went back by himself through the deserted city to the British compound.

The summons from Theodore came at five o'clock in the afternoon. Samuel came into the compound, found each European individually, and told him that Theodore had given orders for them all to pack their belongings and meet him on the Islamgie saddle. Out of the Europeans' more than fifty servants, only half a dozen still remained. They worked quickly in the failing light, tying together bundles of possessions, loading the pack mules that Samuel had brought, saying quick good-bys to warriors who were staying behind. The Europeans themselves, except for Cameron, milled around aimlessly, suddenly lost in the familiar open space between their huts. They stared at one another from a distance, and at last it was Blanc who broke the two-years-long silence. He turned suddenly and strode, as boldly as he could, straight up to Rassam and grasped his hand. He started to speak, changed his mind, then blurted out something less than what he had meant to say: "Wouldn't do to be seen fighting by our saviors, would it?" Still clutching Rassam's hand, he called for Kerens. The young Irishman shook Blanc's hand, and Rassam's. "Jolly good to be friends again," said Kerens, who was still so young that a simple handshake could erase in an instant two years of hatred, and then the three of them took a step backward, looked in astonishment at one another, and wandered away to collect their thoughts.

Cameron, still seeming to hover near death, was loaded carefully onto a stretcher, and the two Ethiopians who would carry it set him casually down in a deep, scummy puddle and walked away. No one moved him. Kerens's mistress, always the image of unhurried modesty, waited with the mules.

"Come, we must hurry," called Samuel from the plaited door. "We must be down before dark." Kerens and Blanc led the servants to the door. Kerens marched quickly through, but Blanc paused at the door, as if he were afraid, after two years, to see the outside world. Then he leaped through. The servants and the mules followed.

Samuel had purposely held back until the last, and he and Rassam were the only ones left at the door. Samuel took Rassam's arm. There was a sense of urgency in his voice: "Master Rassam, I desire a thing of you."

"You have only to ask," said Rassam.

"I have been loyal," said Samuel. "I have never disobeyed an order. I have never failed in a duty to you. I have never asked a thing for myself."

"Samuel, you have been everything a servant could be, and more," said Rassam. "What is it you ask?"

Softly, Samuel said one word: "Release."

"What do you mean?" asked Rassam.

"I would be released from your service." Samuel cast the phrase into the most formal mode of Amharic speech.

"You aren't my slave," said Rassam.

"I am your *balderaba,*" said the wiry old man. "I am yours until you release me. Now, if you will, I would be released."

"Where will you go?" asked Rassam.

"Nowhere. I will stay here."

"It is too dangerous," said Rassam.

"I would stay here," said Samuel. "I am an old man, and I've lived most of my years with the Emperor Theodore. Many of his people left him today, but I am one who would stay."

"You will die," said Rassam. "I can't let you stay."

Tears were falling down Samuel's dusty cheeks. "I would stay."

Rassam looked down at him and saw his desperation. He put his hand on Samuel's shoulder, but couldn't quite bring himself to draw a servant into an embrace. "I release you," he said.

"Thank you," mumbled Samuel. "I am sorry I won't be able to help guide you down the mountain."

Rassam stopped the apology. "I will always remember you with affection."

"And I you," said Samuel.

Rassam started through the door, but Samuel still held his arm. "Another thing I would beg of you, Master Rassam," he said, but where he had been begging before, now he was demanding. "I would beg you not to forget the emperor. To remember his dreams. To keep alive his memory."

"I will," promised Rassam. "I swear it." He had spent the entire afternoon worrying over Napier's mock offer to remain as Ethiopia's civil governor. Mock offer it might be, but once given, he was certain Napier couldn't withdraw it. At the moment, it was the best for which Theodore might hope. Rassam didn't know whether he could sacrifice himself to it or not.

The two men parted, and Rassam hurried after the others.

They found enough horses waiting outside the zigzag gate for everyone, British and servants alike, to ride, though the two men carrying Cameron had no choice but to walk down the long switchback trail to the Islamgie saddle. Rassam took the lead on the way down. Neither Blanc nor Kerens questioned Rassam's leadership: not only was Rassam more familiar with the terrain, but he was, now that they were approaching a relatively governmental situation, their superior in diplomatic rank. At the base of Magdala, they rode past the cattle and sheep that Theodore had sent to Napier. True to their orders, five of the warriors were bringing the animals back to Theodore after Napier had refused them. Rassam knew that the other seven warriors had taken this chance to flee. And that, thought Rassam, looking back at the cattle and sheep, was the final sign. If Theodore's God were to be believed, then Napier was certainly the Light Bringer.

Toward the far end of Islamgie, just before the saddle rose sharply to the Selassie plateau, Rassam made out a large body of Ethiopian warriors, all on foot. A few were perched on higher ground where they could have a view of the British army on Selassie. The rest stood around in a disorganized jumble. Rassam was surprised to see that there were more than fifty of them. The city was empty of loyal warriors, and he had assumed that Theodore was now nearly alone.

As they neared the warriors, Rassam searched for Theodore among them, but he was disappointed. Theodore was sending him down to the English army without a final farewell. For a few moments, Rassam felt cheated; then he became more aware of the Ethiopian warriors, standing squarely across the Royal Road, which at this point was hardly more than a hard-packed line across the flat saddle. They had the look of an unruly, dangerous mob, capable of anything, rather than members of an organized army. They glared at the British party, as if they blamed Rassam, Blanc, and Kerens for the tragedy of the day before. By the time Rassam was fifty yards away, the Ethiopians had stopped milling around. They were all on their feet, watching Rassam and fingering their weapons.

To turn was impossible. Rassam gripped his bridle tightly and moved off the Royal Road to go around them. Trusting in him, his party followed.

Ahead and above him, one of the warriors up on the verge of the Selassie plateau began to chant Theodore's familiar battle cry: *"Alalala-lai."* Rassam felt the fingernails of his bridle hand pressing into his palms. He stared straight ahead into the rising road, but he couldn't help seeing the warrior above him out of the top of his eye. The man was working his matchlock, fiddling with the fuse, taking so much time at it that he must—Rassam prayed, as he hadn't in so many years—be waiting for someone else to join him in murder.

They were past the Ethiopian mob, now. They started up the bank onto the plateau. The man at the top of the rise stopped chanting. Someone else behind Rassam started, faltered nervously, was silent. Rassam spurred his horse lightly. He passed close beside the warrior with the matchlock. The man's braids were still tightly done, and he glared up proudly at Rassam. A punk, with which he would light his matchlock's fuse, smoldered in his hand. Rassam met his flinty eyes for an instant, absorbed the hatred, and rode on. All the European party made it to the plateau. The Anglo-Indian army lay straight ahead, a mile away, but for another fifty yards Rassam could clearly feel the cold impress of a musket barrel on the back of his bare, wet neck, just below his solar helmet.

The Irishmen of the 33rd, the nearest regiment to Magdala, stood to watch as the prisoners approached. Colonel Briggs rode forward to greet them formally, though not particularly happily. He escorted them back through his regiment and waved his hand for a cheer to welcome them. The Irishmen gave a very lukewarm, insipid kind of cheer, which dissolved in seconds into general laughter. Rassam saw tears of anger in Blanc's eyes, tears of laughter in Kerens's.

Briggs escorted them to headquarters, and tents were erected for them near Napier's. The commanding general himself came to enquire after their health, pointedly pretended that Henry Blanc was not there, invited them to dinner, as the situation seemed to demand, and then disappeared.

23

Easter Sunday, April 12, 1868
Magdala

Napier had to be pleased with how the Irishmen of the 33rd Wellington's Own had been tantalized for so long. From a distance he watched
them polishing their weapons with amazing speed, forming into line
before the order was given, and pacing like nervous race horses at the
starting gate. Sir Robert knew he had manipulated them well. They
were ready for their task.

Napier had intended Scott to be Colonel Cooper's replacement, but
Speedy had helped to eliminate that option at the same time he eliminated Napier's need to deal with Cooper. Napier was disappointed, but
that was, after all, one of the random chances that made the game worth
playing. At least Napier could fall back on Briggs. The boy had had a
night to recover some of his lost sleep. He had shaved until his cheeks
were pink, had dressed in a dazzling new uniform he had kept hidden
in his luggage, and at last had abandoned the muslin turban he had
copied from Speedy and assumed a proper solar helmet. He had eaten
a hearty predawn breakfast with Napier and the staff—then had dashed
away and, in full view of the whole army, vomited up everything he'd
eaten. As far as Napier was concerned, that was the best possible sign:
he was as ready as his regiment.

A single company of Madras Sappers, just twenty men, was to go
ahead across Selassie and Islamgie and up the switchback trail to Magdala. Behind the 33rd would come a supporting infantry regiment, the
45th Sherwood Foresters. Then would come mountain batteries and
mortars, which would be positioned near the middle of the Islamgie
saddle. Farther back, a battery of Armstrong guns, the longest-range
cannon in existence, remained near the previous night's campsite; close
to them were the naval rocketeers. Before any men approached the

citadel, the cannons, mortars, and rockets would pulverize it from up to two miles away for half an hour. The 33rd would provide a covering fire while the Sappers rushed forward and blew the main gate. Then it would be up to the 33rd to force an entrance and take the city. No one knew how many warriors remained in Magdala, nor how strong resistance would be.

At six o'clock in the morning, the twenty Sappers—in sparkling scarlet tunics that they had somehow managed to wash and dry during the night, with fresh black puggrees around their forage caps—spread out in a thin skirmishing line across the entire width of Selassie and started southward. Briggs had to struggle to restrain his own impatience, and he left his aides and sergeant majors to restrain the Irishmen. The Sappers dipped out of sight onto Islamgie, and Briggs gave the signal. The bandsmen launched into the regimental theme. The ensign waved the colors, and the 33rd—seven hundred bearded, unwashed Irishmen —was on the move.

They crossed Selassie in fifteen minutes and marched down onto Islamgie. The Sappers and the 33rd were in position at the base of Magdala *amba* at half-past seven. The morning thunderstorm had begun, but a beam of sunlight shone on the stone wall, and when the sheets of rain lessened, the Irishmen could make out the shapes of men standing on top of the wall. Brown water carved rivulets in the face of the *amba* and swirled around their feet; the trail looked perilous.

Exactly on schedule, the artillery began to pound at the city. The cannon shells were invisible, but the rockets made extravagant displays wherever they burst: against the *amba,* on the saddle behind the 33rd, in the clouds, sometimes exactly over the citadel to rain sparks into the city. Through it all the beam of sunlight held firm on Magdala, and three tiny figures, close together, remained absolutely motionless on the wall. And then, in the last minute of the barrage, the gap in the clouds finally responded to a burst of sparks from an errant rocket. The beam of sunlight vanished, and all of Magdala disappeared into the rain.

After precisely thirty minutes, the cannon were suddenly silent, and the Sappers started up the narrow trail. Three minutes later, following the general's perfectly orchestrated plan, the 33rd started up, with Briggs in the lead on his horse and the rest of the regiment slipping on foot through the mud. The going was too rough for the bandsmen to play, and the regiment waded upward in silence except for grunts and curses. One soldier near the front of the file lost his footing and slid over the edge like a boy on a toboggan. For a moment, it seemed he would not stop until he was halfway across Islamgie, but he caught an exposed root fifty feet down and had scrambled back up to the trail by the time the last Irishman had passed. As he fell into line, he began to sing. Men close to him picked up the song before he had finished the first line; before the end of the second, the entire regiment had joined in. It was an eternal song of the Irish regiments, no one knew how old. The verses told the stories of the famous battles of Irish troops in the service of the British and, rarely, in service of themselves. There might be, if the Irish were proud of their upcoming day's work, a new verse added about the battle of Magdala. A chorus ran between each verse:

> Pat may be foolish and sometimes very wrong.
> Paddy's got a temper but it won't last very long.
> Pat is fond of jollity and everybody knows
> There never was a coward where the shamrock grows.

It was half an hour's climb to the top of the trail, and the regiment sang the entire way. They sang with gusto and volume, loud enough to reach back to Napier's headquarters at the far end of Islamgie saddle and through the rain to Theodore, emperor of the Ethiopians, Lion of Judah, standing on the broad wall of John Bell's fortress. Wolde stood so close on Theodore's right side that sometimes, when the rain and wind swayed them, their bodies brushed against each other. Samuel was a few feet away on Theodore's other side. Careful to be nothing more than a servant, he crouched slightly and remained half a step behind. Samuel held a musket, Wolde a sword. In each hand, Theodore held one of the pistols he had received as gifts so long before, from Consul Cameron, the ones engraved with the words, *"Presented to Theodore, Emperor of Ethiopia, by Victoria, Queen of Great Britain and Ireland, for his kindness to her servant Plowden."*

To Wolde Theodore commented, lightly, "Their singing reminds me of an Ethiopian army on the march, how they play their chanting games."

Wolde nodded soberly.

"It isn't anything to worry about," said Theodore, turning on the soothing quality in his voice. "They will conquer us, surely, but we will surrender quickly. We shall not be hurt." He knew he was speaking a lie, but Wolde seemed so small and defenseless, so much the young boy that Kasa had carried in his arms up the switchback trail above the monastic village. Theodore felt absolutely calm now. The thing was done. It was nearly over. He had made his peace.

There were somewhat less than fifty warriors left to Theodore, men who had been with him for a very long time. Some were on the wall, which was ten feet wide across the front of the citadel. Others were below, waiting to leap onto the wall to replace their comrades when they fell. Theodore recognized every one of these men, knew them all by name. For the most part, they were older men, men who had been rescued from slavery by a young *shifta* chieftain and his small band of fierce child monks, men snatched away from Arab slavers in the Sudan, men who had been given new lives by Theodore and who wouldn't leave him now. But Theodore didn't speak to them. He only spoke to little Wolde and tried to soothe the priest's fears.

The British army was vastly superior to the Ethiopian warriors, Theodore knew, but the Europeans wouldn't have the simple time of it they expected. They would surely try to take the main gate, but that would be nearly impossible. During the night, the warriors had filled the zigzag space behind it with stones to a level of five feet. If the British tried to blow the gate down with explosives or a cannon blast, they would do little more than open a space above the level of a man's chest. If soldiers tried to crawl through, they would be slaughtered by Ethiopians firing through rifle slits inside the walls.

It would take courage to storm the wall, even with such a small defending force. Theodore had seen courage during the Friday battle at Aroge, but he wasn't sure it was the kind of courage that would prompt a man to throw himself onto a wall under fire.

Now there was only the waiting. All the warriors except for Theodore, Wolde, and Samuel had taken refuge under the lee of the wall. No one had been hurt, but entire sections of the city had been razed. The bursting sun had exploded directly overhead and rained those taunting sparks down around them. The sun had clashed with the lightning bolts, and the artillery had competed with the thunder.

"B" company of the 33rd regiment hustled up the trail on the heels of the Sappers, while the rest of the 33rd waited below, unable to see the citadel over the top of the cliff. The Sappers and their companion Irishmen threw themselves down in relative security on the lip of the cliff and fired a close, hard volley forward. There were several answering shots, with the feeble, tinny sound of ancient flintlocks, followed by the whisper of harmless pellets far overhead. As the Irish fired a second time, the Sappers rose and hurled themselves toward the wall. One of them slipped in the mud, got almost to his feet, and slumped down. An instant later, the report of the flintlock reached the men below. The man, a fine-skinned old Indian, crawled over the lip and rolled onto his back. His wound was invisible, but he lay perfectly still, with rain dripping into his wide open eyes.

There were more flintlock shots, and a responding Irish volley. "Can't see a bloody t'ing," swore a man at Irion's shoulder. All the men below were craning their necks, as if they could lift their heads the fifty feet they would have needed to see over the cliff.

The Sappers reappeared in a rush and tumbled down to safety. Twenty had gone, but only eight had made it back. The men of "B" company ducked their heads, and the charge at the gate went off in a great hollow sigh. Mud and wood splinters and stone chips filled the air. The sergeant-major of "B" company hoisted himself high enough on his elbows to see the damage, then turned and called down to Briggs. His voice carried faintly, but clearly, as far as Irion's company. "Blasted the gate, sir, sure enough. But there seems to be rubble behind it as high as a man's throat. Doubt if we could force our way through."

Briggs swore silently, and his horse pivoted.

Irion couldn't wait any longer. The cliff face rose nearly straight up from the trail, but there were a few handholds on boulders that protruded out of the mud. He threw himself onto the cliff and pulled at a jagged spine of rock. Someone put a shoulder under his flailing boot. In ten seconds he was standing on the top. Pellets cut through the rain beside him, but he steadied himself against the fear to take a look around. He was in a daze like that of a boy making love for the first time: painfully, supernaturally aware of all the sensations bombarding him, but six inches outside his body, watching and feeling as if it were happening to someone else. The level space between the cliff and the wall was only thirty yards wide. He saw Ethiopians, perhaps a dozen of them, crouched with their firearms on the wall. Closest of all to him were three: an old man with a rifle and a one-armed man with a wide-bladed Ethiopian sword, and in front of them a man in his forties, sitting cross-legged on the outer edge of the wall with a pistol hanging limp in each hand. For a long second, the sitting man's gaze met Irion's. Irion couldn't pull himself away. In the midst of that storm of raindrops and bullets and emotions, no man should be so utterly at peace, so comfortable. Beneath a circlet of badly burned flesh were the same eyes—black, not gray, but still the same eyes—that young Irion, the Maynooth seminarian, had always tried in vain to find in his mental image of Christ.

Something tugged at Irion's arm and spun him down onto his face in the mud. The shoulder of his tunic was torn in a perfect little crease, but there was no pain, and the blood vanished into the rain-soaked scarlet.

He recognized the sound of Briggs's voice and raised his head in that direction. Still far enough down the trail to be safe, the colonel was shouting at him: "Down, you bloody fool. Down." Irion could tell from the desperation on Briggs's face and in his voice that he knew he had lost control of the situation. The gate hadn't blown, individual Irishmen were going off on their own, and Briggs didn't know what to do next. "Down, you bloody fool. Damn you."

Irion remembered the wall. He cupped his mouth and called down to his company, "There's a place where the wall is low enough to hop over, off to the right by fifty yards or so."

"Let's at it," cried someone, and instantly his whole company was clambering up the cliff. Ragged fire burst from the citadel. Irion and his companions were running between the wall and the cliff. An enormous cheer rose behind them, and they knew the entire regiment was following. They sprinted. Their rifles hung loosely in their hands. The man in front of Irion threw out his hands and sprawled in the mud. Irion hurdled him, nearly fell, caught his balance, and ran. The man beside him now was the ensign, waving the pole back and forth to keep the wet regimental colors unfurled.

More shots came from the wall. Another Irishman fell, off to Irion's left. And then, vaguely, he was aware of Briggs's horse at his shoulder, and Briggs leaning down shouting obscenities into his face. Briggs tried to push the horse in front of Irion and cut him off, but Irion swerved sharply behind the horse and kept on running.

He reached the low place in the wall and ducked alone behind a bush. Other Irishmen were close on either side, burrowing down into whatever cover they could find. "Low enough to hop over, Irion?" laughed someone, for the wall was ten feet high. "Hell, it bloody looked it," said Irion, and he took a quick shot at the scattered men along this section of the wall. Muskets fired from the wall and from the bushes. One Ethiopian tumbled, the others ducked out of sight. Irion reloaded, fixed his bayonet, and left the bush. Still in his battle haze, he was peripherally aware of other Irishmen with him, around him, each doing his own little part, each completely isolated but working together with the rest, each one winning the war by himself. It was the Irish way.

Holding his Snyder at waist level, Irion fired again as he sprinted to the wall. Irion's bullet went wild, but someone else's threw a warrior backward out of sight, and there seemed to be a reasonably empty section of the wall. Pressed tightly into the mortared stone, Irion reloaded. Then he turned and threw his hand up: far short. There was a rough outcropping of mortar three feet above the ground, so he scrambled onto it. His fingers were still a foot shy of the top. A dark face leaned out above him. There was a spear. Irion slashed at it with his bayonet. An edge touched his cheek, but he didn't feel any pain. The dark face leaned too far out, and Irion pressed his trigger. The face dissolved, the man rose with the impact and somersaulted over Irion. He clung to the wall, leaned into it, and reloaded. He tried for the top again, but there were no handholds.

Irishmen were firing over his head and cheering him on by name, and Briggs was there on his horse, wandering in slow, confused circles, unsure of what to do. More Irishmen were gathering near this end of the wall: the entire regiment, seven hundred men.

"Colonel, give me a lift," cried Irion. "For God's sake."

Without thinking, Briggs turned his horse into the wall beside Irion. The colonel's face was slack. He did not know what he was doing.

"Lord love you, sir," shouted Irion, but he got no response. He planted his boot on the horse's croup and threw himself upward onto the wall on his back. He rolled onto his belly and surveyed both directions. The wall was almost deserted, just two Ethiopians to one side. He turned his rifle and fired. The nearest fell. The one beyond was already aiming his musket at Irion, but Irion could see from the slow spark, sputtering in the rain, that it was a matchlock and would take a few seconds to discharge. Irion scrambled forward on his knees, parried the barrel with the side of his bayonet just as the powder caught, and felt the burn race across the side of his neck. Before he could drive the point of his bayonet into the man's belly, a Snyder bullet from the ground threw the man off the wall. Irion dropped onto his back and reloaded, then leaped up and looked all around. There wasn't an Ethiopian to be seen.

The ensign was below him, stretching up the regimental colors. Irion took the pole and knelt with it until the ensign, pushed up by dozens of hands, reached the top and stood waving the colors to show the world that this was an Irish wall.

More useless shots whispered around them, but now the whole regiment was on its way over, and Magdala was as Irish as Dublin or Cork.

Theodore had intended to stay on top of the wall until the end, but when the British soldiers came streaming in a shapeless mob up the trail —not at all how he expected Englishmen to fight—he had let Samuel and Wolde draw him away through the rubble to the relative shelter of the first unflattened houses. From that vantage point they watched Theodore's most loyal subjects fall one by one, and they saw the red-coated enemy come swarming like ants over the parapet. The last few Ethiopians fell back together at a dead run through the destruction and stopped to fire back from a cluster of huts near Theodore's shelter. The British soldiers answered them with a loose, bored kind of volley. Several warriors went down, and a few of the British pursued them into the city. Standing still in deep shadow, Theodore, Wolde, and Samuel were not seen, or they were ignored. Wolde was shaking his sword nervously, as if he really would have known how to use it. Theodore was mildly amused at how the tiny, harmless priest had taken up a weapon to protect his emperor. Samuel had a musket, which seemed in his hands to be an imitation of a real weapon, part of the ritual costume that his role in this religious mystery demanded. Wolde looked across at the British, who were shouting and firing their muskets in the air. Somewhere toward the zigzag gate musicians had begun to play. "We have to go," Wolde whimpered. "We can't stay here." His eyes were as round and dull as ostrich eggs.

"We can stay," Theodore said, softly.

"It might be better at the church," Samuel said, with his old man's dignity intact. Theodore could tell that Samuel had no delusions.

"Yes, we will stand at the church," agreed Theodore, and he let Wolde lead them away. They could hear the last resistance across the city, the twanging reports of flintlocks, the hard slaps of the British Snyders. Behind them, all the British soldiers were singing in time to the music of their band. Far away across Islamgie, English cannoneers were firing victory salutes. Wolde kept prancing nervously ahead, tripping over his sword, returning to beg Theodore to hurry, but Theodore and Samuel walked slowly.

Shouts were getting closer. Theodore checked the two pistols to be sure they were properly loaded and primed. He tucked them under his *shama* to protect them from the rain.

They passed the compound of the British prisoners. It had been leveled into the ground by the artillery barrage, and Theodore said a silent prayer of thanks that he had sent them away.

They entered the square of hard-packed mud in front of the church. By some stroke of luck it hadn't been touched by shell or spark. It was a large church, by which Theodore had attempted to demonstrate his piety to a hostile southern empire: low-walled, thatch-roofed, with the near wall open to the elements and with an ostrich-egg cross on top.

They were halfway across the square to the church when shouts erupted behind them. Samuel peeled away from Theodore instantly, dropped to his knee, aimed, and pulled the trigger. But the priming was wet, and the gun did not fire. He stared weakly at it, until a shot from the far end of the square hurled him backward into the mud.

Wolde wasn't a warrior, and it didn't even occur to him to use his sword. He dropped it, seized Theodore by the arm, and tried to half-pull, half-carry him into the church. He stumbled over his sword, lying there in the mud, and fell. He tried to get up. A British shot whistled over his head, and another caught him under the armpit. He tumbled like a rag doll. Theodore stared down at him, then back at the soldiers. There were three of them, all furiously reloading. Theodore stared hard at them until he had drawn their eyes up to his, freezing them with his gaze. One by one, they stopped their reloading and let their weapons hang loose. The emperor turned his back on them and walked away. He slipped one arm under Wolde's back, the other under his knees, and lifted the featherlight body. Wolde was absolutely still, already growing cold. As Theodore stepped slowly toward the gentle darkness of the church, he whispered ancient phrases into dead ears: "God's most cherished," he breathed, with a voice meant to be soothing. "Beloved of the mother of the Lord Iyesus."

The air inside the church was chilly and humid, but the earthen floor was dry. He laid Wolde down gently and stepped away. He placed the muzzle of one of Queen Victoria's pistols to his chest and pulled the trigger. The mechanism was jammed with mud. The pistol didn't fire, and a high wave of doubt nearly took him. But he shut his eyes and put his head down into the wave, and in his mind's eye the wave became the granite face of a great rock spire. He saw a dark cleft near the peak of the spire, and a rope stretching straight down, looking as delicate as a silken thread. In the cleft he saw a vast dome of drum-tight skin over a tiny face with minute, intense black eyes. He heard Madhani's voice, welcoming him with the wavering death keen. With one hand he reached for the basket that bounced at the end of the rope, and with the other he touched the second pistol to his side and put a bullet through his heart.

Every soldier south of the Bashillo was marching across the Islamgie saddle to share in the victory celebration. Packs of leaderless men were already picking through the rubble and pilfering the houses that still stood, hoarding away in their backpacks souvenirs and items of value, fine Oriental carpets and holy Coptic scrolls and blue neck cords from dead warriors. Some of the hearths had been cleared out for cooking, and someone had thrust a bowl of hot, fatty stew and a thick slice of fresh bread into Irion's hands. Irion wore bandages on his neck and his cheek and on his arm under his tunic, almost as if they were medals. The wheel had turned full circle, and he with it: from hero to scapegoat, and back again to hero. His fellow-soldiers forced him to hold court on a pile of bricks, and he had to tell, over and over, for constantly changing audiences, the myth of how he had single-handedly defeated the army of the emperor of the Ethiopians.

Alone, on foot, Brevet Colonel Briggs picked his way down the strip of ground that was marked as a street only by being slightly less littered with debris than the rest of the city. He seemed to be wandering aimlessly.

Irion rose from his pile of bricks to walk after him, and everyone with him started to follow. "Ought to congrat-u-late our young colonel," slurred one Irishman, very drunk on the rum that had appeared miraculously all over the city. "He wan't as brave as our precious lad Geoffrey, but he did a job for himself, too."

"No, I'll go alone, lads," said Irion, waving them down. "I've something to discuss with him. Here—" He tapped his knuckle on a keg of rum. "Have another."

Irion came on the colonel from behind and called to him, but Briggs seemed not to hear. Irion jogged quickly around and faced him, and Briggs barely stopped short of walking into him.

Out of his long experience of wars, Irion had no trouble recognizing the look on Briggs's face. It was the stunned, sleepy look of a man who has glanced, for the first time, into the terrible face of battle, who has felt the gentle flow of bullets near his cheeks and listened to their whispering, deceitful voices. He had learned, as rudely as a man has to, that it is one thing to prance around two hundred yards from the enemy delivering messages and looking dashing in a fine, clean uniform, and quite another to have men bleeding and dying all around and to be in danger of it yourself. Some men let the battle haze show them whatever there is to see. By nature, Irion was such a man. Others struggle against its pull, try to make it fit some old, out-moded image of the world. The colonel was such a man, and if he didn't change, he would never make a soldier.

Briggs searched Irion's face between the bandages, and a glimmer of distant recognition appeared in his gray eyes. "You are the one," he started. His voice was very flat, and he was not speaking to Irion, but rather just identifying Irion to himself. "You are the filthy Irishman from the mutiny at Ada Baga."

"No, sir, not I," Irion said quickly. "On the parapet, sir."

"Ah, you are the Irishman who climbed the wall."

Softly, trying not to frighten the colonel, Irion corrected him again: "I am the Irishman that you helped to climb the wall."

After a pause, Briggs said, "That was foolish. A breach of discipline."

"Aye, sir," said Irion. "But it was a breach of the wall, too. Wasn't it? Sir."

A befuddled grin showed on Briggs's lips, as if he almost, but not quite, understood that Irion had made a joke. He shook his head and tried to concentrate. "Should I court-martial you, or give you a medal?"

"It was a brave deed, helping me so calmly under enemy fire as you did," Irion answered. "If I was commended for a medal, I'd expect you to get one, too. Or even your knighthood."

Briggs blinked. "I need to think. No, I don't want to think at all. I shall sleep. Just lie down a little and sleep for a minute or two." Then, "What is your name?"

"Geoffrey Irion, sir."

"Irion." Slowly, he began to ramble. "They shot my horse from under me, Irion. One of your damned Irish. Some damn potato-eating Irishman. In the middle of all that noise, someone shot my horse, and I went down on my face. I brought that horse from India, rode her all the way from Zula. And one of your people shot her out from under me."

"There were bullets flying everywhere," said Irion, trying to calm the colonel. "I'm sure it was an accident. We're proud to be your regiment."

Briggs looked up sharply. "Do you know how I feel, Irion? How crushed I am?" He actually put out his hands to take Irion's shoulders, but in time he realized that he had called a common soldier by name, that he was about to touch a common man. He recoiled instantly and turned his face away. Inside him, all his training struggled against his emotions. He straightened his shoulders and squeezed his voice back into its distinct, nasal accent. "So, you want a medal?"

Hopefully, for this was exactly what he wanted, Irion said, "I only meant to bring to your attention, sir, that I am no more deserving of one than you. Sir."

"Don't play me for a fool, soldier," said Briggs, but he began to crumble instantly. He pressed his fingertips into his temples. "Leave me alone. Let me sleep."

He started to walk away, but Irion said to his back, "If it makes any difference to you, we are all very well pleased to have a man like you in command."

Briggs turned for just long enough to say, very properly, through his nose, "Why, in heaven's name, would that mean anything to me?" And then he wandered on up the rubble-filled street, looking for a place to curl up out of the rain and forget it all.

None of the musical groups, official or impromptu, inside the city would be denied their part in the celebration, and as the commanding general rode his white charger through the zigzag gate, the city erupted into an immense, bewildering strain of "Hail the Conquering Hero Comes" performed out of step by brass bands and bagpipes, Punjabi reeds and harmonicas and concertinas. Riflemen shot off irregular volleys from the parapets, and artillery units still below with their guns on Islamgie answered from their distance, muted by stone walls and rain.

The Naval Brigade entered Magdala on Napier's heels, and while Napier made a formal speech, Pilbeam slipped away and joined Irion.

"I heard about it all," said Pilbeam, tossing his arm around the smaller man's shoulders and leading him away through the ruined houses. "They said it was you went over the wall first."

"True enough," said Irion. "Clambered up my colonel's horse's ass and flung myself on the savages."

"Killed one or two?"

"Two, I think. It's hard to remember, afterward."

"And a bloody hero you are, Geoffrey. Do you think you'll have a promotion? Or a medal?"

"A medal and the pension that goes with it, I think," said Irion. "I asked the colonel for it, and I think he'll recommend me."

"Coo, you didn't," said Pilbeam.

"I did, Arthur," said Irion, and he stood back and laughed at Pilbeam. "That doesn't sound like you. What did you ever care about medals and heroes?"

Pilbeam fumbled nervously and kicked at a bunch of thatch. "Have you seen my envoy?"

"What do you intend?" asked Irion.

"I've been tasting sulphur and brimstone—*rocket breath*, we call it, my mates and me—since Friday afternoon. I don't think I've brains enough left to have intentions."

"Hasn't there been blood enough?"

"Blood enough," agreed Pilbeam. "I saw him yesterday, and right away I wanted to hurt him. But later all I could remember was the look on his face, a look like a whipped dog. I don't want anything of him, just to see the bastard once more, up close, just to see whether he'll look a man in the eyes."

"He came in with Sir Bob," said Irion. "I watched him carefully, and as soon as he could he sneaked away into the city."

They walked in the direction in which Irion had seen Rassam going, and by luck they found him quickly. Soldiers were walking at random through the square in front of the church, avoiding the three naked bodies that lay on the ground, exposed to the rain. Irion recognized them instantly: the old man, the boy, and the man with Christ's eyes. The old man lay flat on his back with his hands flung out over his head, with a small, round bullet wound in his chest. The one-armed man had been thrown into an awkward posture, his forearm behind his head, his legs spread far apart as if someone had been particularly curious about the fact that, sometime long before, he had been castrated. The man with Christ's eyes lay on his belly. Half his back was the massive crater of the exit of a bullet fired from point-blank range. Looters had stripped all three of them absolutely naked, even down to their *matebs*. The old man had apparently died where he lay, but two shallow, slick troughs in the mud showed how the bodies of the eunuch and the tall man had been dragged into the square from the church. Rassam was kneeling in the mud beside the body of the tall man. His hands were digging into his own knees, his chin was bent down to his chest, and his back was heaving with rhythmic, painful sobs.

Irion watched from the other end of the square. "Is that the man you hate?" he asked.

Pilbeam mumbled, "He seems so small, so weak."

They walked forward and stood over Rassam. He became aware of them and, without looking up, cried out savagely, incoherently, "Haven't you done enough to him? You took his clothes and his dignity. Do you have to take his dreams away, too?"

Pilbeam knelt on one knee beside the tall man. "I'll help you with them, sir," he said, and as he was turning the tall man over and slipping his arms under him, Rassam lifted his head and looked into Pilbeam's eyes. Somehow, Rassam's tear-filled eyes seemed to have been made for misery.

"It's the emperor," said Rassam, struggling to control his breathing. "I remember what he said. He told me, 'One day I think you will see me dead, and while you stand over my corpse it may be that you will curse me. You may say, *"This was a wicked man who shouldn't be buried. Let his remains rot above ground."* But I trust your generosity, Rassam. You will bury me.' Theodore said that to me. I'll remember those words until the day I die."

Pilbeam lifted the dread madman of the mountains and carried him into the church, and while Irion pulled tapestries off the walls of a sunken inner room in the center of the church, Pilbeam carried the other two bodies inside. They wrapped the bodies in the tapestries, and Pilbeam and Irion began to dig three shallow graves, side by side, in the earthen floor of the church with the shovels from their packs.

Rassam retreated into a dark corner, and no one would have known he was there if he hadn't been constantly whimpering. When the graves had been dug and the tapestry-shrouded bodies pushed in, and Pilbeam and Irion, on their knees, were ready to cover them over, Rassam waddled on his knees out of his corner. He meant to grasp Pilbeam's arm in a painful grip, but Pilbeam's arm was too large and his own hand was too small, and all he did was lay his hand against Pilbeam's massive shoulder. "We don't want dreams to fall apart, do we?" Rassam asked. His voice had the giddy, irrational quality of a child directing dolls.

Not understanding, slightly uneasy, Pilbeam answered, "No, sir."

"I cannot stay in Ethiopia," said Rassam. "Though I love it very much. The weather is wonderful. The clean air and the birds and the flowers. Yes, I love Ethiopia, and would stay forever. But I have people waiting for me at home—in England. You understand that, don't you?"

"Yes, I understand."

"Sir Robert's offer is quite generous, but I have people waiting for me in England." He noticed Irion behind him and scrambled quickly to him. "You will stay too, won't you?"

"Aye, if you like," said Irion, softly.

"You can be military governor." Rassam was speaking very quickly now, one word tumbling out after the other. "Be sure to pacify the south. That is the key to Ethiopia. Pacify the south, and then Gabry can be free to stop the slavers in the Sudan, and Engeddah can put down the rebellions in Kwara." He turned suddenly back to Pilbeam. "And you will be governor in my place, won't you?"

"Governor, sir?"

"Governor of Ethiopia. Only until I return, of course. For I will come back and make all the dreams come true, but now I have to leave. I have to leave. To leave."

"Of course, sir," said Pilbeam.

"You will build roads?" asked Rassam. "Schools? Factories? Bridges across the Big Abai, the Takkaze, and the Sobat? You will make the people keep the peace? Stop the slavers?"

"Aye, sir, all those things, and more," said Irion. "It will be another golden age."

"A golden age," breathed Rassam. "That is what he wanted."

"Yes. Don't worry, sir," said Pilbeam.

Rassam wobbled up to his feet. "No, I won't worry," he said. "The dreams will not be lost." As if drunk, he stumbled toward the outside. For the last ten minutes hailstones had been falling, and the square looked as if it were covered with snow. He paused just beyond the thatched eaves. The hailstones drummed against his solar helmet. "I am leaving Ethiopia in good hands," he shouted back, and then he ran across the square, leaving the Irish soldier and the English sailor to shovel dirt over the Lion of Judah, the eunuch-priest, and the loyal old servant.

Epilogue

That night, after all the loot had been removed and the army had returned to its base camp on Selassie, the Sappers fired Magdala. They gathered every Ethiopian body they could find into a row and piled the row high with thatch. They placed explosive charges in the great stone walls. Starting at the church, the Sappers ran through the city with torches. The fire crackled up yellow at the pinnacle, but the bottom, at the level of the wall, glowed a liquid crimson. There were hollow bursts and flashes of brilliant white light as the explosive charges set in the walls began to ignite. Balls of fire shot into the sky and vanished instantly.

The funeral pyre collapsed as quickly as it had burned, and soon Magdala was nothing more than a mass of dimly glowing ash on the peak of a high mountain.

The Bashillo River had swollen so much with the last days' rain that the army had to wait another two days while the Sappers constructed a pontoon bridge. On the fifth day after the battle of Magdala, the entire army had finally assembled on the Dalanta plateau above the north lip of the gorge. The elongated pyramid that the army had formed, broad at Zula and rapier-sharp at Magdala, began to crumble as the veterans of Aroge and Magdala marched northward along that familiar route, dismantled garrisons and depots, collected the servants and tents they had left behind, gathered up the troops who had waited for their lucky comrades to return victorious. After such a success at Aroge and Magdala, it seemed that the return journey should have been far easier than the original, but new difficulties appeared unexpectedly.

The rainy season was picking up tempo. During April, the month that had seen the battle of Magdala, barely four inches of rain fell. May brought five, and June brought seven. The soldiers walked through freezing rains, and the sun seemed to have disappeared entirely. Mules and horses slipped off icy trails. Several careless men froze to death. One by one, the elephants refused to go on, and they were shot and left to rot. With so many baggage animals dying, not all the equipment could be carried back, and much of it was burned at the side of the caravan route. The month of July, when most of the army was making the descent through the steep, narrow defile from Komayli to the salt desert before Zula, brought fourteen inches of rain. More men were carried away by flash floods than had died by accident, murder, or battle.

Most of Ethiopia had been sinking back into anarchy before the British had even contemplated an expedition, but now that Theodore was dead, the *Zemene Mesafint* returned in all its hideous glory. Not only did the Ethiopians begin to fight among themselves for mastery of the country, but, with the impression that the British were retreating, they began to fire at the army from hillsides and to make surprise attacks on baggage trains.

Europeans who traveled alone took their lives in their hands. The 33rd Wellington's Own had spent a night in Ada Baga and early in the morning they marched over that same rise on which they had contrived their famous mutiny. It seemed only fair that something memorable should take place when they passed this way again, and they were not disappointed. As they came over the summit, Brevet Colonel Briggs spied in the distance a tall pole with a round, football-sized object on top. As they came nearer, the object took the form of a human head, wearing a muslin turban. Briggs stopped below the head and studied it. It was sixteen feet up in the air, but it was fresh, and there was no doubt as to whose it was. The sergeant-major who went to lower the pole found Captain Speedy's hands and feet at the base of the pole, wrapped in a scarlet tunic along with the pieces into which his beloved cavalry saber of Damascus steel had been broken.

Briggs buried the pieces without ceremony and sent word back to Napier, who was not greatly distressed when he heard the news.

Napier, who was following a number of marches behind Briggs's 33rd, was at that moment reaching Lake Ashangi. Ibrahim appeared in the bowl with his two hundred men on the morning after Napier's arrival. Napier kept his promise to the petty chieftain and gave him five hundred Brown Bess muskets and enough ammunition, piled up on the shore of the lake in a small Magdala of wooden cases, to last a lifetime. Napier had reasons for the gift, of course, as he had reasons for everything he did—some pragmatic and well thought out, others less so. First, the only hope of ending the anarchy that was tearing apart the empire was for one man—if not an Englishman, then an Ethiopian—to wield so much power that he could crush his neighbors at will. With an arsenal

of Brown Besses, Ibrahim might be the man to fill the void left by
Theodore. And . . . if Ibrahim managed to rule Ethiopia, then in the
future he might be a valuable ally to Great Britain in an empire close
by the sea lanes of the Suez Canal. And . . . Napier simply had a fondness
for the bold, clever, laughing Ibrahim, whose lies had entertained him
so well at their previous meeting, and Napier could think of no better
way to show his appreciation than by giving him the one thing he would
enjoy the most: enough deadly playthings to equip an army.

The Magdala prisoners traveled within their own private military
escort, composed of officers and infantry drawn from different regiments as a sort of honor guard. Wherever the company went, soldiers
and servants stared as if they were animals in a zoo. Blanc's try at
mending a friendship with Rassam and Kerens had not even survived
the crossing of the Bashillo River, and they rode northward as isolated
from one another as they had ever been in Magdala. Kerens had rejected his mistress on the night of their release, and, completely homeless, she had wandered off alone into the rainy wilderness. Kerens had
cried himself to sleep that first night, and then seemed to have exor-
cised her from his memory. Cameron recovered enough strength to
ride a horse, but he remained withdrawn, nursing his shame, tugging
at his beard, dreading his homecoming, not wanting anything but to
crawl into the bush to die.

As Napier had intended, Rassam never gave him any sort of answer
on the offer to remain as civil governor of Ethiopia, and, in fact, they
never saw each other again. Rassam was oblivious to the stares, to the
rain, to nearly everything along the way. He rode with his chin tucked
low and his eyes on the ground, and at every stopping place he hid
himself away in his tent. He had less freedom than he had had at
Magdala; the difference was that now he was his own jailer.

Three days after Napier left Lake Ashangi to the accompaniment of
a military band and a fanatical, joyful Brown Bess salute, Rassam and
his company quietly entered the bowl from the south. It was late on a
black day, with a bitter wind lapping whitecaps out of the lake and
slashing cruel daggers of rain across faces and hands. Servants had
hurried ahead with the baggage train to set up the tents. The lancer
who directed the servants' work was waiting by the road, and he led
Rassam and his company around the lake past the mangrove swamp.
The tents were away from the shore in the shelter of the forest. The
lancer pointed out Rassam's tent to him, and Rassam pulled himself out
of the saddle and walked toward it.

Vaguely, he became aware of men standing between him and the
tent: two pairs of legs; thick, nonmilitary boots; loose trousers. The men
blocked his way to the entrance to the tent. He stopped, let his eyes lift
slowly. Familiar faces; it took a few moments to recognize Paniotti and
Abd-ul-Kerim, unfamiliarly bundled in heavy jackets. Paniotti's hand
lay on Abd-ul-Kerim's shoulder. That light pressure, it seemed, was all

that kept Abd-ul-Kerim from leaping forward and throwing his arms around Rassam. Even in the rain, the golden emblems flashed in the Arab's smile. He shifted anxiously from foot to foot.

"Rassam, my friend," he breathed, but Paniotti's hand gripped suddenly tighter. Like a child obeying some seemingly purposeless order of his father, Abd-ul-Kerim was silent.

Rassam looked at Paniotti. The Greek watched him carefully. Paniotti, Rassam knew, understood everything; Abd-ul-Kerim, nothing.

Rassam turned his shrouded eyes back to Abd-ul-Kerim. "You were in his service," he said, his voice a monotone.

"He was a dreamer, Rassam," said Abd-ul-Kerim. "He was my balloon. I rode with him for a short time. The view was glorious. Now we've lost him, all of us, but we will find other dreamers, new balloons. We must have courage. We will fly again."

The pain was so apparent in Rassam's face that Abd-ul-Kerim lost his words and even his smile. Rassam dropped his head. "I betrayed him," he said. "I had the chance to protect his dreams, and I wasn't man enough. I couldn't. I betrayed him."

He started to step around Abd-ul-Kerim to the entrance to his tent, but Abd-ul-Kerim stopped him with a hard hand on Rassam's arm. "How? I don't understand."

"General Napier offered me the chance to become governor of an Ethiopian colony. With troops to stop the fighting. With teachers and engineers and administrators. I could have done it, with you, with Paniotti. It was everything Theodore wanted. It was what he died for. But I betrayed him. I betrayed us all."

Rassam waited half a minute for Abd-ul-Kerim to speak, but there was only silence. At last, Abd-ul-Kerim dropped his hand from Rassam's arm, and Rassam slipped into the tent.

Late that night, Abd-ul-Kerim came again to Rassam's tent, but Paniotti had followed him there, and like a father easing a sleepwalking child back to bed, led him away. Paniotti and Abd-ul-Kerim departed northward before Rassam was awake in the morning.

Just rewards awaited those who returned safely to England.

An auction of all the exotic loot from the ruins of Magdala raised nearly five thousand pounds, which was distributed, on the basis of rank, to all military personnel who had crossed the Bashillo River.

Robert Napier became the first Baron Napier of Magdala. He eventually retired from the military with the rank of field marshal, and died in 1889. Today, his statue looks down on Englishmen, tourists, and pigeons in Queen's Gate, London.

Briggs was confirmed in his colonelcy and knighted. On his recommendation, Geoffrey Irion received the Victoria Cross and a lifelong pension.

On the advice of her beloved servant Disraeli, Queen Victoria bestowed a gift of five thousand pounds on Rassam and two thousand pounds on Blanc.

Henry Blanc wrote an account of his trials in Africa, in which he painted himself a hero and blamed the entire "Ethiopian imbroglio" on Rassam.

Hormuzd Rassam published his own account, in which he painted himself a hero and castigated Blanc as a very difficult man with whom to live. He resigned his Aden post, married an English wife, resumed Near Eastern archaeology with his patron Layard, and finally retired to Brighton. He was converted to evangelical views, wrote books on archaeology and religion, and had several brushes with the Episcopal church; he died in 1910 at the age of ninety. Among his effects was found a bulky ring bearing the image of a crowned lion holding an intricate crucifix in one paw.

Ibrahim, the self-styled prince of Lasta and Wajerat, was too small a man to fill Theodore's place. Ibrahim, his two hundred warriors, and his five hundred Brown Bess muskets were swallowed up by the greatest coalition of armies that Ethiopia had ever seen. The *Zemene Mesafint* laid its dark hand on the highlands, and all was as it had been before.

ABOUT THE AUTHOR

MASON MCCANN SMITH was born in California in 1952. Since graduating from Pomona College, he has been a newspaper feature writer, graduate student in anthropology, assembly-line worker, key-punch operator, extra and motor-home driver for Hollywood film companies, coordinator of first-aid classes, and administrator of a school for the severely handicapped. He is now at work on a novel about the Comanche Indians.